THE ARTISTRY OF HOLLYWOOD

Jack Lander

MINERVA PRESS
LONDON
MONTREUX LOS ANGELES SYDNEY

THE ARTISTRY OF HOLLYWOOD
Copyright © Jack Lander 1997

All Rights Reserved

No part of this book may be reproduced in any form,
by photocopying or by any electronic or mechanical means,
including information storage or retrieval systems,
without permission in writing from both the copyright owner
and the publisher of this book.

ISBN 1 86106 493 4

First Published 1997 by
MINERVA PRESS
195 Knightsbridge
London SW7 1RE

2nd Impression 1998

Printed in Great Britain for Minerva Press

THE ARTISTRY OF HOLLYWOOD

Contents

Foreword	vii
Looking for Classics	ix
Method of Selection	xii
Order of Selection – The Lander Scale	xv
Order of Selection – Hollywood's Top Two-Fifty	xviii
Film-Making as a Group Activity	xxii
The Entries	xxix
References Quoted in the Text	xxxii
Other Useful References	xxxiv
Acknowledgements	xxxvi
I Hollywood's Top 250 (1997)	**38**
Animated Feature Films	38
Biographical ('Biopics')	49
Comedy (1) – Black Comedy, The Great Clowns, Satirical, and Social Comedy	54
Comedy (2) – 'Screwball' Comedy, Sex Comedy	87
Compendium (Portmanteau) Films	100
Costume Spectacle – Epics, Period Pieces	107
Drama (1: Major Social Issues) – Social Allegory, Social Realism, Pursuit and Concern for Social Justice, Ethnic Conflicts, Films of the 'Counter-Culture'	123

Drama (2: Frictions within Society) – Through the eyes of Youth, Family Tensions, the Sex War, Addictions and Rehabilitation   150

Drama (3: Problems of Power) – Politics and the Services, Prison/Mental Hospital, the Theatre and the Media, 'Moviola'   177

Fantasy – Adventure, Horror and Monster Movies, Science Fiction Movies   200

Literary Adaptations   223

Musicals   226

Romance – Romantic Adventure, Romantic Comedy, Romantic Drama   256

Thrillers – Criminal Investigations, Gangster Melodrama, Psychological Suspense, Spy Melodrama   285

War Films   343

Westerns   357

II Personal Choice   380

III The Film-Makers   402

'Big Shots' (Front Office Executives)   404
Film-Producers   411
Producers   414
Directors   420
Screenwriter-Directors   425
Screenwriters and Authors   427
Cinematographers and Special Effects Creators   443
Contributors to the Art Department   454
Contributors to the Music Department (Composers of Film Scores, Songwriters, Music Directors and Arrangers, Choreographers)   469
Editors   479

IV List of Performers   486

V Alphabetical List of Films   521

Foreword

In her weekly film review in *The Sunday Times* for 16 April 1950, Dilys Powell paid a generous tribute to the film-makers of Hollywood:

> When a film comes over from Hollywood labelled CLASS you can be pretty sure that the piece will be of impeccable craftsmanship. The direction will be assured, the cutting unerring, nobody will question the solidity of the background, the acting will be fluent, everything in short will go off with the proper bang.

The application of all this combined talent did not always result in a work of art. However, in 1940, the knowledgeable and demanding critic of the *New Republic* magazine, Otis Ferguson, used George Cukor's comedy for MGM, *The Philadelphia Story*, to point out that such films

> may help convince some of the more discerning among cultural slugabeds that, when the movies want to turn their hand to anything, they can turn it.

This book is concerned with the better, more creative side of the American movie industry. Without doubt the scandals, the expensive flops, star tantrums, and other turmoil typical of what is now fashionably and derisively termed 'Tinseltown' make more entertaining reading; but here I am attempting to redress the balance somewhat by discussing just over two hundred and fifty of Hollywood's finest films, true classics which make a genuine contribution to the world of fine art.

In reviewing a new anthology of Romantic poetry in *The Sunday Times*, 6 June 1993, A.S. Byatt explains how artistic canons have been formed in literature: "However minor poems may be rendered interesting by contexts, or however well-known poems may be seen in fresh lights, it is possible to recognise great art." Meeting once more the great poems of the great Romantic poets in a comprehensive anthology "makes us understand how canons were formed, and why certain works last and stay alive." Reading this, it occurs to me that what I have been doing in this collection is describing the formation of a collectively derived (certainly not entirely personal) canon of Hollywood films.

This book takes, as the late Basil Wright did in his marvellous history of the cinema (1974), the 'Long View'. In these days of rampant media hype, it is easy to be carried away by the immediate response of journalists of all kinds to films about to be generally released, apart from the mostly irrelevant gossip and articles of human interest that proliferate around them. It is only after a short period of waiting, while the media are concentrating just as intently and just as ephemerally on some new releases, that one can begin to make judgements on the possible lasting value of any one particular film. Many of today's acknowledged classics made little impact when first released, and certainly did not always make a profit at the box office: the list is full of 'sleepers'. Nevertheless, the message is (to those who enjoy not only seeing new films but re-seeing good old ones): "Go on looking for classics!" They seem just as contemporary today as when they were made – in some cases, even more so.

Looking for Classics

Looking for film classics is a perennially fascinating pursuit. In October 1989 David Robinson, the critic and film historian, discussed "classifying the classics" in *The Times*, saying that there was "currently a rage for naming film classics". During the Tokyo Film Festival of that year a gathering of film historians from all over the world attempted to define a film classic for the purposes of preservation and promotion.

Ever since its twentieth anniversary in 1952, the British Film Institute magazine *Sight and Sound* has invited a large international selection of film critics to select their top ten choices from the whole of world film; and it has generally been recognised that an objective assessment is virtually impossible. Bob Baker of *Film Dope* suggested in 1982 that there might be two hundred and forty-seven movies tying for first place, while Gavin Millar, the then critic for the now defunct *Listener*, noted: "I dare say everyone says the same, but there could be a different, equally heartfelt, ten tomorrow."

In the 1992 *Sight and Sound* Top Ten survey published in December of that year, some one hundred directors were also consulted, in addition to the one hundred and thirty critics or so as in the 1982 inquiry. More significant than the collective resulting Top Ten – in which *Citizen Kane* still tops the poll (the directors' as well as the critics'), as it has from 1962 – is the wide range of choice in both lists, which feature many, if not most, of the films in this collection. *Vertigo* and *The Searchers* were both included in the critics' lists for 1982 and 1992, and *Vertigo* is included in the directors' list for 1992.

Singin' in the Rain and *The General* both appeared in the 1982 list, replaced in 1992 by *The Godfather* and *The Godfather II*. It must be remembered that this is a survey of world opinion on world film: selection of Hollywood movies at this level is a high compliment to the respect in which the best of Hollywood film-making is universally held.

Nevertheless, there were, as in 1982, several pungent comments on the subjectivity of the exercise. John Harkness, a Canadian critic, states: "This is how I think today. The list might be different next week." The views of Chris Marker, the French director ("My list, had I time to think of it, would vary from one minute to the next, among the hundreds of films that at one moment, for one reason or another, generally another, were of utmost importance to me"), seem to be reflected in those of Martin Scorsese, the American director: "I can only give five, because even just one more than that opens the floodgates to countless other films."

In this book I have attempted the virtually impossible, restricting myself to the output of Hollywood. I had become somewhat weary of the continual denigration of 'Tinseltown' and its inferior products, of which there are certainly thousands of examples, and the failure to point out the great mass of high-quality films produced by the skill and talent of their many makers of all kinds – directors, performers, cinematographers, cutters, designers, special effects teams, even producers. I attempted to find a value system that would reflect the current reputation of any film, whenever it was made or released. I have described this system in a later section entitled 'Method of Selection' (page xii). There are some difficulties in attributing certain numerical values to entries that were ungraded; but on the whole the method was reasonably objective – in fact, several of the entries I would not have included myself. But as most of the published collections of classics are based on a fundamentally subjective choice, I consider this a great advantage to my method of calculation. The results are published on pages xv and xviii. The chief surprise – mainly because I made the number of showings at the British National Film Theatre from 1975 to 1994 (inclusive) one of my criteria for selection – is that *Chinatown* has tentatively displaced *Citizen Kane* from the lead it has usually retained since 1962. The difference is marginal, however, and does not represent a serious slump in *Citizen Kane*'s reputation. In comparison with the British Film Institute's 1982 list of three hundred and sixty films compiled for the opening of MOMI (the Museum of the Moving Image), as reported by David Robinson in his 1989 article, the list discussed in this book does greater justice to John Huston, who is represented by four major films as director-screenwriter – *The Maltese Falcon*, *The Treasure of the Sierra Madre*, *The Asphalt Jungle* and *The Red Badge of Courage*; as director alone – *Fat City*; as co-screenwriter – *High Sierra*; with an uncredited writing contribution – *The Killers*, 1946, and two performances – *The Treasure of the Sierra Madre* and *Chinatown*.

Method of Selection

The appeal of a true film classic endures, and, like any other enduring work of art, it retains a cutting edge as sharp as any diamond's. A previous attempt at a search for the Hollywood classics had one serious defect: it was based on the establishment of a movie's reputation on sources that have themselves now largely faded from public view. Very recently, there has been the publication of several new assessments to use as criteria to judge a film's current reputation (1996):

- Nicholas Thomas (Ed): *The International Dictionary of Films & Filmmakers* (St James Press, 1990) – the updated version of the *Macmillan Dictionary of Films and Filmmakers*
- Barry Norman: *The 100 Best Films of the Century* (Chapmans, 1992)
- James Monaco *et al.*: *The Virgin Film Guide* (1st Edition, 1992, now already in its 5th Edition, 1996 – claiming to be the "most up-to-date" film guide and using the comprehensive data provided by BASELINE, "the information service for the worldwide entertainment industry")
- The 1992 search by *Sight and Sound* for the world's ten greatest films already mentioned
- Derek Winnert: *Radio Times' Film & Video Guide for 1994* (Hodder & Stoughton, 1993 – massive, practically all-inclusive and very reliable in its gradings)
- David Quinlan: *TV Times' Film & Video Guide* for 1994 (Mandarin Paperbacks, 1993) (now available in a 1996 edition)
- Leonard Maltin: *Movie & Video Guide 1997* Edition (Signet, 1996, the most recent annual revision of a useful publication which first started in 1968)

- *The Motion Picture Guide* (Jay Robert Nash & Stanley Ralph, Ross: Eds) has continued to publish annual extensions, usually employing the same grading system
- John Pym (Ed): *The Penguin Time Out Film Guide* (4th Edition, 1995)

As each of these sources uses different grading systems, I decided, in the interests of consistency, to find the average rating from the five guides as follows:

- *Maltin & Quinlan*, where the maximum rating is 4 points, I allocated points as follows:

    for 4 stars, 1 point   for 3½ stars, .88

    for 3 stars, .75   for 2½ stars, .63

    for 2 stars, .5

- *Winnert, Monaco & Nash-Ross*, where the maximum is 5:

    for 5 stars, 1 point   for 4½ stars, .9

    for 4 stars, .8   for 3½ stars, .7

    for 3 stars, .6   for 2½ stars, .5

    for 2 stars, .4

For inclusion as an individual item in the *St James Press Dictionary* and in *Barry Norman's 100 BEST* I allocated the score of 1.2 points each.

For inclusion in the lists provided to the *Sight and Sound* searches for the *World's Ten Best*:

    for 1982 alone, 1 point

    for 1992 alone, 1.2

    for 1982 and 1992, 1.4

I then evaluated the assessment in the *Penguin Time Out Guide*, 1995 Edition, and the *Variety Movie Guide, 1994* (which are ungraded) in a similar way.

Finally, for each showing at the British National Film Theatre between January 1975 and December 1994 (inclusive), I allocated a bonus of .01 points.

Calculation for the Top Choice, *Chinatown*

Inclusion in the *St James Press Dictionary*	1.2 points
Inclusion in the Barry Norman compendium	1.2
Inclusion in both *Sight and Sound* Surveys	1.4
Maltin****	1.0
Quinlan***	0.75
Winnert*****	1.0
Monaco*****	1.0
Nash-Ross*****	1.0
PTOG	1.0
VMG	1.0
Total	10.55 |//
Average	= 1.055
Add .44 for showings at the NFT	0.44
Grand Total	1.495

Order of Selection – The Lander Scale

Within groups, the films are given in order of grading:

1.40 (+)	*Chinatown, Citizen Kane, Singin' in the Rain*
1.30 (+)	*Some Like It Hot, Stagecoach*
1.29 (+)	*A Night at the Opera*
1.28 (+)	*Casablanca, Double Indemnity*
1.27 (+)	*The Wisard of Oz*
1.25 (+)	*Forty-Second Street*
1.23 (+)	*The Searchers*
1.22 (+)	*Greed, Sunrise, On the Waterfront, Taxi Driver*
1.20 (+)	*King Kong, Meet Me in St Louis, The Big Sleep, High Noon*
1.19 (+)	*The Wild Bunch, The Grapes of Wrath, Psycho*
1.18 (+)	*The Magnificent Ambersons, All About Eve, Red River*
1.16 (+)	*Manhattan*
1.15 (+)	*Rio Bravo, Laura, Love Me Tonight, The Maltese Falcon, Top Hat*
1.14 (+)	*Rear Window, From Here to Eternity, Raging Bull, Bringing Up Baby, The Godfather Part II*
1.13 (+)	*The Adventures of Robin Hood, The Godfather, It Happened One Night*
1.12 (+)	*Annie Hall, Gone with the Wind, To Be Or Not To Be, North by Northwest, All Quiet on the Western Front*
1.11 (+)	*Ninotchka, The Gold Rush, Nashville, The Philadelphia Story, His Girl Friday*
1.10 (+)	*Duck Soup, Sunset Boulevard, Sullivan's Travels, Queen Christina, Vertigo, It's a Wonderful Life, Out of the Past*

1.09 (+)   *The Band Wagon, The General, Modern Times, Bonnie and Clyde*

1.08 (+)   *Apocalypse Now, Touch of Evil, Fort Apache, The Bride of Frankenstein*

1.07 (+)   *Ride the High Country, My Darling Clementine, The Best Years of Our Lives, The Birth of a Nation, Paths of Glory*

1.06 (+)   *The Night of the Hunter, The Public Enemy, White Heat, The Asphalt Jungle, Camille*

1.05 (+)   *The Deer Hunter, In a Lonely Place, On the Town, A Star Is Born, E.T., The Lady Eve, Days of Heaven, Mildred Pierce, The Treasure of the Sierra Madre*

1.04 (+)   *She Wore a Yellow Ribbon, West Side Story, Rebecca, The Big Heat, Blade Runner*

1.03 (+)   *Murder My Sweet, The Lost Weekend, Scarface, Mean Streets, A Streetcar Named Desire, The Outlaw Josey Wales, Invasion of the Body Snatchers, The Big Parade*

1.02 (+)   *Limelight, The Bank Dick, Frankenstein, Marnie, Notorious*

1.01 (+)   *Gentlemen Prefer Blondes, Witness, Missing, Seven Brides for Seven Brothers, The Kid, Shane, Intolerance, Jaws, Mutiny on the Bounty, Shadow of a Doubt, Trouble in Paradise, Bad Day at Black Rock, Hannah and Her Sisters, The Apartment, How Green Was My Valley, Our Hospitality, Pinocchio, Snow White and the Seven Dwarfs*

1.00 (+)   *Mr Smith Goes to Washington, The Graduate, Strangers on a Train, An American in Paris, The Hustler, The Lost Horizon, The Shop Around the Corner, The Last Picture Show, Nothing Sacred*

0.99 (+)   *Letter from an Unknown Woman, They Were Expendable, Ben-Hur, The Birds, City Lights, Rebel without a Cause, I Am a Fugitive from a Chain Gang, Cabaret, The Postman Always Rings Twice, The Thin Man, Gunga Din, Written on the Wind, The Crowd, The Quiet Man*

0.98 (+)   *Body Heat, The Informer, Queen Kelly, The Gold Diggers of 1933, The Navigator, The Old Dark House, David Copperfield, The Manchurian Candidate, To Have and*

	Have Not, Star Wars, Sweet Smell of Success, Dinner at Eight, Mr Deeds Goes to Town, The Awful Truth, Who Framed Roger Rabbit?
0.97 (+)	They Live by Night, The Conversation, The Palm Beach Story, The Shootist, Stage Door, Giant, The King of Comedy, Only Angels Have Wings, The Wind, It's a Gift, One Flew over the Cuckoo's Nest, Swing Time, Fat City, The Ghost and Mrs Muir, All the President's Men, American Graffiti, Close Encounters of the Third Kind, Wuthering Heights
0.96 (+)	Kiss Me Deadly, Dodsworth, Patton, Sherlock Jr., To Kill a Mockingbird, Little Caesar, Wagonmaster, The Miracle of Morgan's Creek, She Done Him Wrong, Twelve o'Clock High, Broken Blossoms, Anatomy of a Murder, Beauty and the Beast, Sons of the Desert
0.95 (+)	Five Easy Pieces, Kramer vs Kramer, Rosemary's Baby, Fury, Raiders of the Lost Ark, The Oxbow Incident, The Right Stuff, Crossfire, The Miracle Worker, Shanghai Express, Adam's Rib, Dumbo, East of Eden, Fantasia, The Little Foxes, America, America, The Good Earth
0.94 (+)	Cat People, Yankee Doodle Dandy, The Scarlet Empress, The Great Dictator, The Southerner, Twelve Angry Men, Way Out West, Gilda, Bambi, Gigi, The Bad and the Beautiful, The Pirate, Spellbound
0.93 (+)	Amadeus, Born Yesterday, The Hunchback of Notre Dame, M*A*S*H, Salvador, The Sea Hawk, The Silence of the Lambs, The Cameraman, All the King's Men, Play Misty for Me, The Man Who Shot Liberty Vallance, The Prisoner of Zenda, Destry Rides Again, Grand Hotel, High Sierra, The Lady from Shanghai
0.92 (+)	Funny Face, The Merry Widow, Of Mice and Men, Mary Poppins, The Killers, The Red Badge of Courage, Young Mr Lincoln, Gun Crazy, Kiss Me Kate, Ace in the Hole, Witness for the Prosecution, Long Day's Journey into Night, Baby Doll
0.918	Do the Right Thing, The Naked City

Schindler's List is also included

Order of Selection – Hollywood's Top Two-Fifty (by genres)

The number in brackets after the name of the film represents the grading order in the total selection (1–250)

Criminal Investigations (Thrillers)
Chinatown (1)
Double Indemnity (8)
The Big Sleep (18)
Laura (28)
The Maltese Falcon (30)
Rear Window (32)
Vertigo (54)
Touch of Evil (62)
In a Lonely Place (76)
Murder My Sweet (89)
Witness (103)
The Thin Man (138)
Kiss Me Deadly (176)
Anatomy of a Murder (187)
Crossfire (197)
Spellbound (219)
The Silence of the Lambs (226)
The Lady from Shanghai (235)
Witness for the Prosecution (246)
The Naked City (250)

Biographical films ('Biopics')
Citizen Kane (2)
Patton (178)
Amadeus (220)
Young Mr Lincoln (242)

Musicals
Singin' in the Rain (3)
The Wisard of Oz (9)
Forty-Second Street (10)
Meet Me in St Louis (17)
Love Me Tonight (29)
Top Hat (31)
The Band Wagon (51)
On the Town (77)
West Side Story (85)
Gentlemen Prefer Blondes (102)
Seven Brides for Seven Brothers (105)
An American in Paris (123)
Cabaret (136)
The Gold Diggers of 1933 (146)
Swing Time (169)
Yankee Doodle Dandy (208)
Gigi (216)
The Pirate (218)
Funny Face (236)
The Merry Widow, 1934 (237)
Mary Poppins (239)
Kiss Me Kate (244)

The Great Clowns (Comedy)
Some Like It Hot (4)
A Night at the Opera (6)
Manhattan (26)
Annie Hall (40)
The Gold Rush (46)
Duck Soup (50)
The General (58)
Limelight (97)
The Bank Dick (98)
The Kid (106)
Our Hospitality (117)
City Lights (133)
The Navigator (147)
It's a Gift (167)

Sherlock Jr. (179)
Sons of the Desert (189)
Way Out West (213)
The Cameraman (227)

Westerns
Stagecoach (5)
The Searchers (11)
High Noon (19)
The Wild Bunch (20)
Red River (25)
Rio Bravo (27)
Fort Apache (63)
Ride the High Country (65)
My Darling Clementine (66)
She Wore a Yellow Ribbon (84)
The Outlaw Josey Wales (94)
Shane (107)
Bad Day at Black Rock (113)
The Shootist (161)
Wagonmaster (182)
The Oxbow Incident (195)
The Man Who Shot Liberty Vallance (230)
Destry Rides Again (232)

Romantic Adventure (Romance)
Casablanca (7)
Out of the Past (56)
To Have and Have Not (151)
Only Angels Have Wings (165)
Shanghai Express (199)

Gilda (214)

Social Realism (Drama)
Greed (12)
On the Waterfront (14)
The Grapes of Wrath (21)
The Treasure of the Sierra Madre (83)
Mean Streets (92)
The Good Earth (206)
The Crowd (141)
The Southerner (211)

Romantic Drama (Romance)
Sunrise (13)
Gone with the Wind (41)
Camille (74)
Rebecca (86)
Letter from an Unknown Woman (127)
Queen Kelly (145)
The Wind (166)
Dodsworth (177)
Broken Blossoms (186)

Social Allegory (Drama)
Taxi Driver (15)
It's a Wonderful Life (55)

Horror and Monster Movies
King Kong (16)
Psycho (22)

The Bride of Frankenstein (64)
Frankenstein (99)
Jaws (109)
The Birds (132)
The Old Dark House (148)
Rosemary's Baby (192)
Cat People (207)

Family Tensions (Drama II)
The Magnificent Ambersons (23)
Mildred Pierce (82)
How Green was My Valley (116)
Written on the Wind (140)
Giant (163)
Kramer vs Kramer (191)
East of Eden (202)
The Little Foxes (204)
America, America (205)
Long Day's Journey into Night (247)

The Theatre and the Media (Drama III)
All About Eve (24)
Sweet Smell of Success (153)
Ace in the Hole (245)

War Films
From Here to Eternity (33)
All Quiet on the Western Front (44)
Apocalypse Now (61)

Paths of Glory (69)
The Deer Hunter (75)
The Big Parade (96)
They Were Expendable (130)
Twelve o'Clock High (185)
The Red Badge of Courage (241)

The Boxing Ring and the Pool Room (Drama III)
Raging Bull (34)
The Hustler (124)
Fat City (170)

Screwball and Sex Comedy
Bringing Up Baby (35)
It Happened One Night (39)
Ninotchka (45)
His Girl Friday (49)
The Lady Eve (80)
The Awful Truth (156)
The Palm Beach Story (160)
She Done Him Wrong (184)
Adam's Rib (200)
Born Yesterday (221)

Gangster Melodrama (Thrillers)
The Godfather Part II (36)
The Godfather (38)
Bonnie and Clyde (60)
The Public Enemy (71)

White Heat (72)
The Asphalt Jungle (73)
The Big Heat (87)
Scarface (91)
Little Caesar (181)
High Sierra (234)
The Killers, 1946 (240)
Gun Crazy (248)

Period Pieces (Costume Spectacle)
The Adventures of Robin Hood (37)
Queen Christina (53)
Mutiny on the Bounty, 1935 (110)
Gunga Din (139)
The Scarlet Empress (209)
The Hunchback of Notre Dame (222)
The Sea Hawk (225)
The Prisoner of Zenda (231)

Satirical and Social Comedy
To Be or Not To Be (42)
Sullivan's Travels (52)
Modern Times (59)
The Apartment (115)
The Graduate (121)
Nothing Sacred (128)
Mr Deeds Goes to Town (155)
The Miracle of Morgan's Creek (183)
The Great Dictator (210)
M*A*S*H (223)

Spy Melodrama (Thrillers)
North by Northwest (43)
Notorious (101)
The Manchurian Candidate (150)

Compendium Films
Nashville (47)
Hannah and Her Sisters (114)
Dinner at Eight (154)
Stage Door (162)
Grand Hotel (233)

Romantic Comedy (Romance)
The Philadelphia Story (48)
Trouble in Paradise (112)
The Shop Around the Corner (126)
The Quiet Man (142)
The Ghost and Mrs Muir (171)

'Moviola' (Drama III)
Sunset Boulevard (51)
A Star Is Born, 1954 (78)
The Bad and the Beautiful (217)

Addiction and Rehabilitation (Drama II)
The Best Years of Our Lives (67)
The Lost Weekend (90)

xx

Epics (Costume Spectacle)
Birth of a Nation (68)
Intolerance (108)
Ben-Hur, 1959 (131)

Pursuit and Concern for Social Justice (Drama I)
The Night of the Hunter (70)
I Am a Fugitive from a Chain Gang (135)
The Informer (144)
They Live by Night (158)
Fury (193)
Twelve Angry Men (212)
Of Mice and Men (238)

Science Fiction Films (Fantasy)
E.T. (79)
Blade Runner (88)
Invasion of the Body Snatchers, 1956 (95)
Star Wars (152)
Close Encounters of the Third Kind (174)

The Sex War (Drama II)
Days of Heaven (81)
A Streetcar Named Desire (93)
Baby Doll (248)

Psychological Suspense (Thrillers)
Marnie (100)
Shadow of a Doubt (111)
Strangers on a Train (122)
The Postman Always Rings Twice (137)
Body Heat (143)
The Conversation (159)
Play Misty for Me (229)

Politics (Drama III)
Missing (104)
Mr Smith Goes to Washington (120)
All the President's Men (172)
The Right Stuff (196)
Salvador (224)
All the King's Men (228)

Animated Features
Pinocchio (118)
Snow White and the Seven Dwarfs (119)
Who Framed Roger Rabbit? (157)
Beauty and the Beast (188)
Dumbo (201)
Fantasia (203)
Bambi (215)

Fantasy Adventure (Fantasy)
The Lost Horizon (125)
Raiders of the Lost Ark (194)

Through the Eyes of Youth (Drama II)
The Last Picture Show (127)
Rebel without a Cause (134)
American Graffiti (173)
To Kill a Mockingbird (180)

Literary Adaptations
David Copperfield (149)
Wuthering Heights (175)

Black Comedy Comedy)
The King of Comedy (164)

Prison/Mental Hospital (Drama II)
One Flew over the Cuckoo's Nest (168)

Films of the 'Counter-Culture' (Drama I)
Five Easy Pieces (190)

Ethnic Conflicts (Drama I)
Do the Right Thing (249)

Film-Making as a Group Activity

Since the beginning of movies, the director has played a predominant role in film-making: D.W. Griffith had been "all things to every finished frame of film" (F. Scott Fitzgerald in *The Last Tycoon*). Such successors as von Stroheim, von Sternberg and, later, Hitchcock all exerted strong personal control over all aspects of their product. In a foreword to von Sternberg's autobiography, *Fun in a Chinese Laundry* (Columbus Books, 1987 Edn), Gary Cooper identifies the dictatorial role that directors assumed in the early days of Hollywood:

> he always wore the rather military gear affected by some directors – breeches, leather boots and a scarf round his neck – so that they could be considered superior to the actors, I suppose... Von Sternberg looked on us all as puppets, with himself pulling the strings... he wouldn't worry very much if we didn't read our speeches exactly as they were written. "Get the sense, the feeling," he would say.

Von Sternberg confirmed this in the autobiography itself:

> An actor is chosen for his fitness to externalise an idea of mine, not an idea of his.

Gerald Kaufman (in *My Life in the Silver Screen*) probably speaks for the average film buff when he says:

> Of course, all those frames crammed with credit titles included the names not only of the hair-stylist and make-up artist but also the lighting cameraman, the editor, the composer of the incidental music, the author of the screenplay, the set designer, and all the others without whom a film of quality would not have been possible. I paid no attention to any of that. I got it into my head

that how a film looked, how a film sounded, and how a film moved were the sole responsibility of the director.

Nevertheless, on the production side, as the industry became established, the general experience was more like that described by Gene Fowler in his account of John Barrymore's arrival in Hollywood:

> What he [John Barrymore] did not know at first and what many other Hollywood invaders have to learn, if not to like, was that a motion picture never is the work of one man. It is the collaboration of many persons concerned with the writing of it, the acting in it, the direction, the photography, the editing, and the distribution. One person is able to spoil a motion picture, and this frequently happens somewhere along the line, but it takes many persons to make the production a good one.

Feature films, as visual drama (exciting spectacle!), need a balance of high visual quality with strong dramatic development. The director plays a key role on both sides of the production relationship – on the dramatic side in joint discussions with producer and editor, and on the visual side, with cinematographer and production designer. It is not surprising then that interested viewers refer to movies as if directors have an almost proprietary right over their product, e.g. Orson Welles' *Citizen Kane*, Fred Zinnemann's *High Noon*, Alfred Hitchcock's *Psycho*, and so on.

This became automatic even to the most discerning critic. James Agee, in his review of *The Spiral Staircase* in the *Nation* of 23 March 1946, modified his generally unfavourable remarks by saying:

> Still, the movie is visually clever; and until some member of the Screenwriters' Guild takes care to correct me – neglecting, as I am doing, such nonentities as the set designer, cameraman, and editor – I will mainly credit Robert Siodmak for that; he merely directed the show.

Barry Norman (in *Talking Pictures*, 1987) also finds it convenient to use the director's name

...as a label, if you like, a sort of shorthand. It saves time and space and makes for easy identification... at the same time pointing out that William Goldman, screenwriter of *Butch Cassidy and the Sundance Kid* and of *All the President's Men*,

> positively hates it... "to give attribution to a director as if he wrote it is loony-tunes time and anybody who's ever been around a movie set knows that the director is at the mercy of the star, at the mercy of the studio, at the mercy of the cameraman – everybody's at everybody else's mercy in a movie. And to single out anyone, whether it's the director or the star or the screenwriter is foolishness. Basically, movies are a group activity but no one wants to know that. We all want to think the stars are cute and the directors are terrific and make up all the visuals. But if the directors do the visuals, why do you pay a cameraman 10,000 dollars a week, which is what a top cameraman gets now? It's because they're worth it, not because they say 'Yessir' to the director."

Goldman included in his *Adventures in the Screen Trade*, 1983, an interview with George Roy Hill, the director of *Butch Cassidy and the Sundance Kid*, in which he declared:

> no director with a poor script that is badly cast can make it work through his direction. On the other hand, if he gets the script right and the actors right, then he can invent, then the rest of it is fun.

The limitations to directors' decision-making are many and not always obvious. Lilian Ross, in her fascinating and devastating record (entitled *Picture*), of the making and final distribution of MGM's *The Red Badge of Courage*, brings out the radical changes which could be imposed on a director's work by the producer and editor, often at the behest of the studio:

> "Once the director is through, you can usually do what you want with a picture." He [Gottfried Reinhardt, the producer] sighed and lit the cigar. "When John [Huston, the director] sees the first cut, he may holler like hell," he said.

Of Margaret Booth (MGM's head cutter, who had worked with the 'wonder boy' Irving Thalberg – on whose personality Scott Fitzgerald based his *The Last Tycoon*), Reinhardt was complimentary and deferential at the same time:

> "Margaret really saves me... she won't work this closely on a picture with all the producers. She feels like a mother to me."

John Huston recognised the authority of this 'grey eminence':

> "That's something if this dame says it's good... people put more stock in what she says than anybody else. She's tough as hell."

From another horse's mouth – so to speak – we hear a similar plaint. Michael Powell, in his frank and often provocative first autobiography, *A Life in Movies*, argues that

> it is very difficult for the general public, and even for the informed public, to realize that making a film is an industrial process and it is perfectly possible to edit, alter and present and have a resounding success without the director having anything more to do with the film from the moment he stops shouting at the actors. These are hard words for the new crop of movie brats, but they are true words. Rex Ingram [with whom Powell had started working on films in Nice] didn't like going into the cutting room and he avoided it as much as possible. Grant Whytock [the editor] told me the other day: "We never allowed directors into the cutting room". Even David Lean, who in my opinion is the greatest editor since D.W. Griffith, would prefer not do the first cut on one of his own great films.

The contribution of the editor to the quality of the final product is too often neglected. Charlton Heston, whose journals from 1956 to 1976, entitled *An Actor's Life*, give a fascinatingly detailed study of day-to-day work on many of the films in which he performed, is very definite on this point:

You have to work in film quite a while before you understand the subtle and shifting responsibility shared by actor, director and editor for the performance finally seen on the screen... It depends in part on the talents and creative authority each of these has, as well as the complexity of the role. Some parts, Shakespeare's for example, absolutely require an initially good performance to work at all. Others, well directed and edited, require from the actor only a chemically effective image on the screen. In any case, you can never tell, watching on the floor during shooting or looking at the dailies, how it will turn out in its final form.

Dede Allen (editor of *Bonnie and Clyde*), also in interview with William Goldman, indicated how editing works, in collaboration with the other processes of film-making:

> It's taking a story, which has been photographed from many different angles, and very often in many different takes, and making it play in the best possible way it can...

James Mason in his autobiography *Before I Forget* describes how he went in briefly for production, and discusses the wider problems of film craftsmanship, among them the necessary collaboration between director and cinematographer, and between director, cinematographer and set designer:

> ...the main function of a director is not to figure out from which angles a sequence may best be photographed nor to figure out which lenses should be used... but it is just as well for the director to develop these skills in case his cameraman is not very bright. No, his main function is to conspire with the actors to create a true happening, to see that there is a common understanding of the value of each sequence and to see that it is expressed with complete credibility as if happening for the first time. Then let the cameraman decide how best to record this happening... It goes without saying that both director and cameraman in consultation with the set

designer have a clear knowledge of the essential basic angles which can be used in each succeeding set...

In directing one of his first films for Gaumont-British in 1934 – *The Night of the Party* – Michael Powell learnt one lesson which was 'plus', a piece of advice from Glen MacWilliams, the veteran American cinematographer:

> He was highly professional. I had been used to doing everything for myself and pushing the unit around at top speed, afraid I couldn't get what I wanted. We fell over each other several times on the first day. Finally he caught me by the arm as I rampaged by. "Mickey! I want a word with you," he said. A word? and lose five seconds? I visibly champed at the bit. He looked at me quizzically. "We've both a job to do and we don't want to get in each other's way. OK?" I saw his point. I said it was OK. I was in a different league. I had learnt my lesson.

In special cases, e.g. *Frankenstein, The Bride of Frankenstein, Jaws, Star Wars, Who Framed Roger Rabbit?*, the make-up and special effects experts make original and inventive contributions which are vital to the quality of the movie. Since what Peter Bogdanovich has called the 'juvenilisation' of the movies (see Barry Norman, *Talking Pictures*), special effects have become the 'be-all and end-all' of the great family blockbusters of recent years. Their creators have become as essential to the production unit as any other member during the golden age of studio production.

A propos Gene Fowler's earlier remark concerning the ability of one person to spoil a movie, this is done most frequently by the superimposition of a totally inappropriate musical score upon the final work; there are examples of this even in this collection of generally superior movies. Effective dramatic scenes may be reduced to over-obvious sentimentality; violent and action scenes adequately conveyed in visual terms may be unnecessarily, even grossly, overemphasised. On the other hand, with proper co-ordination exercised by the director and the producer, collaboration among the leading artists and technicians can produce first-rate works of cinematic art.

In the preface to *The Making of 'Citizen Kane'* (John Murray, 1985), Robert L. Carringer states that he is attempting "to show that the collaborative process provides the best framework for understanding the remarkable achievement that this film represents." Later he points out that it was "especially crucial" for Welles "to have the best talent" in key positions.

> In the making of *Citizen Kane*, he was fortunate to have collaborators who were well qualified, in some instances gifted, and in a few cases truly inspired. *Citizen Kane* is not only Hollywood's greatest film, but it is also, I contend, Hollywood's single most successful instance of collaboration. In a very real sense, the two propositions are synonymous.

The Entries

All the best successes of Hollywood, at least until the 60s, were in the conscious creation of *genres* – slapstick comedy, screwball comedy, 'weepies', Westerns, epics, romance, adventure, gangster movies, horror movies, musicals, spy and combat movies. All these are immediately recognisable to the reader. I have collected like with like, related them briefly to the general development of the genre or sub-genre, then listed them, according to whether they were in black and white or in colour, in alphabetical order.

Under each film entry, I have given a list of leading credits.[1] This is fuller than those given in most books of reference, for it gives the names of art directors/production designers and editors, and a more extended cast list than usual. In this way, credit is not given only to the stars and main character players but also to a host of first-rate, often type-cast, lesser performers who formed the regular stock company of the leading studios. I firmly believe that all the best movies are those made by inspired group work.

I then give an idea of the generally high, though undoubtedly changing, *assessments* of the film in the course of its life (or as Jonathan Miller once called it, its 'after-life'). First comes an example of the kind of review (American or British) that each film received on release. These are not necessarily typical, and are even sometimes downright unfavourable; however, I believe they give some idea of the critical atmosphere of the time, in many cases over twenty years ago, and sometimes as many as fifty or sixty years ago. These critics have also often noticed qualities contributing to the film's lasting value.

---

[1] Film company names have been abbreviated:

AA = Allied Artists; Col = Columbia; MGM = Metro-Goldwyn-Mayer; Par = Paramount; Rep = Republic; RKO = RKO-Radio; TCF = Twentieth Century-Fox; UA = United Artists; Un = Universal; WB = Warner Brothers

Next, I give a selection of current gradings as an indication of the movie's present reputation (1996). To save space, I have coded the author and title; I hope that, with use, these will become instantly recognisable:

StJD   Nicholas Thomas (Ed): *The International Dictionary of Films and Film-makers* (St James Press, 1990)

BN92   Barry Norman: *The 100 Best Films of the Century* (Chapmans, 1992)

S&S82/92   *Sight and Sound*'s 1982 and 1992 searches for the 10 greatest films

LM   Leonard Maltin: *TV Movies and Video Guide, 1997* Edition, Signet, 1996)

DQ   David Quinlan: *'TV Times' Film & Video Guide, 1997* (Mandarin, 1996)

DW   Derek Winnert: *'Radio Times' Film & Video Guide, 1994* (Hodder & Stoughton, 1993)

VFG   James Monaco et al.: *The Virgin Film Guide* (2nd Edition, 1993) (now in 5th Edition, 1996)

MPG   Jay Robert Nash & Stanley Ralph Ross: *The Motion Picture Guide*, from 1985 to date

'Recommendations' under Current Recommendations and Ratings consist of inclusion in the *St James Dictionary* (StJD), the Barry Norman compendium (BN92), and in the *Sight and Sound* surveys of 1982 and 1992 (S&S82/92); and high ratings from the guides: Maltin (LM maximum 4), Quinlan (DQ – maximum 4), Winnert (DW – maximum 5), Monaco (VFG – maximum 5), and Nash-Ross (MPG – maximum 5)

As an example, I give the entry for *Citizen Kane*:

StJD BN92 S&S82/92 LM4 DQ4 DW5 VFG5 MPG5.

I also give an indication of the number of British Film Institute (National Film Theatre) showings:

NFT* =1–9   NFT** =10–19   NFT*** =20–29   NFT**** = 30+

(*Citizen Kane* NFT****)

Finally, for comparison with criticism on release, I give an extract from the summaries and assessments in the *Penguin Time Out Film Guide* (1995 Edition, edited by John Pym), contributed by a group of rigorous, often abrasive, critics who can confirm (or not) the classic status of a film by recognising its enduring qualities.

References Quoted in the Text

General

Don Allen (ed.), *The Book of the Cinema* (Chris Milsome, 1979)
George Bluestone, *Novels into Film* (Johns Hopkins Press, 1957)
Robert L. Carringer, *The Making of 'Citizen Kane'* (John Murray, 1985)
Alastair Cooke (ed.), *Garbo and the Nightwatchman* (rev. edn, Secker & Warburg, 1971)
William Goldman, *Adventures in the Screen Trade* (Macdonald, 1983)
Gerald Kaufman, *My Life in the Silver Screen* (Faber & Faber, 1985)
Lew Keyser, *Hollywood in the Seventies* (Tantivy Press)
Barry Norman, *Talking Pictures* (BBC Books/Hodder & Stoughton, 1987)
Gerald Peary and Roger Shatzkin, *The Modern American Novel and the Movies* (Frederick Ungar, 1978)
Ken Wlaschin, *Bluff Your Way in the Cinema* (Wolfe Publishing Ltd, 1969, reprinted 1974)

Genres

Ivan Butler, *Horror in the Movies* (A.S. Barnes/Thomas Yoseloff, 1979 edn)
Philip French, *Westerns* (Secker & Warburg/BFI, 1977)
Colin McArthur, *Underworld U.S.A.* (Secker & Warburg, 1972)
Robert Ottoson, *A Reference Guide to the American Film Noir, 1940-55* (Methuen/Scarecrow Press, 1981)
Alain Silver and Elizabeth Ward (eds) *Film Noir* (Secker, 1980)

Directors

M.A. Anderegg, *William Wyler* (Twayne, Boston 1979)
Peter Bogdanovich, *John Ford* (Studio Vista, 1968)

Tom Milne, *Rouben Mamoulian* (Thames & Hudson, 1969)
Andrew Sinclair, *John Ford* (Dial Press/James Wade, 1979)
François Truffaut and Helen Scott, *Hitchcock* (Secker & Warburg, 1968)
Josef von Sternberg, *Fun in a Chinese Laundry* (Columbus Books, 1987)

Studios

John Douglas Eames, *The MGM Story* (Octopus, 1975) [2]
Lilian Ross, *Picture* (Gollancz, 1953)
Richard Schickel, *The Disney Version* (Pavilion/ Michael Joseph, rev. edn, 1986)

Miscellaneous

F. Scott Fitzgerald, *Notes On 'The Last Tycoon'* (Grey Walls Press, 1949)
Gene Fowler, *Goodnight, Sweet Prince – The Life and Times of John Barrymore* (Hammond, Hammond & Co., 1949)
Charlton Heston, *The Actor's Life, Journals 1956-76* (Allen Lane, 1979)

---

[2] The first of a copiously illustrated series of OCTOPUS publications giving a chronological account of the total output of various Hollywood studios:
  Clive Hirschhorn's *The Warner Brothers Story*, 1979
  Richard B. Jewell and Vernon Harbin's *The RKO Story*, 1982
  Clive Hirschhorn's *The Universal Story*, 1983
  Ronald Bergan's *The United Artists Story*, 1986
  Clive Hirschhorn's *The Columbia Story*, 1989

Other Useful References

Film Histories

David Cook, *A History of Narrative Film* (Norton & Co, New York, 1981)
Peter Cowie, *A Concise History of the Cinema*, Vols 1 & 2 (Zwemmer-Barnes, 1971)
Peter Cowie, *Eighty Years of Cinema* (The Tantivy Press, 1977)
Thorold Dickinson, *A Discovery of Cinema* (Oxford University Press, 1971)
Jack C. Ellis, *A History of Film* (Prentice-Hall Inc, 1979)
Keith Reader, *The Cinema – A History* (Teach Yourself Books, 1979)
Eric Rhode, *A History of the Cinema from its origins to 1970* (Allen Lane, 1976, paperback edn 1978)
David Robinson, *World Cinema – A Short History* (Eyre Methuen, 1973)
Paul Rotha (with Richard Griffith), *The Film Till Now* (Spring Books, 1967)
Basil Wright, *The Long View* (Secker & Warburg, 1974)

Critical Works

Roy Armes, *Film and Reality* (Pelican Books, 1974)
Raymond Durgnat, *Films and Feelings* (Faber & Faber, 1967)
Robert Gessner, *The Moving Image* (Cassell, 1968)
Siegfried Kracauer, *Nature of Film* (Dennis Dobson, 1961)
V.F. Perkins, *Film as Film* (Penguin 1972)
Richard Roud (ed.), *Cinema – A Critical Dictionary*, Vols I & II (Secker & Warburg, 1980)
François Truffaut, *The Films in My Life* (trans. Leonard Mayhew, Simon & Schuster 1978)
Parker Tyler, *Magic & Myth of the Movies* (Secker & Warburg, 1971)
Robin Wood, *Personal Views – Explorations in Film* (Gordon Fraser, 1976)

Specialist Works (with reference to period or special aspects)

John Baxter, *Hollywood in the Thirties* (Tantivy Press, 1968)
John Baxter, *Hollywood in the Sixties* (Tantivy Press, 1972)
Richard Corliss, *Talking Pictures – Screenwriters of Hollywood* (David Charles, 1975)
Gordon Gow, *Hollywood in the Fifties* (Tantivy Press, 1971)
Graham Greene, *The Pleasure Dome* (Secker & Warburg, 1972)
Charles Higham and Joel Greenberg, *Hollywood in the Forties* (Tantivy Press, 1968)
Charles Higham and Joel Greenberg, *The Celluloid Muse* (Angus & Robertson, 1969)
Pauline Kael, *I Lost it at the Movies* (Jonathan Cape, 1966)
Pauline Kael, *Deeper into Movies* (Little, Brown & Co, 1969)
Pauline Kael, *When the Lights Go Down* (Marian Boyars, 1980, 1st edn 1975)
David Robinson, *Hollywood in the Twenties* (Tantivy Press, 1968)

Reference Works with Selected Film Entries (high-powered recommendations)

Anne Bawden (ed.), *The Oxford Companion to Film* (Oxford UP, 1976)
William Bayer, *The Great Movies* (Hamlyn, 1973)
Leslie Halliwell, *The Filmgoers' Companion* (Granada, 8th Edn, 1984)
Pauline Kael, *Kiss Kiss – Bang Bang* (Calder & Boyars, 1970)
Christopher Lyon (ed.), *The Macmillan Dictionary of Films and Filmmakers*, Vol. 1 – *Films* (Macmillan, 1984)
Danny Peary, *Guide for the Film Fanatic* (Simon & Schuster, 1987)
Roy Pickard, *A Companion to the Movies* (rev. 1979 edn, Frederick Muller)

Acknowledgements

I am indebted to the following publications for quoted extracts of 'Criticism on release',

James Agate, *Around Cinemas – Reviews from* The Tatler (Home & Van Thal, 1946 and 1948)

James Agee, *On Film*, Vol. I (McDowell Obolensky 1958)

George Amberg (ed.), *The New York Times* Film Reviews, (1913-79) (critics Bosley Crowther, Mordaunt Hall, Frank S. Nugent, 'T.M.P.', 'A.D.S.', André Sennwald, 'A.W.', A.H. Walker)

Graham Greene, *The Pleasure Dome* (the Collected Film Criticism, 1935-40, ed. John Russell Taylor), Secker & Warburg, 1972, Oxford paperback, 1980)

Pauline Kael, *Deeper into Movies* – Reviews from *The New Yorker* (Little, Brown & Co, 1969)

Stanley Kauffmann (ed.), *American Film criticism – from the beginnings to* Citizen Kane; Reviews by Heywood Broun, W. Stephen Bush, James Shelley Hamilton, Meyer Levin, Robert E. Sherwood, William Troy, Richard Watts Jr., Edmund Wilson (Liveright, New York, 1972)

Stanley Kauffmann, *A World on Film* – Reviews from *New Republic* (Harper & Row, 1966) and *Figures of Light* – ditto (Harper & Row, 1971)

Pare Lorentz, *Lorentz on Film* – Reviews from *Judge* and *Vanity Fair* (Hopkinson & Blake, New York, 1975)

Paul Rotha (ed.), *Film, Criticism and Caricature – A Selection of contributions by Richard Winnington to the* News Chronicle (Paul Elek, 1975)

Anthony Slide (ed.), *Selected Film Criticism, 1921-30* (The Scarecrow Press, 1982)

François Truffaut, *The Films in My Life - Reviews from Cahiers du Cinema*, trans. Leonard Mayhew, Simon & Schuster, 1978)

Robert Wilson (ed.), *The Film Criticism of Otis Ferguson - Reviews from The New Republic* (Temple University Press, 1971)

I am also indebted to the following archives for access to past issues of journals and periodicals:

The British Film Institute Library (reviews in *Film Weekly* by John Gammie, Leonard Wallace et al.; in *The Monthly Film Bulletin* by 'P.T.D.'; in *Picturegoer* by Lionel Collier, Margaret Hinxman et al.; and in *Sight and Sound* by John Gillett, Du Pré Jones and Herman G. Weinberg)

City of Westminster Public Reference Library (reviews in *The Observer* by Russell Davies and C.A. Lejeune; in *The Sunday Times* by Gavin Lambert, Dilys Powell and Derek Prouse; and in *The Times* by anonymous critics and David Robinson)

I – Hollywood's Top 250 (1997)[3]

Animated Feature Films

It is apt that this collection should begin with animation (which links film most directly to the other visual arts) and also with the work of the Walt Disney studio: in spite of a certain uneasiness about the full-length Disney cartoon films and Disney's attitudes as a creator and as an employer, it produced an abundance of work of artistic and entertainment value. It has become, quite rightly, more popular to refer to the work of Disney's studio under the heading of the leading artists and animators employed, and we must always remember the wealth of inventive talent and skilful craftsmanship which was poured into the studio's products, apart from the provision of delightful entertainment to the world at large.

When *Bambi* was re-released in March 1986, Philip French declared in *The Observer*: "The quintet of full-length cartoon masterworks – *Snow White*, *Pinocchio*, *Fantasia*, *Dumbo* and *Bambi* that the Disney studios produced between 1938 and 1942 stand high among the finest graphic art of this century." *Snow White and the Seven Dwarfs*, 1938 (the first feature-length cartoon film, still capable of attracting and enchanting large family audiences) has defects, e.g. the figures of Snow White herself and of Prince Charming. Possibly the round cuddly animals that cluster round her in the terrifying dark wood might also represent a certain stereotype, but they do defuse an intensely frightening situation very successfully. But all else still appears superlative in terms of popular art – the marvellous 'Crazy Gang' of the dwarfs, the intricate house-cleaning sequence ('Whistle While You Work'), and the scenes of expressionist Gothic horror, very much in the spirit of the Brothers Grimm.

Disney's second full-length feature released in 1940 – *Pinocchio* – seemed even more impressively brilliant than its predecessor.

---

[3] Throughout, before a name or title, '*' denotes the award of an Oscar.

Technically perfect, it also introduced a new element of frank, often terrifying social allegory, in the experiences of a wooden boy puppet striving to become a real human being. The inevitable sentimentality (in the figures of Geppetto, the old woodcarver, and the Blue Fairy) and whimsicality (Cleo the Goldfish and Jiminy Cricket, Pinocchio's 'official conscience') seemed less cloying than before, and the horror more nightmarish than ever (as in the transformation of the loud-mouthed Lampwick into a braying ass and the brutal journey to Pleasure Island in the custody of the sadistic coachman Stromboli. Perhaps the greatest *tour de force* in animated movement was the pursuit by a monster whale, which exploits all the devices of cinematography through ingeniously planned and perfectly executed animation. In retrospect, *Pinocchio* appears to lose human warmth (and, some say, magic) because of its more intellectual concentration.

Fantasia (the audacious, patchy and sometimes irritating venture into classical music presented by Deems Taylor and Leopold Stokowski, the conductor) can also be faulted in many ways, most particularly in the Beethoven *Pastoral Symphony* sequence, where the figures seem uninspired and even cheap (for example, the female centaurs) and the final church procession set to Bach/Gounod's 'Ave Maria'. The treatment of the music was not consistently acceptable: Richard Schickel (in *The Disney Version*, 1968) records criticisms by Igor Stravinsky, the only living composer interpreted. Nevertheless, there are brilliant, exciting and amusing moments, even episodes:

- Dukas' *Sorcerer's Apprentice*, with Mickey Mouse as the central character (the original concept that sparked off the whole compilation);
- the ostrich and hippopotamus ballet, set to Ponchielli's *Dance of the Hours*;
- the volcanic upheavals of the earth's creation in Stravinsky's *Rite of Spring*;
- the delicate pastel shades of Tschaikowsky's *Dance of the Sugar-Plum Fairy*;
- and the Hieronymus Bosch-like witches' sabbath of Mussorgsky's *Night on Bald Mountain* (known in Britain as *A Night on the Bare Mountain*).

Dumbo (released before *Fantasia*, in 1941, though a later work) was shorter than any other Disney feature and less expensive to make:

nevertheless, it is a perfect feature-length cartoon, with the absolutely right amounts of strong visual narrative, humour, song, fantasy and pathos. The baby elephant who learns to fly with his ridiculously big ears is one of Disney's most endearing characters, and he is surrounded by strongly etched and appealing characters (Timothy Mouse, Jim Crow, Stork and the formidable Ringmaster). Amongst the several fascinating set pieces, the 'Pink Elephant' ballet is outstanding.

Bambi, 1942, was larger in scale and beautifully executed, but, in retrospect, possibly no greater an achievement. Here, once more, Disney returns to the life of the forest, concentrating on a fawn's development into a mature leader through all the trials and tribulations of a motherless childhood and youth. The hero has his perky, self-confident helpmate (as in *Pinocchio* and *Dumbo*, in this case a rabbit called Thumper); and the spectacular set-piece, in this case, is the passage of a thunderstorm through the forest – graphically described both visually and dramatically.

For nearly fifty years after this, the world became accustomed to a regular supply of Disney feature-length cartoons, some veering towards the pasteboard and formulaic, others strikingly original and inventive (although still remaining slightly underrated by critics), but always exceptionally well-crafted and aimed perfectly at the hearts and senses of a world audience. It was not until the release of *Beauty and the Beast* in 1991 that critics began to talk of a kind of Disney renaissance, aided by the new computer technology and the artistic enthusiasm of a new generation of animators and songwriters. Compared with *Snow White* and her Prince Charming, the leading characters are lively and real, developing along with the storyline. The *Virgin Film Guide* beautifully sums up the cinematic quality of the new animation techniques: "Using computer wizardry to simulate live-action film techniques like dollies, track and pans, the animation succeeds in creating an uncannily realistic world." And the technique is more than matched by the liveliness of the artistic invention.

In the course of supplying an astonishing variety of animated films to the world market, the Disney studios had often combined live-action with animation; but there is no doubt that this ambitious mixture of techniques reached its highest point in *Who Framed Roger Rabbit?*, 1988, in which the worlds of humans and 'Toons' are fully integrated through the inspired animation of Richard Williams et al.

and the admirably detailed direction of Robert Zemeckis, in what would appear to most of us to be a heart-breaking task. The achievement of Bob Hoskins, acting his part of a jaundiced private-eye reluctantly coming to the aid of the 'hateful' Toons (in thin air) was also phenomenal. Shame that the final, general impression of the work does not live up to the marvellous quality of the separate ingredients!

Bambi, RKO (Disney), 1942 colour

Direction: David Hand Script: Perce Pearce, Larry Morey
(from story by Felix Salten)
Music: Frank Churchill, Edward Plumb
MDir: Alexander Steinert
Sequence Direction: James Algar, Bill Roberts, Norman Wright, Paul Satterfield, Sam Armstrong, Graham Heid
Animation: Milton Kahl, Eric Larson, Joshua Meador, Franklin Thomas, Oliver M. Johnston, Jr.

with voices of Bobby Stewart (Bambi), Peter Behn (Thumper), Stan Alexander (Flower), Cammie King (Phylline), Donnie Dunagan, Hardie Albright, John Sutherland, Tim Davis, Sam Edwards, Sterling Holloway

- Criticism on release

    ...welcome indeed, a touching and beguiling thing, in the master's most felicitous style. Disney has sought after no new forms, pursued no social allegory here. He is happy and relaxed with the things he does best – sketches of wild life, studies of young animals and their endearing ways..What a showman Disney is! How cunningly he uses his little tunes! How wisely he repeats and varies his formal effects! And how surely his instinct guides him to the closing scene, when he shows us a new fawn in the old glade, and the King Stag, ceding his throne to Bambi for the last curtain-fall!

    C.A. Lejeune, *The Observer* 9 August 1942

- Current recommendations and ratings
  StJD BN92 S&S82 LM3½ DW4 VFG4 MPG4 NFT*

    From Disney's richest period, interleaving splendid animation with vulgar Americana. Babycham images occupy only a fraction of the running time in this tale of the adventures of a fawn; the rest is a strikingly impressionistic version of life in the forest and the meadow...

    Andrew Nickolds, PTOG 1995

Beauty and the Beast, Walt Disney Silver Screens Partner IV (Don Hahn), 1991 *colour*

Direction: Kirk Wise, Gary Tronsdale
Script: Linda Woolverton
Art Direction: Brian McEntee
*Songs: Howard Astiman, Alan Menken
Animation: Roger Allers, Ed Ghertner, Lisa Keene, Vera Lanpher, Randy Fullmer, Jim Hillin
Editing: John Carnochan
with voices of Paige O'Hara (Belle), Robby Benson (Beast), Rex Everhart (Maurice), Richard White (Caston), Jesse Corti (Le Fou), Angela Lansbury (Mrs Potts), Jerry Orbach (Lumiere), David Ogden Stiers (Cogsworth/ Narrator), Bradley Michael Pierce (Chip), Hal Smith (Philippe)

- Criticism on release

    Nine months since it became the first animated feature to be nominated for a Best Picture Oscar, this Disney cartoon proves well worth the wait. Belle bravely supplants her inventor father in the Beast's castle. He may be a beast but he isn't a boor, seducing her with a glorious library. When she returns his love and he returns to humanity, he has the appropriate European look of a young Boris Becker. Everything is animated in this dream movie, from the candles to the clocks, with Angela Lansbury extracting every drop out of her performance as a singing teapot. Rarely has there been such a joyous blend of popular music and carefully crafted pictures in a cartoon.

Iain Johnstone, *Sunday Times* 15 November 1992

- Current recommendations and ratings
S&S92 LM3½ DQ4 VFG4½ MPG4½

Disney animation enters the 90s, embraces the stunning technical advances of computer-generated imagery, and updates the traditional dependent heroine – (Beast's) growing relationship with Belle is infinitely touching. His bewitched castle is enlivened by an antic household including a candelabra with the panache of a French *maître d'*, a neurotic clock, and a mother-and-son teapot and cup. The six musical numbers either reveal character or push the action, with 'Be Our Guest' an outstanding example of cartoon choreography. Dazzlingly good.

Brian Case, PTOG 1995

Dumbo, RKO (Disney), 1941 *colour*

Direction: Ben Sharpsteen Script: Joe Grant, Dick Huemer (from the book by Helen Aberson and Harold Pearl

*Songs: Oliver Wallace, Frank Churchill
Lyrics: Ned Washington

Sequence Direction: Norman Ferguson, Wilfred Jackson, Bill Roberts, Jack Kinney, Sam Armstrong

Animation Direction: Arthur Babbitt, Walt Kelly, Ward Kimball, John Lounsbery, Joshua Meador, Fred Moore, Wolfgang Reitherman, Don Towsley, Vladimir Tytla, Cy Young

with voices of Edward Brophy (Timothy Mouse), Herman Bing (Ringmaster), Verna Felton (Elephant), Sterling Holloway (Stork), Cliff Edwards (Jim Crow)

- Criticism on release

    ...the most genial, the most endearing, the most completely precious cartoon feature film ever to emerge from the magical brushes of Walt Disney's wonder-working artists!... Ladeez and gentlemen, see *Dumbo*, a film you will never forget – Mr Disney has crammed it with countless of [his] fanciful delights, (but very wisely) has held the picture to an hour of running time, which is an excellent concession to young children, and has not let any 'horror stuff' slip in.

    Bosley Crowther, *New York Times* 24 October 1941

- Current recommendations and ratings
  LM4 DQ4 DW4 VFG5 MPG5 NFT*

    One of the best of Disney's animated features. The artwork, of course, is magisterial: aerial views of the States, the erecting of the big top in a storm, and the brilliant drunken vision of pink elephants.

    W. Stephen Gilbert, PTOG 1995

Fantasia, RKO (Walt Disney), 1940 *colour*

Production Supervision: Ben Sharpsteen
Sequence Directors: James Algar (*The Sorcerer's Apprentice*), Samuel Amstrong (*Toccata and Fugue, The Nutcracker Suite*), Ford Beebe (*Pastoral Symphony*, with Jim Handley, Hamilton Luske), Norman Ferguson (*Dance of the Hours*, with T. Hee), Wilfred Jackson (*Night on Bald Mountain*), Bill Roberts (*The Rite of Spring*, with Paul Satterfield)

Animation Supervision: Arthur Babbitt (*Pastoral Symphony*, with Oliver Johnston Jr., Ward Kimball, Eric Larson, Fred Moore, Don Towsley, also co-animation on *The Nutcracker Suite*); Joshua Meador (*The Rite of Spring*, with Wolfgang Reitherman); Fred Moore (*The Sorcerer's Apprentice*, with Vladimir Tytla); Vladimir Tytla (*Night on Bald Mountain*)

Script: Joe Grant, Dick Huemer   Musical Direction: Edward Plumb
Editing: Stephen Csillagwith *Leopold Stokowski (conductor and presenter), Deems Taylor (presenter)

- Criticism on release

    ...as a film for everybody to see and enjoy has as a main weakness an absence of story, of motion, of interest – don't get me wrong – it is one of the strange and beautiful things that have happened in the world... the more didactically elevating side [may be forgotten] in the general delight and splendor of its passage.

    Otis Ferguson, *New Republic*, 25 November 1940

- Current recommendations and ratings
  StJD LM3½ DQ4 DW5 VFG4½ MPG5 NFT*

    Only the Dukas *Sorcerer's Apprentice* sequence achieves a respectable kind of success. For the rest, Disney's attempts at the visual illustration of Beethoven & Co – a dubious exercise, anyway – produce Klassical Kitsch of the highest degree – some great sequences for all that, and not to be missed.

    Geoff Brown, PTOG 1995

Pinocchio, RKO (Disney), 1940 *colour*

Direction: Ben Sharpsteen, Hamilton Luske
Script: Ted Sears, Otto Englander, Webb Smith, William Cottrell, Joseph Sabo, Erdman Penner, Aurelius Battaglia (from story by Carlo Collodi)
*Songs: Leigh Hatline, Ned Washington
Music: Paul Smith
Sequence Direction: Bill Roberts, Norman Ferguson, Jack Kinney, Wilfred Jackson, 'T. Hee' (Disney)
Animation Direction: Fred Moore, Milton Kahl, Ward Kimball, Eric Larson, John Lounsbery, Joshua Meador, Franklin Thomas, Don Towsley, Vladimir Tytla, Arthur Babbitt, Wolfgang Reitherman

with voices of Dickie Jones (Pinocchio), Christian Rub (Geppetto), Cliff Edwards (Jiminy Cricket), Evelyn Venable (The Blue Fairy), Walter Catlett (J. Worthington Foulfellow), Frankie Darro (Lampwick), Charles Judels (Stromboli the Coachman), Don Brodie (Barker)

- Criticism on release

    a delight – at times will take your breath away... The fun is in the adventure and the villains; and these are everywhere and lusty... We stay to laugh and feel good and finally admire; and we go away to marvel.

    Otis Ferguson, *New Republic*, March 1940

- Current recommendations and ratings
  StJD S&S92 LM4 DQ4 DW4 VFG5 MPG5 NFT*

    a rum old mixture of the excellent and the awful... Disney orchestrates his queasy material with some stunning animation of a monster whale thrashing about and much delightful background detail... probably shows Disney's virtues and vices more clearly than any other cartoon.

    Geoff Brown, PTOG 1995

Snow White and the Seven Dwarfs, RKO (Walt Disney), 1938 *colour*

Production Supervision: Dave Hand, Ben Sharpsteen
Animation: James Algar, Arthur Babbitt, Norman Ferguson, Wilfred Jackson, Milton Kahl, Ward Kimball, Eric Larson, Hamilton Luske, Joshua Meador, Fred Moore, Wolfgang Reitherman, Bill Roberts, Franklin Thomas, Vladimir Tytla among many others
Music: Frank Churchill, Leigh Harline, Paul Smith
Songs: Larry Morey, Frank Churchill

with voices of: Adriana Caselotti (Snow White), Harry Stockwell (The Prince), Lucille La Verne (The Queen), Scotty Mattraw (Bashful), Roy Atwell (Doc), Pinto Golvig (Sleepy, Grumpy), Otis Harlan (Happy), Billy Gilbert (Sneezy), Moroni Olsen (The Magic Mirror), Stuart Buchanan (The Queen's Coachman), Marion Darlington (bird sounds), The Fraunfelder Family (yodelling)

- Criticism on release

    a fairy-tale, surely the most vivid and gay and sweet in the world; it is done in color, photographed on different

levels to give depth, and it runs almost an hour and a half. Some of the short cartoons have been more of a riot, some have been more tender even. But this is sustained fantasy, the animated cartoon grown up – the animals of course are as uncannily studied and set in motion as they always have been...
    Otis Ferguson, *New Republic*, 26 January 1938

- Current recommendations and ratings
StJD S&S92 DW5 VFG5 MPG5 NFT*

> ...a generally cute fantasy for American kids – *Snow White* almost unbearably winsome, and the anthropomorphic characterisation of the forest creatures soon becomes tiresome. But the animation itself is top-notch, and in a number of darker sequences... Disney's adoption of Expressionist visual devices makes for genuinely powerful drama...
>   Geoff Andrew, PTOG 1995

Who Framed Roger Rabbit?, Touchstone (Robert Watts/ Frank Marshall), 1988 *colour*

Direction: Robert Zemeckis	Script: Jeffrey Price, Peter Seaman (from the book *Who Censored Roger Rabbit?* by Gary K. Wolf)
Camera: Dean Cundey	
Music: Alan Silvestri	
Animation: Richard Williams	Costume Design: Joanna Johnston

Production Design: Elliot Scott, Roger Cain
*Special Effects: Peter Biggs, Brian Morrison, Roger Nichols, David Watkins, Brian Lince, Tony Dunsterville, Brian Warner
*Editing: Arthur Schmidt

with Bob Hoskins, Christopher Lloyd, Joanna Cassidy, Stubby Kaye, Alan Tilvern, Richard Le Parmentier, Joel Silver, and voices of Charles Fleischer (Roger Rabbit), Kathleen Turner (Jessica Rabbit) and Amy Irving (Jessica's singing voice)

- Criticism on release

    ...of course, the animation is brilliantly done; miraculous skill has gone into the union of human and cartoon action... Nevertheless, even at Christmas, I have to speak for the backward minority. And myself. I find *Who Framed Roger Rabbit?* a deplorable development in the possibilities of animation...

    Dilys Powell, *Sunday Times*, 4 December 1988

    What Roger Rabbit achieves is a totally new concept that breathes life into the cartoon characters with stunning 3-dimensional visual effect... a wonderful movie.

    Peter Tipthorp, *Sunday Express*, 4 December 1988

- Current recommendations and ratings
S&S92 LM3½ DQ4 DW4 VFG3 MPG5 NFT*

    Virtually faultless on the technological front, it also excels in terms of a breathless, wisecracking script, deft characterisation (both human and Toon), and rousing action... Supremely entertaining especially for adults.

    Brian Case, PTOG 1995

Biographical ('Biopics')

The films in this genre have been variously described, from Leslie Halliwell's definition as 'sober' films about the life of a real person to Ken Wlaschin's (in *Bluff Your Way in the Cinema*, 1969) as 'glamorous lies' about a real person. The four films discussed here fall somewhere between the extremes of sobriety and glamour, although there may be elements of both in all of them.

John Ford's *Young Mr Lincoln*, 1939 selects an early episode in the life of a future American president (while he was still a lawyer serving on the Springfield, Illinois, circuit) on which to base an inventive and atmospheric evocation of an imagined American past. Henry Fonda's portrayal, as in *The Grapes of Wrath*, made with Ford in the following year, has ironic quality; and Lamar Trotti's script has an admirable fidelity linked with dramatic power.

Citizen Kane, 1941, is about a 'strictly fictional' character (generally recognised to be based on the newspaper tycoon William Randolph Hearst), identifying almost in an autobiographical manner the writer-director (Orson Welles) with the examination of the social and psychological development of its central character through the somewhat slanted memories of his associates, while showing an investigative journalist trying to solve (unsuccessfully) the mystery of 'Rosebud', the tycoon's only true love. Traditionally leading the list of Hollywood achievements and also rated as one of the world's top films, it is difficult to criticise what has become almost a hallowed object – best merely to stand back, admire and enjoy (again and again).

Franklin Schaffner's *Patton*, 1969, a strong revival of military biography, portrayed a military élitist of the Second World War, played by George C. Scott on the edge of extreme neurosis, but with great charisma and power. Coppola's script never glorifies his 'hero', but from the exhibitionistic haranguing of his troops (obscenities and all) at the very beginning, there is no doubt about Patton's single-minded philosophy of all-out offensive, offset to some extent by the paler, more static portrayal of General Omar Bradley's cautious approach by Karl Malden.

Nigel Andrews in his review of Milos Forman's *Amadeus* (*Financial Times* 18 January) defines films about great artists as of two kinds: the hagiographic and the hell-raising; and finds Amadeus "a hellraiser staged like a hagiography". Among critical circles the main concern was whether the movie could match the magnificence of Peter Shaffer's stage play, particularly as first presented at the National Theatre (London), with Paul Scofield as the resentful Salieri and Simon Callow as the repulsive young Mozart. Forman has lost none of the dramatic power of the original, although Tom Hulce's portrait of Mozart suffers from an unprepossessing American accent and perhaps overdoes the giggling moronic side. F. Murray Abraham's portrayal of Salieri, however, is a triumph – sad, tormented, saturnine – and fortunately dominates the film dramatically. The use of the soundtrack is an added bonus – a glorious feast of music beautifully played, always suited to the dramatic development of the theme and provided in a recognisably faithful portrayal of late 18th-century Viennese musical society (in fact, Forman's own Prague stood in for Vienna as the film's location).

Citizen Kane, RKO (George J. Schaefer/Orson Welles), 1941 *bw*

Direction: Orson Welles
Camera: Gregg Toland
Music: Bernard Herrmann
Costume Design: Edward Stevenson
Art Direction: Van Nest Polglase, Perry Ferguson
Editing: Robert Wise, Mark Robson

*Script: Orson Welles, Herman Mankiewicz
Special Effects: Vernon Walker

with Orson Welles, Dorothy Comingore, Joseph Cotten, Everett Sloane, Ray Collins, Ruth Warrick, Agnes Moorehead, William Alland, George Couloris, Harry Shannon, Paul Stewart, Fortunio Bonanova, Alan Ladd (bit) Arthur O'Connell (bit)

- Criticism on release

> ...an all-round class-A production. But the most effective things in it are the creation of Orson Welles' drawing board, not only in story ideas but in plausible, adult dialogue (witty, sardonic, knowledgeable), the impression of life as it actually goes on in the big world, the ready dramatic vigor...
> Otis Ferguson, *New Republic*, 16 June 1941

- Current recommendations and ratings
  StJD BN92 S&S82/92 LM4 DQ4 DW5 VFG5 MPG5 NFT****

    ...still a marvellous movie. A film that gets better with renewed acquaintance.

    Tom Milne, PTOG 1995

Young Mr Lincoln, TCF (Darryl Zanuck/ Kenneth MacGowan), 1939 bw

Direction: John Ford	Script: Lamar Trotti
Camera: Bert Glennon	Music: Alfred Newman
Art Direction: Richard Day, Mark-Lee Kirk	-
Costume Design: Royer	Editing: Walter Thompson

with Henry Fonda, Alice Brady, Margaret Weaver, Arleen Whelan, Richard Cromwell, Donald Meek, Eddie Quillan, Ward Bond, Spencer Charters, Russell Simpson, Charles Halton, Virginia Brissac

- Criticism on release

    another of the strangely honest movies that this year has produced – John Ford deliberately used a slow drawling tempo to fit the subject... Henry Fonda shares top credit – the story demanded a genuinely rustic clumsiness covered with [a] constant implicit dignity. Well, he did it...

    Otis Ferguson, *New Republic*, 21 June 1939

- Current recommendations and ratings
  StJD LM3½ DQ3 DW3 VFG4 MPG4 NFT*

    This first product of the Ford-Fonda partnership – reputedly a favourite not only of Ford but of Eisenstein too – today commands classic status...

    Sheila Johnston, PTOG 1995

Amadeus, Orion (Saul Zaentz), 1984 *colour*

*Direction: Milos Forman *Script: Peter Shaffer (from his
Camera: Miroslav Ondricek   own play)
Music: Mozart, Salieri, Pergolesi Choreography: Twyla Tharp
Production Design: Patrizia von Brandenstein
Costume Design: Theodor Pistek Editing: Nena Danevic

with *F. Murray Abraham, Tom Hulce, Elizabeth Berridge, Simon Callow, Roy Dotrice, Christine Ebersole, Jeffrey Jones

- Criticism on release

    ...Forman of *Amadeus* seems a man reborn, fully alert to the narrative's cinematic potential and wealth of human idiosyncrasies. So many films lie on the screen today looking shrivelled or inert. *Amadeus* sits there resplendent, both stately and supple, a compelling darkly comic story of human glory and human infamy. Shaffer's adaptation of his original play extends far beyond the routine changes needed to transfer theatre to film... Most important of all, Shaffer's story is now propelled through specifically cinematic means: editing techniques play a crucial part in pointing up ironies, puncturing moods, infusing and counterpointing the musical extracts with the unfolding human drama...
    Geoff Brown, *The Times* 18 January 1985

- Current recommendations and ratings
S&S92 LM4 DQ3 DW4 VFG5 MPG4 NFT*

    ...Salieri emerges as the more tragic and sympathetic character, partly because he alone, of all his contemporaries, can appreciate this almost perfect music, and – more importantly, perhaps – because he speaks up for all of us whose talents fall short of our desires. The entire cast speaks in horribly intrusive American accents, but Forman makes some perceptive connections between Mozart's life and work.
    Clancy Sigal, PTOG 1995

Patton/Patton-Lust for Glory (Frank McCarthy), 1970
colour

*Direction: Franklin Schaffner	*Script: Francis Ford Coppola,
Camera: Fred Koenekamp	Edmund H. North
Music: Jerry Goldsmith	2nd Unit Cameramen: Clifford
	Stine, Cecilio Paniagua
*Editing: Marge Fowler	
*Art Direction: Urie McCleary, Gil Parrando	

with *George C. Scott, Karl Malden, Michael Bates, Karl Michael
  Vogler, Edward Binns

- Criticism on release

    ...awesomely impressive – there's so much land and air – and it's so clear – that we seem to be looking at Patton from God's point of view... And, with the picture to himself, George C. Scott gives it all his intensity and his baleful magnetism. We in the audience don't know any more about Patton when *Patton* is over, but we've had quite an exhibition of winking at the liberals while selling your heart to the hawks.
    Pauline Kael, *New Yorker*, 31 January 1970

- Current recommendations and ratings
  LM4 DQ3 DW4 VFG4½ MPG5 NFT*

    As an exercise in biography... marvellous. The film lays bare the roots of Patton's lust for power in his willingness to sacrifice everything to his vaunting ego, a trait which is mirrored in George C. Scott's superb performance.
    Phil Hardy, PTOG 1995

Comedy (1) – Black Comedy, The Great Clowns, Satirical, and Social Comedy

BLACK COMEDY

Tastes in black comedy seem to vary frequently and periodically, and at the moment the one with the highest reputation is Martin Scorsese's *The King of Comedy*, 1983, which is not particularly typical of the director's work. In *The King of Comedy*, Robert De Niro provides another original portrait in a wide repertory of cinematic roles – this time as a prize nerd, Rupert Pupkin, who, incredibly, considers himself worthy of world fame as a stand-up comic and goes to extremes to secure a place on the celebrated Jerry Langford's chat show. Jerry Lewis, who played numerous such nerds in his early film career, plays Langford with extraordinary, unfunny dignity. Pupkin's assistant in the kidnapping to which he resorts is a crazy rich girl, intent on possessing her idol (Langford) as a love object (played rivetingly by Sandra Bernhard). Although directed by Scorsese, who had co-operated with De Niro on several previous hits, including *Taxi Driver* and *Raging Bull*, the movie was a signal flop on release, but has since gained considerably in reputation.

The King of Comedy, TCF (Arnon Milchan), 1983 *colour*

Direction: Martin Scorsese	Script: Paul Zimmerman
Camera: Fred Schuler	Music: Robbie Robertson
Production Design: Boris Leven	
Costume Design: Richard Bruno	Editing: Thelma Schoonmaker

with Robert De Niro, Jerry Lewis, Dianne Abbott, Sandra Bernhard, Ed Herlihy (as himself)

- Criticism on release

   The film is both fascinating and disturbing in its use of comedy as the primary material for what is essentially a story of horror and deformities of the mind and personality. Rupert, a characteristically studied performance by De Niro, with his loud suits and irrepressible cheeriness, is a monster whose eagerness to ingratiate and amuse inspires by turns pity and distaste.

When he finally gets his chance, and we see his act, it is no longer possible to know whether he is funny or not, only that his comedy material is in essence a confession of personal retardation. If Masha's psychological disturbance (as played by Sandra Bernhard) is more extreme in its manifestations, Jerry Lewis's performance as Langford, the entertainer whose private life is misanthropic seclusion, is hardly less unsettling.
David Robinson, *The Times*, 1 July 1983

- Current recommendations and ratings
StJD S&S92 LM3½ DQ2 DW4 VFG4½ MPG4 NFT**

...definitely not a comedy, despite being hilarious, it pays acute homage to Jerry Lewis, while requiring of the man no hint of slapstick infantilism; its uniquely repellent prize nerd is De Niro himself... Creepiest movie of the year in every sense, and one of the best.
Paul Taylor, PTOG 1995

THE GREAT CLOWNS

Film histories show clearly that comedy has been a 'natural' for the movies ever since its beginning as a commercial art, e.g. Lumière's *L'Arroseur Arrosé* – Watering the Gardener (1896). Silent film comedy had great popular appeal, and directors and actors responded with considerable verve and professional expertise. "The studio was an unrivalled school, of comedy, where directors learned new fluid and editing techniques" (David Robinson on 'The Comedy' in *The Book of the Cinema*, 1979). The personalities of the comedians became increasingly more engaging, and ultimately as important as the gags they used, especially in the work of Charles Chaplin, Buster Keaton, and Harold Lloyd. Until the 1950s Keaton had always appeared secondary to Chaplin, but progressively since then caught up with, and has probably now overtaken, him in reputation. But Lloyd obstinately remains very much the 'third genius' of silent film comedy.

Chaplin's first feature-length film, *The Kid*, 1921, still rates high on the Lander Scale (see Order of Selection, pp xv), a typically beguiling mixture of pathos and visual (slapstick) comedy, self-consciously autobiographical in that its story of the Little Tramp's caring for a five-year-old orphan (played with panache by the infant Jackie Coogan) was prompted by the death of Chaplin's own son while only three days old.

The Kid shows the Little Tramp as foster-father, *The Gold Rush*, 1925, as gold prospector, with an idealised heroine (played by Georgia Hale) replacing the orphan as the main centre of his emotional attention and a large number of classic comedy sequences (including the eating of his old boots with relish). The revised 1942 version includes a soundtrack with an amusing narration by Chaplin himself.

In *City Lights*, 1931 (still using titles, but with a soundtrack of his own music and characteristically quirky sound effects), the Little Tramp appears as a sensitive, respectable member of the Great Unwashed, sacrificing himself for the love of a beautiful young blind girl (played by Virginia Cherrill). Visual comedy still dominates the action and, as usual, is beautifully choreographed.

Keaton's output also developed, from the rural comedy *Our Hospitality*, 1923, to his acclaimed masterpiece *The General*, 1926. After that, with the loss of control of production at United Artists with Joseph M. Schenck, Keaton's work declined in quality, although his first film at MGM, *The Cameraman*, 1928, still finds its way into this list of Hollywood's Top Two-Fifty. In *Our Hospitality*, Keaton inherits property in the feuding South, quixotically falling in love with the daughter of a rival clan. Tom Milne admires the "lovingly detailed background and incredibly beautiful visual textures" of this early comedy, characteristic of later masterpieces such as *The General* (review of *The Navigator*, PTOG 1993).

The Navigator, 1924, is the name of an abandoned luxury-liner on which Keaton, as a wimpish playboy, finds himself with the love of his life and ultimately proves himself, as always, without a smile or glimpse of emotion, as a capable, masculine hero. The secret of Keaton's continuing appeal lies in the inventive detail of his 'sight gags' and their perfect execution, even in a deep-water diving suit.

In the same year *Sherlock Jr.* has a delightfully surreal sequence in which, as a cinema projectionist, Keaton becomes part of the film he is showing. Keaton does all his own, well-timed, quite hazardous stunts, as usual. Woody Allen later paid a tribute to this extraordinary comedy by making *The Purple Rose of Cairo*, 1985, employing the same theme.

During recent years, *The General*, 1926 – the name of a Civil War locomotive which the Confederate Keaton prevents from being captured by Federal forces – has gained the reputation of being the greatest silent film comedy of all, rich in sight gags, excitingly edited, beautifully photographed, and with a graceful, touching love story.

In *The Cameraman*, MGM, 1928, one feels (almost unconsciously) the loss of freedom Keaton had enjoyed with Schenck at United Artists: he was never fully able to shape up to becoming a studio employee. However, playing a junior newsreel cameraman falling in love with a film star, he is still immensely inventive and resourceful.

Chaplin's later sound feature, *Limelight*, 1952, includes an outstanding knockabout scene with Keaton: the two comic maestros work together so splendidly that the scene is a crystallisation of this kind of comedy at its finest. The movie as a whole, though, is dominated by pathos: the Little Tramp has become a washed-up music-hall comic and there is a foundling, a desperate young girl (played by an 18-year-old Claire Bloom in her film debut) whom he helps to fulfil her aspiration of becoming a ballet dancer.

Many of the silent stars – Harold Lloyd (most successfully), Charlie Chaplin (reluctantly), Buster Keaton (infrequently and somewhat pathetically) – continued into the sound era, with varying but generally diminished lustre. Stan Laurel – who had understudied Chaplin on two stage tours of the USA by the British Fred Karno company, remaining behind in 1912 and making silent shorts from 1917 – teamed up with a less successful fellow film comic, Oliver Hardy, in 1926, making their first talkie in 1927, heralded by a daffy signature tune. They made a series of Laurel and Hardy perennials during the 1930s and 1940s, of which the two most outstanding were *Sons of the Desert/Fraternally Yours*, 1933 and *Way Out West*, 1936. The first, a development of a silent short, *Their Purple Moment*, is the quintessential Laurel and Hardy classic, where two erring husbands escape from their suspicious wives to join a convention, where Charlie Chase, as the irrepressible practical joker, helps to speed things along until they return home to bitter discovery and faltering explanations. In the second, their version of the old Western story about gold mines and outlaws, every familiar detail of the genre is given a wildly comic treatment with the expected (and always funny) Laurel-and-Hardy routines, plus a softshoe-shuffle dance and a memorable song duo ('In the Blue Ridge Mountains of Virginia').

W.C. Fields' career followed a similar progress from vaudeville (as a juggler) and stage (where he starred in the Ziegfeld Follies and the play *Poppy*), then breaking into silent film but only coming into his own with his slow creaking drawl in sound movies, where he combined the aggressive offensiveness of Groucho Marx with his own despicable vices – chronic mendacity, alcoholism, kleptomania, hatred of women, children and animals. In the supremely characteristic *It's a Gift*, 1934, Fields wrote his own script (as 'Charles Bogle') and played the comic lead, Harold Bissonnette, a henpecked small town grocer, who endures a series of humiliations with grudging and spiteful stoicism, but finally has his triumphant moment of defiant independence.

Fields' performances always had a touch of mad genius: *The Bank Dick/The Bank Detective*, 1940, his masterpiece, self-scripted under the weird name of 'Mahatma Kane Jeeves', reveals this genius in its most controlled, crystallised form. As an old soak (not an unfamiliar role), henpecked by his appalling family (not an unfamiliar position), Fields "gains a fortune... by exploiting his natural idleness, cowardice, gullibility, and cunning" (*The Oxford Companion to Film*, 1972). He is backed up by marvellous performances all round, and there is an hilarious car chase as a climax to the inspired antics.

Sound created a new generation of comedy stars, oustandingly the Marx Brothers, with Groucho's outrageous garrulity ("Mrs Rittenhouse, ever since I've met you I've swept you off my feet"), Chico's idiosyncratic and inconsequential 'Italianese' ("Tutsi-frutsi ice-cream") and, in contrast, Harpo's intransigent dumbness, blond wig, wild eyes, and galloping legs. Their masterpiece, *Duck Soup*, 1933, their last Paramount picture, a political satire of complete zaniness, and *A Night at the Opera*, 1935, a glossier MGM product made for Thalberg and padded with love songs and romantic interest, remain among the greatest film comedies.

Feature-length comedies are generally varied and complex in tone and approach, and are thus difficult to subdivide into convenient sections. The Great Clowns was an inevitable title encompassing the work of Chaplin, Keaton, Laurel and Hardy, Fields, and the Marx Brothers, although in that section I also include *Some Like it Hot*, 1959, not only because Joe E. Brown (one of the old 'giants') had a leading role in it, but also because the performances of the three leading stars – Tony Curtis, Jack Lemmon, Marilyn Monroe – have the quality of incisive caricature that is characteristic of the old film comedians.

In the 1970s, one great clown emerged of the stature of Chaplin, Keaton et al. – a Jewish New Yorker, Allen Stewart Konigsberger (nicknamed 'Woody' because he played jazz clarinet). As a film artist Woody Allen has a social alertness, wit, the appearance of an abstracted puppet (not unlike that of Harpo), and a thorough knowledge of film techniques. These are combined best in *Annie Hall*, 1977, where, like his predecessor, Chaplin, he works his comedy through his relationship with an ideal woman, in this case a 'kooky WASP' with a jumble-sale taste in clothes (played by Diane Keaton). This film is less dominated by gimmickry than his earlier comedies, dealing humorously with two serious themes: the different ethnic origins of the two lovers, and a final clash of cultures. Annie is attracted to the crazy bohemianism of California, whereas Alvy Singer (the Allen figure) remains loyal to the grittier, more submissive realism of New York.

Manhattan, 1979, filmed in a haunting black and white by Gordon Willis, combines the comic persona of Allen with a rhapsodical poem of the 'magic place'. The continually expressive Gershwin music – a co-star of the film, arranged by Tom Pierson with Zubin Mehta and Michael Tilson Thomas as conductors – helps to create an introspective, hypnotic mood, in which Allen's brilliantly comic treatment of angst among New York yuppies fits perfectly.

The Bank Dick/ The Bank Detective (UK), Un (Charles Rogers), 1940 *bw*

Direction: Edward Cline	Script: W.C. Fields (as Mahatma Kane Jeeves)
Camera: Milton Krasner	
Art Direction: Jack Otterson	Musical Direction: Charles Previn
	Editing: Arthur Hilton

with W.C. Fields, Cora Witherspoon, Una Merkel, Jessie Ralph, Franklin Pangborn, Grady Sutton, Russell Hicks

- Criticism on release

> Woolchester Cowperthwaite Fields is among the great one-man shows... His new movie [*The Bank Dick*] was

written by him and mostly directed by him and then stolen by him in the principal part... in between the high points [it] is stiff and static and holds no interest outside of W.C. Fields.

Otis Ferguson, *New Republic*, 30 December 1940

- Current recommendations and ratings
StJD BN92 S&S82 LM4 DQ4 DW5 VFG4½ MPG4 NFT*

...by far the best of Fields' late comedies, with the great man trundling through an impeccably loony scenario of his own devising – totally ramshackle and marvellous.

Geoff Brown, PTOG 1995

The Cameraman, MGM, Lawrence Weingarten), 1928 bw

Direction: Edward Sedgwick
Camera: Elgin Lessley, Reggie Lanning
Titles: Joseph Farnham
Script: Richard Schayer, from story by Clyde Bruckman and Lew Lipton
Editing: Hugh Wynn

with Buster Keaton, Marceline Day, Harold Goodwin, Harry Gibbon, Sidney Bracy, Edward Brophy, Vernon Dent, William Irving

- Criticism on release

Buster Keaton clicks again, and we don't mean perhaps. He's a reformed tintype photographer this time, trying to break into the newsreel service all because his heart aches for the office stenographer. He takes his famous poker face through fire, water and jail for the typewriting lady, and gets all tied up in hard knots trying to scoop a Tong War. Great story, original gags – and Buster's irresistible. See this and bust!

Photoplay, Vol. 34, No.5, October 1928

- Current recommendations and ratings
S&S82/92 LM3 DQ4 DW3 MPG5 NFT*

...the first half of the film [is] a series of gags (collapsing bed, reflex-testing, mixed-up-bathing suits), second-hand enough to have come out of *Nickelodeon*, but the final sequences make up for this disappointment, [finishing with] a delightful piece of film-making within-a-film which is both an insight into Keaton's own logic and also, alas, a sort of epitaph.

Andrew Nickolds, PTOG 1995

City Lights, UA (Charles Chaplin), 1930 *bw*

Direction and Script: Charles Chaplin
Camera: Rollie Totheroh (with Gordon Pollock and Mark Marklatt)
Music: Charles Chaplin   Art Direction: Charles Hall
Editing: Charles Chaplin

with Charles Chaplin, Virginia Cherrill, Harry Myers, Henry Bergman, Hank Mann, Allan Garcia, Robert Parrish (bit), Jean Harlow (bit)

- Criticism on release

    ...if you ever liked Chaplin, you will find that he has done all his old tricks all over again, carefully and painstakingly, and they were funnier than ever to me – I still can see no reason why *City Lights* should be treated with all the solemn pomp of a christening in a corporation laboratory... [it] offers nothing new in the way of direction, lighting, or musical accompaniment... It proves nothing, except that Mr Chaplin is the greatest clown we have, and that's enough.

    Pare Lorentz, *Judge*, 28 February 1931

- Current recommendations and ratings
StJD S&S82/92 LM4 DQ3 VFG4 MPG5 NFT*

    ...edges dangerously close to the weepie wonderland of *Magnificent Obsession* and other lace-handkerchief jobs. This horrid fate is narrowly avoided by bracing doses of slapstick... and Chaplin's supreme delicacy in conveying all shades of human feeling – there are plenty of great moments...

    Geoff Brown, PTOG 1995

Duck Soup, Par (H. Mankiewicz), 1933 bw

Direction: Leo McCarey
Songs: Bert Kalmar and Harry Ruby
Camera: Henry Sharp
Art Direction: Hans Dreier, Wiard Ihnen
Editing: Leroy Stone

Script: Bert Kalmar and Harry Ruby (with Nat Perrin and Arthur Sheekman)

with Groucho, Harpo, Chico and Zeppo Marx, Margaret Dumont, Louis Calhern, Raquel Torres, Edgar Kennedy, Leonid Kinskey, Charles Middleton

- Criticism on release

    ...the latest offering of the Four Marx Brothers is a blurp... their worst concoction... a feeble effort at satirising dictators – the Marx Brothers ought to get wise to the fact that Harpo, and not Groucho, is the genius of the family...

    Meyer Levin, *Esquire*, February 1934

- Current recommendations and ratings
StJD BN92 S&S82/92 LM3½ DQ4 DW5 VFG5 MPG5 NFT*

    ...the greatest of the surreally anarchic threesome's films (foursome here), this is a breathtakingly funny and imaginative spoof of war movie heroics... A masterpiece.

    Geoff Andrew, PTOG 1995

The General, UA (Joseph Schenck/Buster Keaton), 1926 bw

Direction: Buster Keaton and Clyde Bruckman
Script: Buster Keaton, Clyde Bruckman, Al Boasberg and Charles Smith (from *The Great Locomotive Chase* by William Pittinger)
Camera: Bert Haines, J.D. ('Dev') Jennings
Art Direction (and Technical Adviser): Fred Gabourie
Editing: Sherman Kell, Henry Barnes

with Buster Keaton, Marion Mack, Glen Cavender, Jim Farley, Joe Keaton

- Criticism on release

    Buster Keaton shows signs of vaulting ambition in *The General*; he appears to be attempting to enter the 'epic' class. That he fails to get across is due to the scantiness of his material as compared with the length of his films. Two aged locomotives chase each other through the heart of the Civil War zone, and the ingenuity displayed by Buster Keaton in keeping these possibly tedious chases alive is little short of incredible...
    Robert Sherwood, *Life*, 24 February 1927

- Current recommendations and ratings
StJD BN92 S&S82/92 LM3½ DQ4 DW5 MPG5 NFT*

    Keaton's best, and arguably the greatest screen comedy ever made... witty, dramatic, visually stunning, full of subtle, delightful human insights, and constantly hilarious.
    Geoff Andrew, PTOG 1995

The Gold Rush, UA (Charles Chaplin), 1925 bw

Direction: Charles Chaplin (with Charles 'Chuck' Riesner and Harry D'Abbadie D'Arrast)
Script: Charles Chaplin   Camera: Rollie Totheroh, Jack Wilson
Art Direction: Charles Hall   Editing: Harold McGahann

with Charles Chaplin, Mack Swain, Georgia Hale, Henry Bergman

- Criticism on release

    Chaplin's jokes have an unmistakable quality of personal fancy. Furthermore he has made a practice of taking his gags as points of departure for genuine comic situations... by developing [them] with steady logic and vivid imagination – he [also uses them] to help him through the deliberately ironic or pathetic situations which have become more frequent...

    Edmund Wilson, *New Republic*, 2 September 1925

- Current recommendations and ratings
  StJD BN92 S&S82/92 LM4 DQ4 DW5 MPG5 NFT*

    Famous for various imaginative sequences... nevertheless flawed by its mawkish sentimentality – for all its relative dramatic coherence, it's still hard to see how it was ever taken for a masterpiece.

    Geoff Andrew, PTOG 1995

It's a Gift, Par (William LeBaron), 1934 bw

Direction: Norman Z. McLeod Camera: Henry Sharp Art Direction: Hans Dreier, John B. Goodman	Script: Jack Cunningham, W.C. Fields, from play by J.P. McEvoy based on story by 'Charles Bogle' (Fields)

with W.C. Fields, Jean Rouverol, Julian Madison, Kathleen Howard, Tommy Bupp, Tammany Young, Baby LeRoy, Morgan Wallace, Charles Sellon, Josephine Whittell

- Criticism on release

    Perhaps if the W.C. Fields idolaters continue their campaign on his behalf over a sufficient period of years his employers may finally invest him with a production befitting his dignity as a great artist. In the meantime such comparatively journeyman pieces as *It's a Gift* will serve adequately to keep his public satisfied – it permits him to illuminate the third-rate vaudeville katzenjammer of the work with his own irresistible style of humor.

    André Sennwald, *New York Times*, 5 January 1935

- Current recommendations and ratings
  S&S82 LM4 DQ4 DW4 VFG5 MPG5 NFT*

   It's a masterpiece, and Fields' definitive study in the horrors of small-town family life – Fields himself is so curmudgeonly that he almost snatches food from his son's mouth... There's little sentiment (or plot) to provide any relief – easily the most devastating comedy of the 30s.

   Geoff Brown, PTOG 1995

The Kid, AFN (Chaplin), 1921 *bw*

Direction, Script: Charles Chaplin
Camera: Roland (Rollie) Totheroh

with Charles Chaplin, Jackie Coogan (Jr.) Edna Purviance, Carl Miller, Tom Wilson, Henry Bergman, Lita Grey, Charles Riesner, Albert Austin, Jack Coogan Sr, et al.

- Criticism on release

   Such a picture cannot be retold in words. It is a miniature epic of childhood in the comic manner in terms of the screen. There is infinite humor and swift pathos and subtle satire... Millions will enjoy it, and many of those who have stood aloof will have to admit, if only to themselves, the supreme genius of the new Ariel who walks among mortals in the most incongruous shoes that an immortal ever wore.
   Exceptional Photoplays, No.3, January-February 1921

- Current recommendations and ratings
  StJD S&S82/92 LM3½ DQ4 DW4 MPG5 NFT*

   As always, Chaplin's opulent sentimentality is made palatable both by the amazing grace of his pantomimic skills, and the balancing presence of harsh reality: the drama and the intertwining gags are played out amongst garbage, flophouses, a slum world depicted with Stroheim-like detail.

   Geoff Brown, PTOG 1995

Limelight, UA (Charles Chaplin), 1952 bw

Direction and Script: Charles Chaplin	Camera: Karl Struss, Rollie Totheroh
Music: Charles Chaplin, Raymond Rasch, Larry Russell	
Art Direction: Eugene Lourie	Editing: Joe Inge

with Charles Chaplin, Claire Bloom, Sydney Chaplin, Buster Keaton, Nigel Bruce, Norman Lloyd, Marjorie Bennett, Snub Pollard

- Criticism on release

    ...passes the one great test of a work of art – it stays with you and flourishes... As you dwell on it the weaknesses dwindle and you know you cannot rest until you have savoured once more the sweetness and melancholy of its instinctive genius.
    Richard Winnington, *News Chronicle*, 18 October 1952

- Current recommendations and ratings
StJD S&S82/92 LM4 DQ3 FRG4 DW4 MPG4 NFT*

    It's overlong, shapeless, overblown, and... a masterpiece. Few cinema artists have delved into their own lives and emotions with such ruthlessness and with such moving results.
    Geoff Brown, PTOG 1995

Manhattan, UA (Charles H. Joffe), 1979 bw

Direction: Woody Allen	Script: Allen, with Marshall Brickman
Camera: Gordon Willis	
Music: George Gershwin	Editing: Susan E. Morse
Music Direction: Tom Pierson	Art Direction: Mel Bourne
Costume Design: Albert Wolsky, Ralph Lauren	

with Woody Allen, Diane Keaton, Michael Murphy, Mariel Hemingway, Meryl Streep, Anne Byrne, Karen Ludwig

- Criticism on release

    ...it can't, I say, it simply can't match this splendid Gershwin. But it can, it can; the music and the film deserve one another... The film, shot in deeply satisfying black and white, has the nervous tension and the romantic excitement of a beloved city. The characters belong to a well-to-do, restless, intellectual pretentious society... they are held together as a human group by the wit and charm of the figure presented by Mr Allen...

    Dilys Powell, *Sunday Times*, August 1979)

- Current recommendations and ratings
StJD S&S82/92 LM3½ DQ3 DW5 VFG4 MPG5 NFT*

    An edgy social comedy framed as a loving tribute to neurotic New York, overlaid with an evocative Gershwin score; it's funny and sad in exactly the right proportions. Allen could well strive vainly ever to better this film.

    Tom Milne, PTOG 1995

The Navigator, M-C (Joseph M. Schenck), 1924 *bw*

Direction: Buster Keaton, Donald Crisp
Script: Jean Havez, John Mitchell, Clyde Bruckman
Cameraman: Elgin Lessley, Byron Houck

with Buster Keaton, Kathryn McGuire, Frederick Vroom, Noble Johnson

- Criticism on release

    Buster Keaton's sphynx-like face can be seen this week in a nautical film-farce, wherein his wildest emotions are reflected by an occasional upward turn of his right eyebrow... It is funny enough to see this indefatigable stoic as a pampered young man in a wonderful mansion, but it is even more absurd to view his actions when he and his heroine are alone aboard a drifting steamship.

Later he is a sea diver, prodded by a swordfish and caught by the arm of a ravenous octopus – Mr Keaton deserves untold credit for his originality in thinking up most of the funny scenes.
Mordaunt Hall, *New York Times*, 13 October 1924

- Current recommendations and ratings
  StJD S&S82/92 DQ4 DW4 MPG4 NFT*

  Gag for gag, one of the funniest of all Keaton's features as he copes with the snags involved in running a deserted linear single-handed, philosophically accepting that machinery has a malevolent will of its own...
  Tom Milne, PTOG 1995

A Night at the Opera, MGM (Irving Thalberg), 1935 bw

Direction: Sam Wood
Script: George Kaufman, Morris Ryskind, Al Boasberg, from James Kevin McGuinness's story
Camera: Merritt Gerstad
Music: Herbert Stothart
Songs: Arthur Freed, Nacio Herb Brown, Ned Washington, Bronislaw Kaper, Werner Jurmann
Costume Design: Dolly Tree
Art Direction: Cedric Gibbons, Ben Carre
Editing: William Levanway

with Groucho, Harpo and Chico Marx, Margaret Dumont, Kitty Carlisle, Allan Jones, Sig Rumann, Walter Woolf King, Billy Gilbert, Fritz Feld

- Criticism on release
  ...one of the most hilarious collections of bad jokes I've laughed myself nearly sick over... a breakneck crazy business, made violent and living by the presence in it of some impenitently ham and delightful bad boys – their assurance, appetite and vitality are supreme; they are

both great and awful.
Otis Ferguson, *New Republic*, 11 December 1935
- Current recommendations and ratings
StJD S&S82/92 LM4 DQ4 DW4 VFG4 MPG4 NFT***

...a top budget job, opulent and meticulous, with its fair share of vices: this is the first Marx Brothers film where you really feel like strangling the romantic leads. But it has even more virtues...
Geoff Brown, PTOG 1995

Our Hospitality, Metro (Joseph M. Schenck), 1923 *bw*

Direction: Buster Keaton, John Blystone
Script and Titles: Jean Havez, Joseph Mitchell, Clyde Bruckman
Camera: Elgin Lessley, J. ('Dev') Jennings
Art Direction: Fred Gabourie

with Buster Keaton, Natalie Talmadge, Buster Keaton Jr., Joseph Keaton, Kitty Bradbury, Joe Roberts, Leonard Clapham, Craig Ward, Ralph Bushman

- Criticism on release
That stoic comedian, Buster Keaton, has chosen to burlesque the feud drama, in his latest effort. This funny film moves along quietly at the outset, but in the end it gets there, and to our mind it is a mixture that is extremely pleasing, as there is no out-and-out slapstick effect. Natalie Talmadge is quite good in her part, and the rest of the cast are excellent support.
New Times, 10 December 1923

- Current recommendations and ratings
S&S82/92 LM4 DW4 MPG4 NFT*

...[Keaton's] second feature and first full-length masterpiece... The period setting (1831, the early days of rail travel) is made integral to the action, and all the laughs spring directly from the narrative and the characters. Buster's climactic rescue of his sweetheart from a waterfall is one of his most daringly acrobatic and most celebrated gags.

Tony Rayns, PTOG 1995

Sherlock Jr., Metro (Buster Keaton) 1924 bw

Direction: Buster Keaton
Camera: Elgin Lessley, Byron Houck
Art Direction: Fred Gabourie
Script: Clyde Bruckman, Jean Havez, Joseph Mitchell
Costume Design: Clare West

with Buster Keaton, Kathryn McGuire, Joe Keaton, Ward Crane, Jane Conelly

- Criticism on release

    ...about as unfunny as a hospital operating room... There is one piece of business, however, that is well worked out and that is worthy of comment. It is the bit where Buster as a motion picture machine operator in a dream scene walks out of the booth and into the action that is taking place on the screen of the picture that he is projecting. That is clever. The rest is bunk...

    Variety, 28 May 1924

    ...an extremely good comedy which will give you plenty of amusement so long as you permit Mr Keaton to glide into his work with his usual deliberation

    New York Times, 26 May 1924

- Current recommendations and ratings
S&S82/92 LM4 DQ3 DW5 MPG4 NFT*

    ...In an unforgettable sequence, Buster (actually fallen asleep beside the projector) forces his way onto the screen and into the movie he is projecting, only to find himself beset by perils and predicaments as the action around him changes in rapid montage... The timing here is incredible (a technical marvel in fact); even more so in the great chase sequence, a veritable cascade of unbelievably complex gags... It leaves Chaplin standing.

Tom Milne, PTOG 1995

Some Like it Hot, UA (Walter Mirisch, Billy Wilder), 1959 bw

Direction: Buster Keaton	Script: Billy Wilder, I.A.L. Diamond
Camera: Charles Lang	Music: Adolph Deutsch
Art Direction: Edward (Ted) Haworth	
*Costume Design: Orry-Kelly	Editing: Arthur Schmidt
Special Effects: Milt Rice	

with Jack Lemmon, Tony Curtis, Marilyn Monroe, Joe E. Brown, Pat O'Brien, George Raft, Nehemiah Persoff, Joan Shawlee, George E. Stone, Mike Mazurki, Tom Kennedy.

- Criticism on release

    ...very little in the film that is original, but the use of the material is delightful... With easy mastery, [Wilder] has captured much of the scuttling, broad, vaguely surrealistic feeling of the best silent comedies.

    Stanley Kauffmann, *New Republic*, 30 March 1959

- Current recommendations and ratings
  StJD BN92 S&S82/92 LM4 DQ4 DW5 VFG5 MPG5 NFT***
    Still one of Wilder's funniest satires... Deliberately shot in black-and-white to avoid the pitfalls of camp or transvestism, though the best sequences are the gangland ones anyhow.

    Rod McShane, PTOG 1995

Sons of the Desert, MGM (Hal Roach), 1933 bw

Direction: William Seiter
Camera: Kenneth Peach
Choreography: Dave Bennett
Script: Frank Craven, Byron Morgan
Editing: Bert Jordan

with Stan Laurel, Oliver Hardy, Charley Chase (as themselves), Mae Busch, Dorothy Christy, Lucien Littlefield, Billy Gilbert (voice-over)

- Criticism on release

    Let it be said at once that the new Laurel and Hardy enterprise has achieved feature length without benefit of the usual distressing formulae of padding and stretching. It is funny all the way through – Frank Craven is credited with the story, and that might explain its humor, also its sly and irreverent manner with the general subject of fraternal orders. But the expert timing of the gag situations, the technical dexterity which builds big laughs out of low-comedy blue-prints, and the straight playing of Mae Busch and Dorothy Christy as the embattled wives are the real answers. Also Mr Laurel and Mr Hardy.

    'A.D.S.', *New York Times* 12 January 1934

- Current recommendations and ratings
    S&S92 LM3½ DQ4 DW5 VFG4 MPG3½ NFT*

    One of the very finest Laurel and Hardy features... far faster than most of their features, while the duo's essentially childish amiability is beautifully contrasted both with the down-to-earth if somewhat aggressive maturity of their spouses, and with the ghastly mischief wrought by Chase's ever-effervescent convention regular.

    Geoff Andrew, PTOG 1995

Way Out West, Hal Roach (Stan Laurel), 1937 bw

Direction: James W. Horne
Camera: Art Lloyd, Walter Lundin
Art Direction: Arthur I. Royce
Editing: Bert Jordan
Script: Charles Rogers, Felix Adler, James Parrott, from story by Rogers and Jack Jevne
Special Effects: Roy Seawright

with Stan Laurel, Oliver Hardy, James Finlayson, Sharon Lynne, Stanley Fields, Rosina Lawrence

- Criticism on release

    Nature meant them to be anatomical funny men, and there's nothing much any one can do about nature, not even a script writer. *Way Out West* tries to go against it by withholding all but the merest hint of a plot, but anatomy overcomes that. We still chuckle when Ollie falls off a roof, or has a bucket thrust over his head or a lighted candle applied to his trouser-seat. We still splutter when Stan, who is expected to eat a derby hat on a bet, takes a tentative bite, smiles and reaches for the salt and pepper. It is not subtle or witty or clever. It's anatomical humor...
    Frank S. Nugent, *New York Times* 4 May 1937

- Current recommendations and ratings
LM3½ DQ4 DW5 VFG4½ MPG4 NFT*

    Arguably the most assured of Stan and Ollie's features... Some classic moments such as the pair's soft-shoe shuffle outside the saloon, and their vocal duet at the bar on 'The Blue Ridge Mountains of Virginia', as well as a razor-sharp satire of B Western conventions.
    Adrian Turner, PTOG 1995

Annie Hall, UA (Charles H. Joffe), 1977 *colour*

*Direction: Woody Allen
Camera: Gordon Willis
Art Direction: Mel Bourne
*Script: Allen, with Marshall Brickman
Editing: Ralph Rosenblum
Costume Design: Ruth Morley, George Newman, Marilyn Putnam, Ralph Lauren, Nancy McArdle

with Woody Allen, *Diane Keaton, Tony Roberts, Carol Kane, Paul Dewhurst, Janet Margolin, Shelley Duvall, Christopher Walken, Donald Symington, Jeff Goldblum (bit), Sigourney Weaver (bit)

- Criticism on release

> What makes *Annie Hall* the most satisfying of Woody Allen's filmed therapy courses, and the most enlightened comedy we have seen for many months? The secret is in the title, which, for all that it looks like an anagram of something with 'Allen' in it, actually denotes another person: Allen's co-star, whose real name is apparently Hall... *Annie Hall* begins to become itself when its heroine moves in... possibly because it is a post-mortem and not a running diagnosis, this is Woody Allen's most concentrated, still performance...
>
> Russell Davies, *The Observer* 2 October 1977

- Current recommendations and ratings
StJD S&S82/92 LM4 DQ3 DW4 VFG4 MPG4 NFT**

> The one-liners are razor-sharp, the observation of Manhattan manners as keen as mustard, and some of the romantic stuff even quite touching. If you can forgive the fact that it's a ragbag of half-digested intellectual ideas dressed up with trendy intellectual references, you should have a good laugh.
>
> Nigel Floyd, PTOG 1995

SATIRICAL COMEDY

The classics of satirical comedy have similar, clearly delineated targets: Chaplin's *Modern Times*, 1936 and *The Great Dictator*, 1940, tilted against the soullessness of factory conditions and the pompous arrogance of fascist leaders respectively. Although both these films have a serious theme of concern for the 'little fellow' they also have a good assortment of inspired comic set pieces in the Chaplin manner – Charlie's helpless and frantic ballet duos with automatic machinery in *Modern Times*, Adenoid Hynkel (Chaplin's caricature of Adolf Hitler) dancing with a globe of the world, the continuous mismatching at the railway station of a ceremonial red carpet and the train bringing Benzoni Napaloni (Jack Oakie's caricature of Benito Mussolini) for a summit meeting and the two dictators having their barber's chairs alternatively wound up to give a head's advantage during the negotiations in *The Great Dictator*.

Preston Sturges in *The Miracle of Morgan's Creek*, 1944 (miraculously produced during World War II) directed a frontal assault on conventional Puritanism and the fertility cult in American society, deploying with versatile technical skill the talents of Betty Hutton, as the underage (!) whoopee girl, and Eddie Bracken, as the nincompoop fall guy trying to throw a respectable screen over an unwanted pregnancy with astonishing results. Sturges always crowded his screen with characters played by a well-tried, hand-selected company of repertory players, including William Demarest (Hutton's abrasive policeman father), Porter Hall, Alan Bridge, Almira Sessions, Jimmy Conlin, and Esther Howard. Diana Lynn is also surprisingly lively as Hutton's younger sister.

In Billy Wilder's *The Apartment*, 1960, the target is corruption at the upper levels of corporation life. Jack Lemmon plays a run-of-the-mill office worker who gains promotion because of the convenience of his apartment for the illicit liaisons of the higher executives (including Ray Walston). Unfortunately, his compassion for fellow worker Shirley MacLaine, who is being dropped by big boss Fred MacMurray (in a very untypically ruthless role) leads to a clash with the system. The movie effectively combines sharp comedy with serious drama, and, one year after *Some Like it Hot*, convinced the public of Wilder's sure instincts as an innovative film-maker, winning several Oscars at the same time.

Mike Nichols' *The Graduate*, 1967, reflected a favourite theme of protest in the late 60s: the hypocrisy of sexual relations in a contemporary affluent society. An introspective graduate (Dustin Hoffman in his film debut) is seduced by one of his parents' sybaritic friends (Anne Bancroft, a virtuoso performance of sexuality). The dazed Hoffman finds this predatory woman fiercely hostile when he wants to marry her daughter (Katharine Ross). The finale of anarchistic revenge at the daughter's arranged wedding (very popular at the time) seems overwrought today and out of keeping with the measured and subtle satire of the first three-quarters of the film – well written, well acted, well directed, and beautifully photographed (by Robert Surtees).

M*A*S*H is better known of as the long-running TV sitcom series; but Robert Altman's original movie of that name, 1970, still has the power to entertain and shock. It is interesting in that it has two targets on both sides of the fence: it is a strongly anti-war document, but it also attacks the way in which the medicos of this Mobile Army Surgical Hospital during the Korean War react. It's extremely reminiscent of Evelyn Waugh's satire on the lethal frivolity of the 1920s, *Vile Bodies*. The frenzied search for irresponsible play and sex as an antidote to, and distraction from, the reasons for patching up the wounded by Hawkeye (Donald Sutherland), Trapper John (Elliott Gould) and 'Hot Lips' Houlihan (Sally Kellerman) in particular is beautifully represented in wild comedy which can still seem outrageous.

**The Apartment*, UA (Walter Mirisch/Billy Wilder), 1960 bw

*Direction: Billy Wilder *Script: Billy Wilder,
Camera: Joseph La Shelle I.A.L. Diamond
Music: Adolph Deutsch
Art Direction: Alexander Trauner, Edward Boyle
*Editing: Daniel Mandell

with Jack Lemmon, Shirley MacLaine, Fred MacMurray, Ray Walston, Jack Kruschen, Joan Shawlee, Edie Adams

- Criticism on release

    The middle section is perhaps the best... bringing into focus a real feeling for people and atmosphere and taking in its stride a mordant bitter attack on big business firms, their petty internal politics and the men's room humours and infidelities of their executives...
    P.J.D., Monthly Film Bulletin, 1960

- Current recommendations and ratings
  StJD S&S92 LM4 DQ3 DW4 VFG5 MPG4 NFT*

    Diamond-sharp satire with a brilliant performance from Lemmon... Even the cop-out ending... is rather moving, given the delicate skill with which Lemmon and MacLaine commute between comedy and pathos.
    Tom Milne, PTOG 1995

The Great Dictator, UA (Charles Chaplin), 1940 bw

Direction, Script: Charles Chaplin
Camera: Karl Strauss, Rollie Totheroh
Music: Charles Chaplin
Art Direction: J. Russell Spencer
Editing: Willard Nico

with Charles Chaplin, Paulette Goddard, Jack Oakie, Reginald Gardiner, Henry Daniell, Billy Gilbert, Maurice Moscovitch, Emma Dunn, Chester Conklin (bit), Hank Mann (bit)

- Criticism on release

    Chaplin is as acute and perfect verbally as he is in pantomime; he has the splenetic and krauty fustian of the German orator as exactly as Hitler himself. When he says 'Democracy shtoonk, Liberty shtoonk', he crowds out over his collar to the precise degree, and he never misses an opportunity to go from the normal English of the story into this hortatory gibberish, booting his lieutenants around and staring the devil out of everybody, including himself – this is still Chaplin the Great, and growing at his age.
    Otis Ferguson, New Republic, 9 December 1940

- Current recommendations and ratings
  StJD S&S92 LM3½ DQ3 DW4 VFG4 MPG4 NFT*

    The representation of Hitler is vaudeville goonery all the way, but minus the acid wit and inventive energy that Groucho Marx managed in his impersonation of authoritarianism gone berserk in *Duck Soup*...

    Verina Glaessner, PTOG 1995

The Miracle of Morgan's Creek, Par (Preston Sturges), 1943 bw

Direction, Script: Preston Sturges	Camera: John F. Seitz
Music: Leo Shuken, Charles Bradshaw	Editing: Stuart Gilmore
Art Direction: Hans Dreier, Ernst Fegte	Costume Design: Edith Head

with Eddie Bracken, Betty Hutton, Diana Lynn, William Demarest, Brian Donlevy, Akim Tamiroff, Porter Hall, Alan Bridge, Almira Sessions, Esther Howard, J. Parrell MacDonald, Georgia Caine, Torben Meyer, Jimmy Conlin, Chester Gonklin, Byron Foulger, Arthur Hoyt, Jack Norton

- Criticism on release

    [Sturges] plays every twist of his story for sharp realism as well as laughs; his small-town doctor, banker, lawyer and, most notably, Porter Hall as a justice of the peace are bits of comic realism finely graded against the chameleon-like principals... Excepting a few moments when Sturges forces everything too far, the film is beautifully played... Yet the more I think about [it], the less I like it... Cynicism, which gives the film much of its virtue, also has it by the throat...

    James Agee, The Nation, 5 February 1944

- Current recommendations and ratings
    StJD S&S82 LM4 DQ2 DW5 VFG5 MPG5 NFT*

    Great verbal gags and non-sequiturs, fast-paced action, and a thorough irreverence for all things, deemed respectable – politicians, policemen and magistrates included – make it a lasting delight.
    Geoff Andrew, PTOG 1995

Modern Times, UA (Charles Chaplin), 1936 bw

Direction: Charles Chaplin, with Carter De Haven and Henry Bergman
Script, Music Editing: Charles Chaplin   Arrangements: Alfred Newman, David Raksin
Camera: Ira Morgan, Rollie Totheroh
Art Direction: Charles Hall, J. Russell Spencer

with Charles Chaplin, Paulette Goddard, Henry Bergman, Chester Conklin, Hank Mann, Allan Garcia

- Criticism on release

    ...a silent film, with pantomime, printed dialogue and such sound effects as were formerly supplied by the pit band – Chaplin himself is not dated, never will be... he is a first-class buffoon, and I guess the master of our time in dumb show. But this does not make him a first-class picture-maker...
    Otis Ferguson, *New Republic*, 19 February 1936

- Current recommendations and ratings
    StJD BN92 S&S82/92 LM4 DQ3 DW4 VFG4½ MPG4 NFT*

    The last appearance of the Chaplin tramp, before Hitler, Monsieur Verdoux and other personae took over – faces the peril of factory machinery, poverty, starvation and Depression unrest – and just about survives. Chaplin's political and philosophical naivety now seems as remarkable as his gift for pantomime.
    Geoff Brown, PTOG 1995

The Graduate, Embassy (Lawrence Turman), 1967 colour

*Direction: Mike Nichols
Camera: Robert Surtees
Music: Dave Grusin
Art Direction: Richard Sylbert

Script: Calder Willingham, Buck Henry, from Charles Webb's novel)
Songs: Paul Simon
Editing: Sam O'Steen

with Anne Bancroft, Dustin Hoffman, Katharine Ross, William Daniels, Murray Hamilton, Norman Fell, Buck Henry (bit), Richard Dreyfuss (bit)

- Criticism on release

    Mike Nichols' second film... proves that he is a genuine film director – [He] is perceptive, imaginative, witty; he has a shrewd eye, both for beauty and for visual comment – his use of non-verbal sound (something like Antonioni's) does a good deal to fix subliminally the cultural locus...
    Stanley Kauffmann, *New Republic*, 23 December 1967

- Later recommendations and ratings
StJD S&S92 LM4 DQ4 DW5 VFG5 MPG5 NFT*

    Modish, calculated but hugely popular film, which, with the help of an irrelevant but diverting Simon and Garfunkel soundtrack, proved one of the biggest hits of the 60s – very broken-backed... partly because Nichols couldn't decide whether he was making a social satire or a farce.
    Chris Peachment, PTOG 1995

M*A*S*H, TCP (Ingo Preminger), 1970 *colour*

Direction: Robert Altman *Script: Ring Lardner, Jr. (from
Camera: Harold E. Stine   the novel by Richard Hooker)
Music: Johnny Mandel   Editing: Danford Greene
Art Direction: Jack Martin Smith, Arthur Lonergan

with Donald Sutherland, Elliott Gould, Tom Skerritt, Sally Kellerman, Robert Duvall, Jo Ann Pflug, Rene Auberjonois

- Criticism on release

    ...a marvellously unstable comedy, a tough, funny, and sophisticated burlesque of military attitudes – though the setting (a Mobile Army Surgical Hospital) makes it seem a black comedy, it is a cheery black comedy... The silliness of adolescents, compulsively making jokes, seeing the ridiculous in everything is what makes sanity possible here...
    Pauline Kael, *New Yorker*, 24 January 1970

- Current recommendations and ratings
StJD LM4 DQ3 DW4 VFG4½ MPG4 NFT*

    ...shows Altman's stylistic signature in embryonic form: a large number of fast-talking eccentric characters, a series of revealing vignettes rather than a structured plot... and a semi-audible overlapping dialogue. It's frantic, clever fun, but... there's little of the director's muted, unsentimental humanism in evidence.
    Richard Rayner, PTOG 1995

SOCIAL COMEDY

The main difference between 'social' and 'satirical' comedy lies in the emphasis placed on the particular locale in which the social theme is developed as, for instance, in Frank Capra's *Mr Deeds Goes To Town*, 1936, where Gary Cooper's slow-moving but shrewd Longfellow Deeds represents the incorruptibility of the small town (because he is 'pixilated' and 'doodles') pitted against the slick self-seekers of the metropolis, and in William Wellman's *Nothing Sacred*, 1937, where the gullibility of narrow small-townery is contrasted with the knowing exploitation of human misery (in the impending death of an attractive young woman, Hazel Flagg, played by top-star Carole Lombard) by big-town pressmen (represented by the devious reporter Fredric March and his Machiavellian editor Walter Connolly). The biting, cynical script – cruel to both sides – is by ex-reporter and star Hollywood scriptwriter Ben Hecht.

In Preston Sturges's *Sullivan's Travels*, 1941, the locale is Hollywood itself and its theme the 'guilt trips' of certain directors over its concentration on sheer entertainment and neglect of social concerns. Sullivan, the director (played sympathetically by Joel McCrea) brings himself to a pretty pass in his search for elusive 'social significance': in a delightfully tongue-in-cheek prison sequence, he, as part of the convict audience, enjoys the true value of Hollywood's commercial production in the genuine and spontaneous laughter aroused by a Mickey Mouse cartoon. Veronica Lake makes a suitably tomboyish yet glamorous heroine, and, as usual, there is a wonderful welter of small character parts, played by some of Sturges's favourite support players – William Demarest, Robert Warwick, Porter Hall, Franklin Pangborn, Robert Greig (in his familiar portly butler role), Eric Blore (in his familiar diplomatic valet role), Alan Bridge (as a sadistic prison warden – a grim parody, this!) and Byron Foulger.

Ernst Lubitsch's *To Be or Not To Be*, 1942, has the same target as Chaplin's *The Great Dictator* – the pompous tyranny of the Nazis, but replacing the Never-Never Land of satire by a Warsaw theatre during the Occupation, with a detailed study of a repertory company led by an amiable ham actor (Jack Benny) and his seductive wife (Carole Lombard). Benny is very controlled in his central role – this is very much more than a comic vehicle and the whole cast (which includes Felix Bressart, Siegfried Rumann and Lionel Atwill) contribute to the fun and the tension. Tom Dugan's perky yet somehow diffident impersonation of Hitler at the climax is one of the great comic cameos of Hollywood cinema.

That Jewish artists like Chaplin, Lubitsch, Benny and Bressart should, even in the days before the Holocaust, apparently treat a racist dictatorship with entertaining tongue-in-cheek light-heartedness was very surprising at the time, but the splendid ridicule may be all that cruel inhuman group deserve.

Mr Deeds goes to Town, Col (Frank Capra), 1936 bw

*Direction: Frank Capra
Camera: Joseph Walker
Art Direction: Stephen Goosson
Editing: Gene Havlick

Script: Robert Riskin, from story by Clarence Buddington Kelland
Musical Direction: Howard Jackson

with Gary Cooper, Jean Arthur, George Bancroft, Lionel Stander, Raymond Walburn, Douglas Dumbrille, H.B. Warner, Warren Hymer, Ruth Donnelly, Spencer Charters, Emma Dunn, Arthur Hoyt, John Wray, Irving Bacon, Walter Catlett, Franklin Pangborn, Jameson Thomas, Christian Rub

- Criticism on release

    ...every bit as good as its logical predecessor, *It Happened One Night*, possibly better... Everywhere you go in this picture there is someone who is a natural in the part... It is a humdinger and a beauty... more to be seen than heard about.
    Otis Ferguson, *New Republic*, 22 April 1936

- Current recommendations and ratings
LM4 DQ4 DW5 VFG5 MPG5 NFT*

    Before Capra got down to Christmas card morals, he perfected the screwball comedy technique of pursuing common sense to logical ends in a lunatic situation. [This] is one of the best...
    Don MacPherson, PTOG 1995

Sullivan's Travels, Par (Paul Jones), 1941 bw

Direction, Script: Preston Sturges Camera: John F. Seitz
Music: Leo Shuken, Charles Editing: Stuart Gilmore
 Bradshaw
Art Direction: Earl Hedrick

with Joel McCrea, Veronia Lake, William Demarest, Robert Warwick, Franklin Pangborn, Porter Hall, Eric Blore, Esther Howard, Robert Greig, Jimmy Conlin, Chester Conklin, Torben Meyer, Almira Sessions, Alan Bridge, Byron Foulger, Margaret Hayes, J. Farrell MacDonald

- Criticism on release

   ...as an idea it is both original and cute, and handled with a good grasp of satire – [Sullivan] has learned through observation of real hardship that comedy may not be anything so much, but it is all some poor devils have, when they can get it... it is worked up into a story with suspense, odd situations, and a lot of crackle in the lines...
   Otis Ferguson, *New Republic*, 26 January 1942

- Current recommendations and ratings
StJD S&S82/92 LM4 DW5 VFG5 MPG5 NFT*

   Sturges... is putting down the awful liberal solemnities of problem pictures and movies with a message. Whatever, *Sullivan's Travels* is a gem, an almost serious comedy, not taken entirely seriously, with wonderful dialogue, eccentric characterisations, and superlative performances throughout.
   Tom Milne, PTOG 1995

To Be or Not To Be, UA (Alexander Korda), 1942 bw

Direction: Ernst Lubitsch
Camera: Rudolph Maté
Special Effects: Lawrence Butler
Music: Werner Heymann
Costume Design: Irene Gibbons
Script: Edwin Justus Mayer (from story by Lubitsch and Melchior Lengyel)
Art Direction: Vincent Korda
Editing: Dorothy Spencer

with Carole Lombard, Jack Benny, Robert Stack, Lionel Atwill, Felix Bressart, Stanley Ridges, Tom Dugan, Charles Halton, Miles Mander, Frank Reicher, James Finlayson, Halliwell Hobbes, Helmut Dantine

- Criticism on release

    At the beginning of the picture I was a little worried about the propriety of using the agony of Warsaw as a background for farce. But we see almost nothing of the agony, and there is a great deal of very amusing farce – Lubitsch's wit is at any rate first-rate of its kind... Jack Benny as the ham actor asks the Gestapo chief ('Concentration Camp Erhard', played by Sig Rumann) whether he has ever seen Tura, the great Polish tragedian (himself). 'Haf I not?' says the Nazi. 'And vot he did to Shakespeare, ve Germans are doing to Poland!' This brought the house down. There is a charming performance by Carole Lombard, which is, alas, the last we shall have from this gifted player.
    James Agate, *The Tatler*, 1942

- Current recommendations and ratings
StJD BN92 S&S82/92 LM3½ DQ3 DW5 VFG5 MPG5 NFT*

    ...criticised at the time for all its alleged bad taste; but Benny, Lombard and script are all hilarious... It's certainly one of the finest comedies ever to come out of Paramount (sic)...
    Rod McShane, PTOG 1995

Nothing Sacred, UA (David Selznick), 1937 colour

Direction: William Wellman Script: Ben Hecht
Camera: William Howard Greens Music: Oscar Levant
Art Direction: Lyle Wheeler Editing: James Newcom

with Carole Lombard, Fredric March, Charles Winninger, Walter Connolly, Sig Rumann, Monty Woolley, Margaret Hamilton, John Qualen, Hattie McDaniel

- Criticism on release

    I am not altogether pleased with myself for having enjoyed *Nothing Sacred*, but I did enjoy it enormously. It is as callous a bit of satire as I ever remember in the cinema. It describes a newspaper stunt to brighten the last days of a poor country girl, supposedly dying of radium poison. Actually, the film has had the grace to tell us from the beginning that she's not going to die. It is perfectly frank about everything. Callously but brilliantly, it makes game of every kind of emotion...
    C.A. Lejeune, *The Observer*, 6 February 1938

- Current recommendations and ratings
LM3½ DQ3 DW4 VFG5 MPG5 NFT*

    ...sparkling script occasionally loses its way between the satire and the screwball romance, but is even more caustic about newspapermen than *The Front Page*... and provides a welcome antidote to Capracorn in its view of small towns as hellholes to be got out of...
    Tom Milne, PTOG 1995

Comedy (2) – 'Screwball' Comedy, Sex Comedy

'SCREWBALL' COMEDY

'Screwball' Comedy, dating mainly from the 1930s and 1940s, periods of extreme social stress and challenge, typifies Hollywood's unique capacity for delightful escapism in troubled times. This subgenre, based upon loony themes of sex antagonism in sharply ironic contrast to backgrounds of social orthodoxy and seriousness, was one of Hollywood's outstanding inventions. The star quality of its leading performers was one of its essential attributes, as identification with these charmingly dotty, though intelligent, young-mature people provided the essence of this enjoyable, unfortunately often too short at the time, experience in the womb-like dark of the well-attended family cinema.

The casting of Gable and Colbert together in *It Happened One Night* was both fortuitous and inspired, imparting a realistic and leisurely sense of tension to the inevitable development of the somewhat banal plot – poor hard-working reporter meets rich runaway heiress and, in spite of – or because of – their initial mutual hostility, fall deeply and hopelessly in love, to the dismay of each one's immediate associates. The masterly direction of Capra and its popularity with the public, not least in such scenes as the 'Walls of Jericho', signifying the blanket used as a partition in shared sleeping quarters, or the hitchhiking scene where Colbert succeeds, after Gable's failures, by raising her skirt to her knees, ensured the continuance of this genre with well-selected star material for almost another twenty years. It is ironic that Gable, who had been lent to Columbia by MGM "as a form of punishment because, for once, he was making mild waves" (Barry Norman, *Talking Pictures*, 1987), won the only Oscar of his career and went back a bigger star than ever.

The versatile and talented Cary Grant emerged as a leading 'screwball' hero in *The Awful Truth*, 1937, in partnership with Irene Dunne, already well-known as an intelligent performer in all genres. It also introduced Ralph Bellamy in what was to become for him almost a platitude – the stolid, uninspiring, continually put-upon third man. A perfect example of the genre, *The Awful Truth*, was fast, facetious and uncompromising in its sexual hostility, mixing visual and verbal slapstick in about equal amounts in its playful treatment of the serious subject of divorce and remarriage.

Bringing Up Baby, 1938, co-starring Grant with an unlikely screwball heroine, Katharine Hepburn (surprisingly effective as the Lombard-like lead – 'Baby' is her pet leopard, who plays havoc by going off on its own), has often been advanced as Hawks's masterwork, although the later *His Girl Friday* also has a similar claim. It maintains its wild, carefree spirit very well, particularly in scenes involving the marvellous duo and a few other supremely 'batchy' characters (Charlie Ruggles, May Robson, Barry Fitzgerald). The climax in the jail is brilliantly directed, hectic and fun, but too overcrowded to match the previous scenes or the final scene where, slowly and inevitably, we become aware that Grant's patient and punctilious assembly of his giant dinosaur skeleton must be wrecked by Hepburn.

It could be argued that 'screwball' was essentially a 1930s phenomenon: in this respect, *Ninotchka*, 1939, appeared a swansong in Europe, pitting the young-mature Melvyn Douglas, another brilliant screwball hero, against the dourly puritanical Soviet emissary of Greta Garbo, polluting her with capitalist (and parasitic) gaiety and 'making her laugh' (a film event that – at the time – gained considerable publicity for this sophisticated Lubitsch farce scripted by Billy Wilder and Charles Brackett).

For the USA (and Hollywood), however, the troubled peace of the Thirties continued until Pearl Harbor (December 1941): screwball continued to develop, with productions like Hawks' comedy highlight, *His Girl Friday*, 1940, which many would place at the top of his total list of films of all genres, in which Grant plays the role of the high-pressure editor (played previously by Adolphe Menjou in *The Front Page* of 1931) and Rosalind Russell, in a sex change of the role to a female reporter (the part played by Pat O'Brien in the earlier film). In this new adaptation the comedy becomes a breathless farce of sex antagonism, another variation of *The Taming of the Shrew* theme. Russell is marvellous, achieving heights of glamour and wit in this transformed role.

Stanwyck repeated her familiar role of hard-boiled temptress, at first conning then seeking to protect another lovelorn academic (Henry Fonda this time) in *The Lady Eve*, 1941, an example of Preston Sturges's screwball vein. By this time Sturges, at Paramount, could do no wrong as a writer-director: everything he did made money and gained reputation. *The Lady Eve* is as sharp and faultless as a 22 carat diamond. *The Palm Beach Story*, 1942, is rougher and more flawed: as usual Claudette Colbert imparts the right kind of Gallic vivacity, but her partner, Joel McCrea, is perhaps a little too stolid.

American eccentrics abound in a Sturges comedy (just as English ones were to do in post-war Ealing comedies in Britain), and in this *The Palm Beach Story* is no exception, including some of Sturges's finest – for instance, Rudy Vallee's wistfully fastidious millionaire, Hackensacker III, and the ever-delightful Ale and Quail Club.

The classic post-war screwball comedies were both the work of Garson Kanin, writer, and George Cukor, director. The first (co-scripted by Kanin's wife, Ruth Gordon, and featuring the great Tracy-Hepburn team, was *Adam's Rib*, 1949, in which Katharine Hepburn pursued the cause of women against the generally resistant but finally sympathetic masculinity of Spencer Tracy, by defending the disingenuously ingenuous Judy Holliday against the charge of attempting to murder her infuriating husband (Tom Ewell). As Hepburn's husband, played by Tracy, is also a lawyer (representing Ewell), their sex battle takes place both in public (in the courtroom) and in private (at home).

Judy Holliday was the new 'find' in this genre in the early 1950s, short-lived (she died in 1965 at the age of 42) but memorable. She never improved on her scintillating performance, brought from the Broadway stage, in *Born Yesterday*, 1950, playing Billie Dawn, forced by her newly-rich junkman-protector (Broderick Crawford) to make herself 'couth' under the guidance of a vinegary newspaperman (William Holden). Although fairly stage-bound, the Kanin-Gordon dialogue is glorious and Cukor's direction immaculate.

Such heady but superbly controlled performances by stars of the calibre of Lombard, Grant, Hepburn, Stanwyck, Russell and Holliday remained the core of this form of entertainment, being enhanced in the greatest of them by intelligent direction, fast editing, frothy sets, persuasive camerawork and lighting, and a well-etched portrait gallery of eccentric characters encountered on the way.

Adam's Rib (Lawrence Weingarten), 1949 bw

Direction: George Cukor
Camera: George Folsey
Music: Miklos Rozsa
Art Direction: Cedric Gibbons, William Ferrari
Editing: George Boemler
Script: Ruth Gordon, Garson Kanin
Costume Design: Walter Plunkett

with Katharine Hepburn, Spencer Tracy, Judy Holliday, Tom Ewell, David Wayne, Jean Hagen, Clarence Kolb, Hope Emerson, Will Wright

- Criticism on release

    The equality of the sexes and the procedure of American law is most happily burlesqued in this witty comedy. The action is brisk and the interplay of characters extremely good. Katharine Hepburn and Spencer Tracy make a remarkably good comedy team...
    Lionel Collier, *Picturegoer*, 11 March 1950

- Current recommendations and ratings
StJD LM4 DQ4 DW4 VFG3½ MPG3½ NFT*

    ...If Hepburn's feminist arguments are a little on the wild side and too easily bounced off Tracy's paternalistic chauvinism, the script by the Kanins so bristles with wit that it scarcely matters. And in a film in which everybody is acting... the performances (not least from Wayne and Hagen) are matchless.
    Tom Milne, PTOG 1995

The Awful Truth, Col (Leo McCarey), 1937 bw

*Direction: Leo McCarey
Camera: Joseph Walker
Art Direction: Stephen Goosson, Lionel Banks
Editing: Al Clark
Script: Vina Delmar
Musical Direction: Morris Stoloff
Costume Design: Robert Kalloch

with Irene Dunne, Cary Grant, Ralph Bellamy, Alexander D'Arcy, Molly Lamont, Robert Warwick, Claude Allister, Mary Forbes, Alan Bridge, Byron Foulger

- Criticism on release

    The funniest picture of the season... a true director's triumph... In the general taste, motive and final pictorial result, above all in a sense of timing that is delicate and steady as a metronome, you can see the hand of a man who is sufficiently an artist in movies that he can make one out of almost anything, with almost anybody.
    Otis Ferguson, *New Republic*, 1 December 1937

- Current recommendations and ratings
S&S82/92 LM3½ DQ3 DW4 VFG5 MPG5 NFT*

    Zappy, sophisticated screwy comedy... A routine story perhaps, but McCarey transforms it, through his customary affection for his characters and taut pacing, into delightfully effective entertainment...
    Geoff Andrew, PTOG 1995

Born Yesterday, Col (S. Sylvan Simon), 1950 *bw*

Director: George Cukor
Camera: Joseph Walker
Music: Frederick Hollander
Art Direction: William Kiernan, Harry Horner
Editing: Charles Nelson

Script: Albert Mannheimer (from play by Garson Kanin)
Costume Design: Jean Louis

with *Judy Holliday, Broderick Crawford, William Holden, Howard St John

- Criticism on release

> [the] film has lost some of its wit and point on its journey from stage to screen... As it happens it is not the film that matters here; rather it is the playing of Miss Judy Holliday... there is something rich and strange about [her] particular stupidity – doubt insists on intruding and the startled audience has for a moment the monstrous suspicion Billie [Dawn] may be wiser than anyone around her...
>
> Anonymous critic in *The Times*, 30 April 1951

- Current recommendations and ratings
StJD LM3½ DQ4 DW4 VFG4 MPG4 NFT*

> ...screen version still a delight... A very simple idea but enlivened by a sharp witty script and by Cukor's effortless handling of the brilliant performances... Magic.
>
> Geoff Andrew, PTOG 1995

Bringing Up Baby, RKO (Howard Hawks/ Cliff Reid), 1938 bw

Direction: Howard Hawks	Script: Dudley Nichols, Hagar Wilde
Camera: Russell Metty	
Music: Roy Webb	Costume Design: Howard Greer
Editing: George Hively	
Art Direction: Van Nest Polglase, Perry Ferguson	

with Cary Grant, Katharine Hepburn, Charles Ruggles, May Robson, Barry Fitzgerald, Walter Catlett, Fritz Feld, Jack Carson, Ward Bond

- Criticism on release

    ...funny from the word go... Without the intelligence and mercury of [Hepburn's] study, the callous scheming of this bit of fluff would have left all in confusion and the audience howling for her blood. As it is, we merely accept and humor her, as one would a wife. Cary Grant does a nice job of underlining the situation...
    Otis Ferguson, *New Republic*, 16 March 1938

- Current recommendations and ratings
  StJD BN92 S&S82 LM3 DW5 VFG5 MPG5 NFT**

    ...one of the finest screwball comedies ever... Fast, furious, and very, very funny.
    Geoff Andrew, PTOG 1995

His Girl Friday, Col (Howard Hawks), 1940 *bw*

Direction: Howard Hawks
Camera: Joseph Walker
Musical Direction: Morris Stoloff
Art Direction: Lionel Banks
Costume Design: Robert Kalloch
Editing: Gene Havlick

Script: Charles Lederer, with Ben Hecht, uncredited (from the play *The Front Page* by Ben Hecht and Charles MacArthur)

with Cary Grant, Rosalind Russell, Ralph Bellamy, Gene Lockhart, Porter Hall, Ernest Truex, Cliff Edwards, Clarence Kolb, Roscoe Karns, Abner Biberman, Frank Jenks, Regis Toomey, Frank Orth, John Qualen, Billy Gilbert, Edwin Maxwell

- Criticism on release

    ...faster and funnier than many newspaper pictures since *The Front Page* (of which it is a remake): the main trouble is that when they made *The Front Page* the first time, it stayed made.
    Otis Ferguson, *New Republic*, 22 January 1940

- Current recommendations and ratings
StJD BN92 S&S92 LM4 DQ4 DW5 VFG5 MPG5 NFT*

    Perhaps the funniest, certainly the fastest talkie comedy ever made – Hawks transcends the piece's stage origins effortlessly... Quite simply a masterpiece.
    Geoff Andrew, PTOG 1995

It Happened One Night, Col (Harry Cohn), 1934 bw

*Direction: Frank Capra	*Script: Robert Riskin from Samuel Hopkins Adams's story *Night Bus*
Camera: Joseph Walker	
Art Direction: Stephen Goosson	
Editing: Gene Havlick	Costume Design: Robert Kalloch
Musical Direction: Louis Silvers	

with *Clark Gable, *Claudette Colbert, Walter Connolly, Roscoe Karns, Jameson Thomas, Alan Hale, Ward Bond, Arthur Hoyt, Irving Bacon, Charles D. Brown, James Burke

- Criticism on release

    ...better than it has any right to be – better acted, better directed, better written... By changing such types as the usual pooh-bah father and city editor into people with some wit and feeling, by consistently preferring the light touch to the heavy, and by casting actors who are thoroughly up to the work of acting, you can make some rather comely and greenish grasses grow where there was only alkali dust before...

    Otis Ferguson, *New Republic*, 9 May 1934

- Current recommendations and ratings
StJD BN92 S&S82/92 LM4 DQ4 DW5 VFG5 MPG5 NFT*

    Opinions divide about whether the film's comedy and sententious notions about the miserable rich and happy poor have dated, but some of the set pieces definitely haven't aged. Capra's sense of humour is a little like that of Preston Sturges, though less caustic; and the film shows its stars at their best.

    Rod McShane, PTOG 1995

The Lady Eve, Par (Paul Jones), 1941 bw

Direction, Script: Preston Sturges Camera: Victor Milner
Music: Leo Shuken Editing: Stuart Gilmore
Art Direction: Hans Dreier, Ernst Costume Design: Edith Head
  Fegte

with Barbara Stanwyck, Henry Fonda, Charles Coburn, William Demarest, Eugene Pallette, Eric Blore, Melville Cooper, Martha O'Driscoll, Robert Greig, Jimmy Conlin, Alan Bridge, Torben Meyer, Arthur Hoyt, Robert Warwick

- Criticism on release

    They are still asking how he does it, for *The Lady Eve* is his third picture in seven months, and one after the other they have been a delight both to exhibitors and to sit through... Mr Sturges picks his own subjects, writes his own screenplays and puts on his own show... has an appreciation of slapstick and a feeling for people as they are to be found in life – another package that is... the best fun in months.

    Otis Ferguson, *New Republic*, 9 May 1934

- Current recommendations and ratings
  StJD BN92 S&S92 LM3½ DQ3 DW5 VFG5 MPG5 NFT*

    A beguiling ribald sex comedy spattered with characteristic Sturges slapstick... and speech patterns ('Let us be crooked, but never common', urges Sturges's conman). Very nearly perfection and quintessential Sturges.

    Tom Milne, PTOG, 1995

Ninotchka, MGM (Ernst Lubitsch), 1939 bw

Direction: Ernst Lubitsch
Camera: William H. Daniels
Music: Werner Heymann
Art Direction: Cedric Gibbons, Randall Duell
Costume Design: Adrian

Script: Charles Brackett, Billy Wilder, Walter Reisch (from story by Melchior Lengyel)

Editing: Gene Ruggiero

with Greta Garbo, Melvyn Douglas, Ina Claire, Sig Rumann, Felix Bressart, Alexander Granach, Bela Lugosi, Frank Reicher, George Tobias, Mary Forbes, Edwin Maxwell

- Criticism on release

    strikes a wrong note occasionally. But the story gets there, its people are real enough, it has an overall radiance of pleasant but knowing wit... Greta Garbo is the life of it [with] something of a natural style in acting which may take hard work to perfect, but never looks like it...

    Otis Ferguson, *New Republic*, 9 May 1934

- Current recommendations and ratings
  StJD BN92 S&S92 LM3½ DQ4 DW5 VFG5 MPG5 NFT*

    ...not quite the delight history says it is – by the late 30s the famed Lubitsch touch was resembling a heavy blow, the elegant sophistication turning crude and cynical. Yet it's still consistently amusing, and Garbo throws herself into the fray with engaging vigour.

    Geoff Brown, PTOG 1995

The Palm Beach Story, Par (Paul Jones), 1942 bw

Direction, Script: Preston Sturges   Camera: Victor Milner
Music: Victor Young   Costume Design: Irene
Art Direction: Hans Dreier, Ernst
   Fegte
Editing: Stuart Gilmore

with Joel McCrea, Claudette Colbert, Rudy Vallee, Mary Astor, Robert Warwick, Torben Meyer, Jimmy Conlin, William Demarest, Robert Greig, Roscoe Ates, Chester Conklin, Franklin Pangborn, Arthur Hoyt, Alan Bridge, Esther Howard

- Criticism on release

    Mr Sturges, although the fashion among connoisseurs these days, seems just as light-hearted and carefree as a director with no reputation to sustain. If anything, his wit is the nimbler, his fun has a freer range... [the film's] charm lies in the liberty of the camera to digress, comment, fool, beguile and reassemble life to its own pattern
    C.A. Lejeune, *The Observer*, 30 August 1942

- Current recommendations and ratings
  StJD S&S82 LM3½ DQ3 DW5 VFG4½ MPG4 NFT*

    ...few [Sturges'] films were as smoothly accomplished – a knowing satire on the driving force of sex and money... Hilarious, irresistible, impeccably cast.
    Geoff Brown, PTOG 1995

SEX COMEDY

Before Marilyn Monroe there were Jean Harlow and Mae West. Jean Harlow's finest hour was probably in *Dinner at Eight* (see 'Compendium Films' later): Mae West's was probably *She Done Him Wrong*, 1933, adapted from her own play *Diamond Lil*. It derives most of its impact from her bawdy jest and opulent curves, with young Cary Grant providing the right amount of masculine friction. It is an enjoyable tongue-in-cheek version of the kind of sexploitation movie that forced the industry to impose a unique form of self-censorship, the Hays

Code, in the following year. It also was Paramount's financial saviour at a time when its executives were thinking of selling out to MGM.

She Done Him Wrong, Par (William LeBaron), 1933 bw

Direction: Lowell Sherman
Camera: Charles Lang
Songs: Leo Robin, Ralph Rainger
Art Direction: Robert Usher
Costume Design: Edith Head
Script: Mae West, Harvey Thew, John Bright (from Mae West's play, *Diamond Lil*)
Choreography: Harold Hecht
Editing: Alexander Hall

with Mae West, Cary Grant, Owen Moore, Gilbert Roland, Rochelle Hudson, Noah Beery Sr, David Landau, Rafaela Ottiano, Dewey Robinson, Tammany Young, Louise Beavers, Lee Kohmar, Tom Kennedy

- Criticism on release

    ...a pleasant surprise to discover Mae West, swan bed and all, in a movie version of her great play *Diamond Lil*. *She Done Him Wrong* is played straight and to the hilt, and as a result it is good fun... The production itself is surprisingly good; the sets and lighting, and the general direction handled by Lowell Sherman, are way above par... Although definitely a burlesque show, it has a certain beery poignancy and, above all, a gusto about it which makes it a good show.

    Pare Lorentz, *Vanity Fair*, March 1933

- Current recommendations and ratings
  LM4 DQ4 DW4 VFG5 MPG4 NFT*

    West's first starring vehicle and one of her best (i.e. least diluted) movies... West, making her way through ditties like 'I Like a Man What Takes His Time' and 'Frankie and Johnny', keeps most of her double-meanings single. Marvellous stuff.

    Geoff Andrew, PTOG, 1995

Compendium (Portmanteau) Films

There are two main kinds of compendium films: a collection of short stories (of which there are no examples here) and an integrated narrative in which several characters and their lives interact within a complex pattern of development. In reviewing *Grand Hotel*, 1932, Andrew Nickolds refers to it as a film in the 'portmanteau style' and defines this as 'an interwoven group of contrasting stories allowing a bunch of stars to do their familiar turns', a fair description of Irving Thalberg's first great MGM showpiece, featuring Greta Garbo, John Barrymore, Lionel Barrymore, Wallace Beery, Joan Crawford, Jean Hersholt and Lewis Stone. The film's success established MGM's recognisably high production values provided by the director, Edmund Goulding, art director Cedric Gibbons, costume designer Adrian and cameraman William Daniels. From then on the glossiness of quality for which MGM became famous was owed to this grand experiment of an ambitious 'compendium' film concerning the lives of the residents of a Berlin hotel.

Dinner at Eight, 1933, was intended to repeat this success and, according to most of today's critics, is superior to its forerunner. George Cukor's direction has more bite, more wit – but this may also be due to the astringent dialogue from the original stage play by George S. Kaufman and Edna Ferber – and greater pace. Again a sparkling cast, with (once more) Wallace Beery (as a boorish businessman), John Barrymore (as an ageing *roué*), and Lionel Barrymore (as the troubled host). Jean Harlow shines as Beery's vulgar, ambitious wife, Marie Dressler is impressive as a once great actress, Billie Burke does her entertaining twittering as the feather-headed hostess, and the rest of the scintillating cast includes Madge Evans, Edmund Lowe, Lee Tracy, Phillips Holmes, Jean Hersholt (once more), and May Robson.

The compendium in Gregory La Cava's *Stage Door*, 1937, is provided by a bevy of would-be actresses sharing an off-Broadway rooming-house. Like *Dinner at Eight*, it was adapted from a stage play by George S. Kaufman and Edna Ferber, but this time receiving the RKO treatment, under Pandro S. Berman, grainier, more realistic, more *earthy* camerawork (by Robert De Grasse). According to Danny Peary (*Guide for the Film Fanatic*, 1987), "what keeps the film from dating is the camaraderie exhibited" by these inmates, enacted by a "once-in-a-lifetime group of actresses" – Katharine Hepburn, Ginger Rogers (breaking away from Fred Astaire), Lucille Ball (still at the beginning of her career), Ann Miller (the whirlwind dancer), Eve Arden (mistress of the caustic epigram), Gail Patrick (always sickeningly beautiful and successful) and the ingénue, Andrea Leeds. The cast also includes Adolphe Menjou (as a lecherous producer), 'grande dame' Constance Collier, and two masters of camp comedy, Franklin Pangborn and Grady Sutton.

Robert Altman's *Nashville*, 1975 is the compendium film to beat all compendium films, featuring twenty-four major characters, even more country and western songs (many composed by the performers themselves), glimpses of life on the professional circuit, enthusiastic amateurs and fans, and the background of an ecological party's presidential campaign. James Monaco has, quite rightly, suggested (*American Film Now*, 1979) that the more people an Altman movie contains, the better it is. Certainly, *Nashville* is considered to show his thoroughgoing panoramic style at its best. Altman can only put an end to his incessantly inventive plots and sub-plots by the shock of an assassination at the final fund-raising concert, and the ironic bellowing of 'It Don't Worry Me', as the quintessential country and western morale booster, to bring the movie to an end. Planned on the scale of von Stroheim's *Greed* (with an initial eight-hour rough-cut) and similarly doctored down to an ultimate 160-minute release, it still overflows the screen in an amiable excess of quirkiness, fun, satire and music (country and western style).

Woody Allen's *Hannah and Her Sisters*, 1986, is a first-rate seriocomedy in which the Allen persona (in this case a hypochondriac TV writer, Mickey Sachs, who has to confront the threat of terminal cancer) is merely one of the several central characters revolving around three sisters – Hannah (Mia Farrow), Lee (Barbara Hershey), and Holly (Dianne Wiest). The family and love-life relationships are extremely complex, structured around three Thanksgiving dinners, where we meet the parents (Lloyd Nolan and Maureen O'Sullivan), retired entertainers. Mickey was married to Hannah, now married to a financial adviser (Michael Caine), who in turn is attempting to seduce Lee away from a gloomy Swedish sculptor (Max von Sydow). Holly, who sniffs cocaine to console herself for a frustratingly unsuccessful dramatic career, has a brief affair with an architect (Sam Waterston) before dating Mickey (in a riotously disastrous sequence) and ultimately marrying him. Complex enough?

Dinner at Eight, MGM (David O. Selznick), 1933 bw

Direction: George Cukor
Camera: William H. Daniels
Art Direction: Cedric Gibbons
Costume Design: Adrian
Editing: Ben Lewis
Script: Frances Marion, Herman Mankiewicz, Donald Ogden Stewart (from play by George S. Kaufman and Edna Ferber

with Marie Dressler, John Barrymore, Jean Harlow, Lionel Barrymore, Wallace Beery, Lee Tracy, Edmund Lowe, Billie Burke, Madge Evans, Karen Morley, May Robson, Phillips Holmes, Elizabeth Patterson, Jean Hersholt, Louise Closser Hale, Grant Mitchell, Edwin Maxwell, Herman Bing

- Criticism on release

    Like *Grand Hotel*, the novelty and pace accounted for part of its success – this kaleidoscopic cross-section method of storytelling is novel on the stage. It is the very basic principle, however, of moviemaking. The camera can go everywhere... Mr Cukor chose (wisely, considering his unexciting record) to take no chances with directorial experimentation... [showing] close-up shots of characters delivering their lines... This, unfortunately, slows down the pace of the picture...
    Pare Lorentz, *Vanity Fair*, October 1933

- Current recommendations and ratings
LM4 DQ4 DW4 VFG5 MPG5 NFT*

    ...perfect material for Cukor's satirical touch... The laughs are mainly at the expense of the nouveau riche couple, a comedy of manners in which Harlow reveals her natural gift for humour and Beery confirms his status as the definitive boor. But the film

    also reflects the vagaries of the 1930s social scene. Perfect viewing for a wet Saturday afternoon.
    Martyn Auty, PTOG 1995

Grand Hotel, MGM (Irving Thalberg), 1932 bw

Direction: Edmund Goulding
Camera: William H. Daniels
Art Direction: Cedric Gibbons
Costume Design: Adrian
Editing: Blanche Sewell

Script: William Drake (from his translation of Vicki Baum's *Menschen Im Hotel*)

with Greta Garbo, John Barrymore, Joan Crawford, Wallace Beery, Lionel Barrymore, Lewis Stone, Jean Hersholt, Robert McWade, Purnell Pratt, Ferdinand Gottschalk, Rafaela Ottiano, Frank Conroy

- Criticism on release

    ...Edmund Goulding has done an intelligent piece of work, but occasionally it seems as though he relies too much on close-ups. Nevertheless, he has maintained a steady momentum in darting here and there in the busy hostelry and working up to an effective dramatic pitch at the psychological moment. Garbo... is stunning in her early scenes and charming in her love scene with Baron Gaigern, portrayed by John Barrymore with his usual *savoir faire*. [This] does not mean that any aspersion is to be cast at the work of the others in the cast. Miss Crawford, for instance, is splendid...

    Mordaunt Hall, *New York Times*, 13 April 1932

- Current recommendations and ratings
  LM4 DQ4 DW4 VFG5 MPG5 NFT*

    The *Nashville* of its day, *Grand Hotel*'s reputation has outgrown its actual quality, and it is now interesting only as an example of the portmanteau style... Throw in Cedric Gibbons as art director and cameraman William Daniels, and you have the perfect MGM vehicle – dead boring...

    Andrew Nickolds, PTOG 1995

Stage Door, RKO (Pandro S. Berman), 1937 bw

Direction: Gregory La Cava
Camera: Robert De Grasse
Music: Roy Webb
Art Direction: Van Nest Polglase, Carroll Clark
Costume Design: Muriel King

Script: Morris Ryskind, Anthony Veiller, La Cava, uncredited (uc), from play by George Kaufman and Edna Ferber
Editing: William Hamilton

with Katharine Hepburn, Ginger Rogers, Adolphe Menjou, Gail Patrick, Andrea Leeds, Eve Arden, Lucille Ball, Ann Miller, Constance Collier, Samuel S. Hinds, Franklin Pangborn, Jack Carson, Grady Sutton, Katharine Alexander, Ralph Forbes, Mary Forbes, Theodore von Eltz, Pierre Watkin, Frank Reicher

- Criticism on release

    I don't know where you will find so much delight and unspoiled entertainment as in the RKO picture *Stage Door*... As the girls sit around in the boarding-house parlor, swapping thrust and riposte and grousing about the stew, their lives and habits of living are undoubtedly both more brilliant and more warmly generous than life. But while this picture is being reeled off, it is humanly lovely, bright and sad and true – it is a long time since we have seen so much feminine talent so deftly handled...

    Otis Ferguson, *New Republic*, 27 October 1937

- Current recommendations and ratings
LM4 DW5 VFG5 MPG5 NFT*

    ...one of the great sassy-women comedy-dramas of the 30s – the crackling ensemble pieces remain in the memory, expertly timed by La Cava's civilised, generous direction, and localised in lovingly authentic sets beautifully shot by Robert De Grasse.

    Geoff Andrew, PTOG 1995

Hannah and Her Sisters, Orion (Robert Greenhut), 1986
colour

Direction, *Script: Woody Allen   Production Designer: Stuart
Camera: Carlo Di Palma   Wurzel
Costume Design: Jeffrey Kurland   Editing: Susan E. Morse

with Woody Allen, *Michael Caine, Mia Farrow, Carrie Fisher, Barbara Hershey, Lloyd Nolan, Maureen O'Sullivan, Daniel Stern, Max von Sydow, *Dianne Wiest, John Turturro

- Criticism on release

    ...what fools these mortals be, indeed. They are the familiar middle-class and upwardly mobile New Yorkers of Allen's own microcosm, prey to fears, neuroses, fashions, analysts, drugs, lust, alcohol and the latest vogues in books, painting or rock groups. Nobody describes them with a shrewder wit. Allen understands their frail humanity, and loves the losers most of all. Allen is one of those rare clowns with the gift of discovering the universal upon his own doorstep.

    David Robinson, *The Times*, 18 July 1986

- Current recommendations and ratings
BN92 LM3½ DQ3 DW4 VFG4½ MPG5 NFT*

    Wandering in and out of this extended dissection of family love life is Allen himself, playing his familiar nebbish hypochondriac; when a medical crisis brings him uncomfortably close to death, he samples all the different religions, before turning to the Marx Brothers' films as evidence that life is to be enjoyed. It is an articulate, literate film full of humanity and perception about its sometimes less-than-loveable characters, which nonetheless comes down on the side of the best things in life...

    Chris Peachment, PTOG 1995

Nashville, Par (Robert Altman), 1975 colour

Direction: Robert Altman
Camera: Paul Lohmann
Editing: Sidney Levin, Dennis M. Hill
Script: Joan Tewkesbury
Music: Richard Baskin et al. (including *song by Keith Carradine 'I'm Easy')

with Henry Gibson, Michael Murphy, Ned Beatty, Renee Blakley, Keith Carradine, Allan Nicholl, Cristina Gaines, Lily Tomlin, Geraldine Chaplin, Allan Garfield, Karen Black, Gwen Welles, David Hayward, Barbara Harris, Keenan Wynn, Tim Brown, Scott Glen, Jeff Goldblum, David Arkin, David Peel, Richard Baskin (bit), Elliott Gould (as himself) and Julie Christie (as herself)

- Criticism on release

> If *Nashville* in fact has not much to say, it says it at great length, and entertainingly. It all sails along, stopping and starting (the stops mostly look like moments where Altman has admiringly let his artists improvise, with varied effectiveness), maintaining its hold on us by Altman's appreciation of all the oddity of the American scene and its people, and by a cast of consistently excellent performances...
>
> David Robinson, *The Times* 19 September 1975

- Current recommendations and ratings
StJD BN92 S&S82/92 LM4 DW4 VFG5 MPG5 NFT*

> ...a wonderful mosaic, which yields up greater riches with successive viewings, not least in the underrated songs, the superlative performances, and the open-mindedness of Altman's approach to direction. Immensely, exhilaratingly enjoyable.
>
> Tom Milne, PTOG 1995

Costume Spectacle – Epics, Period Pieces

Epics

Epics (or 'blockbusters') are immensely long, vastly expensive, action dramas based on well-known historical, often Biblical, events and personalities, and aimed at wide distribution in the world market. This type of film has been with us from the earliest days of the industry, to begin with in Italy: D.W. Griffith's *The Birth of a Nation* and *Intolerance* were made to demonstrate that Hollywood could do what the Italians had shown themselves capable of. Griffith's films, in fact, had widespread world influence, providing film-makers with a comprehensive 'grammar' of film-making, particularly in the field of editing (montage), but also concerned with all aspects of *mise en scène* and narrative continuity.

In spite of violent protests against its theme *The Birth of a Nation*, 1915, proved a commercial success; even today, when its racist approach to the 'black man' and its powerful defence of Ku Klux Klan activities in the immediate post-Civil War period is even more offensive than it was at the time of issue, we find, on viewing it, a compulsion to watch, putty in the hands of a master film-maker. *The Birth of a Nation* grips with its narrative power, in spite of many defects in its presentation and its bias against the emancipated slaves. Griffith was spurred on by its success to produce an even more ambitious spectacle in *Intolerance*, 1916, welding four stories into one continuous parallel narrative – the fall of Babylon to the Persians, the crucifixion of Christ, the St Bartholomew's Day Massacre, and a contemporary story of last-minute reprieve from execution. The colossal Babylonian sets were perhaps over-grandiose but distinctly memorable. Unfortunately, the film was a 'striking flop' (Roy Armes, *Film and Reality*, 1974), although attendances may have been affected by the fact that the USA entered World War I during its distribution.

Staging a film epic has from the beginning been a very risky financial business. MGM's *Ben-Hur* of 1925 cost $4 million and took three years to complete, beset by troubles throughout, Rex Ingram's first attempt in Italy for Metro being scrapped and only finished after two changes in director and much wasted footage before Ramon Novarro was cast in the lead. The second *Ben-Hur*, 1959, was budgeted at $10m and finally completed for $15m, a high cost ultimately justified by its great popular success, since it grossed nearly $40m. Both versions relied very much on the action sequences – particularly the climactic chariot race, brilliantly filmed by B. Reeves Eason in the first version and by Andrew Marton and Yakima Canutt in the second.

The boom in epics during the late 50s and early 60s became Hollywood's chief response to the challenge of the television small screen, using the latest technical developments, like Robert Surtees's use of a 65mm camera lens in *Ben-Hur*, to provide the 'colossal' entertainment of which Hollywood had always boasted and which was absolutely unobtainable in its glittering, shattering form outside the cinema palaces. Many of the directors commissioned to make these blockbusters – Wyler, for one – had, unlike Cecil B. de Mille (who, ironically, does not rate an undisputed 'classic' among his prolific output for Paramount), little or no experience in this form of production.

It is unlikely that William Wyler was chosen to direct the remake in 1959 because he had been one of the many assistant directors to Fred Niblo in the original: although he had had no previous experience in epic film-making, his technical skill was undoubted and he was known to have "good taste in dealing with highly charged dramatic materials" (M.A. Anderegg, *William Wyler*, 1979). The dialogue was perhaps over-literate (with uncredited contributions from Christopher Fry and Gore Vidal, among others), but the film gained from its frequent and telling references to the living presence of Christ, to whose doctrines the young Jewish hero (played in strong, unsubtle profile by Charlton Heston) is converted. Both versions benefited from excellent performances of Messala, Ben-Hur's former Roman friend become enemy, played in 1925 by Francis X. Bushman and in 1959 by Stephen Boyd.

The Birth of a Nation, Epoch (D.W. Griffith), 1915 bw

Direction: D.W. Griffith
Camera: Billy Bitzer, Karl Brown
Music: Griffith, Joseph Carl Breil
Editing: James E. Smith

Script: Griffith, Frank Woods (from Thomas Dixon's novel *The Klansman*)

with Lillian Gish, Mae Marsh, Elmer Clifton, Henry B. Walthall, Miriam Cooper, Ralph Lewis, Donald Crisp, Eugene Pallette, Raoul Walsh, Sam de Grasse, Wallace Reid, Bessie Love, Elmo Lincoln, Gibson Gowland, Erich von Stroheim (bit)

- Criticism on release

    It would be difficult to overpraise the spectacular part of these reels... Two of the most wonderful pictures ever seen on the screen are Lincoln signing the first call for volunteers and the surrender of Lee to Grant at Appomattox – The weird and mystical garb [of the Ku Klux Klan] has given the director splendid opportunities which he used to the fullest... the audience never fails to respond... On more than one occasion (during the private showing) there were hisses mingled with the applause evoked by the undisguised appeal to racial prejudice.
    W. Stephen Bush, *The Moving Picture World*,
    13 March 1915

- Current recommendations and ratings
  StJD BN92 S&S82/92 LM4 DW4 MPG5 NFT*

    ...remarkable for its technical innovations, and for the truly epic feel... The biggest challenge the film provided for its audience is perhaps to decide when 'ground-breaking, dedicated serious cinematic art' must be reviled as politically reprehensible. The film's explicit glorification of the Ku Klux Klan has never tempered with time.
    Martin Sutton, PTOG 1995

Intolerance, WPC (D.W. Griffith), 1916 bw

Direction, Script: D.W. Griffith
Camera: Billy Bitzer, Karl Brown
Music: Joseph Carl Breil, Griffith
Art Direction: R.E. Wales, with Frank Wortman and Walter L. Hall
Editing: James E. & Rose Smith

with Mae Marsh, Bessie Love, Constance Talmadge, Sam de Grasse, Eugene Pallette, Donald Crisp, Tod Browning, Miriam Cooper, Seena Owen, Elmo Lincoln, Elmer Clifton, Tully Marshall

- Criticism on release

    As a picture *Intolerance* is quite the most marvelous thing which has been put on the screen, but as a theory of life it is trite without being true... The battle before, on and over the walls of Babylon is quite the finest achievement of motion picture art [But] it should be remarked that the genius of this film director does not lie only in the handling of mass effects. Indeed, much of the effectiveness lies in the manner he will drop a big effect to hammer home an interesting detail. In all the technical aspects of screen photography, the picture is remarkable...

    Heywood Broun, *The New York Tribune*,
    7 September 1916

- Current recommendations and ratings
StJD S&S82/92 LM4 DW5 MPG4 NFT*

    ...The thematic approach no longer works (if it ever did); the title cards are stiffly Victorian and sometimes laughingly pedantic; but the visual poetry is overwhelming, especially in the massed crowd scenes.

    Chris Auty, PTOG 1995

Ben-Hur, MGM (Sam Zimbalist), 1959 *colour*

*Direction: William Wyler (with Andrew Marton, Yakima Canutt, Richard Thorpe)
Script: Karl Tunberg (with S.N. Behrman, Christopher Fry, Gore Vidal, all uncredited)
Camera: Robert Surtees
Art Direction: William Horning, Edward Carfagno
Costume Design: Elizabeth Haffenden
Editing: Ralph Winters, John Dunning
*Music: Miklos Rozsa
*Special Effects: A. Arnold Gillespie, Robert MacDonald, Milo Lory

with *Charlton Heston, Jack Hawkins, Stephen Boyd, Haya Harareet *Hugh Griffith, Martha Scott, Sam Jaffe, Cathy O'Donnell, Finlay Currie

- Criticism on release

    There is something in this film for all, and all of us have a hand in making it – indirectly, or to judge by the endless cast list and credits and additional mentions, pretty damned directly, too... For myself, I greatly enjoyed Hugh Griffith's performance as a wily Arabian sheik, and I thought the chariot race superb. But I was disappointed in the gifted William Wyler's inability to lift the religious scenes above the Sunday School level, to put any real excitement into most of the spectacle, or to infuse most of the acting with vitality...

    Stanley Kauffmann, *New Republic* 28 December 1959

- Current recommendations and ratings
S&S92 LM3½ DQ4 DW3 VFG4½ MPG5 NFT**

    Although a bit like a four-hour Sunday school lesson, *Ben-Hur* is not without its compensations, above all, of course, the chariot race (which was directed not by Wyler but by Andrew Marton, and it shows)...

    Scott Meek, PTOG 1995

PERIOD PIECES

A larger number of motion pictures set in a recognisable historical setting do not possess the grand scale of the 'epic', but in their less pretentious way make a strong appeal to audiences with their affectionately – if not always accurately – portrayed period backgrounds. These divide into two main groups: those based on male prowess (often referred to as 'swashbucklers' from the frequent seventeenth century versions), and others, with ambitious, intelligent women at the centre dealing with problems of power.

Queen Christina and *The Scarlet Empress* could both be classified as romantic dramas, because they – the Garbo picture more than the Dietrich one – have a romantic love element that dominates in certain episodes.

Tom Milne, in his study of Mamoulian's work, called *Queen Christina* "carefully scripted [with] moments of genuine distinction", but it is generally associated with two memorable sequences: the lingering, sensuous farewell to the room of Christina's happiness, and the final departure with her lover's corpse on the way to Spain, where she strikes a now-familiar Garbo-esque pose at the prow of the ship. Otis Ferguson (*New Republic* 31 January 1934), however, found that the film reaped "no profit from the fact, that under the ambassadorial mustachios you can perceive the lineaments of Mr John Gilbert." During the viewing of this film, it is impossible to forget that the 'extraordinary attractiveness' of Garbo's screen presence was due to her voice, "low, husky and accented" (Jack Ellis, *History of Film*).

With Dietrich it is an image of convincing perversity (deliberately cultivated by her first – and greatest – director, von Sternberg) in her study of a German foundling who, against all sorts of court intrigue, retains her power as a widowed Tsarina. Although completely studio-bound, owing to von Sternberg's desire for comprehensive control over the product, including, in this case, the arrangement and conducting of the music, together with the editing (shades of Chaplin!) and, in spite of its contemporary reputation as 'pure hokum', it has gained increasing respect as an art film over the years.

The leitmotif of the tolling bell haunts one throughout after the first cruel image of a near-naked man used as a clapper, while the meaningful glances between Dietrich and her leading man, John Lodge, playing Alexei, an "inveterate and opportunistic seducer" (as Robin Wood calls him), punctuate the main development of the plot and provide the blend of savagery and eroticism which are the main features of this baroque drama. Sam Jaffe's performance as the mad Tsar is also suitably over the top. Von Sternberg's artistic conception dominates, although he owes a great deal to his production designers, particularly Peter Ballbusch, for the grotesque and horrifying statues that serve as furniture and decoration for the palace.

One of the earliest sound classics of male prowess is an archetypal sea drama, based on fact, *Mutiny on the Bounty*, produced under Irving Thalberg at MGM and winning the 1935 Academy Award for Best Picture. Three excellent performances – by Laughton as the sadistic and tyrannical Bligh (the most parodied film role at the time!), Gable as the forthright and imperturbable leader of the mutineers, and Franchot Tone as a young officer disillusioned by Bligh's inhuman behaviour – give psychological weight to a beautifully directed, photographed, costumed, and edited historical action film. David O. Selznick's version of Anthony Hope's scintillating Ruritanian adventure – *The Prisoner of Zenda*, 1937 – has been called "the product of a perfect collaborative effort that has created something flawless and timeless" (Jeffrey Richards, in *Radio Times*). Selznick's meticulous faithfulness to a movie's literary origins, linked with tasteful and pacy direction by John Cromwell (with help from W.S. Van Dyke II and George Cukor) and faultless casting – Ronald Colman as the very English double of the kidnapped king, Madeleine Carroll as the graceful, delicately beautiful princess, Douglas Fairbanks Jr. as the charming rogue, Rupert of Hentzau, Raymond Massey as the sardonic 'Black Michael', and on through Mary Astor, C. Aubrey Smith, David Niven downwards – gave the black-and-white version a quality unmatched even in the coloured replica produced for MGM in 1952.

The romantic heroes portrayed by Errol Flynn are amongst the most attractive of Warner Brothers' pre-war period – light-hearted, charming, feckless, an embodiment of the almost facetious chivalry symbolised in Shakespeare's Hotspur, as in *The Adventures of Robin Hood*, 1938, with Flynn as the eponymous hero distinguishing himself in all kinds of presentable ways, but especially in the final exciting duel scene with the ideal 'baddie' of such movies, Basil Rathbone. The film is somewhat of a mish-mash in intention, a mixture of physical adventure with low comedy and idealised romance, but it is vigorously and exhilaratingly executed, artificial but always gripping, with good comic-strip characterisations all round, impressive colour photography and a rousing orchestral score by Warners' most inventive movie composer, Erich Korngold.

Michael Curtiz took over the direction of *Robin Hood* from William Keighley, demonstrating his ability to direct all genres with inspired precision, and was also assigned to *The Sea Hawk*, 1940, a true 'swashbuckler' in which Flynn disports himself admirably as a sixteenth-century patriotic privateer in Elizabethan sword-play and sea battles against the naval might and diplomatic intrigue of Spain. The movie is perfect of its kind, with particularly incisive performances by Claude Rains, as a Spanish intriguer, and Flora Robson as a forthright and vibrant Queen Elizabeth.

These years preceding World War II were distinguished by high-quality films of the boys' adventure type. George Stevens's *Gunga Din*, 1939, remains a fascinating example of its kind with marvellous action scenes, beautifully photographed (by Joseph August), and witty portrayals of Kipling's 'Soldiers Three' by Cary Grant, Douglas Fairbanks Jr., and Victor McLaglen at the centre of the action. Although perhaps not very accurate historically, this is first-rate 'hokum' of the imperial kind, the British Raj depicted with nobility (and some raffishness), the Indian colonials as rebellious and devious, with the exception of the superbly loyal water-carrier, Gunga Din (Sam Jaffe).

Gunga Din's studio, RKO, also produced another high-quality period film in 1939 – William Dieterle's *The Hunchback of Notre Dame*. Best-known for the grotesque make-up and moving performance of Charles Laughton as Quasimodo, the hunchback, it is in fact an interesting study in low medieval life, with fine performances all round (Thomas Mitchell, Cedric Hardwicke, Edmond O'Brien, and the lovely Maureen O'Hara). Dieterle gave an interpretation that was greatly influenced by the masterpieces of the German expressionist cinema, in which he had worked before coming to Hollywood: the photography is inventive and distinctive, with many unusual angles (also by Joseph August).

Gunga Din, RKO (George Stevens), 1939 bw

Direction: George Stevens
Camera: Joseph August
Music: Alfred Newman
Art Direction: Van Nest Polglase, Perry Ferguson
Special Effects: Vernon Walker
Editing: Henry Berman, John Lockert
Script: Fred Guiol (from story by Ben Hecht, Charles MacArthur and William Faulkner, based on Kipling's poem)
Costume Design: Edward Stevenson

with Cary Grant, Victor McLaglen, Douglas Fairbanks Jr., Sam Jaffe, Eduardo Cianelli, Joan Fontaine, Montagu Love, Robert Coote, Abner Biberman, Lumsden Hare

- Criticism on release

    ...to me a sad marker of the decline Hollywood has gone into since the day a few years ago when it could bang out *Lives of a Bengal Lancer* – Cary Grant, Douglas Fairbanks Jr. and Victor McLaglen do nicely in spite of everything, though I regret to say that Sam Jaffe was persuaded to play Gunga Din – the whole mood is irresponsible and wrong... if [it] had been made with the right tongues in the right cheeks it might have passed as a fine burlesque...

    Otis Ferguson, *New Republic*, 22 February 1939

- Current recommendations and ratings
  BN92 LM4 DQ4 DW3 VFG5 MPG5 NFT*

    ...of course one winces a little at the smug colonialist attitudes... All the same this is a pretty spiffing adventure yarn, with some classically staged fights, terrific performances, and not too much stiff upper lip as Kipling's soldiers three go about their rowdy, non-commissioned and sometimes disreputable capers...

    Tom Milne, PTOG 1995

The Hunchback of Notre Dame, RKO (Pandro S. Berman), 1939 bw

Direction: William Dieterle Camera: Joseph August Music: Alfred Newman Art Direction: Van Nest Polglase Editing: William Hamilton, Robert Wise	Script: Sonya Levien, Bruno Frank (from Victor Hugo's novel)

with Charles Laughton, Cedric Hardwicke, Thomas Mitchell, Maureen O'Hara, Edmond O'Brien, Alan Marshal, Walter Hampden, Harry Davenport, Katharine Alexander, George Zucco, Minna Gombell

- Criticism on release

    ...all expense and care and dramatic possibilities considered, ...my candidate for the worst made class-A film of the year. Charles Laughton is effective as usual; the spectacles are spectacular and the sets are good; the main belfry and mob-scene stuff is so near foolproof that it could be crippled only by a superscrupulous application to ham theatricals, but they went at it scrupulously...

    Otis Ferguson, *New Republic*, 22 January 1940

- Current recommendations and ratings
LM3 DQ4 DW4 VFG5 MPG5 NFT*

    ...[Laughton's] hunchback comes across as one of the cinema's most impressive 'grotesque' characterisations. Dieterle directs in a way that reminds you of his background as actor/director in the German expressionist cinema – richly entertaining.

    Tony Rayns, PTOG 1995

Mutiny on the Bounty, MGM (Irving Thalberg/ Frank Lloyd), 1935 *bw*

Direction: Frank Lloyd
Camera: Arthur Edeson
Music: Herbert Stothart,
  Bronislaw Kaper
Art Direction: Cedric Gibbons, A.
  Arnold ('Buddy') Gillespie
	Script: Jules Furthman, Talbot
	  Jennings, Carey Wilson (from
	  the novels by Charles Nordhoff
	  and James Norman Hall
	Editing: Margaret Booth

with Clark Gable, Charles Laughton, Franchot Tone, Henry Stephenson, Dudley Digges, Eddie Quillan, Donald Crisp, Spring Byington, Doris Lloyd, Ian Wolfe, Herbert Mundin

- Criticism on release

    One of the best pictures that have been made – the whole tone of the picture is set by the beauty they have found in ships and described with the true care and knowledge of the craftsman... – by virtue of vivid action... the picture manages to hold [the story] together...

    Otis Ferguson, *New Republic*, 27 November 1935

- Current recommendations and ratings
S&S92 LM4 DQ3 DW4 VFG5 MPG5 NFT*

    An exotic and gripping piece of Hollywood mythology, made with all the technical skill and gloss one associates with Irving Thalberg's MGM...

    Adrian Turner, PTOG 1995

The Prisoner of Zenda, Selznick (David O. Selznick), 1937 bw

Direction: John Cromwell (with George Cukor, W.S. Van Dyke uc) Camera: James Wong Howe Music: Alfred Newman Art Direction: Lyle Wheeler Costume Design: Ernest Dryden	Script: John Balderston, Wells Root, Donald Ogden Stewart (from Edward Rose's play based on Anthony Hope's novel) Special Effects: Jack Cosgrove Editing: Hal C. Kern, James Newcom

with Ronald Colman, Madeleine Carroll, Douglas Fairbanks Jr., Mary Astor, C. Aubrey Smith, Raymond Massey, David Niven, Eleanor Wesselhoeff, Byron Foulger, Montagu Love

- Criticism on release

    ...one of the best things in its class – once the story is accepted, you can see how they worked at it with sincerity and scrupulous care, treating its hokum with dignity. Ronald Colman in the main double role is one reason why the scenes are built into credibility, and Madeleine Carroll... another. Douglas Fairbanks Jr. makes a good ornamental rogue...

    Otis Ferguson, *New Republic*, 15 September 1937

- Current recommendations and ratings
  LM3½ DQ4 DW4 VFG5 MPG5 NFT*

    Easily the best version of Anthony Hope's perennial Ruritanian adventure, often cited as one of the great swashbucklers... Lots of pomp and splendour (especially in the over-indulged Coronation sequence) make Cromwell's elegant direction incline to stateliness, but the swordplay is ripping and Wong Howe's camerawork superb.

    Tom Milne, PTOG 1995

Queen Christina, MGM (Walter Wanger), 1933 bw

Direction: Rouben Mamoulian
Camera: William H. Daniels
Music: Herbert Stothart
Art Direction: Alexander Toluboff
Editing: Blanche Sewell

Script: Salka Viertel, H.M. Harwood, S.N. Behrman, from Margaret R. Levino's story
Costume Design: Adrian

with Greta Garbo, John Gilbert, Ian Keith, Lewis Stone, C. Aubrey Smith, Reginald Owen, Gustav von Seyffertitz, Akim Tamiroff

- Criticism on release

    [Garbo] manages to be a presence, but becomes an empty and futile one, not because it is poor history but because it has nothing satisfactory to give in history's place.

    Otis Ferguson, *New Republic*, 31 January 1934

- Current recommendations and ratings
  LM4 DW5 VFG5 MPG5 NFT**

    ...lifted far above its origins, partly by Mamoulian – who moulds potentially stodgy scenes with his finicky regard to detail; and partly by Garbo herself [who] glides through Mamoulian's winding camera movements with grace, wit and beauty.

    Geoff Brown, PTOG 1995

The Scarlet Empress, Par (Adolph Zukor), 1934 *bw*

Direction: Josef von Sternberg Script: von Sternberg, with Manuel Komroff
Camera: Bert Glennon
Special Effects: Gordon Jennings Costume Design: Travis Banton
Music: von Sternberg, W. Franke Harling, John Leipold
Art Direction: Hans Dreier Statuary: Peter Ballbusch
Ikons and paintings: Richard Kollorsz

with Marlene Dietrich, John Lodge, Sam Jaffe, Louise Dresser, C. Aubrey Smith, Jameson Thomas, Jane Darwell, Edward Van Sloan

- Criticism on release

> ...a bizarre and fantastic historical carnival... not a dramatic photoplay at all, but a succession of overelaborated scenes, dramatized emotional moods and gaudily plotted visual excitements – Mr von Sternberg has at the same time created a barbaric pageant of eighteenth century Russia which is frequently exciting...
>
> 'A.D.S.', *New York Times*, 15 September 1934

- Current recommendations and ratings
  StJD S&S82/92 LM3 DQ3 DW4 VFG5 MPG4

> ...beneath the surface frivolities, it's tough stuff. The decor and costumes, and the *mise en scène* that deploys them, have never been equalled for expressionist intensity.
>
> Tony Rayns, PTOG 1995

The Sea Hawk, WB (Henry Blanke), 1940 *bw*

Direction: Michael Curtiz
Camera: Sol Polito
Music: Erich Wolfgang Korngold
Costume Design: Orry-Kelly
Special Effects: Byron Haskin, H.F. Koenekamp
Script: Howard Koch, Seton I. Miller (from Rafael Sabatini's novel)
Art Direction: Anton Grot
Editing: George Amy

with Errol Flynn, Brenda Marshall, Claude Rains, Flora Robson, Donald Crisp, Henry Daniell, Alan Hale, Una O'Connor, William Lundigan, James Stephenson, Gilbert Roland

- Criticism on release

    ...all historically cockeyed, and the amazing exploits of Mr Flynn, accomplished by him in the most casual and expressionless manner, are quite as incredible as the adventures of Dick Tracy. But Flora Robson makes an interesting Queen Elizabeth, Claude Rains and Henry Daniell play a couple of villainous conspirators handsomely, there is a lot of brocaded scenery and rich Elizabethan costumes and, of course, there is Brenda Marshall to shed a bit of romantic light. And, when you come right down to it, that's about all one can expect in an overdressed 'spectacle' film which derives more from the sword than from the pen.

    New York Times, 23 August 1940

- Current recommendations and ratings
  LM4 DQ4 DW3 VFG5 MPG5 NFT*

    A hugely enjoyable swashbuckler from the days when 'packaging' wasn't such a dirty word and Jack Warner was a master of the art.

    Paul Taylor, PTOG 1995

The Adventures of Robin Hood, WB (Hal Wallis), 1938 colour

Direction: Michael Curtiz, William Keighley
Script: Norman Reilly Raine, Seton I. Miller
Camera: Tony Gaudio, Sol Polito, William Howard Greene
*Music: Erich Wolfgang Korngold *Art Direction: Carl Jules Weyl
Costume Design: Milo Anderson   *Editing: Ralph Dawson

with Errol Flynn, Olivia de Havilland, Claude Rains, Basil Rathbone, Ian Hunter, Eugene Pallette, Alan Hale, Melville Cooper, Una O'Connor, Montagu Love, Patric Knowles, Herbert Mundin

- Criticism on release

    This was a film that was half-made before a shot was in the cameras. Tradition has been working on the script for seven hundred years... It isn't a blustery, carefree thing like the old Fairbanks picture; it is concerned with the taxation troubles of the oppressed Saxons... fine wrath is oddly mixed with riotous Technicolor...

    C.A. Lejeune, *The Observer*, 10 October 1938

- Current recommendations and ratings
  StJD BN92 S&S82 LM3½ DQ4 DW5 VFG5 MPG5 NFT**

    One of the few great adventure movies that you can pretend you are treating the kids to while you are really treating yourself – one of the best examples of what large studio resources could produce. Glorious colour, sumptuous sets, and a brilliantly choreographed, climactic sword fight...

    Scott Meek, PTOG 1995

Drama (1: Major Social Issues) – Social Allegory, Social Realism, Pursuit and Concern for Social Justice, Ethnic Conflicts, Films of the 'Counter-Culture'

Drama refers to all narrative films concerned with serious representations of human conflict; these films are the nearest that Hollywood came to tragedy. They are actually structured by a strong melodramatic content, with violent and sensational episodes to advance the plot which generally culminates in at least a temporary victory of good over evil.

Critics of Hollywood ('Tinseltown') have always underestimated the capacity of the great studios, before their decline, to produce well-presented, riveting movies of this sober kind, although they were generally written to some kind of acceptable formula.

Group 1 deals with films that are concerned with major issues of society as a whole.

SOCIAL ALLEGORY

Hollywood fables about the social conditions of humanity range from the overoptimistic, even cloyingly sentimental, populism of Frank Capra's *It's a Wonderful Life* to the bleakly despairing Orwellian view of Martin Scorsese's *Taxi Driver*. *It's a Wonderful Life*, 1946, is a delightfully Dickensian view of American small-town life, the normal subject matter of Capra's 'corn' – it includes crazy comedy, a psalm to the virtues of domestic life, pathos and melodrama in the theme of the evil persecution of its central character, George Bailey (played by James Stewart in the mode of Jefferson Smith), by the banker, Potter (played as a heartless syndrome by Lionel Barrymore), supernatural comedy in the visitation of an incompetent guardian angel, Clarence Goodbody (cosily played by Henry Travers – one of Hollywood's most appealing character actors), and a nightmare sequence depicting the fate of Bedford Falls without George's creative social sense and altruism, which, naturally, triumphs enthusiastically over evil at the end.

Contrasted with the undiluted cynicism of *Taxi Driver*, 1976, it seems more of a fairy tale than a realistic allegory of modern American life. Scorsese's film has no time for escapist idealism: it depicts rawly and starkly the underbelly of New York life in the 1970s, at the same time identifying the audience with the remorseless, unmitigated anger of the neurotically obsessed central character, depicted by Robert De Niro, in virtuoso partnership with the writer-director Scorsese. This is the anarchistic violence of the finale of *The Graduate* writ large and set in the context not of the decadent upper reaches of suburban society, but of the desperate lower levels of an imprisoned urban population.

It's a Wonderful Life, RKO/Liberty (Frank Capra), 1946 bw

Direction: Frank Capra
Camera: Joseph Walker, Joseph Biroc
Music: Dimitri Tiomkin
Art Direction: Jack Okey
Costume Design: Edward Stevenson
Editing: William Hornbeck

Script: Frances Goodrich, Albert Hackett, Jo Swerling, with Capra (from a story by Philip Van Doren Stern)
Special Effects: Russell A. Cully

with James Stewart, Donna Reed, Lionel Barrymore, Thomas Mitchell, Henry Travers, Beulah Bondi, Frank Faylen, Ward Bond, Gloria Grahame, H.B. Warner

- Criticism on release

> ...a wonderful title for a motion picture about which practically everyone who sees it will agree that it's wonderful entertainment. The film marks Frank Capra's first production since his return from distinguished war service, and he has invested it with the tremendous heart that always stamps his offerings as above average. This couldn't be other than a Capra picture, the humanness of the story the dominant factor at every turn of situation. His direction of the individual characterizations delivered is also distinctively his, and the performances from the starring roles of James Stewart and Donna Reed, down to the smallest bit, are magnificent. When Capra is at his best, no one can top him...
>
> Jack D. Grant, *The Hollywood Reporter*, Vol. 91, No.36, 19 December 1946

- Current recommendations and ratings
  StJD BN92 S&S82/92 LM4 DQ4 DW5 VFG5 MPG5 NFT*

    An extraordinary, unabashed testament to the homely small-town moral values and glossy studio production values that shaped Capra's films so successfully in the late 30s and rapidly disappeared thereafter. Capra has total command of his cast and technical resources, and a touching determination to believe that it is indeed a wonderful life.

    Geoff Brown, PTOG 1995

Taxi Driver, Col (Michael and Julia Phillips), 1976 *colour*

Direction: Martin Scorsese   Script: Paul Schrader
Camera: Michael Chapman   Music: Bernard Herrmann
Art Direction: Charles Rosen Costume Design: Ruth Morley
Special Effects: Dick Smith, Tony Parmalee
Editing: Marcia Lucas, Tom Rolf, Melvin Shapiro

with Robert De Niro, Cybill Shepherd, Jodie Foster, Peter Boyle, Harvey Keitel, Albert Brooks, Leonard Harris, Dianne Abbott, Martin Scorsese (bit)

- Criticism on release

    ...a luridly overwritten melodrama which takes New York as the setting for a kind of Allegory of Our Times. The film has reaped rich rewards at the box office in America (thanks partly to the bloodthirsty finale), but to my mind it is Scorsese's worst film to date...

    Nigel Andrews, *Financial Times* 20 August 1976
    ...the reason why Scorsese's film works so well is that the central figure's decline into mad violence is so well accounted for by temperament and circumstances, and so brilliantly exposed by the performance of Robert De Niro... After the purging binge of bullets, we are left with a public hero in whom a cackling monster still

dwells. We know he is to be feared. But there is nothing we can do about this knowledge. That's what so sinister and frustrating about the film; it transfers Travis's burden of impotent fear and disgust to us.

Russell Davies, *The Observer* 22 August 1976

- Current recommendations and ratings
  StJD BN92 S&S82/92 LM2 DQ4 DW4 VFG5 MPG1 NFT***

...Using, especially, Bernard Herrmann's most menacing score since *Psycho*, Scorsese has set about recreating the landscape of the city in a way that constitutes a truly original and terrifying Gothic canvas. But much more than that: *Taxi Driver* is also, thanks to De Niro's extreme implosive performance, the first film since *Alphaville* to set about a really intelligent appraisal of the fundamental ingredients of contemporary insanity.

David Pirie, PTOG 1995

SOCIAL REALISM

Usually referred to, technically, as 'naturalistic', these films present a superficial truth to nature, often of a pessimistic or depressing kind, their main objectives being to present unpalatable truths about humanity and its systems of social organisation. What is immediately surprising about this group is that three out of seven were distributed under the emblem of the roaring MGM lion, normally associated with high-gloss, technically perfect, escapist entertainment.

Greed, the earliest of this MGM group, had actually been completed when MGM was formed by amalgamation in 1924 and proved something of an embarrassment to the new owners, being about forty-two reels long ("about four times as long as a long film should be", John Douglas Eames in *The MGM Story*, 1975). Six reels were cut by Rex Ingram (with reluctant permission from the director, von Stroheim), but Louis Mayer, the studio's new chief, who was repelled by the whole film, ordered a further drastic cutting to ten reels when it was ultimately issued. Von Stroheim's unremitting attention to detail in the filming of a strong naturalistic novel (Frank Norris's McTeague) – including a gruelling session on location in Death Valley – was never commercially successful, with its three unforgettable but unforgivably grotesque characters, but nevertheless remains an irremovable classic of realist cinema, filmed entirely outside a studio.

The Crowd, written and directed by King Vidor, was produced under the auspices of the young Irving Thalberg and included New York street scenes of exceptional realism, possessing a theme almost as harrowing as that of *Greed* in its story of the struggle of an average young man against the relentless economic forces of society. It had, nevertheless, a surprisingly strong box office appeal. There are two wonderful performances by the leads – Eleanor Boardman, an established star, as the wife, and James Murray, a discovery who never repeated this success in his short acting life, as the husband.

Sidney Franklin was the third director on MGM's *The Good Earth*, 1937, following George Hill, who provided footage on location, and Victor Fleming, who replaced him but had to give up when hospitalised. The film is dedicated to Irving Thalberg, who died while it was being filmed. No one can be completely indifferent to it, and opinions vary greatly, from adulation to denigration. Most agree, however, that Luise Rainer's performance as O-Lan, the dedicated and determined farmer's wife and mother who has to weather drought, a plague of locusts and her husband's fecklessness, received a well-deserved Oscar. There are many spectacular scenes, and a strong sense of Chinese peasant life in close contact with the earth is conveyed in spite of a predominantly Western cast (Paul Muni as the husband, Walter Connolly, Charley Grapewin, and Jessie Ralph as the older generation, and Tilly Losch – the exotic German dancer – as a Chinese temptress). Chinese-Americans (including Keye Luke, best known as Charlie Chan's 'Number One Son') feature in supporting roles.

That Twentieth Century-Fox should be represented by *The Grapes of Wrath* and Warner Brothers by *The Treasure of the Sierra Madre* is no surprise, both studios having a lasting reputation for producing impressive films of social conscience. *The Grapes of Wrath* is generally regarded as the finest of this group, with taut and compelling direction from John Ford and a repertory of first-class performances from a brilliant cast, among whom Henry Fonda, Jane Darwell, Russell Simpson, and John Carradine have become ikonic images of human dignity in adversity and oppression. *The Treasure of the Sierra Madre* is probably its writer-director's greatest achievement, with a remarkable two-generation collaboration between John Huston and his acting father, the veteran Walter Huston (who gained an Oscar), and an interesting idiosyncratic role for Humphrey Bogart as the gold-crazed Dobbs.

The Southerner, 1945, Jean Renoir's third, and best, film made in Hollywood has the quality possessed by his French masterpieces of treating a complex theme with transparent simplicity – the theme of a year of continual endeavour and often tragic frustration in the life of a poor white family trying to grow some cotton in Texas. There is an extraordinary delicacy, tenderness, and openness in the treatment, and the photography (by Lucien Andriot) is almost too lyrically beautiful for its theme. Zachary Scott, demonstrating that he could act outside the role of handsome reptile in which he was normally cast, plays the father with quiet, convincing force. Betty Field also unusually plays a sympathetic role as his warm-hearted wife, attempting to retain respectability and dignity in adversity.

Elia Kazan's *On the Waterfront*, 1954, survives as a great social drama, in spite of many things – not least, Kazan's reputation as an informer to the Un-American Activities Committee (together with the scriptwriter, Budd Schulberg). It is rare that the award of Oscars testifies to the total artistry of a work, but in this case the seven Oscars awarded for all the leading credits were all justified, including the two leads (Marlon Brando, Eve-Marie Saint), the director and scriptwriter, and brilliant cameraman, Boris Kaufman. Leonard Bernstein provided the score, while Lee J. Cobb (as a corrupt union boss) and Rod Steiger (as Brando's shady brother) give excellent performances. All in all, the film is a triumph for the Method style of acting. The story of an inarticulate ex-boxer finding his conscience through love for a woman is both harrowing and moving at times, but ends with a true feeling of tragic catharsis.

These classic black-and-white movies of social realism are all distinguished by superlative camerawork conveying an atmosphere indispensable to the theme:

    William H. Daniels (*Greed*)

    Henry Sharp (*The Crowd*)

    Karl Freund (*The Good Earth*)

    Gregg Toland (*The Grapes of Wrath*)

    Lucien Andriot (*The Southerner*)

Ted McCord (*The Treasure of the Sierra Madre*)
Boris Kaufman (*On the Waterfront*)
Such visual beauty loses much of its quality on the small TV screen, but better seen there than not at all. What we cannot feel grateful for, however, is the tinting of subtly graduated black-and-white photography for commercial videotape distribution.

The irony is that for the older generation black and white meant 'real'; for the younger, colour, as in Martin Scorsese's *Mean Streets*, 1973, has greater realism. It deals with a group of near-stereotypes in such a fresh and interesting way that one experiences the sense of having seen a slice of real life as lived in New York's Little Italy. In the role of an over-mature delinquent, Robert De Niro established himself as 'star material', and the film did no damage to Harvey Keitel's reputation either, in the sympathetically ambiguous role of his young friend who attempts to protect him according to the more conventional code of his Mafia uncle. Scorsese's view of people achieving some kind of individuality against all odds in the worst of all possible environments comes over forcibly in this film, which, though made on a low budget, possesses excellent production values – an intriguing and powerful foretaste of Scorsese's later, better-known achievements. A remarkable piece of realist film-making.

The Crowd, MGM (King Vidor), 1928 *bw*

Direction: King Vidor
Camera: Henry Sharp
Editing: Hugh Wynn
Art Direction: Cedric Gibbons, A. Arnold Gillespie
Script: Vidor (with John V.A. Weaver, Harry Behn)
with Eleanor Boardman, James Murray, Bert Roach, Estelle Clark, Johnny Downs

- Criticism on release

> With restraint and delicacy Eleanor Boardman gives a remarkably good performance [and] a new-found star, James Murray, ably supports her. The story is consistent up until the conclusion and the entire production is smoothed and polished with a beautiful

symmetry by the crafty hand of Mr Vidor. It is a sympathetic and accurate study of a member of our modern army of clerks.... Vidor turns the cold eye of the camera on this barren spectacle with breath-taking results.

       Pare Lorentz, *Judge*, 10 March 1928

- Current recommendations and ratings
StJD S&S82/92 LM4 DW4 MPG5 NFT*

    Certainly one of Vidor's best films, a silent masterpiece which turns a realistically caustic eye on the illusionism of the American dream...

         Tom Milne, PTOG 1995

The Good Earth, MGM (Irving Thalberg, Albert Lewin), 1937 bw

Direction: Sidney Franklin
Camera: Karl Freund
Music: Herbert Stothart
Costume Design: Dolly Tree
Art Direction: Cedric Gibbons, Harry Olivier, Arnold Gillespie
Editing: Basil Wrangell

Script: Talbot Jennings, Tess Slesinger, Claudine West, with Frances Marion (uc), (from Pearl Buck's novel)

with Paul Muni, Luise Rainer, Walter Connolly, Tilly Losch, Charley Grapewin, Jessie Ralph, Soo Yung, Keye Luke, Roland Got, Ching Wah Lee

- Criticism on release

    ...works its characters into the illusion of life, the life into the place and social state of their background with a serene constancy of pitch that is surprising... Photography of exteriors is in keeping and frequently beautiful... And all edited as a movie should be – flexibly, unobtrusively, clarifying the story, joining multiple sequences and bridging over gaps in time or

sense by intercuts and the dissolving fragment that serve
so well here...

Otis Ferguson, New Republic 17 March 1937

- Current recommendations and ratings
  LM4 DQ4 DW4 VFG5 MPG5 NFT*

  A kind of *Lychees of Wrath*, it's a typically lumbering,
  cautious, overblown Thalberg project, saved by Rainer's
  genuinely moving Oscar-winning portrayal of Chinese
  peasantry, and by an immensely spectacular swarm of
  locusts.

Adrian Turner, PTOG 1995

The Grapes of Wrath, TCF (Darryl Zanuck, 1940 bw

*Direction: John Ford
Camera: Gregg Toland
Music: Alfred Newman
Art Direction: Richard Day, Mark-Lee Kirk
Editing: Robert Simpson
Script: Nunnally Johnson (from the novel by John Steinbeck)
Costume Design: Gwen Wakeling

with Henry Fonda, *Jane Darwell, Russell Simpson, Doris Bowden, Charley Grapewin, John Carradine, Eddie Quillan, Darryl Hickman, Zeffie Tilbury, John Qualen, Paul Guilfoyle, Frank Faylen, Ward Bond, Grant Mitchell, Charles D. Brown, Joseph Sawyer, James Flavin, Charles Middleton, Irving Bacon, Tom Tyler, Mae Marsh

- Criticism on release

  The word that comes in most handily for *The Grapes of Wrath* is magnificent – the most mature picture story that has ever been made, in feeling, in purpose and in the use of the medium. Nunnally Johnson's adaptation actually has the good taste to leave out some incidental fireworks Mr Steinbeck didn't. [The movie consists of] a series of great sweeping outdoor shots as beautifully tuned to purpose as anything you've seen...

Otis Ferguson, New Republic, 19 February 1940

- Current recommendations and ratings
  StJD BN92 S&S82/92 LM4 DQ4 DW5 VFG5 MPG5 NFT**

  This classic Ford film..., shot by Gregg Toland with magnificent lyrical simplicity, captures the stark plainness of the migrants, left with innumerable relations and little hope.

  Matthew Hoffman, PTOG 1995

Greed, MGM (inherited from the Goldwyn company/Erich von Stroheim), 1924 *bw*

Direction: Erich von Stroheim
Titles: Joseph Farnham
Art Direction: Richard Day, von Stroheim
Script: von Stroheim, June Mathis (from the novel by Frank Norris)
Camera: Ben Reynolds, William H. Daniels, Ernest Schoedsack
Editing: Frank E. Hull, Joseph Farnham, Rex Ingram, June Mathis

with Gibson Gowland, Zasu Pitts, Jean Hersholt, Chester Conklin

- Criticism on release

  ...in *Greed* there is no scene in the picture, hardly a detail, that is not recognizable to those who have read the book... Atmospherically, [it] is marvelous, [but] entire sequences and important characters have been left out. Thus the story has a choppy quality...

  Robert Sherwood, *Life*, 1 January 1925

- Current recommendations and ratings
  StJD S&S82/92 LM4 DW4 MPG5 NFT**

  ...Von Stroheim's greatest film still survives as a true masterpiece of the cinema – Frank Norris's novel is translated into the cinematic equivalent of, say, Zola at the peak of his powers.

  Geoff Andrew, PTOG 1995

*On the Waterfront, Col (Sam Spiegel), 1954 bw

*Direction: Elia Kazan
*Camera: Boris Kaufman
*Art: Richard Day
Costume Design: Anna Hill Johnstone
*Script: Budd Schulberg
Music: Leonard Bernstein
*Editing: Gene Milford

with *Marlon Brando, *Eva Marie Saint, Karl Malden, Lee J. Cobb, Rod Steiger, Martin Balsam, Leif Erickson, Nehemiah Persoff (bit)

- Criticism on release

> ...as violent and indelible a film record of man's inhumanity to man as has come to light this year... Mr Kazan's direction, his outstanding cast and Mr Schulberg's pithy and punchy dialogue have distinction and terrific impact... movie-making of a rare and high order.
>
> 'A.W.', *New York Times*, 29 July 1954

- Current recommendations and ratings
StJD BN92 S&S92 LM4 DQ4 DW5 VFG4½ MPG5 NFT**

> Superb performances – a memorably colourful script and a sure control of atmosphere make this... powerful stuff... Politics apart, it's pretty electrifying.
>
> Geoff Andrew, PTOG 1995

The Southerner, UA (David L. Loew, Robert Hakim), 1945 bw

Direction: Jean Renoir
Camera: Lucien Andriot
Music: Werner Janssen
Editing: Gregg Tallas
Script: Renoir, Hugo Butler, Nunnally Johnson, with William Faulkner, uc (from the novel by George Sessions Perry)

with Zachary Scott, Betty Field, Beulah Bondi, Bunny Sunshine, Jay Gilpin, Percy Kilbride, Blanche Yurka, Charles Kemper, J. Carrol Naish, Norman Lloyd

- Criticism on release

    I cannot imagine anybody failing to be spellbound by this first successful essay of Franco-American screen collaboration... a fine and beautifully acted film – superb playing of the grandmother by Beulah Bondi...

    Richard Winnington, News Chronicle
1 September 1945

    Physically, exclusive of the players, it is one of the most sensitive and beautiful American-made pictures I have seen. Yet warmly as I respect the picture's whole design and the many good things about it, I saw it with as much regret as pleasure... most of the people were screechingly, unbearably wrong. They didn't walk right, stand right, eat right, sound right or look right...

    James Agee, The Nation 9 June 1945

- Current recommendations and ratings
  StJD LM4 DW4 VFG4½ MPG4 NFT*

    A harsh yet human antidote to traditional Hollywood values about 'real people' – both romantic and realistic in its investigation of courage and freedom, both accurate and impressionistic in its view of 'nature', so that you can smell the river and the dead rain after the flood that almost ends their struggle.

    Chris Wicking, PTOG 1995

The Treasure of the Sierra Madre, WB (Henry Blanke), 1948 *bw*

*Direction, *Script (from the novel by B.S. Traven): John Huston
Camera: Ted McCord   Music: Max Steiner
Art Direction: John Hughes   Editing: Owen Marks
Special Effects: William McGann,
  H.F. Koenekamp

with Humphrey Bogart, *Walter Huston, Tim Holt, Brice Bennett, Alfonso Bedoya, Barton MacLane, Jack Holt, (bit), John Huston (bit), Ann Sheridan (bit), Robert Blake (as Bobby Blake – bit)

- Criticism on release

    Mr Huston has shaped a searching drama of the collision of civilization's vicious greeds with the instinct for self-preservation in an environment where all the barriers are down... But don't let this note of intelligence distract your attention from the fact that Mr Huston is putting it over in a most vivid and exciting action display...

    Bosley Crowther, *New York Times*, 24 January 1948

- Current recommendations and ratings
  StJD BN92 S&S82/92 LM4 DQ4 DW4 VFG5 MPG5 NFT*

    Director Huston tries to yank the basic elements – gold lust in a Mexican wilderness – into the spare eloqence of a fable, but tends to look pretentious rather than profound... There's a quite enjoyable yarn under the hollow laughter.

    Simon Garfield, PTOG 1995

Mean Streets, Taplin-Perry-Scorsese (Jonathan T. Taplin), 1973 *colour*

Direction: Martin Scorsese	Script: Scorsese, Mardik Martin
Camera: Kent Wakeford	
Editing: Sidney Levin	

with Harvey Keitel, Robert De Niro, Amy Robinson, David Proval, Richard Romanus, Cesare Danova, Victor Argo, George Memmoli, Lenny Scaletta, Jeannie Bell

- Criticism on release

    No matter how bleak the milieu, no matter how heartbreaking the narrative, some films are so thoroughly, beautifully realized they have a kind of tonic effect that has no relation to the subject matter. Such a film is *Mean Streets*, the third feature film by Martin Scorsese... It is Scorsese's talent, reflected in his performers, to be able to suggest the mystery of people and place solely in terms of the action... one of the fundamentals of film-making that many directors never grasp.

Vincent Canby, *New York Times* 3 October 1973

- Current recommendations and ratings
StJD BN92 S&S82/92 LM4 DQ3 DW4 VFG4 MPG2½ NFT*

The definitive New York movie, and one of the few to successfully integrate rock music into the structure of film – Scorsese directs with a breathless, head-on energy which infuses the performances, the sharp fast talk, the noise, neon and violence with a charge of adrenalin. One of the best American films of the decade.

Chris Petit, PTOG 1995

PURSUIT AND CONCERN FOR SOCIAL JUSTICE

In films of serious social concern, the drama is often associated with identification with the 'hunted' as a means of intensifying feeling over the social issue. The films in this section mix the following ingredients in varying degrees:

• A near-tract expounding a constructive social idea	In *Fury*, 1936, the irony that an attempted lynching breeds its own kind of ruthless vengeance-seeking in the victim
	In *I Am a Fugitive from a Chain Gang*, 1932, revelation of the cruel and degrading conditions in chain-gang prisons
	In *They Live by Night*, 1949, the exposure of weak but otherwise innocent youngsters to the 'way out' offered by hardened criminals
• An exercise in the re-awakening of social conscience	In *Twelve Angry Men*, 1957, where one doubting juror, by attacking the prejudices of his fellow-jurors, reverses their initial verdict of 'Guilty'

- Nightmarish accounts of relentless pursuit

  In *The Informer*, 1935, of a stupid, materialistic giant who has betrayed his revolutionary friend to the authorities at the time of the Irish Troubles in the 1920s

  In *The Night of the Hunter*, 1955, of two children by a vile perverted priest obsessed with the acquisition of a stolen hoard to do 'God's work'

  In *Of Mice and Men*, 1939 (a chilling yet compassionate morality told with great economy and expertise) of a gentle giant who is liable to slaughter a frailer being for whom he has an uncontrollable passion (Lon Chaney Jr. in his finest screen role)

In all cases but one, the pursuit is physical, confined to a small town in *Fury* and to Dublin in *The Informer*; in the underworld of Middle America in *They Live by Night*; providing a memorable and untypically (for Hollywood) astringent ending to *I Am a Fugitive from a Chain Gang*; hauntingly moving down the Ohio River in *The Night of the Hunter*; and inexorably moving across the vast heartland of Northern America in *Of Mice and Men*. In *Twelve Angry Men*, suitably for a work originally created for TV, the claustrophobic drama unfolds itself entirely in a locked jury room. The 'hunted man', a young Puerto Rican on trial for murder, is never seen, and his representative, Juror No.8, is very soon transformed into a hunter, as he exposes one weakness and prejudice after another of his fellow jurors. All these films are tightly directed and edited with strong emphasis on the visual aspects. Mervyn LeRoy's *I Am a Fugitive* demonstrated his ability to face life starkly as he did in *Little Caesar*. Andrew Sinclair in his *John Ford*, 1979, points out that the visual style of *The Informer* was established before the writing of the script, Dudley Nichols, the scriptwriter, being engaged after the cameraman, Joseph August. Fritz Lang's *Fury* was his first American film and did not meet with Louis Mayer's approval because of its uncompromising realism. In Lewis Milestone's *Of Mice and Men* Aaron Copland's sensitive, versatile musical score makes a real contribution to the film's sometimes lyrical, sometimes brooding, atmosphere. Nicholas Ray's *They Live by Night* was a directorial debut which showed him to be an original, innovative director. *The Night of the Hunter* was Charles Laughton's sole, but highly accomplished, piece of direction, a virtuoso work of lighting and camera angles in the hands of Stanley Cortez. *Twelve Angry Men* indicated what was to be one of Sidney Lumet's strongest points: the translation of powerful stage dramas into an exciting movie version.

In most of these films, among generally effective performances from other members of the cast, the superlative acting of male leads determines the outstanding quality of these films:

- Spencer Tracy in *Fury*, as the innocent victim of a vicious lynch mob who burn down the jail in which he is being held;
- Paul Muni in *I Am a Fugitive*, as another innocent victim, framed in a hold-up and subjected to the suffering and degradation of imprisonment in Georgia of the 1930s under brutal, even sadistic, warders;
- Victor McLaglen in *The Informer*, as the stupid giant trapped by his own greed into the betrayal of a childhood friend;
- Robert Mitchum in *The Night of the Hunter*, as an insane preacher besotted by gold while seeking retribution on all sinners
- Burgess Meredith in *Of Mice and Men*, as the concerned, perplexed friend who attempts to shield the murdering giant from social retribution;
- Henry Fonda in *Twelve Angry Men*, as the young juror with a stubborn conscience gradually undermining the prejudices of the other jury members against a prisoner whose guilt, established by circumstantial evidence, seems unassailable

In *They Live by Night* the performances of the two young leads are both very moving, but in particular Cathy O'Donnell's image remains in the memory as a poignant portrayal of an intelligent, sensitive young woman caught up in the web of crime through her genuine love for a young misguided criminal.

Fury, MGM (Joseph L. Mankiewicz), 1936 bw

Direction, Script (with Bartlett Cormack) (based on story *Mob Rule* by Norman Krasna): Fritz Lang
Camera: Joseph Ruttenberg   Music: Franz Waxman
Art Direction: Cedric Gibbons   Editing: Frank Sullivan
Costume Design: Dolly Tree

with Spencer Tracy, Sylvia Sidney, Walter Abel, Frank Albertson, Walter Brennan, Edward Ellis, Jonathan Hale, Bert Roach, Ward Bond, Clarence Kolb

- Criticism on release

    I doubt if those who see it will carry the whitewash part of it so long in their minds as the straight action of the introduction and middle. [It] has the true creative genius of including little things not germane to the concept but, once you see them, the spit and image of life itself, the macabre sidelights – the kids, the hurled tomato, the women's taunts – that make it not only more likely but more terrible.

    Otis Ferguson, *New Republic*, 10 June 1936

- Current recommendations and ratings
StJD LM3½ DQ4 DW4 VFG4½ MPG5 NFT*

    Lang's first American film – MGM tinkered cravenly with the script all down the line... so not quite the masterpiece of reputation... Still impressive, all the same, especially in the build-up to the lynching sequence.

    Tom Milne, PTOG 1995

I Am a Fugitive from a Chain Gang, WB (Hal Wallis), 1932 bw

Direction: Mervyn LeRoy	Script: Howard J. Green, Sheridan Gibney, Brown Holmes (from the book by Robert E. Burns)
Camera: Sol Polito	
Musical Direction: Leo Forbstein	
Art Direction: Jack Okey	Editing: Walter Holmes
Costume Design: Orry-Kelly	

with Paul Muni, Glenda Farrell, Helen Vinson, Preston Foster, Allen Jenkins, John Wray, Edward Ellis, Berton Churchill, Douglas Dumbrille, Robert Warwick, Charles Middleton, Irving Bacon

- Criticism on release

    I quarrel with the production not because it is savage and horrible, but because each step in an inevitable tragedy is taken clumsily and because each character responsible for the hero's doom is shown more as a caricature than as a person. The men do not seem real. The chain gang certainly does.

    Pare Lorentz, *Vanity Fair*, December 1932

- Current recommendations and ratings
  StJD LM4 DQ4 DW5 VFG4 MPG5 NFT*

    Muni gives a brilliant performance as a regular guy convicted of murder and subjected to the hardships and beatings of a dehumanising chain gang regime... Some of the social commentary now seems a little heavy-handed, but the film still packs a hefty punch. The details of chain gang life are tough and harrowing – and the downbeat ending is a killer.

    Nigel Floyd, PTOG 1995

The Informer, RKO (Cliff Reid/John Ford), 1935 bw

*Direction: John Ford
Camera: Joseph August
*Music: Max Steiner
Costume Design: Walter Plunkett
Editing: George Hively
*Script: Dudley Nichols (from the novel by Liam O'Flaherty)
Art Direction: Van Nest Polglase, Mark-Lee Kirk

with *Victor McLaglen, Preston Foster, Heather Angel, Margot Grahame, Wallace Ford, Una O'Connor, Donald Meek, J.M. Kerrigan, Francis Ford

- Criticism on release

    ...gets off to a beautiful start... For dramatic vigor and beauty of composition there have been few sequences to compare with the one that ends with the camera looking from behind Frankie (the betrayed IRA man – Wallace Ford, excellent) down into the court where the Tans look up with their machine guns – McLaglen at times superb, but he simply does not carry the thing along.

    Otis Ferguson, *New Republic*, 29 May 1935

- Current recommendations and ratings
StJD S&S92 LM4 DQ3 DW4 VFG4½ MPG5 NFT*

    John Ford got the best reviews of his career for this heavy-handed humourless and patronising art film... Today, only Joe August's foggy expressionist camerawork still captures the imagination, but even this becomes enervatingly portentous before long.

    Tom Charity, PTOG 1995

The Night of the Hunter, UA (Paul Gregory), 1955 bw

Direction: Charles Laughton
  (with Denis Sanders)
Camera: Stanley Cortez
Special Effects: Jack Rabin, De Louis Witt
Art Direction: Hildyard Brown

Script: James Agee (with Laughton, uc), (from Davis Grubb's novel)
Music: Walter Schumann
Editing: Robert Golden

with Robert Mitchum, Shelley Winters, Lillian Gish, Billy Chapin, Sally Jane Bruce, James Gleason, Don Beddoe

- Criticism on release

    ...a bizarre adventure; it must be regarded as cruel farce or, better still, as a parable about the relativity of good and evil... The film runs counter to the rules of commercialism; it will probably be Laughton's single experience as a director. It's a pity, for despite failures of style, *The Night of the Hunter* is immensely inventive. It's like a horrifying news item retold by small children.

    François Truffaut, *Cahiers du Cinema*, 1956

- Current recommendations and ratings
StJD S&S82/92 LM3½ DQ4 DW5 VFG4 MPG5 NFT*

    ...Everyone's contribution is equally important. Laughton's deliberately old-fashioned direction throws up a startling array of images... James Agee's script treads a tight path between humour... and suspense. Finally, there's the absolute authority of Mitchum's performance: easy, charming, infinitely sinister.

    Chris Peachment, PTOG 1995

Of Mice and Men, UA (Hal Roach/ Lewis Milestone), 1932 bw

Direction: Lewis Milestone
Camera: Norbert Brodine
Art Direction: Nicolai Remisoff
Editing: Bert Jordan

Script: Eugene Solow (from the play by John Steinbeck)
Music: Aaron Copland

with Burgess Meredith, Lon Chaney Jr., Charles Bickford, Betty Field, Bob Steele, Noah Beery Jr., Roman Bohnen

- Criticism on release

    ...you can put *Of Mice and Men* on the list of the ten best of 1940 - a nice realization of interior and exterior throughout... One undisputed thing is the life in pictures given it by Mr Milestone's subtle use of camera accent to shift the scene within the scene, to anticipate, heighten and release both inward and outward struggle throughout - among the good films of any time...

    Otis Ferguson, *New Republic* 1940

- Current recommendations and ratings
  LM4 DQ3 DW4 MPG5 NFT*

    ...made at the same time as *The Grapes of Wrath* (though released earlier) and matching Ford's harsh lyricism in its evocation of the Depression, the desperation of the migrant farmworkers, their pipedreams of a little place of their own some day. Terrific performances mask much of the novel's naive social philosophy...

    Tom Milne, PTOG 1995

They Live by Night, RKO (John Houseman), 1949 *bw*

Direction: Nicholas Ray
Camera: George E. Diskant
Music: Leigh Harline (with Woody Guthrie, uc)
Art Direction: Albert S. D'Agostino, Al Herman
Editing: Sherman Todd

Script: Charles Schnee, with Ray (from the novel *Thieves Like Us* by Edward Anderson)
Special Effects: Russell A. Culley

with Cathy O'Donnell, Farley Granger, Howard Da Silva, Jay C. Flippen, Helen Craig, Will Wright, Marie Bryant, Ian Wolfe

- Criticism on release

    ...no doubt inspired by the two or three real-life sagas that we've had of 'boy bandits' and their brides, this well-designed motion picture derives what distinction it has from good, realistic production and sharp direction by Nicholas Ray. His sensitive juxtaposing of his actors against highways, tourist camps and bleak motels makes for a vivid comprehension of an intimate personal drama in hopeless flight.

    Bosley Crowther, *New York Times* 4 November 1949

- Current recommendations and ratings
  StJD S&S92 LM3½ DW4 VFG5 MPG4 NFT*

    Ray offers the poetry of doomed romanticism, introducing his outcast lovers with the caption, 'This boy and this girl were never properly introduced to the world we live in'. Passionate, lyrical and imaginative, it's a remarkably assured debut...

    Geoff Andrew, PTOG 1995

Twelve Angry Men, UA (Henry Fonda/ Reginald Rose), 1957 bw

Direction: Sidney Lumet	Script: Reginald Rose (from own TV play)
Camera: Boris Kaufman	
Art Direction: Robert Markell	Music: Kenyon Hopkins
Editing: Doane Harrison	

with Henry Fonda, Lee J. Cobb, Ed Begley, Martin Balsam, Jack Warden, E.G. Marshall, Joseph Sweeney, Edward Binns, John Fiedler, Robert Webber, George Voskovec, Jack Klugman

- Criticism on release

> ...we are present at a deliberation with a strict continuity of time, place and action, and experience intensely the feeling of something being done. It's a triumph of the television style... This movie makes it increasingly difficult to leave as the story unfolds... It's a screenwriter's film, and what an author!
>
> François Truffaut, *Cahiers du Cinema*, 1957

- Current recommendations and ratings
StJD LM4 DQ4 DW4 VFG4 MPG4 NFT*

> ...there is no denying the suitability of [Lumet's] style – sweaty close-ups, gritty monochrome 'realism', one-set claustrophobia – to his subject... But what really transforms the piece from a rather talky demonstration that a man is innocent until proven guilty, is the consistently taut, sweltering atmosphere, created largely by Boris Kaufman's excellent camerawork. The result, however devoid of action, is a strangely realistic thriller.
>
> Geoff Andrew, PTOG 1995

ETHNIC CONFLICTS

Hollywood has made several films which have treated the problem of ethnic relations sympathetically and compassionately (including *To Kill a Mockingbird*, which is discussed later in Through the Eyes of Youth (page 150). Spike Lee's third feature as writer-director, *Do the Right*

Thing, 1989, like all of them, poses the problem without offering any solution. In a multiracial area of New York on a broiling hot Saturday, trouble stirs up between the blacks and the Italian owner of the local pizzeria. From a relatively minor incident the tension mounts until the day ends in a welter of destruction. The presentation and performances are first-rate: Danny Aiello as the basically likeable owner, John Turturro as his bigoted son, Ossie Davis and Ruby Dee – two veteran black performers, and Spike Lee himself as the laid-back delivery boy, who futilely attempts to bring the warring factions together – all are impressively convincing in this comic, dramatic and violent slice of real life.

What can one say of Steven Spielberg's *Schindler's List*, 1993? Too recent to be graded by all the authorities I have used for the other films, it would inevitably rate high in any selection of Hollywood productions. The great master of exciting genre movies has here fulfilled his lasting ambition to produce and direct a 'serious' film, as demonstrated in the earlier *Empire of the Sun*. He has achieved this personal ambition perfectly, in a moving narrative based on one story of the Holocaust. All the elements weld together in a work that was not only appealing to a wide audience, but achieved aesthetic heights within the medium.

*Schindler's List, Un (Steven Spielberg, Branko, Lustig, Gerald R. Malen), 1993 *bw*

*Direction: Steven Spielberg	*Script: Steve Zaillian, with Spielberg, uc (from Thomas Keneally's novel *Schindler's Ark*)
*Camera: Janusz Kaminski	
*Music: John Williams	
*Art Direction: Allan Starski	
Costume Design: Anna Biedrzycki-Sheppard	*Editing: Michael Kahn
with Liam Neeson, Ben Kingsley, Ralph Fiennes, Caroline Goodall, Jonathan Sagalle, Embeth Davidtz, Andrzej Seweryn, Norbert Weisser, Elina Lowenska, Malgoscha Gebel	

- Criticism on release

> Deftly wielding the dollar-driven apparatus of 1990s Hollywood, director Steven Spielberg has achieved

something close to the impossible – a morally serious, aesthetically stunning historical epic that is nonetheless readily accessible to a mass audience – an intensely personal meditation on the nature of heroism and moral choice, rendered in the kind of rich, dreamlike cinematic canvas that only Hollywood can realize...

> James Pallot et al., Eds: *The Motion Picture Guide*,
> 1994 Annual

- Current recommendations and ratings
  LM4 VFG5 MPG5

  ...Spielberg's finest since *Jaws* – a noble achievement and essential viewing...

  > Geoff Andrew, PTOG 1995)

Do the Right Thing, Un (Spike Lee, Monty Ross), 1989 *colour*

Direction and Script: Spike Lee   Camera: Ernest Dickerson
Music: Bill Lee   Production Design: Wynn-Thomas
Costume Design: Ruth Carter   Editing: Barry Alexander Brown
Choreography: Rosie Perez, Otis
  Sallid

with Danny Aiello, Ossie Davis, Ruby Dee, Richard Edson, Giancarlo Esposito, Spike Lee, Bill Nunn, John Turturro, Paul Benjamin, Rosie Perez

- Criticism on release

  ...one terrific movie – the chronicle of a bitter racial confrontation that leaves one man dead and a neighbourhood destroyed. The ending is shattering and maybe too ambiguous for its own good. Yet the telling of this is so buoyant, so fresh, so exact and so moving that one comes out of the theater elated by the display of sheer cinematic wizardry... The movie is packed with idiosyncratic detail of character and event, sometimes very funny and sometimes breathtakingly crude – a remarkable piece of work...

Vincent Canby, *New York Times* 30 June 1989

- Current recommendations and ratings
  LM3 DW4 VFG4½ MPG4 NFT*

...the film – at once stylised and realistic – buzzes throughout with the sheer, edgy bravado that comes from living one's life on the streets. It looks, sounds and feels *right*...

Geoff Andrew, PTOG 1995

FILMS OF THE 'COUNTER-CULTURE'

Such films have difficulty in establishing a permanent sense of artistic achievement, as one cult succeeds another – *Easy Rider*, 1969, and *Midnight Cowboy*, 1969, succeeding *The Wild One*, 1953, and in turn being succeeded by Bob Rafelson's *Five Easy Pieces*, 1970, which drily comments on the dissatisfactions of a man seeking to escape his elegant, musical family to find a real existence in the world of physical labour and mindless pursuits. Confronting his family with a pregnant, demanding and vulgar mistress (observantly played by Karen Black), he firmly and unambiguously chastises the complacent world of art and easy living to which his family belongs without knowing in fact what values to adopt in place of theirs. The film insinuates rather than bludgeons itself into our memory, and there are several memorable performances, particularly by Jack Nicholson in the central role.

Five Easy Pieces, Col/ Bert Schneider (Bob Rafelson, Richard Wechsler), 1970 *colour*

Direction: Bob Rafelson
Camera: Laszlo Kovacs
Music: Bach, Mozart, Chopin
Editing: Gerald Shepard, Christopher Holmes

Script: Adrien Joyce (from a story by Joyce and Rafelson)
Costume Design: Bucky Rous
Production Design: Toby Rafelson

with Jack Nicholson, Karen Black, Billy 'Green' Bush, Susan Anspech, Fannie Flagg, Sally Struthers, Marlena McGuire, Richard Stahl, Lois Smith, Helena Kallianiotes, Toni Basil

- Criticism on release

    Though to hear him in the beginning... you might not guess it, the hero comes of a middle-class musical family where everybody is busy all day with Bach and Mozart. In reaction he drifts, plays the roughneck, spends evenings at the bowling-alley – but all the time guarding himself against entanglements. [His girlfriend, played by Karen Black is a]... bubble-head, demanding, faintly vulgar, incapable of understanding the family setting into which she bores her way... But the text for this tale of solitude... is to be found in his confession and apology and declaration of severance, made with tears to his immobile, speechless, perhaps insensible old father... There are blurred passages, but none in Mr Nicholson's performance.

    Dilys Powell, *Sunday Times* 21 March 1971

- Current recommendations and ratings
StJD LM4 DQ3 DW4 VFG4 MPG5 NFT*

    ...a considered examination of the middle-class patrician American way of life – less a story and more a collection of incidents and character studies, all of which inform each other and extend our understanding of Nicholson's mode of survival: flight.

    Phil Hardy, PTOG 1995

Drama (2: Frictions within Society) – Through the eyes of Youth, Family Tensions, the Sex War, Addictions and Rehabilitation

The films in this second grouping of dramas deal with the disturbing problems of individuals vis-à-vis society: as child or adolescent, as member of a family, as man or woman against the other sex, as addict or as recovering patient. In most cases, the central characters are flawed in some way, but, as viewers, we are persuaded to identify intensely with their vulnerability and rebelliousness against what appear to be overwhelming social odds.

THROUGH THE EYES OF YOUTH

Hollywood studios produced many films in which the centre of interest was a young child, often treated as a star, as, for example, in Shirley Temple films. As they often stressed the performer's precocity, these vehicles had an immediate popular appeal; but the most lasting (as, for example, *The Night of the Hunter* – see Drama 1) have quieter, more subtle contributions by the young performers which form part of the general artistic effect rather than standing out like a silhouette against a greyer background.

The central character in Robert Mulligan's *To Kill a Mockingbird*, 1962 is a widower, Atticus Finch (Gregory Peck), seen through the eyes of his pre-adolescent children, a ten-year-old boy (Philip Alford) and a six-year-old tomboy (Mary Badham). Peck plays an upright liberal lawyer in a small Alabama town: one of the film's themes is clearly anti-racism in his (unsuccessful) defence of a young black who has allegedly raped a white girl and the depiction of the hostility engendered in the community against the Finch family. Another is the children's awe of a neighbour whose apparent mental retardation gives him the reputation of being insane. Robert Duvall's performance in this role (his film debut) is superb, contributing greatly to the eerie atmosphere and ultimately to the education of the children in yet another of life's problems. The camerawork (by Russell Harlan) and music (Elmer Bernstein) contribute unobtrusively to the general poetic effect. Peck's Oscar was not undeserved, but it was unfair in the sense that all other contributors reach an equally high standard.

In general, the public expect tenser, more violent, more melodramatic movies from Hollywood: the movies about youth that have retained the highest reputation are about the problems of adolescence, the most non-conformist, even rebellious, phase in the human life cycle. *Rebel without a Cause*, 1955, in which Dean played a charismatic starring role, after appearing in *East of Eden*, released in the same year, was much more than "a straightforward star vehicle" (Leslie Halliwell, *Filmgoers' Companion*, 1988). It had an extraordinary contemporary resonance: from the opening scene in the police precinct with the probing, ever-moving camera around the young delinquent anti-hero, Nicholas Ray, the director, has his cast acting, and the audience watching, on the edge of their nerves, while the sequence towards the end, where the abandoned old house becomes the 'home' of the restless adolescents (played by Dean and Natalie Wood) has an 'elegance' which, in the words of Raymond Durgnat, *Films and Feelings*, 1967, "evokes the fragile beauty of their love, its dilapidation the 'half-finished' quality of adolescence". Jim Backus provides an irritatingly accurate study as the weak-kneed father. One needs to go no further than this film for the essential Dean persona almost revered by a few generations of adolescents.

Peter Bogdanovich's *The Last Picture Show*, 1971, remains the classic film of this type, less a vehicle of protest and dealing with its theme with greater irony, enhanced by the deliberate choice of the then unfashionable black-and-white photography (brilliantly used by Robert Surtees). Its script is based on a novel by the Texan Larry McMurty (also writer of *Hud* and *Terms of Endearment*). The unprepossessing oil town in 1951 becomes a kind of symbol of narrow-mindedness and repression in the routine lives of teenagers on the brink of being drafted for service in Korea. The romance and excitement for which they yearn is mostly provided by the cinema and desultory adventures in sex. The lads' hero is Sam the Lion – in what all the critics agree is a most beautiful performance by Ben Johnson – owner of the all-night restaurant, pool-hall and cinema, whose premature death deprives them of the fixed centre around which their somewhat purposeless lives revolve. There are other excellent performances, by what would now be considered an all-star cast – Timothy Bottoms, Jeff Bridges, Ellen Burstyn, Cybill Shepherd, Randy Quaid, Cloris Leachman and Eileen Brennan.

In 1973, before making the immensely popular and influential *Star Wars*, George Lucas devised and directed a nostalgic study of the California beat generation of 1962. *American Graffiti* was a very personal movie performed by a group of then unknowns, many of whom also went on to make very big names for themselves – Richard Dreyfuss, Candy Clark, Paul Le Mat, Cindy Williams, and Harrison Ford. At the time of its release its greatest appeal undoubtedly lay in the continuous musical accompaniment of forty-one rock-and-roll hits. Later its lasting success seems to depend much more on the portrayal of the four young male characters – Curt, the budding young intellectual, who eventually becomes the writer on whose work the film is based, the extrovert and ultimately dependable Steve, the macho 'Don Juan' type, Big John, and the awkward, graceless 'born loser', Terry the Toad. The direction is unpretentious but effective, the colour photography (supervised by Haskell Wexler) is highly individual, the script is never banal, and the performances excellent. The movie remains a unique, above-average expression of youth's energy and freshness before being submerged in the full mediocrity of adult life.

The Last Picture Show, BBS (Stephen Friedman), 1971 bw

Direction: Peter Bogdanovich
Camera: Robert Surtees
Production Design: Polly Platt

Script: Bogdanovich, Larry McMurty (from McMurty's novel)
Editing: Donn Cambern

with Timothy Bottoms, Jeff Bridges, Cybill Shepherd, *Ben Johnson, *Cloris Leachman, Ellen Burstyn, Eileen Brennan, Clu Gulager, Sam Bottoms, Sharon Taggart

- Criticism on release

    ...Mr Bogdanovich and Mr McMurtry impose emotions, pitiful or even romantic, on unromantic material. They are romantic, for instance, about the character of Sam the Lion (a beautiful performance by Ben Johnson, one of John Ford's stalwarts)... *The Last Picture Show* doesn't look back with longing... Poolroom, bar, the desolate street where the dust flies and the scraps of paper flap at the passage of trucks on their way to the oil-well somewhere in the flat landscape – the decay of the town is all-pervading... What I find extraordinary in the film is its power to suggest not only the social background but the situations and unspoken desires of its characters...

Dilys Powell, *Sunday Times* 12 March 1972

- Current recommendations and ratings
StJD LM4 DW5 VFG4½ MPG5 NFT*

...where Bogdanovich scores is in his accurate depiction of period and place, so detailed as to be almost tangible, and in the unbridled sympathy he extends to his characters... Superb performances all round add to the charm of this fine, if now unfashionable, film.

Geoff Andrew, PTOG 1995

To Kill a Mockingbird, Un (Alan J. Pakula), 1962 bw

Direction: Robert Mulligan
Camera: Russell Harlan
Music: Elmer Bernstein
Art Direction: Alexander
  Golitzen, Henry Bumstead
Costume Design: Rosemary Odell,
  Viola Thompson

*Script: Horton Foote (from the novel by Harper Lee)
Editing: Aaron Stell

with *Gregory Peck, Mary Badham, Philip Alford, John Megna, Robert Duvall, Frank Overton, Rosemary Murphy, Ruth White, Brock Peters, Estelle Evans, Paul Fix

- Criticism on release

What matters most is Robert Mulligan's robust conception of the children's world, both real and imaginary... combined with the likeable performances of the child actors and Russell Harlan's splendidly atmospheric photography... The over-long courtroom scene falls very flat. Nonetheless, the film is humane, and where it is observing rather than campaigning it reveals considerable talent.

E.S. 'Monthly Film Bulletin', May 1963

- Current recommendations and ratings
  S&S92 LM3½ DQ3 DW4 VFG4 MPG4 NFT**

  ...perhaps we should be grateful that Mulligan merely suffocates with righteousness... The film sits somewhere between the bogus virtue of Kramer's *The Defiant Ones* and Laughton's *Night of the Hunter*, combining racial intolerance with the nightmares of childhood... It looks like a storybook of the Old South, with dappled sunlight and woodwormy porches, and Peck is everyone's favourite uncle...

  Adrian Turner, PTOG 1995

American Graffiti, Un (Coppola), 1973 colour

Direction: George Lucas	Script: Lucas (with Gloria Katz
Camera: Ron Eveslage, Jan	and Willard Huyck)
D'Alquen (with Haskell	Sound Montage: Wallis Murch
Wexler as consultant)	Art Direction: Dennis Clark

with Richard Dreyfuss, Ron Howard, Paul Le Mat, Charlie M. Smith, Cindy Williams, Harrison Ford, Bo Hopkins

- Criticism on release

  George Lucas, the 27-year-old protégé of Francis Ford Coppola... looks back to a nostalgic past necessarily quite recent and, in this case, it must be admitted, still a little undefined... The title aptly describes the rather casual structure of the film, alongside a certain contrivance in packing so much character and incident into the events, of a single night, centred on a drive-in eater, Mel's Burger City, in a spreading but unidentified North Californian town...

  David Robinson, *The Times*, 29 March 1974

- Current recommendations and ratings
  S&S82 LM3½ DQ3 DW4 VFG3 MPG4 NFT*

  The film that launched a thousand careers... Too full of incident to reflect a typical night in reality, it's nevertheless funny, perceptive, pepped up by a great soundtrack, and also something of a text-book lesson in parallel editing as it follows a multitude of adolescents through their various adventures with sex, books, music and cars.

Geoff Andrew, PTOG 1995

Rebel Without a Cause, WB (David Weisbart), 1955 *colour*

Direction: Nicholas Ray
Camera: Ernest Haller
Music: Leonard Rosenman
Editing: William Ziegler
Art Direction: Malcolm Bert

Script: Stewart Stern, with Ray (from Irving Shulman's adaptation of Robert M. Lindner's book)

with James Dean, Natalie Wood, Sal Mineo, Jim Backus, Ann Doran, Rochelle Hudson, William Hopper, Dennis Hopper, Virginia Brissac, Ian Wolfe, Gus Schilling, Almira Sessions

- Criticism on release

  ...convincing, or not, in motivations, this tale of tempestuous kids and their weird ways of conducting their social relations is tense with explosive incidents... To set against [these] is a wistful and truly poignant stretch where Mr Dean and Miss Wood as lonely exiles in their own homes try to pretend they are happy grown-ups in an old mansion. There are some excruciating flashes of accuracy and truth in this film...

  Bosley Crowther, New York Times, 27 October 1955

- Current recommendations and ratings
  StJD S&S82 LM4 DQ4 DW5 VFG4 MPG4 NFT*

  Dean's finest film, hardly surprisingly in that Ray was one of the great 50s directors... What makes the film so powerful is both the sympathy it extends towards all the characters (including the seemingly callous parents) and the precise expressionism of Ray's direction. His use of light, space and motion is continually at the service of the characters' emotions – still the best of the youth movies.

Geoff Andrew, PTOG 1995

FAMILY TENSIONS

John Ford's *How Green was my Valley*, 1941, is a rich, sentimental picture of a Welsh mining family whose traditions and love of the local place are strong but from whom the young narrator, Huw Morgan, has decided to tear himself away to start a new life. Because Ford is a master film-maker, he is able to enchant us into a suspension of our disbelief in the synthetic studio sets and the strange mixture of players – American (Pidgeon, Crisp), English (Loder, Lee, McDowall, Knowles and Lowry) and Irish (O'Hara, Allgood, Fitzgerald and his brother Arthur Shields) to depict what would have been an isolated *Welsh* community. Rhys Williams, who plays Dai Bando the prizefighter, was brought over to coach these polyglot players in the dialect and provides something of the authentic background. The film received the Academy Award for Best Film in 1941, Ford and his cameraman Arthur Miller also receiving Oscars.

Two of the films depicting family relationships in an intensely studied dramatic form deal with monstrous families of privilege – the Hubbards in post-Civil War America (*The Little Foxes*, 1941) and the *Magnificent Ambersons* in the days immediately preceding the First World War. The Hubbards are obsessive self-seekers and, while collectively planning the destruction of a rich sick man for his money, are quite equally prepared to destroy each other to achieve this end. Lilian Hellman adapted her own powerful play to the screen, and William Wyler applied a cool elegant efficiency to its *mise en scène*. Bette Davis, in accordance with her own, rather than Wyler's, view of her character, gives a virtuoso performance of cold-hearted villainy (the sequence in which she allows her husband, played by Herbert Marshall, to die without assistance is much quoted in the critical literature). The other members of the family, in particular those played by Charles Dingle and Dan Duryea, match her performance, while Teresa Wright plays her usual appealing role of intelligent innocence.

The *Magnificent Ambersons* in Orson Welles's film, 1942, are faced with the threat of the automobile which will sweep away the social structure in which they are accustomed to rule. This is a fascinating period piece in addition to being a well-depicted study of the fall of dynastic power (by erosion, not impact). There is something of a toning-down in the experimental approach from *Citizen Kane*; the form more unobtrusively fits the subject. It remains a very interesting technical achievement, however, surviving the mutilation of the end, which Welles did not film and was tacked on to an impressively slow-moving development in a fragmented and hurried close. By the date of its release in 1942, Welles, the 'Wonder Boy' of Hollywood two years previously, had become, like von Stroheim in his later career, the man the moguls loved to hate. Like *Greed*, *The Magnificent Ambersons* shows the fundamental dichotomy between commercialism and art. Many find it a superior film to *Citizen Kane*: quieter, more subtle, a film of moving sequences, especially those with Agnes Moorehead as the tormented self-pitying aunt, and the extraordinary sleigh-riding sequence, which has all the virtues of brilliant open-air camerawork, but was actually filmed in a Hollywood ice-factory.

Mildred Pierce, 1945, a strongly melodramatic 'woman's picture', represents the mother-daughter conflict. Considered by many to be Joan Crawford's finest performance in her later career (she was awarded the Best Actress Oscar for it), she is defied and rejected by a ruthlessly self-seeking daughter (played with all stops out by Ann Blyth). Michael Curtiz at Warner Brothers adapted the *film noir* style to this rather old-fashioned *Stella-Dallas*-type weepie and gave it a completely new look with the help of Anton Grot's art direction, Ernest Haller's camerawork, and Max Steiner's music.

Elia Kazan's *East of Eden*, 1955, deals with a tragic son-father conflict, personified in the dilemma of James Dean, who also featured in *Rebel without a Cause*, released in the same year, and who became a tragic symbol of his generation when he died early in a car accident. *East of Eden* is also a period piece, set during World War I in the Mid-West, and a Biblical allegory stretching in metaphor back to the beginning of time and the Book of Genesis. Kazan's first film as producer-director, it was filmed with superb production values in the new Cinemascope with Ted McCord's varied and atmospheric photography. The acting, apart from Dean, in his first starring role, has an archetypal Biblical resonance, particularly Raymond Massey's stern Jehovah-like father, and Julie Harris, unusually full of reconciling gentleness as the fiancée of Dean's brother (Richard Davalos) – Abel to Dean's Cain.

1956 saw two family blockbusters based on Texan dynasties: George Stevens' *Giant*, which also featured James Dean, in his final role, and Douglas Sirk's *Written on the Wind*. In *Giant* (an appropriate title for a Texan story, from Edna Ferber's novel), the family belongs to a cattle baron (Rock Hudson, with wife Elizabeth Taylor, and sister Mercedes McCambridge). Dean plays a misfit cowhand who falls in love with Southern belle Taylor and is left a small tract of land by McCambridge, which makes him an oil tycoon. This results in a clash between the old values (sympathetically portrayed by Hudson) and the new (intriguingly presented by Dean, even in a lonely and drunken old age). The sense of place is terrific (with photography by William C. Mellor), and although the movie sprawls intricately for over three hours it rarely releases its grip on the viewer.

In *Written on the Wind*, the family belongs to an oil tycoon (Robert Keith) with alcoholic son (Robert Stack) and nymphomaniac daughter (Dorothy Malone). It is clear that their woes are mainly due to self-indulgence inculcated by wealth. Stack marries a New Yorker (Lauren Bacall, another outsider, like Elizabeth Taylor in *Giant*). Rock Hudson again appears, as Stack's best friend, who is eventually suspected of making the wife pregnant. *Written on the Wind* is a steamy melodrama, but made with great style, and, as in *Giant*, has an impressive sense of place (camerawork by Russell Metty).

The next entry portrays the most narcissistically maudlin American family of all: the Tyrone family from Eugene O'Neill's play, *Long Day's Journey into Night*, faithfully and powerfully presented on the screen by Sidney Lumet in 1962. This could equally be considered as a dual study in addiction, with superb performances by Katharine Hepburn as the mother drug-addict and Jason Robards Jr. as drunkard son. The slow relentless, almost documentary, development equally involves the emotions of a once great actor now in decline (Ralph Richardson) and his younger son (Dean Stockwell), from whose viewpoint the tragedy is depicted. A most impressive film, in which the viewer is exposed minute by minute to the raw expression of seismic emotion.

America, America/ The Anatolian Smile, 1963 is a Levantine equivalent of *How Green was my Valley*, more authentic and taken to its logical conclusion, with a long, perhaps over-detailed account of the migration itself – by an Anatolian Greek (Kazan's uncle) through Constantinople to New York in 1896. Kazan's adaptation of his own book and his general approach may have been a little overindulgent, but there are two schools of thought about the movie (you either love or hate it!). The quality of the camerawork (Haskell Wexler) and the splendid performances must be set against the slow pace and occasional *longueurs*.

Kramer vs Kramer, 1979 compensates in its treatment of the subject – the trials and tribulations of a divided family – for its somewhat biased approach: Dustin Hoffman as the father wins over the support of his son (Justin Henry) when the long-suffering mother (Meryl Streep) walks out, although he had previously had no share in the boy's upbringing. Robert Benton's script, which won an Oscar, concentrates on Hoffman's change for the better and the growing affection between him and his son. Inevitably, the mother becomes unsympathetic in spite of all she did before the rift, when Hoffman had little time for his home affairs. Benton also won an Oscar for his direction, as did both Hoffman and Streep for their performances.

America, America/The Anatolian Smile, WB (Elia Kazan), 1963 bw

Direction and Script (from his own book): Elia Kazan
Camera: Haskell Wexler   Music: Manos Hadjidakis
Art Direction: Gene Callahan   Editing: Dede Allen
Costume Design: Anna Hill Johnstone

with Stathis Giallelis, Frank Wolff, Harry Davis, Elena Karam, Estelle Hemsley, Lou Antonio, Salem Ludwig, Linda Marsh, Paul Mann

- Criticism on release

    ...the narrative construction of this lengthy account of the trek of a youth from darkest Asia Minor to the melting pot of New York is achieved with images that have poetic flavor... Along with the truly epic strophes of Manos Hadjidakis's musical score, they develop an assault upon the senses that may leave one completely overwhelmed – if Mr Kazan's pictures weren't so overwhelmingly long and, consequently, so often redundant, it would be – what? Even finer than it is.

New York Times 16 December 1963

- Current recommendations and ratings
S&S82/92 LM4 DW3 MPG4 NFT*

...For once in his career, the director employed little-known actors, with a welcome loss of theatricality – may be seen as one of the peaks of Kazan's career. Certainly, it is one of the finest movies to deal with the plight of those thousands of immigrants who travelled steerage to Ellis Island at the turn of the century.

Geoff Andrew, PTOG, 1995

How Green was my Valley, TCF (Darryl Zanuck), 1941 bw

*Direction: John Ford
*Camera: Arthur C. Miller
Music: Alfred Newman
*Art Direction: Richard Day, Nathan Juran
Script: Philip Dunne (from the novel by Richard Llewellyn)
Costume Design: Gwen Wakeling
Editing: James Clark

with Walter Pidgeon, Maureen O'Hara, *Donald Crisp, Anna Lee, Roddy McDowall, John Loder, Sara Allgood, Barry Fitzgerald, Patric Knowles, Morton Lowry, Arthur Shields, Ann E. Todd, Rhys Williams, Mae Marsh (bit), Irving Pichel (narrator)

- Criticism on release

...isn't the greatest film ever made. It will certainly drive some Welshmen tearing mad, and infuriate some readers of the book, but for all that I believe it to be a fine, gallant picture. Ford... favours a largely silent technique, with a background of Welsh choral singing and the occasional off-screen voice of a narrator... I found myself getting by heart all the details of the cottage – the wall-bed, the geraniums in the window, the blue-and-white plates on the dresser, the pipe smoke rising to the ceiling, the absurdly touching china dog in the hall... It's a pleasure to take time to remember such things among today's urgencies.

C.A. Lejeune, The Observer, 26 April 1942

- Current recommendations and ratings
  S&S82/92 LM4 DQ4 DW4 VFG5 MPG5 NFT*

  The backcloth mining village (impressive as it is) and the babel of accents hardly aid suspension of disbelief in this nostalgic recollection of a Welsh childhood... An elegant and eloquent film, nevertheless, even if the characteristically laconic Fordian poetry seems more contrived here (not least in the uncharacteristic use of an offscreen narration).

  Tom Milne, PTOG 1995

The Little Foxes, RKO (Goldwyn), 1941 bw

Direction: William Wyler
Camera: Gregg Toland
Music: Meredith Willson
Art Direction: Stephen Goosson
Costume Design: Orry-Kelly

Script: Lilian Hellman, Arthur Kober, Dorothy Parker, Alan Campbell (from play by Hellman)
Editing: Daniel Mandell

with Bette Davis, Herbert Marshall, Teresa Wright, Richard Carlson, Patricia Collinge, Dan Duryea, Charles Dingle, Carl Benton Reid, Virginia Brissac, Russell Hicks, Lucien Littlefield, Alan Bridge

- Criticism on release

  ...one of the really beautiful jobs in the whole range of movie-making, and that includes any time or place or name... It was William Wyler who actually made the picture of course; Wyler, as director of the people and the material before him, especially the very good material provided by the scriptmakers,... as assisted by the finest technicians anywhere in the art of set building, by the camera work of Gregg Toland - I do not remember a bad performance...

     Otis Ferguson, *New Republic*, 1 September 1941

- Current recommendations and ratings
  StJD LM3½ DQ4 DW4 VFG3½ MPG5 NFT*

 ...now creaks audibly. But you are unlikely ever to see a better version than this, caressed by Gregg Toland's deep-focus camerawork, embalmed by Wyler's direction and Goldwyn's sumptuous production values, galvanised by some superlative performances...

          Tom Milne, PTOG 1995

Long Day's Journey into Night, TCF (Ely Landau), 1962 bw

Direction: Sidney Lumet (from play by Eugene O'Neill)
Camera: Boris Kaufman   Music: André Previn
Art Direction: Richard Sylbert   Editing: Ralph Rosenblum
Costume Design: Motley

with Katharine Hepburn, Ralph Richardson, Jason Robards, Dean Stockwell

- Criticism on release

 Since the play is essentially unadaptable to film and, anyway, since no real adaptation has been attempted, supply the missing cinema motions by movements of the camera. This not only fails; it is frequently intrusive. His work with the actors is much more successful...

    Stanley Kauffmann, *New Republic*, 24 September 1962

- Current recommendations and ratings
  LM4 DW3 VFG5 MPG5 NFT*

 A straightforward transposition which captures much of the claustrophobic cannibalism of Eugene O'Neill's autobiographical play. Described by him as a play of old sorrow, written in tears and blood, it imposes itself by sheer weight of emotion...

       Tom Milne, PTOG 1995

The Magnificent Ambersons, RKO (George J. Schaefer/ Orson Welles), 1942 bw

Direction: Orson Welles	Script: Welles (from the novel by Booth Tarkington)
Camera: Stanley Cortez	
Special Effects: Vernon Walker	Music: Bernard Herrmann
Art Direction: Mark-Lee Kirk	Costume Design: Edward Stevenson
Editing: Robert Wise (with Mark Robson, uc)	

with Joseph Cotten, Dolores Costello, Tim Holt, Agnes Morehead, Anne Baxter, Ray Collins, Richard Bennett, Erskine Sanford, Gus Schilling

- Criticism on release

 ...rich in ideas that many will want to copy, combined in the service of a story that few will care to imitate... One uncontested fact emerges from this film – Orson Welles has style... one of the few directors who sets his signature on every scene... There is something arrogant and superb, something almost patriarchal, we feel, about the Voice from the void at the end: '...I wrote the story and directed it. My name is Orson Welles.'

    C.A. Lejeune, *The Observer*, 7 March 1943

- Current recommendations and ratings
StJD S&S82/92 LM4 DQ4 DW4 VFG5 MPG5 NFT**

 Hacked about by a confused RKO, Welles's second film still looks a masterpiece, astounding for its almost magical recreation of a gentler age... With immaculate period reconstruction, and virtuoso acting shot in long, elegant takes, it remains the director's most moving film, despite the artificiality of the sentimental tacked-on ending.

      Geoff Andrew, PTOG 1995

Mildred Pierce, WB (Jerry Wald), 1945 bw

Direction: Michael Curtiz
Camera: Ernest Haller
Music: Max Steiner
Art Direction: Anton Grot
Special Effects: Willard Van Enger
Script: Ranald MacDougall (from James M. Cain's novel)
Editing: David Weisbart
Costume Design: Milo Anderson

with *Joan Crawford, Ann Blyth, Zachary Scott, Jack Carson, Eve Arden, Bruce Bennett, George Tobias, Lee Patrick, Moroni Olsen

- Criticism on release

    So they gave Joan Crawford an Academy Award for her performance!... I suppose it possible to admire her exhibition through the trying circumstances of this film, of iron-faced imperturbability. Myself, I found the range of expression with which she greeted divorce, death, remarriage, financial ruin and murder so delicate as to approximate to indifference. The film, a study of mother-love with Ann Blyth as its object and Zachary Scott and Jack Carson as its concomitants, begins admirably with shots of fast secret action in fog, darkness and rain. But don't let that encourage you.

    Dilys Powell, *Sunday Times* April 1946

- Current recommendations and ratings
StJD S&S92 LM3½ DQ3 DW4 VFG5 MPG5 NFT*

    James Cain's novel of the treacherous life in Southern California that sets housewife-turned-waitress-turned successful restaurateur (Crawford) against her own daughter (Blyth) in competition for the love of playboy Zachary Scott is brought fastidiously and bleakly to life by Curtiz's direction, Ernest Haller's camerawork, and Anton Grot's magnificent sets...

    Phil Hardy, PTOG 1995

East of Eden, WB (Elia Kazan), 1955 *colour*

Direction: Elia Kazan
Camera: Ted McCord
Music: Leonard Rosenman
Art Direction: James Basevi, Malcolm Bert
Costume Design: Anna Hill Johnstone
Script: Paul Osborn, Guy Tomajin (from the novel by John Steinbeck)
Editing: Owen Marks

with James Dean, Julie Harris, Raymond Massey, *Jo Van Fleet, Richard Davalos, Burl Ives, Albert Dekker, Tmothy Carey

- Criticism on release

    In terms of human characterisation the narrative is thin; and, stripped of surface ornament and the pretentious gambit of Biblical parallels, fairly unconvincing... [James Dean, an] actor from Broadway, is undoubtedly sensitive and gifted, but he has been so encouraged to imitate Marlon Brando in speech and slouch that his performance is at moments reduced to mere display...

    Gavin Lambert, *Sunday Times*, 10 July 1955

- Current recommendations and ratings
StJD S&S92 LM3½ DQ3 DW4 VFG4½ MPG5 NFT*

    ...as long-winded and bloated as the original... [but] great performances, atmospheric photography and a sure sense of period and place (the Californian farmlands at the time of World War I)...

    Geoff Andrew, PTOG 1995

Giant, WB (George Stevens, Henry Ginsberg), 1956 *colour*

Direction: George Stevens
Camera: William Mellor
Music: Dimitri Tiomkin
Costume Design: Marjorie Best,
Moss Mabry

Script: Fred Guiol, Ivan Moffat
(from Edna Ferber's novel)
Production Design: Boris Leven
Editing: William Hornbeck, Fred
Bohanan, Philip W. Anderson

with Elizabeth Taylor, Rock Hudson, James Dean, Carroll Baker, Jane Withers, Chill Wills, Mercedes McCambridge, Sal Mineo, Dennis Hopper, Earl Holliman

- Criticism on release

    ...in spite of the acting and excellence of certain scenes – the [final] banquet itself is outstanding – in its last third, with a division of interest among the second generation, *Giant* loses impulse; and the final knockdown fight on behalf of racial equality, though I see that it is necessary to establish a change of conscience in the husband, seems an excrescence. Yet the film is an astonishing achievement, evoking the ochre plains alive with cattle, the ruined earth belching oil, the millionaires' palaces and the secret human lives. *Giant* is heroic, a film of creative size, a film to begin a year with. And Mr Stevens has elicited splendid acting performances...

    Dilys Powell, *Sunday Times* January 1957

- Current recommendations and ratings
    StJD LM4 DQ3 DW4 VFG4 MPG4 NFT**

    ...the pace is so plodding, and the general effect so generally unsubtle, that one is left impressed only by the fine landscape photography and Dean's surprisingly convincing portrayal of a middle-aged man. To see the overblown, soft-centred nature of the film, one need only compare it with Sirk's vitriolic account of Texan family life in *Written on the Wind*.

    Geoff Andrew, PTOG 1995

Kramer vs Kramer, Col (Stanley R. Jaffe), 1979 *colour*

*Direction: Robert Benton
Camera: Nestor Almendros
Art Direction: Paul Sylbert
Editing: Jerry Greenberg
*Script: Benton (from the novel by Avery Corman)
Costume Design: Ruth Morley

with *Dustin Hoffman, *Meryl Streep, Jane Alexander, Justin Henry, Howard Duff, George Coe

- Criticism on release

    ...a perceptive, touching, intelligent film about one of the raw sores of contemporary America, the dissolution of the family unit. In refashioning Avery Corman's novel, director-scripter Robert Benton has used a highly effective technique of short, poignant scenes to bring home the message that no one escapes unscarred from the trauma of separation – three-quarters into the film, Streep comes to claim the first-born with the traditional mother's prerogative and a nasty court battle ensues.

    Variety, 1979

- Current recommendations and ratings
LM4 DQ4 DW5 VFG4 MPG4 NFT*

    A real high-class modern weepie – Benton forsakes the eccentric and original delights of his films (*Bad Company*, *The Late Show*) and turns in a very solid and professional domestic melodrama, helped no end by some very fine naturalistic performances...

    Geoff Andrew, PTOG 1995

Written on the Wind, Un (Albert Zugsmith), 1956 colour

Direction: Douglas Sirk
Camera: Russell Metty
Music: Frank Skinner
Art Creation: Alexander Golitzen, Robert Chatworthy
Costume Design: Bill Thomas, Jay A. Morley Jr.
Editing: Russell Schoengarth

Script: George Zuckerman (from Robert Wilder's novel)
Special Effects: Clifford Stine

with Rock Hudson, Lauren Bacall, Robert Stack, Dorothy Malone, Robert Keith, Harry Shannon

- Criticism on release

    ...the best work that has been done in this direction, both visually and intellectually, it is an exact equivalent of a very good 'photo-novel' in color... I would not recommend *Written on the Wind* to the film lover who only goes to see the fifteen or twenty undoubted masterpieces each year, because its naiveté, deliberate or not, and its absurdity would offend him. But the real movie nut, the guy who forgives Hollywood a lot because its films are so alive, will come out ecstatic, dazzled, satisfied for one evening – at least until the next good marital comedy comes along.

    François Truffaut, *Cahiers du Cinema*, 1957

- Current recommendations and ratings
  StJD S&S92 LM3 DQ3 DW3 VFG4½ MPG5 NFT*

    ...one of the quintessential films of the 50s... The acting is dynamite, the melodrama is compulsive, the photography, lighting, and design share a bold disregard for realism. It's not an old movie; it's a film for the future.

    Tony Rayns, PTOG 1995

THE SEX WAR

From the 1950s, two Elia Kazan/Tennessee Williams movies – *A Streetcar Named Desire*, 1951 (which Kazan had previously produced on the Broadway stage in 1947 with Brando and Jessica Tandy) and *Baby Doll* (adapted by Williams from two of his short stories) – were distinguished by superlative performances: Vivien Leigh (replacing Jessica Tandy in the film version of *Streetcar*) winning a well-deserved Oscar in the complex role of Blanche Dubois, moving from refined vulnerability to madness, brought about by the clash between her fading ideals and the brutal realities of her sister's marriage to the primitive Kowalski (a screen performance probably never bettered by Brando in later films). The stagey sets actually make an atmospheric contribution to the steamy claustrophobia of this seedy New Orleans household.

Most film historians remember *Baby Doll*, 1951, with almost reluctant respect. Though not a very likeable film, it has taut direction and editing, atmospheric camerawork, and three outstanding performances by Carroll Baker (the Baby Doll herself), Karl Malden, her deprived and taunted husband, and Eli Wallach as a sexually aggressive, self-assertive Sicilian, who joins with her to bring about her husband's moral collapse.

Terence Malick's *Days of Heaven*, 1978, is difficult to place. Starting as a flight movie, as the young man (Richard Gere), his girlfriend (Brooke Adams), posing as his sister, and his much younger real sister (Linda Manz, who is also the film's narrator) seek casual labour as migrants on a non-mechanised Texan wheat farm, owned by a strange young loner (Sam Shepard in his film debut) – the period is 1915. With Gere's connivance, Adams marries Shepard under the illusion that, after his impending death, she will soon inherit his wealth. Things go awry, however: Adams falls in love with Shepard, and, after Gere has killed Shepard (accidentally), the group take to the road once more. The psychological atmosphere of *Baby Doll* is not far away, but the particular atmosphere of this movie is created by the ravishing camerawork of Nestor Almendros (with the help of the veteran non-conformist cameraman, Haskell Wexler), which at times gives the film an almost Biblical quality. It was Malick's second film – *Badlands* was made four years earlier – and his last, a financial failure, no doubt due to the puzzlement of audiences over a kind of hopeless existentialism, and in spite of its visual glories. Patrick Gibbs, *Daily Telegraph* 1 June 1979 recommended in vain: "One looks forward to his next."

Baby Doll, WB (Elia Kazan), 1956 bw

Direction: Elia Kazan
Camera: Boris Kaufman
Music: Kenyon Hopkins
Costume Design: Anna Hill Johnstone
Editing: Gene Milford

Script: Tennessee Williams (from his own stories)
Art Direction: Richard Sylbert

with Carroll Baker, Karl Malden, Eli Wallach, Mildred Dunnock, Rip Torn

- Criticism on release

    We must take off our hats to Kazan who, throughout *Baby Doll*, succeeds intentionally in filming action that bears no relation at all to the dialogue. The characters think one thing, say another and convey a third... The second time we see *Baby Doll*, we discover a second film which is still richer. Whether it is a work of genius or mere talent, whether decadent or generous, profound or brilliant, *Baby Doll* is fascinating.

    François Truffaut, *Cahiers du Cinema*, 1957

- Current recommendations and ratings
  S&S92 LM3½ DW4 VFG4 MPG2 NFT*

    ...arguably one of Kazan's least ambitious and most successfully realised movies... Condemned by the Legion of Decency upon release, its erotic content now seems tame indeed; but the grotesquely caricatured performances and the evocation of the baking, dusty, indolent homestead make for witty and compelling viewing.

    Geoff Andrew, PTOG 1995

A Streetcar Named Desire, WB (Charles K. Feldman), 1951 bw

Direction: Elia Kazan	Script: Kazan, with Oscar Saul
Camera: Harry Stradling	(from play by Tennessee
Music: Alex North	Williams)
*Art Direction: Richard Day	Costume Design: Lucinda Ballard
Editing: David Weisbart	

with *Vivien Leigh, Marlon Brando, *Kim Hunter, *Karl Malden, Leo Genn

- Criticism on release

    ...theatrically composed settings lit by the fitful glow of neon lights outside and underscored by the despairing beat of the Blues... [It] should be an harrowing experience. It isn't... The transcription of play to film is painlessly professional and loyal to the text... Brando burns with a sullen glow that one will not easily forget.

    Richard Winnington, *News Chronicle* 27 February 1952

- Current recommendations and ratings
  StJD LM4 DQ4 DW5 VFG5 MPG5 NFT*

    ...remains impressive largely because of Brando's superbly detailed performance... Directing with his camera sticking as close to the characters as if they were grouped on the stage, Kazan achieves a sort of theatrical intensity in which the sweaty realism sometimes clashes awkwardly with the stylisation that heightens the dialogue into a kind of poetry...

    Tom Milne, PTOG 1995

Days of Heaven, Par (Bert and Harold Schneider), 1978 colour

Direction, Script: Terence Mallick   Art Direction: Jack Fisk
*Camera: Nestor Almendros   Costume Design: Patricia Norris
Music: Ennio Morricone   Editing: Billy Weber
Special Effects: John Thomas, Mel Merrells

with Richard Gere, Brooke Adams, Sam Shepard, Linda Manz, Bob Wilke, Jackie Shultis, Stuart Margolin

- Criticism on release

    ...the first film to reach London from the Cannes Film Festival, which ended last week, and had, in the competition at least, the highest standard for many a year... had there been an official prize for photography at Cannes, it must have gone to a newcomer to me, Nestor Almendros, helped out by that experienced cameraman Haskell Wexler. Together they provide here a stunningly beautiful series of coloured pictures of the Texan landscape with pictures as wide as you can get, thanks to 70mm film... Following (his first film, *Badlands*) in so many artistic aspects, this second film suggests the arrival of that rarity, a director with an individual style. One looks forward to his next.

    Patrick Gibbs, *Daily Telegraph* 1 June 1979

- Current recommendations and ratings
StJD S&S82/92 LM3½ DQ2 DW4 VFG4½ MPG5 NFT**

    ...a strange fusion of love story, social portrait and allegorical epic, by the director of *Badlands*... Eventually (with a plague-of-locusts climax and the lovers' flight) the narrative collapses, leaving its audience breathlessly suspended between a 90-minute proof that all the bustling activity in the world means nothing, and the perfection of Malick's own perverse desire to catalogue it nonetheless.

    Chris Auty, PTOG 1995

ADDICTION AND REHABILITATION
Among the several good movies dealing with the problem of addiction, the dramatic masterpiece remains Billy Wilder's *The Lost Weekend*, 1945, Hollywood's earliest attempt to deal with alcoholism as a major issue. Its pure economy, almost bleakness, of style still works in its favour. The somewhat extravagant highlights – enforced withdrawal into a downtown 'drying-out' ward and the horrifying appearance of imagined vermin in the drunk's own apartment – gain from contrast with its generally sparse, understated style. The unexpectedly effective performance by Ray Milland (which shocked audiences with its intelligent realism after a decade of light juvenile leads) ensured complete conviction and identification in the harrowing and humiliating experiences of this otherwise intelligent, sensitive man.

In William Wyler's *The Best Years of Our Lives*, 1946, the disorder from which all its main characters (this is also a 'compendium' film) have to recover is the fever of war. The most physically disabled, played by Harold Russell in his only film and himself suffering from the loss of both hands, appears to adjust most readily to new peace-time living. Those played by Fredric March and (particularly) Dana Andrews suffer greater mental strain. Although Richard Griffith, in his Epilogue to Paul Rotha's *The Film Till Now*, 1960, complained that, though "well-made technically", post-World War II films "seldom probed very deeply into the social or other causes of the sicknesses they portrayed". *The Best Years of Our Lives*, based on a blank verse novel by Mackinlay Kantor, deals with relationship problems easily identifiable even today by the audience: it was both a box office and a critical success at the time and is still very much respected for its script, direction, superlative camerawork (Gregg Toland); and the excellent performances all round by, in addition to the leads, Myrna Loy, as March's wife, Teresa Wright as his daughter, Cathy O'Donnell, as Russell's understanding girlfriend, and Hoagy Carmichael, as a philosophical bar pianist, deserve special mention.

Arthur Penn's *The Miracle Worker*, 1962 is a moving tribute to the real-life achievement of Annie Sullivan, who is determined to bring the blind, deaf and rebellious Helen Keller into contact with the outer world. She not only achieves this miracle but helps the very intelligent and individual young girl to become aware of the development of her own personality. The two Oscars won by Anne Bancroft (the teacher) and Patty Duke (the girl) were well deserved; and, although the film remains a basically theatrical experience, it is sensitively directed, powerfully acted and still has a strong meaning for viewers today.

The Best Years of Our Lives, RKO (Samuel Goldwyn), 1946 bw

*Direction: William Wyler
Camera: Gregg Toland
*Music: Hugo Friedhofer
Art Direction: George Jenkins, Perry Ferguson
Costume Design: Irene Sharaff

*Script: Robert E. Sherwood (from the novel by Mackinlay Kantor)
*Editing: Daniel Mandell

with *Fredric March, Dana Andrews, *Harold Russell, Myrna Loy, Teresa Wright, Virginia Mayo, Cathy O'Donnell, Hoagy Carmichael, Gladys George, Roman Bohnen, Ray Collins, Minna Gombell, Steve Cochran, Charles Halton, Don Beddoe, Ray Teal, Erskine Sanford

- Criticism on release

    ...one of the very few American studio-made movies in years that seem to me profoundly pleasing, moving and encouraging... this is a most unusually good screenplay – I can't remember a more thoroughly satisfying job of photography in an American movie, since *Greed* – William Wyler has always seemed to me an exceedingly good and sincere director; he now seems one of the few great ones...

    James Agee, *The Nation* 14 December 1946

- Current recommendations and ratings
StJD BN92 S&S82/92 LM4 DQ3 DW4 VFG5 MPG5 NFT*

    ...one of Wyler's best films – the performances throughout are splendid (including that of Russell, an amateur actor who was himself an amputee), and Gregg

Toland's masterly camerawork serves as a textbook on the proper use of deep focus. Maybe not the masterpiece it would like to be, but a model of fine Hollywood craftsmanship all the same.

Geoff Andrew, PTOG 1995

The Lost Weekend, Par (Charles Brackett), 1945 bw

*Direction: Billy Wilder *Script: Wilder, with Brackett
Camera: John F.Seitz   Music: Miklos Rozsa
Art Direction: Hans Dreier, Earl Costume Design: Edith Head
   Hedrick
Editing: Doane Harrison

with *Ray Milland, Jane Wyman, Philip Terry, Howard Da Silva, Frank Faylen, Doris Dowling, Frank Orth

- Criticism on release

    ...a shatteringly realistic and morbidly fascinating film – an illustration of the drunkard's misery that ranks with the best and most disturbing character studies ever put on the screen... Mr Milland, in a splendid performance, catches all the ugly nature of a 'drunk', yet reveals the inner torment and degradation of a respectable man who knows his weakness and his shame...

    Bosley Crowther, New York Times, 3 December 1945

- Current recommendations and ratings
  StJD LM4 DQ4 DW5 VFG4½ MPG5 NFT*

    ...What makes the film so gripping is the brilliance with which Wilder uses John F. Seitz's camera-work to range from an unvarnished portrait of New York brutally stripped of all glamour... to an almost Wellesian evocation of the alcoholic's inner world, [systematically using] images dominated by huge foreground objects...

    Tom Milne, PTOG 1995

The Miracle Worker, UA/Playfilms (Fred Coe), 1962 bw

Direction: Arthur Penn
Camera: Ernesto Caparros
Music: Laurence Rosenthal
Art Direction: George Jenkins,
　Mel Bourne
Editing: Aram Avakian

Script: William Gibson (from Gibson's own play based on Helen Keller's *The Story of My Life*)
Costume Design: Ruth Morley

with *Anne Bancroft, *Patty Duke, Victor Jory, Inga Swenson, Andrew Prine, Kathleen Comagys

- Criticism on release

    The absolutely tremendous and unforgettable display of physically powerful acting that Anne Bancroft and Patty Duke put on in William Gibson's stage play... is repeated by them in the film made from it by the same producer, Fred Coe, and the same director, Arthur Penn... But because the physical encounters between the two in their strongly graphic roles of trained nurse and deaf-and-blind pupil seem to be more frequent and prolonged than they were in the play and are shown in close-ups, the sheer rough and tumble of the drama becomes more dominant... However, Miss Bancroft's performance does bring to life and reveal a wondrous woman with great humor and compassion as well as athletic skill. And little Miss Duke, in those moments when she frantically pantomimes her bewilderment and desperate groping, is both gruesome and pitiable.

    　　　　Bosley Crowther, *New York Times* 24 May 1962

- Current recommendations and ratings
LM3½ DQ3 DW4 VFG5 MPG5 NFT*

    ...a stunningly impressive piece of work, typically [for Penn] deriving much of its power from the performances... What is in fact astonishing is the way that, while constructing a piece of very carefully directed and intelligently written melodrama, Penn manages to avoid sentimentality or even undue optimism about the value of Helen's education, and the way he achieves such a feeling of raw spontaneity in the acting.

    　　　　　　　　　　Geoff Andrew, PTOG 1995

Drama (3: Problems of Power) – Politics and the Services, Prison/Mental Hospital, the Pool Room and the Boxing Ring, the Theatre and the Media, 'Moviola'

This third group of dramas is concerned with the acquisition and maintenance of power, under the headings detailed in the title.

POLITICS

For Hollywood, politics entails strong melodrama; the forces of good, however weak they appear to be during the telling, finally triumph over the forces of evil. Good, on the whole, means the American Constitution, evil whatever seeks to subvert it.

Mr Smith Goes to Washington, 1939, as the title indicates, takes the success of Capra's previous *Mr Deeds Goes to Town* as its model, and has a similarly strong comic element: in fact, many critics condemned it as a cardboard repetition of the Capra formula. If Mr Smith represents the innocence and honesty of rural America in conflict with the corruption of the big city, it is a theme treated with loving care, particularly from the viewpoint of the worldly but not corrupted urban secretary and reporter (played by Jean Arthur and Thomas Mitchell). The final filibuster of twenty-three hours to expose the graft of the crooked businessman (Edward Arnold) and his bought-up senator (Claude Rains) proclaims Mr Smith (ideally personified in the gawky, gulping charm of James Stewart's portrayal) as the great populist hero of New Deal Hollywood.

Stewart's Mr Smith may be called a study in benevolent demagoguery; there is also a study in malevolent demagoguery: Broderick Crawford's corrupt state governor, Willie Stark, in *All the King's Men*, 1949, deals with state, not federal, politics. Its writer-director, Robert Rossen, gives a pungent, sometimes shocking, picture of the rise and fall of a political demagogue (his career is based on that of Huey Long of Louisiana) and his weak corrupt entourage. Half shot in the studio, half on location (as a concession to Rossen, who also fought justifiably hard to cast the almost unknown Broderick Crawford in the leading role), it has all the Dickensian strengths of drive, intensity and remorseless probing. It also has some Dickensian weaknesses – the need to persuade, the reliance on repetition, distrust of subtlety and implication; it, nevertheless, remains, in Halliwell's words, "an archetypal American political melodrama... [with] excellent performances" by a largely non-star cast.

All the President's Men, 1976, is the celebrated film version of the terrier-like pursuit of the Watergate scandal by two *Washington Post* reporters – Carl Bernstein (Dustin Hoffman) and Bob Woodward (Robert Redford) – scripted by William Goldman and directed by Alan Pakula. The dark mysterious episodes of the investigation (filmed in *film noir* style) are contrasted strongly with the white glare of the newspaper offices and the bluff straightforwardness of the managing editor (played by Jason Robards Jr.). The investigators are not crusaders so much as ambitious, cunning journalists aiming for the Pulitzer Prize; the underlying scepticism ensures that the appeal of the story remains, long past the time when Watergate was a topical cause.

Missing, 1982, the first American Film of Constantin Costa-Gavras has the ironic title of an adaptation from a book called *The Execution of Charles Horman: An American Sacrifice*. The political content is obvious, although the film takes the form of a suspense thriller in the Hitchcock style. However, Costa-Gavras does not repeat Hitchcock's injunction, as for *Psycho*, to see it from the beginning: the dramatic advantage derives from the gradual horrifying discovery of the truth behind Horman's disappearance by his conservative, increasingly concerned father (Jack Lemmon) and his radical, determined wife (Sissy Spacek). The political message is clearly presented in all the South American scenes: the danger of a reactionary backlash against a progressive Socialist state as depicted in the ruthless overthrow of Allende's government in Chile in 1973 (with the suggested collusion of the USA). Brutal details are everywhere, and in one nightmare sequence Spacek, out after curfew, frantically attempts (and just manages) to escape the trigger-happy troops shooting everyone on sight. This is a magnificently realised film, with excellent performances and telling, memorable scenes.

Philip Kaufman's *The Right Stuff*, 1983 is a complex film based on a complex book (by Tom Wolfe). The subject of training astronauts could be treated in a straightforward documentary manner, but ultimately this could be extremely dull. Although this element is not neglected, Kaufman also introduces a fascinating human theme and some forthright political satire. Chuck Yeager (Sam Shepard), a test pilot who helped to make the space program possible, at first views the seven would-be astronauts with some contempt; but their experience not only ennobles them individually but welds them into an intelligent, understanding team full of mutual respect. Even Chuck Yeager admits that they are made of the 'right stuff'. He had not participated himself because of the political dimension and its unworthy 'circus' approach, well depicted in the party given by Vice-President Johnson in Washington at the end of the film. The astronauts are brilliantly depicted by a strong cast; and the other film-makers' contributions are equally outstanding.

As in Costa-Gavras's *Missing*, Oliver Stone's *Salvador*, 1987, transfers a horrified lens to an equally bloody, chaotic shambles in Central America, with a similar criticism of US policy. This time the 'hero' is a dissolute journalist outcast (James Wood – a brilliant portrayal) trying to re-establish himself in his profession by achieving a scoop. His investigations (with an equally disreputable friend, appropriately played by James Belushi) lead to terrifying, confusing experiences which transform him into a committed radical wishing to reveal the truth of all he has seen. Stone collaborated in the script with Robert Boyle, a journalist who seems to have undergone a similar metamorphosis. The film is shocking, disturbing, harrowing, honest and overwhelming: one must be prepared for the continual buffeting of one's senses and total consciousness while viewing.

All the King's Men, Col (Robert Rossen), 1950 bw

Direction: Robert Rossen	Script: Rossen (from the novel by
Camera: Burnett Guffey	Robert Penn Warren)
Music: Louis Gruenberg	Editing: Al Clark, Robert Parrish
Art Direction: Sturges Carne, Louis Diage	
Costume Design: Jean Louis	

with *Broderick Crawford, *Mercedes McCambridge, John Ireland, John Derek, Joanne Dru, Sheppard Strudwck, Will Wright

- Criticism on release

> ...a fascinating but curiously disappointing work – Rossen's staccato factual approach... gives a vital atmospheric view into the political-social atmosphere of the South. He shot the film in all weathers and it gains

enormously. His crowds and locations are real (extras and studio work were cut to the minimum), his angles dramatic and his sound track discriminating and inventive.

Richard Winnington, News Chronicle 15 April

- Current recommendations and ratings
  StJD LM4 DQ3 DW3 VFG5 MPG3½ NFT*

A fine adaptation of Robert Penn Warren's Pulitzer Prize-winning novel, chronicling the rise and fall of Southern demagogue Willie Stark... Given that Stark's relationship with his son builds latterly to some overheated melodrama, the first half of the film is by far the best, but Rossen retains his grip throughout; and the performances [Crawford, Ireland and McCambridge especially] are superb.

Tom Milne, PTOG 1995

Mr Smith Goes to Washington, Col (Frank Capra), 1939 bw

Direction: Frank Capra, with Charles Vidor (2nd unit)
Script: Sidney Buchman (from *story by Lewis Foster)
Camera: Joe Walker   Music: Dimitri Tiomkin
Special Effects: Slavko Vorkapich Costume Design: Robert Kalloch
Art Direction: Lionel Banks
Editing: Gene Havlick, Al Clark

with James Stewart, Jean Arthur, Claude Rains, Thomas Mitchell, Eugene Pallette, Ruth Donnelly, Edward Arnold, Guy Kibbee, Beulah Bondi, H.B. Warner, Harry Carey, Porter Hall, William Demarest, Astrid Allwyn, Jack Carson, Russell Simpson, Alan Bridge, Ann Doran, John Russell, Grant Mitchell, Dorothy Comingore (as Linda Winters)

- Criticism on release

    ...It is a mixture of tough, factual pattern about congressional cloakrooms and pressure groups, and a naive but shameless hooray for the American relic. Politically, the story is eyewash: the machinery of the Senate and the machinery of how it may be used to advantage is shown better than it ever has been. There are some fine lines and there is a whole magazine of nice types, but the occasional humor is dispersed...

Otis Ferguson, *New Republic*, 1 November 1939

- Current recommendations and ratings
  StJD S&S82 LM4 DQ4 DW5 VFG5 MPG5 NFT*

...quintessential Capra – popular with wish-fulfilment served up with such fast-talking comic panache that you don't have time to question its cornball idealism. Scriptwriter Sidney Buchman's crackling dialogue is also lent sharp-tongued conviction by Rains, as the slimy senior senator, Jean Arthur as the hard-boiled dame finally won over by Stewart's honesty, and Harry Carey as the Vice-President.

Nigel Floyd, PTOG 1995

All the President's Men, WB (Walter Coblenz), 1976 *colour*

Direction: Alan Pakula	Script: *William Goldman, from
Camera: Gordon Willis	the book by Carl Bernstein and
Music: David Shire	Bob Woodward
*Art Direction: George Jenkins	Editing: Robert Wolfe

with Dustin Hoffman, Robert Redford, *Jason Robards Jr., Jack Warden, Martin Balsam, Hal Holbrook, Jane Alexander, Ned Beatty

- Criticism on release

...The real star of the film is Jason Robards, formidably yet genially commanding as Ben Bradlee, the *Washington Post*'s Executive Editor. It is a magnificent performance, and the two reporters (played by Hoffman and Redford) must react to it... The investigations, the interviews are conducted, most of them, in darkened rooms - a violent contrast with the newsroom, huge, bleak, not a corner escaping the brutal white light. It is to the newsroom that the two reporters belong. They are the servants of its demand for the pitiless truth...

                Dilys Powell, *Sunday Times* May 1976

- Current recommendations and ratings
  LM4 DQ3 DW4 VFG4 MPG3½ NFT**

  ...remarkably intelligent, working both as an effective thriller (even though we know the outcome of their investigations) and as a virtually abstract charting of the dark corridors of corruption and power...

                  Geoff Andrew, PTOG 1995

Missing, Un/Polygram (Edward and Mildred Lewis), 1982 *colour*

Direction: Constantin Costa-Gavras	Script: Costa-Gavras, Donald Stewart (based on book by Thomas Hauser)
Camera: Ricardo Aronovich	
Music: Vangelis	Production Design: Peter Jamison
Costume Design: Joe I. Tompkins	Editing: Françoise Bonnot
Special Effects: Albert Whitlock	

with Jack Lemmon, Sissy Spacek, Melanie Mayron, John Shea, Charles Cioffi, David Clennon, Richard Venture

- Criticism on release

  ...demonstrates Costa-Gavras's ability to grab you unawares by the lapels and drag you through the labyrinth of intrigue and paranoia that lies beyond the more acceptable corridors of power. He is helped by a strong cast, headed by Jack Lemmon, who picked up the best actor award at Cannes for another detailed variation of his not unfamiliar worm-turning act... As honest Ed and his drop-out daughter-in-law are reconciled, conflicting generations united against the smug establishment, the picture's radical thrust is turned into (or concealed behind) domestic drama... But the movie raises major issues in a usefully provocative way and is far from being anti-American...

Philip French, *The Observer* 30 May 1982

- Current recommendations and ratings
S&S82 LM3½ DW4 VFG4 MPG4 NFT**

...Costa-Gavras' extraordinary first American movie, based on true events during the Chilean coup of 1973... underpins his campaigning content with all the electric atmosphere of a paranoid conspiracy thriller, and ensures that *Missing* will remain the cinematic evocation of a military coup for years to come.

David Pirie, PTOG 1995

The Right Stuff, WB/ Ladd (Irwin Winkler, Robert Chartoff), 1983 *colour*

Direction and Script (based on Tom Wolfe's book): Philip Kaufman	
Camera: Caleb Deschanel	*Music: Bill Conti
Production Designer: Geoffrey Kirkland	*Editing: Glenn Farr, Lisa Fruchtman, Stephen A. Rotter, Tom Rolf, Douglas Stewart
Special Effects: Gary Gutierrez, Jordan Belson	

with Sam Shepard, Scott Glenn, Ed Harris, Dennis Quaid, Fred Ward, Barbara Hershey, Kim Stanley, Veronica Cartwright, Pamela Reed, Scott Paulin

- Criticism on release

...A very American amalgam of the romantic and the cynical, the movie gives a proper account of the excitement of space travel, while holding up the backstage manipulations to ridicule. It celebrates real heroism while lampooning the social machinery that exploits the heroes – a bold, confident picture that makes its points with visual flair and tells us a great deal about the American character and the forces that have been working on it in the post-war era...

                    Philip French, *The Observer* 4 March 1984

- Current recommendations and ratings
  LM3 DQ3 DW4 VFG4 MPG5 NFT**

  ...Kaufman (like Tom Wolfe, whose book *The Right Stuff* this is taken from) is well enough aware of the media circus surrounding the whole project, but still celebrates his magnificent seven's heroism with a rhetoric that is respectful and irresistible.

                      Chris Peachment, PTOG 1995

Salvador, Hemdale (Gerald Green/ Oliver Stone), 1986 colour

Direction: Oliver Stone
Camera: Robert Richardson
Music: Georges Delerue
Editing: Claire Simpson
Script: Stone, Robert Boyle
Special Effects: Yves De Bono
Production Design: Bruno Rubeo
Costume Design: Kathryn Morrison

with James Woods, James Belushi, Michael Murphy, John Savage, Elpidia Carrillo, Tony Plana, Colby Chester, Cynthia Gibb

- Criticism on release

  ...like its central character, disturbingly ambiguous. Both sides in the grisly Salvadorean war are regarded with disfavour. The human condition seems to have reached its nadir... James Woods is much more than a thinking man's Rambo. He redeems the unacceptable anti-hero, giving him courage, compassion, and a conscience that has eluded American officialdom. Stone, screenwriter of *Midnight Express*, and director of *Platoon*, a current American hit about Vietnam, must be regarded as a major new force in American cinema.

                  George Perry, *Sunday Times* 25 January 1987

- Current recommendations and ratings
  StJD LM2½ DW5 VFG4 MPG4 NFT*

  ...The polemic may seem obvious and at times laboured, but the action sequences are brilliant, and the film does achieve a brutal, often very moving, power.

  Richard Rayner, PTOG 1995

PRISON/MENTAL HOSPITAL

In Milos Forman's *One Flew over the Cuckoo's Nest*, 1975, the main theme is the (one-sided) battle for power in a mental hospital between an authoritarian nurse (Louise Fletcher, who gained a Best Actress Oscar) and a disruptive patient, Randle McMurphy, whose mental disorder is a pretence to escape from prison work duties (Jack Nicholson). Nurse Ratchet and McMurphy clash at every point: she is aware that he is trying to release her submissive patients from their terror of her. They get up to all sorts of pranks under his instigation, including the introduction of women into a wild party overnight, which leads to the final unanswerable act of discipline on McMurphy. From the beginning it is apparent that he can never succeed, although he has won the loyal sympathy of the ward, as graphically depicted by an act of destructive violence which allows the giant Chief Bromden (Will Sampson) to escape. The film earned five major Oscars.

*One Flew over the Cuckoo's Nest, UA/ Fantasy Films (Saul Zaentz, Michael Douglas), 1975 *colour*

*Direction: Milos Forman	*Script: Lawrence Hauben, Bo Goldman (from Dale Wasserman's play based on novel by Ken Kesey)
Camera: Haskell Wexler, William A. Fraker, Bill Butler	
Music: Jack Nitzsche	
Production Design: Paul Sylbert	Editing: Richard Chew, Lynzee Klingman, Sheldon Kahn
Costume Design: Annie Guerard Rodgers	

with *Jack Nicholson, *Louise Fletcher, William Redfield, Michael Berryman, Will Sampson, Brad Dourif, Peter Brocco, Dean R. Brooks, Alonzo Brown, Scatman Crothers, Mwako Cumbuka

- Criticism on release

    I'm not at all sure that the terrifying events that Kesey so jauntily describes in his novel would ever have taken place in any mental hospital 10 or 15 years ago, so one must accept the tale as a fictional nightmare of its time – the sixties. The mental hospital... is, I suppose, a metaphor, but is more important as the locale of one more epic battle between a free spirit and a society that cannot tolerate him... Nicholson's flamboyance as an actor here is of an especially productive sort. It doesn't submerge the other actors. It seems to illuminate them – Louise Fletcher (Nurse Ratchet), Will Sampson (Nicholson's deaf-mute Indian sidekick), Brad Dourif as the ward's 'kid' character...

    Vincent Canby, *New York Times* 23 November 1975

- Current recommendations and ratings
  S&S92 LM4 DQ3 DW5 VFG4 MPG5 NFT*

    ...For all the film's painstaking sensitivity and scrupulous chartings of energies and repressions, one longs for more muscle, which only Nicholson consistently provides.

    Chris Petit, PTOG 1995

THE POOL ROOM AND THE BOXING RING

Hollywood's dramas about the sporting world have much in common with their political films, the central character generally fighting to retain his integrity against violent opposition in a dark, usually corrupt world. There is also an additional, near-tragic element when the protagonist is left in isolation (except for a possible girlfriend giving moral support), enabled by his skill and courage alone to break through the crust of monopoly power and prove his own superiority in the world in which he chooses to compete.

It is, therefore, not surprising that Robert Rossen's second great film (with *All the King's Men*) should be in this genre. It is not the least of his achievements that, with *The Hustler*, he effectively erased the memory of Hollywood's former boxing or racing-car classics.

Most of the excitement of *The Hustler* derives from a gigantic duel on the pool table between Eddie Felson, the hustler (Paul Newman), and the reigning champion, Minnesota Fats (Jackie Gleason), but George C. Scott's gambler turned agent also provides a tense element of political drama.

"Of all sports films, movies about the world of boxing have been the most numerous and the most successful. The drama of two men battling it out in front of a cheering crowd is utterly cinematic and easy to follow whether one is a boxing fan or not." (The Siegels, *Guinness Encyclopaedia of Hollywood*, 1990). Neither John Huston's *Fat City*, 1972, nor Martin Scorsese's *Raging Bull*, 1981, fall into the relatively easy pattern of popular boxing films.

Beneath the ironic title of *Fat City* lurks a strange underworld of boxing – not the underworld of fixed fights and gang violence but the underworld of failure, hopelessness, pain, humiliation, and the need for self-delusion to survive. This story involves a strange trio – Stacy Keach's veteran loser who has no choice but to go on dreaming of being a contender, Jeff Bridges' pitifully optimistic nineteen-year-old, and Nicholas Colasanto's well-intentioned but misguided fight manager. The interplay among these three is shown with great humanity and pathos in a modestly effective movie with little of Hollywood's bravado and panache – the work of a quietly confident film-maker, who is master of his theme and technique.

Raging Bull, based on a script by Paul Schrador and Mardik Martin, is an exercise in repulsion. Robert De Niro's portrayal of real-life middleweight champion Jake La Motta is unflattering in the extreme. Many critics have asked why Scorsese and De Niro, among other brilliantly successful collaborations, attempted this and succeeded so well. Was it an attempt to gain sympathy for a 'stupid brute', a 'louse', a 'mean jealous man'? (If so, it soon becomes tedious). Was it to recapture the atmosphere of the period, perfectly achieved in Michael Chapman's austere black-and-white photography? Was it, to show the cinema's unique visual virtuosity in expressing the inarticulate (Nigel Andrews thought so in the *Financial Times*, 20 February 1981)? Or was it, as I suspect, a deliberate act of character alienation in the style of Bertholt Brecht? It is not a film for the squeamish – both images and soundtrack batter the senses and force one into reluctant contact with brutal reality.

The Hustler, TCF (Robert Rossen), 1961 bw

Direction: Robert Rossen
Camera: Eugene Shuftan
Music: Kenyon Hopkins
*Art Direction: Harry Horner
Costume Design: Ruth Morley

Script: Rossen, with Sidney
Carroll (from the novel by
Walter Tevis)
Editing: Dede Allen

with Paul Newman, Jackie Gleason, George C. Scott, Piper Laurie, Myron McCormick, Murray Hamilton, Vincent Gardenia

- Criticism on release

> Besides the pseudo-menace, the script is full of pseudo-meaning. But the execution of the script is extraordinarily good. Rossen, the co-author, has directed with a sure, economical hand. Newman is first-rate – George C. Scott gives his most credible performance, [and] Rossen has skilfully handled Jackie Gleason, as a pool shark
>
> Stanley Kauffmann, *New Republic* 9 October 1961

- Current recommendations and ratings
  StJD LM4 DQ4 DW5 VFG4½ MPG5 NFT*

> It takes defeat, and a longish, dark night of the soul with Laurie, a drunken lame waif of a woman, before [Fast Eddie] can summon the self-respect to return to battle. Rossen allows much space to the essentially concentrated, enclosed scenes of the film, and so it rests solidly on its performances...
>
> Chris *Peachment*, PTOG 1995

Raging Bull, UA (Irwin Winkler, Robert Chartoff), 1980
bw with some colour sequences

Direction: Martin Scorsese	Script: Paul Schrader, Mardik Martin (from the book by Joseph Carter and Peter Savage)
Camera: Michael Chapman	
Production Design: Gene Rudolf	
*Editing: Thelma Schoonmaker	

with *Robert De Niro, Cathy Moriarty, Joe Pesci, Frank Vincent, Nicholas Colasanto

- Criticism on release

    Scorsese was keen to make *Raging Bull* as authentic as possible. The primary reason for filming in monochrome, except for some brief home movie sequences, was to recapture the atmosphere of the old fight newsreels... Great attention has been paid to detail. The fashion changes are faithful. The period sounds of radio music and fight commentators are authentic... The expletives become as commonplace as punctuation, leaving only the most inventive to penetrate the imagination... It is not surprising that De Niro is tipped for an Oscar...

    Nicholas Wapshott, *The Times* 20 February 1981

- Current recommendations and ratings
StJD BN92 S&S92 LM4 DQ3 DW5 VFG4½ MPG5 NFT**

    With breathtaking accuracy, *Raging Bull* ventures still further into the territory Scorsese has mapped in all his films – men and male values – [the fight's] smashing, storyless violence is relentlessly cut with domestic scenes until you learn to flinch in anticipation. The film does more than make you think about masculinity, it makes you see it – in a way that's relevant to all men, not just Bronx boxers...

    Julia Williams, PTOG 1995

Fat City, Col (Ray Stark), 1972 colour

Direction: John Huston
Camera: Conrad Hall
Music: Marvin Hamlisch
Costume Design: Dorothy Jeakins
Editing: Margaret Booth

Script: Leonard Gardner (from his own novel)
Production Design: Richard Sylbert
Special Effects: Paul Stewart

with Stacy Keach, Jeff Bridges, Susan Tyrrell, Candy Clark, Nicholas Colasanto

- Criticism on release

    ...The script's image is one, if not of unrelieved gloom, at least of unrelieved squalor. Everything about the lives of these people is seedy and grubby, and their settings match this down to the last detail... *Fat City* is at once a solid, traditional film, and a very modern film with its flattish cool surface which allows so much to be apparently thrown away without contrived dramatic emphasis, and yet ensures that everything that needs to be understood is understood, all the lights and shadows fall in the right places.

    John Russell Taylor, *Sight and Sound*, Summer 1972

- Current recommendations and ratings
  S&S82/92 LM3 DQ3 DW4 VFG4 MPG4 NFT*

    Marvellous, grimly downbeat study of desperate lives and the escape route people construct for themselves, stunningly shot by Conrad Hall... Beautifully summed up by Paul Taylor as a "masterpiece of skid row poetry"

    Tom Milne, PTOG 1995

The Theatre and the Media

The main characters in *Ace in the Hole*, 1951, and *Sweet Smell of Success* are infinitely corruptible, Wilder's reporter Charles Tatum (Kirk Douglas) because he is bitter with failure, Lehman-Odets' society columnist J.J. Honsegger (Burt Lancaster) because he is rotten with success. Both films were financial flops, no doubt because of their acidly cynical approach to life, from which there is little relief, drumming in the message that ABSOLUTE POWER CORRUPTS ABSOLUTELY. Tatum's power over the man trapped in the cave near Albuquerque is expressed by delaying the rescue operations so that he can revive his own reputation as a 'scoop' journalist; Honsegger's power lies in the destruction overnight of the reputation of leading public figures.

There are melodramatic intensities at the heart of each script: Tatum's ambiguous relationship with the sexually aggressive, frustrated wife of the trapped man (played with impassioned disdain by Jan Sterling) and the final destruction by Honsegger of his lickspittle agent satellite Sidney Falco (Tony Curtis) after he is convinced of the threat to his sister's virtue. In each case, however, the melodramatic core is wrapped round by a strong sense of social reality: there are no concessions in either film to 'romance' or 'sentimentality'. Their lasting interest lies not in these melodramatic plots but in the incisive social comment. It is the portrayal of the 'Big Carnival' on which Wilder concentrates – growing up over the body of a man whose death is directly attributable to the ballyhoo promoted by the delay in rescuing him. It is the nocturnal life of the theatre world off Broadway that gives *Sweet Smell of Success* its distinctively vitriolic flavour (Dilys Powell once referred to its "dreadful authenticity").

'The critic as megalomaniac' is also presented with undiluted acidity in *All About Eve*, 1950, where George Sanders' suave and worldly Addison de Witt also wields cruel and cynical power. But his portrayal does not dominate the film: as a searching study of the brittle, sophisticated world of the Broadway theatre it probes comprehensively into the behaviour and attitudes of playwright (Hugh Marlowe), director (Gary Merrill), and ageing star, Margo Channing (brilliantly played by Bette Davis), whom the determined young actress Eve (incisively played by Anne Baxter) first sycophantically exploits, then ruthlessly attempts to displace. A final impersonal twist at the end turns the tables on her, too. More sympathetic characters are rare (the down-to-earth dresser of Thelma Ritter, the charming and concerned playwright's wife of Celeste Holm), for this view of the theatre world is savagely cynical, as is the generally witty dialogue of writer-director Joseph Mankiewicz.

Ace in the Hole/ The Big Carnival, Par (Billy Wilder), 1951 *bw*

Direction: Billy Wilder
Camera: Charles Lang
Music: Hugo Friedhofer
Art Direction: Earl Hedrick, Hal Pereira
Script: Wilder, with Lesser Samuels and Walter Newman
Editing: Doane Harrison, Arthur Schmidt

with Kirk Douglas, Jan Sterling, Robert Arthur, Porter Hall, Richard Benedict, Ray Teal

- Criticism on release

    ...Billy Wilder, who produced, directed and partly wrote the story, is a skilled machinist. He hardly ever puts a finger wrong. He makes good films that few will distinguish from the hand-made, heart-felt thing, and it is a rare ear that can detect the rattle of the robot innards... This dreadful film is most effectively done. Hard-focus photography, strident sound and the suggestion of sweat and pressure keep the spectator's nerves constantly on the stretch...

    C.A. Lejeune, *The Observer* 17 June 1951

- Current recommendations and ratings
  LM4 DQ4 DW4 VFG4 MPG3½ NFT*

    Wilder ran into charges of bad taste with this acid tale... As a diatribe against all that is worst in human nature, it has moments dipped in pure vitriol ('Kneeling bags my nylons,' snaps Sterling as the victim's wife when invited to be photographed praying for her husband's safety), even though the last reel goes rather astray in comeuppance time.

Tom Milne, PTOG 1995

All About Eve, TCF (Darryl Zanuck), 1950 bw

*Direction and *Script: Joseph Mankiewicz
Camera: Milton Krasner
Art Direction: Lyle Wheeler, George Davis
Music: Alfred Newman
*Costume: Edith Head, Charles LeMaire
Editing: Barbara McLean

with Bette Davis, *George Sanders, Anne Baxter, Celeste Holm, Gary Merrill, Hugh Marlowe, Thelma Ritter, Gregory Ratoff, Marilyn Monroe

- Criticism on release

    ...brilliantly, and I mean brilliantly, played by a Bette Davis unflattered by make-up or lighting. It is the best thing she has done for years, if not in her whole career... Elsewhere the film depends on a quick-fire stream of juicy epigrammatic wisecracks relating to the theatre...

    Richard Winnington, *News Chronicle* 8 December 1950

- Current recommendations and ratings
StJD BN92 S&S82/92 LM4 DQ4 DW5 VFG5 MPG5 NFT*

    ...Mankiewicz's bitchy screenplay makes the most of the situation, being both witty and intelligent. The young Monroe gets to have a stairway entrance (introduced by cynical critic Sanders as a 'graduate of the Copacabana school of acting').

    PTOG 1995

Sweet Smell of Success, UA (James Hill), 1957 bw

Direction: Alexander Mackendrick
Script: Ernest Lehman, Clifford Odets (from Lehman's own story)
Camera: James Wong Howe   Music: Elmer Bernstein
Art Direction: Edward Carrere
Editing: Alan Crosland Jr.

with Burt Lancaster, Tony Curtis, Susan Harrison, Martin Milner, Sam Levene, Emile Meyer, Lurene Tuttle, Edith Atwater

- Criticism on release

    ...inside the cinema, so superbly is the thing done, one's skin crawls with credulous horror. The acting is first-rate, in particular Tony Curtis's performance as the lizard who scurries at the crocodile's call. And a dreadful authenticity is given by the feeling of the place – the smell, you might say, of New York...

    Dilys Powell, *Sunday Times*, 14 July 1957

- Current recommendations and ratings
StJD S&S92 LM3½ DQ4 DW5 VFG4 MPG4 NFT*

    ...[Lancaster's] monster newspaper columnist [is] a figure as evil and memorable as Orson Welles in *The Third Man* or Mitchum in *The Night of the Hunter*. The dark streets gleam with the sweat of fear; Elmer Bernstein's limpid jazz score (courtesy of Chico Hamilton) whispers corruption in the Big City. The screen was rarely so dark or cruel.

    Chris Auty, PTOG 1995

'MOVIOLA'

In the tradition of the Garson Kanin book and the TV series based upon it, the 'Moviola' group consists of films in which Hollywood presents the life of Hollywood itself, the film industry's version of its own backstage story. Several other films reflecting Hollywood mores are not included in this group: *Sullivan's Travels* (already discussed under Social Comedy) and *Singin' in the Rain* (later included under Musicals). The 1954 *A Star Is Born* can also be considered as a splendid musical, but I prefer to give more weight to the always respectful but creative reinterpretation of the original script written for the non-musical 1937 comedy-drama directed by William Wellman. The wonderful songs (by Ira Gershwin and Harold Arlen) are dramatically justifiable as performed by the new young star of the film story, played by an electrifying singing star, Judy Garland, making an effective come-back to the screen after four years. As the film's already established star – Norman Mayne – whose downward curve though drunkenness, degradation, and dignified suicide exactly parallels the rising curve of his young wife, James Mason gives a consistently telling performance (one of the best in his career). The smaller parts are also very well played, with a surprisingly astringent performance by Jack Carson as a resourceful and resentful publicity agent.

Sunset Boulevard is probably the best-known Hollywood film about Hollywood, with fascinating documentary episodes (including a visit to Paramount Studios and an encounter with Cecil B. DeMille playing himself – an excellent performance) interspersed among a series of Gothic scenes involving the doomed relationship between a self-deluded one-time star of the silent era (Gloria Swanson) and the cynical, broke young screenwriter reluctantly driven by his own weak and self-indulgent nature into the role of gigolo (William Holden). The gamut between the legendary atmosphere of the movie past, reinforced by Erich von Stroheim's massive performance as Swanson's ex-director husband now turned valet and the brief appearance of other silent greats, and the near-documentary scenes of contemporary Hollywood is discreetly and tastefully run by scriptwriters Wilder and Brackett (their last collaboration), director Wilder and cameraman John F. Seitz.

John Houseman's and Vincente Minnelli's 'trash masterpiece', *The Bad and the Beautiful*, also uses some exaggeratedly melodramatic situations to approach the so-called 'truth' about Hollywood, uncontrollable temperaments, stereotyped characters, the old cliché 'heartbreak' at the core of the emotional experience, and a brittle self-critical approach that reveals the vulnerability just beneath the thin surface of ruthless egotism. The message of all these films appears to be that success can cripple humanity, and the qualities of stability and integrity required to survive professional success are only exceptionally found among the leading members of the American film industry.

The Bad and the Beautiful, MGM (John Houseman), 1952 bw

Direction: Vincente Minnelli
*Camera: Robert Surtees
*Art Direction: Cedric Gibbons, Edward Carfagno
*Costume Design: Helen Rose
*Script: Charles Schnee (from George Bradshaw's story)
Music: David Raksin
Editing: Conrad Nervig

with Kirk Douglas, Lana Turner, Walter Pidgeon, Dick Powell, Barry Sullivan, *Gloria Grahame, Gilbert Roland, Leo G. Carroll, Paul Stewart, Vanessa Brown, Ivan Triesault, Francis X. Bushman (bit)

- Criticism on release

    In effect, just another behind-the-scenes Hollywood story, set in an artificial world amongst artificial standards of greatness... But in so far as such a subject can be made to seem important, director Minnelli has fulfilled his charge. He shoots, almost infallibly, from the telling angle. He knows how long to hold a scene to the friction of a second. He uses the effect of sound behind sound quite brilliantly...

    C.A. Lejeune, *The Observer* 8 March 1953

- Current recommendations and ratings
  LM3½ DQ3 DW4 VFG5 MPG5 NFT*

    ...Minnelli brings a tougher eye to his story of a young producer's meteoric rise and fall than most directors would have done, and the copious references to actual

people/movies/events anchor the melodrama in a spirit
not unlike that of *Sunset Boulevard*...

Tony Rayns, PTOG 1995

Sunset Boulevard, Par (Charles Brackett), 1950 bw

Direction: Billy Wilder
Camera: John F. Seitz
Special Effects: Gordon Jennings
*Music: Franz Waxman
Song: Jay Livingston, Ray Evans
*Art Direction: Hans Dreier, John Meehan
Editing: Doane Harrison, Arthur Schmidt

*Script: Wilder with Charles Brackett and D.B. Marshman
Costume Design: Edith Head
Editing: Doane Harrison, Arthur Schmidt

with William Holden, Gloria Swanson, Erich von Stroheim, Nancy Olson, Fred Clark, Jack Webb (and Cecil B. DeMille, H.B. Warner, Buster Keaton, Hedda Hopper, and Anna Q. Nilsson as themselves)

- Criticism on release

    ...that rare blend of pungent writing, expert acting, masterly direction and unobtrusively artistic photography which quickly casts a spell over an audience and holds it enthralled to a shattering climax – while all the acting is memorable, one thinks first and mostly of Miss Swanson, of her manifestation of consuming pride, her forlorn despair and a truly magnificent impersonation of Charlie Chaplin...

    'T.M.P.', *New York Times* 11 August 1950

- Current recommendations and ratings
StJD BN92 S&S82/92 LM4 DQ3 DW5 VFG5 MPG5 NFT*

    One of Wilder's finest, and certainly the blackest of all Hollywood's scab-scratching accounts of itself, this establishes its relentless acidity in the opening scene by having the story related by a corpse floating face-down in a Hollywood swimming-pool... The performances are suitably sordid, the direction precise, the camerawork appropriately 'noir', and the memorably sour script sounds bitter-sweet echoes of the Golden Age of Tinseltown...

Geoff Andrew, PTOG 1995

A Star Is Born, WB (Sidney Luft), 1954 *colour*

Direction: George Cukor
Camera: Sam Leavitt
Music: Leonard Gershe
Songs: Ira Gershwin, Harold Arlen
Arranger: Roger Edens
Art Direction: Malcolm Bert
Script: Moss Hart (from a story by William Wellman and Robert Carson)
Choreography: Richard Barstow
Costume Design: Jean Louis, Mary Ann Nyberg, Irene Sharaff
Editing: Folmar Blangsted

with Judy Garland, James Mason, Charles Bickford, Jack Carson, Tommy Noonan, Irving Bacon, Joan Shawlee, Grady Sutton, Louis Jean Heydt, Mae Marsh (bit)

- Criticism on release

    ...one of the grandest heartbreak dramas that have drenched the screen in years... For the Warners and Mr Cukor have really and truly gone to town in giving this hackneyed Hollywood story an abundance of fullness of force – and there is, through it all, a gentle tracing of clever satire of Hollywood, not as sharp as it was in the original, but sharp enough to be stimulating fun.

    Bosley Crowther, New York Times, 12 October 1954

- Current recommendations and ratings
StJD BN92 S&S82/92 LM4 DQ4 DW4 VFG5 MPG5 NFT*

    ...Garland's tremulous emotionalism is here decently harnessed... But the acting honours belong to Mason, whether idly cruising the LA dance-halls for a new woman, sliding into alcoholism, or embarrassing everyone at an Oscar ceremony. He gives a performance which is as good as any actor is ever allowed – a very good wallow.

Chris Peachment, PTOG 1995

Fantasy – Fantasy Adventure, Horror and Monster Movies, Science Fiction Movies

Instead of defining a specific 'adventure' group of movies, this collection deals with them mainly under three headings: Period Pieces (historical adventure), Romantic Adventure (see later, under Romance), and Fantasy Adventure in which the qualities of the adventure – dangerous and exciting episodes experienced by the doughty hero – are set against a completely imagined background which brings it near to fairy-tale or myth.

It is difficult to draw the line between horror and science fiction, as the latter usually possess a strong element of horror, based on repulsion against the new ways of the future or the appearance of alien beings invading the Earth from outer space. (Kingsley Amis's 'Bug-Eyed Monsters' – BEMS). The most important distinction between horror films (which also frequently feature monsters) and science fiction films is the time perspective: horror films deal with the supernatural and grotesque nightmares either encountered in the past or threatening in the present, whereas science fiction suggests prediction, a view into a hostile (?) future, in keeping with the great founders of the genre – Jules Verne and H.G. Wells.

FANTASY ADVENTURE

James Hilton's book, on which Frank Capra's *The Lost Horizon*, 1937, was based, would probably not on its own have made Shangri-La a worldwide expression: this was the work of the film which brought this strange Utopia to life. Perhaps the impressive details of this mythical world do not make such an impact today as they did in 1937. Then, this seemed quite unfamiliar material for Capra, nevertheless confirming his brilliance as a film-maker: it is difficult to fault it. It has superlative craftsmanship, well-judged performances (particularly of Ronald Colman as the visionary diplomat, hijacked to succeed the three-hundred-year-old High Lama, persuasively played by Sam Jaffe, and Margo, as a long-lived beauty desperate to escape the world above the Himalayas), the camerawork (by Capra's usual cameraman, Joseph Walker), the editing, and Dimitri Tiomkin's creative score. This is 'Capracorn' in a refreshingly different guise, but presented with the same kind of cinema magic.

Perhaps 'artistry' is too pretentious a word to apply to Steven Spielberg's *Raiders of the Lost Ark*, 1981 – a very entertaining, very satisfying film, which perfectly combines professionalism with popular taste. The basic approach is very traditional, going back to the physical adventure of the old silent movies, but updated and improved in all sorts of ways. The villains are villains because of their political views, the 'McGuffin' is a religious symbol, the hero and heroine embody virtues that have a strong moral appeal, and technology has enabled special effects and stunts which startle and thrill. The filmmaking is of the highest quality – George Lucas, the producer, and Spielberg, the director, have used the top men in their field – Douglas Slocombe's camerawork, John Williams' music, and Michael Kahn's editing, which won an Oscar. The performances are excellent without exception.

The Lost Horizon, Col (Frank Capra), 1937 bw

Direction: Frank Capra	Script: Robert Riskin (from James Hilton's novel)
Camera: Joseph Walker	
Music: Dimitri Tomkin	*Art Direction: Stephen Goosson
Costume Design: Ernest Dryden	*Editing: Gene Havlick, Gene Milford
Special Effects: Roy Davidson, Ganahl Carson	

with Ronald Colman, Jane Wyatt, Edward Everett Horton, John Howard, Thomas Mitchell, Margo, Isabel Jewell, H.B. Warner, Sam Jaffe

- Criticism on release

    ...a grand adventure film, magnificently staged, beautifully photographed and capitally played – there is no denying the opulence of the production, the impressiveness of the sets, the richness of the costuming, the satisfying attention to large and small detail which makes Hollywood at its best such a generous entertainer...

    Frank S. Nugent, *New York Times* 4 March 1937

- Current recommendations and ratings
  StJD LM4 DQ4 DW4 VFG5 MPG5 NFT*

   ...a full-blown weepie, complete with kitschy sets, admirable if incredibly naive sentiments, and fine acting from Colman. Not at all the sort of film one could make in these considerably more jaundiced times...

   Geoff Andrew, PTOG 1995

Raiders of the Lost Ark, Par (Lucasfilm/Frank Marshall), 1981 *colour*

Direction: Steven Spielberg	Script: Lawrence Kasdan, from a story by Lucas and Philip Kaufman
Camera: Douglas Slocombe, Paul Beetson	
Music: John Williams	Costume Design: Deborah Nadoolman
*Art Direction: Norman Reynolds	
Special Effects: Richard Edlund, Kit West	*Editing: Michael Kahn
Animation: John Van Vliet, Kim Knowton, Garry Waller, Lording Doyle, Scott Caple, Judy Elkins, Sylvia Keuler, Scott Marshal	

with Harrison Ford, Karen Allen, Paul Freeman, Ronald Lacey, John Rhys-Davies, Denholm Elliott

- Criticism on release

   ...the audience is assailed just as much as the hero. Spielberg and editor Michael Kahn fling the action at us in a series of jagged jump-cuts, while on the soundtrack, in Dolby Stereo, the London Symphony Orchestra fiddle and blare their way through John Williams' grandiose music – Spielberg and his executive producer, George Lucas, have aimed their entertainment at the child supposedly lurking in the hearts of all grown-ups, [but] the end result seems more like an exercise in logistics than a piece of personal film-making.

   Geoff Brown, *The Times* 31 July 1981

- Current recommendations and ratings
  StJD S&S92 LM4 DQ3 DW4 VFG4½ MPG5 NFT*

  ...Spielberg's evasion of present day realities in an effort to recapture the sheer childlike fun of moviegoing... What he offers is one long, breathtaking chase of a plot as his pre-World War II superhero, outsize and Bogartian, races to prevent the omnipotent Ark of the Covenant from falling into the hands of Hitler's Nazis. Whether you swallow it or not, see it for a handful of totally unexpected visual jokes, worth the price of admission alone.

  Rod McShane, PTOG 1995

HORROR AND MONSTER MOVIES

Born of nineteenth-century Romanticism (Mary Shelley's *Frankenstein* of 1818 and Bram Stoker's *Dracula* of 1897) and early German Expressionist film (e.g. *The Cabinet of Caligari* and *The Golem* of 1920, and *Nosferatu* of 1922), the two seminal films in this genre were Tod Browning's *Dracula* and James Whale's *Frankenstein* (both produced at Universal in 1931). In spite of a magnificent opening and the archetypal image of Bela Lugosi as the vampire count, Dracula has not retained the magnetism over viewers that *Frankenstein* has. The lumbering destructiveness of Boris Karloff's demented Monster and his "true charnel-house appearance", with his "gaunt features and dark-socketed eyes" (Ivan Butler, *Horror in the Cinema*, 1979 Edn) have become an archetype of the cinema, a performance never equalled in the genre. The galvanisation of the creature in a high tower during a frightening thunderstorm (greatly enhanced by the tormented playing of Colin Clive's 'Frankenstein') is tremendously exciting, as is the final chase and burning of the Monster in an old mill, in spite of the burlesque rendering of some pseudo-Tyrolean villagers. There is also a beautifully tender scene, unaccountably cut from the first showings, where Karloff, in blundering imitation of a floating flower, throws a little girl into the water and awaits anxiously but in vain for her reappearance above the surface. Even the great master of documentary, John Grierson, grudgingly admired the lyricism of this scene.

James Whale attempted something new in any genre film he was given to direct, but his quirky humour and unerring feeling for the grotesque gave his horror films following *Frankenstein* – for example, *The Old Dark House* of 1932 and *The Bride of Frankenstein*, of 1935 (in which the Frankenstein monster was reborn) – unusual quality, aided by his team of inspired craftsmen and exceptional performances from his players. The final result owed as much to Jack Pierce's make-up for the Monster and his bride, the work of the special effects team (especially the brilliant work of John Fulton) and the imaginative camerawork of Arthur Edeson.

The Old Dark House was a formula picture made with great style, using all the Expressionist tricks effectively, creepily perverse and maliciously funny. There are outstanding performances by Boris Karloff, Charles Laughton, Raymond Massey and Ernest Thesiger. Gloria Stuart, Melvyn Douglas and Lilian Bond are above-average representatives of the saner younger generation; and there are some brilliant character studies by unfamiliar members of the cast, particularly Eva Moore as Thesiger's fanatically religious sister and Brember Wills as the craziest of all the crazy Femm household.

Opinions of *The Bride of Frankenstein* greatly vary, from Graham Greene's "pompous, badly acted" film (*The Pleasure Dome*, 1980 Edn) to Angela and Elkan Allen's "about the best horror film ever" (*The Sunday Times Guide to Movies on Television*, 1973) which seems to be the more general opinion. James Whale's use of an accomplished repertory of British actors (Colin Clive once more as the tortured Baron Frankenstein, Ernest Thesiger as the creepy Dr Pretorius, and the superlative Elsa Lanchester as the Bride, whom even Graham Greene credits with the one great moment of excitement, when she awakens to life), his distinctive mixture of Gothic horror with bizarre comedy, his marshalling of the special effects required by the genre – all these combine to make a movie of great character and fascination.

The other archetypal monster of the 1930s (this time, a firmly twentieth-century creation) is *King Kong*. The images of this first (1933) version still haunt the memory, in spite of a recent remake and the presence of several 'corny' episodes and performances in the original. Whenever Kong is on the screen, towering above his human captors, the impression is magical with many unforgettable scenes – holding Fay Wray (a perfect heroine) in the palm of his hand, struggling with prehistoric monsters, crushing a New York elevated train, peering slyly through a bedroom window, swatting planes like flies on top of the Empire State building. Willis O'Brien's device of the giant ape (magnified from the miniature) is effectively anthropomorphic, so that at the end we mourn the crushing death of this vital, educable beast, conquered by Beauty.

With *Cat People*, 1942, we enter a new phase of horror filmmaking. This was the first of an interesting low-budget series produced by Val Lewton, also at RKO, during and just after World War II, a short, but intensely atmospheric film, in which most of the horror is implicit (but always present). The imported French actress Simone Simon is suitably feline and has enough sexuality with intelligence to convince us of the possible transformation into a panther at the onset of sexual jealousy. The script is rich in suggestive detail, and the *mise en scène* is handled economically and inventively by Jacques (son of the great silent film director, Maurice) Tourneur.

Four classics of horror fantasy remain, three belonging to the 1960s – two brilliant exercises in an unusual genre by Alfred Hitchcock, *Psycho*, 1960, and *The Birds*, 1963, and Polanski's gripping, sophisticated study of Satanism, *Rosemary's Baby*, 1968. They are all more in the vein of *Cat People* than of *Dracula*, *Frankenstein* or *King Kong*, the horror being basically psychological rather than physical: teasingly pointed up by Hitchcock in his red herring of a chase at the beginning of *Psycho* ("purposely made on the long side" – Hitchcock to François Truffaut), followed by the brutal shock of the shower murder, after which the ravages of the psychotic murderer (Anthony Perkins) in his Gothic shell of a dwelling dominate the action and attention. Typically, Hitchcock warned against coming to the cinema *after* the film's commencement, which would have spoilt this midway effect; he said nothing of the haunting violence and eeriness of the Bates household, after which one finds it difficult to go home in the dark or to see it in a lonely house. The outstanding quality of *The Birds*, like that of *Vertigo*, has become increasingly apparent in recent years: it exploits a terrifying idea which converts normal creatures to monsters and brings out a basic instinctual anxiety in all human beings regarding their environment. The slow build-up of menace, the everyday nature of the characters and their community life, the clever use of editing in the depiction of the birds' onslaughts, and the equivocal ending – where the central characters are apparently allowed to leave between rows of silently watching birds – all these are typical of Hitchcock's single-minded approach to his theme and the professionalism he demanded from himself and those working with him.

The witches and warlocks of Roman Polanski's film operate in an authentic New York setting and on an apparently ordinary New York couple, played by Mia Farrow and John Cassavetes: they are a lively, sinister lot (as played by Ruth Gordon, Sidney Blackmer, and Ralph Bellamy) and quite capable of being mistaken for cheerful and friendly, if somewhat unconventional, neighbours. The fright induced in us by the young mother's terrifying experiences – not least in the queasy apprehension of her husband's apparent betrayal – have an insidious, haunting quality.

Steven Spielberg's *Jaws*, 1975, marks the return of the monster horror film in an ultra-refined form – the cunning vengeance of the man-eating great white shark is portrayed on a formidable scale in battle with three human protagonists – Roy Scheider (the local police chief), Richard Dreyfuss (a young marine biologist), and Robert Shaw (as Quint, the gnarled old shark-hunter). The realism of the small-town setting offsets the grim symbolic battle waged to a bitter end. This film gave the young Spielberg a worldwide reputation for supreme quality of production.

The Bride of Frankenstein, Un (Carl Laemmle Jr.), 1935 bw

Direction: James Whale
Camera: John Mescall
Special Effects: John Fulton
Art Direction: Charles D. Hall
Make-up: Jack P. Pierce

Script: John Balderston, William Hurlbut
Music: Franz Waxman
Editing: Ted Kent

with Boris Karloff, Colin Clive, Valerie Hobson, Elsa Lanchester, Ernest Thesiger, Dwight Frye, John Carradine, Walter Brennan

- Criticism on release

> For background atmosphere, [and] dramatic invention, *The Bride of Frankenstein* will stand up as one of the best of the year. The episode of the electric storm is an astonishing bit of well-sustained imaginative play – a

great deal of art has gone into the planning and taking of whole portions of this film...

Otis Ferguson, New Republic 29 May 1935

- Current recommendations and ratings
StJD LM4 DQ4 DW5 VFG5 MPG5 NFT*

Tremendous sequel to Whale's own original... What distinguishes the film is less its horror content, which is admittedly low, than the macabre humour and sense of parody. Strong on atmosphere, Gothic sets and expressionist camerawork, it is... a delight from start to finish.

Geoff Andrew, PTOG 1995

Cat People, RKO (Val Lewton), 1942 *bw*

Direction: Jacques Tourneur
Camera: Nicholas Musuraca
Art Direction: Albert S. D'Agostino, Walter E. Keller
Editing: Mark Robson
Script: De Witt Bodeen
Music: Roy Webb

with Simone Simon, Kent Smith, Tom Conway, Jane Randolph, Elizabeth Russell, Jack Holt, Alan Napier

- Criticism on release

Paradoxically enough, one of the least well-done films of the past quarter provided a higher degree of interest than many of its slicker competitors... There are startling scenes, such as the wedding feast interrupted by the women calling Simone 'Sister' in Serbian; the lonely walk through the park in which a woman's hysteria increases with every step; the indoor swimming pool episode...; the kiss that galvanises Simon's face into a bitter smile of neurotic sensuality and which results in violence and death...

Herman G. Weinberg, *Sight and Sound*, Summer 1943

- Current recommendations and ratings
  StJD S&S92 LM3 DQ3 DW4 VFG5 MPG3 NFT*

  First in the wondrous series of B movies in which Val Lewton elaborated his principle of horrors imagined rather than seen... With its chilling set pieces directed to perfection by Tourneur, it knocks Paul Schrader's remake for six, not least because of the care subtly taken to imbue its cat people (Simon Russell) with feline mannerisms...

  Tom Milne, PTOG 1995

Frankenstein, Un (Carl Laemmle Jr.), 1931 bw

Direction: James Whale	Script: Garrett Fort, Francis
Camera: Arthur Edeson	Edward Faragoh, John
Art Direction: Charles D. Hall	Balderston (from the play
Make-up: Jack P. Pierce	*Webling*, after the novel by
Editing: Clarence Kolster, Maurice Pivar	Mary Shelley)
Special Effects: Frank Graves, Kenneth Strickfadden, Raymond Lindsay	

with Colin Clive, Mae Clarke, John Boles, Boris Karloff, Dwight Frye, Edward Van Sloan

- Criticism on release

  ...packed with horrors, but brilliantly produced and distinguished by some excellent acting. Boris Karloff's portrayal is an astonishing piece of work. His make-up alone is masterly, and he depicts the awkwardness, the bewilderment and the fiendish instincts of the creature with restrained power... though exceptionally well made and guaranteed to thrill, it is too gruesome to be recommended without reservations...

  Jon Gammie et al., *Film Weekly* 23 Jan 1932

- Current recommendations and ratings
  StJD BN92 S&S92 LM3 DQ3 DW4 VFG5 MPG4 NFT*

    A stark, solid, impressively stylish film... Karloff gives one of the great performances of all time... The film is unique in Whale's work in that the horror is played absolutely straight, and it has a weird fairytale beauty not matched until Cocteau made *La Belle et le Bête*.

    Tom Milne, PTOG 1995

King Kong, RKO (David Selznick/ Merian C. Cooper/ Ernest Schoedsack), 1933 bw

Direction: Merian C. Cooper, Ernest Schoedsack
Script: Cooper, with James Creelman and Ruth Rose (from a story by Cooper and Edgar Wallace)
Camera: Edward Linden, Vernon Walker, J.O. Taylor
Music: Max Steiner   Costume Design: Walter Plunkett
Art Direction: Carroll Clark, Al Herman, Van Nest Polglase
Special Effects: Willis O'Brien et al.
Editing: Ted Cheeseman

with Fay Wray, Bruce Cabot, Robert Armstrong, Frank Reicher, Noble Johnson, James Flavin, Merian C. Cooper (bit), Ernest Schoedsack (bit)

- Criticism on release

    We have had plays and pictures about monsters before, but never one in which the desired effect depended so completely on the increased dimensions of the monster. Kong is a veritable skyscraper among apes... The photographic ingenuity that was necessary to make all this seem plausible was considerable.

    William Troy, *The Nation*, 21 March 1933

- Current recommendations and ratings
  StJD S&S82/92 LM4 DQ4 DW5 VFG5 MPG5 NFT**

    If this glorious pile of horror-fantasy hokum has lost none of its power to move, excite and sadden, it is in no small measure due to the remarkable technical achievements of Willis O'Brien's animation work, and the superbly matched score of Max Steiner... The throbbing heart of the film lies in the creation of the semi-human simian himself, an immortal tribute to the Hollywood dream factory's ability to fashion a symbol that can express all the contradictory erotic, ecstatic, destructive, pathetic and cathartic buried impulses of 'civilised' man.

Wally Hammond, PTOG 1995

The Old Dark House, Un (Carl Laemmle Jr.), 1932 bw

Direction: James Whale
Camera: Arthur Edeson
Art Direction: Charles D. Ball
Special Effects: John P. Fulton
Editing: Clarence Kolster

Script: Benn W. Levy, R.C. Sherriff (from J.B. Priestley's novel *Benighted*)

with Boris Karloff, Melvyn Douglas, Charles Laughton, Gloria Stuart, Lilian Bond, Ernest Thesiger, Eva Moore, Raymond Massey, Brember Wills, John Dudgeon (Elspeth Dudgeon)

- Criticism on release

...There is a wealth of talent in this production, and while one may wonder, after witnessing the exciting doings, why the motorists who seek refuge in the old dark house did not continue on their way immediately after encountering two or three of the occupants, it must be remembered that Mr [J.B.] Priestley is responsible for their staying and, as the shadow tale adheres quite closely to the book, he is also responsible for the hysteria that prevails during many of the scenes... The current thriller, like *Frankenstein*, had the advantage of being directed by James Whale, who again proves his ability in this direction...

Mordaunt Hall, *New York Times* 28 October 1932

- Current recommendations and ratings
  StJD S&S82 LM3½ DQ4 DW5 VFG5 MPG5 NFT*

    ...a masterly mixture of macabre humour and effectively gripping suspense – what is perhaps most remarkable is the way Whale manages to parody the conventions of the dark house horror genre as he creates them, in which respect the film remains entirely modern.

    Geoff Andrew, PTOG 1995

Psycho, Par (Alfred Hitchcock), 1960 *bw*

Direction: Alfred Hitchcock	Script: Joseph Stefano (from the novel by Robert Bloch)
Camera: John Russell	Music: Bernard Herrmann
Titles and shower sequence: Saul Bass	Editing: George Tomasini
Art Direction: Joseph Hurley, Robert Clatworth	
Costume Design: Helen Colvig	

with Anthony Perkins, Janet Leigh, Martin Balsam, Vera Miles, Frank Albertson, John Gavin, John McIntire, Lurene Tuttle

- Criticism on release

    ...a quiet horror film; punctuated by silences or small sibilant voices, by rain or a shower left running; only now and then, cunningly, the huge eyeballs and the scream... to my relief, this is the felicitous, the mischievous old-style Old-Master Hitchcock...

    Dilys Powell, *Sunday Times* 7 August 1960

- Current recommendations and ratings
  StJD BN92 S&S82/92 LM4 DQ4 DW5 VFG5 MPG5 NFT**

    ...Hitchcock's best film, a stunningly realised (on a relatively low budget) slice of *Grand Guignol* in which the Bates Motel is the arena for much sly verbal sparring and several gruesome murders... The cod-Freudian explanation offered at the conclusion is just so much nonsense, but the real text concerning schizophrenia lies in the tellingly complex visuals. A masterpiece by any standard.

Geoff Andrew, PTOG 1995

The Birds, Un (Alfred Hitchcock), 1963 *colour*

Direction: Alfred Hitchcock
Script: Evan Hunter (from a story by Daphne du Maurier)
Camera: Robert Burks   Special Effects: Ub Iwerks
Sound Consultant: Bernard   Editing: George Tomasini
   Herrmann
Art Direction: Robert Boyle,
   George Milo
Costume Design: Edith Head

with Rod Taylor, Tippi Hedren, Jessica Tandy, Suzanne Pleshette, Charles McGraw, Ethel Griffes

- Criticism on release

   ...Hitchcock's direction has never been so tired, so devoid even at attempts of sardonic realism... He has not even made the most of the beautiful Bodega Bay country in California where this color picture was filmed...
   Stanley Kauffmann, *New Republic* 13 April 1963

   ...what an injustice there is in the generally bad reception! I am convinced that cinema was invented so that such a film could be made... This is an artist's dream; to carry it off requires a lot of art, and you need to be the greatest technician in the world.
   François Truffaut, *Cahiers du Cinema*, 1963

- Current recommendations and ratings
StJD BN92 S&S82/92 LM3 DQ3 DW4 VFG4 MPG3 NFT*

   With death dropping blandly out of a clear sky, this is Hitchcock at his best. Full of subterranean hints as to the ways in which people cage each other, it's fierce and Freudian as well as great cinematic fun...
   Tom Milne, PTOG 1995

Jaws, Un (Richard Zanuck/David Brown), 1975 *colour*

Direction: Steven Spielberg
Camera: Bill Butler, with Rexford Metz (underwater sequences)
*Music: John Williams
Art Direction: Joseph Alves
Special Effects: Robert A. Mattey
Shark footage: Ron Taylor
Script: Peter Benchley, Carl Gottlieb, with Howard Sackler, uncredited (from Benchley's novel)
*Editing: Verna Fields

with Robert Shaw, Richard Dreyfuss, Lorraine Gary, Murray Hamilton, Carl Gottlieb, Peter Benchley (bit)

- Criticism on release

    Jaws has opened everywhere, and the whole country stands agape – three wise men put to sea in a plywood boat, their fast intent to do battle with the monster [shark] – a 'titanic battle', as the handouts quaintly put it. [You wouldn't want to see the film twice, but]... the shocks that director Steven Spielberg produces are well done – of all the civilian-panic pictures so far made it's quite the most economical...

    Russell Davies, *The Observer* 29 December 1975

- Current recommendations and ratings
  StJD S&S82 LM4 DQ4 DW4 VFG4 MPG4 NFT*

    ...Maybe it is just a monster movie reminiscent of all those '50s sci-fi films, but at least it's endowed with intelligent characterisation, a lack of sentimentality (in contrast to, say, *E.T.*), and it really is frightening. And, added to the Ahab/Moby Dick echoes in the grizzled sailor Shaw's obsession with the Great White Shark, there are moments of true darkness...

    Geoff Andrew, PTOG 1995

Rosemary's Baby, Par (William Castle), 1968 colour

Direction: Roman Polanski
Camera: William Fraker
Music: Krzysztof Komeda
Art Direction: Richard Sylbert
Editing: Sam O'Steen, Robert Wyman

Script: Polanski, from the novel by Ira Levin
Make-up: Allan Snyder
Costume Design: Anthea Sylbert

with Mia Farrow, John Cassavetes, *Ruth Gordon, Sidney Blackmer, Ralph Bellamy, Maurice Evans, Elisha Cook Jr., Patsy Kelly, Charles Grodin

- Criticism on release

    Most films that begin feebly finish feebly. *Rosemary's Baby* is an exception. The opening pan along the New York skyline, then down the front of the apartment house, is trite. The first scenes are disappointing – for too long, our only interest is an elderly couple next door [played by Blackmer and Gordon. Then,] as the film begins to jell, Miss Farrow (as Rosemary) begins to hold us... As for Polanski himself, *Rosemary's Baby* seems to settle right in where he wants to live; as a manufacturer of intelligent thrillers, clever and insubstantial...

    Stanley Kauffmann, *New Republic* 15 June 1968

- Current recommendations and ratings
SUD LM4 DQ3 DW4 VFG4 MPG4 NFT*

    A supremely intelligent and convincing adaptation of Ira Levin's Satanist thriller... Although it manages to be frightening, there is little gore or explicit violence; instead, what disturbs is the blurring of reality and nightmare, and the way Farrow is slowly transformed from a healthy, happily-married wife, to a haunted, desperately confused shadow of her former self. Great performances, too, and a marvellously melancholy score by Krzysztof Komeda.

    GEOFF ANDREW, PTOG 1995

SCIENCE FICTION MOVIES

The major concerns of the science fiction classics are: the nature of the earth's relations with aliens from outer space, warfare in outer space (*Invasion of the Body Snatchers*, *Close Encounters of the Third Kind*, and *E.T. – The Extra-terrestrial*), policing of inner cities in the twenty-first century (*Blade Runner*) and global warfare in outer space (*Star Wars*).

The one black-and-white film, Don Siegel's *Invasion of the Body Snatchers*, 1956, still has an edge over the more recent ones in colour. It was a long-term 'sleeper': a low-budget film that now emerges as a masterly novella economically yet impressively scripted and directed. The opening is electrifying, with the distraught young doctor (Kevin McCarthy) striving to get his message through to a clutch of ordinary citizens. The flashback to the 'ordinary' town to which he returned after a holiday is beautifully arranged, with the film returning full circle to the opening scene, except that now we are gravely aware of the source of his 'madness' – the proliferation of huge seed-pods which are gradually taking over the local citizens and reducing them to uncaring, purely functional group minds. The story is told quietly, with small, telling revelations, until the final horrifying discovery and chase – a remarkable film with a strong vein of horror and a great deal of realistic conviction.

In contrast, Steven Spielberg's *Close Encounters of the Third Kind* remains a thoughtful, intriguing plea for interplanetary harmony. Richard Dreyfuss plays a worker who becomes uniquely aware of UFO activity, is drawn irresistibly to Devil's Tower, Wyoming where François Truffaut, as a French scientist, heads a team that has gathered in secret to welcome aliens in a flying saucer and, after the 'encounter', is chosen by the alien leader to accompany him back into outer space. The very accomplished film-makers include Vilmos Zsigmond (camerawork), Douglas Trumbull (special effects) and John Williams (music): a sci-fi movie to appeal to non-sci-fi fans. *The Special Edition*, issued in 1980, shows the spectacular interior of the flying saucer.

At the same time, *Star Wars*, 1977, was being made by Spielberg's associate, George Lucas, the first in a long line of family blockbusters in which special effects play a leading, and mind-blowing, role. It is an epic intergalactic adventure, in which Luke Skywalker (Mark Hamill) seeks to rescue the Princess Leia (Carrie Fisher) from evil, with the help of two robots (C-3PO and R2-D2), Alec Guinness (the sage), and Harrison Ford (the adventurer). Its great popularity spawned two sequels – *The Empire Strikes Back* (directed by Irving Kershner) and *The Return of the Jedi* (directed by Richard Marquand) in 1980 and 1983 respectively.

In Ridley Scott's *Blade Runner*, 1982, Hopalong Cassidy meets Philip Marlowe in Fritz Lang's Metropolis. In a ghetto-like Los Angeles of the future, drenched in acid rain, Rick Deckard (Harrison Ford), a 'blade runner' (eliminator of criminal replicants) chases five replicant outlaws, and falls in love with one (Sean Young) while achieving his objectives regarding the three others, and finally has a near-lethal confrontation with the last (Rutger Hauer). In 1992 a 'director's cut' was issued, omitting the final 'happy ending' of the lovers eloping and taking out the unsatisfactory *film noir* voice-over by Ford in 40s 'shamus' style. The replicants are well played (by Young, Hauer, Joanna Cassidy, Darryl Hannah and Brion James) and the storyline is clear, if a little rudimentary, but the real stars of the movie are the director and the designer, Lawrence G. Paull, who invented this dazzling nightmare of rotting, marauder-haunted streets. *Blade Runner* could be the cinema's "most prophetic blueprint of modern degeneration" (Nigel Andrews, *Financial Times* 26 November 1992)

Carlo Rimbaldi, who produced a charming model for the alien leader in *Close Encounters*, repeated his success on a larger scale in Steven Spielberg's *E.T. – The Extra-Terrestrial*, 1982, the waif-like reptilian creature locked out of his spaceship and yearning to get back home. His mutually educational contact with the human race is made through a suburban Californian family, consisting of an abandoned mother (Dee Wallace) and three children, of whom the younger boy, ten-year-old Elliott (Henry Thomas) is particularly receptive to the alien's appeal. It appears that world audiences fell in love with a being who could just as well have been at the centre of a horror film – a really lovable monster. The film is immaculately fashioned, and Spielberg plays on all the emotions the cinema can arouse – fear, humour, pathos. Even the most determined cynic has to admit surrender to expert manipulation.

Invasion of the Body Snatchers, AA (Walter Wanger), 1956 bw

Direction: Don Siegel	Script: Daniel Mainwaring, with Sam Peckinpah, uncredited (from the novel by Jack Finney)
Camera: Ellsworth Fredricks	
Special Effects: Milt Rice	
Music: Carmen Dragon	
Editing: Robert Eisen	Art Direction: Ted Haworth

with Kevin McCarthy, Dana Wynter, Larry Gates, King Donovan, Carolyn Jones, Whit Bissell, Sam Peckinpah (bit)

- Criticism on release

    This is the most unusual Seal of Merit *Picturegoer* has ever awarded! It goes to a film that has no big name stars (it was made before Fox took over Dana Wynter), no colour, no lavish sets. Made on a shoestring budget, a science-fiction horror film with a depressing ending, [it] proves *Picturegoer*'s point that you don't have to spend a lot of time or money to make a brilliant movie. In its class, it's an outstanding film...

    Margaret Hinxman, Picturegoer 6 October 1956

- Current recommendations and ratings
StJD S&S82/92 LM3½ DQ4 DW4 VFG3½ MPG4 NFT*

    ...this version remains a classic, stuffed with subtly integrated subtexts (postwar paranoia etc.) for those that like that sort of thing, but thrilling and chilling on any level. The late Sam Peckinpah can be spotted in a cameo role as a meter reader, and look out for one of the most sinister kisses ever filmed. You're next!

    Anne Billson, PTOG 1995

Blade Runner, WB (Michael Deeley), 1982 colour

Direction: Ridley Scott
Camera: Jordan Cronenweth
Music: Vangelis
Art Direction: David L. Snyder
Costume Design: Charles Knode, Michael Kaplan
Editing: Terry Rawlings

Script: Hampton Fancher, David Peoples (from a story by Philip K. Dick)
Special Effects: Douglas Trumbull, Richard Yuricich

with Harrison Ford, Rutger Hauer, Sean Young, Edward James Olmos, M. Emmet Walsh, Darryl Hannah, William Sanderson, Brion James, Joseph Turkel, Joanna Cassidy

- Criticism on release

    ...the director Ridley Scott is clearly much less concerned with story than with visual effects, and these certainly offer variety and colour. Even if we question a future (AD 2019) where people still wear lounge suits with revers, read newspapers at lunch counters, and have no more sense than to make robots in forms indistinguishable from themselves, the concept is striking. Los Angeles has become a vast Chinatown. The skies are murky and a perpetual rain beats down. Sophisticated jet-propelled aerial automobiles streak above streets which have been taken over by garbage and marauding gangs. Scene and story alike predict a gloomy future, envisioned out of the most ugly and violent aspects of city streets in our own time.

    David Robinson, *The Times* 10 September 1982

- Current recommendations and ratings
StJD S&S92 LM2½ DQ2 DW5 VFG4 MPG5 NFT***

    ...The script has some superb scenes, notably between Ford and the (android) *femme fatale* Young, while Scott succeeds beautifully in portraying the LA of the future as a cross between a Hong Kong streetmarket and a decaying 200-storey metropolis. But something has gone badly wrong... the android villains are neither menacing nor sympathetic, when ideally they should have been both...

David Pirie, PTOG 1995

Close Encounters of the Third Kind, Col (Julia and Michael Phillips), 1977 *colour*

Direction, Script: Steven Spielberg
*Camera: Vilmos Zsigmond
Art Direction: Joseph Alves
Special Effects: Roy Arbogast, Gregory Jein, Douglas Trumbull, Michael and Richard Yuricich
Music: John Williams
Costume Design: Jim Linn
Editing: Michael Kahn

with Richard Dreyfuss, François Truffaut, Teri Garr, Melinda Dillon, Cary Guffey, Bob Balaban

- Criticism on release

    What in the end will divide the customers into those who find *Close Encounters* an overwhelming experience, charming, spellbinding, spiritually invigorating, and those who accept it as a rollercoaster ride into Oz, a cosmic Disneyland in the sky, is the entry of the strangers from outer space... Perhaps some anticlimax was inevitable, but hardly one of such bathetic dimensions. *Close Encounters of the Third Kind*, like *Star Wars*, is splendid, mindless, holiday entertainment, but awkwardly trailing strands of mystic pretentiousness entwined with nursery nostalgia...

    Alan Brien, *Sunday Times* 19 March 1978)

- Current recommendations and ratings
    StJD S&S82/92 LM4 DQ3 DW4 VFG5 MPG4 NFT*

    There are some awkward touches (Truffaut never ceases to be Truffaut, while some of the comedy scenes are overplayed), but they're small price to pay for the first film in years to give its audience a tingle of shocked emotion that is not entirely based either on fear or on suspense.

David Pirie, PTOG 1995

E.T. - The Extra-Terrestrial, Un (Steven Spielberg, Kathleen Kennedy), 1982 colour

Direction: Steven Spielberg	Script: Melissa Mathison
Camera: Allen Daviau	Music: John Williams
Production Design: James D. Bissell	Special Effects: Industrial Light and Magic
Costume Design: Deborah L. Scott, Carlo Rimbaldi	Editing: Carol Littleton

with Dee Wallace, Henry Thomas, Peter Coyote, Robert MacNaughton, Drew Barrymore, K.C. Martel, Sean Frye, Tom Howell

- Criticism on release

   ...The very cinema is as hushed as a children's party, all eyes on the conjuror. If at this stage inarticulate, E.T. himself is, of course, a finely articulated model of a major modern fantasy: a creature just recognisably human hailing from a far star... The film's instant appeal being to the child in us all, the mood is thus set to make us goggle and giggle over the arts of Mr Spielberg, genial illusionist, whose tricks as a director work like magic. He is our daddy behind the scenes. Every stunt - from extra-sensory perception to levitating bicycles - suspends just the right amount of disbelief to create suspense. And is funny...

   David Hughes, *The Sunday Times* 12 December 1982

- Current recommendations and ratings
  StJD BN92 S&S82/92 LM4 DQ3 DW5 VFG5 MPG4 NFT*

   ...finally seems a less impressive film than *Close Encounters*. This is partly because its first half contains a couple of comedy sequences as vulgar as a Brooke

Bond TV chimps commercial, but more because in reducing the unknowable to the easily lovable, the film sacrifices a little too much truth in favour of its huge emotional punch.

David Pirie, PTOG, 1995

Star Wars, TCF (Gary Kurtz), 1977 *colour*

Direction, Script: George Lucas
*Music: John Williams
*Special Effects: Rick Baker, John Dykstra
*Costume Design: John Mollo, Ron Beck

Camera: Gilbert Taylor
*Art Direction: John Barry
*Editing: Paul Hirsch, Marcia Lucas, Richard Chew

with Mark Hamill, Harrison Ford, Carrie Fisher, Alec Guinness, Peter Cushing, Anthony Daniels, Kenny Baker, Peter Mayhew, James Earl Jones (voice)

- Criticism on release

    ...I had better keep, as they say, a low profile at this moment of time. Not that I dislike *Star Wars* all that much. My complaint about it is that there is not much in it to have an opinion about. The technical standards, I concede, are enormously high. Rockets and space stations have never been made to look so big or so complicated except possibly in Kubrick's *2001*, and not even there was the sense of movement through the galaxy made so whooshingly real... You may say that Alec Guinness's role here dates back to Moses, Merlin or the Old Man of the Sea, but you will not thereby fatten up a thin role. Nor do the twin pally robots appear any the less whimsically conceived when you redub them Don Quixote and Sancho Panza, or Laurel and Hardy.

    Russell Davies, *The Observer* 18 December 1977

- Current recommendations and ratings
  StJD LM3½ DQ3 DW4 VFG5 MPG5 NFT*

Hollywood began in an amusement arcade, so it's appropriate that its most profitable film should be as formally enchanting and psychologically sterile as a Gottlieb Pinball machine – at least 40 years out of date as science fiction, but... nearly 50 years after it was conceived, pulp space fiction is here for the first time presented as a truly viable movie genre... *Star Wars* itself has distinct limitations, but the current return to a cinema of spectacle and wonder is wholly encouraging...

David Pirie, PTOG 1995

Literary Adaptations

A high proportion of all narrative films are adapted from literature of some sort (novels, short stories, plays, autobiographies, and so on), but, in general, to make a successful film the screenwriter uses the original to make his own sort of visual fiction. However, when trying to give a cinematic interpretation of a great work of fiction, there is the need to convey something of the original's literary quality. The two selected – *David Copperfield* and *Wuthering Heights* – both treated the original text with varying degrees of respect: there is a recognisable element of fidelity.

George Cukor's *David Copperfield*, 1935, produced for MGM by David Selznick (a great stickler for fidelity!), not only gained critical praise but was also very good box office. It was one of several studio-made versions of literary classics in which Hollywood invested at the time and one of the most successful, capturing a reasonably faithful Dickensian flavour, and, in spite of what at that time (before *Gone with the Wind*!) might have been considered great length, was never dull for very long. Casting was interesting and, in some cases very original (particularly W.C. Fields as Micawber, and Roland Young as Uriah Heep – both effective 'off-castings'). Selznick was well pleased with the result: it still has the magnetic quality which can also be found in the novel.

Wuthering Heights, 1939, has a high reputation in the William Wyler canon, and it was an unforgettable landmark in the acting careers of its principals (Olivier, Oberon, Robson, Niven). That said, it is difficult to find many reasons for admiring it: today it appears more a facet of Samuel Goldwyn's showmanship than of William Wyler's directorial skill (Goldwyn: "I made *Wuthering Heights*, Wyler only directed it!") The screen adaptation by Ben Hecht and Charles MacArthur is effective within strictly imposed limits, treating the theme as a transcendental love story and cutting the novel virtually in half. The result is a complete misreading of the novel, but Wyler and his cameraman, Gregg Toland, do much in detail to emphasise the atmosphere and some of the dominant images in the book (windows, candles, mastiffs, the crags) trying to be faithful almost by stealth. The film is rich in production values, although the music is too continuous and overemphatic. This film version will inevitably disappoint knowledgeable readers of Emily Brontë's novel, but in search of certain characters and events which "have achieved a mythic life of their own" (George Bluestone, *Novels into Film*, 1957), this is a sometimes very enjoyable film experience.

David Copperfield, MGM (David O. Selznick), 1935 bw

Direction: George Cukor
Camera: Oliver T. Marsh
Music: Herbert Stothart
Art Direction: Cedric Gibbons
Special Effects: Slavko Vorkapich
Editing: Robert J.Kern
Script: Howard Estabrook, Hugh Walpole (from Charles Dickens' novel)
Costume Design: Dolly Tree

with W.C. Fields, Lionel Barrymore, Maureen O'Sullivan, Madge Evans, Edna May Oliver, Lewis Stone, Frank Lawton, Freddie Bartholomew, Elizabeth Allan, Roland Young, Hugh Williams, Basil Rathbone, Jessie Ralph, Elsa Lanchester, Arthur Treacher, Herbert Mundin

- Criticism on release

    ...all [the] omissions merely serve to show how rich the book is, and how skilfully the adaptation has been made since, although half the characters are absent, the whole spirit of the book, Micawber always excepted, is conveyed...

    James Agate, *The Tatler* 16 March 1935

    ...a pretty straight bore...

    Otis Ferguson, *New Republic* 20 February 1935

    ...a gorgeous photoplay which encompasses the rich and kindly humanity of the original so brilliantly that it becomes a screen masterpiece in its own right...

    André Sennwald, *New York Times* 19 January 1935

- Current recommendations and ratings
  S&S82 LM4 DQ4 DW5 VFG5 MPG5 NFT*

    As one might expect from Cukor, an exemplary adaptation of Dickens' classic, condensing the novel's sprawl with careful clarity, and yielding up a host of terrific performances... One of those rare things: a blend of Art and Hollywood that actually works.

Geoff Andrew, PTOG, 1995

Wuthering Heights, UA (Samuel Goldwyn), 1939 *bw*

Direction: William Wyler
*Camera: Gregg Toland
Music: Alfred Newman
Art Direction: James Basevi
Editing: Daniel Mandell
Script: Ben Hecht, Charles MacArthur (from the novel by Emily Brontë)
Costume Design: Omar Kiam

with Merle Oberon, Laurence Olivier, David Niven, Flora Robson, Geraldine Fitzgerald, Hugh Williams, Donald Crisp, Leo G. Carroll, Miles Mander

- Criticism on release

    ...turns out to be among the best pictures made anywhere. Pictures made from novels are usually desperate ventures – some artificiality shows through in the setting... But the closeness with which the story holds together is ultimately the way director, photographer and cutters have used what should be called the moving camera – the camera telling a story...

    Otis Ferguson, *New Republic* 26 April 1939

- Current recommendations and ratings
  LM4 DQ4 DW4 VFG4½ MPG5 NFT*

    Handsomely designed by James Basevi and shot by Gregg Toland, the much-filmed tale of Cathy's passion for Heathcliff succeeds as fulsome melodrama; and while it has little to do with Emily Brontë's sense of environment and pre-Victorian society, it's nevertheless strong on performances – especially Olivier, seen here at the peak of his romantic lead period.

    Martyn Auty, PTOG 1995

Musicals

The musical film is the one superb genre invented and developed by Hollywood, other film industries being quite incapable of imitating or challenging it in this field – unlike the Western (another indigenous form) where the 'Spaghetti Western' proved that the Italians could even outdo the Americans in their own mythology. Warner Brothers were the first to capitalise on the introduction of sound by introducing some trifles of human speech and some memorable songs by one of the most popular vocal entertainers at that time – Al Jolson, in *The Jazz Singer*, 1927 (the film that Jack Warner said had killed his brother, Sam). Apart from the novelty of the sound passages, which have become part of the contemporary folk memory of the world, it is a pretty dreadful film, and its value is mainly archival. The history of the Hollywood musical is punctuated by such innovations, necessary to prevent the popularity of a familiar form efficiently presented from falling into spiritless imitation.

Maurice Chevalier, who was still starring in an MGM musical – *Gigi* – in 1958, first made his mark in a series of Paramount musicals from 1929 onwards, of which *Love Me Tonight*, 1932, is thought to be the finest. The voice and appearance of Jeanette MacDonald always appear as a formidable contrast to the informal charm of Chevalier's performances, but the blend works quite magically in this superb Mamoulian musical, "one of the most enchanting... ever made, the Lubitsch film that Lubitsch never quite pulled off" (Tom Milne, *Rouben Mamoulian*, 1969). Although Chevalier and MacDonald sing most of the Rodgers and Hart numbers, a sparkling cast – Myrna Loy, Charles Butterworth, Charlie Ruggles, C. Aubrey Smith – all join in at times, in their own voices. Mamoulian not only integrates song with action but also uses all available cinematic techniques (except, unfortunately, colour) to expand the confines of the musical beyond its original stage-bound form.

Jeanette MacDonald and Maurice Chevalier appear to similarly excellent advantage in Ernst Lubitsch's *The Merry Widow*, 1934: they have charming songs from the original operetta by Franz Lehar and enough vivacity and humour in their performances to reflect the general wit and verve of Lubitsch's whole production. There are breathtaking ensemble numbers, but also delightful moments of comic intimacy, to which the supporting cast (including George Barbier, Edward Everett Horton and Una Merkel) contribute immeasurably.

The problem of identifying the film musical with its stage origins was faced squarely by the Warner Brothers studio in the 1930s, where the theme usually consisted of 'putting on a show' on Broadway, with all its attendant financial and personal problems. In *Forty-Second Street* and *The Gold Diggers of 1933*, the two classics of this particular sub-genre, the magnificent set-pieces devised and choreographed by the audacious Busby Berkeley are well-known to a TV public, very often extracted from its context for display as a kind of automated ballet. The capacity of film to raise these 'routines' to the level of surrealistic escapism always ends with a return to the 'real' world of the confined theatre with the curtains closing over the proscenium arch and the well-heeled audience applauding (Success after all those weeks of hard grind, worry, romance, jealousy and frustration!). The illusion that such essentially filmic excursions into fantasy could actually be presented on the stage adds to the absurdity and frivolity which were essential ingredients in such entertainments during the Great Depression (and after!). These two Warner Brothers musicals have strong elements of social realism, particularly in *The Gold Diggers of 1933*, where the director, played by Ned Sparks, with a cigar permanently planted in his letter-slot mouth, starkly sums up the purpose of the show: "to make the audience laugh at you starving to death".

The Astaire-Rogers ('Fred and Ginger') musicals at RKO rescued those studios from financial disaster. All have marvellous song-and-dance routines and a kind of feckless comedy, which were perfect antidotes to the grim economic and political background of the 30s. Mark Sandrich's *Top Hat*, 1935 – a confection even more delightful than *The Gay Divorcee*, on which it was modelled – is a first-rate film (to some idolaters, the finest musical ever made) with a gloriously comic cast (Edward Everett Horton, Helen Broderick, Erik Rhode, Eric Blore), a scintillating Irving Berlin score ('Top Hat, White Tie and Tails', 'Isn't it a Lovely Day to be Caught in the Rain', 'Cheek to Cheek' and 'The Piccolino'), archetypal art deco set designs, Hermes Pan choreography and the ethereal Astaire-Rogers song and dance team. *Swing Time*, 1936, the only 'Fred and Ginger' movie directed by George Stevens, also has a marvellous collection of songs (by Dorothy Fields and Jerome Kern – 'A Fine Romance', 'The Way You

Look Tonight', 'Pick Yourself Up', 'Bojangles of Harlem', and 'Never Gonna Dance'), as always, inspired song and dance routines to match them, a witty and romantic script and the two spellbinding leads in one of their very best films providing the menu as before, but with generally superior ingredients, except, possibly, Victor Moore, who hasn't the same imponderable presence as Edward Everett Horton. However, Helen Broderick and Eric Blore are still there, providing astringent and daffy comedy respectively and the film certainly benefits from its handling by a director of character.

The one remaining black-and-white musical, Michael Curtiz's *Yankee Doodle Dandy*, 1942, rests almost completely on James Cagney's performance, singing and dancing, as George M. Cohan, the showman and songwriter. Curtiz has done his usual excellent job of squeezing as much gripping entertainment as possible out of the available material, and Cagney gets more than adequate support from a strong cast, including Joan Leslie as his wife, Walter Huston, Rosemary DeCamp and S.Z. ('Cuddles') Sakall as an endearingly child-like producer. As much of the action takes place around World War I, there is opportunity for jaunty patriotic songs ('Over There', 'Good Old Flag', and the title number, brilliantly rendered by Cagney). The timing of its production is obvious, in the run-up period to World War II, and as an expert piece of 'showbiz' about 'showbiz' it still requires attention, but perhaps does not deserve this place over several other more intriguing musicals.

The kind of talent that flocked to Hollywood during the early years of talkies was custom-made for the musical – talented singers, dancers, comedians, witty scriptwriters, lyricists and composers, many of them recruited from already established (and booming) Broadway productions. The classic Hollywood musical is dominated by a clearly distinguishable group of exceptional personalities: of the twenty-one musicals listed here, ten were created at MGM – seven under the aegis of the great 'maestro', Arthur Freed, once a lyricist for early musical productions such as *The Broadway Melody*, and later assistant producer, as on *The Wizard of Oz*. The partnership of Freed as producer and Vincente Minnelli, a director directly recruited from Broadway, was responsible for five of these outstanding musicals:

- *Meet Me in St Louis*, 1944

    in which Judy Garland is a member of a St Louis family in 1903, the year of the World Fair, with her parents – Mary Astor and Leon Ames, three sisters, including a six-year-old Margaret O'Brien, one brother, and a long-suffering cook, played by the sharp-tongued Marjorie Main. A really great musical, with songs by Hugh Martin and Ralph Blane

- *The Pirate*, 1948

    in which Judy Garland is wooed away from marrying a Caribbean bigwig (Walter Slezak) by a travelling actor (Gene Kelly) pretending to be her dream pirate. Dazzling colour and songs by Cole Porter.

- *An American in Paris*, 1951

    in which Gene Kelly, a poor American artist in Paris dependent upon Nina Foch, meets and falls in love with a French shop girl (Leslie Caron) who feels she ought to marry Georges Guetary. It all ends happily in the midst of a cornucopia of George Gershwin music (including Kelly's 'I Got Rhythm' with the street boys, Guetary's 'Stairway to the Stars', Oscar Levant's playing of the 'Piano Concerto' and Kelly's ballet set to 'An American in Paris').

- *The Band Wagon*, 1953 in which Fred Astaire helps to stage a Broadway show written by Nanette Fabray and Oscar Levant (in an amusing parody of themselves by the writers Betty Comden and Adolph Green) and at first amusingly misdirected by a former avant-garde director (Jack Buchanan). Astaire also clashes, then makes up, with his ballet star (Cyd Charisse). A witty script, wonderful songs (by Howard Dietz and Arthur Schwartz), and scintillating performances by the whole troupe.

- *Gigi*, 1958 n which Louis Jourdain seeks to make the girl he knew, now grown up, his mistress; her grandmother (Hermione Gingold) seems to approve, but Gigi (Leslie Caron) has a mind of her own. The veteran Maurice Chevalier plays Jourdan's roué uncle. Songs by Alan Jay Lerner and Frederick Loewe

Freed also produced the Gene Kelly/Stanley Donen co-directions:

- *On the Town*, 1949 in which three sailors on leave in New York (Gene Kelly, Frank Sinatra and Jules Munshin) become attached to three girlfriends – Sinatra to Betty Garrett, playing a taxi-driver, Brunhilde Esterhazy, Munshin to Ann Miller, a whirlwind dancer (both relatively easily), while Kelly spends most of the film chasing Vera-Ellen ('Miss Turnstiles'). Most of Leonard Bernstein's stage score has been jettisoned, but the added songs, by Comden and Green, the writers, and Roger Edens, associate producer, are very lively.

- *Singin' in the Rain*, 1952 in which Gene Kelly, as silent film star, can make the transition to talkies, whereas his favourite partner on screen, Jean Hagen, cannot, because of her ghastly voice. With the help of his former partner in vaudeville, Donald O'Connor, and a sympathetic producer (Millard Mitchell), Kelly manages to replace Hagen with Debbie Reynolds, first through dubbing her voice, then by a final hilarious act of treachery. Freed must have felt gratified that several of his biggest song hits (with Nacio Herb Brown) from early MGM musicals were used to great effect, particularly in the title number. Still rated as the greatest of all musicals.

Gene Kelly, as leading actor, dancer and choreographer in the Freed-Minnelli *The Pirate* and *An American in Paris*, and later leading actor, dancer, choreographer and co-director in *On the Town* and *Singin' in the Rain*, was obviously a key contributor to MGM musicals in post-war years. Leslie Caron, in her first leading role with him in *An American in Paris*, was later chosen to play the title role in the prestigious *Gigi*. Judy Garland, actress and singer, wife of Minnelli, had starred in the pre-war *The Wizard of Oz* and been directed by her future husband in the wartime *Meet Me in St Louis* (two of the most original and enduringly beautiful of the MGM musicals), before starring with Kelly and being directed by Minnelli in *The Pirate*. Less obvious names are repeated through the credits: Roger Edens, composer, arranger and associate producer (*The Wizard of Oz*, *On the Town*, *Singin' in the Rain*), Conrad Salinger, orchestrator (*Meet Me in St Louis*, *The Pirate*, *On the Town*, *Singin' in the Rain*), Harold Rosson, cameraman (*The Wizard of Oz*, *On the Town*, *Singin' in the Rain*), Betty Comden and Adolph Green, screenwriters and lyricists (*The Band Wagon*, *Singin' in the Rain*, and *On the Town*).

Ironically, one of the perfect later integrated musicals, though made at MGM, was not produced by Freed but by Jack Cummings in

1954 – *Seven Brides for Seven Brothers*. It was directed by a Freed stalwart, however, Stanley Donen; Michael Kidd, the choreographer, had already worked on *The Band Wagon*, as had the co-arranger, Adolph Deutsch. The other co-arranger, Saul Chaplin, sharing his Oscar for this film, was well established at MGM; George Folsey, the cameraman, had also worked on *Meet Me in St Louis*; and the scriptwriters, Frances Goodrich and Albert Hackett, had been responsible for many effective and witty adaptations for that studio, including Hammett's *The Thin Man* and S.N. Behrman's *The Pirate*. The songs in *Seven Brides for Seven Brothers* were fresh and original by an unusual song team, Johnny Mercer and Gene De Paul, while, apart from the two stars, Howard Keel and Jane Powell, already known at this studio and particularly good in this film, the cast seem to have been specially assembled for this vital, exuberant musical. The male dancing, particularly, is phenomenal.

Jack Cummings also produced a sparkling adaptation of Sam and Bella Spewack's Broadway musical, *Kiss Me Kate*, 1953, with nine of Cole Porter's finest songs. There are larger-than-life performances by Howard Keel and Kathryn Grayson, as both the actors and the characters in a production of *The Taming of the Shrew*, inventive choreography by Hermes Pan, wonderful dancing (Ann Miller, Bob Fosse, Tommy Rall, Bobby Van), and two glorious 'hoods' (James Whitmore, Keenan Wynn) yearning for culture ('Brush Up Your Shakespeare').

In spite of the considerable talent at Twentieth-Century Fox since the 1930s (Alice Faye, Carmen Miranda, Betty Grable, the song team of Mack Gordon and Harry Warren), it took the combination of Howard Hawks, Marilyn Monroe and Jane Russell at that studio to produce a really exceptional musical – *Gentlemen Prefer Blondes*, 1953, based on a stage musical adapted from the astringently witty novel by Anita Loos. It has always suffered from comparison with the other films in the Howard Hawks canon, but is in fact a lively and piercing social comedy interspersed with brilliant musical numbers involving Marilyn (at her most piquant) as Lorelei Lee and Jane Russell (at her most provocative) as Dorothy. Considered as a fresh original musical, *Gentlemen Prefer Blondes* retains a new enduring quality.

With Fred Astaire in the lead, Stanley Donen at the helm, and music by Gershwin and Roger Edens, *Funny Face*, 1957, looks very much like an MGM musical, although produced at Paramount. One of the musicals for which Fred, once more, came out of retirement, it is an amusing, at times enchanting, updated version of a Twenties stage musical which had been a hit for him and his sister Adele over thirty years previously. Audrey Hepburn's vulnerable gaminerie makes her fit perfectly into the part of the bookshop heroine become model, and Kay Thompson (in a rare screen appearance as a robust and sophisticated fashion editor) gives a resonantly witty performance.

It was the need for novelty – as always – that prompted the shift from the Freed-style 'integrated musical' (where the songs and dances arise from realistic situations) to the spectacular filmings of successful stage shows, such as *West Side Story* in 1961. Leonard Bernstein's score, which had been greatly truncated on the transfer of *On the Town* to the screen, was triumphantly retained in almost its entirety, with a cast almost fresh to the film musical, the chief exception being Rita Moreno, who had also appeared in *Singin' in the Rain*. The production, with the juvenile vigour appropriate to a modern version of the *Romeo and Juliet* story set against the background of New York street gang warfare, the electrifying virtuosity of the Jerome Robbins choreography, and the use of real locations for the song-and-dance routines, made a strong immediate impact on the box office through its appeal to younger audiences.

A Disney musical with animated inserts (under the inspired direction of Hamilton Luske), *Mary Poppins*, 1964, was intended for, and mainly appeals to, children (of all ages). Julie Andrews had already made her name in *My Fair Lady* on the stage, but had lost the film role to Audrey Hepburn: this is a relatively muted film debut in response (which, nevertheless, won an Oscar). She plays the magical governess (of P.L. Travers's books) of two playful children who have wonderful adventures in Edwardian London, sometimes with chimney sweep Dick Van Dyke, who would be a very amusing companion indeed if it were not for his atrociously synthetic Cockney accent. The songs are full of character, the choreography (by Marc Breaux and Dee Dee Wood) is delightful, Glynis Johns (in the small role of the children's mother) is charming; but the general effect is patchy and sometimes boring (for the less childlike of us).

By the end of the 1960s the revival of the stage-based musical had reached technical perfection but seemed to lack originality in such immaculately presented but glossy creations as *Funny Girl* and *Hello,*

Dolly! Both starred Barbra Streisand whose personality imparted some strength to what had become rather tired and familiar spectacles, made with great expertise. What Streisand lost, Liza Minnelli gained, in *Cabaret*, 1972. This adaptation from the stage (a musical from a play derived from a Christopher Isherwood novella *Goodbye to Berlin*) used the musical element brilliantly both to recreate the atmosphere of, and to crystallise social comment on, Germany in the death-throes of the Weimar Republic in the early 30s, as depicted in the story of Sally Bowles, the fun-loving, guileless, promiscuous, yet ultimately innocent heroine of Isherwood's original. The strengths of the movie are to be found in Minnelli's singing; the decadent and sensual dance routines; the superb revulsion of Joel Grey's all-knowing, leering MC; the jaunty, appealing vulgarity of the Ebb/ Kander songs; the impressive craftsmanship of Bob Fosse, the choreographer-director and of Geoffrey Unsworth, the lighting cameraman. In spite of its undoubted individual appeal, *Cabaret*, nevertheless, was unable to resuscitate a genre which, like the Western, had once represented the highest achievements of Hollywood but now had little popular appeal.

Forty-Second Street, WB (Darryl Zanuck/ Hal Wallis), 1933 bw

Direction: Lloyd Bacon	Script: James Seymour, Rian
Camera: Sol Polito	James (from the novel by
Songs: Al Dubin, Harry Warren	Bradford Ropes)
Choreography: Busby Berkeley	Art Direction: Jack Okey
Costume Design: Orry-Kelly	Editing: Thomas Pratt

with Warner Baxter, Bebe Daniels, George Brent, Ruby Keeler, Dick Powell, Una Merkel, Guy Kibbee, Ginger Rogers, Ned Sparks, Allen Jenkins, Louise Beavers, George E. Stone, Henry B. Walthall, Berkeley (bit), Dubin and Warren (bits)

- Criticism on release

    ...return to the backstage setting for a spectacular musical film, with the difference that it has reason and reality behind it... The lonely figure of the producer (played extremely well by Warner Baxter) dominates it... The choruswork is on the most post-Goldwyn lines, and the musical side is strong, with three real hits...

John Gammie et al., *Film Weekly* 21 April 1933)

- Current recommendations and ratings
StJD LM4 DQ4 DW5 VFG5 MPG5 NFT**

    Seminal backstage musical... Includes some sensationally naughty Busby Berkeley numbers like 'Shuffle Off to Buffalo' and 'Young and Healthy', but it takes a lot to beat Bebe Daniels lolling on a piano as she trills 'You're Getting to be a Habit with Me'...

    Anne Billson, PTOG 1995

The Gold Diggers of 1933, WB (Hal Wallis/Robert Lord), 1933 bw

Direction: Mervyn LeRoy	Script: Erwin Gelsey, James Seymour, David Boehm, Ben Markson (from a play by Avery Hopwood)
Camera: Sol Polito	
Songs: Al Dubin, Harry Warren	
Choreography: Busby Berkeley	
Art Direction: Anton Grot	Costume Design: Orry-Kelly
Editing: George Amy	

with Warren William, Joan Blondell, Aline MacMahon, Ruby Keeler, Dick Powell, Guy Kibbee, Ned Sparks, Ginger Rogers, Sterling Holloway

- Criticism on release

    ...imaginatively staged breezy show, with a story of no greater consequence than is to be found in this type of picture. But it has several humorous episodes and more than once the audience that filled the theatre to the doors applauded the excellent camera work and the artistry of the scenic effects...

    Mordaunt Hall, *New York Times* 8 June 1933

- Current recommendations and ratings
StJD LM3½ DQ4 DW4 VFG5 MPG4 NFT*

Second of the archetypal backstage musicals from Warners (it followed hard on the success of *42nd Street*)... much Depression wisecracking from Blondell, MacMahon and Rogers; but most notable is the vulgar, absurd and wonderfully surreal Berkeley choreography. Great numbers... delirious and delightful.

Geoff Andrew, PTOG 1995

Love Me Tonight, Par (Rouben Mamoulian), 1932 bw

Direction: Rouben Mamoulian
Camera: Victor Milner
Songs: Lorenz Hart, Richard Rodgers
Art Direction: Hans Dreier
Editing: Billy Shea
Costume Design: Travis Banton, Edith Head

Script: Samuel Hoffenstein, Waldemar Young, George Marion Jr. (from a play by Leopold Marchand and Paul Armont)

with Maurice Chevalier, Jeanette MacDonald, Charles Ruggles, Myrna Loy, Charles Butterworth, C. Aubrey Smith, Elizabeth Patterson, Bert Roach

- Criticism on release

    ...should the cries of 'powerful', 'magnificent', 'stupendous' quoted in the papers have kept you away from this picture, you can turn back and find *Love Me Tonight* worth your money. It is a gay, attractive melodious movie... with the aid of a pleasant story, a good musician, talented cast and about a million dollars, [Mamoulian] has done what someone in Hollywood should have done long ago – he has illustrated a musical score...

    Pare Lorentz, *Vanity Fair*, October 1932

- Current recommendations and ratings
    StJD S&S82/92 LM4 DQ4 DW4 VFG5 MPG5 NFT*

A superb musical, outstripping the possible influences of René Clair and Lubitsch... The songs develop the action and characters, the dialogue is witty and rhythmic, and the entire film, with its fine score by Hart and Rodgers, is a charming, tongue-in-cheek fantasy that never descends into syrupy whimsy.

Geoff Andrew, PTOG 1995

The Merry Widow, MGM (Irving Thalberg), 1934 *bw*

Direction: Ernst Lubitsch
Camera: Oliver T. Marsh
Music: Franz Lehar
Art Direction: Cedric Gibbons, Frederic Hope
Choreography: Albertina Rasch

Script: Samson Raphaelson, Ernest Vajda (from Lehar's operetta)
Costume Design: Adrian, Ali Hubert
Editing: Frances Marsh

with Maurice Chevalier, Jeanette MacDonald, Edward Everett Horton, Una Merkel, George Barbier, Minna Gombell, Ruth Channing, Sterling Holloway, Henry Armetta

- Criticism on release

    ...a good show in the excellent Lubitsch manner, heady as the foam on champagne, fragile as mist and as delicately gay as a good-natured censor will permit... [The book suits] the Lubitsch style and the songs which fall to Miss MacDonald and Mr Chevalier have grace and wit. All the sets are consummately lovely... Herr Lubitsch is not the man to crush you under a mountain of spectacle. His sense of humor is impeccable and his taste is faultless. So with his actors...

    André Sennwald, *New York Times* 12 October 1934

- Current recommendations and ratings
StJD LM3 DW3 VFG5 MPG5 NFT*

    Not reviewed in PTOG 1995.

Swing Time, RKO (Pandro S. Berman), 1936 bw

Direction: George Stevens
Camera: David Abel
Songs: Dorothy Fields, Jerome Kern (*Song: 'The Way You Look Tonight')
Art Direction: Van Nest Polglase, Carroll Clark
Choreography: Hermes Pan
Editing: Henry Berman
Script: Howard Lindsay, Allan Scott (from a story by Erwin Gelsey)
Costume Design: Bernard Newman, John Harkrider
Special Effects: Vernon L. Walker

with Fred Astaire, Ginger Rogers, Victor Moore, Helen Broderick, Eric Blore, Betty Furness, George Metaxas, Pierre Watkin

- Criticism on release

    ...the astute film-makers at RKO-RADIO's studio have not forgotten their reliably entertaining formula for an Astaire-Rogers show... of comedy there is a generous portion; of romance the slightest sprinkling; of dancing, in solo, duet and ensemble, a brisk and debonair allotment. Add to these a handsomely modernistic, even impressionistic, series of sets, the usually appreciative photography, and you have a picture that unquestionably will linger for a few weeks at the [Radio City] Music Hall...

    Frank S. Nugent, *New York Times* 28 August 1936

- Current recommendations and ratings
  LM4 DQ4 DW5 VFG5 MPG3½ NFT*

    ...if plot, script and supporters are below par, the score by Jerome Kern and Dorothy Fields is peerless... And nothing Fred and Ginger did together surpasses their lengthy, climactic duet, taking off from 'Never Gonna Dance'...

    W. Stephen Gilbert, PTOG 1995

Top Hat, RKO (Pandro S. Berman), 1935 bw

Direction: Mark Sandrich
Camera: David Abel, Vernon Walker
Songs: Irving Berlin
Music Direction: Max Steiner
Arrangements (uncredited): Edward Powell
Choreography: Hermes Pan, Fred Astaire
Art Direction: Van Nest Polglase, Carroll Clark, Charles Oman (uncredited), Alan Abbott (uncredited)
Costume Design: Bernard Newman
Editing: William Hamilton

Script: Dwight Taylor, Alan Scott (from an adaptation by Karl Noti of a play by Alexander Farago and Laszlo Aladar)

with Fred Astaire, Ginger Rogers, Edward Everett Horton, Helen Broderick, Erik Rhodes, Eric Blore, Lucille Ball (bit)

- Criticism on release

    When *Top Hat* is letting Mr Astaire perform his incomparable magic, or teaming him with the increasingly dexterous Miss Rogers, it is providing the most urbane fun that you will find anywhere on the screen... All the minor players are such skilled comedians that they are able to extract merriment from this none-too-original comedy of errors... worth standing in line for.

    André Sennwald, *New York Times* 30 August 1935

- Current recommendations and ratings
  StJD BN92 S&S92 LM4 DQ4 DW5 VFG5 MPG5 NFT*

    ...with a superlative Irving Berlin score... and equally superlative Hermes Pan routines which spark a distinct sexual electricity between the pair. Oddly enough, the film is almost slavishly patterned on *The Gay*

Divorcee... The reason you don't really notice this – with *Top Hat* readily springing to mind as the archetypal Fred'n'Ginger movie – is the booster given by Van Nest Polglase's stunning 'white Art Deco' designs, which were to set the tone for the series.

Tom Milne, PTOG 1995

Yankee Doodle Dandy, WB (William Cagney), 1942 bw

Direction: Michael Curtiz
Camera: James Wong Howe
Art Direction: Carl Jules Weyl
Choreography: LeRoy Prinz, Seymour Felix, John Boyle
Editing: George Amy
Script: Robert Buckner, Edmund Joseph (from Buckner's story)
Costume Design: Milo Anderson
Arrangements: Ray Heindorf

with *James Cagney, Joan Leslie, Walter Huston, Richard Whorf, George Tobias, Irene Manning, Rosemary DeCamp, Jeanne Cagney, S.Z. Sakall, George Barbier

- Criticism on release

...a loud, fast, skilful stage biography of George M. Cohan, full of songs, dances, choruses, backcloths, patriotism, and James Cagney, who gives a performance of terrific vivacity but less persuasion. The flag-waving, since it is American and not British, can be stomached, and the whole production has a bounce and flounce which, in a kind of sickened way, one cannot but admire.

Dilys Powell, *Sunday Times* October 1942

- Current recommendations and ratings
StJD S&S82 LM4 DQ3 DW4 VFG5 MPG5 NFT*

...everyone remembers Cagney's impersonation, pitched as it is at fever level... This was just the film to bombard American theatres with after Pearl Harbor, full of rousing sentiments and songs... now it seems raucous, vulgar, over long; but if you like slick jobs, this is certainly one of the slickest.

Geoff Brown, PTOG 1995

An American in Paris, MGM (Arthur Freed), 1951
colour

Direction: Vincente Minnelli	*Script: Alan Jay Lerner
*Camera: John Alton, Alfred Gilks	Choreography: Gene Kelly
	Costume Design: Orry-Kelly,
Songs: Ira and George Gershwin	Walter Plunkett, Irene Sharaff
*Arrangements: Johnny Green, Saul Chaplin	Editing: Adrienne Fazan
*Art Direction: Cedric Gibbons, Preston Ames	

with Gene Kelly, Leslie Caron, Oscar Levant, Georges Guetary, Nina Foch

- Criticism on release

    ...spangled with pleasant little patches of amusement and George Gershwin tunes. It is also blessed with Gene Kelly, dancing and singing his way through a minor romantic complication in the usual gaudy Hollywood gay Paree... But the picture takes on its glow of magic when Miss Caron is on the screen. [There is also] a truly cinematic ballet, conceived and performed with taste and talent...

    Bosley Crowther, *New York Times* 5 October 1951

- Current recommendations and ratings
  StJD LM3½ DQ3 DW4 VFG4½ MPG5 NFT*

    ...ludicrously overpraised (especially in Hollywood) and underrated... there are ecstatic moments, like Kelly's jazz eruption into the ballet as Toulouse-Lautrec's Chocolat, his pas de deux with Caron on the river bank, his solo to ''S Wonderful'. And finally of course there is the climactic *American in Paris* ballet [which], besides being colourful, invigorating, ambitious, is also entirely appropriate to Minnelli's interest in his characters' emotions...

    Geoff Andrew, PTOG 1995

The Band Wagon, MGM (Arthur Freed), 1953 colour

Direction: Vincente Minnelli
Camera: Harry Jackson
Songs: Howard Dietz, Arthur Schwartz
Arrangements: Adolph Deutsch, Roger Edens
Art Direction: Cedric Gibbons, Preston Ames

Script: Betty Comden, Adolph Green
Choreography: Michael Kidd
Costume Design: Mary Ann Nyberg
Editing: Albert Akst

with Fred Astaire, Jack Buchanan, Cyd Charisse, Nanette Fabray, Oscar Levant

- Criticism on release

    ...a good lively musical [with] an exciting feeling for movement and rhythm, as indeed we should expect from its director, who has made some of the best musicals to come out of Hollywood in the last ten years. It has even an intelligent and amusing script - I could have done with more edge to the satire on the groaner school of theatre, but Jack Buchanan so agreeably mixes the 'dégagé' man of the world and a knockabout parody of the portentous actor manager that I was consoled.

    Dilys Powell, Sunday Times 10 January 1954

- Current recommendations and ratings
  StJD S&S82/92 LM3½ DQ4 DW4 VFG4½ MPG4 NFT*

    One of Minnelli's best musicals, with an ingenious book... More importantly, it parades a stream of brilliant Howard Dietz-Arthur Schwartz numbers. Astaire is superlative in several items... All this and witty dialogue, too.

    Tom Milne, PTOG 1999

Cabaret, AA (Cy Feuer), 1972 *colour*

*Direction: Bob Fosse
*Camera: Geoffrey Unsworth
Choreography: Bob Fosse
*Arrangements: Ralph Burns
*Editing: David Bretherton
*Art Direction: Jürgen Kiebach, Rolf Zehetbauer
Costume Design: Charlotte Fleming

Script: Jay Presson Allen (from the musical play by Joe Masteroff, based on John Van Druten's play *I Am a Camera* from stories by Christopher Isherwood

with *Liza Minnelli, *Joel Grey, Michael York, Helmut Griem, Fritz Wepper, Marisa Berenson

- Criticism on release

    ...a great movie musical, made, miraculously, without compromise. It's miraculous because the material is hard and unsentimental – it is everything one hopes for and more – the formalized numbers (in the floor show at the Kit Kat Club) are at the center of the movie, are its essence... What dancing there is – which is mostly movement during songs – is marvellous...

    Pauline Kael, *New Yorker*, 19 February 1972

- Current recommendations and ratings
  S&S82 LM3½ DQ3 DW4 VFG4½ MPG5 NFT*

    A maddening mixture... Superbly choreographed by Fosse, the cabaret numbers evoke the Berlin of 1931... so vividly that only an idiot could fail to perceive that something is rotten in the state of Weimar. Doubling as director, Fosse unfortunately... lands the film in a queasy morass of overstatement.

    Tom Milne, PTOG 1995

Funny Face, Par (Roger Edens), 1957 colour

Direction: Stanley Donen
Camera: Ray June
Songs: Ira and George Gershwin, Roger Edens, Leonard Gershe
Art Direction: Hal Pereira, George W. Davis
Choreography: Fred Astaire, Eugene Loring
Script: Leonard Gershe (from his own unproduced musical)
Costume Design: Edith Head, Givenchy
Editing: Frank Bracht
Special Effects: John P. Fulton

with Audrey Hepburn, Fred Astaire, Kay Thompson, Michel Auclair, Robert Flemyng, Dovima, Virginia Gibson

- Criticism on release

   ...when Fred Astaire dances everything is delicate; the large arabesques of action are made up of innumerable tiny gestures of lightning and as precise as the beat of an insect's wing. Astaire makes *Funny Face* plausible... It is with the background of the heroic antique sculpture that Audrey Hepburn displays the drapery of the evening dress... The clothes are dazzling, and she wears them, as she wears her role, with a charm and a wistful composure which add greatly to the pleasures of this gay and lively musical...

   Dilys Powell, *Sunday Times* April 1957

- Current recommendations and ratings
  LM3 DQ4 DW4 VFG4½ MPG3½ NFT*

   The Musical that dares rhyme Sartre with Montmartre... knocks most other musicals off the screen for its visual beauty, its witty panache and its totally uncalculating charm...

   W. Stephen Gilbert, PTOG 1995

Gentlemen Prefer Blondes, TCF (Sol C. Siegel), 1953 *colour*

Direction: Howard Hawks
Camera: Harry Wild Jr.
Special Effects: Ray Kellogg
Choreography: Jack Cole
Songs: Leo Robin, Jule Styne, Harold Adamson, Hoagy Carmichael
Art Direction: Lyle Wheeler, Joseph C. Wright
Script: Charles Lederer (from the musical by Anita Loos and Joseph Fields based on a novel by Loos)
Editing: Hugh S. Fowler
Costume Design: Travilla

with Marilyn Monroe, Jane Russell, Charles Coburn, Elliot Reid, Tommy Noonan, Marcel Dalio, Taylor Holmes, Steven Geray, Norma Varden, Harry Carey Jr., George Chakiris (dancer)

- Criticism on release

    ...an intelligent and pitiless film – Lorelei and Dorothy cease to be merely extravagant personalities and become essences... they are the blonde and the brunette, greed and lust, frigidity and nymphomania... Hawks's comedies, whatever label you put on them, are bright and original, derived more from a nice sense of the absurd than from a sense of commercialism...

    François Truffaut, *Cahiers du Cinema*, 1954

- Current recommendations and ratings
  S&S92 LM3 DQ4 DW5 VFG4 MPG3 NFT*

    A classic musical/social satire, featuring tight script, Hawks' usual humanity of style, and a line-up of sardonic song'n'dance numbers – the Monroe/Russell sexual stereotypes are used ironically to generate a whole range of erotic gambits... Smashing.

    Chris Auty, PTOG 1995

*_Gigi_, MGM (Arthur Freed), 1958 _colour_

*Direction: Vincente Minnelli
*Camera: Joseph Ruttenberg
Songs (incl. *'Gigi'): Alan Jay Lerner, Frederick Loewe
*Arrangements: André Previn
*Art Direction: William Horning, Preston Ames, Cecil Beaton
*Script: Alan Jay Lerner (from the play by Anita Loos based on Colette's novel)
*Editing: Adrienne Fazan
*Costume Design: Cecil Beaton

with Leslie Caron, Maurice Chevalier, Hermione Gingold, Louis Jourdan, Eva Gabor, Isabel Jeans, Jacques Bergerac, John Abbott

- Criticism on release

    Enough of Colette's diamond-sharp exchanges are preserved to give the story a core of character. And round the ironic centre a sparkling, sophisticated web has been spun... Cecil Beaton's designs for the production, both costumes and settings, are at once elegant and exhilarating... I find Vincente Minnelli's direction masterly [and] _Gigi_ strikes me as one of the half-dozen best screen musicals ever made.

    Dilys Powell, _Sunday Times_ 8 February 1958

- Current recommendations and ratings
  LM4 DQ4 DW4 VFG3½ MPG5 NFT*

    Not a Broadway-based musical but a screen original, derived from Colette's short novel set in turn-of-the-century Paris, with famous if vapid songs... the dominating creative contribution comes from Minnelli and Cecil Beaton... the combination of these two visual elitists is really too much... one quickly longs for something solid and vulgar to weigh things down...

    Geoff Brown, PTOG 1995

Kiss Me Kate, MGM (Jack Cummings), 1953 colour

Direction: George Sidney
Camera: Charles Rosher
Songs: Cole Porter
Art Direction: Cedric Gibbons, Urie McCleary
Choreography: Hermes Pan
Special Effects: Warren Newcombe
Script: Dorothy Kingsley (from Sam and Bella Spewack's musical play)
Arrangements: André Previn, Saul Chaplin
Costume Design: Walter Plunkett
Editing: Ralph E. Winters

with Kathryn Grayson, Howard Keel, Ann Miller, Tommy Rall, Bobby Van, Keenan Wynn, James Whitmore, Kurt Kaszner, Bob Fosse, Ron Randell

- Criticism on release

    ...one of the year's more magnificent musical films... a beautifully staged, adroitly acted and superbly sung affair... Loose continuity, combining a play within a play, is one of those baffling carry-overs that just had to be left alone... Under George Sidney's direction, the whole thing moves with zest and grace...

    Bosley Crowther, *New York Times* 6 November 1953

- Current recommendations and ratings
  LM3½ DQ4 DW4 VFG4 MPG4 NFT*

    Cole Porter's amazing score wasn't the only standout when this tricksy backstage/onstage parallel version of *The Taming of the Shrew* first appeared. Contemporary fashion caused Sidney the headache of shooting in both 3-D and 'flat' format... The Chinese box play-within-a-play construction is worked out to a tee...

    Paul Taylor, PTOG 1991

Mary Poppins, Disney (Walt Disney, Bill Walsh), 1964 *colour*

Direction: Robert Stevenson
Camera: Edward Colman
Songs: Richard and Robert Sherman
Art Direction: Carroll Clark, William Tuntke
Special Effects: Peter Ellenshaw, Eustace Lycett, Robert A. Mattey
Animation: Hal Ambro, Oliver M. Johnston, Milt Kahl, Ward Kimball, Eric Larson, John Lounsbery, Hamilton Luske, Cliff Nordberg, Franklin Thomas
Script: Bill Walsh, Don da Gradi (from the books by P.L. Travers)
Music: Irwin Kostal
Editing: Cotton Warburton
Choreography: Marc Breaux, Dee Dee Wood
Costume Design: Tony Walton

with Julie Andrews, Dick Van Dyke, David Tomlinson, Glynis Johns, Hermione Baddeley, Elsa Lanchester, Arthur Treacher, Rita Shaw, Karen Dotrice, Ed Wynn, Jane Darwell

- Criticism on release

    ...This is the genuine Mary Poppins... played superbly by Miss Andrews – it is she, with her unremitting discipline and her disarmingly angelic face who fills this film with a sense of wholesome substance and the serenity of self-confidence... And it is in the performances of the wonders [she brings] that Mr Disney and his people assist in their most felicitous fashion. Flying characters are easy for them. There's nothing at all unusual about sliding a nanny upstairs. And when it comes to surrounding live persons with adorable animated cartoons, they are, of course, past masters. They are close to their best in this film...

    Bosley Crowther, *New York Times* 25 September 1964

- Current recommendations and ratings
  LM4 DQ4 DW4 VFG4 MPG5 NFT*

...the sheer exuberance of Disney's adaptation of P.L. Travers's children's classic should tickle the most jaded fancy. Indeed, the film can hardly contain itself with its catalogue of memorable songs, battery of dance routines, and strong supporting cast...

                              Frances Dickinson, PTOG 1995

Meet Me in St Louis, MGM (Arthur Freed), 1944 *colour*

Direction: Vincente Minnelli
Camera: George Folsey
Songs: Ralph Blane, Hugh Martin
Music Direction: George Stoll
Choreography: Charles Walters
Art Direction: Cedric Gibbons, Jack Martin Smith, Lemuel Ayers
Editing: Albert Akst

Script: Irving Brecher, Fred F. Finkelhoffe (from stories by Sally Benson)
Arrangements: Conrad Salinger
Costume Design: Irene Sharaff

with Judy Garland, Margaret O'Brien, Mary Astor, Lucille Bremer, Leon Ames, Hugh Marlowe, Tom Drake, June Lockhart, Marjorie Main, Harry Davenport, Chill Wills

- Criticism on release

    ...a musical that even the deaf should enjoy. They will miss some attractive tunes (including the sure-fire 'Trolley Song'), but they can watch one of the year's prettiest pictures... Technicolor has seldom been more affectionately used than in its registration of the sober mahoganies and tender muslins and benign gaslights of the period...

                    James Agee, *The Nation* 27 November 1944

- Current recommendations and ratings
StJD S&S82/92 LM4 DQ4 DW4 VFG5 MPG5 NFT**

    Minnelli's captivating musical still comes up fresh as paint... One reason, quite apart from the wit and the characterisations or the skill with which Minnelli integrates the numbers, is that the seismic little shudders of dismay that shake the St Louis family of 1903 – threatened with a move to New York, where father has a better job waiting – seem to hint at the end of an era and the disappearance of a world where such uncomplicated happiness can exist... One of the great musicals.

Tom Milne, PTOG 1995

On the Town, MGM (Arthur Freed), 1949 *colour*

Direction: Stanley Donen, Gene Kelly
Script: Betty Comden, Adolph Green
Songs: Comden, Green, Roger Edens, Leonard Bernstein
*Arrangements: Edens, Lennie Hayton

Camera: Hal Rosson
Editing: Ralph E. Winters
Choreography: Gene Kelly
Art Direction: Cedric Gibbons, Jack Martin Smith
Costume Design: Helen Rose

with Gene Kelly, Frank Sinatra, Vera-Ellen, Ann Miller, Betty Garrett, Jules Munshin, Alice Pearce, Florence Bates, Tom Dugan (bit)

- Criticism on release

    ...wholly cinematic... everything is imagined in terms of movement; the background, with the camera swinging breathlessly after the players, cutting and dissolving from street to street, rooftop to rooftop, joins in the fun – the whole film is dance... has all the gaiety, the vitality and the animal spirits proper to a contemporary popular art.

    Dilys Powell, *Sunday Times* 26 March 1950

- Current recommendations and ratings
StJD S&S82 LM4 DQ4 DW4 VFG4 MPG5 NFT*

    Taking as its premise 'New York, New York, it's a wonderful town', the show looses three 'gobs' on the women (including the imperishable Alice Pearce), the sights, and the nightlife of the town... the most cinematic of film musicals and the most given to dance, *On the Town* is exhilarating brash spectacle, all rip-snorting, wisecracking attack, and maybe just a teensy bit unlikeable.

W. Stephen Gilbert, PTOG 1995

The Pirate, MGM (Arthur Freed), 1948 *colour*

Direction: Vincente Minnelli
Camera: Harry Stradling
Art Direction: Cedric Gibbons, Jack Martin Smith
Choreography: Robert Alton, Gene Kelly
Costume Design: Tom Keogh, Barbara Karinska

Script: Frances Goodrich, Albert Hackett, Joseph Than, Lilian Braun, Anita Loos, Wilkie Mahoney, with Joseph Mankiewicz, uc (from S.N. Behrman's play)
Arrangements: Lennie Hayton, Conrad Salinger

Songs: Cole Porter with Gene Kelly, Judy Garland, Walter Slezak, Gladys Cooper, Reginald Owen, George Zucco, The Nicholas Brothers

- Criticism on release

   ...a dazzling, spectacular extravaganza, shot through with all the colors of the rainbow and then some that are Technicolor patented... It takes this mammoth show some time to generate a full head of steam, but when it gets rolling it's thoroughly delightful... a lopsided entertainment that is wonderfully flamboyant in its high spots and bordering on tedium elsewhere – Gene Kelly is doing some of his fanciest gymnastic dancing in his career... and he's good, very good indeed...

   'T.M.P', *New York Times* 21 May 1948

- Current recommendations and ratings
S&S82/92 LM3 DW4 VFG3½ MPG3½ NFT**
   ...Cole Porter songs, a choreographed camera, vivacious performances, and Minnelli's customarily

camp colour scheme and decor are wonderfully
seductive vehicles for the themes that run obsessively
through all the director's films...

Paul Taylor, PTOG 1995

Seven Brides for Seven Brothers, MGM (Jack Cummings), 1954 *colour*

Direction: Stanley Donen
Camera: George Folsey
Songs: Johnny Mercer, Gene De Paul
Choreography: Michael Kidd
*Arrangements: Adolph Deutsch, Saul Chaplin
Script: Albert Hackett, Frances Goodrich, Dorothy Kingsley (from the story by Stephen Vincent Benet)
Editing: Ralph E. Winters
Art Direction: Cedric Gibbons
Costume Design: Walter Plunkett

with Howard Keel, Jane Powell, Jeff Richards, Russ Tamblyn, Marc Platt, Matt Mattox, Jacques d'Amboise, Virginia Gibson, Julie Newmar, Russell Simpson, Ian Wolfe

- Criticism on release

  ...a wholly engaging, bouncy, tuneful and panchromatic package – a distant relation of *Oklahoma*... This lively fable skilfully blends a warm and comic yarn [with] a melodic score several notches above standard... A thin story line has been enhanced by the contributions of Michael Kidd, whose dance creations are in keeping with the times [1850] and the seemingly unbounded energy of the principals...

  New York Times 23 July 1954

- Current recommendations and ratings
  S&S92 LM4 DW4 VFG4½ MPG5 NFT*

  ...best seen as a dance-fest, with Michael Kidd's acrobatic, *pas d'action* choreography well complemented by ex-choreographer Donen's camera...

it's vigorous and colourful if you can watch the Anscocolor process which also marred *Brigadoon*...

                W. Stephen Gilbert, PTOG 1995

Singin' in the Rain, MGM (Arthur Freed), 1952 *colour*

Direction: Stanley Donen, Gene Kelly
Script: Betty Comden, Adolph Green
Camera: Hal Rosson
Songs: Arthur Freed, Nacio Herb Brown, Betty Comden, Roger Edens
Music Direction: Lennie Hayton
Choreography: Donen, Kelly
Editing: Adrienne Fazan
Arrangements: Conrad Salinger, Wally Heglin, Skip Martin
Art Direction: Cedric Gibbons, Randall Duell
Costume Design: Walter Plunkett

with Gene Kelly, Donald O'Connor, Debbie Reynolds, Jean Hagen, Millard Mitchell, Rita Moreno, Douglas Fowley, Cyd Charisse (dancer)

- Criticism on release

    ...all rather broad and obvious but pleasant and at moments electrifying, as, for instance, in the brilliant main solo dance in the streets through a flood of rain... After Gene Kelly the film belongs almost entirely to Jean Hagen's cunningly balanced disparity between pneumatic-drill voice and glamorous face...

          Richard Winnington, *News Chronicle* 12 April 1952

- Current recommendations and ratings
  StJD BN92 S&S82/92 LM4 DQ4 DW5 VFG5 MPG5 NFT***

    Is there a film clip more often shown than the title number of this most astoundingly popular film? The rest of the movie is great too. It shouldn't be [but somehow] it all comes together... If you've never seen it and don't, you're bonkers.

                    W. Stephen Gilbert, PTOG 1995

West Side Story, UA (Robert Wise), 1961 *colour*

*Direction: Robert Wise, Jerome Robbins
Script: Ernest Lehman (from the musical play by Arthur Laurents)
Songs: Stephen Sondheim, Leonard Bernstein
*Arrangements: Saul Chaplin, Johnny Green, Irwin Kostal, Sid Ramin

*Camera: Daniel Fapp
Choreography: Robbins
*Art Direction: Boris Leven
*Costume Design: Irene Sharaff
*Editing: Thomas Stanford

with Natalie Wood, Richard Beymer, *Rita Moreno, *George Chakiris, Russ Tamblyn, Marni Nixon (vocal dubbing for Wood) Jim Bryant (dubbing for Beymer)

- Criticism on release

    ...For something more than half the film (as with the play) everything meshes so beautifully... that we are led to expect cumulation and a towering conclusion. This does not happen. The weakness of the film is the weakness of the show: its book. It is essentially Robbins' alchemy that uses Bernstein's score, uses the drama and color, and transmutes the fine components into an even finer art...

    Stanley Kauffmann, *New Republic* 23 October 1961

- Current recommendations and ratings
S&S92 LM4 DQ4 DW5 VFG4 MPG4 NFT**

    ...in a state of panic, United Artists brought in Robert Wise to direct the non-musical sequences... more intrigue followed, and finally Robbins was sacked altogether. But before leaving the set, he had completed four song sequences which remain the unchallenged highlights of the film: the whole of the opening sequence ('The Jet Song'), 'America', 'Cool', and 'I Feel Pretty'...

    David Pirie, PTOG 1995

The Wizard of Oz, MGM (Mervyn LeRoy), 1939 *colour*

Direction: Victor Fleming with King Vidor, uc)
Script: Florence Ryerson, Noel Langley, Edgar Allen Woolf (from the story by Frank Baum)
Songs (incl. *'Over the Rainbow'): E.Y. ('Yip') Harburg, Harold Arlen
Special Effects: A. Arnold Gillespie
Camera: Hal Rosson
*Music: Herbert Stothart
Choreography: Bobby Connolly
Art Direction: Cedric Gibbons, William Horning
Editing: Blanche Sewell
Costume Design: Adrian

with Judy Garland, Ray Bolger, Bert Lahr, Jack Haley, Frank Morgan, Billie Burke, Margaret Hamilton, Charley Grapewin, Clara Blandick, Lorraine Bridges (vocal dubbing for Billie Burke)

- Criticism on release

    ...was intended to hit the same audience as *Snow White* and won't fail for lack of trying... The story, of course, has some lovely and wild ideas – men of straw and tin, a cowardly lion, a wizard who isn't a very good wizard – but the picture doesn't know what to do with them, except to be painfully literate and elaborate about everything...

    Otis Ferguson, New *Republic* 20 September 1939

- Current recommendations and ratings
StJD BN92 S&S82/92 LM4 DQ4 DW5 VFG5 MPG5 NFT**

    ...It's hard to imagine now the impact this classic fantasy must have had on a world sliding into war. Garland became a legend at 16. Bolger, Haley and Lahr were immortalised as her three blighted pals. It's still a potent dreamworld. The dubbing and some of the visual effects may creak a bit, but the songs, make-up, costumes and sets are magical...

    W. Stephen Gilbert, PTOG, 1995

Romance – Romantic Adventure, Romantic Comedy, Romantic Drama

The 'romantic melodrama', along with slapstick comedy and the Western, was one of the earliest staple products of Hollywood – the 'woman's picture'. Romance, in Hollywood terms, entailed an (usually) unmarried relationship between 'boy' and 'girl' (man/woman), leading through a precarious and eventful courtship to marriage, or the promise of marriage. The 'weepies' could end in separation or death. The dramatic interest arose from difficulties arising in the relationship, obstacles of any kind (social, psychological, financial), which had to be overcome to reach a 'happy ending'.

During the Thirties the romantic comedy, of which there had been several sparkling examples in the silent era, particularly those starring Clara Bow or Colleen Moore, took on a 'screwball' nature, and most of the classics of Hollywood romantic comedy are of this type (see above, under Comedy). More often than not, romantic melodrama, becoming vehicles for star performers, particularly Garbo and Dietrich, became fused with historical costume drama (see above, under Costume Spectacle). At the same time the romantic adventure developed, with the star couplings taking place in the context of a world of violent physical action, self-sacrifice and achievement.

ROMANTIC ADVENTURE

The first great classic of romantic adventure, Josef von Sternberg's *Shanghai Express*, 1932, was unusual, even unique, in concentrating on the compelling persona of the heroine – Shanghai Lily, a woman of ill fame (played by Marlene Dietrich and charismatically photographed by the superlative Lee Garmes) rather than on her stiff, dislikeable lover (a military doctor, played by Clive Brook, whose charisma has *not* stood the test of time). It is still an exciting film, with sacrifice for love at the centre, exotic costumes and setting, and some powerful performances contributing to the plot, particularly from Warner Oland as a Chinese warlord and Anna May Wong as his resentful mistress. The success of this film encouraged Hollywood to invest in further movies of this type (e.g. Capra's *The Bitter Tea of General Yen* of 1933 and Milestone's *The General Died at Dawn* of 1936) and established the romantic adventure as a popular genre.

In the genre during the 1930s and early 1940s, a conventional relationship, varying individually from film to film, developed, in which although worshipped by the heroes in the grip of the world of physical action, the heroines derive their seriousness and value from the way they come to terms with the masculine code in that external world.

Howard Hawks' *Only Angels Have Wings*, 1939, is set in a small Andean airport run by a freight airline operating on a shoestring. Cary Grant is the hard-boiled boss, apparently sending out his pilots with little concern for their safety. Nevertheless, Jean Arthur, the tough but good woman, soon transfers her affections to him, a move that is confirmed by his reactions to the death of an old friend (Thomas Mitchell), who replaces him on a dangerous flight although his eyesight is failing. Grant has humanity, after all. The relationship of this couple is contrasted with a pilot suspected of cowardice (Richard Barthelmess) and his faithless wife (Rita Hayworth). The claustrophobic atmosphere, mostly confined to Dutchy's (Sig Rumann's) saloon, is well conveyed by a mainly male cast whose ensemble playing is first-rate (also including Allan Joslyn, John Carroll and Noah Beery Jr.).

There is a close connection between two Warner Brothers' romantic adventures – Michael Curtiz's *Casablanca*, 1942, and Howard Hawks' *To Have and Have Not*, 1944 – the second a virtual imitation of the first, providing a star persona in Bogart and using the same set at Warner Brothers (transplanted in the second, for the sake of the story, from Morocco to Martinique).

Much of the action in both these films is reported or implied, although *Casablanca* does have the shooting of an undercover agent (played by Peter Lorre) and *To Have and Have Not* has an extended action sequence in which the hero's fishing boat is used to bring a resistance leader to refuge (not for gun-running, as in Hemingway's original novel). For much of the time we are clamped down in the claustrophobic atmosphere of Rick's cafe in *Casablanca*, or a Martinique dive in *To Have and Have Not*, in which the fascinating love affairs are enacted by Bogart with the beautiful, enigmatic Bergman in *Casablanca* and with an abrasive, provocative Bacall in *To Have and Have Not*.

Casablanca (directed by Michael Curtiz) became the great folk cult film of the TV era, partly through the influence of Woody Allen's affectionate lampoon in *Play It Again, Sam*. The romantic appeal is felt through the sensitively treated detail, particularly the Herman Hupfeld song 'As Time Goes By', and the very gripping final sequence where we discover whether or not Bergman will actually leave Bogart. One must not forget the contribution of Claude Rains as a worldly and cynical Vichy officer who reluctantly aids and abets the lovers, and serves as a philosophical yet bitter commentator on this final scene.

With Charles Vidor's *Gilda*, 1946, the emphasis returned to the heroine: "There Never was a Girl like Gilda!", the posters declaimed when the movie was released. It is a difficult film to assess: basically built to formula but achieving effects and reactions that a pedestrian formula movie could never achieve. Everything, however appalling, is produced with such high quality that it becomes a kind of 'art' film in spite of itself. The performances are well-judged and impressive: Rita Hayworth as the *femme fatale* heroine, Glenn Ford as the tough but oversensitive lover, George Macready as the wryly sinister husband, Joseph Calleia – better remembered as a vicious gangster – as a morose, lowering policeman, a taciturn spider lurking in the centre of his web; even Steven Geray, as a treacherous lavatory attendant, makes his mark. The film is a superb *film noir*, with surprisingly taut direction by Charles (the other) Vidor, ending in the renowned sublimation of a strip routine by Hayworth (Put the Blame on Mame, Boys). The lasting appeal of this movie depends on sublimation – of a low instinctive yearning in us, magnetised by the fascination of its flawless comic-strip realism.

Made at RKO by a team who became renowned for their *films noirs* (Jacques Tourneur, director; Nicholas Musaraca, cameraman; Robert Mitchum and Jane Greer, leads), *Out of the Past/Build My Gallows High*, 1947, was a low-budget movie that could do no wrong. It seemed to have everything this style of film required – amoral, cynical hero, *femme fatale* heroine, murder, intrigue, menacing darkness (with chiaroscuro lighting), a laconic voice-over commentary. Kirk Douglas, in an early role as a vengeful gangster, already shows star quality, but does not outshine the rest of the cast. A remarkable collaborative effort, typical of the RKO studios in the immediate post-war period.

Casablanca, WB (Hal Wallis), 1942 bw

*Direction: , Michael Curtiz
Camera: Arthur Edeson
Music: Max Steiner
Art Direction: Carl Jules Weyl
Costume Design: Orry-Kelly
Song: 'As Time Goes By'
  by Herman Hupfeld
Special Effects: Lawrence Butler,
  Willard Van Enger
	*Script: Howard Koch, Julius and Philip Epstein (from unproduced play *Everybody Comes to Rick's* by Murray Burnett and Joan Alison)
	Editing: Owen Marks (with opening montage by Don Siegel)

with Ingrid Bergman, Humphrey Bogart, Claude Rains, Paul Henreid, Conrad Veidt, Sydney Greenstreet, Peter Lorre, Helmut Dantine, Marcel Dalio, John Qualen, S.Z. Sakall, Leonid Kinskey, Dooley Wilson, Dan Seymour, Jonathan Hale, Torben Meyer, Norma Varden, George Meeker (bit)	

- Criticism on release

    Apparently *Casablanca*, which I must say I liked, is working up a rather serious reputation as a fine melodrama. Why? It is obviously an improvement on one of the world's worst plays, but it is not such an improvement that that is not obvious – Rains, Bogart, Henried, Veidt, Lorre, Sakall, and a coloured pianist whose name I forget were a lot of fun, and Ingrid Bergman was more than that; but even so...

    James Agee, *The Nation* 20 February 1943

- Current recommendations and ratings
StJD BN92 S&S82/92 LM4 DQ4 DW5 VFG5 MPG5 NFT***

    ...at least 70% of its cult reputation is deserved. This was Bogart's greatest type role, as the battered, laconic owner of a night club who meets a girl (Bergman) he left behind in Paris and still loves... There are some great supporting performances, and much of the dialogue has become history.

    David Pirie, PTOG 1995

Gilda, Col (Virginia Van Upp), 1946 bw

Direction: Charles Vidor
Camera: Rudolph Maté
Music: Hugo Friedhofer
Script: Marion Parsonnet(from Jo Eisinger's adaptation of E.A. Ellington's story)
Art Direction: Stephen Goosson, Costume Design: Jean Louis Van Nest Polglase
Choreography: Jack Cole
Editing: Charles Nelson

with Rita Hayworth, Glenn Ford, George Macready, Joseph Calleia, Steven Geray, Joe Sawyer, Gerald Mohr, Robert Scott, Ludwig Donath, Don Douglas

- Criticism on release

    ...one is likely to wonder whether the waters of this expensive film have not been deliberately muddied in order to disguise its shallowness – Miss Hayworth... gives little evidence of a talent that should be commoded or encouraged – Glenn Ford... shows, at least, a certain stamina and poise in the role of the tough young gambler – Charles Vidor, who directed, Virginia Van Upp, who produced for Columbia, and a trio of writers deserve no credit at all. They have made out of Gilda a slow, opaque, unexciting film...

    Bosley Crowther, *New York Times* 15 March 1946

- Current recommendations and ratings
StJD S&S82 LM3 DQ4 DW4 VFG4 MPG4 NFT*

    ...The script is laced with innuendoes and euphemisms – Never has the fear of the female been quite so intense...

    Geoff Samuel, PTOG 1995

Only Angels Have Wings, Col (Howard Hawks), 1939 bw

Direction: Howard Hawks
Camera: Joseph Walker, Elmer Dyer
Music: Dimitri Tiomkin, Manuel Maciste, Morris Stoloff
Art Direction: Lionel Banks
Special Effects: Roy Davidson, Edwin C. Hahn

Script: Jules Furthman, with William Rankin, uc and Eleanore Griffin, uc (from Hawks' own story)
Costume Design: Robert Kalloch
Editing: Viola Lawrence

with Cary Grant, Jean Arthur, Richard Barthelmess, Rita Hayworth, Thomas Mitchell, Sig Rumann, John Carroll, Allan Joslyn, Victor Kilian, Don Barry

- Criticism on release

    ...has everything a good film needs except a good story. It is admirably acted by Mr Cary Grant, Miss Jean Arthur, Mr Thomas Mitchell and Mr Richard Barthelmess (who makes another sombre and impressive return to the screen), and it is quite magnificently directed by Howard Hawks – who made *Scarface...* What does remain in the memory is the setting – drab, dusty, authentic, and a few brilliantly directed scenes, as when a young pilot is trying to land in a ground fog...

    Graham Greene, *The Spectator* 20 October 1939

- Current recommendations and ratings
  S&S92 LM3½ DW4 VFG4 MPG4 NFT*

    ...terrific... epic played out in the confined space of the Dutchman's bar: the more claustrophobic because these men are flyers and need the open sky. If it sounds improbable, it is. Mythical cinema at its best.

    Jane Clarke, PTOG 1995

Out of the Past/Build My Gallows High, RKO (Warren Duff), 1947 bw

Direction: Jacques Tourneur
Camera: Nicholas Musuraca
Music: Roy Webb
Art Direction: Albert S. D'Agostino, Jack Okey
Costume Design: Edward Stevenson
Editing: Samuel E. Beetley

Script: Geoffrey Homes (Daniel Mainwaring), from his own novel)
Special Effects: Russell A. Cully

with Robert Mitchum, Jane Greer, Kirk Douglas, Rhonda Fleming, Richard Webb, Steve Brodie, Virginia Huston, Paul Valentine, Dickie Moore

- Criticism on release

    ...intensely fascinating for a time. And it is made even more galvanic by a smooth realistic style, by fast dialogue and genuine settings in California and Mexico locales. But the pattern and purpose of it is beyond our pedestrian ken... However, as we say, it's very snappy and quite intriguingly played by a cast that has been well and smartly directed by Jacques Tourneur. Robert Mitchum is magnificently cheeky and self-assured as the tangled 'private eye'... And Jane Greer is very sleek as his Delilah...

    Bosley Crowther, *New York Times* 26 November 1947

- Current recommendations and ratings
  StJD S&S82/92 LM3½ DW5 VFG5 MPG5 NFT*

    ...one of the most bewildering and beautiful films ever made. From a traditionally doomed and perversely corrupt world, the mood of obsession was never more powerfully suggested – once seen, never forgotten.

    Don MacPherson, PTOG 1995

Shanghai Express, Par, (Adolph Zukor), 1932 bw

Direction: Josef von Sternberg
*Camera: Lee Garmes
Music: W. Franke Harling
Costume Design: Travis Banton
Script: Jules Furthman (based on a story by Harry Hervey)
Art Direction: Hans Dreier
Editing: von Sternberg (uc)

with Marlene Dietrich, Clive Brook, Warner Oland, Eugene Pallette, Lawrence Grant, Louise Closser Hale, Gustav von Seyffertitz

- Criticism on release

    Novel and arresting drama brilliantly directed by Josef von Sternberg, which at last gives Marlene Dietrich a part worthy of her ability and exotic personality. It is a play of character more than action... The acting is brilliant and there are many scenes of poignant drama and tender sentiment thrown into high relief by the glamorous Oriental.

    Picturegoer, 2 April 1932

- Current recommendations and ratings
  StJD S&S82 LM3 DQ4 DW4 VFG5 MPG4 NFT*

    Von Sternberg, who was forever looking for a new kind of stylisation, said that he intended everything in *Shanghai Express* to have the rhythm of a train. He clearly meant it: the bizarre stop-go cadences of the dialogue delivery are the most blatantly non-naturalistic element, but the overall design and dramatic pacing are equally extraordinary... Dietrich's Shanghai Lily hasn't aged a day, but Clive Brook's stiff-upper-lip British officer (her former lover) now looks like a virtual caricature of the type. None the less, the sincerity and emotional depth with which Sternberg invests their relationship is quite enough to transcend mere style or fashion...

    Tony Rayns, PTOG 1995

To Have and Have Not, WB (Howard Hawks), 1944 *bw*

Direction: Howard Hawks
Camera: Sidney Hickox
Musical Direction: Leo Forbstein
Songs: Johnny Mercer,
  Hoagy Carmichael
Art Direction: Charles Novi

Script: Jules Furthman, William
  Faulkner (from the novel by
  Ernest Hemingway)
Costume Design: Milo Anderson
Editing: Christian Nyby

with Humphrey Bogart, Lauren Bacall, Walter Brennan, Dolores Moran, Hoagy Carmichael, Marcel Dalio, Walter Sande, Sheldon Leonard, Dan Seymour, Walter Molnar, Sir Lancelot

- Criticism on release

    ...just another of these Resistance films from which it is about time we were liberated

    Richard Winnington, *News Chronicle* 10 June 1940

    ...Lauren Bacall, who seems to have something of Dietrich, Lake and Garbo in her make-up, allures dangerously and effectively. Humphrey Bogart is very good and an excellent study of his drunken friend is given by Walter Brennan. I liked, too, Hoagy Carmichael as the pianist in a dubious hotel. There are several good spots in the picture, and it entertains throughout in spite of the rather thin story.

    Lionel Collier, *Picturegoer* 7 July 1945

- Current recommendations and ratings
  StJD S&S82/92 LM3½ DW5 VFG4 MPG4 NFT*

    An unassuming masterpiece – the perfect bridge from the free and open world of *Only Angels Have Wings* to the claustrophobic one of *Rio Bravo*... Bogie and Bacall fell in love while making the film, and their scenes reflect this, giving *To Have and Have Not* a degree of emotional presence that is unusual in the 'bite on the bullet' world of Hawks.

    Phil Hardy, PTOG 1995

Romantic Comedy

Trouble in Paradise, 1932, is generally considered to be the finest of the collaborations between Samson Raphaelson (scriptwriter) and Ernst Lubitsch (director): witty, urbane, upper-class, sophisticated escapism of a very high order. This tale of two jewel thieves delightedly competing with each other in guile and deception, only to acknowledge their mutual appreciation of their mastery in an inevitable 'happy ending', is beautifully played by Herbert Marshall and Miriam Hopkins in the leading roles, and also by a consummate team of practised comedians: Charles Ruggles, Edward Everett Horton and C. Aubrey Smith. One cannot take one's eyes from the screen, as the wit is just as visual as verbal, from the opening shot of a gondolier in Venice singing 'O Sole Mio' as it is revealed that he is helping to dispose of the city's garbage!

Raphaelson's and Lubitsch's accomplished comedies usually deal with the upper classes, however bohemian or wayward they might be. The charming comedy, *The Shop around the Corner*, 1940, deals unashamedly with the lower middle class (although Continental) – the expert American cast are adept, under Lubitsch's direction at creating a fairy-tale Budapest. Outstanding are James Stewart and Margaret Sullavan, who find out that they have been corresponding romantically for years, Frank Morgan as the gruff but intrinsically kindly shopowner, Joseph Schildkraut as the smooth, ingratiating salesman – the villain of the piece – and Felix Bressart, as an understanding, philosophical fellow-worker. In this case MGM's glossy production values enhance the charm of this piece.

The characters and dialogue of *The Philadelphia Story*, 1940, are too close to reality for it to be considered as a 'screwball comedy', which is a kind of crazy fairy tale. Philip Barry's play was set firmly in the high society he knew; his wit reflects on a recognisable group of people, stylised for dramatic purposes, very funny but not fantastic. The best description probably would be 'romantic high comedy'. This movie has all the hallmarks of a durable work of art: inspired direction, generally outstanding production values (worthy of MGM), brilliant performances (particularly by the leads and by Ruth Hussey as a matter-of-fact magazine photographer and Virginia Weidler, as the heroine's uncontrollable younger sister). The dramatic development is slow but sure – not a moment is wasted – and the final replacement of Cary Grant for his stuffy rival in Katharine Hepburn's planned wedding is delightfully climactic and satisfying. James Stewart's Oscar for his role as a caustic, crusading reporter in this film seems more deserved for the series of performances that distinguished his career at this time (notably *Mr Smith Goes to Washington* and *The Shop Around the Corner*).

Joseph Mankiewicz's *The Ghost and Mrs Muir*, 1947 – a strong favourite with NFT audiences in recent years – is the ideal well-fashioned, intelligent Hollywood comedy aimed at an audience that wants original entertainment which takes a familiar form. It is good in a satisfying sort of way, rather than experimental: its originality derives from the idea of a romance between a widow and a ghost. It is easy to identify with Gene Tierney's sympathetic heroine, Rex Harrison – with the creative aid of make-up, lighting and camerawork – brings out the bluff impatience of the seafaring ghost wittily and convincingly, George Sanders plays a well-modulated caddish suitor, and Robert Coote is one of the least infuriating of Hollywood Brits. Very little jars in this accomplished entertainment, except possibly the general tendency to depict 'miniature' British locales on the vast scale of a Californian imagination.

If you are allergic to the conventional virtues of the Irish comedy – folksy humour, the 'blarney', a fiery, red-headed beauty, an epic fist-fight, which sprawls over an unbelievably green landscape (the film was shot mostly on location in west Ireland), a collection of beautifully judged performances, mostly by Irish-Americans, (but Barry Fitzgerald, his brother Arthur Shields, and Jack McGowran are all in the cast), and a somewhat fey rendering of the sex war and clan rivalry – then do not bother to see *The Quiet Man*, 1952. John Ford, in tribute to the land of his origin, provides all these with faultless, relaxed craftsmanship, in a modern fairy tale of an Irish-American boxer (John Wayne, always at his best under Ford's direction), who falls in love with a wilful Irish beauty (Maureen O'Hara) with a resentful brother (Victor McLaglen) and masterfully woos her under the constant vigilance of the unpredictable members of a lively village community. Certainly out of the rut for Ford, and... for that reason, special.

The Ghost and Mrs Muir, TCF (Fred Kohlmar), 1947 bw

Direction: Joseph L. Mankiewicz
Camera: Charles Lang
Music: Bernard Herrmann
Art Direction: Richard Day, George W. Davis
Costume Design: Oleg Cassini
Script: Philip Dunne (from a story by R.A. Dick)
Special Effects: Fred Sersen
Editing: Dorothy Spencer

with Gene Tierney, Rex Harrison, George Sanders, Edna Best, Vanessa Brown, Anna Lee, Robert Coote, Natalie Wood, Isobel Elsom

- Criticism on release

    ...gently humorous and often spanking good entertainment, but only up to a point – [Rex Harrison] has such an ingratiating personality that this compensates in large measure for the lack of characterisation in his role. Gene Tierney plays Mrs Muir in what by now may be called her customary inexpressive style... remains a pleasurable film, despite its failings...

    'T.M.P.', *New York Times* 27 June 1947

- Current recommendations and ratings
LM3½ DQ3 DW4 VFG4 MPG4 NFT**

    ...A hugely charming film... beautifully shot [by Charles Lang], superbly acted, and with a haunting score by Bernard Herrmann.

    Tom Milne, PTOG 1995

The Philadelphia Story, MGM (Joseph Mankiewicz), 1941 bw

Direction: George Cukor
Camera: Joseph Ruttenberg
Music: Franz Waxman
Costume Design: Adrian
Art Direction: Cedric Gibbons, Wade B. Rubottom

Script: Donald Ogden Stewart, with Waldo Salt, uncredited, (from a play by Philip Barry)
Editing: Frank Sullivan

with Katharine Hepburn, Cary Grant, *James Stewart, Ruth Hussey, John Howard, Roland Young, Virginia Weidler, John Halliday, Mary Nash, Henry Daniell

- Criticism on release

    ...the story is no mere vehicle [for Miss Hepburn]. Donald Ogden Stewart is credited with an exceptionally bright job of screenplay writing; George Cukor seems to sit with more authority in his director's chair than he has on many another such occasion of reverential transfer; and to have Cary Grant, James Stewart, Roland Young, Ruth Hussey and John Halliday posted about in key positions is a happy thing for all.

    Otis Ferguson, *New Republic* 30 December 1940

- Current recommendations and ratings
StJD S&S92 LM4 DQ4 DW5 VFG4 MPG5 NFT*

    Cukor and Donald Ogden Stewart's evergreen version of Philip Barry's romantic farce, centering on a socialite wedding threatened by scandal, is a delight from start to finish, with everyone involved working on peak form... Superbly directed by Cukor, the film is a marvel of timing and understated performances, effortlessly transcending its stage origins without ever feeling the need to 'open out' in any way...

    Geoff Andrew, PTOG 1995

The Shop Around the Corner, MGM (Ernst Lubitsch), 1940 *bw*

Direction: Ernst Lubitsch	Script: Samson Raphaelson (from a play by Nikolaus Laszlo)
Camera: William H. Daniels	
Music: Werner Heymann	Editing: Gene Ruggiero
Art Direction: Cedric Gibbons, Wade B. Rubottom	

with James Stewart, Margaret Sullavan, Frank Morgan, Joseph Schildkraut, Sara Haden, Felix Bressart, William Tracy, Inez Courtney, Charles Halton, Edwin Maxwell

- Criticism on release

    ...a pretty kettle of bubbling brew it makes under Mr Lubitsch's deft and tender management, and with a genial company to play it gently, well this side of farce and well that side of seriousness. Possibly the most surprising part of it is the adaptability of the players to Mr Lubitsch's Continental milieu whose splendid evocation is one of the nicest things of the picture...

    Frank S. Nugent, *New York Times* 26 January 1940

- Current recommendations and ratings
LM3½ DW4 VFG5 MPG5 NFT*

    ...a marvellously delicate romantic comedy, finally very moving, with the twisted intrigues among the staff also carrying narrative weight, Morgan's cuckolded proprietor being especially affecting...

    Geoff Andrew, PTOG 1995

Trouble in Paradise, Par (Ernst Lubitsch), 1932 bw

Direction: Ernst Lubitsch
Camera: Victor Milner
Music: W. Franke Harling
Art Direction; Hans Dreier
Editing: Lubitsch (uncredited)

Script: Samson Raphaelson, Grover Jones (from a play by Laszlo Aladar)
Costume Design: Travis Banton

with Miriam Hopkins, Kay Francis, Herbert Marshall, Charles Ruggles, Edward Everett Horton, C. Aubrey Smith, Robert Greig, Leonid Kinskey

- Criticism on release

    The Lubitsch magic is again in evidence... In his slyest and most knowing manner, the master of them all lights upon a slender and less than novel tale... and transforms it into a brilliant excursion into cinema light comedy...

    Richard Watts Jr., *New York Herald Tribune*
    9 November 1932

- Current recommendations and ratings
  StJD BN92 S&S82/92 LM4 DQ3 DW4 VFG5 MPG5 NFT*

    ...spins a wonderful, sophisticated tale in praise of immorality, money and sex – Lubitsch's regular script collaborator Samson Raphaelson never bettered the lethal irony of his dialogue here... And the director's famed 'touch', which can on occasion seem like a thump, remains featherweight and incisive throughout... If ever a film slipped down a treat, this one does.

    Geoff Brown, PTOG 1995

The Quiet Man, RKO/ Argosy (Merian C. Cooper/ John Ford), 1952 *colour*

*Direction: John Ford	Script: Frank S. Nugent, Richard Llewellyn (from Maurice Walsh's story)
*Camera: Winton C. Hoch, Archie Stout	
Music: Victor Young	Costume Design: Adele Palmer
Art Direction: Frank Hotaling	
Editing: Jack Murray	

with John Wayne, Maureen O'Hara, Barry Fitzgerald, Ward Bond, Victor McLaglen, Mildred Natwick, Francis Ford, Eileen Crowe, Arthur Shields, Jack McGowran, May Craig

- Criticism on release

    ...John Ford's feeling for landscape, and for the relation between figures and landscape, has seldom been clearer. *The Quiet Man* reminds us how gifted he is in the handling of players. John Wayne (the American) and Victor McLaglen (the squireen) are always at their best with the director, and Maureen O'Hara, not as a rule an actress of charm, gives a performance of great dash. From Barry Fitzgerald (as the matchmaker) we expect good acting, and once more we get it...

    Dilys Powell, *Sunday Times* June 1952

- Current recommendations and ratings
S&S82/92 LM4 DQ3 DW4 VFG5 MPG5 NFT*

    Ford's flamboyantly Oirish romantic comedy hides a few tough ironies deep in its mistily nostalgic recreation of an exile's dream. But the illusion/ reality theme underlying immigrant boxer Wayne's return from America to County Galway... is soon swamped within a vibrant community of stage-Irish 'types'...

    Paul Taylor, PTOG 1995

ROMANTIC DRAMA

First of all, three great movies of the silent era by three masters of the medium – D.W. Griffith's *Broken Blossoms*, 1919, F.W. Murnau's *Sunrise*, 1927, and Victor Sjöström's *The Wind*, 1928. The audiences of the time no doubt judged the movies on the strength of their narrative quality – the first a story of the brutal murder of a boxer's illegitimate daughter by her father and avenged by a Chinaman who both pities and loves her, the second (based on a story by Hermann Sudermann) concerning the planned murder of his wife by a man enticed by another woman, and the third a story (based on Dorothy Scarborough's novel) of a desperate marriage followed by an attempted rape and an accidental killing. All of the sordid themes were completely transformed by the beauty and imaginativeness of the treatment.

Griffith, one of the great creators of film technique, best known for his monumental epics (see Costume Spectacle above), was not content to make *Broken Blossoms* a straightforward narrative: the use of vertical masking (to stress the isolation of the characters), colour tinting (to vary mood), key lighting (later developed in the German Expressionist cinema), and the poetic use of titles (for instance, 'All the tears of the world washed over his heart', when the Chinaman carries home the dead waif) give it an experimental form that helps to maintain its interest today.

Sunrise may be considered as a basically German film made in Hollywood. After an already distinguished career in the German cinema, Murnau was invited as a prestige director to raise the standard of the Fox studio product. His film is as powerfully atmospheric as Griffith's, although Murnau, somewhat ambitiously, attempts to tell his story without titles, which towards the end tends to slow down the rhythm of the work through the necessary introduction of flashbacks to clear up the mysteries. The Hollywood approach, too, marred the final product by introducing a happy ending and inserting broad comedy scenes which clash with the pervading lyricism. But the performances (particularly by Janet Gaynor as the wife – "radiant", *Oxford Companion to Film*) were strong, and the remarkable city set, by Rochus Gliese, a designer also imported from the German cinema, gave Murnau extraordinary freedom of camera angle and movement.

In a recent review of new videos issued, Geoff Brown (*The Times* 24 September 1994) said of *Sunrise*: "The film is powerful enough to make you wish that talking pictures had never been invented." The same could be said of *The Wind*: the silent film was at its apogee when the sound revolution came. Sjöström's treatment is visually imaginative and evocative. In spite of Lillian Gish's beautiful rendering of the heroine, it is the wanton, destructive and teasing Texan wind which remains the film's compelling leading character.

Erich von Stroheim's *Queen Kelly*, 1928, commands respect but, nevertheless, is an extraordinary oddity, particularly since the typically idiosyncratic African scenes have been added to the fully finished first part. Stopped in mid-production by Joseph Kennedy and Gloria Swanson, its financiers – ostensibly because of the advent of sound, but more probably because of mounting costs (von Stroheim had always been a horrendously extravagant director) – this starring vehicle for Swanson became von Stroheim's swansong! He had always shown enormous interest in visual style, in this case sharing the art direction with Richard Day; the film has great visual momentum, with impressive performances by Gloria Swanson, Walter Byron (as the prince-seducer), and Seena Owen (as his mad wife).

Passing on to the sound era, the story of *Camille*, 1936, the quintessential courtesan wasted by consumption and finally dying in her lover's arms, has many attractive qualities, but seems to be completely dependent upon Garbo's presence, which Ferguson called "simply the most absolutely beautiful thing of a generation". Robert Taylor was less disappointing than Gilbert as the young loyal lover, and there is an extraordinary performance by one of the finest English actors in Hollywood at that time, Henry Daniell, as the jilted Baron: "The duet between him and Camille at the piano is superb" (Ferguson, *New Republic*, 24.3.37). The final sequence of Camille's death in her lover's arms has the same technical finesse and brilliance as the final sequence of *Casablanca*.

Dodsworth, 1936, has several points of interest: it is based on one of Sinclair Lewis's novels (a fruitful source of intelligent and dramatic screenplays); it is one of William Wyler's lesser-known masterpieces made at the Goldwyn Studios; and it is a rare example of a screen romance where the lovers are middle-aged, married, and enjoying extra-marital affairs. The wife (Ruth Chatterton) is more promiscuous than Dodsworth himself (Walter Huston); among her lovers feature characters played by David Niven, Paul Lukas, and Gregory Gaye. The hurt and bewildered Dodsworth finds solace with a sympathetic widow (a lively and attractive Mary Astor, in an unusually appealing role). The scenes between husband and wife have an electric vitality, in tenderness and in violent dispute, Huston in particular giving a truly persuasive performance as opposed to Chatterton's more exhibitionist style.

The mammoth *Gone with the Wind*, 1939, perhaps the greatest romantic melodrama of them all, is partly a Civil War epic and partly a piece of simplistic American social history. It was also a landmark in the history of the movies, not only in its inordinate length (with the provision of an intermission for the weary audience halfway through), but also in its well-publicised search for the right actress to play Scarlett O'Hara, in which practically every leading female star in Hollywood appears to have been involved, initiating an intense interest on the part of the public in the actual process of film-making. Several leading screenwriters, four directors, an experienced and inventive production designer (William Cameron Menzies), a leading film composer (Max Steiner), and a long list of acting credits in major and minor roles help to keep audiences enthralled and on tenterhooks until Gable's final "Frankly, my dear, I don't *give* a damn!" and the final reassertion of Scarlett's fighting spirit in the long last trackback of the camera ("Tomorrow is another day!"). The casting of Vivien Leigh was perfect, that of Leslie Howard perhaps less so, but all the performances of a large experienced cast are at the highest level of Hollywood professionalism.

Laurence Olivier presented, in the enigmatic figure of Maxim de Winter, the 'hero' of Hitchcock's *Rebecca*, 1940, a similarly laconic tortured charm to that he had given to his earlier portrayal of Heathcliff in *Wuthering Heights* and his slightly later portrayal of Darcy in *Pride and Prejudice*. *Rebecca* has enough intrigue, suspense and mayhem to justify the choice of Hitchcock as its director by Selznick, who nevertheless kept a pretty tight rein on Hitchcock's treatment, mainly by insisting on fidelity to the original. The model for *Rebecca* is, of course, *Jane Eyre*, and it is in this sense that the heroine (played with convincing and charming 'gaucherie' by Joan Fontaine) and her fascination with De Winter and the mystery surrounding the death of his first wife (the Rebecca of the title) form the romantic centre of a skilfully presented, well performed, love story, with Gothic horror trappings.

Joan Fontaine also provided an appealing study at the centre of *Letter from an Unknown Woman*, 1948, as the married woman who writes to her former lover, a charming but philandering concert pianist (played by Louis Jourdan) to inform him that her son is really his: the letter recapitulates their love affair, which is shown in flashback and leads to a moving and poignant climax. The style of the director, Max Ophüls (imported from Vienna) is easily distinguishable and very distinctive. The story, set in the Vienna of the early twentieth century, could easily have been novelettish, but is redeemed by the intelligent script (Howard Koch) and the taste and sensitivity of the director. Although made in Hollywood, it has a very Viennese feel about it, reminiscent of Ophüls' first Austrian success, *Liebelei*. Robin Wood (*Personal Views - Explorations in Film*) puts it on the highest artistic level (not 'romantic' like a schoolgirl but 'Romantic' like Keats' poetry).

Broken Blossoms, UA (David Wark Griffith), 1919 bw

Direction: D.W. Griffith
Camera: Billy Bitzer, Karl Brown
Special Effects: Hendrik Sartov
Music: Louis Gottschalk, Griffith

Script: Griffith (from story *The Chink and the Child* by Thomas Burke)
Editing: James Smith

with Lillian Gish, Richard Barthelmess, Donald Crisp, Arthur Howard

- Criticism on release

> I found this little picture as arresting as ever. I know of no other in which so much 'screen beauty' is attained. This, I think, is attributable to the Whistlerian fogs and shadows of the setting, and that dock in Limehouse ever recurring like some pedal point. I once read an Eastern poem of but a single line – 'Oh, these wistaria flowers!' Some of that ache is in the acting of the Chinese boy. The performance of little Lillian Gish still seems to me surpassingly true and moving... In this one picture she ranks with the world's great artists...
>
> James Agate, *The Saturday Review*
> 30 September 1922

- Current recommendations and ratings
  StJD S&S82/92 LM3 DW3 MPG5 NFT*

    ...This is in fact Griffith at his best and worst. On the debit side, some risibly highfalutin titles, some naive attempts to impose wider contexts on what is essentially a fragile short story... and a monotonously simplistic view of the drunken prizefighter father's brutality. On the credit side, though, are stretches of pure Griffith poetry, marvellous use of light and shadow in cameraman Billy Bitzer's evocation of foggy Limehouse, and a truly unforgettable performance from Gish.

    Tom Milne, PTOG 1995

Camille, MGM (Irving Thalberg/David Lewis), 1936 bw

Direction: George Cukor
Camera: William H. Daniels, Karl Freund
Music: Herbert Stothart
Art Direction: Cedric Gibbons
Costume Design: Adrian
Editing: Margaret Booth

Script: Zoe Akins, Frances Marion, James Hilton (from a play by Alexandre Dumas Jr. based on his own novel)

with Greta Garbo, Robert Taylor, Lionel Barrymore, Elizabeth Allan, Henry Daniell, Laura Hope Crews, Jessie Ralph, Lenore Ulric

- Criticism on release

    ...a firm and straight-out piece of film work... The work of Henry Daniell as the Baron in particular is a grand, subtle study of a man bred to pride and cynicism and scorn at war with the human immediacies of impulse. Greta Garbo continues in a form that still distresses the high of brow, with a power and unfailing beauty that are undeniable to all brow levels by the million... the mortal eloquence of the love passages, the renunciation, forced quarrel, last words, etc... simply the most absolutely beautiful thing of a generation.

    Otis Ferguson, *New Republic* 23 March 1937

- Current recommendations and ratings
  StJD S&S82 LM3½ DW4 VFG5 MPG5 NFT**

  MGM's high camp 'funereal' decor, the judicious adaptation of Dumas' play, Cukor's gay sensibility in directing women, and William Daniels' atmospheric photography – all these made *Camille* Garbo's most popular film. Her aura of self-knowledge, inner calm and strength of purpose intermeshed finely with elements of the production to produce a tragedy of love-as-renunciation which was closer in spirit to *Hedda Gabler* than to Dumas...

  Martin Sutton, PTOG 1995

Dodsworth, UA (Samuel Goldwyn), 1936 bw

Direction: William Wyler	Script: Sidney Howard (from his play based on Sinclair Lewis's novel)
Camera: Rudolph Maté	
Music: Alfred Newman	
Art Direction: Richard Day	Costume Design: Omar Kiam
Special Effects: Ray Binger	Editing: Daniel Mandell

with Walter Huston, Ruth Chatterton, Paul Lukas, Mary Astor, David Niven, Gregory Gaye, Marie Ouspenskaya, Odette Myrtal, Kathryn Marlowe, John Payne

- Criticism on release

  ...a very well-made and well-acted film, with an essentially trivial subject... Mr Walter Huston is admirable as the devoted and uncultured husband who is ready to stand almost everything once, even adultery, and who cannot rid himself of the deep sense of responsibility he has accumulated in twenty years of marriage, and Miss Ruth Chatterton presents grimly the fake worldliness, embittered egotism, meanness enough to verge on real evil, of his wife – a little marred by almost incessant music, a relic of the small orchestras which used to accompany silent films... [not justified in *Dodsworth*], where the music sentimentally underlines

emotional situations which have been carefully played
down by the actors and the dialogue writers...
                Graham Greene, *The Spectator* 6 November 1936
• Current recommendations and ratings
  LM4 DQ4 DW4 VFG5 MPG5 NFT*
  Not reviewed in PTOG 1995.

Letter from an Unknown Woman, Un (John Houseman),
1948 bw

Direction: Max Ophüls	Script: Howard Koch, Ophüls
Camera: Franz Planer	(from a story by Stefan Zweig)
Music: Daniele Amfitheatrof	Editing: Ted Kent
Art Direction: Alexander Golitzen	Costume Design: Travis Banton

with Joan Fontaine, Louis Jourdan, Mady Christians, Marcel Journet,
    Art Smith, Howard Freeman

• Criticism on release

    ...fascinating to watch the sure, deft means by which the
    director sidetracks seemingly inevitable clichés and
    holds on to a shadowy tender mood, half buried in the
    past. Here is a fragile filmic charm that is not often or
    easily accomplished and to which the sensitive playing
    of Joan Fontaine is perfectly attuned...
                Richard Winnington, *News Chronicle* 7 January 1950
• Current recommendations and ratings
  StJD S&S82/92 LM3 DW4 VFG5 MPG3½ NFT*

    Of all the cinema's fables of doomed love, none is more
    piercing than this... Ophüls' endlessly elaborate camera
    movements, forever circling the characters or co-opting
    them into larger designs, expose the impasse with
    hallucinatory clarity; we see how these people see each
    other and why they are hopelessly, inextricably stuck.
                            Tony Rayns, PTOG 1995

Queen Kelly, UA (Gloria Swanson/Joseph Kennedy), 1928
bw

Direction and Script: Erich von Stroheim	Costume Design: Max Ree
Camera: Ben Reynolds, Paul Ivano, Gordon Pollock	Art Direction: von Stroheim, Richard Day
Music: Adolph Tandler	Editing: Viola Lawrence

with Gloria Swanson, Walter Byron, Seena Owen, Wilhelm von Brincken, Madge Hunt, Wilson Benge, Tully Marshall

- Criticism on release

    There is no way to give a quotation from a criticism on release as in the case of the other films. It was not released in the usual way: while it was still incomplete, Swanson and Kennedy ordered von Stroheim from the set, ostensibly because of the advent of sound, which made a major silent project a white elephant, but also, predictably, more because of growing dissatisfaction with von Stroheim's notoriously extravagant methods of direction. In 1931 Swanson released the film in Europe, with a superimposed musical score by Adolph Tandler, and a completely inappropriate 'suicide' ending. The version at present shown is a carefully reconstructed version dating from 1985.

- Current recommendations and ratings
  S&S92 LM3½ DQ3 DW3 MPG4 NFT**

    ...Transforming the hackneyed melodramatic plot into an audaciously slow spectacle of lush decor and delirious lighting, the Von conjured up a sensuously detailed world of misguided romanticism and seductive cynicism... The present version, deleting the tacked-on 'suicide' ending, incorporates the two edited reels of African footage (on which Stroheim was working when he was fired) which were rediscovered in 1965, fleshed out by the use of titles and stills. The result is a profoundly flawed vision of what might have been, but riveting none the less.

Geoff Andrew, PTOG 1995

Rebecca, UA (David-Selznick), 1940 bw

Direction: Alfred Hitchcock
*Camera: George Barnes
Music: Franz Waxman
Art Direction: Lyle Wheeler
Script: Robert E. Sherwood, Joan Harrison (from the novel by Daphne du Maurier)
Editing: Hal C. Kern

with Joan Fontaine, Laurence Olivier, George Sanders, Judith Anderson, Nigel Bruce, Gladys Cooper, Reginald Denny, C. Aubrey Smith, Florence Bates, Melville Cooper, Leo G. Carroll

- Criticism on release

    ...Joan Fontaine, quite lovely as a bride, lived a miniature hell every minute [in the first half of the picture], and so did I. After that, things began to go (too late)... Hitchcock's infallible sense of timing and camera effect of suspense opened the window and let some fresh air in. And the cast was right there with him...

    Otis Ferguson, New Republic 8 April 1940

- Current recommendations and ratings
    S&S92 LM4 DQ4 DW5 VFG4 MPG4 NFT*

    ...all the financial advantages of America meant that for the first time he could really explore his technical imagination and create a gripping blend of detective story, gothic romance, and psychological drama... A riveting and painful film.

    Helen Mackintosh, PTOG 1995

*Sunrise, Fox, 1927 bw

Direction: F.W. Murnau
*Camera: Charles Rosher, Karl Struss
Art Direction: Rochus Gliese, Alfred Metsch
Editing: Katherine Hilliker

Script: Carl Mayer (from his novel)
Music: Hugo Riesenfeld

with *Janet Gaynor, George O'Brien, Margaret Livingston, Bodil Rosing, J. Farrell MacDonald

- Criticism on release

  [Fred W. Murnau] is one of the men who has grasped the great possibilities of his craft. *Sunrise* is conceived and written like a symphony. In fact, Murnau sub-titles his picture *A Song of Two Humans*... [The opening] is all done with the careful hand of a man who has a fine feeling, a great understanding of humanity, portrayed by a series of direct pictures that seem beautiful enough to have been struck off by one of the old Flemish masters... One of the most stimulating pictures in the city...

  Pare Lorentz, *Judge* 15 October 1927

- Current recommendations and ratings
  StJD S&S82/92 LM4 DW4 MPG5 NFT**

  ...The tension is allowed to drop in a glorious jazz-age city sequence, and then twisted into breaking-point as a journey of murderous rage is repeated. But its dreamlike realism is also to be enjoyed... Simple, and intense images of unequalled beauty.

  Don MacPherson, PTOG 1995

The Wind, MGM (Victor Sjöström), 1928 bw

Direction: Victor Sjöström
Camera: John Arnold
Art Direction: Cedric Gibbons, Edward Withers
Script: Frances Marion, John Cotton (from Dorothy Scarborough's novel)
Editing: Conrad A. Nervig
with Lillian Gish, Lars Hanson, Montagu Love, Dorothy Cummings, Edward Earle

- Criticism on release

    Victor Seastrom [Sjöström] hammers home his point until one longs for just a suggestion of subtlety... [His] wind comes in a strict continuity, with seldom the impression of a gust. And instead of getting along with the story Mr Seastrom makes his production very tedious by constantly calling attention to the result of the wind... In some of the sequences Miss Gish is dainty and charming and she succeeds in giving one the impression of repressed hysteria. Mr Hanson's acting is excellent throughout...

    Mordaunt Hall, *New York Times* 5 November 1928

- Current recommendations and ratings
StJD S&S92 LM4 DQ3 DW3 MPG5 NFT*

    One of cinema's great masterpieces... Swedish émigré Sjöström directs with immaculate attention to psychological detail, while making perfectly credible the film's transition from low-key comedy of manners to full-blown hysterical melodrama – erotic, beautiful, astonishing, [it] demonstrates such imagination and assurance that it remains, sixty years after it was made, completely modern.

    Geoff Andrew, PTOG, 1995

Gone with the Wind, MGM (David O. Selznick), 1939 *colour*
*Direction: Victor Fleming (with George Cukor, William Cameron Menzies, Sam Wood, uncredited)
*Script: Sidney Howard, with Ben Hecht, uncredited (from the novel by Margaret Mitchell)
*Camera: Ernest Haller, Ray Rennahan (with Lee Garmes, uncredited)
Music: Max Steiner   Costume Design: Walter Plunkett
*Art Direction: William Cameron *Editing: Hal C. Kern, James Menzies, Lyle Wheeler   Newcom

with *Vivien Leigh, Clark Gable, Leslie Howard, Olivia de Havilland, Thomas Mitchell, *Hattie McDaniel, Jane Darwell, Victor Jory, Laura Hope Crews, Ward Bond, Cliff Edwards, Ona Munson, Isabel Jewell, Butterfly McQueen, Harry Davenport, Tom Tyler, Frank Faylen, William Bakewell, Eddie ('Rochester') Anderson, Roscoe Ates, J.M. Kerrigan, Louis Jean Heydt, Paul Hurst, Irving Bacon, George Meeker (bit)

- Criticism on release

    ...stands around on its own foot purely out of size and story complexity... history gives out by the end of the first picture, and to keep things going in the sequel they move from period to personal – with some effect but no total success... their ingenuity in pulling this vast sprawl together was enormous and their public acclaim is deserved. They put enough talent into it to make one good picture – but there they were up to the neck in four years, four million dollars, four hours' running time...
    Otis Ferguson, *New Republic* 22 April 1940

- Current recommendations and ratings
StJD BN92 S&S92 LM4 DQ3 DW5 VFG5 MPG5 NFT**

    What more can one say about this much-loved, much discussed blockbuster? It epitomises Hollywood at its most ambitious (not so much in terms of art, but of middlebrow, respectable entertainment on a polished platter)... It never really confronts the political or historical context of the Civil War, relegating it to a backdrop for the emotional upheavals of Leigh's conversion from bitchy Southern belle to loving wife... yet, although anonymous, it's still remarkably coherent.

Geoff Andrew, PTOG 1995

Thrillers – Criminal Investigations, Gangster Melodrama, Psychological Suspense, Spy Melodrama

'Thriller' remains a necessary though unsatisfactory label for a very wide range of films involving some kind of crime or intrigue described with an element of suspense. My subdivision of the genre into Criminal Investigations ('police' and 'private eye' thrillers), Gangster Melodramas, Psychological Suspense Dramas, and Spy Melodramas is an attempt to recognise those sub-groups (or sub-genres, as they are sometimes called) in which the films have many qualities in common and which can be distinguished from other subgroups by dramatic aim or theme.

The term *Film Noir* should not be used for the categorisation of genres. As Colin McArthur pointed out (in his *Underworld, USA*, 1972): "As applied to films like *The Maltese Falcon*, *The Big Sleep* and other private-eye movies of the forties, the label 'thriller' is perhaps less satisfactory than the French critical term *film noir*, which comments on the mood of the films; though since it comments on a mood rather than a set of conventions making up a genre, it can be applied to individual films, thrillers, gangster films, police documentaries, or even to films in which the crime element is marginal, such as *The Lost Weekend*." Some *films noirs* have already been discussed under other genres – *The Lost Weekend* (Drama – Addiction), Wilder's *Ace in the Hole* and Mackendrick's *Sweet Smell of Success* (Drama – The Press), Wilder's *Sunset Boulevard* (Drama – Moviola) and Charles Vidor's *Gilda* (Romantic Adventure) – but the richest finds will undoubtedly be in the 'thriller' sub-genres.

CRIMINAL INVESTIGATIONS

The starting-point of most of these films was the literary 'whodunits' of the 1920s and 1930s, based on the investigation into a murder by a policeman or amateur detective (sometimes both), with a large number of suspects and the discovery – finally – that the most unexpected was the guilty party. This was a familiar theme in movies of the 1930s, featuring such detectives as The Saint, The Falcon, Charlie Chan, Ellery Queen (badly translated to the screen), Nero Wolfe, and Nick Charles (the miscalled 'Thin Man'). The original *Thin Man*, directed by W.C. Van Dyke for MGM in 1934, dealt with the disappearance of a quirky inventor (the real 'Thin Man' of the title) and a series of puzzling murders set in a wintry New York of penthouses and gangland. Frances Goodrich's and Albert Hackett's lively script was very faithful to Dashiell Hammett's novel: their own contribution included a gathering of suspects at a final dinner party given by Nick and Nora Charles (wittily and engagingly played by William Powell and Myrna Loy) in preparation for the exposure of the murderer (a device which was used consistently in the successful sequels starring the same couple). The movie combined an exciting mystery story with an entertaining screwball comedy in perfect balance.

During the Forties, when themes and performances became blacker, the amateur became a hired private detective (usually known as a private eye or 'shamus'). None of the classics of this genre relies entirely upon formula (it is well-known, for example, that the scriptwriters of *The Big Sleep* were quite confused about one of its murders: see Roger Shatzkin's *Who Cares Who Killed Owen Taylor?* in *The Modern American Novel and the Movies*, edited by Gerald Peary and Roger Shatzkin, 1978). They all make original and significant variations upon the basic theme and, in several cases, so transcend the genre that they become important films of character study in a well-observed social context, for example, *Crossfire*, *Laura*, *Rear Window*, and *Vertigo*.

All these films, except *Rear Window*, are recognised *films noirs* (see Alain Silver and Elizabeth Ward, Eds., *Film Noir*, 1979, and Robert Ottoson, *A Reference Guide to the American Film Noir*, 1940-58, 1981), either for their narrative or visual styles. In each case there is an all-pervading atmosphere of corruption, sadism and violence and an inventive collaboration between director and cameraman in the creation of a sleazy, oppressive, urban night world. *Laura* and *Touch of Evil* have policemen weak in principle ('rogue cops') as central characters, while *The Big Sleep*, *The Lady from Shanghai*, *Laura* and *The Maltese Falcon* have notable *femmes fatales*.

It was *The Maltese Falcon* that set the tone for future private eye *noir* films of the 1940s. John Huston's treatment, which earned him the right to direct this film, was far superior to the previous version and a further adaptation, *Satan Met a Lady* (in 1936), possibly because it was more faithful to the original Dashiell Hammett novel. The pace of the narrative, first-rate photography (by Arthur Edeson), outstanding characterisations by Greenstreet as the obese, belly-giggling Gutman (his movie debut at sixty-one), Lorre (as the epicene

Cairo), and Astor (as the cinema's most fascinatingly ruthless *femme fatale*, Brigid O'Shaughnessy), together with Bogart's charismatic contribution as the private eye, Sam Spade, make this a perfect film of its kind.

Murder My Sweet/Farewell My Lovely, 1944, introduced Raymond Chandler's Philip Marlowe to the screen as *The Maltese Falcon* had Dashiell Hammett's Sam Spade. Played in a new 'tough guy' image by former crooner Dick Powell (rather surprisingly, preferred by Chandler to all other Marlowes), his morality is strictly his own, with no reference to official authority, conventional manners or respectable taste. The script (by John Paxton) renders the 'Chandler-isms' faithfully, the direction (by Edward Dmytryk) is taut and sympathetic, and the atmosphere of sleazy affluence is well captured, while all the convolutions of the storyline – Marlowe seeks a missing girlfriend, Velma, for the brutish, naive Moose Malloy (a fine performance by Mike Mazurki) – are clearly revealed, with the help of Harry J. Wild's inventive camerawork and the performances of a first-rate cast.

Marlowe reappears in Howard Hawks' *The Big Sleep*, 1946, played by Bogart very much in the style of his Sam Spade. Once again cynical badinage cloaks an integrity and sensitivity of which one almost feels ashamed. One major difference between the two portrayals is that, this time, his love is not a self-seeking and conscienceless *femme fatale* but a general's abrasive daughter (played by Lauren Bacall) with a nymphomaniac sister, a gangster ex-husband, and a gift for suggestive repartee. The emphasis of the film is upon character and atmosphere rather than upon plot, which is difficult to follow, not less so because of the need to omit certain references (e.g. homosexuality and pornography) which would have offended the Hays Code.[4] Nevertheless, *The Big Sleep* will always rank high as a Howard Hawks movie, a Bogart-Bacall vehicle, and a tense, exciting *film noir*.

Robert Aldrich's *Kiss Me Deadly*, 1955, is a successful, even great, *film noir*, although by the mid-50s the style had possibly been overworked. Aldrich miraculously achieves the impossible: an original, stylish *film noir* with an implausible plot based on a sequence of existentialist, near-surrealistic events and a crude, private eye anti-

---

[4] See page 98.

hero, Mike Hammer, creation of Mickey Spillane. Aldrich himself avoids crudity, except, possibly, with the ultimate solution to the puzzle, but fortunately Albert Dekker is so expert a villain that the finale is raised to a curious kind of surrealism in keeping with the expression of the whole. *Kiss Me Deadly* is the ideal cult film, because there is so much to fault in it, but more to admire. The atmosphere and characterisation, the movement (so many jump cuts!) and weird camera angles take the viewer right out of this world.

Robert Towne's script to Roman Polanski's *Chinatown*, 1974, is a screen original, and as dense and exciting as any based on Hammett or Chandler. That this film, in recent years, has begun to challenge Orson Welles' *Citizen Kane* as the best-ever made in Hollywood is largely due to the quality of the script and of the performances (John Huston, Faye Dunaway, and, in particular, Jack Nicholson whose J.P. Gittes is a distinctive contribution to the gallery of shady but honest private eyes). Set in 1937, when Los Angeles was a more compact desert city dependent upon a monopoly water supply, the story exploits period values while being sharply modern. The director himself plays a small key role as a knife-wielding hood, as faultlessly handled as the total *mise en scène*.

The 'police thrillers' are as moody and atmospheric as the private eye thrillers – the police detective (Dana Andrews) in *Laura* carries out his investigations in high-bracket penthouse apartments which, though elegant, become almost intolerably claustrophobic during the film; Robert Young's investigations in *Crossfire* of a murder by a soldier moves through a hauntingly seedy night world; in *The Naked City*, two policemen, old and young, pursue their prey through the actual streets and buildings of New York in the spirit of the semi-documentary thrillers developed at Twentieth Century-Fox by March of Time producer Louis De Rochemont, of which *Boomerang* is a classic example; and *Touch of Evil* is set in what Pauline Kael (in *Kiss Kiss – Bang Bang*) has called "the nightmare city" of Venice, California. The themes are equally individual and receive original treatment in each case. *Laura*, 1944, beginning as a witty and elegant whodunit, takes a bizarre turn in the middle when the beautiful eponymous heroine (played by Gene Tierney) is found not to be dead after all, but stunningly alive. The detective in charge of the murder hunt has already become obsessed by her being, so now the narrative becomes a haunting love story as well as a clever murder puzzle. The dialogue is crackling and pungent, and characterisation (in addition to Dana Andrews's impressive performance), particularly by Clifton Webb as an acidulous columnist and Vincent Price as a decadent playboy, is incisive under Preminger's unemotional direction.

For some reason, *Crossfire*, 1947, was considered anti-American: its producer, Adrian Scott, and director, Edward Dmytryk, found themselves under bitter attack during the McCarthy witch-hunt. A beautifully wrought film, thoughtful and tense, it remains memorable less for its plot than for the discovery that the motive for the murder was anti-Semitism (in the original novel by Richard Brooks it was homophobia). Brilliant playing by Robert Ryan, Robert Young, Robert Mitchum, Gloria Grahame, Paul Kelly, Steve Brodie and Sam Levene, a superb script (by John Paxton) and general technical perfection give this police melodrama a timeless quality. The scriptwriter of *The Naked City* (Albert Maltz) was also blacklisted by the Un-American Activities Committee. He brings a strong element of social criticism to a 'police documentary thriller' concerned with the day-by-day probing of two Irish-American police detectives (tetchy, experienced Barry Fitzgerald, callow but imaginative Don Taylor) into the death of a young out-of-town girl, whose parents, against a background of steel girders, inveigh against the evils of the big city. As the murder was carried out by a conspiracy between a corrupt policeman (Ted De Corsia) and a rich layabout (Howard Duff) there is plenty of scope to make attacks on greed and wealth in this 'urban jungle' setting. Perhaps more typical as a Mark Hellinger production than as a film directed by Jules Dassin, it was received with critical acclaim and public approval.

Nearly all of Orson Welles' work, even the Shakespeare films, are *noir*-orientated: *Touch of Evil*, 1958, is the blackest of all these police thrillers, with an unforgettably corrupt world, a massive and monumental 'rogue cop' (Hank Quinlan, played in grotesque make-up by Welles himself), a gallery of bizarre and repellent minor characters, including those portrayed by Akim Tamiroff and Mercedes McCambridge, a complex, puzzling narrative full of violence (murder, bomb explosions, gang-rape), all told with Welles's favourite battery of Expressionist tricks of the trade – angled cameras, low-key lighting, the use of shadows to dominate and menace characters. There is also a conscious attempt to imitate B police movies and an ultimate moral ambiguity as in all the best *film noirs*. By the end of the film the fanatically incorruptible Vargas (Charlton Heston) has gradually lost the viewer's sympathy to the almost understandably corrupt Quinlan who can command devotion from his deputy (Joseph Calleia) and the elusive 'Fate' figure of Tanya (Marlene Dietrich). It is she who delivers, on Quinlan's death in the rubbish-strewn river, the final epitaph ("He was some kind of a man"), before disappearing into the darkness ("Adios!").

Many of the great Hollywood films were made by foreign directors who had already established themselves in their home industry (for example, Roman Polanski's *Chinatown*). A fruitful source of such directors was the Australian film industry: another such film was undoubtedly Peter Weir's *Witness*, 1985, in which Harrison Ford came of age as a leading actor. Weir's reputation for weirdness of theme and Ford's for tough integrity combined splendidly in this police thriller set mainly in a convincingly realised Amish community. Escape into an anachronistic past provides shelter for a cop who has smoked out corruption amongst his colleagues: the lead is given by a young Amish boy who accidentally witnesses a murder in a public lavatory. Kelly McGillis's Amish mother is inevitably attractive, but also, in a sense, alien, and this introduces an intriguing sexual and domestic tangle into a tense thriller plot.

The remaining films of criminal investigation are closely related to 'police' and 'private eye' thrillers, but belong to neither group in their entirety. In *Double Indemnity*, 1944, the story is told (in flashback) by one of the conspiring criminals, Walter Neff, a womanising insurance salesman (Fred MacMurray), although he works and closely identifies himself with the insurance claims officer, Barton Keyes (Edward G. Robinson). The *femme fatale* (Barbara Stanwyck) who seduces him into murdering her husband (Tom Powers) for the insurance is one of the most archetypal in the genre, and Billy Wilder's script (adapted with Raymond Chandler from James Cain's novella) provides a relentless, gripping inevitability to what is basically a brutal morality play. It is beautifully lit in true *noir* style by John F. Seitz and accompanied by moody Miklos Rozsa music. There may be doubts about the inclusion of some movies in this book as classics, but the reputation of this movie among critics and viewers alone makes this a certain choice.

Spellbound, 1945, a relatively early American Hitchcock, is not considered one of the master's great works: the leads – Gregory Peck and Ingrid Bergman – give rather stiff performances, the psychoanalytical approach is somewhat phoney, and the dream sequence is not Dali at his very best. The films that Hitchcock did with Selznick are not first-rank Hitchcock, possibly because two very positive creative personalities did not harmonise perfectly; however, as a whodunit solved in a psychoanalytical setting by psychoanalytical means, *Spellbound* has a kind of distinctiveness, and the supporting players, particularly Leo G. Carroll (one of Hitchcock's favourite stock players) and Michael Chekhov, are very good. Even a 'bad' Hitchcock can be a 'good' movie, because of its technical brilliance.

In Welles's *The Lady from Shanghai* there is also a classic *femme fatale* study in Rita Hayworth's Elsa Bannister; the trapped hero, O'Hara (played by Welles himself), an Irish sailor charged with murder because of his besotted love for her, is driven into investigation to clear himself. The film is best known for its final climactic shooting between Elsa and her serpentine husband (Everett Sloane, one of Welles's original Mercury Company players) in a hall of mirrors, but in fact the whole movie requires closer attention, not only because it is difficult to keep in touch with the storyline, but because there are many other memorable scenes (including a declaration of false love before the giant images of fish in a heated aquarium) and a remarkable integration between the rich kaleidoscope of visual images (photographed by Charles Lawton Jr.) and the moody atmospheric music of Heinz Roemheld.

'Bogie's' performances were unique in the ability to hint at feelings so far below the surface that they can never be brought to light. In his portrayal of the ambiguously violent screenwriter, Dixon Greene, in *In a Lonely Place*, 1950, the capacity to portray hatred based on self-disgust is absolutely vital to this spare, muscular thriller (directed with intense concentration by Nicholas Ray). Did Greene murder the hat-check girl 'in a lonely place' or not? The girl across the way (Gloria Grahame) provides him with an alibi, but she, like others who know him, begins to fear his sometimes illogical fury – in the end, so much that, although she loves him, she must leave him. This is one of Grahame's great performances – and also one of Bogart's. The movie itself is a model of succinctness and power, particularly as it is an allegory as well as an enthralling narrative – the 'lonely place' is also Hollywood in the late 40s.

Hitchcock selected one of his favourite stars, James Stewart, to lead the investigation in two of his most intriguing mystery thrillers – *Rear Window*, 1954, and *Vertigo*, 1958. In the first he plays (with outraged yet helpless charm) the role of a young photographer, immobilised by a broken leg, who gradually and reluctantly begins to identify the activities of a wife-killer opposite (in an apartment block ingeniously constructed in the studio). Grace Kelly, Thelma Ritter, and Raymond Burr give him excellent support. In the second (*Vertigo*), he plays a neurotic ex-policeman turned private eye; this, until the final reels, is essentially an intelligent whodunit, based on a story by Pierre Bouleau and Thomas Narcejac, playing the same kind of sleight of hand with their characters as in Clouzot's *Les Diaboliques*. Hitchcock has said that he reveals the solution of the puzzle concerning the 'two heroines' (played by Kim Novak) because this was less important to his purpose than the irony of the audience being able to observe Stewart's reactions, particularly in the final sequence where he has to overcome his guilt concerning his fear of heights in order to solve the mystery surrounding the girl he thinks he loves. *Vertigo*'s reputation has gained considerably since its first release; it is now recognised as one of Hitchcock's most complex and intriguing films.

Two fascinating crime puzzles take place mostly in the courtroom. Strange that Billy Wilder's *Witness for the Prosecution*, 1957, should have such a high reputation ahead of, say, *Stalag 17*, *Sabrina*, or *The Fortune Cookie*! Based on an Agatha Christie play, it has recognisable faults, particularly a most unlikely plot stressing the mystery, enacted by two-dimensional characters. Wilder makes a good brew-up, though, with a tantalisingly ambiguous American anti-hero (Tyrone Power) and his resourceful German wife (who else but Marlene Dietrich?), and a bravura performance by Charles Laughton as the defence counsel, a truculent patient in the hands of his ministering nurse, played by Laughton's real-life wife, Elsa Lanchester. Alexander Trauner's accurate and atmospheric reproduction of London's Old Bailey received high praise. Much to commend then, but not exactly a masterpiece!

Stewart once more stars in one of the best of Preminger's works, *Anatomy of a Murder*, 1959, which captures the atmosphere of small-town Michigan faithfully and evocatively, while presenting an unusual whodunit theme through a well-recorded, tautly developed court case involving the defence of Ben Gazzara as an army lieutenant charged with murdering a man whom his wife alleges was attempting to rape her. The intimate details of the legal evidence caused quite a stir at the time. Today it seems a leisurely, well-integrated suspense drama with some pleasantly distinctive features: for instance, Saul Bass's introductory credits, Stewart's piano duet with Duke Ellington, and a one-off, fascinating study of a cryptic, understanding judge by a real-life judge, Joseph L. Welch, who had presided over the McCarthy hearings in 1953.

The 1990s produced the most bizarre of criminal investigations on film: Jonathan Demme's *The Silence of the Lambs*, 1991, (adapted from Thomas Harris's best-seller), where, although the horror is coincidental, there is no doubt that Anthony Hopkins's portrayal of an incarcerated serial killer ('Hannibal the Cannibal') will rank among the most memorable of recent movie monsters. As a psychotic psychiatrist his aid is required to read the mind of another serial killer at large ('Buffalo Bill') who clothes himself in the flayed skin of his fat female victims. Sadistically, an FBI agent (Scott Glenn) assigns an attractive woman trainee agent (Jodie Foster) to persuade him to provide clues to the killer's motives and movements. This is an intelligent, well-crafted psychological detective thriller with an unsavoury theme and a lot of excitement for tougher viewers. Hopkins's performance is extraordinary, and Jodie Foster is not far behind: their confrontations are hyper-tense highlights in a very tense film.

Anatomy of A Murder, Col (Otto Preminger), 1959 bw

Direction: Otto Preminger	Script: Wendell Mayes (from the novel by Robert Traver)
Camera: Sam Leavitt	
Music: Duke Ellington	Art Direction: Boris Leven
Credit Titles: Saul Bass	Editing: Louis Loeffler

with James Stewart, Lee Remick, Ben Gazzara, Joseph N. Welch, George C. Scott, Arthur O'Connell, Duke Ellington, Eve Arden, John Conlin, Kathryn Grant

- Criticism on release

    ...Such a virtuoso piece calls for expert direction and playing; and this it gets. Not for a long time has James Stewart subjugated his personal style and mannerisms so completely to the need of a part: Lee Remick is extremely good as the restive frivolous wife, and Ben Gazzara has no equal in conveying the prisoner's veiled but seismic private world. But perhaps the best performance of all comes from Joseph N. Welch [whose] judge is a quaint, dry and superbly discreet showman.

    Derek Prouse, *Sunday Times* 4 October 1959

- Current recommendations and ratings
StJD LM4 DQ3 VFG4½ MPG4 NFT*

    One of Preminger's most compelling and perfectly realised films (with a terrific Duke Ellington score)... it's remarkable for the cool, crystal clear, direction, concentrating on the mechanical processes and professional performances guiding the trial, and for the superb acting... [One suspects] that it was this probing cynicism rather than the 'daring' use of words that caused controversy at the time of release.

    Geoff Andrew, PTOG 1995

The Big Sleep, WB (Howard Hawks), 1946 bw

Direction: Howard Hawks	Script: Jules Furthman, William Faulkner, Leigh Brackett (from the novel by Raymond Chandler)
Camera: Sidney Hickox	
Music: Max Steiner	
Art Direction: Carl Jules Weyl	
Editing: Christian Nyby	Costume Design: Leah Rhodes

with Humphrey Bogart, Lauren Bacall, Martha Vickers, John Ridgeley, Dorothy Malone, Regis Toomey, Bob Steele, Elisha Cook Jr., Charles D. Brown, Louis Jean Heydt, Marc Lawrence

- Criticism on release

    ...the Odysseus of the new world is now the shamus – private dick or eye – put into dour and classical prototype by Humphrey Bogart. I found these dowdy heroics fascinating and I recommend the film wholeheartedly both as entertainment and as a study in social sadism...

    Richard Winnington, *News Chronicle* 1 September 1946

- Current recommendations and ratings
  StJD BN92 S&S82/92 LM4 DQ4 DW5 VFG5 MPG5 NFT**

    One of the finest mainstream noir-thrillers ever made... the story is virtually incomprehensible at points, but who cares when the sultry mood, the incredibly witty and memorable script, and the performances, are so impeccable?

    Geoff Andrew, PTOG 1995

Crossfire, RKO (Dore Schary/Adrian Scott), 1947 *bw*

Direction: Edward Dmytryk Script: John Paxton (from the
Camera: J. Roy Hunt   novel by Richard Brooks)
Music: Roy Webb   Editing: Harry Gerstad
Art Direction: Albert S.
    D'Agostino, Al Herman
with Robert Young, Robert Mitchum, Robert Ryan, Gloria Grahame, Paul Kelly, Sam Levene, Jacqueline White, Steve Brodie, Richard Benedict

- Criticism on release

    ...small (in the trade sense of cost and settings) and courageous... [Ryan] is spine-chilling. [This is a] thriller that insists on being more than a fairy tale. And this realistic slanting somehow adds to the consciousness of the actors...

    Richard Winnington, *News Chronicle*
    16 September 1944

- Current recommendations and ratings
  StJD LM3½ DQ3 DW4 VFG4 MPG4 NFT*

  This ultra-low-budget did what all great B movies do: it broached a subject that 'respectable' movies wouldn't touch... Dmytryk exploits the poverty-row sets for their claustrophobic quality, and introduces 'expressionist' lighting and distorted angles to dramatise the tensions that simmer and finally explode between the characters, GIs back from the war in Europe but not yet discharged... the kind of movie that provoked the McCarthy witch-hunt in Hollywood.

  Tony Rayns, PTOG 1995

Double Indemnity, Par (Joseph Sistrom), 1944 bw

Direction: Billy Wilder	Script: Wilder, Raymond Chandler
Camera: John F. Seitz	(from story by James Cain)
Music: Miklos Rozsa	Editing: Doane Harrison
Art Direction: Hans Dreier, Hal Pereira	
Costume Design: Edith Head	

with Barbara Stanwyck, Fred MacMurray, Edward G. Robinson, Porter Hall, Jean Heather, Tom Powers, Fortunio Bonanova

- Criticism on release

  ...Wilder, from beginning to end the complete master of his story, tells it with consummate economy and packs it with visual subtlety... The idiom is harsh and salty, the deliberately vulgar atmosphere primed with the sultry, cruel passion of shoddy, selfish violent characters. There is a minimum of cliché...

  Richard Winnington, *News Chronicle*
  16 September 1944

- Current recommendations and ratings
  StJD BN92 S&S92 LM4 DQ4 DW5 VFG5 MPG5 NFT***

...certainly one of the darkest thrillers of its time: Wilder presents Stanwyck and MacMurray's attempt at an elaborate insurance fraud as a labyrinth of sexual dominance, guilt, suspicion and sweaty duplicity. Chandler gave the dialogue a sprinkling of characteristic wit, without mitigating any of the overall sense of oppression.

Tony Rayns, PTOG, 1995

In a Lonely Place, Col (Robert Lord, Henry S. Kesler), 1950 bw

Direction: Nicholas Ray	Script: Andrew Solt (from a story by Edmund North, adapted from the novel by Dorothy B. Hughes)
Camera: Burnett Guffey	
Music: George Antheil	
Art Direction: Robert Anderson	
Editing: Viola Lawrence	Costume Design: Jean Louis

with Humphrey Bogart, Gloria Grahame, Frank Lovejoy, Carl Benton Reid, Art Smith, Martha Stewart, Jeff Donnell, Robert Warwick, Morris Ankrum, William Ching

- Criticism on release

    Humphrey Bogart is in top form in his latest independently-made production... and the picture itself is a superior cut of melodrama... The actor plays with such terrific drive that one is content not to pick the characterization apart. Gloria Grahame gives a smoldering portrayal... Mr Bogart had a good team, marshalled by Nicholas Ray, and the result is that *In a Lonely Place* comes off a dandy film.

    'T.M.P.', New York Times 18 May 1950

- Current recommendations and ratings
StJD S&S82/92 LM3 DQ3 DW4 VFG5 MPG5 NFT*

    ...Ray's classic thriller remains as fresh and resonant as the day it was released – an achingly poetic meditation

on pain, distrust and loss of faith, not to mention an admirably unglamorous portrait of Tinseltown...
> Geoff Andrew, PTOG 1995

Kiss Me Deadly, UA (Robert Aldrich), 1955 bw

Direction: Robert Aldrich
Camera: Ernest Laszlo
Music: Frank De Vol
Art Direction: William Glasgow
Editing: Michael Luciano

Script: A.I. Bezzerides, from Mickey Spillane's novel
Songs: De Vol

with Ralph Meeker, Albert Dekker, Paul Stewart, Juano Hernandez, Gaby Rodgers, Maxine Cooper, Cloris Leachman, Jack Lambert, Jack Elam, Fortunio Bonanova, Wesley Addy, Marian Carr, Strother Martin, Marjorie Bennett (bit)

- Criticism on release

    It is pointless to try to sum up the plot... You have to see it a few times before you realize it is very solidly constructed, and that it tells an ultimately quite logical story – the inventiveness is so rich that we don't know what to look at... the images are almost too full, too fertile. Watching a film like this is such an intense experience that we want it to last for hours...
    > François Truffaut, *Cahiers du Cinema*, 1955

- Current recommendations and ratings
StJD S&S82/92 LM3½ DW2 VFG4 MPG4 NFT*

    A key film from the '50s – [Mickey Spillane's hero] acquires new resonance as an example of mankind's mulish habit of meddling with the unknown regardless of consequences. Brilliantly characterised down to the smallest roles, directed with baroque ferocity, superbly shot by Ernest Laszlo in 'film noir' terms, it's a masterpiece of sorts.
    > Tom Milne, PTOG 1995

The Lady from Shanghai, Col (Orson Welles), 1948 bw

Direction: Orson Welles
Camera: Charles Lawton Jr.
Music: Heinz Roemheld
Art Direction: Stephen Goosson, Sturges Carne
Special mirror effects: Lawrence Butler
Script: Welles (from the novel *Before I Die* by Sherwood King)
Editing: Viola Lawrence
Costume Design: Jean Louis

with Orson Welles, Rita Hayworth, Everett Sloane, Glenn Anders, Ted De Corsia, Erskine Sanford, Gus Schilling, Harry Shannon

- Criticism on release

    ...the Wellesian ability to direct a good cast against fascinating backgrounds has never been better displayed in the subtle suggestion of corruption, of selfishness and violence in this group, intermingled with haunting wisps of pathos. Mr Welles could not have done a better job, [but he] certainly could have done better than use himself in the key role of the guileless merchant sailor who is taken in by a woman's winning charm...

    Bosley Crowther, *New York Times* 10 June 1946

- Current recommendations and ratings
StJD BN92 S&S82 LM3 DQ3 DW5 VFG5 MPG3½ NFT*

    ...the principal pleasure of *The Lady from Shanghai* is its tongue-in-cheek approach to story-telling... One intriguing reading of the movie is that it's a commentary on Welles' marriage to Hayworth... the scene in the hall of mirrors, where the temptress's face is endlessly reflected back at him, stands as a brilliant expressionist metaphor for sexual unease and its accompanying loss of identity. Complex, courageous, and utterly compelling.

    Martyn Auty, PTOG 1995

Laura, TCF (Otto Preminger), 1944 bw

Direction: Otto Preminger
*Camera: Joseph La Shelle
Music: David Raksin
Art Direction: Lyle Wheeler, Leland Fuller
Costume Design: Bonnie Cashin
Editing: Louis Loeffler

Script: Jay Dratler, Samuel Hoffenstein, Betty Reinhardt with Ring Lardner Jr., uncredited (from the novel by Vera Caspary)

with Dana Andrews, Gene Tierney, Clifton Webb, Vincent Price, Judith Anderson, Dorothy Adams, James Flavin, Grant Mitchell

- Criticism on release

    ...a thriller of the type which it is now popular to call psychological... a neat job in this contemporary style, proceeding by an exposition of character less banal than usual and making pretty use of suspense and surprise... The story has been well written for the cinema, it is skilfully directed by Otto Preminger, formerly better known as a screen player, [and though] it is not in the class of *The Maltese Falcon* or *Double Indemnity*, shows throughout a nice sense of straightforward cinema technique...

    Dilys Powell, *Sunday Times* December 1944

- Current recommendations and ratings
  StJD BN92 S&S92 LM4 DQ3 DW5 VFG5 MPG5 NFT**

    ...Less investigative thriller than an investigation of that genre's conventions – voyeurism (looking at, and for, Laura), a search for solutions (not just whodunit but whodunwhat), and the race against time (clues and clocks, fantasies and flashbacks) – the plot is deliberately perfunctory, the people deliciously perverse, and the *mise-en-scène* radical.

    Paul Kerr, PTOG 1995

The Maltese Falcon, WB (Hal Wallis), 1941 bw

Direction: John Huston
Camera: Arthur Edeson
Music: Adolph Deutsch
Costume Design: Orry-Kelly
Script: Huston (from the novel by Dashiell Hammett)
Art Direction: Robert Haas
Editing: Thomas Richards

with Humphrey Bogart, Mary Astor, Sydney Greenstreet, Peter Lorre, Gladys George, Elisha Cook Jr., Barton MacLane, Lee Patrick, Jerome Cowan, Ward Bond, James Burke, Walter Huston (bit)

- Criticism on release

    ...the first crime melodrama with finish, speed and bang to come along in what seems ages, and since its pattern is one of the best things Hollywood does, we have been missing it... There is character in the picture and this, as well as the swift succession of its contrived excitements and very shrewd dialogue, is what gives the temporary but sufficient meaning required by its violent fantasy.

    Otis Ferguson, *New Republic* 20 October 1941

- Current recommendations and ratings
  StJD BN92 S&S82/92 LM4 DQ4 DW5 VFG5 MPG5 NFT**

    Huston's first film displays the hallmarks that were to distinguish his later work – the amiably snarling Sam Spade... opened a whole new romantic career for Bogart... What makes it a prototype 'film noir' is the vein of unease missing from the two earlier versions of Hammett's novel. Filmed almost entirely in interiors, it presents a claustrophobic world animated by betrayal, perversion and pain, never quite losing sight of this central abyss darkness, ultimately embodied by Mary Astor's sadly duplicitous siren.

    Tom Milne, PTOG 1995

Murder My Sweet/ Farewell My Lovely, RKO, (Adrian Scott), 1944 bw

Direction: Edward Dmytryk
Camera: Harry J. Wild
Music: Roy Webb
Art Direction: Albert S. D'Agostino, Carroll Clark
Special Effects: Vernon Walker
Editing: Joseph Noriega

Script: John Paxton, from Raymond Chandler's novel *Farewell My Lovely*
Costume Design: Edward Stevenson

with Dick Powell, Claire Trevor, Anne Shirley, Otto Kruger, Mike Mazurki, Miles Mander, Douglas Walton, Ralf Harolde, Don Douglas, Esther Howard, Dewey Robinson

• Criticism on release

...The picture preserves most of the faults and virtues of the book. I suppose a lot that I like about it is not really good except by comparison with the deadly norm... nevertheless, I enjoyed the romanticism of the picture and its hopefulness and energy and much of its acting, that of Miles Mander, Claire Trevor, Ralf Harolde and Dick Powell especially. Even its messiness and semi-accomplishment made me feel better about it than about the much better-finished, more nearly unimpeachable, but more academic and complacent, *Double Indemnity*.

James Agee, *The Nation* 16 December 1944

• Current recommendations and ratings
LM3½ DQ4 DW5 VFG5 MPG5 NFT*

...Powell is surprisingly good as Marlowe, certainly more faithful to the writer's conception than Bogart was in *The Big Sleep*, while the supporting cast make the most of John Paxton's superb dialogue. And Harry Wild's chiaroscuro camerawork is the true stuff of 'noir'...

Geoff Andrew, PTOG 1995

The Naked City, Un (Mark Hellinger), 1948 bw

Direction: Jules Dassin	Script: Albert Maltz, Marvin Wald
*Camera: William H. Daniels	Costume Design: Grace Houston
Music: Miklos Rozsa, Frank Skinner	*Editing: Paul Weatherwax
Art Direction: John De Cuir	

with Barry Fitzgerald, Don Taylor, Howard Duff, Dorothy Hart, Ted De Corsia, Arthur O'Connell, Frank Conroy

- Criticism on release

    Before he became a movie producer and was still just a newspaper scribe, Mr Hellinger went for Manhattan in a blissfully uninhibited way – for its sights and sounds and restless movements, its bizarre people and its equally bizarre smells... Now, in his final motion-picture, [thanks to] the actuality filming the seams of a none-too-good whodunnit are rather cleverly concealed...

    Bosley Crowther, *New York Times* 5 March 1948

- Current recommendations and ratings
StJD LM3½ DQ4 DW4 VFG4 MPG4 NFT*

    Despite its reputation, a rather overrated police-procedure thriller which has gained its seminal status simply by its accent on ordinariness and by its adherence to the ideal of shooting on location – thanks be then to Ted De Corsia as the killer, adding a touch of real nastiness to the admittedly well-constructed final chase.

    Geoff Andrew, PTOG 1995

Spellbound, UA (David Selznick), 1945 bw

Direction: Alfred Hitchcock	Script: Ben Hecht (from the novel
Camera: George C.Barnes	*The House of Dr Edwardes* by
*Music: Miklos Rozsa	Francis Beeding)
Art Direction: John Ewing	Editing: William Ziegler, Hal C.
Dream Sequences: Salvador Dali	Kern

with Ingrid Bergman, Gregory Peck, Michael Chekhov, Leo G. Carroll, Rhonda Fleming, Steven Geray, Norman Lloyd, Wallace Ford, Regis Toomey, Irving Bacon, Victor Kilian

- Criticism on release

    ...a fine film – the firm texture of the narration, the flow of continuity and dialogue, the shock of the unexpected, the scope of image – all are happily here... Mr Peck is also a large contributor. His performance, restrained and refined, is precisely the proper counter to Miss Bergman's exquisite role... A rare film.

    Bosley Crowther, *New York Times* 2 November 1945

- Current recommendations and ratings
LM3½ DQ3 DW4 VFG4 MPG4 NFT**

    In 1945, Freud & Co were beginning to have a profound influence on American thinking, so... Hitchcock decided to 'turn out the first picture on psychoanalysis'... But *Spellbound* is also a tale of suspense, and Hitchcock embellishes it with characteristically brilliant twists... The imagery is sometimes overblown, but there are moments, especially towards the end, when the images and the ideas really work together.

    Helen Mackintosh, PTOG 1995

The Thin Man, MGM (Hunt Stromberg), 1934 bw

Direction: W.S. Van Dyke	Script: Albert Hackett, Frances Goodrich (from the novel by Dashiell Hammett)
Camera: James Wong Howe	
Music: William Axt	
Art Direction: Cedric Gibbons	Costume Design: Dolly Tree
Editing: Robert J. Kern	

with William Powell, Myrna Loy, Maureen O'Sullivan, Nat Pendleton, Porter Hall, Minna Gombell, Harold Huber, Cesar Romero, Edward Brophy, Edward Ellis, Douglas Fowley, Bert Roach

- Criticism on release

    ...leans frankly on Hammett's novel for its effects... But on the whole it was thoroughly well-conceived and carried out – a strange mixture of excitement, quips, and hard-boiled (but clever and touching) sentiment. It is a good movie and should not be missed.

    Otis Ferguson, *New Republic* 4 July 1934

- Current recommendations and ratings
  StJD LM4 DQ4 DW4 VFG4½ MPG4 NFT*

    ...With Powell and Loy fitting the parts to perfection, the film draws happy doodles around the mystery of the missing scientist. What enchants, really, is the relationship between Nick and Nora as they live an eternal cocktail hour... in a marvellous blend of marital familiarity and constant courtship, pixilated fantasy and childlike wonder...

    Tom Milne, PTOG 1995

Touch of Evil, Un (Albert Zugsmith), 1958 bw

Direction: Orson Welles
Camera: Russell Metty
Music: Henry Mancini
Art Direction: Alexander Golitzen, Robert Clatworthy
Script: Welles (from the novel *Badge of Evil* by Whit Masterson)
Costume Design: Bill Thomas
Editing: Virgil Vogel, Aaron Stell

with Charlton Heston, Janet Leigh, Orson Welles, Joseph Calleia, Akim Tamiroff, Marlene Dietrich, Dennis Weaver, Ray Collins, Mercedes McCambridge, Lalo Rios, Zsa Zsa Gabor (bit), Keenan Wynn (bit), Joseph Cotten (bit)

- Criticism on release

  [from] a woefully poor little detective novel, Welles has given himself the role of a brutal and greedy policeman, an ace investigator, very well known. Since he works only by intuition, he uncovers murderers without bothering about proof... There is a fierce battle between [him and an American policeman on his honeymoon, Charlton Heston]. Heston finds proof against Welles while Welles manufactures proof against him... the sympathetic character is led to commit an underhand act in order to undo the monster...

  François Truffaut, *Cahiers du Cinema*, 1958

- Current recommendations and ratings
  StJD S&S82/92 LM4 DQ4 DW5 VFG5 MPG5 NFT*

  ...A sweaty thriller conundrum on character and corruption, justice and the law, worship and betrayal, it plays havoc with moral ambiguities... Set in the backwater border hell-hole of Los Robles, inhabited almost solely by patented Wellesian grotesques, it's shot to resemble a nightscape from Kafka.

  Paul Taylor, PTOG 1995

Witness for the Prosecution, UA (Arthur Hornblow Jr.), 1957 bw

Direction: Billy Wilder
Camera: Russell Harlan
Art Direction: Alexander Trauner
Music: Matty Malneck
Costume Design: Edith Head, Joe King

Script: Wilder, Harry Kurnitz, Larry Marcus (from Agatha Christie's play and novel)
Editing: Daniel Mandell

with Tyrone Power, Marlene Dietrich, Charles Laughton, Elsa Lanchester, John Williams, Henry Daniell, Ian Wolfe, Una O'Connor, Torin Thatcher, Francis Compton

- Criticism on release

    ...comes off extraordinarily well. This results mainly from Billy Wilder's splendid staging of some splintering court-room scenes and a first-rate performance by Charles Laughton in the defense-attorney role – Tyrone Power has his ups as the accused man, Marlene Dietrich hits her high points as his wife... Miss Lanchester is delicious as [the] maidenly henpecking nurse. The added dimensions of Mr Laughton bulge this black-and-white drama into a hit.

    Bosley Crowther, *New York Times* 7 February 1958

- Current recommendations and ratings
  LM4 DQ4 DW4 VFG4½ MPG3½ NFT*

    The undisputed star of this courtroom drama is Alexander Trauner's magnificent recreation of the Old Bailey – Tyrone Power is surprisingly good as the man accused of murdering his mistress, but the swift twists and turns of Ms Christie's plot soon drain Dietrich's and Laughton's roles of any dramatic credibility.

    Phil Hardy, PTOG 1995

Chinatown, Par (Robert Evans), 1974 *colour*

Direction: Roman Polanski	Script: Robert Towne
Camera: John Alonzo	Music: Jerry Goldsmith
Art Direction: Richard Sylbert	Costume Design: Anthea Sylbert
Special Effects: Logan Frazee	Editing: Sam O'Steen

with Jack Nicholson, Faye Dunaway, John Huston, Perry Gomez, John Hillerman, Darrell Zwerling, Diane Ladd, Roy Jenson, Roy Roberts, Roman Polanski

- Criticism on release

    ...Roman Polanski's consummate new private eye thriller – Chinatown is also Chandlertown; and still a pretty good place to set a movie... 'Forget it, Jake, it's only Chinatown,' says someone. It is a line with a nice sense of movie history behind it, and that true Chandlerian feeling of the darkness out there and the long drop over the edge... *Chinatown* brings the private eye mystery bounding back because it keeps its sense of the past within itself, playing none of those cute, boring audience games with nostalgia...

    Penelope Houston, *The Times* 9 August 1974

- Current recommendations and ratings
  StJD BN92 S&S82/92 LM4 DQ3 DW5 VFG5 MPG5 NFT****

    Classic detective film, with Nicholson's JJ Gittes moving through the familiar world of the Forties 'film noir'... [his] peculiar vulnerability is closer to Chandler's concept of Philip Marlowe than many screen Marlowes, and the sense of time and place (the formation of LA in the '30s) is very strong. Directed by Polanski in bravura style, it is undoubtedly one of the great films of the 70s

    PTOG 1995

Rear Window, Par (Alfred Hitchcock), 1954 *colour*

Direction: Alfred Hitchcock
Camera: Robert Burks
Music: Franz Waxman
Art Direction: Hal Pereira
Editing: George Tomasini

Script: John Michael Hayes (from the novel by Cornell Woolrich)
Costume Design: Edith Head

with James Stewart, Grace Kelly, Wendell Corey, Thelma Ritter, Raymond Burr, Judith Evelyn, Kathryn Grant

- Criticism on release

    ...the plot seems more slick than profound... yet I am convinced that this film is the most important of all the seventeen Hitchcock has made in Hollywood, one of those rare films without imperfection or weakness, which concedes nothing... What could have been a dry and academic gamble, an exercise in cold virtuosity turns out to be a fascinating spectacle.
    François Truffaut, *Cahiers du Cinema* 1954

- Current recommendations and ratings
StJD S&S82/92 LM4 DQ4 DW5 VFG5 MPG5 NFT*

    There is suspense enough, of course, but the important thing is the way that it is filmed; the camera never strays from inside Stewart's apartment, and every shot is closely aligned with his point of view. And what this relentless monomaniac witnesses is everyone's dirty linen: suicide, broken dreams and cheap death. Hitchcock has nowhere else... given us so disturbing a definition of what it is to watch the 'silent film' of other people's lives.
    Chris Peachment, PTOG 1995

The Silence of the Lambs, Orion (Edward Saxon, Kenneth Litt, Ron Bozman), 1991 *colour*

*Direction: Jonathan Demme	*Script: Ted Tally (from Thomas Harris's novel)
Camera: Tak Fujimoyo	
Music: Howard Shore	Production Design: Kristi Zea
Editing: Craig McKay	Costume Design: Colleen Moore

with *Jodie Foster, *Anthony Hopkins, Scott Glenn, Ted Levine, Anthony Heald, Brooke Smith, Charles Napier, Diane Baker, Kasi Lemmons, Roger Corman

- Criticism on release

    If *The Silence of the Lambs* had been an ineptly made schlock-horror film about two serial killers – one of whom skins his victims whereas the other eats his – it would have been easy for the audience to laugh it off as a piece of 'grand guignol'. After all, the cinema has long fed on the deeds of such men, from Jack the Ripper to the Boston Strangler. But what makes this new film creepy and unsettling and even questionable as an entertainment is that it's so persuasively done. It is Clarice Starling who makes the whole edifice of the film credible... Jodie Foster has an eagle-eyed integrity and a presence so rooted in reality that if she were to state that the Martians had landed, you would feel constrained to believe her. This is one of America's outstanding actresses...

    Iain Johnstone, *Sunday Times* 2 June 1991

- Current recommendations and ratings
S&S92 LM3½ DQ3 DW4 VFG4½ MPG4½ NFT*

    In its own old-fashioned way, satisfying... Understandably, much has been made of Hopkins' hypnotic Lecter, but the laurels must go to Levine's killer, admirably devoid of camp overstatement, and to Foster... a vulnerable but pragmatic intelligence bent on achieving independence...

    Geoff Andrew, PTOG 1995

Vertigo, Par (Alfred Hitchcock), 1958 colour

Direction: Alfred Hitchcock
Camera: Robert Burks
Music: Bernard Herrmann
Special Effects: John P. Fulton
Art Direction: Hal Pereira, Henry Bumstead
Editing: George Tomasini

Script: Alec Coppel, Samuel Taylor (from the novel *D'entre Les Morts* by Pierre Boileau and Thomas Narcejac)
Costume Design: Edith Head

with James Stewart, Kim Novak, Barbara Bel Geddes, Tom Helmore, Henry Jones, Ellen Corby, Lee Patrick, Konstantin Shayne

- Criticism on release

> I greatly admire Hitchcock. I enjoy thrillers. I appreciate the massive skill of technicians as well as director... which has created so solid a picture of the insecurity of the opulent... As you might hope from the authors of *Les Diaboliques* and *Les Jouves* (Boileau and Narcejac), the plot is a brilliant box of devilish tricks. Yet the film disappoints – it needs the touch of the harsh and squalid...
>
> Dilys Powell, *Sunday Times* 10 August 1958

- Current recommendations and ratings
StJD S&S82/92 LM4 DQ4 DW4 VFG5 MPG5 NFT*

> James Stewart is excellent as the neurotic detective employed by an old pal to trail his wandering wife... Hitchcock gives the game away about halfway through the movie, and focuses on Stewart's strained psychological stability; the result inevitably involves a lessening of suspense... the bleakness is perhaps a little hard to swallow, but there's no denying that this is the director at the very peak of his powers, while Novak is a revelation. Slow but totally compelling.
>
> Geoff Andrew, PTOG 1995

Witness, Par (Edward B. Peldman), 1985 colour

Direction: Peter Weir
Camera: John Beale
Music: Maurice Jarre
Production Design: Stan Jolley
Costume Design: Shari Feldman, Dallas Doman
*Script: Earl W. Wallace, William Kelley (from story by Kelley, Wallace and Patricia Wallace)
Special Effects: John R. Elliott
*Editing: Thom Noble

with Harrison Ford, Kelly McGillis, Josef Sommer, Lukas Haas, Jan Rubes, Alexander Godunov, Patti LuPone, Danny Glover, Brent Jennings, Angus MacInnes

- Criticism on release

  ...a movie of up-market visuals, down-market thriller plot: as if Vermeer had been hired to shoot an Ellery Queen mystery. The images gleam with beauty; the murder story stomps along from one duff mystification to another... Weir's great talent is for weird... and *Witness* thrives best, like an exotic weed, in the surreal crack in cultural cohesion between Ford's big-city roughneck and the prim and pristine community in which he tries, for most of the film, to camouflage himself... The movie moves to a climax of thick-eared predictability as the villains descend on the wheatfield with shotgun and mean looks, set for last-reel mayhem. But if you lie back and think of Flemish painting and of Ford's mimetic mastery, you will have an entertaining time.

  Nigel Andrews, *Financial Times* 24 May 1985

- Current recommendations and ratings
  StJD S&S92 LM3 DQ4 DW4 VFG4½ MPG4 NFT*

  ...Powerful, assured, full of beautiful imagery and thankfully devoid of easy moralising, it also offers a performance of surprising skill and sensitivity from Ford.

  Richard Rayner, PTOG 1995

GANGSTER MELODRAMAS

The classic gangster films of the 1930s were 'rise and fall' melodramas, reminiscent of Shakespeare's *Richard III* and *Macbeth*, where the erstwhile executioner becomes the eventual victim. Sympathy for the central character throughout the film was sharply corrected by the moral purgations of the conclusion, with its warning that ruthless violence can rebound upon itself. Of the three classic gangster careers of the 1930s – Tony Camonte's in *Scarface*, 1932, Rico's in *Little Caesar*, 1930, and Tom Powers' in *The Public Enemy*, 1931 – it is Paul Muni's memorable portrayal of the ape-killer of *Scarface* that makes the strongest impact today, possibly because the whole film, redolent of its time, has fewer outdated passages than *Little Caesar* or *The Public Enemy*.

Rich in characterisation and imagery, *Scarface* has a strange consistency of atmosphere, a dark parody of realism – which haunts and excites. After a time, the relentless movement of the plot gives way to attention to detail – Gaffney (Boris Karloff) shot while bowling, Guino (George Raft) flipping his coin (a gesture now immortalised as the emblem of the 'hood'), Camonte's sister (Ann Dvorak) stepping it out in the dance hall.

Nevertheless, the images of Edward G. Robinson's Rico and James Cagney's Tom Powers have a visual incisiveness which raises the films in which they are embedded above the tendentious dullness of some of their scenes. Their death scenes are phenomenal, providing models for all gangster epics, but never equalled – "Is this the end of little Rico?" and Powers's corpse delivered as a gruesome parcel on the doorstep of his mother's house.

Raoul Walsh's *High Sierra*, 1941, (a decade later) approaches the final end of a gangster from quite a different angle: Bogart does not go out with a bang but with a whimper. 'Mad Dog' Roy Earle (played by an unusually sensitive Humphrey Bogart), a coldly professional gangster sprung from jail to carry out one last 'caper', is a very moving character, near-tragic also, but with a greater emphasis on compassion. He loses out on his good intentions with a crippled girl (Joan Leslie); he has to suffer the immature selfishness of his confederates (Arthur Kennedy, Scott Brady, Cornel Wilde); enduring loyalty comes only from a hard-bitten moll (Ida Lupino); and he finally meets Nemesis in a shoot-out with cops among the peaks of the Sierra Nevada. The quality of the script (John Huston helping

W.R. Burnett to adapt his own novel) is rare; the camerawork (by Tony Gaudio) is first-rate (superlative in the final sequence); the performances are excellent, the direction and editing taut and convincing – one of Walsh's major films, a work of art with a few forgivable blemishes.

The post-war gangster movies gain from the application of qualities that became characteristic of *film noir*: the sense of futility, the prevalence of self-deception, the knowledge that nothing will ever go right, the visual style (incorporating favourite Expressionist techniques – angled cameras, low-key lighting), city streets in the rain at night, the setting of sleazy urban dives. Of Robert Siodmak's *The Killers*, 1946, Tony Rayns (PTOG 1993) says: "If anyone still doesn't know what is signified by the critical term *film noir*, then *The Killers* provides an exhaustive definition." This adaptation of an Ernest Hemingway short story about a young Swedish-American boxer enticed by a gang boss's sultry mistress (Albert Dekker, Ava Gardner) into a web of crime uses a series of flashbacks (another favourite *film noir* technique) to probe the causes of the mysterious killing graphically described in the opening scene. This was Burt Lancaster's film debut as the boxer; Ava Gardner was a superb 'bitch goddess'; Miklos Rozsa's dramatic score became almost symbolical of this kind of thriller; and Mark Hellinger began an impressive, though unfortunately brief, career as producer at Universal after his earlier creative career at Warners (including *High Sierra*).

In Raoul Walsh's retrospective *White Heat*, 1949, James Cagney's gangster 'hero' dies with an almighty bang: "Made it, Ma – Top of the world!" he cries on top of a refinery, as it explodes all round him. Throughout the movie, this psychotic master-criminal (as he conceives himself), fixated on a power-mad mother (marvellously played by Margaret Wycherley), batters himself irresistibly into our sympathies, so that the undercover cop (Edmond O'Brien) who wins his confidence in jail, in order to betray him, appears as a kind of Judas. An expert and experienced director, Walsh, in this movie, not only has the advantage of a great star on top form, but the very finest craftsmanship available to Warner Brothers at that time: he tells the story at a cracking pace with the utmost impact.

Joseph H. Lewis's *Gun Crazy*, 1949, is a near-perfect B movie by a director who never failed to achieve a high quality in spite of low budgets. After *Bonnie and Clyde*, it is difficult to appreciate how innovative this movie was, and how seminal it remains: its young 'gun-crazy' duo (Peggy Cummins, John Dall) never achieved star status or even widespread recognition; and, until recently, both critics and the public were unprepared to consider such 'genre' movies on the level of more serious A productions. However, this is a little gem of film-making (script by Millard Kaufman from a Mackinlay Kantor story, camerawork by Russell Harlan, music by Victor Young). There is also fine support playing from Barry Kroeger, Morris Carnovsky and Don Beddoe.

The great W.R. Burnett, masterly exponent of gangster drama since *Little Caesar*, provides the superb material for *The Asphalt Jungle*, 1950, with the great John Huston as writer-director at the top of his form. The plot concerns a beautifully executed jewel robbery, which fails in the end because of the various foibles of the gang members – a wonderful assortment of well-etched characters: the mastermind (Sam Jaffe), the dumb ox leader (Sterling Hayden, a much undervalued actor), the oily fence (Louis Calhern), the family-man dynamiter (Anthony Caruso), and the hunchbacked driver (James Whitmore). All the *noir* qualities are there, superbly assembled, including a frisky Marilyn Monroe (in an early role as Calhern's kept woman) and Jean Hagen (in a finely shaded performance as a moll). A rare pure masterpiece from MGM.

The third of the post-war gangster movies is a Fritz Lang film with possibly the highest reputation among his American movies – *The Big Heat*, 1953. It is told with great intensity but with perfect control, the only possible excess being the hurling of boiling hot coffee into his mistress's face by a repulsive hood (the two characters are played by Gloria Grahame and Lee Marvin). The incident appears to be a later, much less inhibited, example of the masculine brutality first shockingly portrayed in *Public Enemy* by James Cagney's squashing a grapefruit in the face of his moll. *The Big Heat* depicts the pursuit by a morally relentless cop of the gangsters who, in an attempt to prevent his exposing their corruption, had killed his wife by placing a bomb in his car. Glenn Ford's rendering of this role and Gloria Grahame's as a woman gradually discovering the right in his cause to her own cost are particularly impressive among the generally very effective performances; and Lang's first-rate filmcraft and control of the medium reaches a brilliant and sustained height throughout the movie.

Bonnie and Clyde stands on its own. Ostensibly reviving the gangster epic of the 1930s, it represents a remarkable shift in moral standpoint. Using a fable of the real 1930s, Penn reconstructs a myth for the 1960s and 1970s – one cannot somehow imagine the attractive couple, played by Warren Beatty and Faye Dunaway, without the personal accoutrements of the bathroom (and the TV ad): deodorant, aftershave, and the unisex hairdo. Compare them with contemporary photographs of the originals! The physical glamorisation is accompanied by a moral glamorisation: vicious acts are given a heroic twist, and the message of the ending is no longer "There goes an enemy of society", but "What a waste of lively young charm!" No wonder the younger generation of 1967 took this film to their hearts, for it made them feel both good and rejected. Technically, in every department, it is a perfect film, and has all the glossy production values of the superior Hollywood product.

The Godfather is "a popular masterpiece" (Lew Keyser, *Hollywood in the Seventies*). The qualities that made this complex, powerful film appealing to critics and public alike are many and apparent: direction that never sacrifices the total effect for the immediate, the intriguing link between the public murders and the private family concerns, first-rate acting on a mythic level (particularly by Brando and Pacino), memorable images and compositions (the photography is by Gordon Willis), and a feeling, as with *Citizen Kane*, that we are seeing lived before us the mainsprings of motive and feeling – however destructive of society – which have made the North American continent a vital, competitive, capitalist community. The apparently respectable family surface makes the acts of Machiavellian power-seeking and treachery even more horrifying. Generally considered as even more impressive, Francis Ford Coppola's sequel, *The Godfather Part II*, 1974, also scripted by Coppola with Mario Puzo, continues the story of Michael Corleone (Al Pacino) who has taken over the fortunes of the 'family' from his incapacitated father, Vito. It also flashes back and forth between this 'contemporary' narrative and the career of young Vito (Robert De Niro replacing Marlon Brando) in Sicily and New York at the turn of the century. The sense of continuity and inevitability is overpowering, with Coppola pulling out all the stops with the performers (including a unique cameo study from drama teacher Lee Strasberg as a Jewish gangster) and the whole production team, many of whom had worked with him on the first *Godfather* (for example, Gordon Willis, camera, and Nino Rota, music).

The Asphalt Jungle, MGM (Arthur Hornblow Jr.), 1950 bw

Direction: John Huston
Camera: Hal Rosson
Music: Miklos Rozsa
Art Direction: Cedric Gibbons, Randall Duell
Editing: George Boemler

Script: Huston, with Ben Maddow (from the novel by W.R. Burnett)

with Sterling Hayden, Louis Calhern, Sam Jaffe, Jean Hagen, James Whitmore, John McIntire, Marc Lawrence, Anthony Caruso, Marilyn Monroe, Dorothy Tree

- Criticism on release

    ...a gangster movie turned inside out... hopes and fears, weaknesses and strengths, loyalties and treacheries... supply the film's tension – Huston vitiated his detachment by a sentimentality that becomes positively mawkish in the long drawn-out finale. But on the way he has given us some crisp characterisation delineated in exciting movie technique... perhaps the best robbery staged in Hollywood...

    Richard Winnington, 7 October 1950

- Current recommendations and ratings
  StJD S&S82/92 LM3½ DQ4 DW4 VFG5 MPG5 NFT*

    A classic heist movie, and one of Huston's finest... a taut, unsentimental study in character and relative morality. Beautifully shot by Harold Rosson, played to perfection by a less than starry cast, and directed in admirably forthright fashion by Huston...

    Geoff Andrew, PTOG 1995

The Big Heat, Col (Jerry Wald/Robert Arthur), 1953 bw

Direction: Fritz Lang
Camera: Charles Lang Jr.
Music: Daniele Amfitheatrof
Costume Design: Jean Louis
Editing: Charles Nelson

Script: Sydney Boehm (from the novel by William P. McGivern)
Art Direction: Robert Peterson

with Glenn Ford, Gloria Grahame, Lee Marvin, Alexander Scourby, Jocelyn Brando, Jeanette Nolan, Carolyn Jones, Dan Seymour

- Criticism on release

    ...well worth looking at for those with the stomach for violence (it has an X certificate); exciting, made with cold savage skill, played for all it is worth by Glenn Ford and Gloria Grahame.

    Dilys Powell, *Sunday Times* May 1954

- Current recommendations and ratings
StJD S&S92 LM3 DQ3 DW4 VFG4 MPG4 NFT**

    ...Lang strips down William R. McGivern's novel to essentials, giving the story narrative drive as efficient and powerful as a handgun. The dialogue is functional. Every shot is composed with economy and exactitude, no act gratuitous...

    Wally Hammond, PTOG 1995

Gun Crazy/Deadly Is the Female, Un (Frank & Maurice King), 1950 bw

Direction: Joseph H. Lewis
Camera: Russell Harlan
Music: Victor Young
Costume Design: Norma

Script: Mackinlay Kantor, Millard Kaufman (from Kantor's story)
Production Design: Gordon Wiles
Editing: Harry Gerstad

with Peggy Cummins, John Dall, Barry Kroeger, Morris Carnovsky, Annabel Shaw, Harry Lewis

- Criticism on release

    ...basically on a par with the more humdrum pulp fiction... The plot as episodic as familiar. In all fairness to Mr Kantor's idea, the actual script which he wrote with Millard Kaufman is a fairly literate business... The dialogue is quite good and the photography is first-rate. In fact, director Joseph H. Lewis has kept the whole thing zipping along at a colorful tempo which deserves a much better outlet. The main drawbacks are the stars themselves, who look more like fugitives from a 4-H Club than from the law...

    'H.H.T', *New York Times* 25 August 1950

- Current recommendations and ratings
S&S82/92 LM3½ DQ4 DW4 MPG2 NFT*

    ...sees Lewis – one of the very finest B movie directors – firing on all cylinders... Far more energetic than *Bonnie and Clyde* – the most famous of its many progeny – its intensity borders on the subversive and surreal.

    Geoff Andrew, PTOG 1995

High Sierra, WB (Hal Wallis/Mark Hellinger), 1941 *bw*

Direction: Raoul Walsh
Camera: Tony Gaudio
Music: Adolph Deutsch
Special Effects: Byron Haskin, H.F. Koenekamp
Costume Design: Milo Anderson
Editing: Jack Killifer

Script: John Huston, W.R. Burnett (from Burnett's novel)
Art Direction: Ted Smith

with Humphrey Bogart, Ida Lupino, Alan Curtis, Arthur Kennedy, Joan Leslie, Henry Travers, Henry Hull, Barton MacLane, Cornel Wilde, Minna Gombell, Elizabeth Risdon, Jerome Cowan, John Eldredge, Donald MacBride, Isabel Jewell, Paul Harvey

- Criticism on release

    ...one of the rare times a good action story has had naturally within it some of the elements of the fates and the furies which are the material of tragedy, this is a picture that lives on the screen. In the middle of it is Humphrey Bogart, whose conception and rock-bound maintenance of the hard-handed, graying and bitter ex-con is not only one of the finest productions of character in any story of men in action but the whole vertebrate structure of this one. There are of course the other good character actors, down to the dog and up to the rather difficult and well done part of Ida Lupino, writing and direction gauged to the stern demands of the true movie... and a setting that is as much a tribute to the original conception as to the eloquent, flexible camera setups of Tony Gaudio...

    Otis Ferguson, *New Republic* 31 March 1941

- Current recommendations and ratings
  StJD LM3 DQ3 DW4 VFG4 MPG4 NFT*

    A momentous gangster movie... terrific performances, camerawork and dialogue, with Walsh... giving it something of the memorable melancholy of a Peckinpah Western.

    Tom Milne, PTOG 1995

The Killers, Un (Mark Hellinger), 1946 bw

Direction: Robert Siodmak
Camera: Elwood ('Woody') Bredell
Music: Miklos Rozsa
Art Direction: Jack Otterson, Martin Obzina
Costume Design: Vera West

Script: Anthony Veiller, with John Huston, uncredited (from story by Ernest Hemingway)
Editing: Arthur Hilton

with Burt Lancaster, Ava Gardner, Edmond O'Brien, Albert Dekker, Sam Levene, John Miljan, Donald MacBride, Virginia Christine, Vince Barnett, Jeff Corey, Charles D. Brown, William Conrad, Charles McGraw, Jack Lambert

- Criticism on release

    ...starts off with Ernest Hemingway's brilliant, frightening story, then spends the next hour or so highlighting all that the story so much more powerfully left in the dark... [The film story is] a comparative letdown, but it... is better movie – good bars, fierce boxing, nice stuff for several minor players... There is a good strident journalistic feeling for tension, noise, sentiment and jazzed-up realism, all well manipulated by Robert Siodmak, which is probably chiefly to the credit of the producer, Mark Hellinger...

    James Agee, *The Nation* 14 September 1946

- Current recommendations and ratings
  StJD LM4 DQ3 DW4 VFG5 MPG4 NFT*

    If anyone still does not know what is signified by the critical term 'film noir', then *The Killers* provides an exhaustive definition... After the brilliant opening murder scene, what follows is a series of flashbacks as Edmond O'Brien's insurance investigator looks into the circumstances of Lancaster's death. Ava Gardner is an admirably tacky *femme fatale*, and her fickleness/faithfulness provides the not very surprising dénouement. Worth attention as a 40s thriller, but more than that as a prime example of post-war pessimism and fatalism.

Tony Rayns, PTOG 1995

Little Caesar, WB (Darryl Zanuck/Hal Wallis), 1930 bw

Direction: Mervyn LeRoy	Script: Robert Lee, Francis Edward Faragoh, Darryl Zanuck (from the novel by W.R. Burnett)
Camera: Tony Gaudio	
Musical Direction: Erno Rapee	
Art Direction: Anton Grot	
Costume Design: Earl Luick	Editing: Ray Curtiss

with Edward G. Robinson, Douglas Fairbanks Jr., Glenda Farrell, Sidney Blackmer, Thomas Jackson, George E. Stone

- Criticism on release

   ...by pushing into the background the usual romantic conventions of the theme and concentrating on characterization rather than on plot, [*Little Caesar*] emerges not only as an effective and rather chilling melodrama, but also as what is sometimes described as a Document... It is, of course, Mr Robinson's film, but the lesser roles are capably handled. That increasingly competent actor, the younger Douglas Fairbanks, is particularly good...

   Richard Watts Jr., *The New York Herald Tribune*
   10 January 1931

- Current recommendations and ratings
StJD LM3½ DQ4 DW4 VFG4 MPG4 NFT*

   Though it looks somewhat dated now, there's no denying the seminal importance of this classic adaptation of W.R. Burnett's novel. Robinson - vain, cruel, jealous and vicious - is superb... Like many early talkies, the film often in fact errs on the slow side, at least in terms of dialogue; but the parallels with Capone, Tony Gaudio's photography, and LeRoy's totally unrepentant tone ensure that it remains fascinating.

   Geoff Andrew, PTOG 1995

The Public Enemy, WB (Darryl Zanuck), 1931 *bw*

Direction: William Wellman
Camera: J.D. ('Dev') Jennings
Music Direction: David Mendoza
Costume Design: Earl Luick
Script: Kubec Glasmon, John Bright, Harvey Thew
Art Direction: Max Parker
Editing: Edward McCormick

with James Cagney, Jean Harlow, Edward Woods, Joan Blondell, Mae Clarke, Donald Cook, Beryl Mercer, Leslie Fenton, Frankie Darro

- Criticism on release

  ...another gang picture, [but] with a definite idea and a great deal of sadistic, bloody glee in it, as well as some of the best direction of the year... I fear [the star] will be playing one gangster after another because of his work in this production. His name is James Cagney and, while you may not remember him, he has been doing excellent work in the playhouses for several years without excessive praise or reward. He is a good actor...

  Pare Lorentz, *Judge* 16 May 1931

- Current recommendations and ratings
  StJD S&S92 LM3½ DW5 VFG4½ MPG5 NFT*

  ...the film is badly let down by the performances of Harlow as a classy moll, and Cook and Mercer as Cagney's brother and mother (the latter coming across as a simpering moron). But Cagney's energy and Wellman's gutsy direction carry the day, counteracting the moralistic sentimentality of the script and indelibly etching the star on the memory as a definitive gangster hero.

  Geoff Andrew, PTOG 1995

Scarface, UA (Howard Hughes/Howard Hawks), 1932 bw

Direction: Howard Hawks
Camera: Lee Garmes, L. William O'Connell
Music: Adolph Tandler, Gus Arnheim
Art Direction: Harry Olivier
Editing: Edward Curtis
Script: Ben Hecht, Seton I. Miller, John Lee Mahin, W.R. Burnett (from the novel by Armitage Trail)
Costume Design: Patricia Norris

with Paul Muni, Ann Dvorak, George Raft, Boris Karloff, Karen Morley, Osgood Perkins, Vince Barnett, Tully Marshall, C. Henry Gordon, Edwin Maxwell, Henry Armetta, Hank Mann, Paul Fix

- Criticism on release

    ...as a film, *Scarface* is as good as any gangster film that has been made. It is more brutal, more cruel, more wholesale than any of its predecessors and, by that much, nearer to the truth. It is built with more solid craftsmanship, it is better directed and better acted... The only really troublesome weaknesses in the story are in the extraneous moralizing speeches...

    James Shelley Hamilton, *National Board of Review Magazine* March 1932

- Current recommendations and ratings
StJD S&S92 LM3½ DQ4 DW4 VFG5 MPG5 NFT*

    ...this Howard Hughes production was the one unflawed classic the tycoon was involved with. Hawks and head screenwriter Ben Hecht were after an equation between Capone and the Borgias; they provided so much contentious meat for the censors amid the violent crackle of Chicago gangland warfare that they managed to slip a subsidiary incest theme through unnoticed. Two years' haggling ended with the subtitles *Shame of a Nation* being added, and a hanging finale being substituted for the shootout – happily restored – which closes proceedings with forceful poetry. Unmissable...

    Paul Taylor, PTOG 1995

White Heat, WB (Louis F. Edelman), 1949 bw

Direction: Raoul Walsh
Camera: Sid Hickox
Music: Max Steiner
Art Direction: Edward Carrere
Special Effects: Roy Davidson, H.F. Koenekamp
Script: Ivan Goff, Ben Roberts (from Virginia Kellogg's novel)
Costume Design: Leah Rhodes
Editing: Owen Marks

with James Cagney, Virginia Mayo, Edmond O'Brien, Margaret Wycherley, Steve Cochran, John Archer, Wally Cassell, Fred Clark, Paul Guilfoyle

- Criticism on release

   ...James Cagney reappears in a part of the kind which made him famous, a gangster part. As the killer with what the film calls 'a fierce psychopathic devotion to his mother', he gives his usual easy, beautifully shaded performance, the director [Raoul Walsh] has seen to it that the audience never has time to lose interest in the record of murder, and the screenwriters have seen to it that death and savagery dominate the tale... Today death by the dozen is the entertainment of the people.

   Dilys Powell, *Sunday Times* November 1949

- Current recommendations and ratings
StJD S&S92 LM3½ DQ4 DW5 VFG5 MPG5 NFT*

   ...the fitting climax of the '30s gangster movie.

   Phil Hardy, PTOG 1995

Bonnie and Clyde, WB (Warren Beatty), 1967 colour

Direction: Arthur Penn
*Camera: Burnett Guffey
Music: Charles Strouse
Costume Design: Theodora Van
  Runkle
Editing: Dede Allen

Script: David Newman, Robert
  Benton
Art Direction: Dean Tavoularis

with Warren Beatty, Faye Dunaway, Michael J. Pollard, Gene Hackman, *Estelle Parsons, Denver Pyle, Dub Taylor, Gene Wilder

- Criticism on release

    ...Penn treats killing as killing; his actors don't just fall down, they die. Still he understands the romantic connections between outlawry and space... Burnett Guffey's color camerawork articulates these feelings; he combines the starkness of East Texas and the Midwest with haunting, almost picturesque quality... Dede Allen's editing gives a long melancholy sweep to some sequences but also gives a terrible flesh-thumping impact to the gunfights...

    Stanley Kauffmann, *New American Review*
    2 January 1968

- Current recommendations and ratings
StJD BN92 S&S82/92 LM4 DQ4 DW5 VFG4 MPG4 NFT*

    ...inevitably met with some grudging devaluation. But it's still great: half comic fairy-tale, half brutal fact... With its weird landscape of dusty, derelict towns and verdant highways, stunningly shot by Burnett Guffey in muted tones of green and gold, it has the true quality of folk legend.

    Tom Milne, PTOG 1995

The Godfather, Par (Albert S. Ruddy), 1972 *colour*

Direction: Francis Ford Coppola
Camera: Gordon Willis
Music: Nino Rota
Art Direction: Dean Tavoularis
Costume Design: Anna Hill Johnstone
*Script: Coppola, with Mario Puzo (from the novel by Puzo)
Editing: William Reynolds, Peter Zinner

with *Marlon Brando, Al Pacino, James Caan, Robert Duvall, Sterling Hayden, Richard Castellano, John Marley, Richard Conte, Diane Keaton, Talia Shire, John Cazale

- Criticism on release

    Coppola has stayed very close to the book's greased-lightning sensationalism and yet has made a movie with the spaciousness and strength that popular novels such as Dickens' used to have... It offers a wide, startlingly vivid view of a Mafia dynasty. The abundance is from the book; the quality of feeling is Coppola's...

    Pauline Kael, *New Yorker* 18 March 1972

- Current recommendations and ratings
  StJD BN92 S&S82/92 LM4 DQ4 DW5 VFG5 MPG5 NFT*

    An everyday story of Mafia folk, incorporating severed horses' heads in the bed and a number of heartwarming family occasions... Mario Puzo's novel was brought to the screen in bravura style by Coppola... Its soap operatics should never have been presented separately from Part II.

    Geoff Andrew, PTOG 1995

The Godfather Part II, Par (Francis Ford Coppola, Gary Frederickson, Fred Roos), 1974 *colour*

*Direction (and *Script, with Mario Puzo, from Puzo's novel): Francis Ford Coppola
Camera: Gordon Willis
*Music: Nino Rota, Carmine Coppola
Costume Design: Theodora Van Runkle
Special Effects: A.D. Flowers, Joe Lombardi
*Production Design: Dean Tavoularis
Editing: Peter Zinner, Barry Malkin, Richard Marks

with Al Pacino, Robert Duvall, Diane Keaton, *Robert De Niro, Talia Shire, John Cazale, Lee Strasberg, Troy Donahue, Harry Dean Stanton, James Caan, Michael V. Gazzo

- Criticism on release

    ...the film the director would have liked to have made from Mario Puzo's novel the first time round... Clearly it is by some way the more subtle piece of cinema and worth at least some of its half a dozen Oscars. But one has to say straight away that it is not as viscerally exciting and that it has both dull and confusing patches... Even so – and one must emphasise this – the film is a definitive achievement. It is an epic about the underbelly of America that says far more than *The Great Gatsby*, for instance, ever did... *Longueurs* there are, but *Godfather II* remains the one sequel that's arguably better than the original.

    Derek Malcolm, *The Guardian* 15 May 1975

- Current recommendations and ratings
StJD BN92 S&S82/92 LM4 DQ4 DW5 VFG5 MPG5 NFT*

    Far superior to *The Godfather*... The basic theme here... becomes, by the time of Michael's absolute control over a nationwide criminal empire, an aggressive obsession with power for power's sake, so warped and ruthless that the Don is reduced to killing family and friends... In 1977, acknowledging the awkwardnesses resulting from the split into two films, Coppola re-edited them into a chronological whole for TV, adding almost an hour of previously unseen footage.

Anne Billson, PTOG 1995

PSYCHOLOGICAL SUSPENSE

This is basically Hitchcock territory. In the initial (English) phase of his career, Alfred Hitchcock had attempted and also often succeeded in creating works in most genres, but, once established in Hollywood in the early 1940s, he had become known as a 'master of suspense' because of his English masterpieces of the late 1930s.

Whatever his theme, his main aim became to use his total technical expertise to create films that kept the audience on the edge of their seats for most of the film. We have already discussed *Psycho* as a horror film; *Rear Window* and *Vertigo* may be considered as original developments of the detective story, and later we shall discuss two of his spy thrillers *Notorious* and *North by Northwest*.

In *Shadow of a Doubt*, 1943, and *Strangers on a Train*, 1951, the suspense derives from the question: how long before the members of a law-abiding society can be released from the threat of a killer/killers intimately associated with them?

In *Shadow of a Doubt*, Hitchcock cast Joseph Cotten as the handsome, softly-spoken, plausible 'Merry Widow' murderer Charlie, whose niece and namesake (Teresa Wright) is attracted and becomes devoted to him, only to be shocked into the hidden truth at the end. This *doppelgänger* story is set against the background of ordinary family life in a small rural town, brought to life with complete authenticity with the help of Thornton Wilder's dialogue.

In *Strangers on a Train*, Farley Granger stars as the self-satisfied tennis champion, Guy, who finds himself manoeuvred into a reluctant compact with Bruno, a pampered amoral socialite (played with a sinister charm by Robert Walker) to commit each other's murder. The dramatic tension arises from the fact that Bruno carries out his pledge, whereas Guy does not. After the long takes of *Rope*, Hitchcock reverts to being 'the virtuoso of the scissors' (as in the expert cross-cutting between Bruno's attempts to retrieve a vital clue – a cigarette lighter that has fallen down a deep drain, and Guy's straining to win a vital match). There are also ingenious devices by which Hitchcock depicts critical stages of the action – the murder seen in the victim's fallen spectacles, the cataclysmic final sequence culminating in the crash of a runaway carousel. A film utterly without moral significance, *Strangers on a Train* is ensured its place as a classic suspense thriller.

Even when Hitchcock was not involved in the making, his work acted as an inevitable criterion of its worth in employing suspense techniques: no greater compliment could be paid than the label 'Hitchcockian'. Billy Wilder's *Double Indemnity*, 1944, was almost matched in this respect by Tay Garnett's *The Postman Always Rings Twice*, 1946, also based on a James Cain novel and untypically produced at MGM. The story of the murder of a complaisant husband by two uncontrollably passionate lovers and the retribution meted out to them had already been made in Italy (Visconti's magnificent *Ossessione*, 1942) and was not easy to get past the Breen Office[5], but the final version starring a charismatic couple (John Garfield and Lana Turner) succeeded in meeting the censors' requirements while remaining extraordinarily erotic – much more so than the much more explicit American sequel made by Bob Rafaelson in 1981. Except for Cecil Kellaway, as the amiable cuckold, the performances are suitably abrasive and in atmosphere, particularly those of Hume Cronyn and Leon Ames as the almost gleeful agents of justice.

Hitchcock's *Marnie*, 1964, is the story of a beautiful blonde (Tippi Hedren in a role originally intended for Grace Kelly), who is both a compulsive thief and liar, profoundly disturbed. Her employer (Sean Connery) blackmails her into marrying him when he catches her robbing his safe; continually rejected by her, he makes a Freudian exploration into her childhood to discover the source of her disturbance, which becomes particularly critical during thunderstorms. Marnie needs to establish a *true* identity which would explain her fear and hatred of men. Hitchcock, as usual, manipulates his audience with self-assurance, almost arrogance: even the obviousness of the back projections and the climactic painted backcloth, he asserted, were deliberately made relevant to the main theme – that of alienation. Hitchcock's work never lacked a refreshing touch of sardonic humour.

---

[5] Joseph Breen succeeded Will Hays as chief administrator of the Production Code in 1945

Clint Eastwood's directorial debut, *Play Misty for Me*, 1971, introduced the theme of the male whose indulgence in casual sex leads him to a near-fatal relationship with an obsessed woman bent on sole possession. Eastwood himself plays the disc jockey, whose confidence in his power over women is cataclysmically shattered by the effect of a 'one night stand' on a psychotic fan (Jessica Walter, a memorable performance). The film is entertaining, but also shocking and frightening.

Gene Hackman's performance as Harry Caul, the guilt-ridden surveillance expert, dominates *The Conversation*, 1974, which Francis Ford Coppola made after the phenomenal success of *The Godfather*. This is to his credit, although it had little public support. It is an excellent thriller, unusual and taut, but also more than a thriller, just as Graham Greene's 'entertainments' are more than entertainments. Although his memory is haunted by a murder caused by 'his recordings', Caul purports to care little about the purposes to which his work is put: he just wishes to produce a perfect technical job. When he picks up the fragmentary conversation of a strolling couple (Cindy Williams and Frederic Forrest), he begins to suspect ultimately that by handing over the tapes to the rich and powerful husband (Robert Duvall) the tragedy will be repeated. The 'Hitchcockian' suspense story is, however, less important than the study of Caul's demoralisation and breakdown (the main theme).

Lawrence Kasdan's *Body Heat*, 1982, is a highly self-conscious revival of the *film noir* in colour (which seems a contradiction in terms; but *noir* always meant the dramatic atmosphere as much as the chiaroscuro camerawork). Viewers will have no difficulty in recognising the doomed hero and the scheming female of *Double Indemnity*, *Out of the Past* and *The Postman Always Rings Twice*, the labyrinth of relationships into which they descend with no thread to lead the way back. William Hurt as an overconfident lawyer and Kathleen Turner (her screen debut) are ideal in the lead parts of this tale of a conspiracy to murder in a heat-ridden Florida. Symbolic clues are always present in the twisting narrative; but Lawrence Kasdan, writer as well as director, and Carol Littleton, editor, make doubly sure that every stage of the lovers' fate is marked clearly and starkly; the surprise ending should be no surprise either. John Barry's 'mood indigo' score fits the atmosphere perfectly.

The Postman Always Rings Twice, MGM (Carey Wilson), 1946 bw

Direction: Tay Garnett
Camera: Sidney Wagner
Music: George Bassman
Art Direction: Cedric Gibbons, Randall Duell
Script: Harry Ruskin, Niven Busch (from James Cain's novel)
Costume Design: Irene, Marion Herwood Keyes
Editing: George White

with Lana Turner, John Garfield, Cecil Kellaway, Hume Cronyn, Leon Ames, Audrey Totter, Alan Reed

- Criticism on release

>...mainly a terrible misfortune from start to finish. I except chiefly the shrewd performances of Hume Cronyn and Leon Ames, as lawyers. I say it with all respect for the director, Tay Garnett, and with all sympathy for the stars, Lana Turner and John Garfield. It seems to have been made in a depth of seriousness incompatible with material, complicated by a paralysis of fear of the front office – The attitude is almost 100 per cent contemptuous of organised justice and is accepted as such, with evident pleasure, by the audience...
>
> James Agee, *The Nation* 11 May 1946

- Current recommendations and ratings
LM4 DQ4 DW4 VFG5 MPG5 NFT*

>...The plot gathers slack latterly; but this is only a minor flaw in a film, more gray than 'noir', whose strength is that it is cast as a bleak memory in which, from the far side of paradise, condemned man surveys the age-old trail through sex, love and disillusionment.
>
> Tom Milne, PTOG 1995

Shadow of a Doubt, Un (Jack Skirball), 1943 *bw*

Direction: Alfred Hitchcock
Camera: Joseph Valentine
Music: Dimitri Tiomkin
Art Direction: John E. Goodwin, Robert Boyle
Script: Thornton Wilder, Sally Benson, Alma Reville
Editing: Milton Carruth

with Joseph Cotten, Teresa Wright, Macdonald Carey, Patricia Collinge, Henry Travers, Hume Cronyn, Wallace Ford, Irving Bacon

- Criticism on release

    ...Thornton Wilder, Sally Benson and Alma Reville have drawn a graphic and affectionate outline of a small-town American family which an excellent cast has brought to life and Mr Hitchcock has manifested completely in his naturalistic style... As the progressively less charming Uncle Charlie, Joseph Cotten plays with smooth, insinuating ease while injecting a harsh and bitter quality which nicely becomes villainy...

    Bosley Crowther, *New York Times* 13 January 1943

- Current recommendations and ratings
  S&S92 LM3½ DQ4 DW4 VFG4½ MPG5 NFT*

    One of Hitchcock's finest films of the 40s... not only psychologically intriguing... but a sharp dissection of middle American life... Funny, gripping and expertly shot by Joe Valentine. It's a small but memorable gem.

    Geoff Andrew, PTOG 1995

Strangers on a Train, WB (Alfred Hitchcock), 1951 bw

Direction: Alfred Hitchcock
Camera: Robert Burks
Special Effects: H.F. Koenekamp
Music: Dimitri Tiomkin
Art Direction: Ted Haworth
Editing: William H. Ziegler

Script: Raymond Chandler, Czenzi Ormonde, Whitfield Cook (from the novel by Patricia Highsmith)
Costume Design: Leah Rhodes

with Farley Granger, Robert Walker, Ruth Roman, Leo G. Carroll, Patricia Hitchcock, Laura Elliott, Howard St. John, Jonathan Hale, Marion Lorne, Norma Varden

- Criticism on release

    ...the tempo has diminished and the flaws of logic obtrude... Robert Walker gives a polished and chilling performance throughout the film... the action finally resolves into a race against time... confirms Hitchcock's utter dependence on his script – in this case the best he has had for years – and a basic superficiality which prevents him from developing the psychological conflicts his characters do no more than suggest...

    Richard Winnington, *News Chronicle* September 1951

- Current recommendations and ratings
  StJD S&S92 LM4 DQ4 DW3 VFG5 MPG5 NFT*

    Hitchcock didn't use much of Raymond Chandler's original script, because Chandler was too concerned with the characters' motivation. In place of that, Hitchcock erects a web of guilt around Granger... and structures his film around a series of set pieces, ending with a paroxysm of violence on a circus carousel...

    Phil Hardy, PTOG 1995

Body Heat, WB (Fred T. Gallo), 1981 colour

Direction, Script: Lawrence Kasdan
Camera: Richard H. Kline
Costume Design: Renie Conley
Music: John Barry
Editing: Carol Littleton

with William Hurt, Kathleen Turner, Richard Crenna, Ted Danson, J.A. Preston, Mickey Rourke, Kim Zimmer

- Criticism on release

    [The] plot is immediately recognizable as a reworking of Billy Wilder's *Double Indemnity*... But Kasdan has added a slick double-twist ending (of the sort associated with the novels of Boileau and Narcejac), and he handles the narrative and conventions with great skill. There is the heightened, deliberately literary dialogue, the plaintive, bluesy saxophone on the soundtrack, the sweet smell of corruption... The acting is uniformly excellent and Richard Kline's fine photography, of blindingly brilliant days and dark nights pierced with pools of baleful light, reflects the characters' moral climate...

    Philip French, *The Observer* 24 January 1982

- Current recommendations and ratings
  StJD LM3 DQ4 DW4 VFG3½ MPG4 NFT**

    ...whether the movie-movie cleverness becomes as stifling as the atmosphere Kasdan casts over his sunstruck night people is all down to personal taste, but there's no denying the narrative confidence that brings the film to its unfashionably certain double-whammy conclusion.

    Paul Taylor, PTOG 1995

The Conversation, Par (Francis Ford Coppola), 1974 *colour*

Direction and Script: Francis Ford Coppola
Camera: Bill Butler
Production Design: Dean Tavoularis
Editing: Walter Murch, Richard Chew

Music: David Shire

with Gene Hackman, John Cazale, Allen Garfield, Frederic Forrest, Cindy Williams, Michael Higgins, Elizabeth MacRae, Teri Garr, Harrison Ford

- Criticism on release

   ...What Coppola's film does is to show how this very assignment, the long-distance eavesdropping on the couple in the square, educates Harry out of his shoulder-shrugging fatalism, acquainting him in the nastiest possible way with the full awfulness of what he is doing for a living. So the film is fundamentally a morality... I must say it is good to see the director of *The Godfather* putting the proceeds of that vastly overrated epic of mumble-and-bang to such good and articulate use.

   Russell Davies, *The Observer* 11 July 1974

- Current recommendations and ratings
  LM4 DW4 VFG5 MPG4 NFT*

   ...A bleak and devastatingly brilliant film.

   Tom Milne, PTOG 1995

Marnie, Un (Alfred Hitchcock), 1964 *colour*

Direction: Alfred Hitchcock
Camera: Robert Burks
Music: Bernard Herrmann
Costume Design: Edith Head

Script: Jay Presson Allen (from Winston Graham's novel)
Production Design: Robert Boyle
Editing: George Tomasini

with Tippi Hedren, Sean Connery, Diane Baker, Martin Gabel, Louise Latham, Bob Sweeney, Alan Napier

- Criticism on release

    ...looking at his new film, I find the casting of this psychological thriller about a compulsive thief extremely cunning... For the resourceful, fastidious, frigid thief he needs a cool symbol; and there is Tippi Hedren, burnished, elegant, with the tiny pout of the small amused mouth... For the man who falls in love with the girl and means to save her Hitchcock needs a sardonically masculine symbol; and there is Sean Connery, trailing Bondish clouds of sexual arrogance, a man who can afford to bide his time... And the whole film develops as a matter of the precise planning, with the actors, too, moving in prearranged patterns. It isn't one of the director's continuously heart-in-mouth works... But you don't get away from it.

    Dilys Powell, *Sunday Times* July 1964

- Current recommendations and ratings
  S&S82/92 LM3 DQ3 DW4 VFG4 MPG2½ NFT***

    ...it's as sour a vision of male-female interaction as *Vertigo*, though far less bleak and universal in its implications. That said, it's still thrilling to watch, lush, cool and oddly moving...

    Geoff Andrew, PTOG 1995

Play Misty for Me, Un/ Malpaso (Robert Daley), 1971 *colour*

Direction: Clint Eastwood	Script: Jo Heims, Dean Riesner
Camera: Bruce Surtees	(from a story by Jo Harris)
Music: Dee Barton	Art Direction: Alexander Golitzen
Costume Design: Helen Colvig, Brad Whitney	Editing: Carl Pingitore

with Clint Eastwood, Jessica Walter, Donna Mills, John Larch, Jack Ging, Irene Hervey, James McEachin, Clarice Taylor, Don Siegel, Duke Everts

- Criticism on release

    ...sad that this film with its locale and some of its moods out of *Vertigo* and its central obsessional action almost an inversion of Preminger's wonderful *Laura* should echo so briefly in the imagination... I think the fault lies with Clint Eastwood the director, who has made too many easy decisions about events, about the management of the atmosphere, about the treatment of the performances – including the rather inexpressive one of Clint Eastwood the actor, who is asked to bear witness to a quality of inwardness that his better directors have yet had the temerity to ask of him...

    Roger Greenspun, *New York Times* 4 November 1971

- Current recommendations and ratings
StJD LM3 DQ4 DW4 VFG3½ MPG3½ NFT*

    ...A highly enjoyable thriller made under the influence of Siegel (who contributes a memorable cameo as a bartender,... poor Eastwood is driven into a corner like a mesmerised rabbit, unable to find a way out of the impasse without driving one of his two jealous women over the edge. From there it's but a step to... a splendid all-stops-out finale.

    Tom Milne, PTOG 1995

SPY MELODRAMA

The spy hunt was one of Hitchcock's favourite themes, the three English masterpieces in this genre – *The Man Who Knew Too Much*, *The Thirty-Nine Steps*, and *The Lady Vanishes* – giving him an international reputation that resulted in his invitation to Hollywood.

Notorious and *North by Northwest* both feature Cary Grant, Hollywood's greatest light comedian, which reminds us that Hitch always gave us laughter – sometimes black, sometimes tremulous – mixed up with the thrills. Although the cynical American federal agent in *Notorious* and the harassed 'fall guy' in *North by Northwest* both operate within the recognised Grant persona, there is sufficient variety in the two roles to match the different atmospheres in which they work.

Notorious, 1946, is a quietly effective Hitchcock movie: script by Ben Hecht, a performance by Ingrid Bergman that is far more assured than in *Spellbound*, an unforgettable (because human) master spy in Claude Rains, the extraordinary, even embarrassing, choice of uranium as the ultimate objective of the spying process (what Hitch himself called a 'McGuffin' – no matter what it was in reality), the use of familiar objects as images of suspense (here a key stolen by Bergman from Rains whom she has married to serve Grant's purposes), and a bitter and moving love story at the centre. Truffaut's judgement, stated in an interview with Hitchcock, that this was his favourite among the black-and-white pictures is an impressive tribute to this film by an outstanding film-maker and critic (François Truffaut, *Hitchcock*, 1967).

The later *North by Northwest*, 1959, is somehow richer, more varied and more picaresque. The situation is also more appropriate to Grant's comic style, reaching a climax in the Mount Rushmore sequence where his tenuous grip on the stony face of a presidential image is trampled on by Leonard (Martin Landau), valet-bodyguard to arch-enemy Vandamm (played by James Mason, with a subtlety and elegance equal to that of Claude Rains in *Notorious*). Both films have a long sensuous embrace, with even less discretion in *North by Northwest*, made during a more permissive period. The classical sequence of the pursuit of Grant by a crop-spraying plane in a vast expanse of open prairie is one of Hitchcock's most wonderfully realised pieces of wordless action, a 'must' in the instruction given at all film schools for editing, camerawork and direction (and pre-planning). The artfully calculated rhythm has all the artlessness of great art.

John Frankenheimer's *The Manchurian Candidate*, 1962, approaches the problem from a different direction, the suspense (just as skilfully created as in any Hitchcock spy thriller) being subordinated to a 'real-life' idea of political significance: the role of brain-washing in the assassination of a leading political figure (in this case a liberal senator) and the techniques of control which governments can exercise over their subjects (or, in this case, prisoners). This gives *The Manchurian Candidate* an Orwellian quality in the relationship between the soldier brainwashed in North

Korea to carry out assassinations (Laurence Harvey) and the regular officer, similarly brainwashed, who is more conscious of the process of betrayal (a remarkable, serious portrayal by Frank Sinatra). In addition to the element of prophecy, there is gripping political and psychological melodrama, particularly in the manipulations of the soldier's monstrous right-wing mother (Angela Lansbury).

The Manchurian Candidate, UA (Howard C. Koch/ George Axelrod), 1962 bw

Direction: John Frankenheimer
Camera: Lionel Lindon
Music: David Amram
Editing: Ferris Webster
Script: George Axelrod (from the novel by Richard Condon)
Art Direction: Richard Sylbert
Costume Design: Moss Mabry

with Frank Sinatra, Laurence Harvey, Janet Leigh, Angela Lansbury, Henry Silva, James Gregory, John McGiver, Khigh Dhiegh

- Criticism on release

    ...an insolent, heartless thriller... [Frankenheimer is] less concerned than Hitchcock with tension; and though he may be more involved psychologically with his characters, he doesn't take you into the same close, frightening physical contact... If the word 'cold' had in this context no derogatory sense I should say I coldly recommended this film.

    Dilys Powell, *Sunday Times* November 1962

- Current recommendations and ratings
StJD LM3½ DQ4 DW4 VFG5 MPG3½ NFT*

    ...Frankenheimer's version of Richard Condon's tragically prophetic novel looks even better now than it did then. Its greatest virtue lies in its brilliant balancing acts: political satire and nail-biting thriller, the twin lunacies of the Right and Left, and the outrageously funny dialogue during the parallel courtships set against the sadness of the unlovable Shaw's predicament.

Among a marvellous cast... Lansbury stands out. An Iron Lady to savour, for a change. A masterpiece.

Brian Case, PTOG 1995

Notorious, RKO (Alfred Hitchcock), 1946 bw

Direction: Alfred Hitchcock
Camera: Ted Tetzlaff
Art Direction: Albert S. D'Agostino, Carroll Clark
Editing: Theron Worth
Script: Ben Hecht
Music: Roy Webb
Costume Design: Edith Head

with Cary Grant, Ingrid Bergman, Claude Rains, Louis Calhern, Leopoldine Konstantin, Reinhold Schunzel, Moroni Olsen, Ivan Triesault, Antonio Moreno, Charles D. Brown

- Criticism on release

  ...one of the most absorbing pictures of the year... [its] distinction is the remarkable blend of love story with expert 'thriller' that it represents... Actually, the 'thriller' elements are familiar and commonplace, except in so far as Mr Hitchcock has galvanized them into life... But the rare quality of the picture is in the uncommon character of the girl and in the drama of her relations with the American intelligence man...

  Bosley Crowther, *New York Times* 16 August 1946

- Current recommendations and ratings
  StJD S&S82/92 LM3½ DQ3 DW4 VFG4 MPG5 NFT*

  One of Hitchcock's finest films of the 40s... Suspense there is, but what really distinguishes the film is the way its smooth, polished surface illuminates a sickening tangle of self-sacrifice, exploitation, suspicion, and emotional dependence. Grant, in fact, is the least sympathetic character in the dark, ever-shifting relationships on view, while Rains, oppressed by a cigar-chewing, possessive mother and deceived by all around him, is treated with great generosity. Less war thriller than black romance...

  Geoff Andrew, PTOG 1995

North by Northwest, MGM (Alfred Hitchcock), 1959 colour

Direction: Alfred Hitchcock
Camera: Robert Burks
Music: Bernard Herrmann
Special Effects: A. Arnold
  Gillespie, Lee LeBlanc

Script: Ernest Lehman
Credit Titles: Saul Bass
Editing: George Tomasini
Art Direction: Robert Boyle,
  William Horning, Merrill Pye

with Cary Grant, Eva Marie Saint, James Mason, Leo G. Carroll, Jessie Royce Landis, Martin Landau, Philip Ober, Josephine Hutchinson

- Criticism on release

    ...a suspenseful and delightful Cook's Tour of some of the more photogenic spots in the United States. Although they are involved in lightning-fast romance and some loose intrigue, it is all done in brisk, genuinely witty and sophisticated style... Cary Grant, a veteran member of the Hitchcock acting varsity, was never more at home than in this role of the advertising-man-on-the-lam. In casting Eva Marie Saint as his romantic *vis-à-vis*, Mr Hitchcock has plumbed some talents not shown by the actress heretofore...

    A.H. Weiler, *New York Times* 7 August 1959

- Current recommendations and ratings
  StJD S&S82/92 LM4 DQ4 DW5 VFG4 MPG5 NFT**

    ...treads a bizarre tightrope between sex and repression, nightmarish thriller and urbane comedy. Cary Grant is truly superb as the light-hearted advertising executive who's abducted, escapes, and then is hounded across America trying to find out what's going on and slowly being forced to assume another man's identity... All in all, an improbable classic.

    Helen Mackintosh, PTOG 1995

War Films

A 'war' (or, as the Americans call it, 'combat') movie is based upon the heroic but confused actions of battle and upon the psychology of the serving soldier. The battle sequences in these six films vary in length and significance, dominating *All Quiet on the Western Front* and *The Red Badge of Courage*, providing major dramatic sequences in *The Big Parade*, starkly exemplifying the anti-general theme of *Paths of Glory*, providing a spectacular climax to *From Here to Eternity* (which ends with the traumatic Japanese attack on Pearl Harbor) and providing significant emotive interludes to two dramas of the Vietnam War (*The Deer Hunter, Apocalypse Now*).

King Vidor's *The Big Parade*, 1925, excellently combines these essential ingredients, romance and comedy intermingled with action-packed battle sequences, depicting the harsher aspects of trench warfare in France during World War I, seen from the American viewpoint. The hero is not a dedicated patriot, but a playboy type (John Gilbert) who is seen both courting a French peasant girl (Renée Adorée) and experiencing the horrors and comradeship of war. He returns after the war, minus a leg, to marry the girl. The action sequences, especially the operation at Belleau Wood, are strong and exciting. The movie is concerned more with experience than message, although Vidor has stated that he made it as an anti-war film. In fact, it became an impressive and original romantic vehicle for its star.

Lewis Milestone's *All Quiet on the Western Front*, 1930, in its portrayal of the baptism of a group of very young, very raw German recruits in the same trench warfare (seen from the other side), makes a much stronger indictment of war in its terrifying impact upon humanity. Its detailed concern with the ordinary soldier, together with the shock of viewing vividly reconstructed battle scenes from the viewpoint of the participants, derive both from Remarque's powerful novel and the brilliance of Milestone's *mise en scène*. Lew Ayres makes a visually impressive central character (note his performance when cooped up with a French corpse in a shell-hole and during the macabre sequence of the bombardment in the churchyard), and there is a massively realistic, comic and moving performance by Louis Wolheim as the veteran Katszinsky.

John Ford apparently enjoyed his war service in the Navy more than making Hollywood films, and only undertook the filming of W.L. White's documentary account of MTBs (Motor Torpedo Boats) operating in the Pacific because of his admiration for Captain Bulkeley (Brickley in the movie, played magnificently by Robert Montgomery, himself a serving Naval officer during the war). The late Lindsay Anderson, himself a fine film-maker, was a passionate advocate of this film: "John Ford did not want to make *They Were Expendable*, 1945, but once he agreed, he did his very best. And he made a masterpiece." (see his book *About John Ford*). It contains scenes of action, but it is not chauvinistic or flag-waving; rather it is a moving elegy of resignation and stoicism in defeat. Even the brief love interlude (between John Wayne and Donna Reed) is tinged with sadness and regret, and the film as a whole records American withdrawals from the Pacific after Pearl Harbor. Ford generously but honestly records the realism, courage, devotion and loyalty of his MTB crews, not only with telling performances from Montgomery (as the commander) and Wayne (as his Number 2), but also from Marshall Thompson, Cameron Mitchell and a whole host of Ford stalwarts, including Ward Bond and Russell Simpson. Joseph August, who did the camerawork on *The Informer*, also served as a Navy photographer and his lyrical, exhilarating camerawork adds immeasurably to the film's quality.

Henry King's *Twelve o'Clock High*, 1949 is a perfect piece of collaborative film-making between the director, the star (Gregory Peck), and the talented team of film-makers at the Twentieth Century-Fox studios in the late 40s and early 50s. It is concerned with the physical and mental strain of flying in bombers during the saturation attacks on German-occupied Europe during World War II. Set entirely within an American air base in Britain, it has the unity of place, time and action which distinguished the great Greek tragedies. King's treatment is tasteful and largely un-melodramatic, observing the clash between discipline and popularity, and the sad irony of a commander (Gregory Peck) who himself cracks under the strain of driving his men to their limits. There is only one battle sequence, but this is essentially a psychological drama – perceptive and powerful. Dean Jagger's Oscar for Supporting Actor was well deserved as the quiet, thoroughly human adjutant-narrator.

The Red Badge of Courage, 1945, based on one of the finest literary achievements in American fiction – Stephen Crane's novel of 1895 – while expressing indignation at the stupidities and excesses of war, particularly between those sharing a similar language and culture, is more concerned with the compassion for the young males plunged into fear of immediate death, crucial self-reliance and experiences of human suffering that was also the major concern of *All Quiet on the Western Front*. The young hero, played by Audie Murphy, goes through the sequences of hell like a sleepwalker in a familiar, seemingly innocent countryside.

Fred Zinnemann's *From Here to Eternity*, was best known at the time of its release for providing Frank Sinatra with his first serious dramatic role as the misfit Private Maggio, and what were considered then as very frank love scenes between Burt Lancaster (as Sergeant Warden, a single-minded professional) and Deborah Kerr (hitherto considered rather prim), as an officer's wife. This adaptation of a novel by regular soldier turned novelist, James Jones, certainly brings the phrase 'brutal, licentious soldiery' to mind. Many of the scenes have a raw authenticity, particularly the scenes of the brutal beating of Maggio in the stockade and the killing of the sadistic 'Fatso' (Ernest Borgnine) by the bugler Prewitt (Montgomery Clift) in a knife duel. Clift may seem somewhat oversensitive as the stubborn bugler (possibly a modified self-portrait of the novelist himself); but the performances generally ring true, and it remains an excellent, perhaps unique, portrayal of the psychology of the serving soldier in peacetime, culminating in the Pearl Harbor attack, when the whole garrison springs into frantic, desperate action.

Stanley Kubrick's *Paths of Glory*, 1957, (a bitterly angry film) places more emphasis on the brutal ironies of war than on compassion for the doomed participants. The cruel tragedy of a defeated French detachment from which the intransigently chauvinistic General Mireau (George Macready) has a number of soldiers selected by lot for trial for cowardice is seen very much from the point of view of headquarters, where a forthright colonel (Kirk Douglas) takes on the role of defending officer, and corrupt General Broulard (Adolphe Menjou) cynically plans how he should replace Mireau, later to be court-martialled for ordering the opening of fire on his own soldiers. Kubrick's attitude is never ambiguous: this is not only horror but horror emanating from evil.

A large-scale treatment of the Vietnam theme, from the point of view of three working-class recruits – seen both at home and on campaign in the manner of Tolstoy's *War and Peace* – Michael Cimino's *The Deer Hunter*, 1978, is a highly emotional, even at times harrowing, movie. The three Pennsylvanian steel workers (impeccably played by Robert De Niro, Christopher Walken, and John Savage) undergo devastating changes in a baptism of fire in a futile war, particularly in their treatment as prisoners by the Vietcong. This is contrasted vividly with the early scenes of a wedding in a Russian immigrant community and the deer hunt with friends before departing for the war. The film is lavish, highly stylised (it is presented in three formal acts (the departure, the war experience, the return); and Vilmos Zsigmond's images of war and peace are stunning.

Another grand-scale version of the Vietnam débâcle, Francis Ford Coppola's *Apocalypse Now*, 1979, is a grandiose, operatic film transplanting Joseph Conrad's *Heart of Darkness* from imperialism in tropical Africa to the American military intervention in Vietnam. Although basically ambitious, even pretentious, hokum, it is compulsively watchable and masterly film-making, a virtual feast until the final enigmatic sequences with the lonely desperate philosophy of the megalomaniac Kurtz (an excellent performance by Marlon Brando), whom the protagonist, a military hit-man hired by the CIA (Martin Sheen), seeks to kill in the 'heart of darkness', Kurtz's stronghold in a decaying Buddhist temple on a jungle riverbank.

All Quiet on the Western Front, Un (Carl Laemmle Jr.), 1930 bw

*Direction: Lewis Milestone	Dialogue Direction: George Cukor
Script: Dell Andrews, Maxwell Anderson, George Abbott (from the novel by Erich Maria Remarque)	Music: David Broekman
	Special Effects: Frank H. Booth
	Art Direction: Charles D. Hall, W.R. Schmitt
Camera: Arthur Edeson, Karl Freund, Tony Gaudio	Editing: Edgar Adams, Milton Carruth, Maurice Pivar

with Lew Ayres, Louis Wolheim, John Wray, Slim Summerville, Russell Gleason, Ben Alexander, William Bakewell, Beryl Mercer, Vince Barnett, Edwin Maxwell, Fred Zinnemann (bit)

- Criticism on release

    ...I wish it had been a better movie... there is no doubt that it will be successful, but if two writers (Maxwell Anderson and George Abbott) and a director (Lewis Milestone)... had been allowed money and opportunity to produce an original work, the result would have been far more exciting. What they have done has power, but it is spread all over the place...

    Pare Lorentz, *Judge* 24 May 1930

- Current recommendations and ratings
StJD BN92 S&S92 LM4 DQ4 DW5 VFG5 MPG5 NFT*

    ...renowned as the classic anti-war movie... the film's strength now derives less from its admittedly powerful but highly simplistic utterances about war as waste than from a generally excellent set of performances (Ayres especially) and an almost total reluctance to follow normal plot structure...

    Geoff Andrew, PTOG 1995

The Big Parade, MGM (Irving Thalberg), 1925 bw

Direction: King Vidor
Camera (with tinted sequences): John Arnold
Music: William Axt, David Mendoza
Art Direction: Cedric Gibbons, James Basevi

Script: Harry Behn (from a play by Joseph Farnham based on the story by Laurence Stallings)
Editing: Hugh Wynn

with John Gilbert, Renée Adorée, Karl Dane, Tom O'Brien, Hobart Bosworth, Claire Adams

- Criticism on release

    I could not detect a single flaw in *The Big Parade*, not one error of taste, or of authenticity; [it] can be ranked among the few genuinely great achievements of the screen... [Vidor] has made war scenes that actually resemble war... Although the war scenes are naturally predominant the picture is essentially a love story - and a superbly stirring one at that...

    Robert E. Sherwood, *Life* 10 December 1925

- Current recommendations and ratings
  StJD LM4 MPG5 NFT*

    Time has not dealt altogether kindly with Vidor's silent blockbuster... Too much of it is plain embarrassing... Yet even if it romanticizes the true horrors beyond all recognition, there is undeniable power in Vidor's vision of a doughboy's episodic odyssey through the vast landscape of war. One is never left in any doubt that he was, even then, a major talent.

    Tom Milne, PTOG 1995

From Here to Eternity, Col (Harry Cohn/Buddy Adler), 1953 bw

*Direction: Fred Zinnemann
*Camera: Burnett Guffey
Music: George Duning
*Editing: William Lyon

*Script: Daniel Taradash (from the novel by James Jones)
Art Direction: Gary Odell

with Burt Lancaster, Deborah Kerr, *Frank Sinatra, Montgomery Clift, *Donna Reed, Ernest Borgnine, Philip Ober, Jack Warden, Claude Akins, Jean Willes, Joan Shawlee

- Criticism on release

    ...a shining example of truly professional movie-making... the team of scenarist, director, producer and cast has managed to transfer convincingly the muscularity of the basically male society with which the book dealt; the poignancy and futility of the love lives of the professional soldiers involved, as well as the indictment of commanding officers whose selfishness can break men devoted to soldiering... Credit Fred Zinnemann with an expert directorial achievement in maintaining [the] various involvements on equal and lucid levels...

    'A.W.', *New York Times* 6 August 1953

- Current recommendations and ratings
  StJD LM4 DQ4 DW4 VFG5 MPG5 NFT**

    ..besides Burnett Guffey's crisp monochrome camerawork and Daniel Taradash's taut screenplay, it's the performances that stay in the memory, particularly those of Clift and Sinatra. Zinnemann's flat direction does produce its dull moments, though...

    Geoff Andrew, PTOG 1995

Paths of Glory, UA (James E. Harris), 1957 bw

Direction: Stanley Kubrick	Script: Kubrick, with Calder Willingham, Jim Thompson (from novel by Humphrey Cobb)
Camera: George Krause	
Music: Gerald Fried	
Art Direction: Ludwig Reiber	
	Editing: Eva Kroll
with Kirk Douglas, Adolphe Menjou, Ralph Meeker, George Macready, Timothy Carey, Richard Anderson, Emile Meyer, Joseph Turkel	

- Criticism on release

> ...will never be released in France, not as long as there are soldiers around, in any case. It's a shame, because it is very beautiful from a number of points of view. It is admirably directed, even better than *The Killing*, with very many fluid long shots. The splendid camera work captures the plastic style of that epoch – we think of the war as it was pictured in the photographs of *L'Illustration*... an important film that establishes the talent and energy of a new American director...
>
> François Truffaut, *Cahiers du Cinema*, 1958

- Current recommendations and ratings
StJD BN92 S&S82/92 LM4 DQ3 DW5 VFG5 MPG5 NFT*

> Unusually trenchant for its time... Kubrick's first prestige movie bitterly attacks the role of the French military authorities in World War I through an account of the court-martial and execution of three blameless privates... the film is politically and emotionally anchored in Kirk Douglas' astonishingly successful performance as the condemned men's defender. One measure of the film's effectiveness is that it was banned in France on political grounds for eighteen years.
>
> Tony Rayns, PTOG 1995

The Red Badge of Courage, MGM (Gottfried Reinhardt), 1951 bw

Direction: John Huston
2nd Unit Direction: Andrew Marton
Camera: Hal Rosson
Art Direction: Cedric Gibbons, Hans Peters
Script: Huston, with Albert Band (from the novel by Stephen Crane)
Music: Bronislaw Kaper
Editing: Ben Lewis

with Audie Murphy, Bill Maudlin, Arthur Hunnicutt, John Dierkes, Royal Dano, Douglas Dick, Andy Devine, Glenn Strange, Whit Bissell

- Criticism on release

    ...one of the most remarkable war films ever made... Directly inspired by the wonderful Civil War photographs of Matthew Brady, [it] excels in pictorial representation of, let it be admitted, a highly picturesque war. [It] inducts you into the heat and chaos of battle in a way that hasn't been equalled since *All Quiet on the Western Front*.

    Richard Winnington, *News Chronicle*
    16 November 1951

- Current recommendations and ratings
  LM3½ DQ3 DW5 VFG5 MPG5 NFT*

    ...The fragments that remain, linked by a voice-over commentary drawn from the novel, nevertheless exhibit a remarkable delicacy and depth of feeling that sometimes (as in the death of the Tall Soldier) approximates the visionary quality of the novel. And visually, with Harold Rosson's camerawork lovingly recreating the harsh, dustily faded textures of Matthew Brady's Civil War pictures, it looks absolutely superb.

    Tom Milne, PTOG 1995

They Were Expendable, MGM (John Ford/ Cliff Reid), 1945 bw

Direction: John Ford, with Robert Montgomery, uc	Script: Frank Wead (from W.L. White's book)
Camera: Joseph H. August	Music: Herbert Stothart
Art Direction: Cedric Gibbons, Malcolm Brown	Editing: Frank E. Hull, Douglas Biggs
Special Effects: A. Arnold Gillespie	

with Robert Montgomery, John Wayne, Donna Reed, Jack Holt, Ward Bond, Marshall Thompson, Cameron Mitchell, Leon Ames, Louis Van Heydt, Charles Trowbridge, Robert Barrat, Russell Simpson, Alan Bridge, Tom Tyler

- Criticism on release

    For what seems half of the dogged, devoted length of *They Were Expendable* all you have to watch is men getting on or off PT boats, and other men watching them do so. But this is made so beautiful and so real that I could not feel one foot of the film was wasted... Visually, and in detail, and in nearly everything he does with people, I think it is John Ford's finest movie. Another man who evidently learned a tremendous amount through the war is Robert Montgomery whose sober, light, sure performance is, so far as I can remember, the one perfection to turn up in movies during the year.

    James Agee, *The Nation* 5 January 1946

- Current recommendations and ratings
S&S82/92 LM4 DQ3 DW4 VFG5 MPG5 NFT*

    ...The tugs of docu-drama, emotionalism and sheer timing produced a major work of surprisingly downbeat romanticism... A curious movie, whose premises Ford would obsessively rework in his subsequent cavalry pictures, with the luxury of historical distance.

    Paul Taylor, PTOG 1995

Twelve o'Clock High, TCF (Darryl F. Zanuck), 1949 bw

Direction: Henry King
Camera: Leon Shamroy
Music: Alfred Newman
Art Direction: Lyle Wheeler,
  Maurice Ransford

Script: Sy Bartlett, Beirne Lay
  (from their own novel)
Editing: Barbara McLean

with Gregory Peck, Hugh Marlowe, Gary Merrill, Millard Mitchell,
  *Dean Jagger, Robert Arthur, Paul Stewart

- Criticism on release

    Two things strike me about *Twelve o'Clock High* – two things, I mean, quite apart from the fact that it is a fine, an adult and a memorable film. The first is that it marks a changing attitude on the part of the American cinema towards the war. The second is that it displays for once the strength of the talking film – as well as, now and then, the weaknesses. The emotions are concentrated in the characters and development of a group of American airmen... Once or twice [it] talks too much... But, on the other hand, it makes effective play with its silences... Gregory Peck, to whom these moments fall here, handles them like the good actor he is...

    Dilys Powell, *Sunday Times* 12 February 1950

- Current recommendations and ratings
  LM4 DQ4 DW4 VFG4½ MPG5 NFT*

    Along with *The Gunfighter* (also directed by the erratic but undervalued King), one of Peck's best performances... King's control, the electric tension and the performances all hold firm

    Tom Milne, PTOG 1995

Apocalypse Now, UA/ Omni Zoetrope (Francis Ford Coppola), 1979 colour

Direction and Script (with John Milius and Michael Herr):
 F.F. Coppola
Camera: Vittorio Storaro
Music: Carmine Coppola,
 F.F. Coppola
Costume Design: Charles James
Production Design: Dean
 Tavoularis
Editing: Richard Marks

with Marlon Brando, Martin Sheen, Robert Duvall, Frederic Forrest, Albert Hall, Sam Bottoms, Dennis Hopper, Harrison Ford

- Criticism on release

  Mr Coppola and Mr Milius have attempted to update Conrad, who really doesn't need updating... The Marlow character is now a battle-scarred Special Services officer [whose] adventures as he travels upriver in the small patrol boat provided by the Army... are often spellbinding – Vittorio Storaro, who photographed *Last Tango in Paris*, among other fine films, is responsible for the extraordinary camerawork that almost, but not quite, saves *Apocalypse Now* from its profoundly anticlimactic intellectual muddle.

  Vincent Canby, *New York Times* 15 August 1979

- Current recommendations and ratings
  StJD BN92 S&S82/92 LM3½ DQ3 DW4 VFG4 MPG3½ NFT**

  ...a film of great effects (a flaming bridge, Wagnerian strikes) and considerable pretension (quotes from T.S. Eliot?)... The casting of Brando is perhaps the acid-test: brilliant as movie-making, but it turns Vietnam into a vast trip into a war of the Imagination.

  Chris Auty, PTOG 1995

The Deer Hunter, Un (Barry Spikings, Michael Deeley, Michael Cimino, John Peverall), 1978 *colour*

*Direction: Michael Cimino
Camera: Vilmos Zsigmond
Music: Stanley Myers
Special Effects: Fred Cramer
Art Direction: Ron Hobbs, Kim Swados
Costume Design: Eric Seelig

Script: Deric Washburn, from a story by Cimino, Washburn, Louis Garfinkle and Quinn H. Redeker
Editing: Peter Zinner

with Robert De Niro, John Cazale, John Savage, Christopher Walken, Meryl Streep, George Dzundza, Chuck Aspegren, Shirley Stoler

- Criticism on release

    Among the considerable achievements of Michael Cimino's *The Deer Hunter* is the fact that the film remains intense, powerful and fascinating for more than three hours. The picture is a long, sprawling epic-type in many ways more novel than motion picture. It employs literary references stylistically, forecasting events which will happen in the film. It is a brutal work... Throughout the film various ceremonies and cultural rituals are explored, compared and juxtaposed – the wedding, the game and the deer hunt. It is up to the viewer to decide how these rituals fit together and it is a big comprehension demand... Still, the film is ambitious and it succeeds on a number of levels, and it proves that Cimino is an important director...

    Variety, 1978

- Current recommendations and ratings
  StJD S&S92 LM4 DQ4 DW4 VFG4½ MPG5 NFT*

    ...probably one of the great films of the decade... it proposes De Niro as a Ulyssean hero tested to the limit by war. Moral imperatives replace historical analysis, social rituals become religious sacraments, and the sado-masochism of the central (male) love affair is icing on a Nietzschean cake.

Ideally, though, it should prove as gruelling a test of its audience's moral and political conscience as it seems to have been for its makers.

Chris Auty, PTOG 1995

Westerns

John Ford does not dominate the Western in the same way that Hitchcock does the suspense thriller. There is also Howard Hawks and, later, Sam Peckinpah, and several other directors with one masterpiece to their name. However, Ford is a key figure in the genre: in 1939 – a vintage year for the kind of high-gloss entertainment provided by Hollywood – his *Stagecoach* set a new style and standard for the Western using high production values and breaking away from crude melodrama, chases and gunfights, and adding characterisation, location poetry and the world of myth.

In the same year, Joe Pasternak at Universal produced a marvellous tongue-in-cheek Western – *Destry Rides Again* – starring James Stewart (still in his early, mainly light comedy, days) and Marlene Dietrich (singing her glorious 'Boys in the Back Room'). Although essentially comic and romantic, it has enough authentic toughness to make it a true Western.

Nevertheless, it was *Stagecoach* which exerted the most potent influence over future Westerns, with its group of twilight characters travelling through hostile Indian country and experiencing birth, love, struggle, conversion and death, and culminating in one of the most gripping shoot-outs in film history, with the Ringo Kid (John Wayne) seeking revenge for the killing of his younger brother.

Except for an outstanding *noir* Western, *The Oxbow Incident* of 1943, the genre hung fire until after the war. Twentieth Century combined its interest in films of social concern with a Western background in Lamar Trotti's adaptation of Walter van Tilburg Clark's novel of an unjust lynching of three strangers (one a Mexican, thus introducing the theme of racialism). William Wellman's treatment has a claustrophobic atmosphere imparted by the imaginative studio sets. Although filmed on a modest budget, it has a wealth of excellent players, including all the leads and two studies of unbalanced hatred by Jane Darwell and Frank Conroy. "Oppressive and powerful" seems a reasonable summary of the critical opinion, and in many ways it is an extraordinary film to come out of the Hollywood studios during wartime.

Almost immediately after the war, Ford staged a comeback in this genre with what is now considered one of his finest films, *My Darling Clementine*, 1946, with Henry Fonda's Marshal Earp preparing a near-military manoeuvre against the Clantons at dawn near the OK Corral. This is a quintessential Western, with tender and perceptive community scenes, the Monument Valley rock shapes, outstanding performances from the whole cast (even, somewhat surprisingly, from Victor Mature as a doom-laden Doc Halliday), atmospheric black-and-white photography from Joe MacDonald, and a gradual *accelerando* of pace from the teasingly slow beginning to the exciting finale.

The first of John Ford's 'cavalry trilogy', *Fort Apache*, 1948, has recently re-established itself. On release this portrayal by Henry Fonda of a snobbish, embittered ex-general demoted to commander of a frontier post, was considered a waste of the kind of talent that had created ikonic figures in *Young Mr Lincoln* and *The Grapes of Wrath*. Now, it appears to be the first impressive study of an inhuman, even menacing, character of the kind for which he became quite renowned (*Once Upon a Time in the West*). The film also features John Wayne, who plays his second-in-command, a dedicated professional who knows his men, the terrain, and the enemy. A human conflict is inevitable, but the best man wins. *Fort Apache* is a masterwork based on a mythical American past, which scores in the domestic scenes – the ordinary background of cavalry life – almost more than it does in the brilliantly depicted action scenes.

The archetypal John Wayne also appeared in a Howard Hawks masterpiece, *Red River*, 1948, closely followed by the second (and best) of the 'cavalry trilogy', *She Wore a Yellow Ribbon*, 1949. In *Red River* he was a harsh cattleman foster-father, forced into a long cattle drive with his resentful ward (Montgomery Clift – in his first, impressive, screen appearance), in *She Wore a Yellow Ribbon* an ageing and widowed cavalry officer on the verge of reluctant retirement, coping with Indian raids with variable help from bucolic Sergeant Quincannon, played by Victor McLaglen. This time it is the Ford film that is in colour, but the cinematography of *Red River* – by Russell Harlan – is by no means inferior for its purpose to the glowing Technicolor photography of Winton Hoch in *She Wore a Yellow Ribbon*. By now the Wayne 'persona' was well established under any director: suspicious of too much talk, too stoic and too proud to reveal his own inner tenderness publicly, impatient with treachery and guile, often fretting under the mistaken commands of short-sighted authority.

The third movie in the 'cavalry trilogy', *Rio Grande*, does not make it into the Top Two-Fifty category, but Ford's *Wagonmaster*,

1950, does. Called by some a 'muted' John Ford Western (as if he were directing a perfect pastiche of his own work), its leisurely, expansive movement has familiar ingredients – the Mormon wagon train, the hired leader who knows his terrain like the palm of his hand (Ben Johnson in his first starring role), the spiteful, callous outlaw tribe, the boozy, degenerate camp followers, and the marvellous sequences of landscape images photographed on an epic scale by Bert Glennon. Familiarity with the subject and its treatment certainly has not led to contempt, rather a feeling of relaxed naturalness.

Before Ford's next great Western, *The Searchers* (also shot in colour by Hoch), two inevitable imitations of the Ford-style Western appeared, made with all the expected high professionalism of the Fifties: Fred Zinnemann's *High Noon*, 1952, (about a marshal in a border town threatened by outlaws) and George Stevens' *Shane*, 1953, (about frontier settlers threatened by outlaws). *High Noon* first made its impact through the somewhat haggard performance of Gary Cooper and the quiet sincerity of Grace Kelly's Quaker wife, together with the haunting ballad music by Dimitri Tiomkin ('Do not forsake me, oh my darlin'!'), and the minute-by-minute tension building up as the marshal awaits his confrontation with the outlaws newly released from jail. The addition of a kind of allegory referring to appeasement became fashionable during the Vietnam War, but it is the film's interest as a first-class traditional Western that remains. The popularity of *Shane* has always been greater than its critical reputation. It perfectly embodies all the characteristics of the ideal folk myth: Alan Ladd's angelic and existentialist hero, Jean Arthur's beautifully realised portrait of "an unfulfilled Pioneer mother" (Philip French in *Westerns*, 1973), Van Heflin's harassed settler and Jack Palance's almost abstract figure of evil. Loyal Griggs's work in Technicolor must be amongst the most lushly beautiful to be seen in the whole genre.

John Sturges's *Bad Day at Black Rock*, 1954, has a contemporary but also archetypal Western theme, with Spencer Tracy as the one-armed avenger stirring up the guilt and menace of a remote Western farming community. Also, it is a drama of pursuit and social concern, for it is the murder of a Japanese-American army comrade which is the cause of the stranger's visit. According to Philip French, this is one of the most striking of what he calls the 'post-Westerns', using the recently devised Cinemascope screen with great artistry.

John Ford's *The Searchers*, 1956, is even more of a Western for the connoisseur. Filmed with sure artistic feeling, it tells the story of Ethan Edwards, a 'loner' (Ford's own description – see Peter Bogdanovich, *John Ford*, 1967), tracking down his niece who was kidnapped by Indians during an Indian raid and massacre. His intense loathing of Indians contributes to the emotional intensity of the chase; Ethan's alienated personality (well portrayed by John Wayne) gives a tragic essence to what is essentially a taut pursuit story. This is one of Ford's most personal and serious films.

Hollywood's 'high noon' of this traditional frontier style came at the end of the 1950s. In 1956 Howard Hawks' *Rio Bravo*, a slow rich Western, with its group of oddly assorted characters uniting in the face of a violent threat (including Dean Martin as a drunken deputy, Walter Brennan as a garrulous old-timer, Ricky Nelson as a young cowhand intent on proving his manhood, and Angie Dickinson as a sexy saloon singer, Feathers) nevertheless pivots around the traditional events of the small-town Western with Wayne as a sheriff attempting to keep the desperado in jail until the marshal arrives.

In Ford's *The Man Who Shot Liberty Vallance*, 1962, we have a preview of the modern (less heroic, more 'realistic') Western. The man reputed to have shot the primitive and vicious outlaw, Liberty Vallance (Lee Marvin), is a dude lawyer, Ransom Stoddart (James Stewart), who then goes on to make his career in the world of politics. The man who actually shot Vallance was Tom Doniphon, a gunfighter of the Old West (John Wayne), rival for the hand of the girl Stoddart marries (Vera Miles). The story is told in flashback to the local newspaper editor (Edmond O'Brien) by Senator Stoddart, returning to Shinbone with his wife for Tom's funeral. Ford thus emphasises the latent chivalry of the Old West while raucously denigrating the world of Eastern politics. As usual with Ford, the film has outstanding production values, with beautiful camerawork by William Clothier.

Sam Peckinpah became the master of the 'anti-Western'. Although *The Wild Bunch*, his best-known picture, crystallises his attitudes and techniques within itself, the earlier *Ride the High Country* (or *Guns in the Afternoon*, as it is called in Britain) 1962, is one of the finest of all Westerns, reflecting the traditions of the genre but treating them with a new and bolder realism. Dealing with two ageing Westerners (Joel McCrea and Randolph Scott) coming to terms with the decline from the physical peak of their youth in the context of the ageless frontier we know from countless 'horse operas', it symbolises the almost imperceptible collapse of the American Dream.

The *Wild Bunch*, 1969, a bitter study of the kind of gunfighters that made up *The Magnificent Seven*, but this time on the wrong side of the law (and justice) at the tag-end of the great era of the West, depicts with brutal candour the vile and violent side of the heroics, culminating in a bloodthirsty massacre and the ironic triumph of the bounty-hunters lumping the bodies of their prey to the border on the backs of mules. This movie set the final seal on the 'post-Western', after which the restoration of the old Western seemed virtually impossible. Amongst general lack of interest in the Western during the 1970s, Clint Eastwood – never forgetting what he owed to his portrayal of the 'Man Without a Name' in Sergio Leone's wonderful 'Spaghetti Westerns' – revived the genre originally and effectively in *High Plains Drifter* and, particularly, *The Outlaw Josey Wales*, 1976. Typically a tale of revenge, it tells of an outlaw seeking to avenge the murder of his wife and children by Union guerilas during the Civil War. Chief Dan George scores a hit as one of his many strange supporters, an old Cherokee with an endearingly wry slant on life. The movie is long and sometimes dull perhaps, but it is a labour of love that restores a new sympathetic quality to Eastwood's laconic anti-hero.

The appeal of Don Siegel's *The Shootist*, 1976, is by no means reduced by the knowledge that John Wayne, as John Bernard Books, a veteran gunfighter dying of cancer, is virtually playing himself, reflecting his courage, his manly individualism and the many major roles in past Westerns. Books's final days are harassed by young would-be ace gunslingers trying to beat him to the draw and his attraction to a beautiful widow (Lauren Bacall) in whose lodgings he spends his last days. There is a climactic shoot-out, but, on the whole, this is a lyrical work mourning the passing of an era (the date is 1901) and of the giant frontiersmen celebrated in a half century of films. It is fitting that the old doctor who diagnoses the fatal disease is played by another of the cinema's great cowboy heroes, James Stewart.

Destry Rides Again, Un (Joe Pasternak), 1939 bw

Direction: George Marshall
Camera: Hal Mohr
Music: Frank Skinner
Songs: Frank Loesser, Frederick Hollander
Art Direction: Jack Otterson, Martin Obzina
Script: Felix Jackson, Gertrude Purcell, Henry Myers (from the novel *The Sheriff of Dyke's Hole* by Max Brand)
Editing: Milton Carruth
Costume Design: Vera West

with James Stewart, Marlene Dietrich, Brian Donlevy, Charles Winninger, Una Merkel, Mischa Auer, Irene Hervey, Allen Jenkins, Warren Hymer, Billy Gilbert, Samuel S. Hinds, Jack Carson, Virginia Brissac

- Criticism on release

   ...Western melodrama at its best directed with subtlety yet incorporating all the usual rough-house stuff put over with unabated vigour... A free for all between Dietrich and Una Merkel must be seen to be believed. James Stewart has not given a better performance... Altogether a very enjoyable picture [which] should put Marlene Dietrich right back on the movie map...

   Lionel Collier, *Picturegoer* 13 April 1940

- Current recommendations and ratings
LM4 DQ4 DW5 VFG4 MPG3½ NFT*

   Marvellous comedy Western... What is remarkable about the film is the way it combines humour, romance, suspense and action so seamlessly [with individual scenes... indelibly printed on the memory]. Flawless performances, pacy direction and a snappy script place it head and shoulders above virtually any other spoof oater.

   Geoff Andrew, PTOG 1995

Fort Apache, RKO/Argosy (John Ford/Merian C. Cooper), 1948 bw

Direction: John Ford	Script: Frank S. Nugent (from a story by James Warner Bellah)
Camera: Archie Stout	
Music: Richard Hageman	Special Effects: David Koehler
Art Direction: James Basevi	Editing: Jack Murray
Costume Design: Michael Meyers, Ann Peck	

with Henry Fonda, John Wayne, Shirley Temple, Ward Bond, John Agar, George O'Brien, Irene Rich, Victor McLaglen, Anna Lee, Pedro Armendariz, Dick Foran, Guy Kibbee, Mae Marsh, Hank Worden

- Criticism on release

    ...a salty and sizzling visualization of regimental life at a desert fort, of strong masculine personality and of racing battles beneath the withering sun. For, of course, Mr Ford is a genius at directing this sort of thing and Frank S. Nugent has ably supplied him with a tangy and workable script – Henry Fonda is withering as the colonel, fiercely stubborn and stiff with gallantry, and John Wayne is powerful as his captain, forthright and exquisitely brave...

    Bosley Crowther, *New York Times* 26 June 1948

- Current recommendations and ratings
  S&S82/92 LM3 DQ4 DW4 VFG5 MPG5 NFT**

    ...West Point stiffness [the Custer-like Fonda] meets the more organic Western community of an isolated Arizona outpost, and inflexible notions of duty lead inexorably to disaster, historically written as glory.

    Paul Taylor, PTOG 1995

High Noon, UA (Stanley Kramer), 1952 bw

Direction: Fred Zinnemann
Camera: Floyd Crosby
Music: Dimitri Tiomkin
*Song, 'Do Not Forsake Me,Oh My Darlin'' - Tiomkin, Ned Washington
Script: Carl Foreman (from the story *The Tin Star* by John Cunningham)
Art Direction: Rudolph Sternad
*Editing: Harry Gerstad, Elmo Williams

with *Gary Cooper, Grace Kelly, Thomas Mitchell, Katy Jurado, Lloyd Bridges, Otto Kruger, Lon Chaney Jr., Henry Morgan, Lee Van Cleef, Harry Shannon

- Criticism on release

   ...futile to mourn the tragi-ironic ending that would have made this an outstanding film. Allowing for the tritenesses and the monotonous ageing Cooper front there is some fine tension and consistently high craftsmanship.

   Richard Winnington, *News Chronicle* 3 May 1952

- Current recommendations and ratings
  StJD BN92 S&S82/92 LM4 DQ4 DW4 VFG5 MPG5 NFT*

   A Western of stark, classical lineaments... Writer Carl Foreman, who fetched up on the HUAC blacklist[6], leaves it open whether the marshal is making a gesture of sublime, arrogant futility - as his bride (Kelly), a Quaker opposed to violence, believes - or simply doing what a man must. *High Noon* won a fistful of Oscars, but in these days of pasteboard screen machismo, it's worth seeing simply as the anatomy of what it took to make a man before the myth turned sour.

   Sheila Johnston, PTOG 1995

---

[6] i.e. found guilty of Communist sympathies by the House Un-American Activities Committee operating Senator McCarthy's witch-hunt

The Man Who Shot Liberty Vallance, Par (Willis Goldbeck), 1962 bw

Direction: John Ford
Camera: William Clothier
Music: Cyril Mockridge, Alfred Newman
Art Direction: Hal Pereira, Eddie Imazu
Editing: Otho Lovering

Script: Willis Goldbeck, James Warner Bellah (from a story by Dorothy M. Johnson)
Costume Design: Edith Head

with James Stewart, John Wayne, Vera Miles, Lee Marvin, Edmond O'Brien, Andy Devine, Ken Murray, John Carradine, Jeanette Nolan, John Qualen, Woody Strode, Strother Martin, Lee Van Cleef, Denver Pyle, Anna Lee (bit)

- Criticism on release

    ...handled with consummate professionalism by such top hands as John Ford, director, James Stewart and John Wayne. But time has made their vehicle creaky. Their basically honest, rugged and mature saga has been sapped of a great deal of effect by an obvious, overlong and garrulous anticlimax. But [Ford's] vignettes of the brawling life of Shinbone on a Saturday night; the ravenous diners on giant, fried steaks; the tinny music and clatter of a saloon; the tinkling sounds of a cantina near the desert; and a raucous local election are the authentic sights and sounds of a pioneer community...

    A.H. Weiler, *New York Times* 24 May 1962

- Current recommendations and ratings
StJD S&S82/92 LM4 DQ3 DW4 VFG3 MPG3 NFT*

    Ford's purest and most sustained expression of the familiar themes of the passing of the Old West, the conflict between untamed wilderness and the cultivated garden, and the power of myth...

    Nigel Floyd, PTOG 1995

My Darling Clementine, TCF (Samuel G. Engel), 1946 bw

Direction: John Ford
Camera: Joe MacDonald
Music: Cyril Mockridge
Art Direction: James Basevi, Lyle Wheeler
Costume Design: Rene Hubert
Editing: Dorothy Spencer

Script: Samuel G. Engel, Winston Miller (from a story by Sam Hellman based on *Wyatt Earp, Frontier Marshal* by Stuart Lake)

with Henry Fonda, Linda Darnell, Victor Mature, Walter Brennan, Tim Holt, Cathy Downs, Ward Bond, Alan Mowbray, John Ireland, Grant Withers, Roy Roberts, Jane Darwell, Russell Simpson, Francis Ford, J. Farrell MacDonald

- Criticism on release

    Seven years ago John Ford's classic *Stagecoach* snuggled very close to fine art in this genre. And, now, by George, he's almost matched it... every scene, every shot is the product of a keen and sensitive eye, an eye which has deep comprehension of the beauty of rugged people and a rugged world... When he catches a horseman or stagecoach thumping across the scrubby wastes, the magnificence of nature – the sky and desert – dwarf the energies of man...

    Bosley Crowther, *New York Times* 4 December 1946

- Current recommendations and ratings
StJD BN92 S&S82/92 LM4 DQ4 VFG5 MPG5 NFT*

    For viewers, the film's greatness (and enjoyability) rests not in the accuracy of the final shootout, but in the orchestrated series of incidents – the drunken Shakespearean actor, Earp's visit to the barber, the dance in the unfinished church – which give meaning to the shootout...

    Phil Hardy, PTOG 1995

The Oxbow Incident/ Strange Incident, TCF (Darryl Zanuck/Lamar Trotti), 1943 bw

Direction: William Wellman	Script: Lamar Trotti (from the novel by Walter van Tilburg Clark)
Camera: Arthur C. Miller	
Music: Cyril Mockridge	
Costume Design: Earl Luick	Art Direction: Richard Day, James Basevi
	Editing: Allen McNeil

with Henry Fonda, Dana Andrews, Anthony Quinn, William Eythe, Henry Morgan, Jane Darwell, Harry Davenport, Frank Conroy, Marc Lawrence, Francis Ford, Paul Hurst, Frank Orth, Almira Sessions, Margaret Hamilton, Victor Kilian

- Criticism on release

    ...it is hard to imagine a picture with less promise commercially... It shows a tragic violation of justice with little backlash to sweeten the bitter draught... It also points a moral, bluntly and unremittingly, to show the horror of mob rule... Willam Wellman has directed the picture with a realism that is as sharp and cold as a knife, [and] an all-round excellent cast has played the film brilliantly...

    Bosley Crowther, New York Times 10 May 1943

- Current recommendations and ratings
StJD LM4 DW4 VFG5 MPG5 NFT*

    A solemn, somewhat simplistically liberal Western – a decidedly uncelebratory portrait of the frontier spirit.

    Geoff Andrew, PTOG 1995

Red River, UA (Charles Feldman/Howard Hawks), 1948 bw

Direction: Howard Hawks
Camera: Russell Harlan
Music: Dimitri Tiomkin
Art Direction: John Arensma
Script: Borden Chase, Charles Schnee (from a story by Chase)
Editing: Christian Nyby

with John Wayne, Montgomery Clift, Joanne Dru, Walter Brennan, Coleen Gray, John Ireland, Harry Carey, Harry Carey Jr., Noah Beery Jr., Paul Fix, Tom Tyler (bit), Glenn Strange (bit), Shelley Winters (bit)

- Criticism on release

  ...[Clift's performance], an extremely tough one, easily holds its own for authenticity among a bunch of old-time westerners like John Wayne, Walter Brennan, Noah Beery Jr., and Harry Carey... The story develops along the lines of two personal conflicts: the personal fight between a couple of men who at once love and are bitterly hostile to each other, and the broader struggle against exhaustion, hunger, rain, drought, border gangs and Indians. It is told with enormous gusto and strong film sense against magnificent natural backgrounds...

  C.A. Lejeune, *The Observer* 28 November 1948

- Current recommendations and ratings
  StJD BN92 S&S82/92 LM4 DQ4 DW5 VFG5 MPG5 NFT*

  ...a sheer delight that works on many levels: an examination of Wayne's heroic image... another variation of Hawks' perennial concern with the theme of self-respect and professionalism, and being part of 'the group', [and] an intimate epic celebrating the determination to establish civilisation in the wilderness... Immaculately shot by Russell Harlan, perfectly performed by a host of Hawks regulars, and shot through with dark comedy, it's probably the finest Western of the 40s.

  Geoff Andrew, PTOG 1995

Stagecoach, UA (Walter Wanger), 1939 bw

Direction: John Ford, with Yakima Canutt (2nd Unit)
Script: Dudley Nichols (from the story *Stage to Lordsburg* by Ernest Haycox)
Camera: Bert Glennon
Art Direction: Alexander Toluboff
Editing: Dorothy Spencer, Walter Reynolds
Special Effects: Ray Binger
Costume Design: Walter Plunkett
Music: Richard Hageman, John Leipold, Leo Shuken, W. Franke Harling, Louis Gruenberg (adapted from seventeen American folk tunes of the 1880s)

with John Wayne, Claire Trevor, *Thomas Mitchell, George Bancroft, Andy Devine, Louise Platt, Tim Holt, John Carradine, Donald Meek, Berton Churchill, Tom Tyler

- Criticism on release

    ...In one superbly expansive gesture, [John Ford] has swept aside the years of artifice and talkie compromise and has made a motion picture that sings a song of camera. It moves, and how beautifully it moves, across the plains of Arizona, skirting the skyreaching mesas of Monument Valley, beneath the piled-up cloudbanks which every photographer dreams about... Here, in a sentence, is a movie of the grand old school, a genuine rib-thumper and a beautiful sight to see...

    Frank Nugent, *New York Times* 3 March 1939

- Current recommendations and ratings
StJD BN92 S&S82/92 LM4 DQ4 DW5 VFG5 MPG5 NFT**

    Impossible to overstate the influence of Ford's magnificent film, generally considered to be the first modern Western. Shot in the Monument Valley which Ford was later to make his own, it also initiated Wayne's extraordinarily fertile partnership with the director, and established in embryo much of the mythology explored and developed in Ford's subsequent Westerns...

    Nigel Floyd, PTOG 1995

Wagonmaster, RKO/ Argosy (John Ford/ Merian C.Cooper), 1950 bw

Direction: John Ford	Script: Frank S. Nugent, Patrick Ford (from John Ford's concept)
Camera: Bert Glennon	
Music: Richard Hageman	
Art Direction: James Basevi	Special Effects: Jack Caffee
Costume Design: Wesley V. Jefferies, Adele Parmenter	Editing: Jack Murray

with Ben Johnson, Harry Carey Jr., Joanne Dru, Ward Bond, Charles Kemper, Jane Darwell, Alan Mowbray, James Arness, Jim Thorpe, Ruth Clifford, Russell Simpson, Francis Ford, Kathleen O'Malley, Hank Worden

- Criticism on release

    [Mr Ford] is not deviating greatly from his own time-tested formula... Naturally, the overpoweringly rugged terrain, the menacing killers and a tribe of touchy Navajos are not conducive to a peaceful trek – Despite all these hurdles, romance, which is kept in a decidedly minor key, is permitted to flower, so that at the journey's end the young trail-blazers appear to be altar-bound, too. Ben Johnson... is handsome, natural, laconic and sits a horse well in the title role, [but] the 'star' is the vast, colorful Utah locale in which a portion of it was filmed.

    'A.W.', *New York Times* 19 June 1950

- Current recommendations and ratings
S&S82/92 LM3 DQ3 DW3 VFG4 MPG5 NFT*

    Another Fordian epic positing the American community as the sum of its bands of outsiders... A moral tale, but with a refreshing lack of rhetoric in its poetry...

    Paul Taylor, PTOG 1995

Bad Day at Black Rock, MGM (Dore Schary), 1954 colour

Direction: John Sturges	Script: Millard Kaufman, Don McGuire (from a story by Howard Breslin)
Camera: William C. Mellor	
Art Direction: Cedric Gibbons, Malcolm Browne	Music: André Previn
Editing: Newell Kimlin	

with Spencer Tracy, Robert Ryan, Anne Francis, Dean Jagger, Walter Brennan, Ernest Borgnine, Lee Marvin

- Criticism on release

    ...has a classical economy of form. It has a beginning, a development, a climax, a summing-up. And the story itself, with beautiful craftsmanship, balances character and action... I could not wish for a better cast – nor for a more convincing picture of sun-cracked desolation: the photography, in Eastman colour, is splendid...

    Dilys Powell, *Sunday Times* 13 March 1955

- Current recommendations and ratings
StJD LM3½ DQ3 VFG4 MPG5 NFT*

    ...Nicely put together by Sturges, its suspense derives largely from the excellent performances and imaginative use of the 'scope frame by cameraman William C. Mellor.

    Geoff Andrew, PTOG 1993

The Outlaw Josey Wales, WB/Malpaso (Robert Dalex), 1976 *colour*

Direction: Clint Eatwood	Script: Philip Kaufman, Sonia Chemus (from Forrest Carter's *Gone to Texas*)
Camera: Bruce Surtees	
Music: Jerry Fielding	
Production Design: Tambi Larsen	Editing: Ferris Webster

with Clint Eastwood, Chief Dan George, Sondra Locke, Bill McKinney, John Vernon, Paula Trueman, Sam Bottoms, Will Sampson, Geraldine Keams

- Criticism on release

    ...a thoroughly likeable Western. I even thought we were going to get through without any mishandling of the horses – until, nearly at the end, there was a ferocious fall. Or was the victim a model? I certainly hope so; for the rest the riders very properly took the falls themselves. The script is witty as well as humane (the comments given to Chief Dan George are as lively as his performance). The landscape looks magnificent in Bruce Surtees's camerawork, and Clint Eastwood can be congratulated on his direction of the narrative as well as his own un-showy, astringent playing.

    Dilys Powell, Sunday Times 8 August 1976

- Current recommendations and ratings
LM2½ DQ4 DW5 VFG5 MPG5 NFT**

    A remarkable film which sets out as a revenge Western – [But slowly] it becomes the story of a man who (re)discovers his role as family man, as he befriends Indians and various strays and leads them to a paradise of sorts where they can forget their individual pasts... After a period of directorial uncertainty, the film demonstrated Eastwood's ability to recreate his first starring role, as the Man with No Name of the Italian Westerns, and to subtly undercut it through comedy and mockery.

    Phil Hardy, PTOG 1995

Ride the High Country/ Guns in the Afternoon, MGM
(Richard E. Lyons), 1962 *colour*

Direction: Sam Peckinpah	Script: N.B. Stone Jr.
Camera: Lucien Ballard	Music: George Bassman
Art Direction: George W. Davis, Leroy Coleman	
Editing: Frank Santillo	

with Randolph Scott, Joel McCrea, Mariette Hartley, Edgar Buchanan, Ronald Starr, R.G. Armstrong, James Drury, Warren Oates, L.Q. Jones

- Criticism on release

    ...an almost perfectly realised little film – full of intelligence, quiet charm and thorough understanding of its materials... The two ex-lawmen are tough but creaking vestiges of the old days, virtually useless in a territory that no longer needs their simple talents... With this film Peckinpah displays not mere competence, but imagination and promise...

    DuPré Jones, *Sight and Sound*, Summer 1962

- Current recommendations and ratings
StJD S&S82/92 LM4 DW4 VFG5 MPG5 NFT*

    Peckinpah's superb second film, a nostalgic lament for the West in its declining years, with a couple of great set pieces (the bizarre wedding in the mining camp, the final shootout among the chickens). Affectionately funny [but] also achieving an almost biblical grandeur... Truly magnificent camerawork from Lucien Ballard.

    Tom Milne, PTOG 1995

Rio Bravo, WB (Howard Hawks), 1959 colour

Direction: Howard Hawks	Script: Jules Furthman, Leigh
Camera: Russell Harlan	Brackett (from a story by
Music: Dimitri Tiomkin	Barbara Hawkes McCampbell)
Songs: Tiomkin (with lyrics by	Art Direction: Leo Kuter
Paul Francis Webster)	Editing: Folmar Blangsted
Costume Design: Marjorie Best	

with John Wayne, Dean Martin, Angie Dickinson, Walter Brennan, Ricky Nelson, Ward Bond, John Russell, Claude Akins, Bob Steele, Harry Carey Jr.

- Criticism on release

    ...a long, leisurely affair which mixes most of the standard ingredients - very black villains, a stalwart sheriff hero, a frightened community - and erupts suddenly into fierce action whose very terseness makes it all the more effective. Aided by clear-cut characterisation, the old Western myths survive through Hawks' deceptively relaxed direction; and the atmosphere of his little town is enhanced, by a precise geographical placing of the action.

    John Gillett, *Sight and Sound*, Summer-Autumn 1959

- Current recommendations and ratings
StJD S&S82/92 LM3½ DQ3 DW4 VFG4 MPG4 NFT**

    Arguably Hawks' greatest film, a deceptively rambling chamber Western made in response to the liberal homilies of *High Noon*... Little of the film is shot outdoors, with a subsequent increase in claustrophobic tension, while Hawks peppers the generally relaxed and easy narrative - which even takes time out to include a couple of songs for Dino and Ricky - with superb set pieces... Beautifully acted, wonderfully observed, and scripted with enormous wit and generosity.

    Geoff Andrew, PTOG 1995

The Searchers, WB (Merian Cooper/C.V.Whitney), 1956) *colour*

Direction: John Ford
Camera: Winton Hoch
Music: Max Steiner
Art Direction: Frank Hotaling, James Basevi
Costume Design: Frank Beetson, Ann Peck
Script: Frank Nugent (from the novel by Alan LeMay)
Song: Stan Jones
Editing: Jack Murray

with John Wayne, Jeffrey Hunter, Vera Miles, Ward Bond, Natalie Wood, Hank Worden, Henry Brandon, Harry Carey Jr., Olive Carey, John Qualen, Antonio Moreno

- Criticism on release

    ...This has so many mysterious undertones that detract from the wonderful action. And wonderful it is! For here is John Ford, the master Western-maker, near the top of his form... The search (for two nieces abducted by Indians after a massacre) stretches into years of relentless trekking and disappointment... The film has the typical Ford sweep and grandeur, laced with folksy details of frontier living, with its humours and tragedies.

    Margaret Hinxman et al., *Picturegoer* 11 August 1956

- Current recommendations and ratings
StJD BN92 S&S82/92 LM4 DQ4 DW5 VFG5 MPG5 NFT**

    A marvellous Western... There is perhaps some discrepancy in the play between Wayne's heroic image and the pathological outsider he plays here (forever excluded from home, as the doorway shots at beginning and end suggest), but it hardly matters, given the film's visual splendour and muscular poetry...

    Tom Milne, PTOG 1995

Shane, Par (George Stevens), 1953 colour

Direction: George Stevens
*Camera: Loyal Griggs
Special Effects: Gordon Jennings
Art Direction: Hal Pereira, Walter Tyler
Editing: William Hornbeck, Tom McAdoo
Script: A.B. Guthrie, Jack Sher (from the novel by Jack Shaefer)
Costume Design: Edith Head
Music: Victor Young

with Alan Ladd, Jean Arthur, Van Heflin, Jack Palance, Brandon De Wilde, Ben Johnson, Edgar Buchanan, Emile Meyer, Elisha Cook Jr., John Dierkes, Ellen Corby

- Criticism on release

    ...an exceptional Western film... the Wyoming of seventy years ago; a place of conflict and growth; primitive, brutal, opulent and breathtakingly beautiful... The realism of the fights matches that of the Settlement – bare and crude – utterly void of gilded saloons, can-can girls, debonair gamblers or singing cowboys... It adds up to quite a film.

    Richard Winnington, *News Chronicle*
    4 September 1953

- Current recommendations and ratings
  StJD BN92 LM4 DQ3 DW4 VFG4 MPG5 NFT*

    Stevens' classic Western, with its inflated reputation, looks as if it were self-consciously intended as a landmark film right from the start... But the slow pace and persistent solemnity reduce tension, prefiguring the portentous nature of Stevens' later work. That said, the cast is splendid, and both the emotional tensions between Ladd and Arthur, and the final confrontation with Palance, are well handled.

    Geoff Andrew, PTOG 1995

She Wore a Yellow Ribbon, RKO (Merian C. Cooper/John Ford), 1949 *colour*

Direction: John Ford
*Camera: Winton Hoch
Music: Richard Hageman
Art Direction: James Basevi
Costume Design: Michael Meyers, Ann Peck
Script: Frank Nugent, Laurence Stallings (from a story by James Warner Bellah)
Editing: Jack Murray

with John Wayne, Joanne Dru, John Agar, Victor McLaglen, Ben Johnson, Harry Carey Jr., George O'Brien, Mildred Natwick, Tom Tyler, Arthur Shields, Noble Johnson

- Criticism on release

    This new John Ford work is a splendid example of the sort of thing the cinema has always done best; something, moreover, that only the cinema can do, a combination of effects and materials in which it is unique... This, you feel, is really a story with roots in the nation, not just a fiction snatched out of the busy air... Even apart from the yellow ribbon, the colour, though occasionally bloodshot, is frequently significant, and gives us magnificent cloud effects over tawny rock-chimneys, distant blue ranges, milky green rivers, and lightning snaking down venomously from a jagged sky...

    C.A. Lejeune, *The Observer* 16 April 1950

- Current recommendations and ratings
StJD BN92 S&S82 LM3½ DQ4 DW4 VFG4 MPG4, NPT**

    The centrepiece of Ford's cavalry trilogy (flanked by *Fort Apache* and *Rio Grande*)... structured around a series of ritual incidents rather than narrative conflicts... Winton Hoch's Technicolor cinematography of Monument Valley (modelled at Ford's insistence on Remington pictorialism) won him an Oscar.

    Paul Taylor, PTOG 1995

The Shootist, De Laurentiis/ Par (M.J. Frankovich, William Self), 1976 *colour*

Direction: Don Siegel	Script: Miles Hood Swarthout, Scott Hale (from Glendon Swarthout's novel)
Camera: Bruce Surtees	
Music: Elmer Bernstein	
Production Design: Robert Boyle	Special Effects: Augie Lohman
Costume Design: Moss Mabry, Luster Bayless, Edna Taylor	
with John Wayne, Lauren Bacall, Ron Howard, James Stewart, Richard Boone, Hugh O'Brian, Bill McKinney, Harry Morgan, John Carradine, Sheree North, Scatman Crothers	

- Criticism on release

> ...Don Siegel, the director, has used an ironic story about the new and old West, written by Glendon Swarthout, for his own unfocused purposes... The iron comes straight and coated with molasses... This is not to say that *The Shootist* is a bad picture. It is often funny. It is sometimes telling. And John Wayne, James Stewart and Lauren Bacall all possess that particular mystery of performance that allows them to touch us even when they are ridiculous. But Mr Siegel's lack of form and fidelity to his own story means that, as the movie proceeds, even those things that are charming turn to lead.
>
> Richard Eder, *New York Times* 12 August 1976

- Current recommendations and ratings
  LM3½ DQ4 DW4 VFG4 MPG4 NFT*

> From the opening montage of clips from Wayne's earlier films to the final superb shootout in a cavernous saloon, Siegel's film is a subtle, touching valedictory tribute to both Wayne and the Western in general... The performances are uniformly excellent, Bruce Surtees' photography is infused with an appropriately wintry feel, and Siegel handles both pace and tone beautifully...
>
> Geoff Andrew, PTOG 1995

The Wild Bunch, WB (Phil Feldman), 1969 *colour*

Direction: Sam Peckinpah
Camera: Lucien Ballard
Music: Jerry Fielding
Art Direction: Edward Carrere
Editing: Louis Lombardo

Script: Peckinpah, Walon Green (from the story by Green and Roy N. Sickner)
Costume Design: Gordon Dawson

with William Holden, Ernest Borgnine, Robert Ryan, Edmond O'Brien, Warren Oates, Jaime Sanchez, Ben Johnson, Emilio Fernandez, Strother Martin, L.Q. Jones, Albert Dekker, Bo Hopkins

- Criticism on release

    Lately [the Western] is becoming an arena for exaltation in gore with perhaps a fade-out nod to virtue – a Theater of Cruelty on the cheap... In the hands of Sam Peckinpah, the matter becomes more complex because he is such a gifted director that I don't see how one can avoid using the word 'beautiful' about his work... This is not merely a matter of big vistas and stirring gallops and silhouettes against the sky, although Peckinpah understands all about them. It is a matter of the kinetic beauty in the very violence that his film lives and revels in...

    Stanley Kauffmann, *New Republic* 19 July 1969

- Current recommendations and ratings
  StJD BN92 S&S82/92 LM4 DQ3 DW5 VFG5 MPG5 NFT**

    ...Though he spares none of the callousness and brutality of Holden and his gang, Peckinpah nevertheless presents their macho code of loyalty as a positive value in a world increasingly dominated by corrupt railroad magnates and their mercenary killers (Holden's old buddy Ryan)... In purely cinematic terms, the film is a savagely beautiful spectacle, Lucien Ballard's superb cinematography complementing Peckinpah's darkly elegiac vision.

    Nigel Floyd, PTOG 1995

II – Personal Choice

In attempting to make an objective selection, I preferred measuring *current reputations* (1996) to attempting to measure *intrinsic aesthetic value* – a supremely difficult, if not impossible, task. Inevitably, because the method does not claim to be perfect, there are some discrepancies: the films with the highest reputation are not necessarily the 'best' films. However, I find very little to object to in the list of HOLLYWOOD'S TOP TWO-FIFTY. But there are some regrets (concerning about thirty omissions), either owing to the decision to limit the choice (which arbitrarily excluded all films scoring below .918) or because of a subjective conviction that a few films have been generally underrated or even unfairly neglected. Among those right on the margin, I believe the following are enduring classics: Joseph Mankiewicz's *Julius Caesar* and Robert Altman's *The Player* (both .917), Elia Kazan's *Boomerang*, George Cukor's *Holiday* and Jean Negulesco's *Johnny Belinda* (all .916), Henry King's *The Gunfighter* (.914), Nicholas Ray's *Johnny Guitar* (.913), and Tod Browning's *Freaks* (.912).

Julius Caesar, 1953, would be justified as the finest Shakespearean adaptation made in Hollywood, outpacing Warners' 1935 *A Midsummer Night's Dream*, MGM's 1936 *Romeo and Juliet*, and Orson Welles's 1948 *Macbeth* for Republic. Mankiewicz's *Julius Caesar* has marvellous protagonists in James Mason's Brutus and John Gielgud's Cassius; Marlon Brando's Marc Antony is refreshingly original (even with his Method style of delivery); the dramatic tension is maintained magnificently; and Shakespeare's text is treated with the greatest of respect (the producer John Houseman had worked on a Mercury Players production with Orson Welles in 1937).

The Player, 1992, brings 'Moviola' waspishly up to date, in a kaleidoscopic comedy thriller, Altman-style, deploying a huge cast of players, including irresistible Whoopi Goldberg as a suspicious policewoman, and a richly explored Tinseltown setting. It is one of the very best of recent Hollywood productions.

Boomerang, 1947, was one of the excellent group of documentary thrillers made at Twentieth-Century Fox in the immediate post-war period (the producer was Louis de Rochemont, previously responsible for the superlative *March of Time* newsreel features). Not only does it pose an intriguing puzzle – not so much whodunit (we never know the answer to that), but how can the crusading lawyer (Dana Andrews) with the help of a conscientious police chief (Lee J. Cobb), both threatened by removal from office after the impending election, prove that the murder suspect (Arthur Kennedy) did not do it? Based on a real-life case, it has a startling and cathartic climax. *Holiday*, 1937, based, like *The Philadelphia Story*, on a play by Philip Barry, stars Cary Grant and Katharine Hepburn (before *Bringing Up Baby*). Amidst the delightful social comedy, there is the suggestion of a slightly darker theme – the unhappiness of the sensitive rich – towards which Lew Ayres, as Hepburn's escapist brother, contributes a memorable performance. Cukor directed many near-perfect films, and this is as near-perfect as you can get.

Johnny Belinda, 1948, a bleak romance centred upon an unwanted deaf-mute – played magnificently by Jane Wyman in an exceptionally strong character role (for which she won an Oscar) – is set in the bleak atmosphere of a New England seaboard farming community. The direction by Jean Negulesco is surprisingly and effectively austere, and Ted McCord's camerawork fits the gloomy mood of the film admirably. Lew Ayres, again, gives a strong (though not macho) performance as a sympathetic young doctor who suffers from being the girl's only ally in this hostile environment.

The Gunfighter, 1950 – directed by Henry King and starring Gregory Peck – is a worthy companion-piece to their *Twelve o'Clock High* of the previous year. Observing all the unities – of time, place and action – recommended to Greek tragedy, it tells of the death of the Old West in tragic form, through the doomed attempt of a worn-out old gunfighter to see his alienated wife and son once more. Focused on the hotel room where he is staying, visited by an old associate, now sheriff – played, as if on buskins, by Millard Mitchell – the drama unfolds in a kind of hopeless claustrophobia, beautifully conveyed in the camerawork of Arthur C. Miller.

Johnny Guitar, 1954, is another extraordinary (even weird) Western, with the emotive spectacle of Joan Crawford as Vienna, the owner of a desert saloon grappling with an embittered ranch-owner, Emma Small (Mercedes McCambridge) over love and land. The men involved – played by Sterling Hayden as Johnny Guitar (an intelligent, controlled performance) and Scott Brady as the Dancin' Kid, the bone of contention between Vienna and Emma – play absolute second fiddle. The *Virgin Movie Guide* calls it Crawford's way of "thanking her many lesbian friends", whereas Geoff Brown in the *Penguin Time Out Guide* refers to a "hypnotic Freudian web of shifting relationships". Ray uses all the normal Western conventions, but transforms them into a complex and flamboyant costume spectacle.

Freaks, 1932, was MGM's – and Tod Browning's – attempt to follow Universal on to the *Dracula* and *Frankenstein* bandwagon. It was banned from cinema circuits for years, on the pretext of Browning's treatment of the circus performers in the title who play the main roles. Viewing it over sixty years later, they appear sympathetic in comparison with the more normal humans, in particular the loathsome trapeze artist Cleopatra (Olga Baclanova), on whom they wreak a terrible revenge.

The films I consider to be underrated according to the criteria adopted are: Charles Chaplin's *Monsieur Verdoux* (.893), Martin Ritt's *Hud* (.891), Stanley Kubrick's *The Killing* (.884), George Abbott and Stanley Donen's *The Pajama Game* (.883), Alfred Hitchcock's *The Wrong Man* (.877), Martin Scorsese's *Alice Doesn't Live Here Anymore* (.869), Ted Tetzlaff's *The Window* (.860), Stanley Kubrick's *Spartacus* (.853), Robert Wise's *The Set-Up* (.843), and Vincente Minnelli's *Father of the Bride* (.841).

Monsieur Verdoux, 1947, has always provoked controversy, but, viewed as adult black comedy made with an acid tongue planted firmly in the cheek, it is without doubt one of Chaplin's most sophisticated and polished films. It depicts a mild charming man who is, in fact, a serial killer concentrating on wealthy widows (a combination of Landru, 'Bluebeard' and 'Brides in the Bath' Smith). Martha Raye's exuberant performance as the most vulgar French widow ever, who refuses to succumb to his treatment, is exhilarating.

Hud, 1963, is a contemporary 'anti-Western', in which the main unruly character – played by Paul Newman – is an unpleasant combination of rebellious attitudes and selfish behaviour (a kind of latter-day James Dean). He is completely at loggerheads with his father (Melvyn Douglas), who is bitterly disappointed with Hud's complete lack of the old frontier virtues. The antagonism is viewed from the stance of, and in relationship to, two other characters – a frustrated housekeeper (Patricia Neal) and the young nephew who mistakenly idolises him (Brandon de Wilde). It has a strong script (based on a Larry McMurty novel), taut, intelligent direction by Ritt, and scintillating black-and-white photography by James Wong Howe.

The Killing, 1956, is a highly artificial, structured 'caper' movie: tough Sterling Hayden sets up a racetrack robbery with a strange assortment of fellow robbers (Jay C. Flippen, Ted de Corsia, Joseph Sawyer, Elisha Cook Jr. – whose scene with his demanding, contemptuous wife played by Marie Windsor is a little gem – and Timothy Carey). The robbery is seen in a series of episodes viewed by the participants in turn, punctuated by a shot of horses in the starting-gate. The ending is strongly reminiscent of *The Treasure of the Sierra Madre*, with the hard-won 'killing' blown from a case at the airport (just on the verge of success!). It is said that this film inspired Quentin Tarantino to make his much more violent and gory *Reservoir Dogs* (with all the advantages of colour).

The Pajama Game, 1957 – a favourite brainchild of Broadway veteran George Abbott (the co-screenwriter, co-producer and co-director of the movie) – this lovely plebeian musical owes a great deal to its stage origins, including many of the original cast – John Raitt, Carol Haney, and Eddie Foy Jr. – who made few other contributions to the Hollywood musical. The popular star, Doris Day, is at her best as a union organiser who compromises her case by falling in love with the boss. Charming songs (Richard Adler/ Jerry Ross), original choreography (Bob Fosse), and inventive camerawork (Harry Stradling), intelligent direction by Abbott and Stanley Donen make this a distinctive and entertaining film.

The Wrong Man, 1956, is the most serious of Hitchcock's films – entirely gripping, with the breathtaking suspense that is the hallmark of the master, but with little humour and a rigorous recording of an impersonal police procedure, in which mistaken identity provides its own ruthless logic. Henry Fonda is perfectly cast as the hapless bass player charged with a crime he did not commit – haggard, sensitive, puzzled, having to endure the shock of his wife's madness before the final, long-delayed acquittal. Hitchcock never used actual locations to such fine effect – the result is a plea for social justice rather than a superbly entertaining thriller. That Hitchcock avoided his normal brief appearance (which serves as a kind of signature to his other films) indicates that he felt this one was possibly of a higher order.

Alice Doesn't Live Here Anymore, 1974, seems almost too charming, too laid-back at times, to be a Scorsese movie. The story of a widowed mother (Ellen Burstyn – who received an Oscar) taking to the road to find her way back into a singing career, and who finds true love instead with a Californian farmer (Kris Kristofferson), could have been unbearably sentimental, but Scorsese's sense of realism, the gritty dialogue (script by Robert Getchell), the sharp playing of an awkward young son (Alfred Lutter, excellent), an abrasive fellow waitress (Diane Ladd – nominated for an Oscar), and the owner of Mel's Diner (Vic Tayback) help to keep this movie's feet on the ground.

The Window, 1947, is a small masterpiece. Made on a low budget for RKO, everything about it is quality. The script (adapted by Mel Dinelli from Cornell Woolrich) is spare but incisive. Tetzlaff's experience as cameraman greatly helped the direction of a first-rate cast on an authentic New York tenement location. The tale of a young lad (Bobby Driscoll), whose report of a witnessed murder is dismissed as fanciful fantasy, until his parents (Arthur Kennedy, Barbara Hale) are faced with the threat of their son's own possible murder, is made even more gripping by brilliant editing (Frederic Knutson – nominated for an Oscar).

In spite of the millions of dollars spent on Hollywood epics, no really satisfactory epic remains. *Spartacus*, 1960, is the most consistently interesting, with few weak passages. Kirk Douglas (co-producer) is the perfect embodiment of the gladiator leading a revolt against his Roman masters, especially Marcus Crassus (a steely Laurence Olivier). Charles Laughton (as Crassus's political opponent), Jean Simmons (as the gladiator's wife), Tony Curtis (as Crassus's toyboy), Peter Ustinov (in an Oscar-winning portrayal as the slave-owner) – all contribute tellingly to the Roman atmosphere; and there is plenty of action. The panoramic scenes endemic to all epics seem to have greater significance in relation to the characters and drama than usual.

The Set-Up, 1949, is another classic B picture from RKO, with a powerful performance from Robert Ryan as the ageing boxer who stubbornly wins a fight, to the chagrin of his manager (George Tobias) who has 'set up' the fight for Ryan to lose – without telling him – with a gangster (Alan Curtis). Robert Wise's success as producer-director of blockbuster musicals such as *West Side Story* and *The Sound of Music* is still well in the future: his direction here is stark and uncompromising, resulting (with the ruthless black-and-white camerawork of Milton Krasner) in some of the most harrowing fight scenes in cinema (only surpassed by Martin Scorsese and Michael Chapman in *Raging Bull*).

Father of the Bride, 1950, is based on a witty adaptation by Frances Goodrich and Albert Hackett of a very amusing novel by Edward Streeter. Minnelli directs in a truly comic spirit, not too realistically and firmly taking sides with the harassed father (Spencer Tracy) as he proceeds through the protocol of a fashionable marriage, ending in complete exhaustion and near-bankruptcy. Tracy plays comedy subtly and pointedly, and captures our sympathies entirely. He is supported by an excellent cast (including Joan Bennett, as his wife, and Elizabeth Taylor as the bride).

A certain number of films gaining relatively low scores on this assessment deserve a much higher reputation. These are: Clarence Brown's *Intruder in the Dust* (.819), Henry Hathaway's *Call Northside 777* (.809), Robert Siodmak's *The Dark Mirror* (.801), Otto Preminger's *Advise and Consent* (.798), Norman Taurog's *The Adventures of Tom Sawyer* (.796), Sam Taylor's and Fred Newmeyer's *Safety Last* (.795), Wolfgang Reitherman's, Hamilton Luske's and Clyde Geronimi's *One Hundred and One Dalmatians* (.792), Bruce Beresford's *Tender Mercies* (.783), Clint Eastwood's *Bird* (.779), Charles Walters' *High Society* (.760), and John Farrow's *Alias Nick Beal* (.738).

In the manner of West End theatres advertising their product, I have selected glowing extracts from three recent film guides: *The Penguin Time Out Guide*, Derek Winnert's *Radio Times Film and Video Guide*, and *The Virgin Film Guide*.

Intruder in the Dust, 1949

- By far the best of the race prejudice cycle of the 40s (Tom Milne, PTOG)
- ...admirable version of the William Faulkner novel... a model of how to shoot a novel (Winnert)
- ...the lack of big name stars is, if anything, a plus in making this one of the most powerful movies ever made about racism (VFG)

Call Northside 777, 1948

- What finally impresses... is Stewart's gradual development from sceptical scoop-hunter to a committed crusader for justice (Geoff Andrew, PTOG)
- Hathaway... achieves a pungent whiff of reality through the naturalistic performances and by filming on real locations (Winnert)
- ... one of the most impressive semi-documentary noir thrillers (VFG)

The Dark Mirror, 1946

- What really makes it work is Siodmak's firm grasp of mood and suspense (Geoff Andrew, PTOG)
- An excellent suspenseful mystery, admirably directed from an absorbing script (Winnert)
- De Havilland's finest hour (VFG)

Advise and Consent, 1962

- ...still grips like a vice thanks to the skill with which Preminger's stunning *mise en scène* absorbs documentary detail (Tom Milne, PTOG)
- Superb political drama with a powerful array of character actors (Winnert)
- Preminger's touch is more precise and cautious than usual... a more realistic, if less humane, portrait of the Senate than *Mr Smith Goes to Washington* (VFG)

The Adventures of Tom Sawyer, 1938

- ...does capture the sense of a lazy Mississippi summer and much of the spirit of the book (Tom Milne, PTOG)
- Selznick's thoroughly enjoyable version of Mark Twain's children's favourite (Winnert)
- ...excellent Selznick production (VFG)

Safety Last, 1923 [7]

- ...one of Lloyd's best thriller comedies. The skyscraper climbing sequence is one of the cleverest and famous in silent movies (Winnert)
- Not reviewed in PTOG or VFG

One Hundred and One Dalmatians, 1961

- Disney at his finest... brilliant entertainment (Roger Parsons, PTOG)
- ...well above par for the studio's latterday course... Cruella (De Vil) is a memorable villainess (Winnert)
- Throughout the story are subtle visual elements creating an atmosphere that transcends mere cartoon reality (VFG)

Tender Mercies, 1982

- ...offers an attractive if unassuming alternative to the Hollywood mainstream... bears more resemblance to, say, the films of Wenders (or even, at a stretch, Ozu) than to commercial Hollywood, though it grips from start to finish. Beautiful. (Geoff Andrew, PTOG)
- Oscar-winning Duvall is superb... Gentle, minor-key film is an all-round little winner though it was quiet at the box-office (Winnert)
- ...episodic gem (VFG)

---

[7] Harold Lloyd still obstinately remains very much the third genius of silent comedy – his reputation has never caught up with Chaplin's or Keaton's.

Bird, 1988

- At last American cinema has done black music proud. Unforgettable. (Brian Case, PTOG)
- Eastwood's outstanding film about renowned American 40s black jazz saxophonist Charlie Parker is truly a labour of love... the ultimate tribute and a great credit to Clint (Winnert)
- In a remarkable directorial effort, Eastwood shows a great flair for atmosphere and composition and presents a nuanced, complex, human portrait of Parker's talents, obstacles, virtues and failings (VFG)

High Society, 1956 [8]

- ...scores over the original only in the score... many pleasures ('S.G.', PTOG)
- Classy musical remake of *The Philadelphia Story* – an acid social comedy reworked as a plush showcase for the 3 stars (Winnert)
- Cole Porter's score sits on it like a champagne bubble on a vat of flat beer (VFG)

Alias Nick Beal/The Contact Man, 1949

- An undeservedly neglected film which should rank high on the list of Farrow's best... a model screenplay (by Jonathan Latimer) of precision and construction (Chris Wicking, PTOG)
- Imaginative fantasy/gangster film version of *Faust*, with creepily on-form Milland (Winnert)
- Not reviewed in VFG

---

[8] Devalued as a film because it is always compared to the great romantic comedy *The Philadelphia Story*, on which it is based, it nevertheless remains an outstanding musical.

Names in CAPITAL LETTERS represent *film-makers* and *performers* already referred to in the credit lists

Animated Feature

One Hundred and One Dalmatians, WALT DISNEY, 1961 colour

Direction: WOLFGANG REITHERMAN, HAMILTON LUSKE, Clyde Geronimi
Script: Bill Peet (from Dodie Smith's book)
Production Design: Ken Anderson
Music: George Bruns

Animation: Hal Ainbro, Les Clark, Eric Cleworth, Blaine Gibson, Bill Kell, Hal King, Eric Larson, JOHN LOUNSBERY, Dick Lucas, Cliff Norberg, John Sibley, Art Stevens, Julius Svendson, FRANKLIN THOMAS
Editing: Donald Halliday, Roy M. Brewer Jr.

with the voices of ROD TAYLOR, Lisa Davis, Cate Bauer, Frederic Worlock, J. Pat O'Malley, Betty Lou Gerson, Martha Wentworth, TOM CONWAY, George Pelling

Biographical Pictures ('Biopics')

Bird, Malpaso (CLINT EASTWOOD), 1988 colour

Direction: CLINT EASTWOOD
Camera: Jack N. Green
Special Effects: Joe Day
Script: Joel Oliansky
Music: Lenni Niehaus
Editing: Joel Cox

with Forest Whitaker, Diane Venora, Michael Zelniker, Samuel E. Wright, Keith David, Michael Guire, James Handy, Damon Whitaker, Morgan Nagler, Arlen Dean Snyder

Comedy (1) – Black Comedy

Monsieur Verdoux, UA (CHARLES CHAPLIN), 1947 *bw*

Direction, Script and Music: CHARLES CHAPLIN	Editing: WILLARD NICO
Camera: ROLAND TOTHEROH, Curt Courant, Wallace Chewing	Art Direction: John Beckman

with CHARLES CHAPLIN, Mady Correll, Allison Roddan, Roland Lewis, Audrey Betz, Martha Raye, ISOBEL ELSOM, WILLIAM FRAWLEY

Comedy (1) – The Great Clowns

Safety Last (HAL ROACH/Harold Lloyd), 1923 *bw*

Direction: Sam Taylor and Fred Newmeyer	Art Direction and Editing: FRED GUIOL
Script: Harold Lloyd, Sam Taylor, Tim Whelan, HAL ROACH	
Camera: Walter Lundin	

with Harold Lloyd, Mildred Davis, Noah Young

Comedy (1) – Social Comedy

Father of the Bride, MGM (PANDRO S. BERMAN), 1950 *bw*

Direction: Vincente Minnelli
Camera: JOHN ALTON
Art Direction: CEDRIC GIBBONS,
  Leonid Vasian
Costume Design: HELEN ROSE,
  WALTER PLUNKETT
Music: ADOLPH DEUTSCH
Script: FRANCES GOODRICH,
  ALBERT HACKETT (from
  Edward Streeter's novel)
Editing: FERRIS WEBSTER

with SPENCER TRACY, Joan Bennett, Elizabeth Taylor, DON TAYLOR, BILLIE BURKE, LEO G. CARROLL, MORONI OLSEN, MELVILLE COOPER, TAYLOR HOLMES, Paul Harvey

Costume Spectacle – Epics

Spartacus, Un (Edward Lewis/KIRK DOUGLAS), 1960 *colour*

Direction: STANLEY KUBRICK
*Camera: RUSSELL METTY
*Art Direction: ALEXANDER
  GOLITZEN, Eric Orbom
Costume Design: BILL THOMAS,
  John Arlington Valles
Script: DALTON TRUMBO (from
  Howard Fast's novel)
Music: ALEX NORTH
Editing: ROBERT LAWRENCE

with KIRK DOUGLAS, LAURENCE OLIVIER, JEAN SIMMONS, CHARLES LAUGHTON, TONY CURTIS, *Peter Ustinov, John Gavin, NINA FOCH, Herbert Lom, JOHN DALL, Woody Strode, JOHN IRELAND, CHARLES MCGRAW

Drama (1) – Social Allegory

Alias Nick Beal/ The Contact Man, Par (Endre Bohm), 1949 bw

Direction: John Farrow	Script: JONATHAN LATIMER (from Mindret Lord's story)
Camera: LIONEL LINDON	
Art Direction: HANS DREIER, Franz Bochelm	Music: FRANZ WAXMAN
	Editing: Edna Warren

with RAY MILLAND, THOMAS MITCHELL, Audrey Totter, GEORGE MACREADY, Geraldine Wall, Henry O'Neill, FRED CLARK, Darryl Hickman, KING DONOVAN, Nestor Paiva

Drama (1) – Ethnic Conflicts

Intruder in the Dust, MGM (CLARENCE BROWN), 1949 bw

Direction: CLARENCE BROWN	Script: Ben Maddow (from WILLIAM FAULKNER's novel)
Camera: ROBERT SURTEES	
Music: ADOLPH DEUTSCH	Editing: ROBERT J. KERN
Art Direction: CEDRIC GIBBONS, RANDALL DUELL	

with DAVID BRIAN, Claude Jarman Jr., ELIZABETH PATTERSON, Juano Hernandez, PORTER HALL, Charles Kemper, WILL GEER

Drama (1) – Pursuit and Concern for Social Justice

The Wrong Man, WB (ALFRED HITCHCOCK), 1956 bw

Direction: ALFRED HITCHCOCK	Script: MAXWELL ANDERSON, Angus McPhail (from ANDERSON's book)
Camera: ROBERT BURKS	
Music: BERNARD HERRMANN	
Art Direction: PAUL SYLBERT, William L. Kuehl	Editing: GEORGE TOMASINI

with HENRY FONDA, VERA MILES, Anthony Quayle, Harold J. Stone, Esther Minciotti, Charles Cooper, NEHEMIAH PERSOFF

Drama (1) – Films of the 'Counter-Culture'

Alice Doesn't Live Here Anymore, WB (David Susskind, Audrey Mass), 1975 *colour*

Direction: MARTIN SCORSESE	Script: Robert Getchell
Camera: Kent Wakeford	Music: Richard La Salle
Production Design: TOBY RAFELSON	Editing: MARCIA LUCAS

with *ELLEN BURSTYN, Kris Kristofferson, Alfred Lutter, Billy 'Green' Bush, DIANE LADD, Leila Goldoni, HARVEY KEITEL, Lana Bradbury, Vic Tayback, JODIE FOSTER

Drama (2) – Through the Eyes of Youth

The Window, RKO (Frederic Ullman, Jr.), 1949 *bw*

Direction: TED TETZLAFF Script: Mel Dinelli (from
Camera: William Steiner   CORNELL WOOLRICH's
Music: ROY WEBB   novella)
Art Direction: WALTER KELLER, Special Effects: RUSSELL A.
    Sam Corso   CULLY
                             Editing: Frederic Knutson
with Barbara Hale, ARTHUR KENNEDY, Bobby Driscoll, PAUL STEWART, RUTH ROMAN, Anthony Ross, RICHARD BENEDICT

Drama (3) – Politics

Advise and Consent, Col (OTTO PREMINGER), 1962 *colour*

Direction: OTTO PREMINGER
Camera: SAM LEAVITT
Music: JERRY FIELDING
Costume Design: Hope Bryce
Editing: LOUIS LOEFFLER
Script: WENDELL MAYES (from Allen Drury's novel)
Production Designer: LYLE WHEELER

with HENRY FONDA, CHARLES LAUGHTON, Don Murray, WALTER PIDGEON, Peter Lawford, George Grizzard, GENE TIERNEY, FRANCHOT TONE, LEW AYRES, BURGESS MEREDITH

Drama (3) – The Boxing Ring

The Set-Up, RKC (Richard Goldstone), 1949 *bw*

Direction: ROBERT WISE
Camera: MILTON KRASNER
Art Direction: ALBERT S. D'AGOSTINO, JACK OKEY
Script: Art Cohn (from verse novel by JOSEPH MONCURE MARCH)
Editing: Roland Gross

with ROBERT RYAN, Audrey Totter, GEORGE TOBIAS, Alan Baxter, WALLACE FORD

Drama (3) 'Moviola'

The Player, Guild (DAVID BROWN, Michael Tolkin), 1992 *colour*

*Direction: ROBERT ALTMAN Camera: Jean Lepine Production Design: Stephen Altman	*Script: Michael Tolkin (from his novel) Music: Thomas Newman Editing: Geraldine Peroni, Maysie Hoy

with Tim Robbins, Greta Scacchi, FRED WARD, Whoopi Goldberg, Peter Gallagher, Brion James, Vincent D'Onofrio, DEAN STOCKWELL, Bruce Willis, Lily Tomlin, et al.

Fantasy

Freaks, MGM (TOD BROWNING), 1932 *bw*

Direction: TOD BROWNING Camera: Merritt Gerstad Editing: BASIL WRANGELL	Script: WILLIS GOLDBECK, Leon Gordon, EDGAR ALLAN WOOLF, AL BOASBERG (from a story by Ted Robbins)

with WALLACE FORD, Leila Hyams, Olga Baclanova, ROSCOE ATES, Henry Victor, Harry Earles, Daisy Earles

Literary Adaptations

Julius Caesar, MGM (JOHN HOUSEMAN), 1953 bw

Direction and Script (from SHAKESPEARE): JOSEPH MANKIEWICZ
Camera: JOSEPH RUTTENBERG
Art Direction: CEDRIC GIBBONS, EDWARD CARFAGNO
Music: MIKLOS ROSZA
Costume Design: Herschel McCoy
Editing: JOHN DUNNING

with MARLON BRANDO, JAMES MASON, JOHN GIELGUD, LOUIS CALHERN, EDMOND O'BRIEN, Greer Garson, GEORGE MACREADY, DEBORAH KERR, Alan Napier

The Adventures of Tom Sawyer, Selznick (William H. Wright), 1938 colour

Direction: Norman Taurog
Camera: JAMES WONG HOWE, Wilfred M. Cline
Editing: Margaret Clancy
Script: John V.A. Weaver (from Mark Twain's novel)

with Tommy Kelly, Jackie Moran, Ann Gillis, MAY ROBSON, WALTER BRENNAN, VICTOR JORY, VICTOR KILIAN

Musicals

High Society, MGM (SOL C.SIEGEL), 1956 *colour*

Directon: CHARLES WALTERS
Camera: Paul C. Vogel
Songs: COLE PORTER
Arrangements: JOHNNY GREEN, SAUL CHAPLIN
Art Direction: CEDRIC GIBBONS, HANS PETERS
Special Effects: A. ARNOLD GILLESPIE
Script: John Patrick (from Philip Barry's play *The Philadelphia Story*)
Choreography: CHARLES WALTERS
Costume Design: HELEN ROSE
Editing: RALPH E. WINTERS

with Bing Crosby, GRACE KELLY, FRANK SINATRA, CELESTE HOLM, John Lund, LOUIS CALHERN, SIDNEY BLACKMER, Louis Armstrong

The Pajama Game, WB (GEORGE ABBOTT, STANLEY DONEN), 1957 *colour*

Direction: George Abbott, Stanley Donen
Camera: Harry Stradling
Songs: Richard Adler, Jerry Ross
Choreography: BOB FOSSE
Costume Design: Jean Eckart
Script: ABBOTT, with Richard Bissell (from their musical and Bissell's novel *Seven and a Half Cents*)
Art Direction: MALCOLM BERT
Editing: WILLIAM ZIEGLER

with Doris Day, John Raitt, Carol Haney, Eddie Foy Jr., Reta Shaw, Barbara Nichols, Thelma Pelish

Romantic Comedy

Holiday, Col (Everett Riskin), 1938 *bw*

Direction: GEORGE CUKOR
Camera: FRANZ PLANER
Music: Sidney Cutner
Art Direction: STEPHEN GOOSSON, LIONEL BANKS
Script: DONALD OGDEN STEWART, Sidney Buchman (from a play by Philip Barry)
Editing: Otto Meyer, AL CLARK

with KATHARINE HEPBURN, CARY GRANT, Doris Nolan, EDWARD EVERETT HORTON, RUTH DONNELLY, LEW AYRES, Henry Kolker, Binnie Barnes, HENRY DANIELL

Romantic Drama

Johnny Belinda, WB (JERRY WALD), 1948 *bw*

Direction: Jean Negulesco
Camera: TED MCCORD
Music: MAX STEINER
Editing: DAVID WEISBART
Script: Irmgard von Cube, Allen Vincent (from the play by Elmer Harris)
Art Direction: ROBERT HAAS

with *JANE WYMAN, LEW AYRES, CHARLES BICKFORD, AGNES MOOREHEAD, Stephen McNally, JAN STERLING, Rosalind Ivan, DAN SEYMOUR

Tender Mercies, EMI (HORTON FOOTE, ROBERT DUVALL), 1983 *colour*

Direction: Bruce Beresford
Camera: Russell Boyd
Art Direction: Jeannine Oppewell
Script: HORTON FOOTE
Music: George Dreyfus
Editing: William Anderson

with *ROBERT DUVALL, Tess Harper, Betty Buckley, Wilford Brimley, Ellen Barkin

Thrillers – Criminal Investigations

Boomerang, TCF (Louis de Rochemont), 1947 bw

Direction: ELIA KAZAN	Script: Richard Murphy
Camera: NORBERT BRODINE	Music: DAVID BUTTOLPH
Editing: Harmon Jones	Art Direction: RICHARD DAY

with DANA ANDREWS, JANE WYATT, LEE J. COBB, Cara Williams, ARTHUR KENNEDY, SAM LEVENE, TAYLOR HOLMES, ROBERT KEITH, ED BEGLEY

Call Northside 777, TCF (Otto Lang), 1948 bw

Direction: Henry Hathaway	Script: Jerry Cady, JAY DRATLER (from articles by James McGuire in the *Chicago Times*)
Camera: JOE MACDONALD	
Art Direction: LYLE WHEELER, MARK-LEE KIRK	Special Effects: DICK SMITH, FRED SERSEN
Costume Design: Kay Nelson	
Editing: J. Watson Webb	

with JAMES STEWART, RICHARD CONTE, LEE J. COBB, Helen Walker, Betty Garde, Kazia Orzazewski, Joanna de Burgh, Howard Smith, MORONI OLSEN, JOHN MCINTIRE

The Dark Mirror, Un (NUNNALLY JOHNSON), 1946 bw

Direction: ROBERT SIODMAK	Script: NUNNALLY JOHNSON (from the novel by Vladimir Pozner)
Camera: MILTON KRASNER	
Music: DIMITRI TIOMKIN	Production Design: Duncan Cramer
Special Effects: J. ('DEV') JENNINGS, Paul K. Lerpae	Editing: Ernest Nims
Costume Design: IRENE SHARAFF	

with OLIVIA DE HAVILLAND, LEW AYRES, THOMAS MITCHELL, Richard Long, Charles Evans, Garry Owen

Gangster Melodrama

The Killing, UA (JAMES B. HARRIS), 1956 bw

Direction: STANLEY KUBRICK	Script: KUBRICK, JIM THOMPSON (from Lionel White's novel *Clean Break*)
Camera: LUCIEN BALLARD	
Music: GERALD FRIED	
Costume Design: Rudy Harrington	Art Direction: Ruth Sobotka Kubrick
Editing: Betty Steinberg	

with STERLING HAYDEN, COLEEN GRAY, Vince Edwards, JAY C. FLIPPEN, Marie Windsor, TED DE CORSIA, ELISHA COOK JR., JOSEPH SAWYER, TIMOTHY CAREY

Westerns

The Gunfighter, TCF (NUNNALLY JOHNSON), 1950 bw

Direction: HENRY KING	Script: William Bowers, William Sellers, NUNNALLY JOHNSON, André de Toth (from a story by Bowers)
Camera: ARTHUR MILLER	
Music: ALFRED NEWMAN	
Art Direction: LYLE WHEELER, Robert Irvine	

with GREGORY PECK, Helen Westcott, MILLARD MITCHELL, Jean Parker, KARL MALDEN, Skip Homeier, Anthony Ross, VERNA FELTON, ELLEN CORBY, Richard Jaeckel

Hud, Par (Martin Ritt, Irving Ravetch), 1963 bw

Direction: Martin Ritt	Script: Irving Ravetch, Harriet Frank (fromLARRY MCMURTY's novel, *Horseman Pass By*)
*Camera: JAMES WONG HOWE	
Music: ELMER BERNSTEIN	
Art Direction: HAL PEREIRA, TAMBI LARSEN	Special Effcts: Paul K. Lerpae
Costume Design: EDITH HEAD	

with PAUL NEWMAN, *MELVYN DOUGLAS, *Patricia Neal, BRANDON DE WILDE, WHIT BISSELL, Val Avery

Johnny Guitar, Republic (Herbert Yates), 1954 *colour*

Direction: NICHOLAS RAY	Script: Philip Yordan (from Roy Chanslor's novel)
Camera: HARRY STRADLING	
Music: VICTOR YOUNG	Production Design: John McCarthy Jr.
Special Effects: Howard Lydecker, Theodora Lydecker	Editing: Richard L. Van Enger
Costume Design: Sheila O'Brien	

with JOAN CRAWFORD, STERLING HAYDEN, MERCEDES MCCAMBRIDGE, Scott Brady, WARD BOND, Ben Cooper, ERNEST BORGNINE, JOHN CARRADINE, ROYAL DANO, Frank Ferguson

III – The Film-Makers

Even when restricted to the 250 films dealt with in this book, listing the leading film-makers is a complex business. The list covers the whole gamut of Hollywood production: a great movie can emerge from any studio and be made by any skilful and coherent group of film-makers. Naturally some lead the field, but there are many more examples of film-makers' work where one particular contribution stands out from all the rest, where there was a particularly happy combination of achievement by all involved. In most cases, at the time it just seemed a job well done, but over the years reputations solidify or evaporate. Consciousness of the classic status of certain productions and the outstanding work poured into them grows, becoming more definite in the appreciation of the general public.

Many of the names in the following lists do not appear in other references. However, for most of the names, further biographical detail may be found in the following useful reference works:

Tim Cawkwell and John H. Smith (Eds), *The World Encyclopaedia of Film* (Studio Vista, 1972)

Ephraim Katz, *The International Film Encyclopaedia* (Pan-Macmillan Edition, 1994)

Ann Lloyd and Graham Fuller (Eds), *The Illustrated Who's Who of the Cinema* (Consultant Editor – Arnold Dessert, Orbis Publishing, London, 1983)

Roger Manvell (ed.), *The International Encyclopaedia of Film* (Michael Joseph, 1972)

David Thomson, *A Biographical Dictionary of the Cinema* (André Deutsch Books Edition, 1994)

John Walker (ed.), *Halliwell's Filmgoers' Companion* (Grafton Books, 11th Edition, 1995)

The following specialist reference works can also be recommended:

DIRECTORS

David Quinlan, *Illustrated Directory of Film Directors* (Batsford, 1983)

PERFORMERS

David Quinlan, *Illustrated Directory of Film Stars* (Batsford, 1986)

David Shipman, *The Great Movie Stars – The Golden Years* (Hamlyn, 1970)

David Shipman, *The Great Movie Stars – The International Years* (Angus & Robertson, 1972)

David Quinlan, *Illustrated Directory of Film Character Actors* (B.T. Batsford, 1985, reprinted 1989)

'Big Shots' (Front Office Executives)

Hortense Powdermaker (*The Hollywood Dream Factory*, 1951):

> Mr Big Shot, the head of a large studio, has a reputation for imposing his will and authority on everyone in the studio. And yet his desire for power over people is not the whole story, for he has a deep and strong interest in the production of movies; and *the output of his studio includes some unusual and excellent pictures as well as the run-of-the-mill.*

BARNEY BALABAN (14): President of Paramount, 1936-64 (with Y. Frank Freeman as Studio Head 1938–59)

1941	*The Lady Eve, Sullivan's Travels*
1942	*The Palm Beach Story*
1944	*The Miracle of Morgan's Creek, Double Indemnity*
1945	**The Lost Weekend*
1950	*Sunset Boulevard*
1951	*Ace in the Hole/The Big Carnival*
1953	*Shane*
1954	*Rear Window*
1957	*Funny Face*
1958	*Vertigo*
1960	*Psycho*
1964	*The Man Who Shot Liberty Vallance*

HARRY COHN (14): President and Head of Production at Columbia, 1924-58

1934	**It Happened One Night*
1936	*Mr Deeds Goes to Town*
1937	*The Awful Truth, The Lost Horizon*
1939	*Mr Smith Goes to Washington, Only Angels Have Wings*
1940	*His Girl Friday*
1946	*Gilda*
1948	*The Lady from Shanghai*
1950	**All the King's Men, In a Lonely Place*
1950	*Born Yesterday*
1952	**From Here to Eternity*
1953	*The Big Heat*

B.G. ('Buddy') DE SYLVA (6): Head of Production at Paramount, 1941–5
    1941   *The Lady Eve, Sullivan's Travels*
    1942   *The Palm Beach Story*
    1944   *The Miracle of Morgan's Creek, Double Indemnity*
    1945   **The Lost Weekend*

WALT DISNEY (6): Head of Disney Studios and Disney Enterprises, 1928-66
    1938   *Snow White and the Seven Dwarfs*
    1940   *Pinocchio, Fantasia*
    1941   *Dumbo*
    1942   *Bambi*
    1964   *Mary Poppins* (live action)

WILLIAM FOX (1): Executive Head, Fox Film Corporation, 1915-30
    1927   *Sunrise*

SAMUEL GOLDWYN (4): Head of Samuel Goldwyn Productions, 1923-59
    1936   *Dodsworth*
    1936   *Wuthering Heights*
    1941   *The Little Foxes*
    1946   **The Best Years of Our Lives*

HOWARD HUGHES (2)
- Independent producer, 1925–32
  Scarface
- Executive Head of RKO, 1948–55:
  She Wore a Yellow Ribbon

CARL LAEMMLE Jr. (4): Head of Production and Producer at Universal, 1929-36
    1930   **All Quiet on the Western Front*
    1931   *Frankenstein*
    1932   *The Old Dark House*
    1935   *The Bride of Frankenstein*

LOUIS B. MAYER (28): Studio Head at Metro-Goldwyn-Mayer from its foundation in 1924 until ousted in conflict with Dore Schary in 1951

1924 *Greed* (a Goldwyn production drastically cut in 1924)
1925 *The Big Parade*
1928 *The Crowd, The Wind, The Cameraman*
1932 *Grand Hotel*
1933 *Queen Christina, Dinner at Eight*
1934 *The Thin Man, The Merry Widow*
1935 **Mutiny on the Bounty, David Copperfield,*
 A Night at the Opera
1936 *Fury*
1937 *The Good Earth*
1939 *Ninotchka, The Wizard of Oz*
1940 *The Philadelphia Story, The Shop around the Corner*
1944 *Meet Me in St Louis*
1945 *They Were Expendable*
1946 *The Postman Always Rings Twice*
1948 *The Pirate*
1949 *Adam's Rib, On the Town*
1950 *The Asphalt Jungle*
1951 **An American in Paris, The Red Badge of Courage*

WALTER MIRISCH (3): Vice-President in charge of production for the Mirisch Company Inc.
1959 *Some Like It Hot*
1960 **The Apartment*
1961 **West Side Story*

HAL ROACH (3): Head of Hal Roach Productions
1933 *Sons of the Desert*
1937 *Way Out West*
1939 *Of Mice and Men*

GEORGE SCHAEFER (2): Studio Head at RKO, 1938–42
1941 *Citizen Kane*
1942 *The Magnificent Ambersons*

DORE SCHARY (14)
- Head of Production at RKO, 1947–8:
 1947 *Crossfire, Out of the Past*
 1948 *Fort Apache*

- Head of Production at MGM, 1948-51:
  1949 *Adam's Rib, On the Town*
  1950 *The Asphalt Jungle*
  1951 **An American in Paris*, *The Red Badge of Courage*
- Studio Head at MGM, replacing Louis B. Mayer, 1951-6:
  1952 *Singin' in the Rain, The Bad and the Beautiful*
  1953 *The Band Wagon, Kiss Me Kate*
  1954 *Seven Brides for Seven Brothers, Bad Day at Black Rock*

JOSEPH M. SCHENCK (10)

- Chairman of United Artists, 1922-33:
  1923 *Our Hospitality*
  1924 *The Navigator, Sherlock Jr.*
  1925 *The Gold Rush*
  1926 *The General* (also co-prod)
  1930 *The Gold Rush*
  1932 *Scarface*
- President of Twentieth Century, 1933-5, and Chairman of Twentieth Century-Fox, 1935-41:
  1939 *Young Mr Lincoln*
  1940 *The Grapes of Wrath*
  1941 **How Green Was My Valley*

DAVID O. SELZNICK (8)

- Head of Production at RKO, 1931-3:
  1933 *King Kong*
- Producer at MGM:
  1933 *Dinner at Eight*
- Temporary head of production at MGM, replacing Thalberg in 1935:
  1935 *David Copperfield*
- President of Selznick International, 1936-57:
  1937 *Nothing Sacred* (released through United Artists)
  1939 **Gone with the Wind* (joint venture with MGM)
  1940 **Rebecca* (through UA)
  1945 *Spellbound* (through UA)
  1946 *Notorious* (through RKO)

SOL C. SIEGEL (5)
- Producer under Darryl F. Zanuck at Twentieth Century-Fox, 1947–56:
  1953   *Gentlemen prefer Blondes*
- Head of Production at MGM, 1958–62:
  1958   **Gigi*
  1959   **Ben-Hur, North by Northwest*
  1961   *Ride the High Country*

SPYROS SKOURAS (8): Producer of Twentieth Century-Fox, 1942–62 (with Darryl F. Zanuck as Head of Production until 1956)
  1943   *The Oxbow Incident*
  1944   *Laura*
  1946   *My Darling Clementine*
  1947   *The Ghost and Mrs Muir*
  1949   *Twelve o'Clock High*
  1950   **All About Eve*
  1953   *Gentlemen Prefer Blondes*
  1961   *The Hustler*

IRVING THALBERG (10): Head of Production at MGM, 1924–36, with long periods of absence through illness during the last years of his short career: replaced temporarily by Walter Wanger in 1933 and by David O. Selznick in 1935; see relevant entries)
  1924   *Greed* (revised version)
  1925   *The Big Parade*
  1928   *The Crowd, The Wind, The Cameraman*
  1934   *The Thin Man, The Merry Widow*
  1935   **Mutiny on the Bounty, A Night at the Opera*
  1936   *Camille* (died before completion)

HAL B. WALLIS (9)
- Producer under Darryl F. Zanuck at Warner Brothers, 1930–3:
  1930   *Little Caesar*
  1932   *I am a Fugitive from a Chain Gang*
  1933   *Forty-Second Street, The Gold Diggers of 1933* (co-prod with Robert Lord)

- Head of Production at Warner Brothers, 1933–44:

  1938   *The Adventures of Robin Hood* (co-prod with Henry Blanke)
  1940   *The Sea Hawk*
  1941   *The Maltese Falcon*
  1942   **Casablanca, Yankee Doodle Dandy*

WALTER WANGER (3)

- Temporary Head of Production at MGM, replacing Thalberg, in 1933:

  1933   *Queen Christina*

- Independent producer (releasing through United Artists):

  1939   *Stagecoach*

- Independent producer (releasing through Allied Artists):

  1956   *Invasion of the Body Snatchers*

JACK WARNER (24): Studio Head at Warner Brothers, 1927–67

1931   *Little Caesar, The Public Enemy*
1932   *I am a Fugitive from a Chain Gang*
1933   *Forty-Second Street, The Gold Diggers of 1933*
1938   *The Adventures of Robin Hood*
1940   *The Sea Hawk*
1941   *The Maltese Falcon, High Sierra*
1942   *Yankee Doodle Dandy*
1943   **Casablanca*
1944   *To Have and To Hold*
1945   *Mildred Pierce*
1946   *The Big Sleep*
1948   *The Treasure of the Sierra Madre*
1949   *White Heat*
1951   *Strangers on a Train, A Streetcar Named Desire*
1954   *A Star Is Born*
1955   *East of Eden, Rebel without a Cause*
1956   *Giant*
1959   *Rio Bravo*
1963   *America, America*

DARRYL F. ZANUCK (16)
- Head of Production at Warner Brothers, 1929–33:
  1931 *Little Caesar* (also co-scripted, with Francis Edward Faragoh and Robert Lee), *The Public Enemy*
  1932 *I am a Fugitive from a Chain Gang*
  1933 *Forty-Second Street*
- Head of Production at Twentieth Century, 1933, then Twentieth Century-Fox, 1934–56:
  1939 *Young Mr Lincoln*
  1940 *The Grapes of Wrath*
  1941 **How Green Was My Valley*
  1943 *The Oxbow Incident*
  1944 *Laura*
  1946 *My Darling Clementine*
  1947 *The Ghost and Mrs Muir*
  1949 *Twelve o'Clock High* (also prod.)
  1950 **All About Eve* (also prod.)
  1953 *Gentlemen Prefer Blondes*
- Independent producer, 1956–62 and Executive President at Twentieth Century-Fox, 62–71, with his son Richard as Head of Production:
  1970 *M*A*S*H*, **Patton*

RICHARD ZANUCK (3)
- Head of Production under his father Darryl at Twentieth Century-Fox, 1962–71:
  1970 *M*A*S*H*, **Patton*
- Independent producer with David Brown, 1972–88:
  1975 *Jaws*

ADOLPH ZUKOR (7): President of Paramount Pictures, 1916–35, with Jesse Lasky as Head of Production, 1916–32
  1932 *Love Me Tonight, Shanghai Express, Trouble in Paradise*
  1933 *Duck Soup, She Done Him Wrong*
  1934 *The Scarlet Empress, It's a Gift*

Filmmaker Producers

Hortense Powdermaker's 1951 analysis of the power structure of the "Hollywood Dream Factory" strikes a very familiar chord and is still relevant today, and no more so than in her description of the power of the producer.

> The producer's power is not limited to control of the writer and the contents of the script. He has authority over the casting, and his judgement in cutting, one of the most important aspects of movie making, supersedes that of the director. It is the producer's OK which is necessary for the work of the composer, scene designer and everyone else connected with the production of the movie.

Important film-makers sought to become producers to concentrate power in their own hands during the creation process. It is a sign of high prestige when a director, screenwriter, a director-screenwriter, or sometimes a star performer, provides enough finance or gains the authority to produce the film for himself. Such prestigious film-makers include: [9]

Robert Aldrich (1): *Kiss Me Deadly*, 1955 – Pr., also Dir

Robert Altman (1): *Nashville*, 1975 – Pr., also Dir-Scr.

Warren Beatty (1): *Bonnie and Clyde*, 1967 – Pr., also Perf.

CHARLES BRACKETT (2): *The Lost Weekend*, 1945 – Pr., also Co-Scr.; *Sunset Boulevard*, 1950 – Pr., also Co-Scr.

FRANK CAPRA. (3): *Mr Deeds Goes to Town*, 1936 – Pr., also Dir.; *Mr Smith Goes to Washington*, 1939 – Pr., also Dir.; *It's a Wonderful Life*, 1946 – Pr., also Dir.)

CHARLES CHAPLIN (6): *The Kid*, 1921 – Pr. also Dir-Scr.; *The Gold Rush*, 1925 – Pr., also Dir-Scr.; *City Lights*, 1930 – Pr. also Dir-Scr.; *Modern Times*, 1936 – Pr., also Dir-Scr.; *The Great Dictator*, 1940 – Pr., also Dir-Scr.; *Limelight*, 1952 – Pr., also Dir-Scr.

Michael Cimino (1): *The Deer Hunter*, 1978 – Co-Pr., also Dir.

---

[9] In the following lists of filmmakers capital letters are used to indicate more than one contribution.

MERIAN C. COOPER (6): *King Kong*, 1933 – Co-Pr., also Co-Dir.; *Fort Apache*, 1948 – Co-Pr.; *She Wore a Yellow Ribbon*, 1949 – Co-Pr.; *Wagonmaster*, 1950 – Co-Pr.; *The Quiet Man*, 1952 – Co-Pr.; *The Searchers*, 1956 – Co-Pr.

FRANCIS FORD COPPOLA (4): *American Graffiti*, 1973 – Co-Pr.; *The Conversation*, 1974 – Pr., also Dir-Scr.; *The Godfather Part II*, 1974 – Co-Pr., also Dir-Co-Scr.; *Apocalypse Now*, 1979 – Co-Pr., also Dir-Co-Scr.

Henry Fonda (1): *Twelve Angry Men*, 1957 – Co-Pr., also Perf.

JOHN FORD (6): The Informer, 1935 – Co-Pr., also *Dir.; *They Were Expendable*, 1945 – Co-Pr., also Dir.; *Fort Apache*, 1948 – Co-Pr., also Dir.; *She Wore a Yellow Ribbon*, 1949 – Co-Pr., also Dir.; *Wagonmaster*, 1950 – Co-Pr., also Dir.; *The Quiet Man*, 1952 – Co-Pr., also Dir.

Willis Goldbeck (1): *The Man Who Shot Liberty Vallance*, 1962 – Pr., also Co-Scr.

D.W. GRIFFITH (3): *The Birth of a Nation*, 1915 – Pr., also Dir-Scr.; *Intolerance*, 1916 – Pr., also Dir-Scr.; *Broken Blossoms*, 1919 – Pr., also Dir-Scr.

HOWARD HAWKS (8): *Scarface*, 1932 – Co-Pr., also Dir.; *Bringing Up Baby*, 1938 – Co-Pr., also Dir.; *Only Angels Have Wings*, 1939 – Pr., also Dir.; *His Girl Friday*, 1940 – Pr., also Dir.; *To Have and Have Not*, 1944 – Pr., also Dir.; *The Big Sleep*, 1946 – Pr., also Dir.; *Red River*, 1948 – Co-Pr., also Dir.; *Rio Bravo*, 1959 – Pr., also Dir.

ALFRED HITCHCOCK (8): *Notorious*, 1946 – Pr., also Dir.; *Strangers on a Train*, 1951 – Pr., also Dir.; *Rear Window*, 1954 – Pr., also Dir.; *Vertigo*, 1958 – Pr., also Dir.; *North by Northwest*, 1959 – Pr., also Dir.; *Psycho*, 1960 – Pr., also Dir.; *The Birds*, 1963 – Pr., also Dir.; *Marnie*, 1964 – Pr., also Dir.

Nunnally Johnson (1): *The Grapes of Wrath*, 1940 – Co-Pr., also Scr.

ELIA KAZAN (3): *East of Eden*, 1955 Pr., also Dir.; *Baby Doll*, 1956 – Pr., also Dir.; *America, America*, 1963 Pr., also Dir.

BUSTER KEATON (3): Sherlock Jr., 1924 – Co-Pr., also Dir. and Perf.; *The Navigator*, 1924 – Co-Pr., also Co-Dir. and Perf.; *The General*, 1926 – Co-Pr., also Co-Dir. and Perf.

Burt Lancaster (1): *Sweet Smell of Success*, 1957 – Co-Pr., also Perf.

Stan Laurel (1): *Way Out West*, 1937 – Co-Pr., also Perf.

Frank Lloyd (1): *Mutiny on the Bounty*, 1935 – Pr., also Dir.

ERNST LUBITSCH (4): *Trouble in Paradise*, 1932 – Pr., also Dir.; *Ninotchka*, 1939 – Pr., also Dir.; *The Shop Around the Corner*, 1940 – Pr., also Dir.; *To Be or Not To Be*, 1942 – Co-Pr., also Dir.

Leo McCarey (1): *The Awful Truth*, 1937 – Pr., also Dir.

Rouben Mamoulian (1): *Love Me Tonight*, 1932 – Pr., also Dir.

Lewis Milestone (1): *Of Mice and Men*, 1939 – Pr., also Dir.

OTTO PREMINGER (2): *Laura*, 1944 – Pr., also Dir.; *Anatomy of a Murder*, 1959 – Pr., also Dir.

Bob Rafelson (1): *Five Easy Pieces*, 1970 – Co-Pr., also Dir.

Reginald Rose (1): *Twelve Angry Men*, 1957 – Co-Pr., also Scr.

ROBERT ROSSEN (2): *All the King's Men*, 1950 Pr., also Dir-Scr.; *The Hustler*, 1961 – Pr.: also Dir. and Co-Scr.

Ernest Schoedsack (1): *King Kong*, 1933 – Co-Pr., also Co-Dir.

Victor Sjöström (1): *The Wind*, 1928 – Pr., also Dir.

GEORGE STEVENS (3): *Gunga Din*, 1939 – Pr., also Dir.; *Shane*, 1953 – Pr., also Dir.; *Giant*, 1956 – Co-Pr., also Dir.

Gloria Swanson (1): *Queen Kelly*, 1928 – Co-Pr., also Perf.

Lamar Trotti (1): *The Oxbow Incident*, 1943 – Pr., also Scr.

KING VIDOR (2): *The Big Parade*, 1925 – Pr., also Dir.; *The Crowd*, 1928 – Pr., also Dir. and Co-Scr.

Erich von Stroheim (1): *Greed*, 1924 – Co-Pr., also Dir.

Bill Walsh (1): *Mary Poppins*, 1964 – Pr., also Co-Scr.

ORSON WELLES (3): *Citizen Kane*, 1941 – Pr., also Dir. and Perf.; *The Magnificent Ambersons*, 1942 – Pr., also Dir.; *The Lady from Shanghai*, 1948 – Pr., also Dir. and Perf.

BILLY WILDER (3): *Ace in the Hole*, 1951 – Pr., also Dir-Co-Scr.; *Some Like it Hot*, 1959 – Pr., also Dir-Co-Scr.; *The Apartment*, 1960 – *Pr., also Dir-Co-Scr.

Robert Wise (1): *West Side Story*, 1961 – *Pr., also *Co-Dir.

Producers

> Lesser Gods, but Colossal...
>
> Hortense Powdermaker

Combining the duties of producer with any creative function in a movie must be very taxing. Many find the tasks of production wearing in themselves, e.g, Albert S. Ruddy, the producer of *The Godfather* said, "Show me a relaxed producer and I'll show you a failure." (*Halliwell's Filmgoers' Companion*, 1990).

Hortense Powdermaker again:

> [As the various departments] became increasingly more efficient, the producer, instead of becoming less important, which would have been the natural evolution, became more powerful and took on the function of representing the front office in the never-ending struggle between the business and creative aspects of production. The producers do not always see themselves in this light... they, as well as the executives, are often not content to be businessmen controlling artists, they want to be artists too. Because they have so little understanding of the creative role it is easy for them to think they are playing it. The producer may mistake his power, to control the content of the movie and the people who work on it, for creativity. This situation creates more problems than would a clear-cut struggle between artists and businessmen, each sticking to his own role...

Powdermaker's depiction of the various types of producer also seems very perceptive:

> Producers, like other people, get their jobs in different ways, and there are various kinds, some typical and others exceptional. Mr Good Judgment, the college graduate of good sense and confidence in it, is most exceptional. Mr Scoop, with his fanatical devotion to movies and humanitarianism, even though limited by his standards of the newspaper scoop, is not typical. The

majority of producers of A pictures are well represented by Mr Mediocre, who has been a Hollywood producer for a long time and who works completely according to formula; by Mr Kowtow, clever and intelligent but lacking in self-confidence and courage; by Mr Persistence, conscientious and a hard worker but with no unusual talent; and Mr Schizo, a man in conflict, who works in a constant state of panic and without direction...

How far one can recognise these types in the list given below depends upon one's (unlikely) knowledge of the rather shadowy but influential supervisors of the ceremonies.

Buddy Adler (1): *From Here to Eternity*, 1953 – *Pr., Col.

Robert Arthur (1): *The Big Heat*, 1953 – Co-Pr., Col.

George Axelrod (1): *The Manchurian Candidate*, 1962 – Pr. UA

PANDRO S. BERMAN (5): *Top Hat*, 1935 – Pr., RKO; *Swing Time*, 1936 – Pr. RKO; *Stage Door*, 1937 – Pr., RKO; *Gunga Din*, 1939 – Pr. RKO; *The Hunchback of Notre Dame*, 1939 – Pr. RKO

Paul Bern (1): Grand Hotel, 1932 – Pr., MGM

HENRY BLANKE (3): *The Sea Hawk*, 1940 – Pr. WB; *The Maltese Falcon*, 1941 – Pr., WB; *The Treasure of the Sierra Madre*, 1948 – Pr., WB

Ron Bozman (1): *The Silence of the Lambs*, 1991 – Co-Pr., Orion

David Brown (1): *Jaws*, 1975 – Co-Pr., Un

William Cagney (1): *Yankee Doodle Dandy*, 1942 – Pr., WB

WILLIAM CASTLE (2): *The Lady from Shanghai*, 1948 – Co-Pr., Col; *Rosemary's Baby*, 1968 – Pr., Par

Robert Chartoff (1): *Raging Bull*, 1980 – Co-Pr., UA

Walter Coblenz (1): *All the President's Men*, 1976 – Pr., WB

Fred Coe (1): *The Miracle Worker*, 1962 – Pr., UA

JACK CUMMINGS (2): *Kiss Me Kate*, 1953 – Pr., MGM; *Seven Brides for Seven Brothers*, 1954 – Pr., MGM

ROBERT DALEY (2): *Play Misty for Me*, 1971 – Pr., Un; *The Outlaw Josey Wales*, 1976 – Pr. WB

MICHAEL DEELEY (2): *The Deer Hunter*, 1978 – Pr., Un; *Blade Runner*, 1982 – Co-Pr., WB

Michael Douglas (1): *One Flew over the Cuckoo's Nest*, 1975 – *Pr., UA

Warren Duff (1): *Out of the Past*, 1947 – Pr., RKO

Louis F. Edelman (1): *White Heat*, 1949 – Pr., WB

Roger Edens (1): *Funny Face*, 1957 – Pr., Par

Samuel C. Engel (1): *My Darling Clementine*, 1946 – Pr., TCF

Robert Evans (1): *Chinatown*, 1974 – Pr., Par

CHARLES S. FELDMAN (2): *Red River*, 1948 – Co-Pr., UA; *A Streetcar Named Desire*, 1951 – Pr., WB

Edward S. Feldman (1): *Witness*, 1985 – Pr., Par

Phil Feldman (1): *The Wild Bunch*, 1969 – Pr., WB

Cy Feuer (1): *Cabaret*, 1972 – Pr., AA

M.J. Frankovich (1): *The Shootist*, 1976 – Co-Pr., Par

Gary Frederickson (1): *The Godfather Part II*, 1974 – Co-Pr., Par

ARTHUR FREED (7): *Meet Me in St Louis*, 1944 – Pr., MGM; *The Pirate*, 1948 – Pr., MGM; *On the Town*, 1949 – Pr., MGM; *An American in Paris*, 1951 – *Pr., MGM; *Singin' in the Rain*, 1952 – Pr., MGM; *The Band Wagon*, 1953 – Pr., MGM; *Gigi*, 1958 – Pr., MGM

Stephen J. Friedman (1): *The Last Picture Show*, 1971 – Pr., Col

Fred T. Gallo (1): *Body Heat*, 1981 – Pr., WB

Henry Ginsberg (1): *Giant*, 1956 – Co-Pr., WB

Robert Greenhut (1): *Hannah and Her Sisters*, 1986 – Pr., Orion

Paul Gregory (1): *The Night of the Hunter*, 1955 – Pr., UA

Robert Hakim (1): *The Southerner*, 1945 – Pr., UA

James E. Harris (1): *Paths of Glory*, 1957 – Pr., UA

Harold Hecht (1): *Sweet Smell of Success*, 1957 – Co-Pr., UA

MARK HELLINGER (3): *High Sierra*, 1941 – Co-Pr., WB; *The Killers*, 1946 – Pr., Un; *The Naked City*, 1948 – Pr., Un

James Hill (1): *Sweet Smell of Success*, 1957 – Co-Pr., UA

ARTHUR HORNBLOW JR. (2): *The Asphalt Jungle*, 1950 – Pr., MGM; *Witness for the Prosecution*, 1957 – Pr., UA

JOHN HOUSEMAN (3): *Letter from an Unknown Woman*, 1948 – Pr., Un; *They Live by Night*, 1949 – Pr., RKO; *The Bad and the Beautiful*, 1952 – Pr., MGM

Stanley Jaffe (1): *Kramer vs Kramer*, 1979 – *Pr., Col
CHARLES H. JOFFE (2): *Annie Hall*, 1977 – Pr., UA; *Manhattan*, 1979 – Pr., UA
PAUL JONES (3): *The Lady Eve*, 1941 – Pr., Par; *Sullivan's Travels*, 1941 – Pr., Par; *The Palm Beach Story*, 1942 – Pr., Par
Joseph Kennedy (1): *Queen Kelly*, 1928 – Co-Pr.
Kathleen Kennedy (1): *E.T.*, 1982 – Co-Pr., Un
Frank and Maurice King (1): *Gun Crazy*, 1950 – Pr., Un
Fred Kohlmar (1): *The Ghost and Mrs Muir*, 1947 – Pr., TCF
Alexander Korda (1): *To Be or Not To Be*, 1942 – Co-Pr., UA
Stanley Kramer (1): *High Noon*, 1952 – Pr., UA
GARY KURTZ (2): *American Graffiti*, 1973 – Co-Pr., Un; *Star Wars*, 1977 – Pr., TCF
Ely Landau (1): *Long Day's Journey into Night*, 1962 – Pr., TCF
WILLIAM LE BARON (2): *She Done Him Wrong*, 1933 – Pr., Par; *It's a Gift*, 1934 – Pr., Par
Mervyn LeRoy (1): *The Wizard of Oz*, 1939 – Pr., MGM
David Lewis (1): *Camille*, 1936 – Pr., MGM
Val Lewton (1): *Cat People*, 1942 – Pr., RKO
Kenneth Litt (1): *The Silence of the Lambs*, 1991 – Co-Pr., Orion
David Loew (1): *The Southerner*, 1945 – Co-Pr., UA
ROBERT LORD (2): *The Gold Diggers of 1933* – Pr., WB; *In a Lonely Place*, 1950 – Pr., Col
Sidney Luft (1): *A Star Is Born*, 1954 – Pr., WB
Richard E. Lyons (1): *Ride the High Country*, 1962 – Pr., MGM
Frank McCarthy (1): *Patton*, 1970 – Pr., MGM
Kenneth MacGowan (1): *Young Mr Lincoln*, 1939 – Pr., MGM
Herman Mankiewicz (1): *Duck Soup*, 1933 – Pr., Par
JOSEPH MANKIEWICZ (2): *Fury*, 1936 – Pr., MGM; *The Philadelphia Story*, 1940 – Pr., MGM
FRANK MARSHALL (2): *Raiders of the Lost Ark*, 1981 – Pr., Par; *Who Framed Roger Rabbit*, 1988 – Pr., Touchstone
Arnon Milchan (1): *The King of Comedy*, 1983 – Pr., TCF
Alan Pakula (1): *To Kill a Mockingbird*, 1962 – Pr., Un
Joe Pasternak (1): *Destry Rides Again*, 1939 – Pr., Un

John Peverall (1): *The Deer Hunter*, 1978 – Co-Pr., Un
MICHAEL AND JULIA PHILLIPS (2): *Taxi Driver*, 1976 – Pr., Col; *Close Encounters of the Third Kind*, 1977 – Pr., Col
Ingo Preminger (1): *M*A*S*H*, 1970 – Pr., TCF
CLIFF REID (3): *The Informer*, 1935 – Co-Pr., RKO; *Bringing Up Baby*, 1938 – Co-Pr., RKO; *They Were Expendable*, 1945 – Co-Pr., MGM
Charles Rogers (1): *The Bank Dick*, 1940 – Pr., Un
Albert S. Ruddy (1): *The Godfather*, 1972 – Pr., Par
Edward Saxon (1): *The Silence of the Lambs*, 1991 – Co-Pr., Orion
BERT SCHNEIDER (2): *Five Easy Pieces*, 1970 – Co-Pr., Col; *Days of Heaven* – Co-Pr., Par
Harold Schneider (1): *Days of Heaven*, 1978 – Co-Pr., Par
ADRIAN SCOTT (2): *Murder My Sweet*, 1944 – Pr., RKO; *Crossfire*, 1947 – Pr., RKO
William Self (1): *The Shootist*, 1976 – Co-Pr., WB
S. Sylvan Simon (1): *Born Yesterday*, 1950 – Pr., Col
Joseph Sistrom (1): *Double Indemnity*, 1944 – Pr., 1944
Jack Skirball (1): *Shadow of a Doubt*, 1943 – Pr., Un
Sam Spiegel (1): *On the Waterfront*, 1954 – Pr., Col
Barry Spikings (1): *The Deer Hunter*, 1978 – Pr., Un
Ray Stark (1): *Fat City*, 1972 – Pr., Col
Hunt Stromberg (1): *The Thin Man*, 1934 – Pr., MGM
Jonathan T. Taplin (1): *Mean Streets*, 1973 – Pr., TPS
Lawrence Turman (1): *The Graduate*, 1967 – Pr., UA
Virginia van Upp (1): *Gilda*, 1946 – Pr., Col
JERRY WALD (2): *Mildred Pierce*, 1945 – Pr., WB; *The Big Heat*, 1953 – Co-Pr., Col
Robert Watts (1): *Who Framed Roger Rabbit?*, 1988 – Co-Pr., Touchstone
Richard Wechsler (1): *Five Easy Pieces*, 1970 – Co-Pr., Col
LAWRENCE WEINGARTEN (2): *The Cameraman*, 1928 – Pr., MGM; *Adam's Rib*, 1949 – Pr., MGM
David Weisbart (1): *Rebel without a Cause*, 1955 – Pr., WB
C.V. Whitney (1): *The Searchers*, 1956 – Co-Pr., WB

Carey Wilson (1): *The Postman Always Rings Twice*, 1946 – Pr., MGM

Irwin Winkler (1): *Raging Bull*, 1980 – Co-Pr., UA

SAUL ZAENTZ (2): *One Flew over the Cuckoo's Nest*, 1975 – Co-Pr., UA; *Amadeus*, 1984 – Pr., Orion

Sam Zimbalist (1): *Ben-Hur*, 1959 – Pr., MGM

ALBERT ZUGSMITH (2): *Written on the Wind*, 1956 – Pr., Un; *Touch of Evil*, 1958 – Pr., Un

Directors

D = direction
Co- = in co-operation with another or others
uc = uncredited

Robert Aldrich (1): *Kiss Me Deadly*, 1955 – D
ROBERT ALTMAN (2): *M*A*S*H*, 1970 – D; *Nashville*, 1975 – D
Lloyd Bacon (1): *Forty-Second Street*, 1933 – D
Henry Bergman (1): *Modern Times*, 1936 – Co-D
John Blystone (1): *Our Hospitality*, 1923 – D
YAKIMA CANUTT (2): *Stagecoach*, 1939 – 2nd unit D; *Ben-Hur*, 1959 – 2nd unit D
FRANK CAPRA (5): *It Happened One Night*, 1934 – *D; *Mr Deeds Goes to Town*, 1936 – *D; *The Lost Horizon*, 1937 – D; *Mr Smith Goes to Washington*, 1939 – D; *It's a Wonderful Life*, 1946 – D
Michael Cimino (1): *The Deer Hunter*, 1978 – D and Co-Story
Edward Cline (1): *The Bank Dick*, 1940 – D
Merian C. Cooper (1): *King Kong*, 1933 – Co-D
Donald Crisp (1): *The Navigator*, 1924 – Co-D
John Cromwell (1): *The Prisoner of Zenda*, 1937 – D
GEORGE CUKOR (8): *Dinner at Eight*, 1933 – D; *David Copperfield*, 1935 – D; *Camille*, 1936 – D; *Gone with the Wind*, 1939 – Co-D, uc; *The Philadelphia Story*, 1940 – D; *Adam's Rib*, 1949 – D; *Born Yesterday*, 1950 – D; *A Star Is Born*, 1954 – D
MICHAEL CURTIZ (5): *The Adventures of Robin Hood*, 1938 – Co-D; *The Sea Hawk*, 1940 – D; *Casablanca*, 1942 – *D; *Yankee Doodle Dandy*, 1942 – D; *Mildred Pierce*, 1945 – D
Harry D'Abbadie D'Arrast (1): *The Gold Rush*, 1925 – Co-D
Jules Dassin (1): *The Naked City*, 1948 – D
Carter De Haven (1): *Modern Times*, 1936 – Co-D
Jonathan Demme (1): *The Silence of the Lambs*, 1991 – D
William Dieterle (1): *The Hunchback of Notre Dame*, 1939 – D
EDWARD DMYTRYK (2): *Murder My Sweet*, 1944 – D; *Crossfire*, 1947 – D

STANLEY DONEN (4): *On the Town*, 1949 – Co-D; *Singin' in the Rain*, 1952 – Co-D; *Seven Brides for Seven Brothers*, 1954 – D; *Funny Face*, 1957 – D

B. Reeves ('Breezy') Eason (1): *Gone with the Wind*, 1939 – 2nd unit D, uc

CLINT EASTWOOD (2): *Play Misty for Me*, 1971 – D; *The Outlaw Josey Wales*, 1976 – D

VICTOR FLEMING (2): *The Wizard of Oz*, 1939 – D; *Gone with the Wind*, 1939 – *Co-D

JOHN FORD (13): *The Informer*, 1935 – *D; *Stagecoach*, 1939 – D; *Young Mr Lincoln*, 1939 – D; *The Grapes of Wrath*, 1940 – D; *How Green Was My Valley*, 1941 – *D; *They Were Expendable*, 1945 – D; *My Darling Clementine*, 1946 – D; *Fort Apache*, 1948 – D; *She Wore a Yellow Ribbon*, 1949 – D; *Wagonmaster*, 1950 – D; *The Quiet Man*, 1952 – D; *The Searchers*, 1956 – D; *The Man Who Shot Liberty Vallance*, 1962 – D

MILOS FORMAN (2): *One Flew over the Cuckoo's Nest*, 1975 – *D; *Amadeus*, 1984 – D

Bob Fosse (1): *Cabaret*, 1972 – *D

John Frankenheimer (1): *The Manchurian Candidate*, 1962 – D

Sidney Franklin (1): *The Good Earth*, 1937 – D

Tay Garnett (1): *The Postman Always Rings Twice*, 1946 – D

Edmund Goulding (1): *Grand Hotel*, 1932 – D

HOWARD HAWKS (9): *Scarface*, 1032 – D; *Bringing Up Baby*, 1938 – D; *Only Angels Have Wings*, 1939 – D; *His Girl Friday*, 1940 – D; *To Have and Have Not*, 1944 – D; *The Big Sleep*, 1946 – D; *Red River*, 1948 – D; *Gentlemen Prefer Blondes*, 1953 – D; *Rio Bravo*, 1959

ALFRED HITCHCOCK (11): *Rebecca*, 1940 – D; *Shadow of a Doubt*, 1943 – D; *Spellbound*, 1945 – D; *Notorious*, 1946 – D; *Strangers on a Train*, 1951 – D; *Rear Window*, 1954 – D; *Vertigo*, 1958 – D; *North by Northwest*, 1959 – D; *Psycho*, 1960 – D; *The Birds*, 1963 – D; *Marnie*, 1964 – D

James W. Horne (1): *Way Out West*, 1937 – D

ELIA KAZAN (5): *A Streetcar Named Desire*, 1951 – D; *On the Waterfront*, 1954 – *D; *East of Eden*, 1955 – D; *Baby Doll*, 1956 – D; *America, America*, 1963 – D

BUSTER KEATON (4): *Our Hospitality*, 1923 – Co-D; *The Navigator*, 1924 – Co-D; *Sherlock Jr.*, 1924 – D; *The General*, 1926 – Co-D
William Keighley (1): *The Adventures of Robin Hood*, 1938 – Co-D
GENE KELLY (2): *On the Town*, 1949 – Co-D; *Singin' in the Rain*, 1952 – Co-D
Gregory La Cava (1): *Stage Door*, 1937 – D
Charles Laughton (1): *The Night of the Hunter*, 1955 – D and Co-S, uc
MERVYN LEROY (3): *Little Caesar*, 1931 – D; *I Am a Fugitive from a Chain Gang*, 1932 – D; *The Gold Diggers of 1933* – D
Joseph H. Lewis (1): *Gun Crazy*, 1950 – D
Frank Lloyd (1): *Mutiny on the Bounty*, 1935 – D
ERNST LUBITSCH (5): *Trouble in Paradise*, 1932 – D; *The Merry Widow*, 1934 – D; *The Shop Around the Corner*, 1939 – D; *Ninotchka*, 1939 – D; *To Be or Not To Be*, 1942 – D
SIDNEY LUMET (2): *Twelve Angry Men*, 1957 – D; *Long Day's Journey into Night*, 1962 – D
LEO MCCAREY (2): *Duck Soup*, 1933 – D; *The Awful Truth*, 1937 – D
Alexander Mackendrick (1): *Sweet Smell of Success*, 1957 – D
Norman Z. McLeod (1): *It's a Gift*, 1934 – D
ROUBEN MAMOULIAN (2): *Love Me Tonight*, 1932 – D; *Queen Christina*, 1933 – D
George Marshall (1): *Destry Rides Again*, 1939 – D
ANDREW MARTON (2): *The Red Badge of Courage*, 1951 – 2nd unit D; *Ben-Hur*, 1959 – 2nd unit D
LEWIS MILESTONE (2): *All Quiet on the Western Front*, 1930 – D; *Of Mice and Men*, 1939 – D
VINCENTE MINNELLI (6): *Meet Me in St Louis*, 1944 – D; *The Pirate*, 1948 – D; *An American in Paris*, 1951 – D; *The Bad and the Beautiful*, 1952 – D; *The Band Wagon*, 1953 – D; *Gigi*, 1958 – *D
Robert Mulligan (1): *To Kill a Mockingbird*, 1962 – D
F.W. Murnau (1): *Sunrise*, 1927 – D
Mike Nichols (1): *The Graduate*, 1967 – *D
Alan J. Pakula (1): *All the President's Men*, 1976 – D

ARTHUR PENN (2): *The Miracle Worker*, 1962 - D; *Bonnie and Clyde*, 1967 - D

OTTO PREMINGER (2): *Laura*, 1944 - D; *Anatomy of a Murder*, 1959 - D

Bob Rafelson (1): *Five Easy Pieces*, 1970 - D

NICHOLAS RAY (3): *They Live by Night*, 1949 - D; *In a Lonely Place*, 1950 - D; *Rebel without a Cause*, 1955 - D

Charles ('Chuck') Riesner (1): *The Gold Rush*, 1925 - Co-D

Jerome Robbins (1): *West Side Story*, 1961 - *Co-D

Mark Sandrich (1): *Top Hat*, 1935 - D

Franklin Schaffner (1): *Patton*, 1970 - *D

Ernest Schoedsack (1): *King Kong*, 1933 - Co-D

Ridley Scott (1): *Blade Runner*, 1982 - D

Edward Sedgwick (1): *The Cameraman*, 1928 - D

William Seiter (1): *Sons of the Desert*, 1933 - D

Lowell Sherman (1): *She Done Him Wrong*, 1933 - D

DON SIEGEL (3): *Casablanca*, 1942 - montage sequence; *Invasion of the Body Snatchers*, 1956 - D; *The Shootist*, 1976 - D

Robert Siodmak (1): *The Killers*, 1946 - D

Douglas Sirk (1): *Written on the Wind*, 1956 - D

Victor Seastrom (Sjöström) (1): *The Wind*, 1928 - D

GEORGE STEVENS (4): *Swing Time*, 1936 - D; *Gunga Din*, 1939 - D; *Shane*, 1953 - D; *Giant*, 1956 - D

Robert Stevenson (1): *Mary Poppins*, 1964 - D

John Sturges (1): *Bad Day at Black Rock*, 1954 - D

Richard Thorpe (1): *Ben-Hur*, 1959 - *Co-2nd unit D

JACQUES TOURNEUR (2): *Cat People*, 1942 - D; *Out of the Past*, 1947 - D

Gary Tronsdale (1): *Beauty and the Beast*, 1991 - Co-D

W.S. ('Woody') Van Dyke (1): *The Thin Man*, 1934 - D

CHARLES VIDOR (2): *Mr Smith Goes to Washington*, 1939 - 2nd unit D; *Gilda*, 1946 - D

JOSEF VON STERNBERG (2): *Shanghai Express*, 1932 - D; *The Scarlet Empress*, 1934 - D

RAOUL WALSH (2): *High Sierra*, 1941 - D; *White Heat*, 1949 - D

Peter Weir (1): *Witness*, 1985 – D

WILLIAM WELLMAN (3): *The Public Enemy*, 1931 – D; *Nothing Sacred*, 1937 – D; *The Oxbow Incident*, 1943 – D

JAMES WHALE (3): *Frankenstein*, 1931 – D; *The Old Dark House*, 1932 – D; *The Bride of Frankenstein*, 1935 – D

Kirk Wise (1): *Beauty and the Beast*, 1991 – Co-D

ROBERT WISE (2): *The Magnificent Ambersons*, 1942 – Co-D, uc; *West Side Story*, 1961 – Co-D

SAM WOOD (2): *A Night at the Opera*, 1935 – D; *Gone with the Wind*, 1939 – Co-D, uc

WILLIAM WYLER (5): *Dodsworth*, 1936 – D; *Wuthering Heights*, 1939 – D; *The Little Foxes*, 1941 – D; *The Best Years of Our Lives*, 1946 – *D; *Ben-Hur*, 1959 – D

Robert Zemeckis (1): *Who Framed Roger Rabbit?*, 1998 – D

FRED ZINNEMANN (2): *High Noon*, 1952 – D; *From Here to Eternity*, 1953 – *D

Screenwriter-Directors

S = Screenplay
D = Direction
Co- = in co-operation with another or others
uc = uncredited

WOODY ALLEN (3): *Annie Hall*, 1977 – D and Co-S; *Manhattan*, 1979 – D and Co-S; *Hannah and Her Sisters*, 1986 – D and S

ROBERT BENTON (2): *Bonnie and Clyde*,1967 – Co-S; *Kramer vs Kramer*, 1979 – D and S

Peter Bogdanovich (1): *The Last Picture Show*, 1971 – D and Co-S

Clyde Bruckman (1): *The General*, 1926 – Co-D and Co-S

CHARLES CHAPLIN (6): *The Kid*, 1921 – D and S; *The Gold Rush*, 1925 – D and S; *City Lights*, 1930 – D and S; *Modern Times*, 1936 – D and S; *The Great Dictator*, 1940 – D and S; *Limelight*, 1952 – D and S

FRANCIS FORD COPPOLA (5): *Patton*, 1970 – Co-S; *The Godfather*, 1974 – D and *Co-S; *The Conversation*, 1974 – D and S; *The Godfather Part II*, 1976 – *D and *Co-S; *Apocalypse Now*, 1979 – D and S

D.W. GRIFFITH (3): *The Birth of a Nation*, 1915 – D and S; *Intolerance*, 1916 – D and S; *Broken Blossoms*, 1919 – D and S

JOHN HUSTON (7): *High Sierra*, 1941 – Co-S; *The Killers*, 1946 – Co-S, uc; *The Maltese Falcon*, 1941 – D and S; *The Treasure of the Sierra Madre*, 1948 – *D and *S; *The Asphalt Jungle*, 1950 – D and Co-S; *The Red Badge of Courage*, 1951 – D and Co-S; *Fat City*, 1972 – D

LAWRENCE KASDAN (2): *Raiders of the Lost Ark*, 1981 – Co-S; *Body Heat*, 1981 – D and S

Stanley Kubrick (1): *Paths of Glory*, 1957 – D and Co-S

FRITZ LANG (2): *Fury*, 1936 – D and Co-S; *The Big Heat*, 1953 – D

GEORGE LUCAS (2): *American Graffiti*, 1973 – D and Co-S; *Star Wars*, 1977 – D and Co-S

Terence Mallick (1): *Days of Heaven*, 1978 – D and S

JOSEPH MANKIEWICZ (2): *The Ghost and Mrs Muir*, 1947 – D; *All About Eve*, 1950 – *D and *S

Max Ophüls (1): *Letter from an Unknown Woman*, 1948 – D and Co-S

SAM PECKINPAH (3): *Invasion of the Body Snatchers*, 1956 – Co-S, uc; *Ride the High Country*, 1962 – D; *The Wild Bunch*, 1969 – D and Co-S

ROMAN POLANSKI (2): *Rosemary's Baby*, 1968 – D and S; *Chinatown*, 1974 – D

Jean Renoir (1): *The Southerner*, 1945 – D and Co-S

ROBERT ROSSEN (2): *All the King's Men*, 1950 – D and S; *The Hustler*, 1961 – D and Co-S

MARTIN SCORSESE (3): *Mean Streets*, 1973 – D and Co-S; *Taxi Driver*, 1976 – D; *Raging Bull*, 1980 – D

STEVEN SPIELBERG (5): *Jaws*, 1975 – D; *Close Encounters of the Third Kind*, 1977 – D and S; *Raiders of the Lost Ark*, 1981; *E.T.*, 1982 – D; *Schindler's List*, 1993 – D

Oliver Stone (1): *Salvador*, 1986 – D and Co-S

PRESTON STURGES (4): *The Lady Eve*, 1941 – D and S; *Sullivan's Travels*, 1941 – D and S; *The Palm Beach Story*, 1942 – D and S; *The Miracle of Morgan's Creek*, 1943 – D and S

KING VIDOR (3): *The Big Parade*, 1925 – D; *The Crowd*, 1928 – D and S; *The Wizard of Oz*, 1939 – Co-D, uc

ERICH VON STROHEIM (2): *Greed*, 1924 – D and Co-S; *Queen Kelly*, 1928 – D and Co-S

ORSON WELLES (4): *Citizen Kane*, 1941 – D and Co-S; *The Magnificent Ambersons*, 1942 – D and S; *The Lady from Shanghai*, 1948 – D and S; *Touch of Evil*, 1958 – D and S

BILLY WILDER (8): *Ninotchka*, 1939 – Co-S: *Double Indemnity*, 1944 – D and Co-S; *The Lost Weekend*, 1945 – *D and *Co-S; *Sunset Boulevard*, 1950 – D and Co-S; *Ace in the Hole*, 1951 – D and Co-S; *Witness for the Prosecution*, 1957 – D and Co-S; *Some Like it Hot*, 1959 – D and Co-S; *The Apartment*, 1960 – *D and *Co-S

Screenwriters and Authors

Hortense Powdermaker, 1951:

> The script is the basic raw material from which a movie is made. If it is weak or shoddy, a good picture cannot be made from it, any more than a strong bridge could be constructed with poor steel. The importance of the script to the finished movie cannot be overestimated.

AS = screenplay based on the adaptation of another work
OS = original screenplay
Uc = uncredited
Co- = in co-operation with other writers

George Abbott (1): *All Quiet on the Western Front*, 1930 , Co-AS

Helen Aberson (1): *Dumbo*, 1941 – Co-Story base

Samuel Hopkins Adams (1): *It Happened One Night*, 1934 – Story base, *Night Bus*

Felix Adler (1): *Destry Rides Again*, 1939 – Co-AS

James Agee (1): *The Night of the Hunter*, 1955 – Co-AS

Zoe Akins (1): *Camille*, 1936 – Co-AS

Laszlo Aladar (1): *Top Hat*, 1935 – Co-Play base

Joan Alison (1): *Casablanca*, 1942 – Co-Play base

JAY PRESSON ALLEN (2): *Marnie*, 1964 – AS; *Cabaret*, 1972 – AS

Edward Anderson (1): *They Live by Night*, 1949 – Novel base, *Thieves Like Us*

Maxwell Anderson (1): *All Quiet on the Western Front*, 1930 – Co-AS

Dell Andrews (1): *All Quiet on the Western Front*, 1930 – Co-AS

Paul Armont (1): *Love Me Tonight*, 1932 – Co-Play base

George Axelrod (1): *The Manchurian Candidate*, 1962 – AS

JOHN BALDERSTON (3): *Frankenstein*, 1931 – Co-AS; *The Bride of Frankenstein*, 1935 – Co-OS; *The Prisoner of Zenda*, 1937 – Co-AS

Albert Band (1): *The Red Badge of Courage*, 1951 – Co-AS

Philip Barry (1): *The Philadelphia Story*, 1940 – Play base

Sy Bartlett (1): *Twelve o'Clock High*, 1949 – Co-AS and Co-Novel base

Aurelius Battaglia (1): *Pinocchio*, 1940 – Co-AS

Frank Baum (1): *The Wizard of Oz*, 1939 – Story base

HARRY BEHN (2): *The Big Parade*, 1925 – AS; *The Crowd*, 1928 – Co-OS

S.N. BEHRMAN (3): *Queen Christina*, 1933 – Co-AS; *The Pirate*, 1948 – Play base; *Ben-Hur*, 1959 – Co-AS, uc

JAMES WARNER BELLAH (3): *Fort Apache*, 1948 – Story base; *She Wore a Yellow Ribbon*, 1949 – Story base; *The Man Who Shot Liberty Vallance*, 1962 – Co-AS

Peter Benchley (1): *Jaws*, 1975 – Co-AS and Novel base

Stephen Vincent Benet (1): *Seven Brides for Seven Brothers*, 1954 – Story base

SALLY BENSON (2): *Shadow of a Doubt*, 1943 – Co-AS; *Meet Me in St Louis*, 1944 – Story base

Henry Bergman (1): *Modern Times*, 1936 – Co-OS

Carl Bernstein (1): *All the President's Men*, 1976 – Co-Story base

A.I. Bezzerides (1): *Kiss Me Deadly*, 1955 – AS

Roger Bloch (1): *Psycho*, 1960 – Novel base

AL BOASBERG (2): *The General*, 1926 – Co-AS; *A Night at the Opera*, 1935 – Co-AS

De Witt Bodeen (1): *Cat People*, 1942 – OS

David Boehm (1): *The Gold Diggers of 1933*, 1933 – Co-AS

Sydney Boehm: *The Big Heat*, 1953 – AS

Pierre Boileau (1): *Vertigo*, 1958 – Co-Novel base, *D'Entre Les Morts*

CHARLES BRACKETT (3): *Ninotchka*, 1939 – Co-AS; *The Lost Weekend*, 1945 – Co-AS; *Sunset Boulevard*, 1950 – Co-OS

LEIGH BRACKETT (2): *The Big Sleep*, 1946 – Co-AS; *Rio Bravo*, 1959 – Co-AS

George Bradshaw (1): *The Bad and the Beautiful*, 1952 – Story base

Max Brand (1): *Destry Rides Again*, 1939 – Novel base

Lilian Braun (1): *The Pirate*, 1948 – Co-AS

Irving Brecher (1): *Meet Me in St Louis*, 1944 – Co-AS

Howard Bresley (1): *Bad Day at Black Rock*, 1954 – Story base

MARSHALL BRICKMAN (2): *Annie Hall, 1977 – Co-OS; Manhattan, 1979 – Co-OS

JOHN BRIGHT (2): The Public Enemy, 1931 – Co-AS and Story base; She Done Him Wrong, 1933 – Co-AS

Emily Brontë (1): Wuthering Heights, 1939 – Novel base

Richard Brooks (1): Crossfire, 1947 – Novel base

CLYDE BRUCKMAN (4): Our Hospitality, 1923 – Co-OS; Sherlock Jr., 1924 – Co-OS; The Navigator, 1924 – Co-OS; The General, 1926 – Co-AS

Sidney Buchman (1): Mr Smith Goes to Washington, 1939 – AS

Robert Buckner (1): Yankee Doodle Dandy, 1942 – Story base

Thomas Burke (1): Broken Blossoms, 1919 – Story base, The Chink and the Child

Murray Burnett (1): Casablanca, 1942 – Co-Play base

W.R. BURNETT (3): Little Caesar, 1930 – Novel base; Scarface, 1932 – Co-AS; High Sierra, 1941 – Co-AS and Novel base

Robert Burns (1): I Am a Fugitive from a Chain Gang, 1932 – Story base

Niven Busch (1): The Postman Always Rings Twice, 1946 – Co-AS

Hugo Butler (1): The Southerner, 1945 – Co-AS

JAMES CAIN (2): Double Indemnity, 1944 – Story base; The Postman Always Rings Twice, 1946 – Story base

Alan Campbell (1): The Little Foxes, 1941 – Co-AS

Sidney Carroll (1): The Hustler, 1961 – Co-AS

Robert Carson (1): A Star Is Born, 1954 – Co-Story base

Forrest Carter (1): The Outlaw Josey Wales, 1976 – Story base

Joseph Carter (1): Raging Bull, 1980 – Co-Story base

Vera Caspary (1): Laura, 1944 – Novel base

RAYMOND CHANDLER (4): Double Indemnity, 1944 – Co-AS; Murder My Sweet, 1944 – Novel base, Farewell My Lovely; The Big Sleep, 1946 – Novel base; Strangers on a Train, 1951 – Co-AS

Borden Chase (1): Red River, 1948 – Co-AS and Novel base

Sonia Chemus (1): The Outlaw Josey Wales, 1976 – Co-AS

Agatha Christie (1): Witness for the Prosecution, 1957 – Novel and Play base

Humphrey Cobb (1): *Paths of Glory*, 1957 – Novel base

Colette (1): *Gigi*, 1958 – Novel base

Carlo Collodi (1): *Pinocchio*, 1940 – Novel base

BETTY COMDEN (3): *On the Town*, 1949 – Co-OS; *Singin' in the Rain*, 1952 – Co-OS; *The Band Wagon*, 1953 – Co-OS

Richard Condon (1): *The Manchurian Candidate*, 1962 – Novel base

Joseph Conrad (1): *Apocalypse Now*, 1979 – Novel base, *Heart of Darkness*

Whitfield Cook (1): *Strangers on a Train*, 1951 – Co-AS

Alec Coppel (1): *Vertigo*, 1958 – Co-AS

Bartlett Cormack (1): *Fury*, 1936 – Co-AS

Avery Corman (1): *Kramer vs Kramer*, 1979 – Novel base

John Cotton (1): *The Wind*, 1928 – Co-AS

William Cottrell (1): *Pinocchio*, 1940 – Co-AS

Stephen Crane (1): *The Red Badge of Courage*, 1951 – Novel base

Frank Craven (1): *Sons of the Desert*, 1933 – Co-OS

James Creelman (1): *King Kong*, 1933 – Co-AS

James Cunningham (1): *It's a Gift*, 1934 – Co-AS

John Cunningham (1): *High Noon*, 1952 – Story base

Don da Gradi (1): *Mary Poppins*, 1964 – Co-AS

Carter De Haven (1): *Modern Times*, 1936 – Co-OS

Vina Delmar (1): *The Awful Truth*, 1937 – AS

I.A.L. DIAMOND (2): *Some Like It Hot*, 1959 – Co-OS; *The Apartment*, 1960 – Co-OS

Philip Dick (1): *Blade Runner*, 1982 – Novella base, *Do Androids Dream of Electric Sheep?*

R.A. Dick (1): *The Ghost and Mrs Muir*, 1947 – Story base

Thomas Dixon (1): *Birth of a Nation*, 1915 Novel base, *The Klansman*

William Drake (1): *Grand Hotel*, 1932 – AS and translated play base, from Vicki Baum's novel, *Menschen im Hotel*

Jay Dratler (1): *Laura*, 1944 – Co-AS

Alexandre Dumas Fils (1): *Camille*, 1936 Play and Novel base, *La Dame aux Camellias*

DAPHNE DU MAURIER (2): *Rebecca*, 1940 – Novel base; *The Birds*, 1963 – Story base

PHILIP DUNNE (2): *How Green Was My Valley*, 1941 – AS; *The Ghost and Mrs Muir*, 1947 – AS

Jo Eisinger (1): *Gilda*, 1946 – Co-AS

E.A. Ellington (1): *Gilda*, 1946 – Story base

Samuel Engel (1): *My Darling Clementine*, 1946 – Co-AS

Otto Englander (1): *Pinocchio*, 1940 – Co-AS

Julius and Philip Epstein (1): *Casablanca*, 1942 – Co-AS

Howard Estabrook (1): *David Copperfield*, 1935 – Co-AS

Hampton Fancher (1): *Blade Runner*, 1982 – Co-AS

Alexander Farago (1): *Top Hat*, 1935 – Co-Play base

FRANCIS EDWARD FARAGOH (2): *Little Caesar*, 1930 – Co-AS, uc; *Frankenstein*, 1931 – Co-AS

Joseph Farnham (1): *The Big Parade*, 1925 – Play base

WILLIAM FAULKNER (3): *To Have and Have Not*, 1944 – Co-AS; *The Southerner*, 1945 – Co-AS, uc; *The Big Sleep*, 1946 – Co-AS

EDNA FERBER (2): *Dinner at Eight*, 1933 – Co-Play base; *Stage Door*, 1937 – Co-Play base

Joseph Fields (1): *Gentlemen Prefer Blondes*, 1953 – Co-Play base

W.C. FIELDS (2): *It's a Gift*, 1934 – Co-AS and Co-Story base, as Charles Bogle; *The Bank Dick*, 1940 – OS, as Mahatma Kane Jeeves

Fred F. Finkelhoffe (1): *Meet Me in St Louis*, 1944 – Co-AS

Horton Foote (1): **To Kill a Mockingbird*, 1962 – AS

Patrick Ford (1): *Wagonmaster*, 1950 – Co-AS

Carl Foreman (1): *High Noon*, 1952 – AS

Garrett Fort (1): *Frankenstein*, 1931 – Co-AS

Lewis Foster (1): **Mr Smith Goes to Washington*, 1939 – Story base, *The Gentleman from Montana*

Bruno Frank (1): *The Hunchback of Notre Dame*, 1939 – Co-AS

Christopher Fry (1): *Ben-Hur*, 1959 – Co-AS, uc

JULES FURTHMAN (6): *Shanghai Express*, 1932 – Co-AS; *Mutiny on the Bounty*, 1935 – Co-AS; *Only Angels Have Wings*, 1939 – Co-AS; *To Have and Have Not*, 1944 – Co-AS; *The Big Sleep*, 1946 – Co-AS; *Rio Bravo*, 1959 – Co-AS

Leonard Gardner (1): *Fat City*, 1972 – AS and Novel base

Louis Garfinkle (1): *The Deer Hunter*, 1976 – Co-Story base
ERWIN GELSEY (2): *The Gold Diggers of 1933* – Co-AS; *Swing Time*, 1936 – Story base
Leonard Gershe (1): *Funny Face*, 1957 – Co-AS
Sheridan Gibney (1): *I Am a Fugitive from a Chain Gang*, 1932 – Co-AS
William Gibson (1): *The Miracle Worker*, 1962 – AS and Novel base
Kubec Glasmon (1): *The Public Enemy*, 1931 – Co-AS
Ivan Goff (1): *White Heat*, 1949 – Co-AS
Willis Goldbeck (1): *The Man Who Shot Liberty Vallance*, 1962 – Co-AS
Bo Goldman (1): *One Flew over the Cuckoo's Nest*, 1975 – Co-AS
William Goldman (1): *All The President's Men*, 1976 – AS
FRANCES GOODRICH (4): *The Thin Man*, 1934 – Co-AS; *It's a Wonderful Life*, 1946 – Co-AS; *The Pirate*, 1948 – Co-AS; *Seven Brides for Seven Brothers*, 1954 – Co-AS
Ruth Gordon (1): *Adam's Rib*, 1949 – Co-OS
Carl Gottlieb (1): *Jaws*, 1975 – Co-AS
Winston Graham (1): *Marnie*, 1964 – Novel base
JOE GRANT (2): *Fantasia*, 1940 – Co-OS; *Dumbo*, 1941 – Co-AS
ADOLPH GREEN (3): *On the Town*, 1949 – Co-OS; *Singin' in the Rain*, 1952 – Co-OS; *The Band Wagon*, 1953 – Co-OS
Howard J. Green (1): *I Am a Fugitive from a Chain Gang*, 1932 – Co-AS
Walon Green (1): *The Wild Bunch*, 1969 – Co-AS and Story base
Eleanore Griffin (1): *Only Angels Have Wings*, 1939 – Co-OS, uc
Davis Grubb (1): *The Night of the Hunter*, 1955 – Novel base
FRED GUIOL (2): *Gunga Din*, 1939 – AS; *Giant*, 1956 – Co-AS
A.B. Guthrie (1): *Shane*, 1953 – Co-AS
ALBERT HACKETT (4): *The Thin Man*, 1934 – Co-AS; *It's a Wonderful Life*, 1946 – Co-AS; *The Pirate*, 1948 – Co-AS; *Seven Brides for Seven Brothers*, 1954 – Co-AS
Scott Hale (1): *The Shootist*, 1976 – Co-AS
James Norman Hall (1): *Mutiny on the Bounty*, 1935 – Co-Novel base

DASHIELL HAMMETT (2): *The Thin Man*, 1934 – Novel base; *The Maltese Falcon*, 1941 – Novel base
Jo Harris (1): *Play Misty for Me*, 1971 – Story base
Thomas Harris (1): *The Silence of the Lambs*, 1991 – Novel base
Joan Harrison (1): *Rebecca*, 1940 – Co-AS
Moss Hart (1): *A Star Is Born*, 1954 – AS
H.M. Harwood (1): *Queen Christina*, 1933 – Co-AS
Lawrence Hauben (1): *One Flew over the Cuckoo's Nest*, 1975 – Co-AS
JEAN C. HAVEZ (3): *Our Hospitality*, 1923 – Co-OS; *Sherlock Jr.*, 1924 – Co-OS; *The Navigator*, 1924 – Co-OS
John Michael Hayes (1): *Rear Window*, 1954 – AS
BEN HECHT (9): *Scarface*, 1932 – Co-AS; *Queen Christina*, 1933 – Co-AS, uc; *Nothing Sacred*, 1937 – OS; *Gunga Din*, 1939 – Co-Story base; *Wuthering Heights*, 1939 – Co-AS; *Gone with the Wind*, 1939 – Co-AS, uc; *His Girl Friday*, 1940 – Co-Play base; *Spellbound*, 1945 – Co-AS; *Notorious*, 1946 – OS
Jo Heims (1): *Play Misty for Me*, 1971 – Co-AS
Lilian Hellman (1): *The Little Foxes*, 1941 – Co-AS and Play base
Sam Hellman (1): *My Darling Clementine*, 1946 – Story base
ERNEST HEMINGWAY (2): *To Have and Have Not*, 1944 – Novel base; *The Killers*, 1946 – Story base
Buck Henry (1): *The Graduate*, 1967 – Co-AS
Michael Herr (1): *Apocalypse Now*, 1979 – Co-AS
Harry Hervey (1): *Shanghai Express*, 1932 – Story base
Patricia Highsmith (1): *Strangers on a Train*, 1951 – Novel base
JAMES HILTON (1): *Camille*, 1936 – Co-AS; *The Lost Horizon*, 1937 – Novel base
SAMUEL HOFFENSTEIN (2): *Love Me Tonight*, 1932 – Co-AS; *Laura*, 1944 – Co-AS
Brown Holmes (1): *I Am a Fugitive from a Chain Gang*, 1932 – Co-AS
Richard Hooker (1): *M*A*S*H*, 1970 – Novel base
Anthony Hope (1): *The Prisoner of Zenda*, 1937 – Novel base
Avery Hopwood (1): *The Gold Diggers of 1933* – Play base

SIDNEY HOWARD (2): *Dodsworth*, 1936 – AS; **Gone with the Wind*, 1939 – Co-AS
DICK HUEMER (2): *Fantasia*, 1940 – Co-OS; *Dumbo*, 1941 – Co-AS
Dorothy B. Hughes (1): *In a Lonely Place*, 1950 – Novel base
Victor Hugo (1): *The Hunchback of Notre Dame*, 1939 – Novel base
Evan Hunter (1): *The Birds*, 1963 – AS
William Hurlbut (1): *The Bride of Frankenstein*, 1935 – Co-OS
Willard Huyck (1): *American Graffiti*, 1973 – Co-OS
Christopher Isherwood (1): *Cabaret*, 1972 – Story base, *Sally Bowles*
Felix Jackson (1): *Destry Rides Again*, 1939 – Co-AS
Rian James (1): *Forty-Second Street*, 1933 – Co-AS
TALBOT JENNINGS (2): *Mutiny on the Bounty*, 1935 – Co-AS; *The Good Earth*, 1937 – Co-AS
Jack Jevne (1): *Way Out West*, 1937 – Co-Story base
Dorothy M. Johnson (1): *The Man Who Shot Liberty Vallance*, 1962 – Story base
NUNNALLY JOHNSON (2): *The Grapes of Wrath* – 1940 AS; *The Southerner*, 1945 – Co-AS
Grover Jones (1): *Trouble in Paradise*, 1932 – Co-AS
James Jones (1): *From Here to Eternity*, 1953 – Novel base
Edmund Joseph (1): *Yankee Doodle Dandy*, 1942 – Co-AS
'Adrien Joyce' (Carol Eastman) (1): *Five Easy Pieces*, 1970 – AS and Co-Story base
Bert Kalmar (1): *Duck Soup*, 1933 – Co-OS, also Lyrics
GARSON KANIN (2): *Adam's Rib*, 1949 – Co-OS; *Born Yesterday*, 1950 – Play base
MACKINLAY KANTOR (2): *The Best Years of Our Lives*, 1946 – Novella base; *Gun Crazy*, 1950 – Co-AS and Story base
Gloria Katz (1): *American Graffiti*, 1973 – Co-OS
GEORGE S. KAUFMAN (3): *Dinner at Eight*, 1933 – Co-Play base; *A Night at the Opera*, 1935 – Co-AS; *Stage Door*, 1937 – Co-Play base
MILLARD KAUFMAN (2): *Gun Crazy*, 1950 – Co-AS; *Bad Day at Black Rock*, 1954 – Co-AS

Clarence Buddington Kelland (1): *Mr Deeds Goes to Town* – Story base

William Kelley (1): *Witness*, 1985 – Co-AS and Co-Story base

Ken Kesey (1): *One Flew over the Cuckoo's Nest*, 1975 – Novel base

Sherwood King (1): *The Lady from Shanghai*, 1948 – Novel base

DOROTHY KINGSLEY (2): *Kiss Me Kate*, 1953 – AS; *Seven Brides for Seven Brothers*, 1954 – Co-AS

Rudyard Kipling (1): *Gunga Din*, 1939 – Poem base

Arthur Kober (1): *The Little Foxes*, 1941 – Co-AS

HOWARD KOCH (3): *The Sea Hawk*, 1940 – Co-AS; *Casablanca*, 1942 – Co-AS; *Letter from an Unknown Woman*, 1948 – Co-AS

Manuel Komroff (1): *The Scarlet Empress*, 1934 – Co-OS

Norman Krasna (1): *Fury*, 1936 – Co-Story base

Harry Kurnitz (1): *Witness for the Prosecution*, 1957 – Co-AS

Stuart N. Lake (1): *My Darling Clementine*, 1946 – Book base, *Wyatt Earp, Frontier Marshal*

Noel Langley (1): *The Wizard of Oz*, 1939 – Co-AS

RING LARDNER JR. (2): *Laura*, 1944 – Co-AS, uc; **M*A*S*H*, 1970 – AS

Nikolaus Laszlo (1): *The Shop Around the Corner*, 1940 – Play base

Arthur Laurents (1): *West Side Story*, 1961 – Musical play base

Beirne Lay Jr. (1): *Twelve O'clock High*, 1949 – Co-AS and Co-Novel base

CHARLES LEDERER (2): *His Girl Friday*, 1940 AS; *Gentlemen Prefer Blondes*, 1953 – AS

Harper Lee (1): *To Kill a Mockingbird*, 1962 – Novel base

Robert Lee (1): *Little Caesar*, 1930 – Co-AS

ERNEST LEHMAN (3): *Sweet Smell of Success*, 1957 – Co-AS and Story base; *North by Northwest*, 1959 – OS; *West Side Story*, 1961 – AS

Alan LeMay (1): *The Searchers*, 1956 – Novel base

MELCHIOR LENGYEL (2): *Ninotchka*, 1939 – Story base; *To Be or Not To Be*, 1942 – Co-Story base

ALAN JAY LERNER (2): *An American in Paris*, 1951 – OS; **Gigi*, 1958 – AS

Sonya Levien (1): *The Hunchback of Notre Dame*, 1939 – Co-AS
Ira Levin (1): *Rosemary's Baby*, 1968 – Novel base
Margaret R. Levino (1): *Queen Christina*, 1933 – Story base
Robert M. Lindner (1): *Rebel without a Cause* – Novel base
Howard Lindsay (1): *Swing Time*, 1936 – Co-AS
Ben Lipton (1): *The Cameraman*, 1928 – Co-Story base
RICHARD LLEWELLYN (2): *How Green Was My Valley*, 1941 – Novel base; *The Quiet Man*, 1952 – Co-AS
ANITA LOOS (3): *The Pirate*, 1948 – Co-AS; *Gentlemen Prefer Blondes*, 1953 – Novel and Co-Play base; *Gigi*, 1958 – Play base
CHARLES MACARTHUR (3): *Wuthering Heights*, 1939 – Co-AS; *Gunga Din*, 1939 – Co-Story base; *His Girl Friday*, 1940 – Co-Play base, *The Front Page*
Barbara Hawkes McCampbell (1): *Rio Bravo*, 1959 – Story base
Gordon McDonnell (1): *Shadow of a Doubt*, 1943 – Story base
J.P. McEvoy (1): *It's a Gift*, 1934 – Play base
William McGivern (1): *The Big Heat*, 1953 – Novel base
James Kevin McGuinness (1): *A Night at the Opera*, 1935 – Story base
Don McGuire (1): *Bad Day at Black Rock*, 1955 – Co-AS
Larry McMurty (1): *The Last Picture Show*, 1971 – Novel base and Co-AS
Ben Maddow (1): *The Asphalt Jungle*, 1950 – Co-AS
John Lee Mahin (1): *Scarface*, 1932 – Co-AS
Wilkie Mahoney (1): *The Pirate*, 1948 – Co-AS
DAVID MAINWARING (Geoffrey Homes) (2): *Out of the Past*, 1947 – AS and Novel base, *Build My Gallows High*; *Invasion of the Body Snatchers*, 1956 – AS
Albert Maltz (1): *The Naked City*, 1948 – Co-AS
HERMAN MANKIEWICZ (2): *Dinner at Eight*, 1933 – Co-AS; *Citizen Kane*, 1941 – Co-OS
Albert Mannheimer (1): *Born Yesterday*, 1950 AS
Leopold Marchand (1): *Love Me Tonight*, 1932 – Co-Play base

FRANCES MARION (4): *The Wind*, 1928 – Co-AS; *Dinner at Eight*, 1933 – Co-AS; *Camille*, 1936 – Co-AS; *The Good Earth*, 1937 – Co-AS, uc

George Marion Jr. (1): *Love Me Tonight*, 1932 – Co-AS

Ben Markson (1): *The Gold Diggers of 1933* – Co-AS

D.M. Marshman Jr. (1): **Sunset Boulevard*, 1950 – Co-AS

MARDIK MARTIN (2): *Mean Streets*, 1973 – Co-OS; *Raging Bull*, 1980 – Co-AS

Charles Masteroff (1): *Cabaret*, 1972 – Musical comedy base

Whit Masterson (1): *Touch of Evil*, 1958 – Novel base

June Mathis (1): *Greed*, 1924 – Co-AS

Melissa Mathison (1): *E.T.*, 1982 – OS

Carl Mayer (1): *Sunrise*, 1927 – AS

Edwin Justus Mayer (1): *To Be or Not To Be*, 1942 – AS

John Milius (1): *Apocalypse Now*, 1979 – Co-AS

SETON I. MILLER (3): *Scarface*, 1932 – Co-AS; *The Adventures of Robin Hood*, 1938 – Co-AS; *The Sea Hawk*, 1940 – Co-AS

Winston Miller (1): *My Darling Clementine*, 1946 – Co-AS

JOSEPH A. MITCHELL (3): *Our Hospitality*, 1923 – Co-OS; *The Navigator*, 1924 – Co-OS; *Sherlock Jr.*, 1924 – Co-OS

Margaret Mitchell (1): *Gone with the Wind*, 1939 – Novel base

Ivan Moffat (1): *Giant*, 1956 – Co-AS

Larry Morey (1): *Bambi*, 1942 – Co-AS

Byron Morgan (1): *Sons of the Desert*, 1933 – Co-OS

Henry Myers (1): *Destry Rides Again*, 1939 – Co-AS

Thomas Narcejac (1): *Vertigo*, 1958 – Co-Novel base, *D'entre Les Morts*

David Newman (1): *Bonnie and Clyde*, 1967 – Co-OS

Walter Newman (1): *Ace in the Hole*, 1951 – Co-OS

DUDLEY NICHOLS (3): **The Informer*, 1935 – AS; *Bringing Up Baby*, 1938, – Co-AS; *Stagecoach*, 1939 – AS

Charles Nordhoff (1): *Mutiny on the Bounty*, 1935 – Co-Novel base

Frank Norris (1): *Greed*, 1924 – Novel base, *McTeague*

EDMUND H. NORTH (2): *In a Lonely Place*, 1950 – Co-AS; **Patton*, 1970 – Co-AS

Karl Noti (1): *Top Hat*, 1935 – Story base

FRANK S. NUGENT (5): *Fort Apache*, 1948 – AS; *She Wore a Yellow Ribbon*, 1949 – Co-AS; *Wagonmaster*, 1950 – Co-AS; *The Quiet Man*, 1952 – Co-AS; *The Searchers*, 1956 – AS

Clifford Odets (1): *Sweet Smell of Success*, 1957 – Co-AS

Liam O'Flaherty (1): *The Informer*, 1935 – Novel base

Eugene O'Neill (1): *Long Day's Journey into Night*, 1962 – Play base

Czenzi Ormonde (1): *Strangers on a Train*, 1951 – Co-AS

Paul Osborn (1): *East of Eden*, 1955 – Co-AS

Dorothy Parker (1): *The Little Foxes*, 1941 – Co-AS

James Parrott (1): *Way Out West*, 1937 – Co-AS

Marion Parsonnet (1): *Gilda*, 1946 – Co-AS

Fred Pasley (1): *Scarface*, 1932 – Co-AS

JOHN PAXTON (2): *Murder My Sweet*, 1944 – AS; *Crossfire*, 1947 – AS

Perce Pearce (1): *Bambi*, 1942 – Co-AS

Harold Pearl (1): *Dumbo*, 1941 – Co-Story base

Erdman Penner (1): *Pinocchio*, 1940 – Co-AS

David Peoples (1): *Blade Runner*, 1982 – Co-AS

Nat Perrin (1): *Duck Soup*, 1933 – Co-OS

George Sessions Perry (1): *The Southerner*, 1945 – Novel base

Jeffrey Price (1): *Who Framed Roger Rabbit?*, 1988 – Co-AS

Gertrude Purcell (1): *Destry Rides Again*, 1939 – Co-AS

MARIO PUZO (2): *The Godfather*, 1972 – Co-AS and Novel base; *The Godfather Part II*, 1974 – Co-AS and Novel base

Norman Reilly Raine (1): *The Adventures of Robin Hood*, 1938 – Co-AS

William Rankin (1): *Only Angels Have Wings*, 1939 – Co-AS, uc

SAMSON RAPHAELSON (3): *Trouble in Paradise*, 1932 – Co-AS; *The Merry Widow*, 1934 – Co-AS; *The Shop Around the Corner*, 1940 – AS

Quinn H. Redeker (1): *The Deer Hunter*, 1978 – Co-Story base

Betty Reinhardt (1): *Laura*, 1944 – Co-AS

Walter Reisch (1): *Ninotchka*, 1939 – Co-AS

Erich Maria Remarque (1): *All Quiet on the Western Front*, 1930 – Novel base

Alma Reville (1): *Shadow of a Doubt*, 1943 – Co-OS

ROBERT RISKIN (3): **It Happened One Night*, 1934 – AS; *Mr Deeds Goes to Town*, 1936 – AS; *The Lost Horizon*, 1937 – AS

Ben Roberts (1): *White Heat*, 1949 – Co-AS

Charles Rogers (1): *Way Out West*, 1937 – Co-AS

Wells Root (1): *The Prisoner of Zenda*, 1937 – Co-AS

Bradford Ropes (1): *Forty-Second Street*, 1933 – Novel base

Edward Rose (1): *The Prisoner of Zenda*, 1937 – Play base

Reginald Rose (1): *Twelve Angry Men*, 1957 – AS and TV Play base

Ruth Rose (1): *King Kong*, 1933 – Co-AS

Harry Ruby (1): *Duck Soup*, 1933 – Co-OS, also music

Harry Ruskin (1): *The Postman Always Rings Twice*, 1946 – Co-AS

Florence Ryerson (1): *The Wizard of Oz*, 1939 – Co-AS

MORRIS RYSKIND (2): *A Night at the Opera*, 1935 – Co-OS; *Stage Door*, 1937 – Co-AS

Rafael Sabatini (1): *The Sea Hawk*, 1940 – Novel base

Joseph Sabo (1): *Pinocchio*, 1940 – Co-AS

Waldo Salt (1): *The Philadelphia Story*, 1940 – Co-AS, uc

Felix Salten (1): *Bambi*, 1942 – Novel base

Lesser Samuels (1): *Ace in the Hole*, 1951 – Co-OS

Oscar Saul (1): *A Streetcar Named Desire*, 1951 – Co-AS

Peter Savage (1): *Raging Bull*, 1980 – Co-Story base

Dorothy Scarborough (1): *The Wind*, 1928 – Novel base

Jack Schaefer (1): *Shane*, 1953 Novel base

CHARLES SCHNEE (3): *Red River*, 1948 – Co-AS; *They Live by Night*, 1948 – Co-AS; **The Bad and the Beautiful*, 1952 – AS

PAUL SCHRADER (2): *Taxi Driver*, 1976 – OS; *Raging Bull*, 1980 – Co-AS

ALAN SCOTT (2): *Top Hat*, 1935 – Co-AS; *Swing Time*, 1936 – Co-AS

Peter Seaman (1): *Who Framed Roger Rabbit?*, 1988 – Co-AS

JAMES SEYMOUR (2): *Forty-Second Street*, 1933 – Co-AS; *The Gold Diggers of 1933* – Co-AS

Peter Shaffer (1): *Amadeus*, 1984 – AS and Play base
Arthur Sheekman (1): *Duck Soup*, 1933 – Co-OS
Mary Wollstonecraft Shelley (1): *Frankenstein*, 1931 – Novel base
Jack Sher (1): *Shane*, 1953 – Co-AS
ROBERT E. SHERWOOD (2): *Rebecca*, 1940 – Co-AS; *The Best Years of Our Lives*, 1946 – AS
Irving Shulman (1): *Rebel without a Cause*, 1955 – Adaptation
Tess Slesinger (1): *The Good Earth*, 1937 – Co-AS
Charles Smith (1): *The General*, 1926 – Co-AS
Webb Smith (1): *Pinocchio*, 1940 – Co-AS
Eugene Solow (1): *Of Mice and Men*, 1939 – AS
Andrew Solt (1): *In a Lonely Place*, 1950 – Co-AS
Samuel and Bella Spewack (1): *Kiss Me Kate*, 1953 – Musical comedy base
Mickey Spillane (1): *Kiss Me Deadly*, 1955 – Novel base
LAURENCE STALLINGS (2): *The Big Parade*, 1925 – Story base; *She Wore a Yellow Ribbon*, 1949 – Co-AS
Joseph Stefano (1): *Psycho*, 1960 – AS
JOHN STEINBECK (3): *Of Mice and Men*, 1939 – Play base; *The Grapes of Wrath*, 1940 – Novel base; *East of Eden*, 1955 – Novel base
Philip Van Doren Stern (1): *It's A Wonderful Life*, 1946 – Story base
Stewart Stern (1): *Rebel without a Cause*, 1955 – Co-AS
DONALD OGDEN STEWART (3): *Dinner at Eight*, 1933 – Co-AS; *The Prisoner of Zenda*, 1937 – Co-AS; *The Philadelphia Story*, 1940 – Co-AS
N.B. Stone Jr. (1): *Ride the High Country*, 1962 – OS
Hermann Sudermann (1): *Sunrise*, 1927 – Novel base
Glendon Swarthout (1): *The Shootist*, 1976 – Novel base
Miles Hood Swarthout (1): *The Shootist*, 1976 – Co-AS
Jo Swerling (1): *It's a Wonderful Life*, 1946 – Co-AS
Ted Tally (1): *The Silence of the Lambs*, 1991 – AS
Daniel Taradash (1): *From Here to Eternity*, 1953 – AS
Booth Tarkington (1): *The Magnificent Ambersons*, 1942 – Novel base
Dwight Taylor (1): *Top Hat*, 1935 – Co-AS

Samuel Taylor (1): *Vertigo*, 1958 – Co-AS
Walter Tevis (1): *The Hustler*, 1961 – Novel base
Joan Tewkesbury (1): *Nashville*, 1975 – OS
Joseph Than (1): *The Pirate*, 1948 – Co-AS
HARVEY THEW (2): *The Public Enemy*, 1931 – Co-AS; *She Done Him Wrong*, 1934 – Co-AS
Jim Thompson (1): *Paths of Glory*, 1957 – Co-AS
Guy Tomajin (1): *East of Eden*, 1955 – Co-AS, uc
Robert Towne (1): **Chinatown*, 1974 – OS
Armitage Trail (1): *Scarface*, 1932 – Novel base
B.S. Traven (1): *The Treasure of the Sierra Madre*, 1948 – Novel base
Robert Traver (1): *Anatomy of a Murder*, 1959 – Novel base
P.L. Travers (1): *Mary Poppins*, 1964 – Story base
LAMAR TROTTI (2): *Young Mr Lincoln*, 1939 – OS; *The Oxbow Incident*, 1943 – AS
Karl Tunberg (1): *Ben-Hur*, 1959 – Co-AS
ERNEST VAJDA (2): *Dinner at Eight*, 1933 – Co-AS; *The Merry Widow*, 1934 – Co-AS
John Van Druten (1): *Cabaret*, 1972 – Play base, *I Am a Camera*
Anthony Veiller (1): *The Killers*, 1946 – Co-AS
Gore Vidal (1): *Ben-Hur*, 1959 – Co-AS, uc
Salka Viertel (1): *Queen Christina*, 1933 – Co-AS and Co-Story base
Marvin Wald (1): *The Naked City*, 1948 – Co-AS and Story base
Earl W. Wallace (1): *Witness*, 1985 – Co-AS and Co-Story base
Patricia Wallace (1): *Witness*, 1985 – Co-Story base
Hugh Walpole (1): *David Copperfield*, 1935 – Co-AS
Bill Walsh (1): *Mary Poppins*, 1964 – Co-AS
Maurice Walsh (1): *The Quiet Man*, 1952 – Story base
Robert Penn Warren (1): *All the King's Men*, 1950 – Novel base
Deric Washburn (1): *The Deer Hunter*, 1978 – AS and Co-Story base
Frank ('Spig') Wead (1): *They Were Expendable*, 1945 – AS
John V.A. Weaver (1): *The Crowd*, 1928 – Co-OS
Charles Webb (1): *The Graduate*, 1967 – Novel base

Peggy Webling (1): *Frankenstein*, 1931 – Play base
Claudine West (1): *The Good Earth*, 1937 – Co-AS
Mae West (1): *She Done Him Wrong*, 1934 – Co-AS and Play base, *Diamond Lil*
William L. White (1): *They Were Expendable*, 1945 – Book base
Hagar Wilde (1): *Bringing Up Baby*, 1938 – Co-AS and Story base
Robert Wilder (1): *Written on the Wind*, 1956 – Novel base
Thornton Wilder (1): *Shadow of a Doubt*, 1943 – Co-AS
TENNESSEE WILLIAMS (2): *A Streetcar Named Desire*, 1951 – Co-AS and Play base; *Baby Doll*, 1956 – AS and Story base
CALDER WILLINGHAM (2): *Paths of Glory*, 1957 – Co-AS; *The Graduate*, 1967 – Co-AS
Carey Wilson (1): *Mutiny on the Bounty*, 1935 – Co-AS
Frank Woods (1): *The Birth of a Nation*, 1915 – Co-AS
Bob Woodward (1): *All the President's Men*, 1976 – Co-Story base
Edgar Allan Woolf (1): *The Wizard of Oz*, 1939 – Co-AS
Cornell Woolrich (1): *Rear Window*, 1954 – Novel base
Linda Woolverton (1): *Beauty and the Beast*, 1991 – AS
Waldemar Young (1): *Love Me Tonight*, 1932 – Co-AS
Darryl Zanuck (1): *Little Caesar*, 1930 – Co-AS
Paul Zimmerman (1): *The King of Comedy*, 1983 – OS
George Zuckerman (1): *Written on the Wind*, 1956 – AS
Stefan Zweig (1): *Letter from an Unknown Woman*, 1948 – Story base

Cinematographers and Special Effects Creators

C = Cinematography
Co- = in co-operation with another
Spec.Effs = Special visual effects
uc = uncredited

L.B. Abbott (1): *Patton*, 1970 – Co-Spec.Effs

David Abel (1): *Top Hat*, 1935 – Co-C

NESTOR ALMENDROS (2): **Days of Heaven*, 1978 – C; *Kramer vs Kramer*, 1979 – C

John Alonzo (1): *Chinatown*, 1974 – C

John Alton (1): **An American in Paris*, 1951 – Co-C

Lucien Andriot (1): *The Southerner*, 1945 – C

Roy Arbogast (1): *Close Encounters of the Third Kind*, 1977 – Co-Spec.Effs

JOHN ARNOLD (2): *The Big Parade*, 1925 – C; *The Wind*, 1928 – C

Richard Aronovich (1): *Missing*, 1982 – Co-C

JOSEPH AUGUST (4): *The Informer*, 1935 – C; *Gunga Din*, 1939 – C; *The Hunchback of Notre Dame*, 1939 – C; *They Were Expendable*, 1945 – C

Rick Baker (1): *Star Wars*, 1977 – Co-Spec.Effs

LUCIEN BALLARD (2): *Ride the High Country*, 1962 – C; *The Wild Bunch*, 1969 – C

GEORGE C. BARNES (2): **Rebecca*, 1940 – C; *Spellbound*, 1945 – C

Paul Beetson (1): *Raiders of the Lost Ark*, 1981 – Co-C

Jordan Belson (1): *Missing*, 1983 – Co-C

Peter Biggs (1): **Who Framed Roger Rabbit?*, 1988 – Co-Spec.Effs

RAY BINGER (2): *Dodsworth*, 1936 – Spec.Effs; *Stagecoach*, 1939 – Spec.Effs

Joseph Biroc (1): *It's a Wonderful Life*, 1946 – Co-C

BILLY BITZER (3): *Birth of a Nation*, 1915 – Co-C; *Intolerance*, 1916 – Co-C; *Broken Blossoms*, 1919 – Co-C

Elwood ('Woody') Bredell (1): *The Killers*, 1946 – C

Norbert Brodine (1): *Of Mice and Men*, 1939 – C

KARL BROWN (3): see BILLY BITZER

ROBERT BURKS (6): *Strangers on a Train*, 1951 – C; *Rear Window*, 1954 – C; *Vertigo*, 1958 – C; *North by Northwest*, 1959 – C; *The Birds*, 1963 – C; *Marnie*, 1964 – C

BILL BUTLER (3): *The Conversation* 1974 – C; *Jaws*, 1975 – Co-C, *One Flew over the Cuckoo's Nest*, 1975 – Co-C

LAWRENCE BUTLER (3): *To Be or Not To Be*, 1942 – Spec.Effs; *Casablanca*, 1942 – Co-Spec.Effs; *The Lady from Shanghai*, 1948 – Spec. (Mirror) Effs

Jack Caffee (1): *Wagonmaster*, 1950 – Spec.Effs

Ernesto Caparros (1): *The Miracle Worker*, 1962 – Spec.Effs

Ganahl Carson (1): *The Lost Horizon*, 1937 – Co-Spec.Effs

MICHAEL CHAPMAN (2): *Taxi Driver*, 1976 – C; *Raging Bull*, 1980 – C

William Clothier (1): *The Man Who Shot Liberty Vallance*, 1962 – C

Edward Colman (1): *Mary Poppins*, 1964 – C

STANLEY CORTEZ (2): *The Magnificent Ambersons*, 1942 – C; *The Night of the Hunter*, 1955 – C

Fred Cramer (1): *The Deer Hunter*, 1979 – Spec.Effs

Jordan Cronenweth (1): *Blade Runner*, 1982 – C

Floyd Crosby (1): *High Noon*, 1952 – C

RUSSELL A. CULLY (2): *It's a Wonderful Life*, 1946 – Spec.Effs; *They Live by Night*, 1946 – Spec.Effs

Dean Cundey (1): *Who Framed Roger Rabbit?*, 1988 – C

Jan D'Alquen (1): *American Graffiti*, 1973 – Co-C

WILLIAM H. DANIELS (8): *Greed*, 1924 – Co-C; *Grand Hotel*, 1932 – C; *Dinner at Eight*, 1933 – C; *Queen Christina*, 1933 – C; *Camille*, 1936 – C; *Ninotchka*, 1939 – C; *The Shop Around the Corner*, 1940 – C; **The Naked City*, 1948 – C

Allen Daviau (1): *E.T.*, 1982 – C

ROY DAVIDSON (2): *The Lost Horizon*, 1937 – Co-Spec.Effs; *Only Angels Have Wings*, 1939 – Co-Spec.Effs

Robert De Grasse (1): *Stage Door*, 1937 – C

Caleb Deschanel (1): *The Right Stuff*, 1983 – C

Carlo Di Palma (1): *Hannah and Her Sisters*, 1986 – C

George E. Diskant (1): *They Live by Night*, 1949 – C

Tony Dunsterville (1): *Who Framed Roger Rabbit?*, 1988 – *Co-Spec.Effs

Elmer Dyer (1): *Only Angels Have Wings*, 1939 – Co-C

John Dykstra (1): *Star Wars*, 1977 – Co-Spec.Effs

ARTHUR EDESON (6): *All Quiet on the Western Front*, 1930 – Co-C; *Frankenstein*, 1931 – C; *The Old Dark House*, 1932 – C; *Mutiny on the Bounty*, 1935 – C; *The Maltese Falcon*, 1941 – C; *Casablanca*, 1942 – C

Richard Edlund (1): *Raiders of the Lost Ark*, 1981 – Co-Spec.Effs

Ron Eveslage (1): *American Graffiti*, 1973 – Co-C

Daniel Fapp (1): *West Side Story*, 1961 – C

GEORGE FOLSEY (3): *Meet Me in St Louis*, 1944 – C; *Adam's Rib*, 1949 – C; *Seven Brides for Seven Brothers*, 1954 – C

WILLIAM A. FRAKER (2): *Rosemary's Baby*, 1968 – C; *One Flew over the Cuckoo's Nest*, 1975 – Co-C

Ellsworth Fredricks (1): *Invasion of the Body Snatchers*, 1956 – C

KARL FREUND (3): *All Quiet on the Western Front*, 1930 – Co-C; *Camille*, 1936 – Co-C; *The Good Earth*, 1937 – C

JOHN P. FULTON (3): *The Old Dark House*, 1932 – Spec.Effs; *The Bride of Frankenstein*, 1935 – Spec.Effs; *Funny Face*, 1957 – Spec.Effs

LEE GARMES (3): *Shanghai Express*, 1932 – *C; *Scarface*, 1932 – Co-C; *Gone with the Wind*, 1939 – *Co-C, uc

TONY GAUDIO (4): *All Quiet on the Western Front*, 1930 – Co-C; *Little Caesar*, 1930 – C; *The Adventures of Robin Hood*, 1938 – Co-C; *High Sierra*, 1941 – C

Merritt Gerstad (1): *A Night at the Opera*, 1935 – C

Alfred Gilks (1): *An American in Paris*, 1951 – *Co-C

A. ARNOLD ('Buddy') GILLESPIE (4): *The Wizard of Oz*, 1939 – Spec.Effs; *They Were Expendable*, 1945 – Spec.Effs; *Ben-Hur*, 1959 – *Co-Spec.Effs; *North by Northwest*, 1959 – Co-Spec.Effs

BERT GLENNON (4): *The Scarlet Empress*, 1934 – C; *Stagecoach*, 1939 – C; *Young Mr Lincoln*, 1939 – C; *Wagonmaster*, 1950 – C

Frank Graves (1): *Frankenstein*, 1931 – Co-Spec.Effs

WILLIAM HOWARD GREENE (2): *Nothing Sacred*, 1937 – C; *The Adventures of Robin Hood*, 1938 – Co-C

Loyal Griggs (1): *Shane*, 1953 – *C

BURNETT GUFFEY (4): *In a Lonely Place*, 1950 – C; *All the King's Men*, 1950 – C; *From Here to Eternity*, 1953 – *C; *Bonnie and Clyde*, 1967 – *C

Gary Gutierrez (1): *Missing*, 1983 – Co-Spec.Effs

Edwin C. Hahn (1): *Only Angels Have Wings*, 1939 – Co-Spec.Effs

Bert Haines (1): *The General*, 1926 – Co-C

Conrad Hall (1): *Fat City*, 1972 – C

ERNEST HALLER (3): *Gone with the Wind*, 1939 – *Co-C; *Mildred Pierce*, 1945 – C; *Rebel without a Cause*, 1955 – C

RUSSELL HARLAN (5): *Red River*, 1948 – C; *Gun Crazy*, 1950 – C; *Witness for the Prosecution*, 1957 – C; *Rio Bravo*, 1959 – C; *To Kill a Mockingbird*, 1962 – C

Byron Haskin (1): *The Sea Hawk*, 1940 – Co-Spec.Effs

SIDNEY HICKOX (3): *To Have and Have Not*, 1944 – C; *The Big Sleep*, 1946 – C; *White Heat*, 1949 – C

WINTON C. HOCH (3): *She Wore a Yellow Ribbon*, 1949 – *C; *The Quiet Man*, 1952 – Co-C; *The Searchers*, 1956 – C

BYRON HOUCK (2): *The Navigator*, 1924 – Co-C; *Sherlock Jr.*, 1924 – Co-C

JAMES WONG HOWE (4): *The Thin Man*, 1934 – C; *The Prisoner of Zenda*, 1937 – C; *Yankee Doodle Dandy*, 1942 – C; *Sweet Smell of Success*, 1957 – C

J. Roy Hunt (1): *Crossfire*, 1947 – C

Industrial Light and Magic (1): *E.T.*, 1982 – Spec.Effs

Paul Ivano (1): *Queen Kelly*, 1928 – Co-C

Ub Iwerks (1): *The Birds*, 1963 – Spec.Effs

Harry Jackson (1): *The Band Wagon*, 1953 – C

GORDON JENNINGS (3): *The Scarlet Empress*, 1934 – Spec.Effs; *Sunset Boulevard*, 1950 – Spec.Effs; *Shane*, 1953 – Spec.Effs

J.D. ('Dev') JENNINGS (3): *Our Hospitality*, 1923 – Co-C; *The General*, 1926 – Co-C; *The Public Enemy*, 1931 – C

Ray June (1): *Funny Face*, 1957 – C

BORIS KAUFMAN (4): *On the Waterfront*, 1954 – *C; *Baby Doll*, 1956 – C; *Twelve Angry Men*, 1957 – C; *Long Day's Journey into Night*, 1962 – C

Ray Kellogg (1): *Gentlemen Prefer Blondes*, 1953 – Spec.Effs

Richard H. Kline (1): *Body Heat*, 1981 – C

Fred Koenekamp (1): *Patton* – Co-C

H.F. KOENEKAMP (3): *The Sea Hawk*, 1940 – Co-Spec.Effs; *The Treasure of the Sierra Madre*, 1948 – Co-Spec.Effs; *Strangers on a Train*, 1951 – Spec.Effs

Laszlo Kovacs (1): *Five Easy Pieces*, 1970 – C

MILTON KRASNER (2): *The Bank Dick*, 1940 – C; *All About Eve*, 1950 – C

George Krause (1): *Paths of Glory*, 1957 – C

CHARLES B. LANG (5): *She Done Him Wrong*, 1933 – C; *The Ghost and Mrs Muir*, 1947 – C; *Ace in the Hole*, 1951 – C; *The Big Heat*, 1953 – C; *Some Like it Hot*, 1959 – C

JOSEPH LA SHELLE (2): *Laura*, 1944 – *C; *The Apartment*, 1960 – C

Ernest Laszlo (1): *Kiss Me Deadly*, 1955 – C

Charles Lawton Jr. (1): *The Lady from Shanghai*, 1948 – C

SAM LEAVITT (2): *A Star Is Born*, 1954 – C; *Anatomy of a Murder*, 1959 – C

Lee LeBlanc (1): *North by Northwest*, 1959 – Co-Spec.Effs

ELGIN LESSLEY (4): *Our Hospitality*, 1923 – Co-C; *The Navigator*, 1924 – Co-C; *Sherlock Jr.*, 1924 – Co-C; *The Cameraman*, 1928 – Co-C

Edward Linden (1): *King Kong*, 1933 – Co-C

Lionel Lindon (1): *The Manchurian Candidate*, 1962 – C

Raymond Lindsay (1): *Frankenstein*, 1931 – Co-Spec.Effs

Art Lloyd (1): *Way Out West*, 1937 – Co-C

Augie Lohman (1): *The Shootist*, 1976 – Spec.Effs

Paul Lohmann (1): *Nashville*, 1975 – C

Milo Lory (1): *Ben-Hur*, 1959 – *Co-Spec.Effs

Walter Lundin (1): *Way Out West*, 1937 – Co-C

Eustace Lycett (1): *Mary Poppins*, 1964 – Co-Spec.Effs

TED MCCORD (2): *The Treasure of the Sierra Madre*, 1948 – C; *East of Eden*, 1955 – C

Joe MacDonald (1): *My Darling Clementine*, 1946 – C

Robert MacDonald (1): *Ben-Hur*, 1959 – *Co-Spec.Effs

William McGann (1): *The Treasure of the Sierra Madre*, 1948 – Co-Spec.Effs

Reggie Manning (1): *The Cameraman*, 1928 – Co-C

Mark Marklatt (1): *City Lights*, 1930 – Co-C

OLIVER T. MARSH (2): *The Merry Widow*, 1934 – C; *David Copperfield*, 1935 – C

RUDOLPH MATÉ (3): *Dodsworth*, 1936 – C; *To Be or Not To Be*, 1942 – C; *Gilda*, 1946 – C

ROBERT A. MATTEY (2): *Mary Poppins*, 1964 – Co-Spec.Effs; *Jaws*, 1975 – Spec.Effs

William C. Mellor (1): *Bad Day at Black Rock*, 1954 – C

John Mescall (1): *The Bride of Frankenstein*, 1935 – C

RUSSELL METTY (3): *Bringing Up Baby*, 1938 – C; *Written on the Wind*, 1956 – C; *Touch of Evil*, 1958 – C

Rexford Metz (1): *Jaws*, 1975 – Co-C, underwater photography

ARTHUR C. MILLER (2): *How Green Was My Valley*, 1941 – *C; *The Oxbow Incident*, 1943 – C

VICTOR MILNER (4): *Love Me Tonight*, 1932 – C; *Trouble in Paradise*, 1932 – C; *The Lady Eve*, 1941 – C; *The Palm Beach Story*, 1942 – C

HAL MOHR (2): *Queen Kelly*, 1928 – Co-C; *Destry Rides Again*, 1939 – C

Ira Morgan (1): *Modern Times*, 1936 – Co-C

Brian Morrison (1): *Who Framed Roger Rabbit?*, 1988 – *Co-Spec.Effs

NICHOLAS MUSURACA (2): *Cat People*, 1942 – C; *Out of the Past*, 1947 – C

Warren Newcombe (1): *Kiss Me Kate*, 1953 – Spec.Effs

Roger Nichols (1): *Who Framed Roger Rabbit?*, 1988 – *Co-Spec.Effs

Willis O'Brien (1): *King Kong*, 1933 – Spec.Effs

L. William O'Connell (1): *Scarface*, 1932 – Co-C

Miroslav Ondricek (1): *Amadeus*, 1984 – C

Cecilio Paniagua (1): *Patton*, 1970 – Co-C

Tony Parmalee (1): *Taxi Driver*, 1976 – Co-Spec.Effs

Kenneth Peach (1): *Sons of the Desert*, 1933 – C
Franz Planer (1): *Letter from an Unknown Woman*, 1949 – C
SOL POLITO (5): *I Am a Fugitive from a Chain Gang*, 1932 – C; *The Gold Diggers of 1933* – C; *Forty-Second Street*, 1933 – C; *The Adventures of Robin Hood*, 1938 – Co-C; *The Sea Hawk*, 1940 – C
GORDON POLLOCK (2): *Queen Kelly*, 1928 – Co-C; *City Lights*, 1931 – Co-C
Jack Rabin (1): *The Night of the Hunter*, 1955 – Co-Spec.Effs
Ray Rennahan (1): *Gone with the Wind*, 1939 – *Co-C
BENJAMIN REYNOLDS (2): *Greed*, 1924 – Co-C; *Queen Kelly*, 1928 – Co-C
MILT RICE (2): *Invasion of the Body Snatchers*, 1956 – Spec.Effs; *Some Like it Hot*, 1959 – Spec.Effs
CHARLES ROSHER (2): *Sunrise*, 1927 – *Co-C; *Kiss Me Kate*, 1953 – C
HAL ROSSON (5): *The Wizard of Oz*, 1939 – C; *On the Town*, 1949 – C; *The Asphalt Jungle*, 1950 – C; *The Red Badge of Courage*, 1951 – C; *Singin' in the Rain*, 1952 – C
John L. Russell (1): *Psycho*, 1960 – C
JOSEPH RUTTENBERG (3): *Fury*, 1936 – C; *The Philadelphia Story*, 1940 – C; *Gigi*, 1958 – *C
Hendrik Sartov (1): *Broken Blossoms*, 1919 – Spec.Effs
Ernest Schoedsack (1): *Greed*, 1924 – Co-C
Fred Schuler (1): *The King of Comedy*, 1983 – C
John Seale (1): *Witness*, 1985 – C
Roy Seawright (1): *Way Out West*, 1937 – Spec.Effs
JOHN F. SEITZ (5): *Sullivan's Travels*, 1941 – C; *The Miracle of Morgan's Creek*, 1943 – C; *Double Indemnity*, 1944 – C; *The Lost Weekend*, 1945 – C; *Sunset Boulevard*, 1950 – C
Fred Sersen (1): *The Ghost and Mrs Muir*, 1947 – Spec.Effs
Leon Shamroy (1): *Twelve o'Clock High*, 1949 – C
HENRY SHARP (3): *The Crowd*, 1928 – C; *Duck Soup*, 1933 – C; *It's a Gift*, 1934 – C
Eugene Shuftan (Eugen Schüfftan) (1): *The Hustler*, 1961 – C
George Slocombe (1): *Raiders of the Lost Ark*, 1981 – Co-C

Dick Smith (1): *Taxi Driver* – Co-Spec.Effs
Paul Stewart (1): *Fat City*, 1972 – C
Clifford Stine (1): *Patton*, 1970 – Co-C
Harold E. Stine (1): *M*A*S*H*, 1970 – C
Vittorio Storaro (1): *Apocalypse Now*, 1979 – *C
ARCHIE STOUT (2): *Fort Apache*, 1948 – C; *The Quiet Man*, 1952 – Co-C
HARRY STRADLING (2): *The Pirate*, 1948 – C; *A Streetcar Named Desire*, 1951 – C
Kenneth Strickfadden (1): *Frankenstein*, 1931 – Co-Spec.Effs
KARL STRUSS (3): *Sunrise*, 1927 – *Co-C; *The Great Dictator*, 1940 – Co-C; *Limelight*, 1952 – Co-C
BRUCE SURTEES (3): *Play Misty for Me*, 1971 – C; *The Outlaw Josey Wales*, 1976 – C; *The Shootist*, 1976 – C
ROBERT SURTEES (4): *The Bad and the Beautiful*, 1952 – *C; *Ben-Hur*, 1959 – *C; *The Graduate*, 1967 – C; *The Last Picture Show*, 1971 – C
Gilbert Taylor (1): *Star Wars*, 1977 – C
J.O. Taylor (1): *King Kong*, 1933 – Co-C
Ron Taylor (1): *Jaws*, 1975 – Co-Spec.Effs
Ted Tetzlaff (1): *Notorious*, 1946 – C
John Thomas (1): *Days of Heaven*, 1978 – Co-Spec.Effs
GREGG TOLAND (5): *Wuthering Heights*, 1939 – *C; *The Grapes of Wrath*, 1940 – C; *Citizen Kane*, 1941 – C; *The Little Foxes*, 1941 – C; *The Best Years of our Lives*, 1946 – C
ROLAND ('Rollie') TOTHEROH (6): *The Kid*, 1921 – C; *The Gold Rush*, 1925 – C; *City Lights*, 1930 – Co-C; *Modern Times*, 1936 – Co-C; *The Great Dictator*, 1941 – Co-C; *Limelight*, 1952 – Co-C
DOUGLAS TRUMBULL (2): *Close Encounters of the Third Kind*, 1977 – Co-Spec.Effs; *Blade Runner*, 1982 – Co-Spec.Effs
Geoffrey Unsworth (1): *Cabaret*, 1972 – *C
Joseph Valentine (1): *Shadow of a Doubt*, 1953 – C
WILLARD VAN ENGER (2): *Casablanca*, 1942 – Co-Spec.Effs; *Mildred Pierce*, 1945 – Co-Spec.Effs

Slavko Vorkapich (2): *David Copperfield*, 1935 – Spec.Effs; *Mr Smith Goes to Washington*, 1939 – Spec.Effs

Sidney Wagner (1): *The Postman Always Rings Twice*, 1946 – C

Kent L. Wakeford (1): *Mean Streets*, 1973 – C

Joseph ('Joe') Walker (8): *It Happened One Night*, 1934 – C; *Mr Deeds Goes to Town*, 1936 – C; *The Awful Truth*, 1937 – C; *The Lost Horizon*, 1937 – C; *Only Angels Have Wings*, 1939 – C; *Mr Smith Goes to Washington*, 1939 – C; *His Girl Friday*, 1940 – C; *It's A Wonderful Life*, 1946 – Co-C

Vernon Walker (6): *King Kong*, 1933 – Co-C; *Top Hat*, 1935 – Co-C; *Swing Time*, 1936 – Spec.Effs; *Citizen Kane*, 1941 – Spec.Effs; *The Magnificent Ambersons*, 1942 – Spec.Effs; *Notorious*, 1946 – Spec.Effs

Brian Warner (1): *Who Framed Roger Rabbit?*, 1988 – *Co-Spec.Effs

David Watkins (1): *Who Framed Roger Rabbit?*, 1988 – *Co-Spec.Effs

Kit West (1): *Raiders of the Lost Ark*, 1981 – Co-Spec.Effs

Haskell Wexler (3): *America, America*, 1963 – C; *American Graffiti*, 1973 – Co-C; *One Flew over the Cuckoo's Nest*, 1975 – Co-C

Albert Whitlock (1): *Missing*, 1982 – Spec.Effs

Harry Wild Jr. (2): *Murder My Sweet* 1946 – C; *Gentlemen Prefer Blondes*, 1953 – C

Gordon Willis (5): *The Godfather*, 1972 – C; *The Godfather Part II*, 1974 – C; *All the President's Men*, 1976 – C; *Annie Hall*, 1977 – C; *Manhattan*, 1979 – C

Jack Wilson (1): *The Gold Rush*, 1925 – Co-C

De Louis Witt (1): *The Night of the Hunter*, 1955 – Co-Spec.Effs

Michael Yuricich (1): *Close Encounters of the Third Kind*, 1977 – Co-Spec.Effs

Richard Yuricich (2): *Close Encounters of the Third Kind*, 1977 – Co-Spec.Effs; *Blade Runner*, 1982 – Co-Spec.Effs

Vilmos Zsigmond (2): *Close Encounters of the Third Kind*, 1977 – *C; *The Deer Hunter*, 1978 – C

NOTES

Billy Bitzer (with the help of Karl Brown) worked exclusively for D.W. Griffith, as did Rollie Totheroh for Chaplin and Elgin Lessley for Keaton. Many other cinematographers also worked in the early Hollywood industry (in the 1910s:

> Lucien Andriot, Joseph August, George Barnes, Norbert Brodine, William H. Daniels, Arthur Edeson, George Folsey, Lee Garmes, Tony Gaudio, Bert Glennon, Sidney Hickox, James Wong Howe, Oliver T. Marsh, Arthur C. Miller, Victor Milner, Hal Mohr, Sol Polito, Ray Rennahan, Charles Rosher, Hal Rosson, Joseph Ruttenberg, John F. Seitz, Archie Stout, Karl Struss, Joseph Walker

Joseph August, Arthur Edeson and Tony Gaudio were among the co-founders of the American Society of Cinematographers – the A.S.C. – in 1918.

George Barnes helped to shape the career of Gregg Toland (recruited to the industry in the 1920s): he, in turn, helped to train Robert Surtees.

Others joining the industry *in the 1920s* were:

> John Alton, Floyd Crosby, Karl Freund (from Germany, where he was the leading cinematographer at the time), William Howard Greene, Ernest Haller, Ray June, Charles Lang Jr., Ted McCord, Leon Shamroy, Henry Sharp, Ted Tetzlaff (who became a director in the 1940s), Joseph Valentine

Successive generations arrived, *from the 1930s*:

> Lucien Ballard, Stanley Cortez (brother of Ricardo Cortez, the star), Russell Harlan (formerly a stunt man), Milton Krasner, Charles Lawton Jr., Rudolph Maté (from the European cinema, later a director), William C. Mellor, Russell Metty, Franz Planer (from Germany)

From the 1940s:

> Joseph Biroc, Willam Clothier, Daniel Fapp, Burnett Guffey (previously a camera operator), Winton C. Hoch, Boris Kaufman (from Europe, brother of the Russian director, Dziga Vertov), Joseph La Shelle, Joe

MacDonald, Harry Stradling (in France and Britain in the 1930s)

From the 1950s:

Robert Burks (previously a special effects expert for Warner Brothers, then mainly lighting cameraman for Hitchcock in the 1950s and 60s), Ellsworth Fredricks, Sam Leavitt, Haskell Wexler (concentrating on camerawork after more general contributions)

From the 1960s and 70s:

Nestor Almendros (Spanish-American), Bill Butler, Michael Chapman, Jordan Cronenweth, William A. Fraker, Richard Kline, Bruce Surtees, Gordon Willis, Vilmos Zsigmond (from Hungary)

Several, from early on, began to develop specialisms and innovatory techniques: William Daniels became known as 'Garbo's cameraman'; Lee Garmes lit Dietrich in a dreamy, romantic aura for von Sternberg in the 1930s, and developed techniques such as the 'crab dolly' and the 'north light'. George Folsey was a pioneer in soft black-and-white lighting, and John Seitz in low-key intensive lighting. Hal Mohr developed the use of dollies and booms, while Russell Metty was a specialist in complex crane shots. Gregg Toland became renowned as the master of 'deep focus' as in *Wuthering Heights*, *Citizen Kane*, and *The Best Years of Our Lives*.

Contributors to the Art Department

AD = Art Direction (Production Design)
Cost = Costume Design
Anim = Animation
Co- = in co-operation with others
uc = uncredited

Alan Abbott (1): *Top Hat*, 1935 – Co-AD, uc

ADRIAN (Gilbert Adrian) (8): *Grand Hotel*, 1932 – Cost; *Dinner at Eight*, 1933 – Cost; *Queen Christina*, 1933 – Cost; *The Merry Widow*, 1934 – Cost; *Camille*, 1936 – Cost; *Ninotchka*, 1939 – Cost; *The Wizard of Oz*, 1939 – Cost; *The Philadelphia Story*, 1940 – Cost

JAMES ALGAR (3): *Snow White and the Seven Dwarfs*, 1938 – Co-Anim; *Fantasia*, 1940 – Co-Anim; *Bambi*, 1942 – Co-Anim

Roger Allers (1): *Beauty and the Beast*, 1991 – Co-Anim

JOSEPH ALVES (2): *Jaws*, 1975 – AD; *Close Encounters of the Third Kind*, 1977 – AD

PRESTON AMES (3): **An American in Paris*, 1951 – *Co-AD; *The Band Wagon*, 1953 – Co-AD; *Gigi*, 1958 – *Co-AD

MILO ANDERSON (5): *The Adventures of Robin Hood*, 1938 – Cost; *High Sierra*, 1941 – Cost; *Yankee Doodle Dandy*, 1942 – Cost; *To Have and Have Not*, 1944 – Cost; *Mildred Pierce*, 1945 – Cost

John Arensma (1): *Red River*, 1948 – AD

SAMUEL ARMSTRONG (3): *Fantasia*, 1940 – Seq. Dir.; *Dumbo*, 1941 – Co-Anim; *Bambi*, 1942 – Co-Anim

Lemuel Ayers (1): *Meet Me in St Louis*, 1944 – Co-AD

ARTHUR BABBITT (4): *Snow White and the Seven Dwarfs*, 1938 – Co-Anim; *Fantasia*, 1940, – Co-Anim; *Pinocchio*, 1940 – Co-Anim; *Dumbo*, 1941 – Co-Anim

Lucinda Ballard (1): *A Streetcar Named Desire*, 1951 – Cost

Peter Ballbusch (1): *The Scarlet Empress*, 1934 – Statuary

LIONEL BANKS (4): *The Awful Truth*, 1937 – Co-AD; *Only Angels Have Wings*, 1939 – AD; *Mr Smith Goes to Washington*, 1939 – AD; *His Girl Friday*, 1940 – AD

TRAVIS BANTON (6): *Love Me Tonight*, 1932 – Cost; *Trouble in Paradise*, 1932 – Cost; *Shanghai Express*, 1934 – Cost; *The Scarlet Empress*, 1934 – Cost; *Nothing Sacred*, 1937 – Cost; *Letter from an Unknown Woman*, 1948 – Cost

John Barry (1): *Star Wars*, 1977 – *Co-AD

JAMES BASEVI (9): *The Big Parade*, 1925 – Co-AD; *Wuthering Heights*, 1939 – AD; *The Oxbow Incident*, 1943 – Co-AD; *My Darling Clementine*, 1946 – Co-AD; *Fort Apache*, 1948 – AD; *She Wore a Yellow Ribbon*, 1949 – AD; *Wagonmaster*, 1950 – AD; *East of Eden*, 1955 – Co-AD; *The Searchers*, 1956 – Co-AD

SAUL BASS (5): *Vertigo*, 1958 – Titles; *Anatomy of a Murder*, 1959 – Titles; *North by Northwest*, 1959 – Titles; *Psycho*, 1960 – Titles; *West Side Story*, 1961 – Titles

Luster Bayless (1): *The Shootist*, 1976 – Co-Cost

Cecil Beaton (l): *Gigi*, 1958 – *Co-AD and *Cost

Ron Beck (1): **Star Wars*, 1977 – *Co-Cost

Ford Beebe (1): *Fantasia*, 1940 – Seq. Dir.

Frank Beetson (1): *The Searchers*, 1956 – Co-Cost

MALCOLM BERT (3): *East of Eden*, 1955 – Co-AD; *A Star Is Born*, 1954 – AD; *Rebel without a Cause*, 1955 – AD

MARJORIE BEST (2): *Giant*, 1956 – Co-Cost; *Rio Bravo*, 1959 – Co-Cost

Anna Biedrzicki-Sheppard (1): *Schindler's List*, 1993 – Cost

James D. Bissell (1): *E.T.*, 1982 – AD

Jerry Bos (1): *The Night of the Hunter*, 1955 – Cost

MEL BOURNE (3): *The Miracle Worker*, 1962 – Co-AD; *Annie Hall*, 1977 – AD; *Manhattan*, 1979 – AD

Edward Boyle (1): *The Apartment*, 1960 – *Co-AD

Robert Boyle (4): *Shadow of a Doubt*, 1943 – Co-AD; *North by Northwest*, 1959 – Co-AD; *The Birds*, 1963 – Co-AD; *Marnie*, 1964 – AD

Hildyard Brown (1): *The Night of the Hunter*, 1955 – AD

MALCOLM BROWNE (2): *They Were Expendable*, 1945 – Co-AD; *Bad Day at Black Rock*, 1954 – Co-AD

Richard Bruno (1): *The King of Comedy*, 1983 – Cost

HENRY BUMSTEAD (2): *Vertigo*, 1958 – Co-AD; *To Kill a Mockingbird*, 1962 – Co-AD

Roger Cain (1): *Who Framed Roger Rabbit?*, 1988 – Co-AD

Gene Callahan (1): *America, America*, 1963 – AD

EDWARD CARFAGNO (2): *The Bad and the Beautiful*, 1952 – *Co-AD; *Ben-Hur*, 1959 – *Co-AD

Sturges Carne (2): *The Lady from Shanghai*, 1948 – AD; *All the King's Men*, 1949 – AD

Ben Carre (1): *A Night at the Opera*, 1935 – Co-AD

Edward Carrere (3): *White Heat*, 1949 – AD: *Sweet Smell of Success*, 1957 – AD; *The Wild Bunch*, 1969 – AD

Bonnie Cashin (1): *Laura*, 1944 – Cost

Oleg Cassini (1): *The Ghost and Mrs Muir*, 1947 – Cost

CARROLL CLARK (6): *King Kong*, 1933 – Co-A; *Top Hat*, 1935 – Co-AD; *Swing Time*, 1936 – Co-AD; *Stage Door*, 1937 – Co-AD; *Murder My Sweet*, 1944 – Co-AD; *Mary Poppins*, 1964 – Co-AD

Dennis Clark (1): *American Graffiti*, 1973 – AD

ROBERT CLATWORTHY (3): *Written on the Wind*, 1956 – Co-AD; *Touch of Evil*, 1958 – Co-D; *Psycho*, 1960 – Co-AD

Leroy Coleman (1): *Ride the High Country*, 1962 – Co-AD

HELEN COLVIG (2): *Psycho*, 1960 – Cost; *Play Misty for Me*, 1971 – Co-Cost

Renie Conley (1): *Body Heat*, 1981 – Cost

ALBERT D'AGOSTINO (6): *Cat People*, 1942 – Co-AD; *Murder My Sweet*, 1944 – Co-AD; *Notorious*, 1946 – Co-AD; *Crossfire*, 1947 – Co-AD; *Out of the Past*, 1944 – Co-AD; *They Live by Night*, 1949

Salvador Dali (1): *Spellbound*, 1945 – Dream Sequence

GEORGE W. DAVIS (4): *The Ghost and Mrs Muir*, 1947 – Co-AD; *All About Eve*, 1950 – Co-AD; *Funny Face*, 1957 – Co-AD; *Ride the High Country*, 1962 – Co-AD

Gordon Dawson (1): *The Wild Bunch*, 1969 – Cost

RICHARD DAY (10): *Greed*, 1924 – Co-AD; *Queen Kelly*, 1928 – Co-AD; *Dodsworth*, 1936 – AD; *Young Mr Lincoln*, 1939 – Co-AD; *The Grapes of Wrath*, 1940 – Co-AD; *How Green Was My Valley*, 1941 – *Co-AD; *The Oxbow Incident*, 1943 – Co-AD; *The Ghost *and Mrs Muir*, 1949 – Co-AD; *A Streetcar Named Desire*, 1951 – *AD; *On the Waterfront*, 1954 – *AD

John de Cuir (1): *The Naked City*, 1948 – AD

Hubert de Givenchy (1): *Funny Face*, 1957 – Co-Cost

Louis Diage (1): *All the King's Men*, 1949 – Co-AD

Leslie Dilley (1): *Star Wars*, 1977 – *Co-AD

Dallas Doman (1): *Witness*, 1985 – Co-Cost

HANS DREIER (13): *Shanghai Express*, 1932 – AD; *Love Me Tonight*, 1932 – AD; *Trouble in Paradise*, 1932 – AD; *Duck Soup*, 1933 – Co-AD; *The Scarlet Empress*, 1934 – AD; *It's a Gift*, 1934 – Co-AD; *The Lady Eve*, 1941 – Co-AD; *Sullivan's Travels*, 1941 – Co-AD; *The Palm Beach Story*, 1942 – Co-AD; *The Miracle of Morgan's Creek*, 1943 – Co-AD; *Double Indemnity*, 1944 – Co-AD; *The Lost Weekend*, 1945 – Co-AD; *Sunset Boulevard*, 1950 – *Co-AD

Ernest Dryden (1): *The Prisoner of Zenda*, 1937 – Cost

RANDALL DUELL (4): *Ninotchka*, 1939 – Co-AD; *The Postman Always Rings Twice*, 1946 – Co-AD; *The Asphalt Jungle*, 1950 – Co-AD; *Singin' in the Rain*, 1952 – Co-AD

John Ewing (1): *Spellbound*, 1945 – AD

ERNST FEGTE (3): *The Lady Eve*, 1941 – Co-AD; *The Palm Beach Story*, 1942 – Co-AD; *The Miracle of Morgan's Creek*, 1943 – Co-AD

Shari Feldman (1): *Witness*, 1985

NORMAN FERGUSON (4): *Snow White and the Seven Dwarfs*, 1938 – Co-Anim; *Pinocchio*, 1940 – Co-Anim; *Fantasia*, 1940 – Co-Anim; *Dumbo*, 1941 – Co-Anim

PERRY FERGUSON (4): *Bringing Up Baby*, 1938 – Co-AD; *Gunga Din*, 1939 – Co-AD; *Citizen Kane*, 1941 – Co-AD; *The Best Years of Our Lives*, 1946 – Co-AD

William Ferrari (1): *Adam's Rib*, 1949 – Co-AD

Jack Fisk (1): *Days of Heaven*, 1978 – AD

Charlotte Fleming (1): *Cabaret*, 1972 – Cost

Leland Fuller (1): *Laura*, 1944 – Co-AD

Randy Fullman (1): *Beauty and the Beast*, 1991 – Co-Anim

Fred Gabourie (1): *The General*, 1926 – AD and Technical Adviser

Ed Ghertner (1): *Beauty and the Beast*, 1991 – Co-Anim

CEDRIC GIBBONS (32): *The Big Parade*, 1925 – Co-AD; *The Crowd*, 1928 – Co-AD; *The Wind*, 1928 – Co-AD; *Grand Hotel*, 1932 – AD; *Dinner at Eight*, 1933 – AD; *The Merry Widow*, 1934 – Co-AD; *The Thin Man*, 1934 – AD; *A Night at the Opera*, 1935 – Co-AD; *Mutiny on the Bounty*, 1935 – Co-AD; *David Copperfield*, 1935 – AD; *Fury*, 1936 – AD; *Camille*, 1936 – AD; *The Good Earth*, 1937 – Co-AD; *Ninotchka*, 1939 – Co-AD; *The Wizard of Oz*, 1939 – Co-AD; *The Philadelphia Story*, 1940 – AD; *The Shop Around the Corner*, 1940 – Co-AD; *Meet Me in St Louis*, 1944 – Co-AD; *They Were Expendable*, 1945 – Co-AD; *The Postman Always Rings Twice*, 1946 – Co-AD; *The Pirate*, 1948 – Co-AD; *Adam's Rib*, 1949 – Co-AD; *On the Town*, 1949 – Co-AD; *The Asphalt Jungle*, 1950 – Co-AD; *An American in Paris*, 1951 – *Co-AD; *The Red Badge of Courage*, 1951 – Co-AD; *The Bad and the Beautiful*, 1952 – *Co-AD; *Singin' in the Rain*, 1952 – Co-AD; *The Band Wagon*, 1953 – Co-AD; *Kiss Me Kate*, 1953 – Co-AD; *Seven Brides for Seven Brothers*, 1954 – AD; *Bad Day at Black Rock*, 1954 – Co-AD

A. ARNOLD (Buddy) GILLESPIE (4): *The Crowd*, 1928 – Co-AD; *Mutiny on the Bounty*, 1935 – Co-AD; *The Good Earth*, 1937 – Co-AD; *The Wizard of Oz*, 1939 – Co-AD

William Glasgow (1): *Kiss Me Deadly*, 1955 – AD

Rochus Gliese (1): *Sunrise*, 1927 – AD

ALEXANDER GOLITZEN (5): *Letter from an Unknown Woman*, 1948 – Co-AD; *Written on the Wind*, 1956 – Co-AD; *Touch of Evil*, 1958 – Co-AD; *To Kill a Mockingbird*, 1962 – Co AD; *Marnie*, 1964 – Co-AD

JOHN E. GOODMAN (2): *It's a Gift*, 1934 – Co-AD; *Shadow of a Doubt*, 1943 – Co-AD

STEPHEN GOOSSON (6): *It Happened One Night*, 1934 – AD; *Mr Deeds Goes to Town*, 1936 – AD; *The Awful Truth*, 1937 – AD; *The Little Foxes*, 1941 – AD; *Gilda*, 1946 – AD; *The Lady from Shanghai*, 1948 – Co-AD

ANTON GROT (4): *Little Caesar*, 1930 – AD; *The Gold Diggers of 1933*, 1933 – AD; *The Sea Hawk*, 1940 – AD; *Mildred Pierce*, 1945 – AD

Robert Haas (1): *The Maltese Falcon*, 1941 – AD

Elizabeth Haffenden (1): *Ben-Hur* 1939 – *Cost

CHARLES D. HALL (7): *The Gold Rush*, 1925 – AD; *All Quiet on the Western Front*, 1930 – AD; *City Lights*, 1930 – AD; *Frankenstein*, 1931 – AD; *The Old Dark House*, 1932 – AD; *The Bride of Frankenstein*, 1935 – AD; *Modern Times*, 1936 – Co-AD

Walter L. Hall (1): *Intolerance*, 1916 – Co-AD, uc

Jim Handley (1): *Fantasia*, 1940 – Co-Anim

John Harkrider (1): *Swing Time*, 1936 – Co-Cost

EDWARD (TED) HAWORTH (3): *Strangers on a Train*, 1951 – AD; *Invasion of the Body Snatchers*, 1956 – AD; *Some Like it Hot*, 1959 – AD

EDITH HEAD (18): *Love Me Tonight*, 1932 – Co-Cost; *She Done Him Wrong*, 1933 – Cost; *The Lady Eve*, 1941 – Cost; *Travels*, 1941 – Cost; *The Miracle of Morgan's Creek*, 1943 – Cost; *Double Indemnity*, 1944 – Cost; *The Lost Weekend*, 1945 – Cost; *Notorious*, 1946 – Cost; *Sunset Boulevard*, 1950 – Cost; *All About Eve*, 1950 – Co-Cost; *Shane*, 1953 – Cost; *Rear Window*, 1954 – Co-Cost; *Witness for the Prosecution*, 1957 – Co-Cost; *Funny Face*, 1957 – Cost; *Vertigo*, 1958 – Cost; *The Man Who Shot Liberty Vallance*, 1962 – Cost; *The Birds*, 1963 – Cost; *Marnie*, 1964 – Cost

EARL HEDRICK (3): *Sullivan's Travels*, 1941 – Co-AD; *The Lost Weekend*, 1945 – Co-AD; *Ace in the Hole*, 1951 – Co-AD

'T. HEE' (Walt Disney) (2): *Pinocchio*, 1940 – Co-Anim; *Fantasia*, 1940 – Co-Anim

Graham Heid (1): *Bambi*, 1942 – Co-Anim

AL HERMAN (3): *King Kong*, 1933 – Co-AD; *Crossfire*, 1947 – Co-AD; *They Live by Night*, 1949 – Co-AD

Jim Hillin (1): *Beauty and the Beast*, 1991 – Co-Anim

Ron Hobbs (1): *The Deer Hunter*, 1978 – Co-AD

FREDERIC HOPE (3): *Dinner at Eight*, 1933 – Co-AD; *The Merry Widow*, 1934 – Co-AD; *Camille*, 1936 – Co-AD

HARRY HORNER (2): *Born Yesterday*, 1950 – Co-AD; *The Hustler*, 1961 – AD

WILLIAM HORNING (5): *The Wizard of Oz*, 1939 – Co-AD; *Gigi*, 1958 – *Co-AD; *Ben-Hur*, 1959 – *Co-AD

FRANK HOTALING (2): *The Quiet Man*, 1952 – AD; *The Searchers*, 1956 – Co-AD

Grace Houston (1): *The Naked City* 1948 – Cost

Ali Hubert (1): *The Merry Widow*, 1934 – Co-Cost

Rene Hubert (1): *My Darling Clementine*, 1946 – Cost

John Hughes (1): *The Treasure of the Sierra Madre*, 1948 – AD

Joseph Hurley (1): *Psycho*, 1960 – Co-AD

Wiard Ihnen (1): *Duck Soup*, 1933 – Co-AD

Eddie Imazu (1): *The Man Who Shot Liberty Vallance*, 1962 – Co-AD

'IRENE' (Irene Gibbons) (3): *The Palm Beach Story*, 1942 – Cost; *To Be or Not To Be*, 1942 – Cost; *The Postman Always Rings Twice*, 1946 – Co-AD

WILFRED JACKSON (4): *Snow White and the Seven Dwarfs*, 1938 – Co-Anim; *Pinocchio*, 1940 – Co-Anim; *Fantasia*, 1940 – Co-Anim; *Dumbo*, 1941 – Co-Anim

Dorothy Jeakins (1): *Fat City*, 1972 – Cost

GEORGE JENKINS (3): *The Best Years of Our Lives*, 1946 – Co-AD; *The Miracle Worker*, 1962 – Co-AD; *All the President's Men*, 1976 – *AD

Joanna Johnston (1): *Who Framed Roger Rabbit?*, 1988 – Cost

OLIVER JOHNSTON JR. (2): *Fantasia*, 1940 – Co-Anim; *Bambi*, 1942 – Co-Anim

ANNA HILL JOHNSTONE (4): *On the Waterfront*, 1954 – Cost; *East of Eden*, 1955 – Cost; *America, America*, 1963 – Cost; *The Godfather*, 1972 – Cost

Stan Jolley (1): *Witness*, 1985 – AD

Nathan Juran (1): *How Green Was My Valley*, 1941 – *Co-AD

MILTON KAHL (3): *Snow White and the Seven Dwarfs*, 1938 – Co-Anim; *Pinocchio*, 1940 – Co-Anim; *Bambi*, 1942 – Co-Anim

ROBERT KALLOCH (5): *It Happened One Night*, 1934 – Cost; *The Awful Truth*, 1937 – Cost; *Only Angels Have Wings*, 1939 – Cost: *Mr Smith Goes to Washington*, 1939 – Cost; *His Girl Friday*, 1940 – Cost

Michael Kaplan (1): *Blade Runner*, 1982 – Co-Cost

Barbara Karinska (1): *The Pirate*, 1948 – Co-Cost

Lisa Keene (1): *Beauty and the Beast*, 1991 – Co-Anim

Walter E. Keller (1): *Cat People*, 1942 – Co-AD

Walt Kelly (1): *Dumbo*, 1941 – Co-Anim

Tom Keogh (1): *The Pirate*, 1948 – Co-Cost

Marion Harwood Keyes (1): *The Postman Always Rings Twice*, 1946 – Co-Cost

OMAR KIAM (2): *Dodsworth*, 1936 – Cost; *Wuthering Heights*, 1939 – Cost

Jürgen Kiebach (1): *Cabaret*, 1972 – *Co-AD

WARD KIMBALL (4): *Snow White and the Seven Dwarfs*, 1938 – Co-Anim; *Pinocchio*, 1940 – Co-Anim; *Fantasia*, 1940 – Co-Anim; *Dumbo*, 1941 – Co-Anim

Joe King (1): *Witness for the Prosecution*, 1957 – Co-Cost

Muriel King (1): *Stage Door*, 1937 – Cost

JACK KINNEY (2): *Pinocchio*, 1940 – Co-Anim; *Dumbo*, 1941 – Co-Anim

MARK-LEE KIRK (4): *The Informer*, 1935 – Co-AD; *Young Mr Lincoln*, 1939 – Co-AD; *The Grapes of Wrath*, 1940 – Co-AD; *The Magnificent Ambersons*, 1942 – AD

Geoffrey Kirkland (1): *The Right Stuff*, 1983 – AD

Charles Knode (1): *Blade Runner*, 1982 – Co-AD

Richard Kollorsz (1): *The Scarlet Empress*, 1934 – Ikons and Paintings

Vincent Korda (1): *To Be or Not To Be*, 1942 – AD

Jeffrey Kurland (1): *Hannah and Her Sisters*, 1986 – Cost

Leo Kuter (1): *Rio Bravo*, 1959 – AD

Samuel Lange (1): *Mr Deeds Goes to Town*, 1936 – Cost

Vera Lanpher (1): *Beauty and the Beast*, 1991 – Co-Anim

Tambi Larsen (1): *The Outlaw Josey Wales*, 1976 – AD

ERIC LARSON (4): *Snow White and the Seven Dwarfs*, 1938 – Co-Anim; *Pinocchio*, 1940 – Co-Anim; *Fantasia*, 1940 – Co-Anim; *Bambi*, 1942 – Co-Anim

RALPH LAUREN (2): *Annie Hall*, 1977 – Co-Cost; *Manhattan*, 1979 – Co-Cost

Charles LeMaire (1): *All About Eve*, 1950 – Co-Cost

BORIS LEVEN (4): *Giant*, 1956 – AD; *Anatomy of a Murder*, 1959 – AD; *West Side Story*, 1961 – *AD; *The King of Comedy*, 1981 – AD

Jim Linn (1): *Close Encounters of the Third Kind*, 1977 – Cost

Arthur Lonergan (1): *M*A*S*H*, 1970 – Co-AD

JEAN LOUIS (6): *Gilda*, 1946 – Cost; *The Lady from Shanghai*, 1948 – Cost; *All the King's Men*, 1950 – Cost; *In a Lonely Place*, 1950 – Cost; *The Big Heat*, 1953 – Cost; *A Star Is Born*, 1954 – Co-Cost

JOHN LOUNSBERY (3): *Snow White and the Seven Dwarfs*, 1938 – Co-Anim; *Pinocchio*, 1940 – Co-Anim; *Fantasia*, 1940 – Co-Anim

EUGENE LOURIE (2): *The Southerner*, 1945 – AD; *Limelight*, 1952 – AD

EARL LUICK (3): *Little Caesar*, 1930 – Cost; *The Public Enemy*, 1931 – Cost; *The Oxbow Incident*, 1943 – Cost

HAMILTON LUSKE (3): *Snow White and the Seven Dwarfs*, 1938 – Co-Anim; *Pinocchio*, 1940 – Co-Dir; *Fantasia*, 1940 – Co-Anim

MOSS MABRY (2): *Giant*, 1956 – Co-Cost; *The Shootist*, 1976 – Cost

Nancy McArdle (1): *Annie Hall*, 1977 – Co-Cost

URIE MCCLEARY (2): *Kiss Me Kate*, 1953 – Co-AD; *Patton*, 1970 – *Co-AD

Robert Markell (1): *Twelve Angry Men*, 1957 – AD

JOSHUA MEADOR (5): *Snow White and the Seven Dwarfs*, 1938 – Co-Anim; *Pinocchio*, 1940 – Co-Anim; *Fantasia*, 1946 – Co-Anim; *Dumbo*, 1941 – Co-Anim; *Bambi*, 1942 – Co-Anim

John Meehan (1): *Sunset Boulevard*, 1950 – *Co-AD

Willam Cameron Menzies (1): *Gone with the Wind*, 1939 – *Co-AD

MICHAEL MEYERS (2): *Fort Apache*, 1948 – Co-Cost; *She Wore a Yellow Ribbon*, 1949 – Co-Cost

George Milo (1): *The Birds*, 1963 – Co-AD

John Mollo (1): *Star Wars*, 1977 – Co-Cost

Colleen Moore (1): *The Silence of the Lambs*, 1991 – Cost

FRED MOORE (4): *Snow White and the Seven Dwarfs*, 1938 – Co-Anim; *Pinocchio*, 1940 – Co-Anim; *Fantasia*, 1940 – Co-Anim; *Dumbo*, 1941 – Co-Anim

Jay A. Morley Jr. (1): *Written on the Wind*, 1956 – Co-AD

RUTH MORLEY (5): *The Hustler*, 1961 – Cost; *The Miracle Worker*, 1962 – Cost; *Taxi Driver*, 1976 – Cost; *Annie Hall*, 1977 – Co-Cost; *Kramer vs Kramer*, 1979 – Cost

Kathryn Morrison (1): *Salvador*, 1986 – Cost

Motley (1): *Long Day's Journey into Night*, 1962 – Cost

Deborah Nadoolman (1): *Raiders of the Lost Ark*, 1981 – Cost

BERNARD NEWMAN (2): *Top Hat*, 1935 – Cost; *Swing Time*, 1936 – Co-Cost

George Newman (1): *Annie Hall*, 1977 – Co-AD

Norma (1): *Gun Crazy*, 1950 – Cost

Patricia Norris (1): *Days of Heaven*, 1978 – Cost

Charles Novi (1): *To Have and Have Not*, 1944 – AD

MARY ANN NYBERG (2): *The Band Wagon*, 1953 – Cost; *A Star Is Born*, 1954 – Co-Cost

MARTIN OBZINA (2): *Destry Rides Again*, 1939 – Co-AD; *The Killers*, 1946 – Co-AD

Gary Odell (1): *From Here to Eternity*, 1953 – AD

Rosemary Odell (1): *To Kill a Mockingbird*, 1962 – Co-Cost

JACK OKEY (4): *I Am a Fugitive from a Chain Gang*, 1932 – AD; *Forty-Second Street*, 1933 – AD; *It's a Wonderful Life*, 1946 – AD; *Out of the Past*, 1947 – Co-AD

HARRY OLIVIER (2): *Scarface*, 1932 – AD; *The Good Earth*, 1937 – Co-AD

Charles Oman (1): *Top Hat*, 1935 – Co-AD, uc

ORRY-KELLY (9): *I Am a Fugitive from a Chain Gang*, 1932 – Cost; *Forty-Second Street*, 1933 – Cost; *The Gold Diggers of 1933*, – Cost; *The Sea Hawk*, 1940 – Cost; *The Little Foxes*, 1941 – Cost; *The Maltese Falcon*, 1941 – Cost; *Casablanca*, 1942 – Cost; *An American in Paris*, 1951 – Co-Cost; *Some Like it Hot*, 1959 – *Cost

JACK OTTERSON (3): *Destry Rides Again*, 1939 – Co-AD; *The Bank Dick*, 1940 – AD; *The Killers*, 1946 – Co-AD

Adele Palmer (1): *The Quiet Man*, 1952 – Cost

Max Parker (1): *The Public Enemy*, 1931 – AD

Gil Parrando (1): *Patton*, 1970 – *Co-AD

ANN PECK (3): *Fort Apache*, 1948 – Co-Cost; *She Wore a Yellow Ribbon*, 1949 – Co-Cost; *The Searchers*, 1956 – Co-Cost

HAL PEREIRA (7): *Double Indemnity*, 1944 – Co-AD; *Ace in the Hole*, 1951 – Co-AD; *Shane*, 1953 – Co-AD; *Rear Window*, 1954 – AD; *Vertigo*, 1958 – Co-AD; *Funny Face*, 1957 – Co-AD; *The Man Who Shot Liberty Vallance*, 1962 – Co-AD

Hans Peters (1): *The Red Badge of Courage*, 1951 – Co-AD

ROBERT PETERSON (2): *In a Lonely Place*, 1950 – AD; *The Big Heat*, 1953 – AD

JACK PIERCE (2): *Frankenstein*, 1931 – Make-Up; *The Bride of Frankenstein*, 1935 – Make-Up

Polly Platt (1): *The Last Picture Show*, 1971 – AD

WALTER PLUNKETT (9): *King Kong*, 1933 – Cost; *The Informer*, 1935 – Cost; *Stagecoach*, 1939 – Cost; *Gone with the Wind*, 1959 – Cost; *The Hunchback of Notre Dame*, 1939 – Cost; *Adam's Rib*, 1949 – Cost; *An American in Paris*, 1951 – *Co-Cost; *Singin' in the Rain*, 1952 – Cost; *Kiss Me Kate*, 1953 – Cost

VAN NEST POLGLASE (9): *King Kong*, 1933 – Co-AD; *Top Hat*, 1935 – Co-AD; *The Informer*, 1935 – Co-AD; *Swing Time*, 1936 – Co-AD: *Bringing Up Baby*, 1938 – Co-AD; *Gunga Din*, 1939 – Co-AD; *The Hunchback of Notre Dame*, 1929 – AD; *Citizen Kane*, 1941 – Co-AD; *Gilda*, 1946 – Co-AD

Marilyn Putnam (1): *Annie Hall*, 1977 – Co-AD

Merrill Pye (1): *North by Northwest*, 1959 – Co-AD

Toby Rafelson (1): *Five Easy Pieces*, 1975 – AD

Maurice Ransford (1): *Twelve o'Clock High*, 1949 – Co-AD

Ludwig Reiber (1): *Paths of Glory*, 1957 – AD

WOLFGANG REITHERMAN (4): *Snow White and the Seven Dwarfs*, 1938 – Co-Anim; *Pinocchio*, 1940 – Co-Anim; *Fantasia*, 1940 – Co-Anim; *Dumbo*, 1941 – Co-Anim

NORMAN REYNOLDS (2): *Star Wars*, 1977 – *Co-AD; *Raiders of the Lost Ark*, 1981 – AD

LEAH RHODES (3): *The Big Sleep*, 1946 – Cost; *White Heat*, 1949 – Cost; *Strangers on a Train*, 1951 – Cost

CARLO RIMBALDI (2): *Close Encounters of the Third Kind*, 1977 model work; *E.T.*, 1982 – model work, E.T. creation

BILL ROBERTS (5): *Snow White and the Seven Dwarfs*, 1938 – Co-Anim; *Pinocchio*, 1940 – Co-Anim; *Fantasia*, 1940 – Co-Anim; *Dumbo*, 1941 – Co-Anim; *Bambi*, 1942 – Co-Anim

AGGIE GUERARD RODGERS (2): *American Graffiti*, 1973 – Cost; *One Flew over the Cuckoo's Nest*, 1975 – Cost

HELEN ROSE (2): *On the Town*, 1949 – Cost; *The Bad and the Beautiful*, 1950 – *Cost

Charles Rosen (1): *Taxi Driver*, 1976 – AD

Bucky Rous (1): *Five Easy Pieces*, 1970 – Cost

Arthur I. Royce (1): *Way Out West*, 1937 – AD

Royer (1): *Young Mr Lincoln*, 1939 – Cost

Bruno Rubeo (1): *Salvador*, 1936 – AD

WADE B. RUBOTTOM (2): *The Philadelphia Story*, 1940 – Co-AD; *The Shop Around the Corner*, 1940 – Co-AD

Gene Rudolf (1): *Raging Bull*, 1980 – AD

PAUL SATTERFIELD (2): *Fantasia*, 1940 – Co-Anim; *Bambi*, 1942 – Co-Anim

W.R. Schmitt (1): *All Quiet on the Western Front*, 1930 – Co-AD

Deborah L. Scott (1): *E.T.*, 1982 – Co-Cost

Elliot Scott (1): *Who Framed Roger Rabbit?*, 1988 – Co-AD

Eric Seelig (1): *The Deer Hunter*, 1978 – Cost

IRENE SHARAFF (5): *Meet Me in St Louis*, 1944 – Cost; *An American in Paris*, 1951 – *Co-Cost; *The Best Years of Our Lives*, 1946 – Cost; *A Star Is Born*, 1954 – Co-Cost; *West Side Story*, 1961 – *Cost

JACK MARTIN SMITH (4): *Meet Me in St Louis*, 1944 – Co-AD; *The Pirate*, 1948 – Co-AD; *On the Town*, 1949 – Co-AD; *M*A*S*H*, 1970 – Co-AD

Rose Smith (1): *Intolerance*, 1916 – Co-AD

Ted Smith (1): *High Sierra*, 1941 – AD

Allan Snyder (1): *Rosemary's Baby*, 1968 – Make-Up

David L. Snyder (1): *Blade Runner*, 1982 – AD

J. RUSSELL SPENCER (2): *Modern Times*, 1936 – Co-AD; *The Great Dictator*, 1940 – AD

Allen Starski (1): *Schindler's List*, 1993 – AD

Rudolph Sternad (1): *High Noon*, 1952 – AD

EDWARD STEVENSON (6): *Gunga Din*, 1939 – Cost; *Citizen Kane*, 1941 – Cost; *The Magnificent Ambersons*, 1942 – Cost; *Murder My Sweet*, 1944 – Cost; *It's a Wonderful Life*, 1946 – Cost; *Out of the Past*, 1947 – Cost

Kim Swados (1): *The Deer Hunter*, 1978 – Co-AD

ANTHEA SYLBERT (2): *Rosemary's Baby*, 1968 – Cost; *Chinatown*, 1974 – Cost

PAUL SYLBERT (2): *One Flew over the Cuckoo's Nest*, 1975 – AD; *Kramer vs Kramer*, 1979 – AD

RICHARD SYLBERT (7): *Baby Doll*, 1956 – AD; *The Manchurian Candidate*, 1962 – AD; *Long Day's Journey into Night*, 1962 – AD; *The Graduate*, 1967 – AD; *Rosemary's Baby*, 1968 – AD; *Fat City*, 1972 – AD; *Chinatown*, 1974 – AD

DEAN TAVOULARIS (5): *Bonnie and Clyde*, 1967 – AD; *The Godfather*, 1972 – AD; *The Godfather Part II*, 1974 – *AD; *The Conversation*, 1974 – AD; *Apocalypse Now*, 1979 – AD

Edna Taylor (1): *The Shootist*, 1976 – Co-Cost

BILL THOMAS (2): *Written on the Wind*, 1956 – Co-AD; *Touch of Evil*, 1958 – AD

FRANKLIN THOMAS (3): *Snow White and the Seven Dwarfs*, 1938 – Co-Anim; *Pinocchio*, 1940 – Co-Anim; *Bambi*, 1942 – CoAnim

Viola Thompson (1): *To Kill a Mockingbird*, 1962 – Co-Cost

ALEXANDER TOLUBOFF (2): *Queen Christina*, 1933 – Co-AD; *Stagecoach*, 1939 – AD

DON TOWSLEY (3): *Pinocchio*, 1940 – Co-Anim; *Fantasia*, 1940 – Co-Anim; *Dumbo*, 1941 – Co-Anim

ALEXANDER TRAUNER (2): *The Apartment*, 1960 – *Co-AD; *Witness for the Prosecution*, 1957 – AD

(William) Travilla (1): *Gentlemen Prefer Blondes*, 1953 – Cost

DOLLY TREE (4): *The Thin Man*, 1934 – Cost; *David Copperfield*, 1935 – Cost; *Fury*, 1936 – Cost; *The Good Earth*, 1937 – Cost

William Tuntke (1): *Mary Poppins*, 1964 – Co-AD

Walter Tyler (1): *Shane*, 1953 – Co-AD

VLADIMIR TYTLA (4): *Snow White and the Seven Dwarfs*, 1938 – Co-Anim; *Pinocchio*, 1940 – Co-Anim; *Fantasia*, 1940 – Co-Anim; *Dumbo*, 1941 – Co-Anim

Robert Usher (1): *She Done Him Wrong*, 1933 – AD

THEODORA VAN RUNKLE (2), *Bonnie and Clyde*, 1967 – Cost; *The Godfather Part II*, 1974 – Cost

Pamela von Brandenstein (1): *Amadeus*, 1984 – AD

ERICH VON STROHEIM (2): *Greed*, 1924 – Co-AD; *Queen Kelly*, 1928 – Co-AD

GWEN WAKELING (2): *The Grapes of Wrath*, 1940 – Cost; *How Green Was My Valley*, 1941 – Cost

R.E. Wales (1): *Intolerance*, 1916 – Co-AD

TONY WALTON (2): *The Pirate*, 1948 – Co-Cost; *Mary Poppins*, 1964 – Cost

VERA WEST (2): *Destry Rides Again*, 1939 – Cost; *The Killers*, 1946 – Cost

CARL JULES WEYL (4): *The Adventures of Robin Hood*, 1938 – *AD; *Casablanca*, 1942 – AD; *Yankee Doodle Dandy*, 1942 – AD; *The Big Sleep*, 1946 – AD

LYLE WHEELER (9): *The Prisoner of Zenda*, 1937 – Co-AD; *Nothing Sacred*, 1937 – Co-AD; *Gone with the Wind*, 1939 – *Co-AD; *Rebecca*, 1940 – AD; *Laura*, 1944 – Co-AD; *My Darling Clementine*, 1946 – Co-AD; *Twelve o'Clock High*, 1949 – Co-AD; *All About Eve*, 1950 – Co-AD; *Gentlemen Prefer Blondes*, 1953 – Co-AD

Brad Whitney (1): *Play Misty for Me*, 1971 – Co-Cost

Richard Williams (1): *Who Framed Roger Rabbit?*, 1988 – Anim

Edward Withers (1): *The Wind*, 1928 – Co-AD

Albert Wolsky (1): *Manhattan*, 1979 – Co-Cost

Frank Wortman (1): *Intolerance*, 1916 – Co-AD, uc

Joseph C. Wright (1): *Gentlemen Prefer Blondes*, 1953 – Co-AD

Norman Wright (1): *Bambi*, 1942 – Co-Anim

Stuart Wurzel (1): *Hannah and Her Sisters*, 1981 – AD

Cy Young (1): *Dumbo*, 1941 – Co-Anim

Rolf Zehetbauer (1): *Cabaret*, 1972 – *Co-AD

Patricia Zipprodt (1): *The Graduate*, 1967 – Cost

NOTE

Albert Agostino (at RKO), Hans Dreier (at Paramount), Cedric Gibbons (at MGM), Hal Pereira (at Paramount), Van Nest Polglase (at RKO), and Lyle Wheeler (at TCF from 1944), all have high scores because, apart from their creative work, they also became heads of their respective art departments, automatically gaining a mention in the credits. In the case of a co-operative effort, the collaborator probably made the more significant contribution.

Contributors to the Music Department (Composers of Film Scores, Songwriters, Music Directors and Arrangers, Choreographers)

M = composer of film score
Lyrs = writer of song lyrics
SongM = composer of song music
Songs = a writer of lyrics and a composer of song music
MDir = music director
Arr = arranger, orchestration
Chor = choreographer
Uc = uncredited
Co- = in co-operation with others

Harold Adamson (1): *Gentlemen Prefer Blondes*, 1953 – Co-Lyrs

Robert Alton (1): *The Pirate*, 1948 – Co-Chor

DANIELE AMFITHEATROF (2): *Letter from an Unknown Woman*, 1948 – M; *The Big Heat*, 1953 – M

David Amram (1): *The Manchurian Candidate*, 1962 – M

George Antheil (1): *In a Lonely Place*, 1950 – M

HAROLD ARLEN (2): *The Wizard of Oz*, 1939 – SongM; *A Star Is Born*, 1954 – Song M

Gus Arnheim (1): *Scarface*, 1932 – Co-M

Howard Ashman (1): *Beauty and the Beast*, 1991 – Lyrs

FRED ASTAIRE (2): *Top Hat*, 1935 – Co-Chor; *Funny Face*, 1957 – Co-Chor

WILLIAM AXT (2): *The Big Parade*, 1925 – Co-M; *The Thin Man*, 1934 – M

CONSTANTIN BAKALEINIKOFF (2): *Notorious*, 1946; *Crossfire*, 1947 – M

John Barry (1): *Body Heat*, 1981 – M

Richard Barstow (1): *A Star Is Born*, 1954 – Chor

Dee Barton (1): *Play Misty for Me*, 1971 – M

Richard Baskin (1): *Nashville*, 1975 – M

GEORGE BASSMAN (2): *The Postman Always Rings Twice*, 1946 – M; *Ride the High Country*, 1962 – M

David Bennett (1): *Sons of the Desert*, 1933 – Chor

BUSBY BERKELEY (2): *Forty-Second Street*, 1933, – Chor; *The Gold Diggers of 1933*, 1933 – Chor

Irving Berlin (1): *Top Hat*, 1935 – Songs

ELMER BERNSTEIN ('Bernstein West') (3): *Sweet Smell of Success*, 1957 – M; *To Kill a Mockingbird*, 1962 – M; *The Shootist*, 1976 – M

LEONARD BERNSTEIN ('Bernstein East') (3): *On the Town*, 1949 – Co-SongM; *On the Waterfront*, 1954 – M; *West Side Story*, 1961 – SongM

Ralph Blane (1): *Meet Me in St Louis*, 1944 – Lyrs

John Boyle (1): *Yankee Doodle Dandy*, 1942 – Co-Chor

CHARLES BRADSHAW (2): *Sullivan's Travels*, 1941 – Co-M; *The Miracle of Morgan's Creek*, 1943 – Co-M

Marc Breaux (1): *Mary Poppins*, 1964 – Co-Chor

JOSEPH CARL BREIL (2): *The Birth of a Nation*, 1915 – Co-M; *Intolerance*, 1916 – Co-M

David Broekman (1): *All Quiet on the Western Front*, 1930 – M

NACIO HERB BROWN (2): *A Night at the Opera*, 1935 – Co-SongM; *Singin' in the Rain*, 1952 – Co SongM

Ralph Burns (1): **Cabaret*, 1972 – Arr

HOAGY CARMICHAEL (2): *To Have and Have Not*, 1944 – Songs; *Gentlemen Prefer Blondes*, 1953 – Co-SongM

CHARLES CHAPLIN (4): *City Lights*, 1930 – M; *Modern Times*, 1936 – M; *The Great Dictator*, 1940 – M; *Limelight*, 1952 – *Co-M and Chor

SAUL CHAPLIN (4): *An American in Paris*, 1951 – *Co-Arr; *Kiss Me Kate*, 1953 – Co-Arr; *Seven Brides for Seven Brothers*, 1954 – *Co-Arr; *West Side Story*, 1961 – *Co-Arr

FRANK CHURCHILL (3): *Snow White and the Seven Dwarfs*, 1938 – Co-M and SongM; *Dumbo*, 1941 – *Co-M and SongM; *Bambi*, 1942 – Co-M and SongM

George M. Cohan (1): *Yankee Doodle Dandy*, 1942 – Songs

JACK COLE (3): *Gilda*, 1946 – Chor; *Gentlemen Prefer Blondes*, 1953 – Chor; *Some Like it Hot*, 1959 – Chor

BETTY COMDEN (2): *On the Town*, 1949 – Co-Lyrs; *Singin' in the Rain*, 1952 – Co-Lyrs

Bobby Connolly (1): *The Wizard of Oz*, 1939 – Chor

Bill Conti (1): *The Right Stuff*, 1983 – M

Aaron Copland (1): *Of Mice and Men*, 1939 – M

CARMINE COPPOLA (2): *The Godfather Part II*, 1974 – *Co-M; *Apocalypse Now*, 1979 – Co-M

Francis Ford Coppola (1): *Apocalypse Now*, 1979 – Co-M

Georges Delerue (1): *Salvador*, 1986 – M

Gene De Paul (1): *Seven Brides for Seven Brothers*, 1954 – SongM

ADOLPH DEUTSCH (6): *The Maltese Falcon*, 1941 – M; *High Sierra*, 1941 – M; *The Band Wagon*, 1953 – Co-Arr; *Seven Brides for Seven Brothers*, 1954 – Co-Arr; *Some Like it Hot*, 1959 – M; *The Apartment*, 1960 – M

Frank De Vol (1): *Kiss Me Deadly*, 1955 – M

Howard Dietz (1): *The Band Wagon*, 1953 – Lyrs

STANLEY DONEN (2): *On the Town*, 1949 – Co-Chor; *Singin' in the Rain*, 1952 – Co-Chor

AL DUBIN (2): *Forty-Second Street*, 1933 – Lyrs; *The Gold Diggers of 1933* – Lyrs

George Duning (1): *From Here to Eternity*, 1953 – M

Fred Ebb (1): *Cabaret*, 1972 – Lyrs

ROGER EDENS (5): *On the Town*, 1949 – Co-SongM and *Co-Arr; *Singin' in the Rain*, 1952 – Co-SongM; *The Band Wagon*, 1953 – Co-Arr; *A Star Is Born*, 1954 – Arr; *Funny Face*, 1957 – Co-SongM

Duke Ellington (1): *Anatomy of a Murder*, 1959 – M

JERRY FIELDING (2): *The Wild Bunch*, 1969 – M; *The Outlaw Josey Wales*, 1976 – M

Dorothy Fields (1): *Swing Time*, 1936 – Lyrs including: *Song, 'The Way You Look Tonight'

LEO FORBSTEIN (2): *I Am a Fugitive from a Chain Gang*, 1932 – MDir; *To Have and Have Not*, 1944 – MDir

ARTHUR FREED (2): *A Night at the Opera*, 1935 – Lyrs; *Singin' in the Rain*, 1952 – Lyrs

Gerald Fried (1): *Paths of Glory*, 1957 – M

HUGO FRIEDHOFER (3): *The Best Years of our Lives*, 1946 – M; *Gilda*, 1946 – M; *Ace in the Hole*, 1951 – M

LEONARD GERSHE (2): *A Star Is Born*, 1954 – M; *Funny Face*, 1957 – Co-SongM

GEORGE GERSHWIN (3): *An American in Paris*, 1951 – M and SongM; *Funny Face*, 1957 – Co-SongM; *Manhattan*, 1979 – M

IRA GERSHWIN (2): *A Star Is Born*, 1954 – Lyres; *Funny Face*, 1957 – Co-Lyrs

Jerry Goldsmith (1): *Chinatown*, 1974 – M

Louis Gottschalk (1): *Broken Blossoms*, 1919 – Co-M

ADOLPH GREEN (2): *On the Town*, 1949 – Co-Lyrs; *Singin' in the Rain*, 1952 – Co-Lyrs

JOHNNY GREEN (2): **An American in Paris*, 1951 – Co-Arr; *West Side Story*, 1961 – Co-Arr

D.W. GRIFFITH (2): *The Birth of a Nation*, 1915 – Co-M; *Intolerance*, 1916 – Co-M; *Broken Blossoms*, 1919 – Co-M

Louis Gruenberg (1): *All the King's Men*, 1950 – M

David Grusin (1): *The Graduate*, 1967 – M

Woody Guthrie (1): *They Live by Night*, 1949 – Co-M, uc

Manos Hadjidakis (1): *America, America*, 1963 – M

RICHARD HAGEMAN (4): **Stagecoach*, 1939 – Co-M; *Fort Apache*, 1948 – M; *She Wore a Yellow Ribbon*, 1949 – M; *Wagonmaster* 1950 – M

Marvin Hamlisch (1): *Fat City*, 1972 – M

E.Y. ('Yip') Harburg (1): *The Wizard of Oz*, 1939 – Lyrs

LEIGH HARLINE (2): *Snow White and the Seven Dwarfs*, 1938 – Co-M; *Pinocchio*, 1940 – SongM, including *Song: 'When You Wish Upon a Star'

W. FRANKE HARLING (5): *Shanghai Express*, 1932 – M: *Trouble in Paradise*, 1932 – M; *The Scarlet Empress*, 1934 – Co-M; **Stagecoach*, 1939 – Co-M; *They Live by Night*, 1949 – Co-M

Lorenz Hart (1): *Love Me Tonight*, 1932 – Lyrs

Marvin T. Hatley (1): *Way Out West*, 1937 – M

LENNIE HAYTON (2): *On the Town*, 1949 – *Co-Arr; *Singin' in the Rain*, 1952 – MDir

Harold Hecht (1): *She Done Him Wrong*, 1933 – Chor

Wally Heglin (1): *Singin' in the Rain*, 1952 – Co-Arr

BERNARD HERRMANN (9): *Citizen Kane*, 1941 – M; *The Magnificent Ambersons*, 1942 – M; *The Ghost and Mrs Muir*, 1947 – M; *Vertigo*, 1958 – M; *North by Northwest*, 1959 – M; *Psycho*, 1960 – M; *The Birds*, 1963 – Sound consultant; *Marnie*, 1964 – M; *Taxi Driver*, 1976 – M

WERNER HEYMANN (3): *Ninotchka*, 1939 – M; *The Shop Around the Corner*, 1940 – M; *To Be or Not To Be*, 1942 – M

FREDERICK HOLLANDER (2): *Destry Rides Again*, 1939 – SongM; *Born Yesterday*, 1950 – M

KENYON HOPKINS (3): *Baby Doll*, 1956 – M; *Twelve Angry Men*, 1957 – M; *The Hustler*, 1961 – M

Herman Hupfeld (1): *Casablanca*, 1942 – Song: 'As Time Goes By'

Howard Jackson (1): *Mr Deeds Goes to Town*, 1936 – MDir

Werner Janssen (1): *The Southerner*, 1945 – M

Maurice Jarre (1): *Witness*, 1985 – M

Stan Jones (1): *The Searchers*, 1956 – Title song

Walter Jurmann (1): *A Night at the Opera* – Co-SongM

Bert Kalmar (1): *Duck Soup*, 1933 – Lyrs

John Kander (1): *Cabaret*, 1972 – SongM

BRONISIAW KAPER (3): *Mutiny on the Bounty*, 1935 M; *A Night at the Opera*, 1935 – Co-SongM; *The Red Badge of Courage*, 1951 – M

GENE KELLY (4): *The Pirate*, 1948 – Co-Chor; *On the Town*, 1949 – Chor; *An American in Paris*, 1951 – Chor; *Singin' in the Rain*, 1952 – Co-Chor

Jerome Kern (1): *Swing Time*, 1936 – SongM

MICHAEL KIDD (2): *The Band Wagon*, 1953 – Chor; *Seven Brides for Seven Brothers*, 1954 – Chor

Krzysztof Komeda (1): *Rosemary's Baby*, 1968 – M

ERICH WOLFGANG KORNGOLD (2): *The Adventures of Robin Hood*, 1938 – M; *The Sea Hawk*, 1940 – M

Irwin Kostal (2): *West Side Story*, 1961 – *Co-Arr; *Mary Poppins*, 1964 – M

Franz Lehar (1): *The Merry Widow*, 1934 – SongM

JOHN LEIPOLD (2): *The Scarlet Empress*, 1934 – Co-M; *Stagecoach*, 1939 – *Co-M

Alan Jay Lerner (1): *Gigi*, 1958 – Lyrs – including *Song: 'Gigi'

Oscar Levant (1): *Nothing Sacred*, 1937 – M
Frank Loesser (1): *Destry Rides Again*, 1939 – Lyrs
Frederick Loewe (1): *Gigi*, 1958 – SongM – including *Song: 'Gigi'
Eugene Loring (1): *Funny Face*, 1957 – Co-Chor
Manuel Maciste (1): *Only Angels Have Wings*, 1939 – Co-M
Matt Malneck (1): *Witness for the Prosecution*, 1957 – M
Henry Mancini (1): *Touch of Evil*, 1958 – M
Johnny Mandel (1): *M*A*S*H*, 1970 – M
Hugh Martin (1): *Meet Me in St Louis*, 1944 – SongM
Skip Martin (1): *Singin' in the Rain*, 1952 – Co-Arr
David Mendoza (1): *The Big Parade*, 1925 – Co-M
Alan Menken (1): *Beauty and the Beast*, 1991 – SongM
JOHNNY MERCER (3): *Laura*, 1944 – Lyrs; *To Have and Have Not*, 1944 – Lyrs; *Seven Brides for Seven Brothers*, 1954 – Lyrs
CYRIL MOCKRIDGE (3): *The Oxbow Incident*, 1943 – M; *My Darling Clementine*, 1946 – M; *The Man Who Shot Liberty Vallance*, 1962 – M
Larry Morey (1): *Snow White and the Seven Dwarfs*, 1938 – Lyrs
Ennio Morricone (1): *Days of Heaven*, 1978 – M
Wallis Murch (1): *American Graffiti*, 1973 – sound montage
Stanley Myers (1): *The Deer Hunter*, 1978 – M
ALFRED NEWMAN (10): *Dodsworth*, 1936 – M; *The Prisoner of Zenda*, 1937 – M; *The Hunchback of Notre Dame*, 1939 – M; *Wuthering Heights*, 1939 – M; *Young Mr Lincoln*, 1939 – M; *Gunga Din*, 1939 – M; *The Grapes of Wrath*, 1940 – M; *How Green Was My Valley*, 1941 – M; *Twelve o'Clock High*, 1949 – M; *All About Eve*, 1950 – M
Jack Nitzsche (1): *One Flew over the Cuckoo's Nest*, 1975 – M
Marni Nixon (1): *West Side Story*, 1961 – vocal dubbing for Natalie Wood
Alex North (1): *A Streetcar Named Desire*, 1951 – M
HERMES PAN (2): *Top Hat*, 1935 – Co-Chor; *Swing Time*, 1936 – Chor
Tom Pierson (1): *Manhattan*, 1979 – MDir
EDWARD PLUMB (2): *Fantasia*, 1940 – MDir; *Bambi*, 1942 – Co-M

COLE PORTER (2): *The Pirate*, 1948, – Songs; *Kiss Me Kate*, 1953 – Songs

ANDRÉ PREVIN (4): *Kiss Me Kate*, 1953 – Co-Arr and MDir; *Bad Day at Black Rock*, 1954 – M; *Gigi*, 1958 – *Arr and MDir; *Long Day's Journey into Night*, 1962 – M

Charles Previn (1): *The Bank Dick*, 1940 – MDir

Ralph Rainger (1): *She Done Him Wrong*, 1933 – SongM

DAVID RAKSIN (2): *Laura*, 1944 – M and SongM; *The Bad and the Beautiful*, 1952 – M

Sid Ramin (1): *West Side Story*, 1961 – *Co-Arr

Erno Rapee (1): *Little Caesar*, 1930 – MDir

Raymond Rasch (1): *Limelight*, 1952 – *Co-M

Hugo Riesenfeld (1): *Sunrise*, 1927 – M

Jerome Robbins, (1): *West Side Story*, 1961 – Chor

Robbie Robertson (1): *The King of Comedy*, 1983 – M

LEO ROBIN (2): *She Done Him Wrong*, 1933 – Lyrs; *Gentlemen Prefer Blondes*, 1953 – Co-Lyrs

Richard Rodgers (1): *Love Me Tonight*, 1932 – SongM

Heinz Roemheld (1): *The Lady from Shanghai*, 1948 – M

LEONARD ROSENMAN (2): *East of Eden*, 1955 – M; *Rebel without a Cause*, 1955 – M

Laurence Rosenthal (1): *The Miracle Worker*, 1962 – M

NINO ROTA (2): *The Godfather*, 1972 – M; *The Godfather Part II*, 1974 – *Co-M

MIKLOS ROZSA (8): *Double Indemnity*, 1944 – M; *The Lost Weekend*, 1945 – M; *Spellbound*, 1945 – *M; *The Killers*, 1946 – M; *The Naked City*, 1948 – Co-M; *Adam's Rib*, 1949 – M; *The Asphalt Jungle*, 1950 – M; *Ben-Hur*, 1959 – *M

Harry Ruby (1): *Duck Soup*, 1933 – SongM

Larry Russell (1): *Limelight*, 1952 – *Co-M

CONRAD SALINGER (2): *Meet Me in St Louis*, 1944 – Arr; *Singin' in the Rain*, 1952 – Co-Arr

Walter Schumann (1): *The Night of the Hunter*, 1955 – M

Arthur Schwartz (1): *The Band Wagon*, 1953 – SongM

Richard and Robert Sherman (1): *Mary Poppins*, 1964 – Songs

DAVID SHIRE (2): *All the President's Men*, 1974 – M; *The Conversation*, 1974 – M

Howard Shore (1): *The Silence of the Lambs*, 1991 – M

LEO SHUKEN (4): *Stagecoach*, 1939 – *Co-M; *Sullivan's Travels*, 1941 – M; *The Lady Eve*, 1941 – M; *The Miracle of Morgan's Creek*, 1943 – M

Louis Silvers (1): *It Happened One Night*, 1934 – MDir

Alan Silvestri (1): *Who Framed Roger Rabbit?*, 1988 – M

Paul Simon (1): *The Graduate*, 1967 – Songs

FRANK SKINNER (3): *Destry Rides Again*, 1939 – M; *The Naked City*, 1940 – Co-M; *Written on the Wind*, 1956 – M

PAUL SMITH (2): *Snow White and the Seven Dwarfs*, 1938 – Co-M; *Pinocchio*, 1940 – Co-M

Stephen Sondheim (1): *West Side Story*, 1961 – Lyrs

MAX STEINER (10): *King Kong*, 1933 – M; *The Informer*, 1935 – *M; *Top Hat*, 1935 – MDir; *Gone with the Wind*, 1939 – M; *Casablanca*, 1942 – M; *Mildred Pierce*, 1945 – M; *The Big Sleep*, 1946 – M; *The Treasure of the Sierra Madre*, 1948 – M; *White Heat*, 1949 – M; *The Searchers*, 1956 – M

Alexander Steinert (1): *Bambi*, 1942 – MDir

MORRIS STOLOFF (3): *The Awful Truth*, 1937 – MDir; *Only Angels Have Wings*, 1939 – Co-M; *His Girl Friday*, 1940 – MDir

George Stoll (1): *Meet Me in St Louis*, 1944 – MDir

HERBERT STOTHART (8): *Queen Christina*, 1933 – M; *David Copperfield*, 1935 – M; *Mutiny on the Bounty*, 1935 – Co-M; *A Night at the Opera*, 1935 – M; *Camille*, 1936 – M; *The Good Earth*, 1937 – M; *The Wizard of Oz*, 1939 – *M; *They Were Expendable*, 1945 – M

Charles Strouse (1): *Bonnie and Clyde*, 1967 – M

Jule Styne (1): *Gentlemen Prefer Blondes*, 1953 – Co-SongM

Adolph Tandler (1): *Scarface*, 1932 – Co-M

Twyla Tharp (1): *Amadeus*, 1984 – Chor

DIMITRI TIOMKIN (10): *The Lost Horizon*, 1937 – M; *Mr Smith Goes to Washington*, 1939 – M; *Only Angels Have Wings*, 1939 – Co-M; *Shadow of a Doubt*, 1943 – M; *It's a Wonderful Life*, 1946 – M; *Red River*, 1948 – M; *Strangers on a Train*, 1951 – M; *High

Noon, 1952 – *M and *SongM; *Giant*, 1956 – M; *Rio Bravo*, 1959 – M and SongM

VANGELIS (2): *Missing*, 1982 – M; *Blade Runner*, 1982 – M

Josef von Sternberg (1): *The Scarlet Empress*, 1934 – Co-M

Oliver Wallace (1): *Dumbo*, 1941 – *Co-M

Charles Walters (1): *Meet Me in St Louis*, 1944 – Chor

HARRY WARREN (2): *Forty-Second Street*, 1933 – SongM; *The Gold Diggers of 1933* – SongM

NED WASHINGTON (4): *A Night at the Opera*, 1935 – Co-Lyrs; *Pinocchio*, 1940 – including Lyrs: *Song: 'When You Wish upon a Star'; *Dumbo*, 1941 – Lyrs; *High Noon*, 1952 – *Lyrs, Title Song

FRANZ WAXMAN (7): *The Bride of Frankenstein*, 1935 – M; *Fury*, 1936 – M; *Rebecca*, 1940 – M; *The Philadelphia Story*, 1940 – M; *To Have and Have Not*, 1945 – M, uc; *Sunset Boulevard*, 1950 – *M; *Rear Window*, 1954 – M

ROY WEBB (7): *Stage Door*, 1937 – M; *Bringing Up Baby*, 1938 – M; *Cat People*, 1942 – M; *Murder My Sweet*, 1944 – M; *Notorious*, 1946 – M; *Crossfire*, 1947 – M; *Out of the Past*, 1947 – M

Paul Francis Webster (1): *Rio Bravo*, 1959 – Lyrs

JOHN WILLIAMS (6): *Jaws*, 1975 – *M; *Close Encounters of the Third Kind*, 1977 – M; *Star Wars*, 1977 – *M; *Raiders of the Lost Ark*, 1981 – M; *E.T.*, 1982 – *M; *Schindler's List*, 1993 – *M

Meredith Willson (1): *The Little Foxes*, 1941 – M

Dee Dee Wood (1): *Mary Poppins*, 1964 – Co-Chor

VICTOR YOUNG (4): *The Palm Beach Story*, 1942 – M; *Gun Crazy*, 1950 – M; *The Quiet Man*, 1952 – M; *Shane*, 1953 – M

NOTES

There are several film composers in this list who can justifiably be called maestros. Over one-third (eighty-six films) of Hollywood's Top Two-Fifty were scored by just eleven composers and arrangers – Alfred Newman, Max Steiner, Dimitri Tiomkin, Bernard Herrmann, Miklos Rozsa, Herbert Stothart, Franz Waxman, Roy Webb, Adolph Deutsch, W. Franke Harling, and John Williams. Newman (always expressive but sometimes too obviously over-emotional), Steiner (original, versatile and prolific, from *King Kong* to *The Searchers*), and Dimitri Tiomkin (with his Russian love for the grand theme, and rich orchestration) lead the field with ten contributions. Not far behind come Herrmann (starting magnificently with Orson Welles's two masterpieces, providing atmospheric and exciting music and sound to Hitchcock's finest films and ending in startling form with Martin Scorsese's *Taxi Driver*), Rozsa (one of Korda's Hungarian 'court' in London and Hollywood), then providing intense, dramatic scores from *Double Indemnity* to the 1959 *Ben-Hur*, for which he gained an Oscar and Herbert Stothart (composing tuneful, evocative, appropriate scores for MGM in the 1930s and 40s).

Franz Waxman's seven contributions include an Oscar-winning score for *Sunset Boulevard* and an uncredited score for *To Have and Have Not*, while Roy Webb, working steadily at RKO, provided excellent scores that have probably not been adequately acknowledged. Deutsch's six contributions include two superb sets of arrangements for two MGM musicals – *The Band Wagon* and *Seven Brides for Seven Brothers*.

Deutsch's collaborator on the last-named musical – for which they gained an Oscar – Saul Chaplin, was involved the scoring of three other outstanding musicals, two of which also gained Oscars for their arrangements – *An American in Paris* and *West Side Story*. It is sometimes forgotten how important a brilliant orchestration is for the final superb effort of this distinctive Hollywood genre.

John Williams emerges as the modern maestro of the Spielberg era. No need to remind oneself of the scores for *Jaws* and *Star Wars*, but the tasteful, un-melodramatic scoring of *Schindler's List*, for which an Oscar was also awarded, is an interesting departure that testifies to the artistry of this great film composer.

Editors

The editors (or 'cutters') have been unjustifiably ignored until recent years. They are now recognised as one of the most creative group of contributors to the final copy shown to the general public (see Film-Making As a Group Activity).

Edgar Adams (1): *All Quiet on the Western Front*, 1930 – Co-Ed

ALBERT AKST (2): *Meet Me in St Louis*, 1944 – Ed; *The Band Wagon*, 1953 – Ed

DEDE ALLEN (3): *The Hustler*, 1961 – Ed; *America, America*, 1963 – Ed; *Bonnie and Clyde*, 1967 – Ed

GEORGE AMY (3): *The Gold Diggers of 1933* – Ed; *The Sea Hawk*, 1940 – Ed; *Yankee Doodle Dandy*, 1942 – Ed

Philip Anderson (1): *Giant*, 1956 – Co-Ed

Aram Avakian (1): *The Miracle Worker*, 1962 – Ed

Henry Barnes (1): *The General*, 1926 – Co-Ed

Samuel E. Beetley (1): *Out of the Past*, 1947 – Ed

HENRY BERMAN (2): *Swing Time*, 1936 – Ed; *Gunga Din*, 1939 – Co-Ed

Douglas Biggs (1): *They Were Expendable*, 1945 – Co-Ed

FOLMAR BLANGSTED (2): *A Star Is Born*, 1954 – Ed; *Rio Bravo*, 1959 – Ed

GEORGE BOEMLER (2): *Adam's Rib*, 1949 – Ed; *The Asphalt Jungle*, 1950 – Ed

Fred Bonahan (1): *Giant*, 1956 – Co-Ed

Françoise Bonnot (1): *Missing*, 1982 – Ed

MARGARET ('Maggie') BOOTH (3): *Mutiny on the Bounty*, 1935 – Ed; *Camille*, 1936 – Ed; *Fat City*, 1972 – Ed

Frank Bracht (1): *Funny Face*, 1957 – Ed

David Bretherton (1): *Cabaret*, 1972 – *Ed

Donn Cambern (1): *The Last Picture Show*, 1971 – Ed

John Carnochan (1): *Beauty and the Beast*, 1991 – Ed

MILTON CARRUTH (3): *All Quiet on the Western Front*, 1930 – Co-Ed; *Destry Rides Again*, 1939 – Ed; *Shadow of a Doubt*, 1963 – Ed

CHARLES CHAPLIN (2): *City Lights*, 1930 – Ed; *Modern Times*, 1936 Ed

Ted Cheeseman (1): *King Kong*, 1933 – Ed

RICHARD CHEW (3): *The Conversation*, 1974 – Co-Ed; *One Flew over the Cuckoo's Nest*, 1971 – Co-Ed; *Star Wars*, 1977 – Co-Ed

Alan Crosland, Jr. (1): *Sweet Smell of Success*, 1957 – Ed

Stephen Csillag (1): *Fantasia*, 1940 – Ed

Edward Curtis (1): *Scarface*, 1932 – Ed

Ray Curtiss (1): *Little Caesar*, 1932 – Ed

Nina Danevic (1): *Amadeus*, 1984 – Ed

Ralph Dawson (1): *The Adventures of Robin Hood*, 1938 – *Ed

John Dunning (1): *Ben-Hur*, 1959 – *Co-Ed

Robert S. Eisen (1): *Invasion of the Body Snatchers*, 1956 – Ed

Joseph Farnham (1): *Greed*, 1924 – Co-Ed

Glenn Farr (1): *The Right Stuff*, 1983 – Co-Ed

ADRIENNE FAZAN (3): *An American in Paris*, 1951 – Ed; *Singin' in the Rain*, 1952 – Co-Ed; *Gigi*, 1958 – *Co-Ed

VERNA FIELDS (2): *American Graffiti*, 1973 – Co-Ed; *Jaws*, 1975 – *Ed

HUGH S. FOWLER (2): *Gentlemen Prefer Blondes*, 1953 – Ed; *Patton*, 1970 – *Ed

Lise Fruchtman (1): *The Right Stuff*, 1983 – Co-Ed

HARRY GERSTAD (3): *Crossfire*, 1947 – Ed; *Gun Crazy*, 1950 – Co-Ed; *High Noon*, 1952 – *Co-Ed

STUART GILMORE (4): *The Lady Eve*, 1941 Ed; *Sullivan's Travels*, 1941 – Ed; *The Palm Beach Story*, 1942 – Ed; *The Miracle of Morgan's Creek*, 1943 – Ed

Robert Golden (1): *The Night of the Hunter*, 1955 – Ed

Jerry Greenberg (1): *Kramer vs Kramer*, 1979 – Ed

Danford Greene (1): *M*A*S*H*, 1970 – Ed

Alexander Hall (1): *She Done Him Wrong*, 1933 – Ed

WILLIAM HAMILTON (3): *Top Hat*, 1935 – Ed; *Stage Door*, 1937 – Ed; *The Hunchback of Notre Dame*, 1939 – Co-Ed

DOANE HARRISON (5): *Double Indemity*, 1944 – Ed; *The Lost Weekend*, 1945 – Ed; *Sunset Boulevard*, 1950 – Co-Ed; *Ace in the Hole*, 1951 – Ed; *Twelve Angry Men*, 1957 – Ed

GENE HAVLICK (5): *It Happened One Night*, 1934 – Ed; *Mr Deeds Goes to Town*, 1936 – Ed; *The Lost Horizon*, 1937 – *Co-Ed; *Mr Smith Goes to Washington*, 1939 – Ed; *His Girl Friday*, 1940 – Ed

Dennis Hill (1): *Nashville*, 1975 – Co-Ed

Katherine Hilliker (1): *Sunrise*, 1927 – Ed

ARTHUR HILTON (2): *The Bank Dick*, 1940 – Ed; *The Killers*, 1946 – Ed

Paul Hirsch (1): *Star Wars*, 1977 – Co-Ed

GEORGE HIVELY (2): *The Informer*, 1935 – Ed; *Bringing Up Baby*, 1938 – Ed

Christopher Holmes (1): *Five Easy Pieces*, 1970 – Co-Ed

Walter Holmes (1): *I Am a Fugitive from a Chain Gang*, 1932 – Ed

WILLIAM HORNBECK (3): *It's a Wonderful Life*, 1946 – Ed; *Shane*, 1953 – Co-Ed; *Giant*, 1956 – Co-Ed

FRANK E. HULL (2): *Greed*, 1924 – Co-Ed; *They Were Expendable*, 1945 – Co-Ed

Joe Ince (1): *Limelight*, 1952 – Ed

Rex Ingram (1): *Greed*, 1924 – Co-Ed

BERT JORDAN (3): *Sons of the Desert*, 1933 – Ed; *Way Out West*, 1937 – Ed; *Of Mice and Men*, 1939 – Ed

MICHAEL KAHN (2): *Raiders of the Lost Ark*, 1981 – *Ed; *Schindler's List*, 1993 – *Ed

Sheldon Kahn (1): *One Flew over the Cuckoo's Nest*, 1975 – Co-Ed

Sherman Kell (1): *The General*, 1926 – Co-Ed

TED KENT (2): *Bride of Frankenstein*, 1935 – Ed; *Letter from an Unknown Woman*, 1948 – Ed

HAL C. KERN (4): *Nothing Sacred*, 1937 – Co-Ed; *The Prisoner of Zenda*, 1937 – Co-Ed; *Gone with the Wind*, 1939 – *Co-Ed; *Rebecca*, 1940 – Co-Ed

ROBERT J. KERN (2): *The Thin Man*, 1934 – Ed; *David Copperfield*, 1935 – Ed

Jack Killifer (1): *High Sierra*, 1941 – Ed

Newell Kimlin (1): *Bad Day at Black Rock*, 1954 – Ed

Lynzee Klingman (1): *One Flew over the Cuckoo's Nest*, 1975 – Co-Ed

Clarence Kolster (1): *Frankenstein*, 1931 – Co-Ed

Eva Kroll (1): *Paths of Glory*, 1957 – Ed

VIOLA LAWRENCE (4): *Queen Kelly*, 1928 – Ed; *Only Angels Have Wings*, 1939 – Ed; *The Lady from Shanghai*, 1948 – Ed; *In a Lonely Place*, 1950 – Ed

William Levanway (1): *A Night at the Opera*, 1935 – Ed

SIDNEY LEVIN (2): *Mean Streets*, 1973 – Ed; *Nashville*, 1975 – Co-Ed

BEN LEWIS (2): *Dinner at Eight*, 1933 – Ed; *The Red Badge of Courage*, 1951 – Ed

CAROL LITTLETON (2): *Body Heat*, 1981 – Ed; *E.T.*, 1982 – Ed

John Lockert (1): *Gunga Din*, 1939 – Co-Ed

LOUIS LOEFFLER (2): *Laura*, 1944 – Ed; *Anatomy of a Murder*, 1959 – Ed

Louis Lombardo (1): *The Wild Bunch*, 1969 – Ed

Otho Lovering (1): *The Man Who Shot Liberty Vallance*, 1962 – Ed

MARCIA LUCAS (3): *American Graffiti*, 1973 – Co-Ed; *Taxi Driver*, 1976 – Co-Ed; *Star Wars*, 1977 – Co-Ed

Michael Luciano (1): *Kiss Me Deadly*, 1955 – Ed

William Lyon (1): *From Here to Eternity*, 1953 – *Ed

Tom McAdoo (1): *Shane*, 1953 – Co-Ed

Edward McCormick (1): *The Public Enemy*, 1931 – Ed

Harold McGahann (1): *The Gold Rush*, 1925 – Ed

Craig McKay (1): *The Silence of the Lambs*, 1991 – Ed

BARBARA MCLEAN (2): *Twelve o'Clock High*, 1949 – Ed; *All About Eve*, 1950 – Ed

Allen McNeil (1): *The Oxbow Incident*, 1943 – Ed

Barry Malkin (1): *The Godfather Part II*, 1974 – Co-Ed

DANIEL MANDELL (6): *Dodsworth*, 1936 – Ed; *Wuthering Heights*, 1939 – Ed; *The Little Foxes*, 1941 – Ed; *The Best Years of Our Lives*, 1946 – *Ed; *Witness for the Prosecution*, 1959 – Ed; *The Apartment*, 1960 – Ed

OWEN MARKS (4): *Casablanca*, 1942 – Ed; *The Treasure of the Sierra Madre*, 1948 – Ed; *White Heat*, 1949 – Ed; *East of Eden*, 1955 – Ed

RICHARD MARKS (2): *The Godfather Part II*, 1974 – Co-Ed; *Apocalypse Now*, 1979 – Co-Ed

Frances Marsh (1): *The Merry Widow*, 1934 – Ed

June Mathis (1): *Greed*, 1924 – Co-Ed

GENE MILFORD (3): *The Lost Horizon*, 1937 – *Co-Ed; *On the Waterfront*, 1954 – *Ed; *Baby Doll*, 1956 – Ed

SUSAN MORSE (2): *Manhattan*, 1979 – Ed; *Hannah and Her Sisters*, 1986 – Ed

Walter Murch (1): *The Conversation*, 1974 – Co-Ed

JACK MURRAY (5): *Fort Apache*, 1948 – Ed; *She Wore a Yellow Ribbon*, 1949 – Ed; *Wagonmaster*, 1950 – Ed; *The Quiet Man*, 1952 – Ed; *The Searchers*, 1956 – Ed

CHARLES NELSON (3): *Gilda*, 1946 – Ed; *Born Yesterday*, 1950 – Ed; *The Big Heat*, 1953 – Ed

CONRAD NERVIG (2): *The Wind*, 1928 – Ed; *The Bad and the Beautiful*, 1952 – Ed

JAMES NEWCOM (4): *Nothing Sacred*, 1937 – Co-Ed; *The Prisoner of Zenda*, 1937 – Co-Ed; *Gone with the Wind*, 1939 – *Co-Ed; *Rebecca*, 1940 – Co-Ed

Willard Nico (1): *The Great Dictator*, 1940 – Ed

Thom Noble (1): *Witness*, 1985 – Ed

Joseph Noriega (1): *Murder My Sweet*, 1944 – Ed

CHRISTIAN NYBY (3): *To Have and Have Not*, 1944 – Ed; *The Big Sleep*, 1946 – Ed; *Red River*, 1948 – Ed

SAM O'STEEN (3): *The Graduate*, 1967 – Ed; *Rosemary's Baby*, 1968 – *Co-Ed; *Chinatown*, 1974 – Ed

Richard Parrish (1): *All the King's Men*, 1950 – Co-Ed

Carl Pingitore (1): *Play Misty for Me*, 1971 – Ed

MAURICE PIVAR (2): *All Quiet on the Western Front*, 1930 – Co-Ed; *Frankenstein*, 1931 – Co-Ed

Thomas Pratt (1): *Forty-Second Street*, 1933 – Ed

Terry Rawlings (1): *Blade Runner*, 1982 – Ed

Walter Reynolds (1): *Stagecoach*, 1939 – Co-Ed

William H. Reynolds (1): *The Godfather*, 1972 – Co-Ed

Thomas Richards (1): *The Maltese Falcon*, 1941 – Ed

MARK ROBSON (3): *Citizen Kane*, 1941 – Co-Ed; *The Magnificent Ambersons*, 1942 – Co-Ed, uc; *Cat People*, 1942 – Ed

TOM ROLF (2): *Taxi Driver*, 1976 – Co-Ed; *The Right Stuff*, 1983 – Co-Ed

RALPH ROSENBLUM (2): *Long Day's Journey into Night*, 1962 – Ed; *Annie Hall*, 1977 – Ed

GENE RUGGIERO (2): *Ninotchka*, 1939 – Ed; *The Shop Around the Corner*, 1940 – Ed

Frank Santillo (1): *Ride the High Country*, 1962 – Ed

ARTHUR SCHMIDT (4): *Sunset Boulevard*, 1950 – Co-Ed; *Ace in the Hole*, 1951 – Co-Ed; *Some Like it Hot*, 1959 – Ed; *Who Framed Roger Rabbit?*, 1988 – *Ed

BLANCHE SEWELL (3): *Grand Hotel*, 1932 – Ed; *Queen Christina*, 1933 – Ed; *The Wizard of Oz*, 1939 – Ed

Melvin Shapiro (1): *Taxi Driver*, 1976 – Co-Ed

Billy Shea (1): *Love Me Tonight*, 1932 – Ed

Gerald Shepard (1): *Five Easy Pieces*, 1970 – Co-Ed

Don Siegel (1): *Casablanca*, 1942 – opening montage

Claire Simpson (1): *Salvador*, 1986 – Ed

Robert Simpson (1): *The Grapes of Wrath*, 1940 – Ed

JAMES SMITH (3): *The Birth of a Nation*, 1915 – Ed; *Intolerance*, 1916 – Co-Ed; *Broken Blossoms*, 1919 – Ed

Rose Smith (1): *Intolerance*, 1916 – Co-Ed

DOROTHY SPENCER (4): *Stagecoach*, 1939 – Co-Ed; *To Be or Not To Be*, 1942 – Ed; *My Darling Clementine*, 1946 – Ed; *The Ghost and Mrs Muir*, 1947 – Ed

Thomas Stanford (1): *West Side Story*, 1961, – *Ed

AARON STELL (2): *Touch of Evil*, 1958 – Co-Ed; *To Kill a Mockingbird*, 1962 – Ed

Douglas Stewart (1): *The Right Stuff*, 1983 – Co-Ed

LeRoy Stone (1): *Duck Soup*, 1933 – Ed

FRANK SULLIVAN (2): *Fury*, 1936 – Ed; *The Philadelphia Story*, 1940 – Ed

Gregg Tallas (1): *The Southerner*, 1945 – Ed

Walter Thompson (1): *Young Mr Lincoln*, 1939 – Ed

Sherman Todd (1): *They Live by Night*, 1949 – Ed

GEORGE TOMASINI (6): *Rear Window*, 1954 – Ed; *Vertigo*, 1958 – Ed; *North by Northwest*, 1959 – Ed; *Psycho*, 1960 – Ed; *The Birds*, 1963 – Ed; *Marnie*, 1964 – Ed

Virgil Vogel (1): *Touch of Evil*, 1958 – Co-Ed

JOSEF VON STERNBERG (2): *Shanghai Express*, 1932 – Ed, uc; *The Scarlet Empress*, 1934 – Ed, uc

Slavko Vorkapich (1): *Mr Smith Goes to Washington*, 1939 – montage

Paul Weatherwax (1): *The Naked City*, 1948 – *Ed

Billy Weber (1): *Days of Heaven*, 1978 – Ed

FERRIS WEBSTER (2): *The Manchurian Candidate*, 1962 – Ed; *The Outlaw Josey Wales*, 1976 – Ed

David Weisbart (1): *A Streetcar Named Desire*, 1951 – Ed

George White (1): *The Postman Always Rings Twice*, 1946 – Ed

Elmo Williams (1): *High Noon*, 1953 – Co-Ed

RALPH E. WINTERS (3): *On the Town*, 1949 – Ed; *Seven Brides for Seven Brothers*, 1954 – Ed; *Ben-Hur*, 1959 – *Co-Ed

ROBERT WISE (3): *The Hunchback of Notre Dame*, 1939 – Co-Ed; *Citizen Kane*, 1941 – Co-Ed; *The Magnificent Ambersons*, 1942 – Co-Ed

Robert L. Wolfe (1): *All the President's Men*, 1976 – Ed

Theron Worth (1): *Notorious*, 1946 – Ed

Robert Wyman (1): *Rosemary's Baby*, 1968 – Co-Ed

HUGH WYNN (2): *The Big Parade*, 1925 – Ed; *The Crowd*, 1928 – Ed

WILLIAM H. ZIEGLER (3): *Spellbound*, 1945 – Ed; *Strangers on a Train*, 1951 – Ed; *Rebel without a Cause*, 1955 – Ed

PETER ZINNER (3): *The Godfather*, 1972 – Co-Ed; *The Godfather Part II*, 1974 – Co-Ed; *The Deer Hunter*, 1978 – *Ed

IV – List of Performers

This is an alphabetical list of all performers who appeared in two or more of the films treated in this collection (capital letters for more than two appearances):

> L = Male and female leads (including 'The Stars')
> LS = Leading support players
> S = Support players

F. Murray Abraham (2): *All the President's Men*, 1976 – S; *Amadeus*, 1984 – LS

Edie Adams (2): *The Apartment*, 1960 – S; *Days of Heaven*, 1978 – S

John Agar (2): *Fort Apache*, 1948 L; *She Wore a Yellow Ribbon*, 1949 – L

Claude Akins (2): *From Here to Eternity*, 1953 – S; *Rio Bravo*, 1959 – S

Frank Albertson (2): *Fury*, 1936 – S; *Psycho*, 1960 – S

Jane Alexander (2): *All the President's Men*, 1976 – S; *Kramer vs Kramer* – LS

Katharine Alexander (2): *Stage Door*, 1937 – S; *The Hunchback of Notre Dame*, 1939 – S

Elizabeth Allan (2): *David Copperfield*, 1935 – LS; *Camille*, 1936 – LS

WOODY ALLEN (3): *Annie Hall*, 1977 – L; *Manhattan*, 1979 – L; *Hannah and Her Sisters*, 1986 – L

LEON AMES (3): *Meet Me in St Louis*, 1944 – LS; *They Were Expendable*, 1945 – S; *The Postman Always Rings Twice*, 1946 – LS

Judith Anderson (2): *Rebecca*, 1940 – LS; *Laura*, 1944 – LS

DANA ANDREWS (3): *The Oxbow Incident*, 1943 – L; *Laura*, 1944 – L; *The Best Years of Our Lives*, 1946

EVE ARDEN (3): *Stage Door*, 1937 – LS; *Mildred Pierce*, 1945 – LS; *Anatomy of a Murder*, 1959 – LS

JEAN ARTHUR (4): *Mr Deeds Goes to Town*, 1936 – L; *Only Angels Have Wings*, 1939 – L; *Mr Smith Goes to Washington*, 1939 – L; *Shane*, 1953 – L

Robert Arthur (2): *Twelve o'Clock High*, 1946 – S; *Ace in the Hole*, 1951 – S

FRED ASTAIRE (4): *Top Hat*, 1935 – L; *Swing Time*, 1936 – L; *The Band Wagon*, 1953 – L; *Funny Face*, 1957 – L

MARY ASTOR (5): *Dodsworth*, 1936 – LS; *The Prisoner of Zenda*, 1937 – LS; *The Maltese Falcon*, 1941 – L; *The Palm Beach Story*, 1942 – LS; *Meet Me in St Louis*, 1944 – LS

Roscoe Ates (2): *Gone with the Wind*, 1939 – S; *The Palm Beach Story*, 1942 – S

IRVING BACON (8): *I Am a Fugitive from a Chain Gang*, 1932 – S; *It Happened One Night*, 1934 – S; *Mr Deeds Goes to Town*, 1936 – S; *Gone with the Wind*, 1939 – S; *The Grapes of Wrath*, 1940 – S; *Shadow of a Doubt*, 1943 – S; *Spellbound*, 1945 – S; *A Star Is Born*, 1954 – S

Carroll Baker (2): *Baby Doll*, 1956 – L; *Giant*, 1956 – LS

Diane Baker (2): *Marnie*, 1964 – S; *The Silence of the Lambs*, 1991 – S

William Bakewell (2): *All Quiet on the Western Front*, 1930 – LS; *Gone with the Wind*, 1939 – S

Lucille Ball (2): *Top Hat*, 1935 – S; *Stage Door*, 1937 – LS

MARTIN BALSAM (4): *On the Waterfront*, 1954 – S; *Twelve Angry Men*, 1957 – LS; *Psycho*, 1960 – LS; *All the President's Men*, 1976 – LS

Anne Bancroft (2): *The Miracle Worker*, 1962 – *L; *The Graduate*, 1967 – L

George Bancroft (2): *Mr Deeds Goes to Town*, 1936 – LS; *Stagecoach*, 1939 – LS

George Barbier (2): *The Merry Widow*, 1934 – LS; *Yankee Doodle Dandy*, 1942 – S

VINCE BARNETT (3): *All Quiet on the Western Front*, 1930 – S; *Scarface*, 1932 – S; *The Killers*, 1946 – S

John Barrymore (2): *Grand Hotel*, 1932 – L; *Dinner at Eight*, 1933 – L

LIONEL BARRYMORE (4): *Grand Hotel*, 1932 – LS; *Dinner at Eight*, 1933 – LS; *David Copperfield*, 1935 – LS; *Camille*, 1936 – LS

Richard Barthelmess (2): *Broken Blossoms*, 1919 – L; *Only Angels Have Wings*, 1939 – LS

Florence Bates (2): *Rebecca*, 1940 – S; *On the Town*, 1949 – S

Anne Baxter (2): *The Magnificent Ambersons*, 1942 – L; *All About Eve*, 1950 – L

Ned Beatty (2): *Nashville*, 1975 – LS; *All the President's Men*, 1976 – S

Louise Beavers (2): *Forty-Second Street*, 1933 – S; *She Done Him Wrong*, 1933 – S

Don Beddoe (2): *The Best Years of Our Lives*, 1946 – S; *The Night of the Hunter*, 1955 – S

NOAH BEERY JR. (3): *Only Angels Have Wings*, 1919 – S; *Of Mice and Men*, 1939 – S; *Red River*, 1948 – S

Wallace Beery (2): *Grand Hotel*, 1932 – L; *Dinner at Eight*, 1933 – L

RALPH BELLAMY (3): *The Awful Truth*, 1937 – LS; *His Girl Friday*, 1940 – LS; *Rosemary's Baby*, 1968 – LS

Richard Benedict (2): *Crossfire*, 1947 – S; *Ace in the Hole*, 1951 – S

Marjorie Bennett (2): *Limelight*, 1952 – S; *Kiss Me Deadly*, 1955 – S

HENRY BERGMAN (4): *The Kid*, 1921 – S; *The Gold Rush*, 1925 – S; *City Lights*, 1930 – S; *Modern Times*, 1936 – S

INGRID BERGMAN (3): *Casablanca*, 1942 – L; *Spellbound*, 1945 – L; *Notorious*, 1946 – L

Abner Biberman (2): *Gunga Din*, 1939 – S; *His Girl Friday*, 1940 – S

Charles Bickford (2): *Of Mice and Men*, 1939 – LS; *A Star Is Born*, 1954 – LS

Herman Bing (2): *Dinner at Eight*, 1933 – S; *Dumbo*, 1941 – S, the voice of the ringmaster

Edward Binns (2): *Twelve Angry Men* – S; *Patton*, 1970 – S

WHIT BISSELL (3): *The Red Badge of Courage*, 1951 – S; *Invasion of the Body Snatchers*, 1956 – S; *The Manchurian Candidate*, 1962 – S

Karen Black (2): *Five Easy Pieces*, 1970 – L; *Nashville*, 1975 – LS

Sidney Blackmer (2): *Little Caesar*, 1930 – LS; *Rosemary's Baby*, 1968 – LS

Joan Blondell (2): *The Public Enemy*, 1931 – LS; *The Gold Diggers of 1933* – LS

ERIC BLORE (4): *Top Hat*, 1935 – S; *Swing Time*, 1936 – S; *The Lady Eve*, 1941 – S; *Sullivan's Travels*, 1941 – S

MONTE BLUE (3): *The Birth of a Nation*, 1915 – S; *Intolerance*, 1916 – S; *The Palm Beach Story*, 1942 – S

HUMPHREY BOGART (7): *High Sierra*, 1941 – L; *The Maltese Falcon*, 1941 – L; *Casablanca*, 1941 – L; *To Have and Have Not*, 1944 – L; *The Big Sleep*, 1946 – L; *The Treasure of the Sierra Madre*, 1948 – L; *In a Lonely Place*, 1950 – L

Roman Bohnen (2): *Of Mice and Men*, 1939 – S; *The Best Years of Our Lives*, 1946 – S

FORTUNIO BONANOVA (3): *Citizen Kane*, 1941 – S; *Double Indemnity*, 1944 – S; *Kiss Me Deadly*, 1955 – S

WARD BOND (13): *It Happened One Night*, 1934 – S; *Bringing Up Baby*, 1938 – S; *Young Mr Lincoln*, 1939 – S; *Gone with the Wind*, 1939 – S; *The Grapes of Wrath*, 1940 – S; *The Maltese Falcon*, 1941 – S; *They Were Expendable*, 1945 – LS; *My Darling Clementine*, 1946 – LS; *Fort Apache*, 1948 – LS; *Wagonmaster*, 1950 – LS; *The Quiet Man*, 1952 – LS; *The Searchers*, 1956 – LS; *Rio Bravo*, 1959 – LS

Beulah Bondi (2): *Mr Smith Goes to Washington*, 1939 – S; *The Southerner*, 1945 – LS

ERNEST BORGNINE (3): *From Here to Eternity*, 1953 – LS; *Bad Day at Black Rock*, 1954 – LS; *The Wild Bunch*, 1969 – LS

SAM BOTTOMS (3): *The Last Picture Show*, 1971 – S; *The Outlaw Josey Wales*, 1975 – S; *Apocalypse Now*, 1979 – S

MARLON BRANDO (4): *A Streetcar Named Desire*, 1951 – L: *On the Waterfront*, 1954 – *L; *The Godfather*, 1972 – *L; *Apocalypse Now*, 1979 – L

WALTER BRENNAN (7): *The Bride of Frankenstein*, 1935 – S; *Fury*, 1936 – S; *To Have and Have Not*, 1944 – LS; *My Darling Clementine*, 1946 – LS; *Red River*, 1948 – LS; *Bad Day at Black Rock*, 1954 – LS; *Rio Bravo*, 1959 – LS

FELIX BRESSART (3): *Ninotchka*, 1939 – S; *The Shop Around the Corner*, 1939 – S; *To Be or Not To Be*, 1942 – S

ALAN BRIDGE (8): *The Awful Truth*, 1937 – S; *Mr Smith Goes to Washington*, 1939 – S; *The Little Foxes*, 1941 – S; *The Lady Eve*, 1941 – S; *Sullivan's Travels*, 1941 – S; *The Palm Beach Story*, 1942 – S; *The Miracle of Morgan's Creek*, 1943 – S; *They Were Expendable*, 1945 – S

Jeff Bridges (2): *The Last Picture Show*, 1971 – L; *Fat City*, 1972 – L

VIRGINIA BRISSAC (4): *Destry Rides Again*, 1939 – S; *Young Mr Lincoln*, 1939 – S; *The Little Foxes*, 1941 – S; *Rebel without a Cause*, 1955 – S

Helen Broderick (2): *Top Hat*, 1935 – LS; *Swing Time*, 1936 – LS

Steve Brodie (2): *Crossfire*, 1947 – LS; *Out of the Past*, 1947 – LS

EDWARD BROPHY (3): *The Cameraman*, 1928 – S; *The Thin Man*, 1934 – S; *Dumbo*, 1941 – S, voice of Timothy Mouse

CRARLES D. BROWN (5): *It Happened One Night*, 1934 – S; *The Grapes of Wrath*, 1940 – S; *The Big Sleep*, 1946 – S; *The Killers*, 1946 – S; *Notorious*, 1946 – S

Vanessa Brown (2): *The Ghost and Mrs Muir*, 1947 – S; *The Bad and the Beautiful*, 1952 – S

Nigel Bruce (2): *Rebecca*, 1940 – LS; *Limelight*, 1952 – LS

Edgar Buchanan (2): *Shane*, 1953 – LS; *Ride the High Country*, 1962 – LS

BILLIE BURKE (3): *Dinner at Eight*, 1933 – LS; *It's a Gift*, 1934 – S; *The Wizard of Oz*, 1939 – LS

JAMES BURKE (3): *It Happened One Night*, 1934 – S; *The Scarlet Empress*, 1934 – S; *The Maltese Falcon*, 1941 – S

James Caan (2): *The Godfather*, 1972 – LS; *The Godfather Part II*, 1974 – S

Bruce Cabot (2): *King Kong*, 1933 – LS; *Fury*, 1936 – LS

JAMES CAGNEY (3): *The Public Enemy*, 1932 – L; *Yankee Doodle Dandy*, 1942; *White Heat*, 1949 – L

LOUIS CALHERN (3): *Duck Soup*, 1931 – LS; *Notorious*, 1946 – LS; *The Asphalt Jungle*, 1950 – LS

Harry Carey (2): *Mr Smith Goes to Washington*, 1939 – S; *Red River*, 1948 – S

HARRY CAREY JR. (6): *Red River*, 1948 – S; *She Wore a Yellow Ribbon*, 1949 – LS; *Wagonmaster*, 1950 – LS; *Gentlemen Prefer Blondes*, 1953 – S; *The Searchers*, 1956 – S; *Rio Bravo*, 1959 – S

Timothy Carey (2): *East of Eden*, 1955 – S; *Paths of Glory*, 1957 – S

Hoagy Carmichael (2): *To Have and Have Not*, 1944 – LS; *The Best Years of Our Lives*, 1946 – LS

Leslie Caron (2): *An American in Paris*, 1951 – L; *Gigi*, 1958 – L

JOHN CARRADINE (5): *The Bride of Frankenstein*, 1935 – S; *Stagecoach*, 1939 – LS; *The Grapes of Wrath*, 1940 – LS; *The Man Who Shot Liberty Vallance*, 1962 – S; *The Shootist*, 1976 – S

LEO C. CARROLL (6): *Wuthering Heights*, 1939, – S; *Rebecca*, 1940 – S; *Spellbound*, 1945 – LS; *Strangers on a Train*, 1951 – S; *The Bad and the Beautiful*, 1952 – S; *North by Northwest*, 1959 – LS

JACK CARSON (6): *Stage Door*, 1937 – S; *Bringing Up Baby*, 1938 – S; *Mr Smith Goes to Washington*, 1939 – S; *Destry Rides Again*, 1939 – S; *Mildred Pierce*, 1945 – LS; *A Star Is Born*, 1954 – LS

Joanna Cassidy (2): *Blade Runner*, 1982 – LS; *Who Framed Roger Rabbit?*, 1988 – LS

WALTER CATLETT (3): *Mr Deeds Goes to Town*, 1936, – S; *Bringing Up Baby*, 1938 – S; *Pinocchio*, 1940 – S, the voice of J. Worthington Foulfellow

JOHN CAZALE (4): *The Godfather*, 1972 – S; *The Conversation*, 1974 – S; *The Godfather Part II*, 1974 – S; *The Deer Hunter*, 1978 – S

George Chakiris (2): *Gentlemen Prefer Blondes*, 1953 – S; *West Side Story*, 1961 – *LS

Lon Chaney Jr. (2): *Of Mice and Men*, 1939 – LS; *High Noon*, 1952 – LS

CHARLES CHAPLIN (6): *The Kid*, 1921 – L; *The Gold Rush*, 1925 – L; *City Lights*, 1930 – S; *Modern Times*, 1936 – L; *The Great Dictator*, 1940 – L; *Limelight*, 1952 – L

Cyd Charisse (2): *Singin' in the Rain*, 1952 – LS; *The Band Wagon*, 1953 – L

SPENCER CHARTERS (4): *Mr Deeds Goes to Town*, 1936 – S; *The Prisoner of Zenda*, 1937 – S; *Young Mr Lincoln*, 1939 – S; *The Hunchback of Notre Dame*, 1939 – S

MAURICE CHEVALIER (3): *Love Me Tonight*, 1932 – L; *The Merry Widow*, 1934 – L; *Gigi*, 1958 – L

Berton Churchill (2): *I Am a Fugitive from a Chain Gang*, 1932 – S; *Stagecoach*, 1939 – S

Fred Clark (2): *White Heat*, 1949 – S; *Sunset Boulevard*, 1950 – LS

Mae Clarke (2): *The Public Enemy*, 1931 – LS; *Frankenstein*, 1931 – L

Montgomery Clift (2): *Red River*, 1948 L; *From Here to Eternity*, 1953 – L

Elmer Clifton (2): *The Birth of a Nation*, 1915 – S; *Intolerance*, 1916 – S

Colin Clive (2): *Frankenstein*, 1931 – L; *The Bride of Frankenstein*, 1935 – L

Lee J. Cobb (2): *On the Waterfront*, 1954 – LS; *Twelve Angry Men*, 1957 – LS

Charles Coburn (2): *The Lady Eve*, 1941 – LS; *Gentlemen Prefer Blondes*, 1953 – LS

Steve Cochran (2): *The Best Years of Our Lives*, 1946 – S; *White Heat*, 1949 – LS

Nicholas Colasanto (2): *Fat City*, 1972 – LS; *Raging Bull*, 1980 – LS

Claudette Colbert (2): *It Happened One Night*, 1934 – *L; *The Palm Beach Story*, 1942 – L

Constance Collier (2): *Intolerance*, 1916 – S; *Stage Door*, 1937 – LS

Patricia Collinge (2): *The Little Foxes*, 1941 – LS; *Shadow of a Doubt*, 1943 – LS

RAY COLLINS (4): *Citizen Kane*, 1941 – S: *The Magnificent Ambersons*, 1942 – S; *The Best Years of Our Lives*, 1946 – S; *Touch of Evil*, 1958 – S

Ronald Colman (2): *The Lost Horizon*, 1937 – L; *The Prisoner of Zenda*, 1937 – L

Dorothy Comingore (2): *Mr Smith Goes to Washington*, 1939 – bit as Linda Winters; *Citizen Kane*, 1941 – LS

CHESTER CONKLIN (6): *Greed*, 1924 – S; *Modern Times*, 1936 – S; *The Great Dictator*, 1940 – S; *Sullivan's Travels*, 1941 – S; *The Palm Beach Story*, 1942 – S; *The Miracle of Morgan's Creek*, 1943 – S

JIMMY CONLIN (5): *The Lady Eve*, 1941 – S; *Sullivan's Travels*, 1941 – S; *The Palm Beach Story*, 1942 – S; *The Miracle of Morgan's Creek*, 1943 – S; *Anatomy of a Murder*, 1959 – S

WALTER CONNOLLY (3): *It Happened One Night*, 1934 – LS; *Nothing Sacred*, 1937 – LS; *The Good Earth*, 1937 – LS

FRANK CONROY (3): *Grand Hotel*, 1932 – S; *The Oxbow Incident*, 1943 – S; *The Naked City*, 1948 – S

ELISHA COOK JR. (4): *The Maltese Falcon*, 1941 – S; *The Big Sleep*, 1946 – S; *Shane*, 1955 – S; *Rosemary's Baby*, 1968 – S

Gary Cooper (2): *Mr Deeds Goes to Town*, 1936 – L; *High Noon*, 1952 – *L

Gladys Cooper (2): *Rebecca*, 1940 – S; *The Pirate*, 1948 – LS

MELVILLE COOPER (3): *The Adventures of Robin Hood*, 1938 – S; *Rebecca*, 1940 – S; *The Lady Eve*, 1941 – S

Miriam Cooper (2): *The Birth of a Nation*, 1915 – LS; *Intolerance* 1916 – S

Robert Coote (2): *Gunga Din*, 1939 – S; *The Ghost and Mrs Muir*, 1947 – S

Ellen Corby (2): *Shane*, 1953 – S; *Vertigo*, 1958 – S

JOSEPH COTTEN (4): *Citizen Kane*, 1941 – L; *The Magnificent Ambersons*, 1942 – L; *Shadow of a Doubt*, 1943 – L; *Touch of Evil*, 1958 – S, cameo

Jerome Cowan (2): *High Sierra*, 1941 – S; *The Maltese Falcon*, 1941 – S

Broderick Crawford (2): *All the King's Men*, 1949 – *L; *Born Yesterday*, 1950 – L

Joan Crawford (2): *Grand Hotel*, 1932 – LS; *Mildred Pierce*, 1945 – L

Laura Hope Crews (2): *Camille*, 1936 – LS; *Gone with the Wind*, 1939 – LS

DONALD CRISP (7): *The Birth of a Nation*, 1915 – S; *Intolerance*, 1916 – S; *Broken Blossoms*, 1919 – LS, *Mutiny on the Bounty*, 1935 – LS; *Wuthering Heights*, 1939 – S; *The Sea Hawk*, 1940 – LS; *How Green Was My Valley*, 1941 – *LS

Hume Cronyn (2): *Shadow of a Doubt*, 1943 – S; *The Postman Always Rings Twice*, 1946 – LS

Scatman Crothers (2): *One Flew over the Cuckoo's Nest*, 1975 - S; *The Shootist*, 1976 - S

Tony Curtis (2): *Sweet Smell of Success*, 1957 - L; *Some Like it Hot*, 1959 - L

Esther Dale (2): *Fury*, 1936 - S; *The Awful Truth*, 1937 - S

MARCEL DALIO (3): *Casablanca*, 1942 - S; *To Have and Have Not*, 1944 - S; *Gentlemen Prefer Blondes*, 1953 - S

HENRY DANIELL (6): *Camille*, 1936 - LS; *The Awful Truth*, 1937 - S; *The Sea Hawk*, 1940 - S; *The Great Dictator*, 1940 - LS; *The Philadelphia Story*, 1940 - S; *Witness for the Prosecution*, 1957 - S

Helmut Dantine (2): *To Be or Not To Be*, 1942 - S; *Casablanca*, 1942 - S

Alexander D'Arcy (2): *The Prisoner of Zenda*, 1937 - S; *The Awful Truth*, 1937 - S

Frankie Darro (2): *The Public Enemy*, 1931 - S; *Pinocchio*, 1940 - S, the voice of Lampwick

JANE DARWELL; (7): *The Scarlet Empress*, 1934 - S; *Gone with the Wind*, 1939 - S; *The Grapes of Wrath* 1940 - *LS; *The Oxbow Incident*, 1943 - LS; *My Darling Clementine*, 1946 - S; *Wagonmaster*, 1950 - LS; *Mary Poppins*, 1964 - S

Howard Da Silva (2): *The Lost Weekend*, 1945 - LS; *They Live by Night*, 1949 - LS

HARRY DAVENPORT (4): *Gone with the Wind*, 1939 - S; *The Hunchback of Notre Dame*, 1939 - S; *The Oxbow Incident*, 1943 - S; *Meet Me in St Louis*, 1944 - LS

Bette Davis (2): *The Little Foxes*, 1941 - L; *All About Eve*, 1950 - L

Ted De Corsia (2): *The Lady from Shanghai*, 1948 - S; *The Naked City*, 1948 - LS

Sam De Grasse (2): *The Birth of a Nation*, 1915 - S; *Intolerance*, 1916 - S

Olivia de Havilland (2): *The Adventures of Robin Hood*, 1938 - L; *Gone with the Wind*, 1939 - L

ALBERT DEKKER (4): *The Killers*, 1946 - LS; *East of Eden*, 1955 - S; *Kiss Me Deadly*, 1955 - LS; *The Wild Bunch*, 1969 - S

WILLIAM DEMAREST (5): *Mr Smith Goes to Washington*, 1939 – S; *The Lady Eve*, 1941 – LS; *Sullivan's Travels*, 1941 – S; *The Palm Beach Story*, 1942 – S; *The Miracle of Morgan's Creek*, 1943 – LS

ROBERT DE NIRO (5): *Mean Streets*, 1973 – L; *The Godfather Part II*, 1974 – *L; *The Deer Hunter*, 1978 – L; *Raging Bull*, 1980 – L; *The King of Comedy*, 1983 – L

ANDY DEVINE (3): *Stagecoach*, 1939 – S; *The Red Badge of Courage*, 1951 – S; *The Man Who Shot Liberty Vallance*, 1962 – S

John Dierkes (2): *The Red Badge of Courage*, 1951 – S; *Shane*, 1953 – S

MARLENE DIETRICH (4): *Shanghai Express*, 1932 – L; *The Scarlet Empress*, 1934 – L; *Destry Rides Again*, 1939 – L; *Touch of Evil*, 1958 – S, cameo

Brian Donlevy (2): *Destry Rides Again*, 1939 – LS; *The Miracle of Morgan's Creek*, 1943 – S, cameo

Ruth Donnelly (2): *Mr Deeds Goes to Town*, 1936 – S; *Mr Smith Goes to Washington*, 1939 – S

King Donovan (2): *Singin' in the Rain*, 1952 – S; *Invasion of the Body Snatchers*, 1956 – S

Ann Doran (2): *Mr Smith Goes to Washington*, 1939 – S; *Rebel without a Cause*, 1955 – S

Don Douglas (2): *Murder My Sweet*, 1946 – S; *Gilda*, 1946 – S

KIRK DOUGLAS (4): *Out of the Past*, 1947 – LS; *Ace in the Hole*, 1951 – L; *The Bad and the Beautiful*, 1952 – L; *Paths of Glory*, 1957 – L

Melvyn Douglas (2): *The Old Dark House*, 1932 – L; *Ninotchka*, 1939 – L

RICHARD DREYFUSS (4): *The Graduate*, 1967 – S, bit; *American Graffiti*, 1973 – L; *Jaws*, 1975; *Close Encounters of the Third Kind*, 1977 – L

JOANNE DRU (4): *Red River*, 1948 – L; *All the King's Men*, 1949 – L; *She Wore a Yellow Ribbon*, 1949 – L; *Wagonmaster*, 1950 – L

Howard Duff (2): *The Naked City*, 1948 – L; *Kramer vs Kramer*, 1979 – LS

Tom Dugan (2): *To Be or Not To Be*, 1942 – S; *On the Town*, 1949 – S

Douglas Dumbrille (2): *I Am a Fugitive from a Chain Gang*, 1932 – S; *Mr Deeds Goes to Town*, 1936 – S

Margaret Dumont (2): *Duck Soup*, 1933 – LS; *A Night at the Opera*, 1935 – LS

Faye Dunaway (2): *Bonnie and Clyde*, 1967 – L; *Chinatown*, 1974 – L

Emma Dunn (2): *Mr Deeds Goes to Town*, 1936 – S; *The Great Dictator*, 1940 – S

ROBERT DUVALL (5): *To Kill a Mockingbird*, 1962 – LS; *M*A*S*H*, 1970 – LS; *The Godfather*, 1972 – LS; *The Godfather Part II*, 1974 – LS; *Apocalypse Now*, 1979 – LS

Shelley Duvall (2): *Nashville*, 1975 – LS; *Annie Hall*, 1977 – LS

Clint Eastwood (2): *Play Misty for Me*, 1971 – L; *The Outlaw Josey Wales*, 1976 – L

CLIFF EDWARDS (4): *Gone with the Wind*, 1939 – S; *His Girl Friday*, 1940 – S; *Pinocchio*, 1940 – S, voice of Jiminy Cricket; *Dumbo*, 1941 – S, voice of Jim Crow

EDWARD ELLIS (3): *I Am a Fugitive from a Chain Gang*, 1932 – S; *The Thin Man*, 1934 – S; *Fury*, 1936 – S

Madge Evans (2): *Dinner at Eight*, 1933 – LS; *David Copperfield*, 1935 – L

DOUGLAS FAIRBANKS JR. (3): *Little Caesar*, 1930 – L; *The Prisoner of Zenda*, 1937 – L; *Gunga Din*, 1939 – L

Glenda Farrell (2): *Little Caesar*, 1930 – LS; *I Am a Fugitive from a Chain Gang*, 1932 – LS

Mia Farrow (2): *Rosemary's Baby*, 1968 – L; *Hannah and Her Sisters*, 1986 – L

FRANK FAYLEN (3): *Gone with the Wind*, 1939 – S; *The Grapes of Wrath*, 1940 – S; *The Lost Weekend*, 1945 – S

Fritz Feld (2): *A Night at the Opera*, 1935 – S; *Bringing Up Baby*, 1938 – S

Betty Field (2): *Of Mice and Men*, 1930 – L; *The Southerner*, 1945 – L

W.C. FIELDS (3): *It's a Gift*, 1934 – L; *David Copperfield*, 1935 – LS; *The Bank Dick*, 1940 – L

James (Jimmy) Finlayson (2): *Way Out West*, 1937 – S; *To Be or Not To Be*, 1942 – S

Carrie Fisher (2): *Star Wars*, 1977 – L; *Hannah and Her Sisters*, 1986 – L

BARRY FITZGERALD (4): *Bringing Up Baby*, 1938 – LS; *How Green Was My Valley*, 1941 – LS; *The Naked City*, 1948 – LS; *The Quiet Man*, 1952 – LS

PAUL FIX (3): *Scarface*, 1932 – S; *Red River*, 1948 – S; *To Kill a Mockingbird*, 1962 – S

JAMES FLAVIN (3): *King Kong*, 1933 – S; *The Grapes of Wrath*, 1940 – S; *Laura*, 1944 – S

Errol Flynn (2): *The Adventures of Robin Hood*, 1938, – L; *The Sea Hawk*, 1940 – L

HENRY FONDA (7): *Young Mr Lincoln*, 1939 – L; *The Grapes of Wrath*, 1940 – L; *The Lady Eve*, 1941 – L; *The Oxbow Incident*, 1943 – L; *My Darling Clementine*, 1946 – L; *Fort Apache*, 1948 – L; *Twelve Angry Men*, 1957 – L

JOAN FONTAINE (3): *Gunga Din*, 1939 – L; *Rebecca*, 1940 – L; *Letter from an Unknown Woman*, 1948 – L

MARY FORBES (3): *Stage Door*, 1937 – S; *The Awful Truth*, 1937 – S; *Ninotchka*, 1939 – S

FRANCIS FORD (7): *The Informer*, 1935 – S; *Stagecoach*, 1939 – S; *Young Mr Lincoln*, 1939 – S; *The Oxbow Incident*, 1943 – S; *My Darling Clementine*, 1946 – L; *Wagonmaster*, 1950 – S; *The Quiet Man*, 1952 – S

Glenn Ford (2): *Gilda*, 1946 – L; *The Big Heat*, 1953 – L

HARRISON FORD (7): *American Graffiti*, 1973 – S; *The Conversation*, 1974 – S; *Star Wars*, 1977 – LS; *Apocalypse Now*, 1979 – S; *Raiders of the Lost Ark*, 1981 – L; *Blade Runner*, 1982 – L; *Witness*, 1983 – L

Paul Ford (2): *The Naked City*, 1948 – S; *All the King's Men*, 1949 – S

WALLACE FORD (3): *The Informer*, 1935 – S; *Shadow of a Doubt*, 1943 – S; *Spellbound*, 1945 – S

Jodie Foster (2): *Taxi Driver*, 1976 – LS; *The Silence of the Lambs*, 1991 –*L

Preston Foster (2): *I Am a Fugitive from a Chain Gang*, 1932 – LS; *The Informer*, 1935 – LS

BYRON FOULGER (4): *The Awful Truth*, 1937 – S; *The Prisoner of Zenda*, 1937 – S; *Sullivan's Travels*, 1941 – S; *The Miracle of Morgan's Creek*, 1943 – S

Dwight Frye (2): *Frankenstein*, 1931 – S; *The Bride of Frankenstein*, 1935 – S

CLARK GABLE (3): *It Happened One Night*, 1934 – *L; *Mutiny on the Bounty*, 1935 – L; *Gone with the Wind*, 1939 – L

GRETA GARBO (4): *Grand Hotel*, 1932 – L; *Queen Christina*, 1933 – L; *Camille*, 1936 – L; *Ninotchka*, 1939 – L

Allen Garfield (2): *The Conversation*, 1974 – LS; *Nashville*, 1975 – LS

JUDY GARLAND (4): *The Wizard of Oz*, 1939 – *L; *Meet Me in St Louis*, 1944 – L; *The Pirate*, 1948 – L; *A Star Is Born*, 1954 – L

Teri Garr (2): *The Conversation*, 1974 – S; *Close Encounters of the Third Kind*, 1977 – LS

Gladys George (2): *The Maltese Falcon*, 1941, – S; *The Best Years of Our Lives*, 1946 – S

STEVEN GERAY (4): *Spellbound*, 1945 – S; *Gilda*, 1946 – S; *All About Eve*, 1950 – S; *Gentlemen Prefer Blondes*, 1953 – S

BILLY GILBERT (6): *Sons of the Desert*, 1933 – S, voice-over; *A Night at the Opera*, 1935 – S; *Snow White and the Seven Dwarfs*, 1938 – S, voice of Sneezy; *Destry Rides Again*, 1939 – S; *His Girl Friday*, 1940 – S; *The Great Dictator*, 1940 – S

John Gilbert (2): *The Big Parade*, 1925 – L; *Queen Christina*, 1933 – L

LILLIAN GISH (5): *The Birth of a Nation*, 1915 – L; *Intolerance*, 1916 – L; *Broken Blossoms*, 1919 – L; *The Wind*, 1928 – L; *The Night of the Hunter*, 1955 – L

SCOTT GLENN (3): *Nashville*, 1975 – LS; *The Right Stuff*, 1983 – LS; *The Silence of the Lambs*, 1991 – LS

Paulette Goddard (2): *Modern Times*, 1936 – L; *The Great Dictator*, 1940 – L

Jeff Goldblum (2): *Nashville*, 1975 – LS; *Annie Hall*, 1977 – S, bit

MINNA GOMBELL (5): *The Thin Man*, 1934 – S; *The Merry Widow*, 1934 – S; *The Hunchback of Notre Dame*, 1939 – S; *High Sierra*, 1941 – S; *The Best Years of Our Lives*, 1946 – S

Elliott Gould (2): *M*A*S*H*, 1970 – L; *Nashville*, 1975 – S, as himself

Gibson Gowland (2): *The Birth of a Nation*, 1915 – S; *Greed*, 1924 – L

GLORIA GRAHAME (4): *Crossfire*, 1947 – S; *In a Lonely Place*, 1950 – LS; *The Bad and the Beautiful*, 1952 – *LS; *The Big Heat*, 1953 – LS

Farley Granger (2): *They Live by Night*, 1949 – L; *Strangers on a Train*, 1951 – L

CARY GRANT (9): *She Done Him Wrong*, 1933 – LS; *The Awful Truth*, 1937 – L; *Bringing Up Baby*, 1938 – L; *Gunga Din*, 1939 – L; *Only Angels Have Wings*, 1939 – L; *His Girl Friday*, 1940 – L; *The Philadelphia Story*, 1940 – L; *Notorious*, 1946 – L; *North by Northwest*, 1959 – L

Kathryn Grant (2): *Rear Window*, 1954 – S; *Anatomy of a Murder*, 1959 – S

CHARLES (Charley) GRAPEWIN (3): *The Good Earth*, 1937 – LS; *The Wizard of Oz*, 1939 – S; *The Grapes of Wrath*, 1940 – LS

Sydney Greenstreet (2): *The Maltese Falcon*, 1941 – LS; *Casablanca*, 1942 – S

James Gregory (2): *The Naked City*, 1948 – S; *The Manchurian Candidate*, 1962 – S

ROBERT GREIG (5): *Love Me Tonight*, 1932 – S; *Trouble in Paradise*, 1932 – S; *The Lady Eve*, 1941 – S; *Sullivan's Travels*, 1941 – S; *The Palm Beach Story*, 1942 – S

Paul Guilfoyle (2): *The Grapes of Wrath*, 1940 – S; *White Heat*, 1949 – S

Gene Hackman (2): *Bonnie and Clyde*, 1967 – LS; *The Conversation*, 1974 – L

JEAN HAGEN (3): *Adam's Rib*, 1949 – LS; *The Asphalt Jungle*, 1950 – LS; *Singin' in the Rain*, 1952 – LS

ALAN HALE (3): *It Happened One Night*, 1934 – S; *The Adventures of Robin Hood*, 1938 – LS; *The Sea Hawk*, 1940 – LS

JONATHAN HALE (3): *Fury*, 1936 – S; *Casablanca*, 1942 – S; *Strangers on a Train*, 1951 – S

Louise Closser Hale (2): *Shanghai Express*, 1932 – S; *Dinner at Eight*, 1933 – S

PORTER HALL (7): *The Thin Man*, 1934 – S; *Mr Smith Goes to Washington*, 1939 – S; *His Girl Friday*, 1940 – S; *Sullivan's Travels*, 1941 – S; *The Miracle of Morgan's Creek*, 1943 – S; *Double Indemnity*, 1944 – S; *Ace in the Hole*, 1951 – S

CHARLES HALTON (5): *The Prisoner of Zenda*, 1937 – S; *Young Mr Lincoln*, 1939 – S; *The Shop Around the Corner*, 1939 – S; *To Be or Not To Be*, 1942 – S; *The Best Years of Our Lives*, 1946 – S

MARGARET HAMILTON (3): *Nothing Sacred*, 1937 – S; *The Wizard of Oz*, 1939 – S; *The Oxbow Incident*, 1943 – S

MURRAY HAMILTON (3): *The Hustler*, 1961 – S; *The Graduate*, 1967 – S; *Jaws*, 1975 – S

Oliver Hardy (2): *Sons of the Desert*, 1933 – L; *Way Out West*, 1937 – L

JEAN HARLOW (3): *City Lights*, 1931 – S, bit; *The Public Enemy*, 1931 – L; *Dinner at Eight*, 1933 – L

Sterling Hayden (2): *The Asphalt Jungle*, 1950 – L; *The Godfather*, 1972 – LS

RITA HAYWORTH (3): *Only Angels Have Wings*, 1939 – LS; *Gilda*, 1946 – L; *The Lady from Shanghai*, 1948 – L

Tippi Hedren (2): *The Birds*, 1963 – L; *Marnie*, 1964 – L

KATHARINE HEPBURN (5): *Stage Door*, 1937 – L; *Bringing Up Baby*, 1938 – L; *The Philadelphia Story*, 1940 – L; *Adam's Rib*, 1949 – L; *Long Day's Journey into Night*, 1962 – L

Barbara Hershey (2): *The Right Stuff*, 1983 – LS; *Hannah and Her Sisters*, 1986 – LS

JEAN HERSHOLT (3): *Greed*, 1924 – LS; *Grand Hotel*, 1932 – LS; *Dinner at Eight*, 1933 – LS

Irene Hervey (2): *Destry Rides Again*, 1939 – LS; *Play Misty for Me*, 1971 – LS

Charlton Heston (2): *Touch of Evil*, 1958 – L; *Ben-Hur*, 1959 – *L

LOUIS JEAN HEYDT (4): *Gone with the Wind*, 1939 – S; *They Were Expendable*, 1945 – S; *The Big Sleep*, 1946 – S; *A Star Is Born*, 1954 – S

Russell Hicks (2): *The Bank Dick*, 1940 – S; *The Little Foxes*, 1941 – S

Samuel S. Hinds (2): *Stage Door*, 1937 – S; *Destry Rides Again*, 1939 – S

DUSTIN HOFFMAN (3): *The Graduate*, 1967 – L; *All the President's Men*, 1976 – L; *Kramer vs Kramer*, 1979 – L

WILLIAM HOLDEN (3): *Sunset Boulevard*, 1950 – L; *Born Yesterday*, 1950 – L; *The Wild Bunch*, 1969 – L

Judy Holliday (2): *Adam's Rib*, 1949 – LS; *Born Yesterday*, 1950 – L

STERLING HOLLOWAY (4): *The Gold Diggers of 1933*, 1933 – S; *The Merry Widow*, 1934 – S; *Dumbo*, 1941 – S, voice of Stork; *Bambi*, 1942 – S, voice

JACK HOLT (3): *Cat People*, 1942 – S; *They Were Expendable*, 1945 – S; *The Treasure of the Sierra Madre*, 1948 – S, bit

TIM HOLT (4): *Stagecoach*, 1939 – LS; *The Magnificent Ambersons*, 1942 – L; *My Darling Clementine*, 1946 – LS; *The Treasure of the Sierra Madre*, 1948 – LS

Bo Hopkins (2): *The Wild Bunch*, 1969 – S; *American Graffiti*, 1973 – S

DENNIS HOPPER (3): *Rebel without a Cause*, 1955 – S; *Giant*, 1956 – LS; *Apocalypse Now*, 1979 – LS

EDWARD EVERETT HORTON (4): *Trouble in Paradise*, 1932 – LS; *The Merry Widow*, 1934 – LS; *Top Hat*, 1935 – LS; *The Lost Horizon*, 1937 – LS

ESTHER HOWARD (4): *Sullivan's Travels*, 1941 – S; *The Palm Beach Story*, 1942 – S; *The Miracle of Morgan's Creek*, 1943 – S; *Murder My Sweet*, 1944 – S

John Howard (2): *The Lost Horizon*, 1937 – LS; *The Philadelphia Story*, 1940 – LS

Ron Howard (2): *American Graffiti*, 1973 – LS; *The Shootist*, 1976 – LS

ARTHUR HOYT (5): *It Happened One Night*, 1934 – S; *Mr Deeds Goes to Town*, 1936 – S; *The Lady Eve*, 1941 – S; *The Palm Beach Story*, 1942 – S; *The Miracle of Morgan's Creek*, 1943 – S

Rochelle Hudson (2): *She Done Him Wrong*, 1933 – LS; *Rebel without a Cause*, 1955 – LS

Rock Hudson (2): *Giant*, 1956 – L; *Written on the Wind*, 1956 – L

Paul Hurst (2): *Gone with the Wind*, 1939 – S; *The Oxbow Incident*, 1943 – S

John Huston (2): *The Treasure of the Sierra Madre*, 1948 – S, cameo; *Chinatown*, 1974 – LS

WALTER HUSTON (4): *Dodsworth*, 1936 – L; *The Maltese Falcon*, 1941 – S, cameo; *Yankee Doodle Dandy*, 1942 – LS; *The Treasure of the Sierra Madre*, 1948 – LS

Warren Hymer (2): *Mr Deeds Goes to Town*, 1936 – S; *Destry Rides Again*, 1939 – S

JOHN IRELAND (3): *My Darling Clementine*, 1946 – LS; *Red River*, 1948 – LS; *All the King's Men*, 1949 – L

SAM JAFFE (5): *The Scarlet Fortress*, 1934 – LS; *The Lost Horizon*, 1937 – LS; *Gunga Din*, 1939 – LS; *The Asphalt Jungle*, 1950 – LS; *Ben-Hur*, 1959 – LS

Dean Jagger (2): *Twelve o'Clock High*, 1946 – *LS; *Bad Day at Black Rock*, 1954 – LS

ALLEN JENKINS (3): *I Am a Fugitive from a Chain Gang*, 1932 – S; *Forty-Second Street*, 1933 – S; *Destry Rides Again*, 1939 – S

ISABEL JEWELL (3): *The Lost Horizon*, 1937 – S; *Gone with the Wind*, 1939 – S; *High Sierra*, 1941 – S

BEN JOHNSON (5): *She Wore a Yellow Ribbon*, 1949 – LS; *Wagonmaster*, 1950 – L; *Shane*, 1953 – LS; *The Wild Bunch*, 1969 – LS; *The Last Picture Show*, 1971 – *LS

NOBLE JOHNSON (3): *The Navigator*, 1924 – S; *King Kong*, 1933 – S; *She Wore a Yellow Ribbon*, 1949 – S

Carolyn Jones (2): *The Big Heat*, 1953 – LS; *Invasion of the Body Snatchers*, 1956 – LS

L.Q. Jones (2): *Ride the High Country*, 1962 – S; *The Wild Bunch*, 1969 – S

Victor Jory (2): *Gone with the Wind*, 1939 – LS; *The Miracle Worker*, 1962 – LS

Louis Jourdan (2): *Letter from an Unknown Woman*, 1948 – L; *Gigi*, 1958 – L

BORIS KARLOFF (4): *Frankenstein*, 1931 – L; *Scarface*, 1932 – LS; *The Old Dark House*, 1932 – LS; *The Bride of Frankenstein*, 1935 – L

ROSCOE KARNS (4): *I Am a Fugitive from a Chain Gang*, 1932 – S; *It Happened One Night*, 1934 – S; *His Girl Friday*, 1940 – S; *It's a Wonderful Life*, 1946 – S

BUSTER KEATON (7): *Our Hospitality*, 1923 – L; *Sherlock Jr.*, 1924 – L; *The Navigator*, 1924 – L; *The General*, 1926 – L; *The Cameraman*, 1928 – L; *Sunset Boulevard*, 1950 – S, cameo; *Limelight*, 1952 – S, cameo

DIANE KEATON (4): *The Godfather*, 1972 – LS; *The Godfather Part II*, 1974 – LS; *Annie Hall*, 1977 – *L; *Manhattan*, 1979 – L

JOE KEATON (3): *Our Hospitality*, 1923 – S; *Sherlock Jr.*, 1924 – S; *The General*, 1926 – S

Howard Keel (2): *Kiss Me Kate*, 1953 – L; *Seven Brides for Seven Brothers*, 1954 – L

Ruby Keeler (2): *Forty-Second Street*, 1933 – L; *The Gold Diggers of 1933*, 1933 – L

Harvey Keitel (2): *Mean Streets*, 1973 – L; *Taxi Driver*, 1976 – LS

GENE KELLY (4): *The Pirate*, 1948 – L; *On the Town*, 1949 – L; *An American in Paris*, 1951 – L; *Singin' in the Rain*, 1952 – L

Grace Kelly (2): *High Noon*, 1952 – L; *Rear Window*, 1954 – L

Charles Kemper (2): *The Southerner*, 1945 – S; *Wagonmaster*, 1950 – S

TOM KENNEDY (3): *Forty-Second Street*, 1933 – S; *She Done Him Wrong*, 1933 – S; *Some Like it Hot*, 1959 – S

J.M. Kerrigan (2): *The Informer*, 1935 – S; *Gone with the Wind*, 1939 – S

GUY KIBBEE (4): *Forty-Second Street*, 1933 – LS; *The Gold Diggers of 1933*, 1933 – LS; *Mr Smith Goes to Washington*, 1939 – LS; *Fort Apache*, 1948 – S

VICTOR KILIAN (3): *Only Angels Have Wings*, 1939 – S; *The Oxbow Incident*, 1943 – S; *Spellbound*, 1945 – S

LEONID KINSKEY (3): *Trouble in Paradise*, 1932 – S; *Duck Soup*, 1933 – S; *Casablanca*, 1942 – S

Patric Knowles (2): *The Adventures of Robin Hood*, 1938 – LS; *How Green Was My Valley*, 1941 – LS

Clarence Kolb (2): *His Girl Friday*, 1940 – S; *Adam's Rib*, 1949 – S

Otto Kruger (2): *Murder My Sweet*, 1944 – LS; *High Noon*, 1952 – LS

Alan Ladd (2): *Citizen Kane*, 1941 – S, bit; *Shane*, 1953 – L

Jack Lambert (2): *The Killers*, 1946 – S; *Kiss Me Deadly*, 1955 – S

BURT LANCASTER (3): *The Killers*, 1946 – L; *From Here to Eternity*, 1953 – L; *Sweet Smell of Success*, 1957 – L

ELSA LANCHESTER (4): *David Copperfield*, 1935 – S; *The Bride of Frankenstein*, 1935 – LS; *Witness for the Prosecution*, 1957 – LS; *Mary Poppins*, 1964 – S

Angela Lansbury (2): *The Manchurian Candidate*, 1962 – LS; *Beauty and the Beast*, 1991 – S, voice of Mrs Potts

CHARLES LAUGHTON (4): *The Old Dark House*, 1932 – L; *Mutiny on the Bounty*, 1935 – L; *The Hunchback of Notre Dame*, 1939 – L; *Witness for the Prosecution*, 1957 – LS

Stan Laurel (2): *Sons of the Desert*, 1933 – L; *Way Out West*, 1937 – L

MARC LAWRENCE (3): *The Oxbow Incident*, 1943 – S; *The Big Sleep*, 1946 – S; *The Asphalt Jungle*, 1950 – S

Cloris Leachman (2): *Kiss Me Deadly*, 1955 – LS; *The Last Picture Show*, 1971 – *LS

ANNA LEE (4): *How Green Was My Valley*, 1941 – L; *The Ghost and Mrs Muir*, 1947 – LS; *Fort Apache*, 1948 – LS; *The Man Who Shot Liberty Vallance*, 1962 – S, bit

JANET LEIGH (3): *Touch of Evil*, 1958 – L; *Psycho*, 1960 – L; *The Manchurian Candidate*, 1962 – L

Vivien Leigh (2): *Gone with the Wind*, 1939 – *L; *A Streetcar Named Desire*, 1951 – *L

JACK LEMMON (3): *Some Like it Hot*, 1959 – L; *The Apartment*, 1960 – L; *Missing*, 1982 – L

Joan Leslie (2): *High Sierra*, 1941 – LS; *Yankee Doodle Dandy*, 1942 – L

Oscar Levant (2): *An American in Paris*, 1951 – LS; *The Band Wagon*, 1953 – LS

SAM LEVENE (3): *The Killers*, 1946 – S; *Crossfire*, 1947 – S; *Sweet Smell of Success*, 1959 – LS

Elmo Lincoln (2): *Birth of a Nation*, 1915 – S; *Intolerance*, 1916 – S

Lucien Littlefield (2): *Sons of the Desert*, 1933 – S; *The Little Foxes*, 1941 – S

NORMAN LLOYD (3): *The Southerner*, 1945 – S; *Spellbound*, 1945 – S; *Limelight*, 1952 – S

Carole Lombard (2): *Nothing Sacred*, 1937 – L; *To Be or Not To Be*, 1942 – L

Peter Lorre (2): *The Maltese Falcon*, 1941 – LS; *Casablanca*, 1942 – LS

Bessie Love (2): *The Birth of a Nation*, 1915 – S; *Intolerance*, 1916 – LS

MONTAGU LOVE (4): *The Wind*, 1928 – S; *The Prisoner of Zenda*, 1937 – S; *The Adventures of Robin Hood*, 1938 – S; *Gunga Din*, 1939 – S

MYRNA LOY (3): *Love Me Tonight*, 1932 – LS; *The Thin Man*, 1934 – L; *The Best Years of Our Lives*, 1946 – L

Donald MacBride (2): *High Sierra*, 1941 – S; *The Killers*, 1946 – S

MERCEDES MCCAMBRIDGE (3): *All the King's Men*, 1949 – LS; *Giant*, 1956 – LS; *Touch of Evil*, 1958 – S, cameo

JOEL MCCREA (3): *Sullivan's Travels*, 1941 – L; *The Palm Beach Story*, 1942 – L; *Ride the High Country*, 1962 – L

Hattie McDaniel (2): *Nothing Sacred*, 1937 – S; *Gone with the Wind*, 1939 – *LS

Jeanette MacDonald (2): *Love Me Tonight*, 1932 – L; *The Merry Widow*, 1934 – L

J. FARRELL MACDONALD (4): *Sunrise*, 1927 – S; *Sullivan's Travels*, 1941 – S; *The Miracle of Morgan's Creek*, 1943 – S; *My Darling Clementine*, 1946 – S

Charles McGraw (2): *The Killers*, 1946 – S; *The Birds*, 1963 – S

Kathryn McGuire (2): *Sherlock Jr.*, 1924 – L; *The Navigator*, 1924 – L

John McIntire (2): *The Asphalt Jungle*, 1950 – S; *Psycho*, 1960 – S

Bill McKinney (2): *The Outlaw Josey Wales*, 1976 – S; *The Shootist*, 1976 – S

VICTOR MCLAGLEN (5): *The Informer*, 1935 – *L; *Gunga Din*, 1939 – L; *Fort Apache*, 1948 – LS; *She Wore a Yellow Ribbon*, 1949 – LS; *The Quiet Man*, 1952 – LS

BARTON MACLANE (3): *High Sierra*, 1941 – S; *The Maltese Falcon*, 1941 – S; *The Treasure of the Sierra Madre*, 1948 – S

Fred MacMurray (2): *Double Indemnity*, 1944 – L; *The Apartment*, 1960 – LS

George Macready (2): *Gilda*, 1946 – LS; *Paths of Glory*, 1957 – LS

KARL MALDEN (4): *A Streetcar Named Desire*, 1951 – *LS; *On the Waterfront*, 1952 – LS; *Baby Doll*, 1956 – L; *Patton*, 1970 – LS

Dorothy Malone (2): *The Big Sleep*, 1946 – S; *Written on the Wind*, 1956 – LS

MILES MANDER (3): *Wuthering Heights*, 1939 – S; *To Be or Not To Be*, 1942 – S; *Murder My Sweet*, 1944 – S

HANK MANN (4): *City Lights*, 1910 – S; *Scarface*, 1932 – S; *Modern Times*, 1936 – S; *The Great Dictator*, 1940 – S

Fredric March (2): *Nothing Sacred*, 1937 – L; *The Best Years of Our Lives*, 1946 – L

HUGH MARLOWE (3): *Meet Me in St Louis*, 1944 – LS; *Twelve o'Clock High*, 1946 – LS; *All About Eve*, 1950 – LS

MAE MARSH (7): *The Birth of a Nation*, 1915 – L; *Intolerance*, 1916 – L; *The Grapes of Wrath*, 1940 – S; *How Green Was My Valley*, 1941 – S; *Fort Apache*, 1948 – S; *A Star Is Born*, 1954 – S; *The Searchers*, 1956 – S

Herbert Marshall (2): *Trouble in Paradise*, 1932 – L; *The Little Foxes*, 1941 – L

Tully Marshall (2): *Intolerance*, 1916 – S; *Scarface*, 1932 – S

STROTHER MARTIN (4): *The Asphalt Jungle*, 1950 – S; *Kiss Me Deadly*, 1955 – S; *The Man Who Shot Liberty Vallance*, 1962 – S; *The Wild Bunch*, 1969 – S

LEE MARVIN (3): *The Big Heat*, 1953 – LS; *Bad Day at Black Rock*, 1954 – LS; *The Man Who Shot Liberty Vallance*, 1962 – LS

The Marx Brothers (Chico, Groucho, Harpo) (2): *Duck Soup* (with Zeppo), 1933 – L; *A Night at the Opera*, 1935 – L

James Mason (2): *A Star Is Born*, 1954 – L; *North by Northwest*, 1959 – LS

RAYMOND MASSEY (3): *The Old Dark House*, 1932 – LS; *The Prisoner of Zenda*, 1937 – LS; *East of Eden*, 1955 – LS

EDWIN MAXWELL (6): *All Quiet on the Western Front*, 1930 – S; *Scarface*, 1932 – S; *Dinner at Eight*, 1933 – S; *Ninotchka*, 1939 – S; *The Shop Around the Corner*, 1939 – S; *His Girl Friday*, 1940 – S

Virginia Mayo (2): *The Best Years of Our Lives*, 1946 – LS; *White Heat*, 1949 – LS

Mike Mazurki (2): *Murder My Sweet*, 1944 – S; *Some Like it Hot*, 1959 – S

DONALD MEEK (3): *The Informer*, 1935 – S; *Stagecoach*, 1939 – S; *Young Mr Lincoln*, 1939 – S

George Meeker (2): *Gone with the Wind*, 1939 – S; *Casablanca*, 1942 – S

Ralph Meeker (2): *Kiss Me Deadly*, 1955 – L; *Paths of Glory*, 1957 – LS

Adolphe Menjou (2): *Stage Door*, 1937 – LS; *Paths of Glory*, 1957 – LS

Beryl Mercer (2): *All Quiet on the Western Front*, 1930 – S; *The Public Enemy*, 1931 – S

UNA MERKEL (4): *Forty-Second Street*, 1933 – LS; *The Merry Widow*, 1934 – LS; *Destry Rides Again*, 1939 – LS; *The Bank Dick*, 1940 – LS

Gary Merrill (2): *Twelve o'Clock High*, 1946 – LS; *All About Eve*, 1950 – LS

EMILE MEYER (3): *Shane*, 1953 – S; *Sweet Smell of Success*, 1957 – S; *Paths of Glory*, 1957 – S

TORBEN MEYER (5): *The Lady Eve*, 1941 – S; *Sullivan's Travels*, 1941 – S; *The Palm Beach Story*, 1942 – S; *Casablanca*, 1942 – S; *The Miracle of Morgan's Creek*, 1943 – S

Charles Middleton (2): *Duck Soup*, 1933 – S; *The Grapes of Wrath*, 1940 – S

VERA MILES (3): *The Searchers*, 1956 – L; *Psycho*, 1960 – LS; *The Man Who Shot Liberty Vallance*, 1962 – L

ANN MILLER (3): *Stage Door*, 1937 – LS; *On the Town*, 1949 – LS; *Kiss Me Kate*, 1953 – LS

Sal Mineo (2): *Rebel without a Cause*, 1955 – LS; *Giant*, 1956 – LS

GRANT MITCHELL (4): *Dinner at Eight*, 1933 – S; *Mr Smith Goes to Washington*, 1939 – S; *The Grapes of Wrath*, 1940 – S; *Laura*, 1944 – S

Millard Mitchell (2): *Twelve o'Clock High*, 1946 – LS; *Singin' in the Rain*, 1952 – LS

THOMAS MITCHELL (7): *The Lost Horizon*, 1937 – LS; *Stagecoach*, 1939 – *LS; *Only Angels Have Wings*, 1939 – LS; *Mr Smith Goes to Washington*, 1939 – LS; *Gone with the Wind*, 1939 – LS; *The Hunchback of Notre Dame*, 1939 – LS; *High Noon*, 1952 – LS

MARILYN MONROE (4): *The Asphalt Jungle*, 1950 – S; *All About Eve*, 1950 – S; *Gentlemen Prefer Blondes*, 1953 – L; *Some Like it Hot*, 1959 – L

Agnes Moorehead (2): *Citizen Kane*, 1941 – LS; *The Magnificent Ambersons*, 1942 – LS

Antonio Moreno (2): *Notorious*, 1946 – S; *The Searchers*, 1956 – S

Rita Moreno (2): *Singin' in the Rain*, 1952 – S; *West Side Story*, 1961 – *LS

Frank Morgan (2): *The Wizard of Oz*, 1939 – LS; *The Shop Around the Corner*, 1940 – LS

HENRY MORGAN (3): *The Oxbow Incident*, 1943 – S; *High Noon*, 1952 – S; *The Shootist*, 1976 – S

Karen Morley (2): *Scarface*, 1932 – LS; *Dinner at Eight*, 1933 – LS

Alan Mowbray (2): *My Darling Clementine*, 1946 – S; *Wagonmaster*, 1950 – S

HERBERT MUNDIN (3): *David Copperfield*, 1935 – S; *Mutiny on the Bounty*, 1935 – S; *The Adventures of Robin Hood*, 1938 – S

PAUL MUNI (3): *Scarface*, 1932 – L; *I Am a Fugitive from a Chain Gang*, 1932 – L; *The Good Earth*, 1937 – L

MICHAEL MURPHY (3): *Nashville*, 1975 – LS; *Manhattan*, 1979 – LS; *Salvador*, 1986 – LS

Mildred Natwick (2): *She Wore a Yellow Ribbon*, 1949 – S; *The Quiet Man*, 1952 – S

JACK NICHOLSON (3): *Five Easy Pieces*, 1970 – L; *Chinatown*, 1974 – L; *One Flew over the Cuckoo's Nest*, 1976 – *L

DAVID NIVEN (3): *Dodsworth*, 1936 – LS; *The Prisoner of Zenda*, 1937 – LS; *Wuthering Heights*, 1939 – LS

Jeanette Nolan (2): *The Big Heat*, 1953 – LS; *The Man Who Shot Liberty Vallance*, 1962 – S

Tommy Noonan (2): *Gentlemen Prefer Blondes*, 1953 – LS; *A Star Is Born*, 1954 – LS

JACK NORTON (3): *The Bank Dick*, 1940 – S; *The Palm Beach Story*, 1942 – S; *The Miracle of Morgan's Creek*, 1943 – S

Warren Oates (2): *Ride the High Country*, 1962 – LS; *The Wild Bunch*, 1969 – LS

Philip Ober (2): *From Here to Eternity*, 1953 – S; *North by Northwest*, 1959 – S

EDMOND O'BRIEN (5): *The Hunchback of Notre Dame*, 1939 – LS; *The Killers*, 1946 – LS; *White Heat*, 1949 – LS; *The Man Who Shot Liberty Vallance* – LS; *The Wild Bunch*, 1969 – LS

GEORGE O'BRIEN (3): *Sunrise*, 1927 – L; *Fort Apache*, 1948 – S; *She Wore a Yellow Ribbon*, 1949 – S

ARTHUR O'CONNELL (3): *Citizen Kane*, 1941 – S, bit; *The Naked City*, 1948 – S; *Anatomy of a Murder*, 1959 – LS

UNA O'CONNOR (6): *David Copperfield*, 1935 – S; *The Bride of Frankenstein*, 1935 – S; *The Informer*, 1935 – S; *The Adventures of Robin Hood*, 1938 – S; *The Sea Hawk*, 1940 – S; *Witness for the Prosecution*, 1957 – S

CATHY O'DONNELL (3): *The Best Years of Our Lives*, 1946 – LS; *They Live by Night*, 1949 – L; *Ben-Hur*, 1959 – LS

MAUREEN O'HARA (3): *The Hunchback of Notre Dame*, 1939 – L; *How Green Was My Valley*, 1941 – L; *The Quiet Man*, 1952 – L

Laurence Olivier (2): *Wuthering Heights*, 1939 – L; *Rebecca*, 1940 – L

MORONI OLSEN (3): *Snow White and the Seven Dwarfs*, 1938 – S, voice of the magic mirror; *Mildred Pierce*, 1945 – S; *Notorious*, 1946 – S

FRANK ORTH (3): *His Girl Friday*, 1940 – S; *The Oxbow Incident*, 1943 – S; *The Lost Weekend*, 1945 – S

MAUREEN O'SULLIVAN (3): *The Thin Man*, 1934 – LS; *David Copperfield*, 1935 – L; *Hannah and Her Sisters*, 1986 – LS

Rafaela Ottiano (2): *Grand Hotel*, 1932 – S; *She Done Him Wrong*, 1933 – S

Reginald Owen (2): *Queen Christina*, 1933 – LS; *The Pirate*, 1948 – LS

Seena Owen (2): *Intolerance*, 1916 – S; *Queen Kelly*, 1928 – LS

Al Pacino (2): *The Godfather*, 1972 – LS; *The Godfather Part II*, 1974 – LS

EUGENE PALLETTE (6): *The Birth of a Nation*, 1915 – S; *Intolerance*, 1916 – S; *Shanghai Express*, 1932 – LS; *The Adventures of Robin Hood*, 1938 – LS; *Mr Smith Goes to Washington*, 1939 – LS; *The Lady Eve*, 1941 – LS

FRANKLIN PANGBORN (5): *Mr Deeds Goes to Town*, 1936 – S; *Stage Door*, 1937 – S; *The Bank Dick*, 1940 – S; *Sullivan's Travels*, 1941 – S; *The Palm Beach Story*, 1942 – S

LEE PATRICK (3): *The Maltese Falcon*, 1941 – LS; *Mildred Pierce*, 1945 – S; *Vertigo*, 1958 – S

Elizabeth Patterson (2): *Love Me Tonight*, 1932 – S; *Dinner at Eight*, 1933 – S

GREGORY PECK (3): *Spellbound*, 1945 – L; *Twelve o'Clock High*, 1946 – L; *To Kill a Mockingbird*, 1962 – *L

NEHEMIAH PERSOFF (3): *The Naked City*, 1948 – S; *On the Waterfront*, 1954 – S; *Some Like it Hot*, 1959 – S

Walter Pidgeon (2): *How Green Was My Valley*, 1941 – LS; *The Bad and the Beautiful*, 1952 – LS

DICK POWELL (4): *Forty-Second Street*, 1933 – L; *The Gold Diggers of 1933*, 1933 – L; *Murder My Sweet*, 1944 – L; *The Bad and the Beautiful*, 1952 – L

Denver Pyle (2): *The Man Who Shot Liberty Vallance*, 1962 – S; *Bonnie and Clyde*, 1967 – S

JOHN QUALEN (7): *Nothing Sacred*, 1937 – S; *His Girl Friday*, 1940 – S; *The Grapes of Wrath*, 1940 – S; *Casablanca*, 1942 – S; *The Searchers*, 1956 – S; *Anatomy of a Murder*, 1959 – S; *The Man Who Shot Liberty Vallance*, 1962 – S

EDDIE QUILLAN (3): *Mutiny on the Bounty*, 1935 – S; *Young Mr Lincoln*, 1939 – S; *The Grapes of Wrath*, 1940 – S

George Raft (2): *Scarface*, 1932 – LS; *Some Like it Hot*, 1959 – LS

CLAUDE RAINS (5): *The Adventures of Robin Hood*, 1938 – LS; *Mr Smith Goes to Washington*, 1939 – LS; *The Sea Hawk*, 1940 – LS; *Casablanca*, 1942 – LS; *Notorious*, 1946 – LS

JESSIE RALPH (4): *David Copperfield*, 1935 – S; *Camille*, 1936 – LS; *The Good Earth*, 1937 – LS; *The Bank Dick*, 1940 – LS

Basil Rathbone (2): *David Copperfield*, 1935 – S; *The Adventures of Robin Hood*, 1938 – LS

DONNA REED (3): *They Were Expendable*, 1945 – LS; *It's a Wonderful Life*, 1946 – L; *From Here to Eternity*, 1953 – *LS

FRANK REICHER (4): *King Kong*, 1933 – S; *Stage Door*, 1937 – S; *Ninotchka*, 1939 – S; *To Be or To Be*, 1942 – S

Carl Benton Reid (2): *The Little Foxes*, 1941 – S; *In a Lonely Place*, 1950 – LS

Thelma Ritter (2): *All About Eve*, 1950 – LS; *Rear Window*, 1954 – LS

BERT ROACH (4): *The Crowd*, 1928 – S; *Love Me Tonight*, 1932 – S; *The Thin Man*, 1934 – S; *Fury*, 1936 – S

Jason Robards Jr. (2): *Long Day's Journey into Night*, 1962 – LS; *All the President's Men*, 1976 – *LS

Roy Roberts (2): *My Darling Clementine*, 1946 – S; *Chinatown*, 1974 – S

Dewey Robinson (2): *She Done Him Wrong*, 1933 – S; *Murder My Sweet*, 1944 – S

Edward G. Robinson (2): *Little Caesar*, 1930 – L; *Double Indemnity*, 1944 – L

Flora Robson (2): *Wuthering Heights*, 1939 – LS; *The Sea Hawk*, 1940 – LS

May Robson (2): *Dinner at Eight*, 1933 – S; *Bringing Up Baby*, 1938 – LS

GINGER ROGERS (5): *Forty-Second Street*, 1933 – LS; *The Gold Diggers of 1933*, 1933 – LS; *Top Hat*, 1935 – L; *Swing Time*, 1936 – L; *Stage Door*, 1937 – L

GILBERT ROLAND (3): *She Done Him Wrong*, 1933 – LS; *The Sea Hawk*, 1940 – S; *The Bad and the Beautiful*, 1950 – LS

Christian Rub (2): *Mr Deeds Goes to Town*, 1936 – S; *Pinocchio*, 1940 – S, voice of Geppetto

CHARLES (Charlie) RUGGLES (3): *Love Me Tonight*, 1932 – LS; *Trouble in Paradise*, 1932 – LS; *Bringing Up Baby*, 1938 – LS

SIEGFRIED (Sig) RUMANN (5): *A Night at the Opera*, 1935 – LS; *Nothing Sacred*, 1937 – LS; *Only Angels Have Wings*, 1939 – LS; *Ninotchka*, 1939 – LS; *To Be or Not To Be*, 1942 – LS

John Russell (2): *Mr Smith Goes to Washington*, 1939 – S; *Rio Bravo*, 1959 – S

ROBERT RYAN (3): *Crossfire*, 1947 – LS; *Bad Day at Black Rock*, 1954 – LS; *The Wild Bunch*, 1969 – LS

Eva Marie Saint (2): *On the Waterfront*, 1954 – *LS; *North by Northwest*, 1959 – L

Howard St John (2): *Born Yesterday*, 1950 – S; *Strangers on a Train*, 1951 – S

S.Z. 'Cuddles' Sakall (2): *Yankee Doodle Dandy*, 1942 – S; *Casablanca*, 1942 – S

Will Sampson (2): *One Flew over the Cuckoo's Nest*, 1975 – LS; *The Outlaw Josey Wales*, 1976 – S

GEORGE SANDERS (3): *Rebecca*, 1940 – LS; *The Ghost and Mrs Muir*, 1947 – LS; *All About Eve*, 1950 – *LS

ERSKINE SANFORD (3): *The Magnificent Ambersons*, 1942 – S; *The Best Years of Our Lives*, 1946 – S; *The Lady from Shanghai*, 1948 – S

John Savage (2): *Salvador*, 1976 – LS; *The Deer Hunter*, 1978 – LS

JOSEPH SAWYER (3): *The Informer*, 1935 – S; *The Grapes of Wrath*, 1940 – S; *Gilda*, 1946 – S

GUS SCHILLING (3): *The Magnificent Ambersons*, 1942 – S; *The Lady from Shanghai*, 1948 – S; *Rebel without a Cause*, 1955 – S

GEORGE C. SCOTT (3): *Anatomy of a Murder*, 1959 – LS; *The Hustler*, 1961 – LS; *Patton*, 1970 – *L

ALMIRA SESSIONS (4): *Sullivan's Travels*, 1941 – S; *The Miracle of Morgan's Creek*, 1943 – S; *The Oxbow Incident*, 1943 – S; *Rebel without a Cause*, 1955 – S

DAN SEYMOUR (3): *Casablanca*, 1942 – S; *To Have and Have Not*, 1944 – S; *The Big Heat*, 1953 – S

HARRY SHANNON (4): *Citizen Kane*, 1941 – S; *The Lady from Shanghai*, 1948 – S; *High Noon*, 1952 – S; *Written on the Wind*, 1956 – S

JOAN SHAWLEE (4): *From Here to Eternity*, 1953 – S; *A Star Is Born*, 1954 – S; *Some Like it Hot*, 1959 – S; *The Apartment*, 1960 – S

Sam Shepard (2): *Days of Heaven*, 1978 – LS; *The Right Stuff*, 1983 – LS

ARTHUR SHIELDS (3): *How Green Was My Valley*, 1941 – S; *She Wore a Yellow Ribbon*, 1949 – S; *The Quiet Man*, 1952 – S

Talia Shire (2): *The Godfather*, 1972 – S; *The Godfather Part II*, 1974 – LS

RUSSELL SIMPSON (7): *Mr Smith Goes to Washington*, 1939 – S; *Young Mr Lincoln*, 1939 – S; *The Grapes of Wrath*, 1940 – S; *They Were Expendable*, 1945 – S; *My Darling Clementine*, 1946 – S; *Wagonmaster*, 1950 – S; *Seven Brides for Seven Brothers*, 1954 – S

FRANK SINATRA (3): *On the Town*, 1949 – LS; *From Here to Eternity*, 1953 – *LS; *The Manchurian Candidate*, 1962 – L

Everett Sloane (2): *Citizen Kane*, 1941 – LS; *The Lady from Shanghai*, 1948 – LS

Art Smith (2): *Letter from an Unknown Woman*, 1948 – S; *In a Lonely Place*, 1950 – S

C. AUBREY SMITH (6): *Love Me Tonight*, 1932 – S; *Trouble in Paradise*, 1932 – S; *Queen Christina*, 1933 – S; *The Scarlet Empress*, 1934 – S; *The Prisoner of Zenda*, 1937 – S; *Rebecca*, 1940 – S

Ned Sparks (2): *Forty-Second Street*, 1933 – LS; *The Gold Diggers of 1933* – LS

Robert Stack (2): *To Be or Not To Be*, 1942 – LS; *Written on the Wind*, 1956 – S

Barbara Stanwyck (2): *The Lady Eve*, 1941 – L; *Double Indemnity*, 1944 – L

BOB STEELE (3): *Of Mice and Men*, 1939 – S; *The Big Sleep*, 1946 – S; *Rio Bravo*, 1959 – S

JAMES STEWART (10): *Destry Rides Again*, 1939 – L; *Mr Smith Goes to Washington*, 1939 – L; *The Shop Around the Corner*, 1940 – L; *The Philadelphia Story*, 1940 – *L; *It's a Wonderful Life*, 1946 – L;

Rear Window, 1954 – L; *Vertigo*, 1958 – L; *Anatomy of a Murder*, 1959 – L; *The Man Who Shot Liberty Vallance*, 1962 – L; *The Shootist*, 1976 – LS

PAUL STEWART (4): *Citizen Kane*, 1941 – S; *Twelve o'Clock High*, 1946 – S; *The Bad and the Beautiful*, 1952 – S; *Kiss Me Deadly*, 1955 – LS

GEORGE E. STONE (3): *Little Caesar*, 1930 – S; *Forty-Second Street*, 1933 – S; *Some Like it Hot*, 1959 – S

LEWIS STONE (3): *Grand Hotel*, 1932 – LS; *Queen Christina*, 1933 – LS; *David Copperfield*, 1935 – LS

Glenn Strange (2): *Red River*, 1948 – S; *The Red Badge of Courage*, 1951 – S

MERYL STREEP (3): *The Deer Hunter*, 1978 – LS; *Manhattan*, 1979 – LS; *Kramer vs Kramer*, 1979 – *LS

GRADY SUTTON (3): *Stage Door*, 1937 – S; *The Bank Dick*, 1940 – S; *A Star Is Born*, 1954 – S

Gloria Swanson (2): *Queen Kelly*, 1928 – L; *Sunset Boulevard*, 1950 – L

Russ Tamblyn (2): *Seven Brides for Seven Brothers*, 1954 – LS; *West Side Story*, 1961 – L

AKIM TAMIROFF (3): *Queen Christina*, 1933 – S; *The Miracle of Morgan's Creek*, 1943 – S, cameo; *Touch of Evil*, 1938 – LS

Rod Taylor (2): *Giant*, 1956 – S; *The Birds*, 1963 – L

Ray Teal (2): *The Best Years of Our Lives*, 1946 – S; *Ace in the Hole*, 1951 – S

Ernest Thesiger (2): *The Old Dark House*, 1932 – LS; *The Bride of Frankenstein*, 1935 – LS

JAMESON THOMAS (3): *It Happened One Night*, 1934 – S; *The Scarlet Empress*, 1934 – S; *Mr Deeds Goes to Town*, 1936 – S

Gene Tierney (2): *Laura*, 1944 – L; *The Ghost and Mrs Muir*, 1947 – L

GEORGE TOBIAS (4): *Ninotchka*, 1939 – S; *The Hunchback of Notre Dame*, 1939 – S; *Yankee Doodle Dandy*, 1942 – S; *Mildred Pierce*, 1945 – S

REGIS TOOMEY (3): *His Girl Friday*, 1940 – S; *Spellbound*, 1945 – S; *The Big Sleep*, 1946 – S

SPENCER TRACY (3): *Fury*, 1936 – L; *Adam's Rib*, 1949 – L; *Bad Day at Black Rock*, 1954 – L

HENRY TRAVERS (3): *High Sierra*, 1941 – S; *Shadow of a Doubt*, 1943 – LS; *It's a Wonderful Life*, 1946 –

Arthur Treacher (2): *David Copperfield*, 1935 – S; *Mary Poppins*, 1964 – S

Claire Trevor (2): *Stagecoach*, 1939 – L; *Murder My Sweet*, 1944 – L

Ivan Triesault (2): *Notorious*, 1946 – S; *The Bad and the Beautiful*, 1952 – S

Kathleen Turner (2): *Body Heat*, 1981 – L; *Who Framed Roger Rabbit?*, 1988 – S, voice of Jessica Rabbit

Lana Turner (2): *The Postman Always Rings Twice*, 1946 – L; *The Bad and the Beautiful*, 1952 – L

John Turturro (2): *Hannah and Her Sisters*, 1986 – S; *Do the Right Thing*, 1989 – S

TOM TYLER (6): *Stagecoach*, 1939 – S; *Gone with the Wind*, 1939 – S; *The Grapes of Wrath*, 1940 – S; *They Were Expendable*, 1945 – S; *Red River*, 1948 – S; *She Wore a Yellow Ribbon*, 1949 – S

Lenore Ulric (2): *Camille*, 1946 – S; *Notorious*, 1946 – S

Lee Van Cleef (2): *High Noon*, 1952 – S; *The Man Who Shot Liberty Vallance*, 1962 – S

Edward Van Sloan (2): *Frankenstein*, 1931 – LS; *The Scarlet Empress*, 1934 – S

NORMA VARDEN (4): *Casablanca*, 1942 – S; *Stangers on a Train*, 1951 – S; *Gentlemen Prefer Blondes*, 1953 – S; *Witness for the Prosecution*, 1957 – S

Gustav von Seyffertitz (2): *Shanghai Express*, 1932 – S; *Queen Christina*, 1933 – S

Christopher Walken (2): *Annie Hall*, 1977 – S; *The Deer Hunter*, 1978 – LS

Henry B. Walthall (2): *The Birth of a Nation*, 1915 – LS; *Forty-Second Street*, 1933 – S

JACK WARDEN (3): *From Here to Eternity*, 1953 – S; *Twelve Angry Men*, 1957 – LS; *All the President's Men*, 1976 – LS

H.B. WARNER (4): *Mr Deeds Goes to Town*, 1936 – S; *The Lost Horizon*, 1937 – S; *Mr Smith Goes to Washington*, 1939 – S; *Sunset Boulevard*, 1950 – S, cameo, as himself

ROBERT WARWICK (7): *I Am a Fugitive from a Chain Gang*, 1932 – S; *The Awful Truth*, 1937 – S; *The Adventures of Robin Hood*, 1938 – S; *The Lady Eve*, 1941 – S; *Sullivan's Travels*, 1941 – S; *The Palm Beach Story*, 1942 – S; *In a Lonely Place*, 1950 – S

Pierre Watkin (2): *Swing Time*, 1936 – S; *Stage Door*, 1937 – S

JOHN WAYNE (10): *Stagecoach*, 1939 – L; *They Were Expendable*, 1945 – LS; *Fort Apache*, 1948 – LS; *Red River*, 1948 – L; *She Wore a Yellow Ribbon*, 1949 – L; *The Quiet Man*, 1952 – L; *The Searchers*, 1956 – L; *Rio Bravo*, 1959 – L; *The Man Who Shot Liberty Vallance*, 1962 – L; *The Shootist*, 1976 – L

ORSON WELLES (3): *Citizen Kane*, 1941 – L; *The Lady from Shanghai*, 1948 – L; *Touch of Evil*, 1958 – L

James Whitmore (2): *The Asphalt Jungle*, 1950 – LS; *Kiss Me Kate*, 1953 – S

Cindy Williams (2): *American Graffiti*, 1973 – LS; *The Conversation*, 1974 – LS

Hugh Williams (2): *David Copperfield*, 1935 – LS; *Wuthering Heights*, 1939 – LS

Chill Wills (2): *Way Out West*, 1937 – S; *Meet Me in St Louis*, 1944 – S

Charles Winninger (2): *Nothing Sacred*, 1937 – LS; *Destry Rides Again*, 1939 – LS

Shelley Winters (2): *Red River*, 1948 – S; *The Night of the Hunter*, 1955 – LS

IAN WOLFE (5): *Mutiny on the Bounty*, 1935 – S; *They Live by Night*, 1949 – S; *Seven Brides for Seven Brothers*, 1954 – S; *Rebel without a Cause*, 1955 – S; *Witness for the Prosecution*, 1957 – S

NATALIE WOOD (4): *The Ghost and Mrs Muir*, 1947 – S; *Rebel without a Cause*, 1955 – L; *The Searchers*, 1956 – L; *West Side Story*, 1961 – L

HARRY WOODS (4): *I Am a Fugitive from a Chain Gang*, 1932 – S; *The Scarlet Empress*, 1934 – S; *My Darling Clementine*, 1946 – S; *She Wore a Yellow Ribbon*, 1949 – S

HANK WORDEN (5): *Fort Apache*, 1948 – S; *Red River*, 1948 – S; *Wagonmaster*, 1950 – S; *The Quiet Man*, 1952 – S; *The Searchers*, 1956 – S

JOHN WRAY (3): *All Quiet on the Western Front*, 1930 – S; *I Am a Fugitive from a Chain Gang*, 1932 – S; *Mr Deeds Goes to Town*, 1936 – S

TERESA WRIGHT (3): *The Little Foxes*, 1941 – L; *Shadow of a Doubt*, 1943 – L; *The Best Years of Our Lives*, 1946 – L

Will Wright (2): *Adam's Rib*, 1949 – S; *They Live by Night*, 1949 – S

KEENAN WYNN (3): *Kiss Me Kate*, 1953 – S; *Touch of Evil*, 1958 – S, cameo; *Nashville*, 1975 – S, bit

Roland Young (2): *David Copperfield*, 1935 – LS; *The Philadelphia Story*, 1940 – LS

Tammany Young (2): *She Done Him Wrong*, 1933 – S; *It's a Gift*, 1934 – S

George Zucco (2): *The Hunchback of Notre Dame*, 1939 – S; *The Pirate*, 1948 – LS

NOTES

Hortense Powdermaker, 1951:

> Stars do not fall into any single category. Among them are handsome men and beautiful women, and those with just pleasant, everyday faces, tough heroes and gentle ones, straight comedians and song-and-dance ones, character actors, all ages from children to those past middle age, actors with great talent and those with very little. To stay on top for a long period, the actors must appeal to both sexes and male stars do this more often than female.

The above list may seem a little strange to most moviegoers, as it is based on the number of appearances made in Hollywood's Top Two-Fifty by any player, whether a star, juvenile lead, leading support player, or just playing a bit part; it shows very clearly one of the difficulties in recognising the true artistry of Hollywood.

It was mainly through the work of its players that the public became aware of the attraction, even magnetism, of the cinema. The generally unknown writers, cameramen, art directors, composers, and editors listed previously were essential to the artistic effect of the final movies but it was the knowledge of stars and instantly recognisable character actors that familiarised audiences with Hollywood artistry. Hollywood's attitude towards its actors and actresses was continuously schizophrenic: the build up of the star system was above all a supremely successful commercial operation. Movies often became star vehicles and these were not always the best of films in a general sense.

This accounts for the fact that the films credited are not always those that contain the best-known of the stars' performances, and also for the fact that many of the best-known stars appear in only one or two of the greatest films, for example Bette Davis and Barbara Stanwyck – both very powerful actresses who could attract huge audiences to very ordinary, even mediocre, films.

The male and female leads who rate the highest number of credits in this collection are:

MALE LEADS
James Stewart, John Wayne (10)
Cary Grant (9)
Humphrey Bogart, Henry Fonda, Harrison Ford (7)
Robert De Niro (5)

FEMALE LEADS
Lillian Gish, Katharine Hepburn, Ginger Rogers (5)

This seems to bear out the Powdermaker thesis (male stars stay at the top more often than female).

An unusually equal number of male stars and female stars score 4 each:

MALE LEADS
Fred Astaire, Marlon Brando, Joseph Cotten, Kirk Douglas, Richard Dreyfuss, Gene Kelly, Dick Powell (4)

FEMALE LEADS
Jean Arthur, Marlene Dietrich, Joanne Dru, Greta Garbo, Judy Garland, Marilyn Monroe, Natalie Wood (4)

Powdermaker's emphasis on the wide variety of performers who can become stars would allow us to include Boris Karloff and Charles Laughton (with 4 each). As brilliant character actors they would normally fall into the category of Leading Support Players, who can at times reach star status:

MALE LEADING SUPPORT PLAYERS

Ward Bond (13)

Walter Brennan, Donald Crisp, Thomas Mitchell (7)

Harry Carey Jr., Jack Carson (6)

Robert Duvall, Sam Jaffe, Ben Johnson, Victor McLaglen, Edmond O'Brien, Claude Rains, Siegfried (Sig) Rumann (5)

Martin Balsam, Lionel Barrymore, Albert Dekker, Barry Fitzgerald, Tim Holt, Edward Everett Horton, Walter Huston, Karl Malden (4)

FEMALE LEADING SUPPORT PLAYERS

Jane Darwell (7)

Mary Astor (5)

Gloria Grahame, Diane Keaton, Elsa Lanchester, Anna Lee, Una Merkel, Jessic Ralph (4)

The Hollywood studios also employed an army of less prominent but regularly cast character actors and actresses, who became very familiar to audiences a very different way. Often stereotyped, they were chosen to play a recognisable role, taken in relatively small doses but always played immaculately. Any repertory company that could rely on such players to play minor roles with consistent flourish would consider itself exceedingly fortunate.

MALE SUPPORT PLAYERS

Irving Bacon, Alan Bridge (8)

Francis Ford, Porter Hall, John Qualen, Russell Simpson, Robert Warwick (7)

Leo G. Carroll, Chester Conklin, Henry Daniell, Billy Gilbert, Edwin Maxwell, Eugene Pallette, C. Aubrey Smith, Tom Tyler (6)

FEMALE SUPPORT PLAYERS

Mae Marsh (a star of silent days) (7)

Una O'Connor (6)

Charles D. Brown, John Carradine, Jimmy Conlin, William Demarest, Robert Greig, Charles Halton, Arthur Hoyt, Torben Meyer, Franklin Pangborn, Ian Wolfe, Hank Worden (5)

Eric Blore, John Cazale, Spencer Charters, Ray Collins, Elisha Cook Jr., Harry Davenport, Byron Foulger, Steven Geray, Louis Jean Heydt, Roscoe Karns, Montagu Love, J. Farrell MacDonald, Grant Mitchell, Frank Reicher, Bert Roach, Erskine Sanford, Harry Shannon, Paul Stewart, George Tobias, H.B. Warner, Harry Woods (4)

Minna Gombell (5)

Virginia Brissac, Esther Howard, Almira Sessions, Joan Shawlee, Norma Varden (4)

Alan Bridge, Chester Conklin, Jimmy Conlin, William Demarest, Byron Foulger, Robert Greig, Porter Hall, Esther Howard, Arthur Hoyt, J. Farrell MacDonald, Torben Meyer, Franklin Pangborn, Almira Sessions, and Robert Warwick were all members of the Preston Sturges stock company.

The scores of Francis Ford, Mae Marsh, Russell Simpson, Tom Tyler, and Hank Worden are all high because they regularly played in films directed by John Ford.

V – Alphabetical List of Films

	Page
Ace in the Hole/The Big Carnival, Par 1951	191, 192
Adam's Rib, MGM 1949	89, 90
The Adventures of Robin Hood, WB 1938	113, 122
The Adventures of Tom Sawyer, UA 1938	387, 396
Advise and Consent, Col 1962	385, 386, 394
Alias Nick Beal/The Contact Man, Par 1949	385, 388, 390
Alice Doesn't Live Here Anymore, WB 1974	382, 384, 393
All About Eve, TCF 1950	191, 193
All Quiet on the Western Front, Un 1930	343, 345, 347
All the King's Men, Col 1950	177, 179, 186
All the President's Men, WB 1976	178, 181
Amadeus, Orion 1984	49, 52
America, America/The Anatolian Smile, WB 1963	159
American Graffiti, Un 1973	151, 154
An American in Paris, MGM 1951	231, 241
Anatomy of a Murder, Col 1959	292, 293
Annie Hall, UA 1977	59, 74
The Apartment, UA 1960	75, 76
Apocalypse Now, UA 1979	343, 346, 354
The Asphalt Jungle, MGM 1950	315, 317
The Awful Truth, Col 1937	87, 91
Baby Doll, WB 1956	169, 170
The Bad and the Beautiful, MGM 1952	195, 196
Bad Day at Black Rock, MGM 1954	359, 371

Bambi, Disney 1941	38, 40, 41
The Band Wagon, MGM 1953	230–232, 242
The Bank Dick, Un 1940	58, 59
Beauty and the Beast, Disney 1991	40, 42
Ben-Hur, MGM 1959	107–109, 111
The Best Years of Our Lives, RKO 1946	173, 174
The Big Heat, Col 1953	315, 318
The Big Parade, MGM 1925	343, 348
The Big Sleep, WB 1946	285–287, 294
Bird, Malpaso 1988	388, 389
The Birds, Un 1963	205, 212
The Birth of a Nation, Epoch 1915	107, 109
Blade Runner, WB 1982	215–216, 218
Body Heat, WB 1981	331, 335
Bonnie and Clyde, WB 1967	314, 316, 326
Boomerang, TCF 1947	299, 380–381, 399
Born Yesterday, Col 1950	89, 92
The Bride of Frankenstein, Un 1935	204, 206
Bringing Up Baby, RKO 1938	88, 93, 381
Broken Blossoms, D.W. Griffith 1919	272, 275
Cabaret, AA 1972	234, 243
Call Northside 775, TCF 1948	385–386, 399
The Cameraman, MGM 1928	56–57, 60
Camille, MGM 1936	273, 276
Casablanca, WB 1942	257, 259
Cat People, RKO 1942	205, 207
Chinatown, Par 1974	288, 290, 308
Citizen Kane, RKO 1941	49, 50, 157
City Lights, UA 1930	56, 61
Close Encounters of the Third Kind, Col 1977	215–216, 219
The Conversation, Par 1974	31, 36
Crossfire, RKO 1947	288–289, 295

The Crowd, MGM 1928   127, 128, 129

The Dark Mirror, Un 1946   386, 399
David Copperfield, MGM 1935   223, 224
Days of Heaven, Par 1978   169, 172
The Deer Hunter, Un 1978   343, 346, 355
Destry Rides Again, Un 1937   357, 362
Dinner at Eight, MGM 1933   98, 100, 102
Dodsworth, UA 1936   273, 277
Do the Right Thing, Un 1989   146, 147
Double Indemnity, Par 1944   290, 296
Duck Soup, Par 1933   58, 62
Dumbo, Disney 1941   38, 40, 43

East of Eden, WB 1955   151, 157, 165
E.T. – the Extra-Terrestrial, Un 1982   215, 216, 220

Fantasia, Disney 1940   38–40, 44
Fat City, Col 1972   187, 190
Father of the Bride, MGM 1950   382, 385, 391
Five Easy Pieces, Col 1970   148, 149
Fort Apache, RKO 1948   358, 363
Forty-Second Street, WB 1933   227, 234
Frankenstein, Un 1931   203–205, 208
Freaks, MGM 1932   380, 382, 395
From Here to Eternity, Col 1953   343, 345, 349
Funny Face, Par 1957   232, 244
Fury, MGM 1936   136–138, 139

The General, UA 1926   55–57, 63
Gentlemen Prefer Blondes, TCF 1953   232, 245
The Ghost and Mrs Muir, TCF 1947   266, 267
Giant, WB 1956   158, 166

Gigi, MGM 1958	226, 230, 231, 246
Gilda, Col 1946	258, 260
The Godfather, Par 1972	316–317, 327
The Godfather Part II, Par 1974	316, 328
The Gold Diggers of 1933; WB 1933	227, 235
The Gold Rush, UA 1925	56, 63
Gone with the Wind, MGM 1939	223, 283
The Good Earth, MGM 1937	127–128, 130
The Graduate, UA 1967	76, 80
Grand Hotel, MGM 1932	100, 103
The Grapes of Wrath, TCF 1940	127–128, 131
The Great Dictator, UA 1940	75, 77
Greed, MGM 1924	101, 126–128, 132
Gun Crazy, Un 1950	314, 318
The Gunfighter, TCF 1950	380–381, 400
Gunga Din, RKO 1939	114, 115
Hannah and Her Sisters, Orion 1986	101, 195
High Noon, UA 1952	359, 364
High Sierra, WB 1941	313–314, 319
High Society, MGM 1956	388, 397
His Girl Friday, Col 1940	9), 94
Holiday, Col 1938	380–381, 398
How Green Was My Valley, TCF 1941	156, 159, 160
Hud, Par, 1963	382, 400
The Hunchback of Notre Dame, RKO 1939	114, 116
The Hustler, TCF 1961	186–187, 188
I Am a Fugitive from a Chain Gang, WB 1932	136–137, 140
In a Lonely Place, Col 1950	291, 297
The Informer, RKO 1935	137–138, 141
Intolerance, Wark 1916	107, 110
Intruder in the Dust, MGM 1949	385–386, 392

Invasion of the Body Snatchers, AA 1956	215, 217
It Happened One Night, Col 1934	87, 95
It's a Gift, Par 1934	58, 64
It's a Wonderful Life, RKO 1946	123, 124
Jaws, Un 1975	206, 213
Johnny Belinda, WB 1948	381, 398
Johnny Guitar, Republic 1954	382, 401
Julius Caesar, MGM 1953	380, 396
The Kid, First National 1921	55–56, 65
The Killers, Un, 1946	314, 321
The Killing, UA 1956	382–383, 400
King Kong, RKO 1933	204–205, 209
The King of Comedy, TCF 1983	54
Kiss Me Deadly, UA 1955	287–288, 298
Kiss Me Kate, MGM 1953	232, 247
Kramer vs Kramer, Col 1979	159, 167
The Lady Eve, Par 1941	88, 89, 96
The Lady from Shanghai, Col 1948	286, 291, 299
The Last Picture Show, Col 1971	151, 152
Laura, TCF 1944	286, 288, 300
Letter from an Unknown Woman, Un 1948	275, 278
Limelight, UA 1952	57, 66
Little Caesar, WB 1930	137, 313, 315, 322
The Little Foxes, RKO 1941	156, 161
Long Day's Journey into Night, TCF 1962	158, 162
The Lost Horizon, Col 1937	200, 201
The Lost Weekend, Par 1945	173, 175
Love Me Tonight, Par 1932	226, 236
The Magnificent Ambersons, RKO 1942	156–157, 163

The Maltese Falcon, WB 1941 — 285–287, 301
The Man Who Shot Liberty Vallance, Par 1962 — 360, 365
The Manchurian Candidate, UA 1962 — 339, 340
Manhattan, UA 1979 — 59, 66
Marnie, Un 1964 — 330, 336
Mary Poppins, Disney 1964 — 233, 248
*M*A*S*H*, TCF 1970 — 76, 81
Mean Streets, Taplin-Perry-Scorsese 1973 — 129, 135
Meet Me in St Louis, MGM 1944 — 231–232, 249
The Merry Widow, MGM 1934 — 226, 237
Mildred Pierce, WB 1945 — 157, 164
The Miracle of Morgan's Creek, Par 1943 — 75, 78
The Miracle Worker, UA 1962 — 173, 176
Missing, Un 1982 — 178–179, 182
Mr Deeds Goes to Town, Col 1936 — 81, 83
Mr Smith Goes to Washington, Col 1939 — 177, 180
Modern Times, UA 1936 — 75, 79
Monsieur Verdoux, UA 1947 — 382, 390
Murder My Sweet, RKO 1944 — 287, 302
Mutiny on the Bounty, MGM 1935 — 113, 117
My Darling Clementine, TCF 1946 — 357, 366

The Naked City, Un 1948 — 288–289, 303
Nashville, Par 1975 — 101, 106
The Navigator, UA 1924 — 56, 67
A Night at the Opera, MGM 1935 — 58, 68
The Night of the Hunter, UA 1955 — 137–139, 142
Ninotchka, MGM 1939 — 88, 97
North by Northwest, MGM 1959 — 329, 338–339, 342
Nothing Sacred, UA 1937 — 81, 86
Notorious, RKO 1946 — 329, 338–339, 341

Of Mice and Men, UA 1939	137, 138, 143
The Old Dark House, Un 1932	204, 210
On the Town, MGM 1949	230–233, 250
On the Waterfront, Col 1954	128–129, 133
One Flew over the Cuckoo's Nest, UA 1975	185
One Hundred and One Dalmatians, Disney 1961	385, 387, 389
Only Angels Have Wings, Col 1939	257, 261
Our Hospitality, Metro 1923	56, 69
Out of the Past/Build My Gallows High, RKO 1947	258, 262
The Outlaw Josey Wales, WB 1976	361, 371
The Oxbow Incident, TCF 1943	357, 367
The Pajama Game, WB 1957	382–383, 397
The Palm Beach Story, Par 1942	89, 98
Paths of Glory, UA 1957	343, 345, 350
Patton, TCF 1970	49, 53
The Philadelphia Story, MGM 1940	265, 268
Pinocchio, Disney 1940	38–40, 45
The Pirate, MGM 1948	229–232, 251
Play Misty for Me, Un 1971	331, 337
The Postman Always Rings Twice, MGM 1946	330–331, 332
The Prisoner of Zenda, UA 1937	113, 118
Psycho, Par 1960	178, 205, 211
The Public Enemy, WB 1931	313, 315, 323
Queen Christina, MGM 1933	112, 119
Queen Kelly, UA 1928	273, 289
The Quiet Man, RKO 1952	271, 275, ~~279~~
Raging Bull, UA 1980	54, 187, 189, 385
Raiders of the Lost Ark, Par 1981	201, 202
Rear Window, Par 1954	286, 292, 309
Rebecca, UA 1940	274, 280

Rebel without a Cause, WB 1955	151, 155
The Red Badge of Courage, MGM 1951	343, 345, 351
Red River, UA 1948	364, 368
Ride the High Country/Guns in the Afternoon, MGM 1962	360, 373
The Right Stuff, WB 1983	178, 183
Rio Bravo, WB 1959	360, 374
Rosemary's Baby, Par 1968	205, 214
Safety Last, Hal Roach 1923	385, 387, 390
Salvador, Hemdale 1986	179, 184
Scarface, UA 1932	261, 313, 324
The Scarlet Empress, Par 1934	112, 120
Schindler's List, Un 1993	146
The Set-Up, RKO 1949	382, 384, 394
The Sea Hawk, WB 1940	114, 121
The Searchers, WB 1956	359–360, 375
Seven Brides for Seven Brothers, MGM 1954	232, 252
Shadow of a Doubt, Un 1943	329, 333
Shane, Par 1953	359, 376
Shanghai Express, Par 1932	256, 263
She Done Him Wrong, Par 1933	98, 99
She Wore a Yellow Ribbon, RKO 1949	358, 377
Sherlock Jr., Metro 1924	56, 70
The Shootist, Par 1976	361, 378
The Shop Around the Corner, MGM 1940	265–266, 269
The Silence of the Lambs, Orion 1991	293, 310
Singin' in the Rain, MGM 1952	195, 231, 233, 253
Snow White and the Seven Dwarfs, Disney 1938	38, 40, 46
Some Like it Hot, UA 1959	58, 71
Sons of the Desert/Fraternally Yours, MGM 1933	57, 72
The Southerner, UA 1945	128, 133
Spartacus, Un 1960	382, 384, 391
Spellbound, UA 1945	290–291, 304

Stage Door, RKO 1937   100, 104
Stagecoach, UA 1939   357, 366, 369
A Star Is Born, WB 1954   195, 198
Star Wars, TCF 1977   215, 221
Strangers on a Train, WB 1951   329–330, 334
A Streetcar Named Desire, WB 1951   169, 171
Sullivan's Travels, Par 1941   82, 84
Sunrise, Fox 1927   272, 281
Sunset Boulevard, Par 1950   195, 197
Sweet Smell of Success, UA 1957   191, 194, 285
Swing Time, RKO 1936   227, 238

Taxi Driver, Col 1976   54, 123, 125
Tender Mercies, EMI 1983   385, 387, 398
They Live by Night, RKO 1949   136–138, 144
They Were Expendable, MGM 1945   344, 352
The Thin Man, MGM 1934   232, 285, 305
To Be or Not To Be, UA 1942   82, 85
To Have and Have Not, WB 1944   257, 264
To Kill a Mockingbird, Un 1962   145, 150, 153
Top Hat, RKO 1935   227, 239
Touch of Evil, Un 1958   286–289, 306
The Treasure of the Sierra Madre, WB 1948   127–129, 134
Trouble in Paradise, Par 1932   265, 270
Twelve Angry Men, UA 1957   136–138, 145
Twelve o'Clock High, TCF 1949   344, 353

Vertigo, Par 1958   205, 286, 292, 311

Wagonmaster, RKO 1950   358, 370
Way Out West, MGM 1937   57, 73
West Side Story, UA 1961   233, 254
White Heat, WB 1949   314, 325

Who Framed Roger Rabbit?, Touchstone 1988	41, 47
The Wild Bunch, WB 1969	360, 361, 379
The Wind, MGM 1928	272–273, 282
The Window, RKO 1949	382, 384, 393
Witness, Par 1985	290, 312
Witness for the Prosecution, UA 1957	292, 307
The Wizard of Oz, MGM 1939	236, 239, 263
Written on the Wind, Un 1956	165, 174–175
The Wrong Man, WB 1957	390, 402
Wuthering Heights, UA 1939	230–232
Yankee Doodle Dandy, WB 1942	235, 248
Young Mr Lincoln, TCF 1939	54, 57, 365